Since 2004, internat⋯ ⋯ ⋯as
placed ove⋯ ⋯ ⋯ the
past ⋯ ⋯ ⋯mes.
This ⋯ writes
within.

Proclaimed the pre-eminent voice in paranormal fiction by critics, Kenyon has helped pioneer – and define – the current paranormal trend that has captivated the world and continues to blaze new trails that blur traditional genre lines.

With more than 25 million copies of her books in print in over 100 countries, her current series include: The Dark-Hunters, League, Lords of Avalon, Chronicles of Nick, and Belador Code.

Visit Sherrilyn Kenyon online:

www.darkhunter.com | www.sherrilynkenyon.co.uk

www.facebook.com/AuthorSherrilynKenyon

www.twitter.com/KenyonSherrilyn

Praise for Sherrilyn Kenyon:

'A publishing phenomenon . . . [Sherrilyn Kenyon] is the reigning queen of the wildly successful paranormal scene'
Publishers Weekly

'Kenyon's writing is brisk, ironic and relentlessly imaginative. These are not your mother's vampire novels'
Boston Globe

'Whether writing as Sherrilyn Kenyon or Kinley MacGregor, this author delivers great romantic fantasy!'
New York Times bestselling author Elizabeth Lowell

D0299977

Dark Bites

SHERRILYN KENYON

piatkus

PIATKUS

First published in the US in 2014 by St Martin's Press, New York
First published in Great Britain in 2014 by Piatkus

A CIP catalogue record for this book
is available from the British Library.

ISBN 978-0-349-40140-9

Printed and bound by
CPI Group (UK) Ltd, Croydon, CR0 4YY

Papers used by Piatkus are from well-managed forests
and other responsible sources.

MIX
Paper from
responsible sources
FSC® C104740

Copyright Acknowledgments

To you, the reader, for taking these adventures with me. And as always, to my family and friends who tolerate my many hours of solitude while I work, and who keep me sane whenever I emerge from the rabbit hole. And as always, to my peeps at SMP for all their hard work and for making these adventures possible. Y'all rock!

DARK
BITES

CONTENTS

House of the Rising Son

July 20, 12,252 BC

"How do they look?"

The daeve demon, Caleb Malphas, turned away from the sparring soldiers at the delicate, emotionless voice of the goddess he served. As was her wont, she'd appeared silently and suddenly behind him—something that was always disconcerting to a warrior who didn't like anyone or anything at his back.

With long, dark brown hair, flawless skin, and vivid greenish-gold eyes, Bathymaas was exquisitely beautiful, but as cold-blooded as any creature he'd ever known. The embodiment of justice, she wasn't supposed to have any type of emotion or feeling. . . .

And she didn't. However, she was as kind as she was ruthless, and fair beyond his comprehension.

Malphas glanced back at the four soldiers who were training in the large arena in front of him. "Not bad. They might actually survive a few battles."

His dark humor was lost on a goddess who had no understanding of it. Luckily, she didn't get sarcasm, either, therefore she never took offense to his. It made serving her a lot less painful for him, and it was the primary reason he'd agreed to help her assemble her team of elite protectors who would be charged with keeping her peoples safe.

She brushed a stray piece of hair back from her face. "We still need two more to represent the Atlanteans. Have you any suggestions?"

"There's an Atlantean champion who's been making a name for himself during games and festivals. Galenus of Didimosia. I was planning to test and then invite him to join our merry crew later today."

"Have you seen him fight?"

Malphas nodded. "Two days ago. He beat back six larger opponents at one time, during an exhibition match. He is impressive, and given the way he savored the fight and victory, he should make a good addition to our group."

"May I go with you?"

"Of course, my lady. I would be highly honored."

Inclining her head to him, she walked away with a grace that would rival his own beloved Lilliana's. That comparison made him involuntarily flinch as vivid memories surged to stab him with painful regrets. Unwilling to go there with his thoughts, Malphas returned to the men he was training to protect this fragile world from the very kind of tragedy he, himself, had gone through.

You *should have* been there, brother. It was incredible! They came at me like giant mountainous beasts, wanting only my blood and bones to eat, and I beat them back, single-handedly. When I won the fight . . . this incredible shout went up through the amphitheater like raucous thunder." Cupping his hands around his mouth, Galenus demonstrated the sound.

Aricles smiled at his twin's exuberance while Galenus went on to illustrate his expert sword skills that had won his tournament two days ago. "You know what would really impress me, Galen?"

His brother froze with a frown in the middle of his mock sword stroke. "What?"

"Help with laying down the fertilizer in my field."

Galenus scoffed indignantly as he climbed up on the fence and grimaced. "How can you stand it here? I hate farming and tending animals and fields. . . . You should come with me next time and participate in the games. Together we'd be invincible . . . and win enough money to make the king himself look like a pauper."

Aricles paused to wipe the sweat from his brow with his forearm before he cut the cord on a fresh batch of manure. Unlike his brother, who was dressed in noble finery to rival a prince's chiton and chlamys, he was shirtless with only a short brown breechcloth and worn leather shoes to cover him while he worked. Even so, sweat rolled down his back and plastered his short, reddish-brown hair to his head. "It's not so bad here. Father needs the help."

"Bah! He has plenty of servants for that. Why work us like dogs in the heat of summer? We were born to be better than this."

Disagreeing completely, Aricles hoisted the barrel up on his shoulder to carry it to where he'd left off covering the plants. "There's nothing wrong or undignified about a good day's labor. You should try it sometime."

"Says the man covered in cow shit."

Aricles threw a handful of it at his brother. It landed in the middle of his chest, staining his stark white chiton.

"Ugh! That's disgusting, Ari! I can't believe you did that."

Laughing, Aricles began spreading it around the sprouting plants. He'd never understand his brother's love of or need for war. Personally, he hated conflict and fighting. He'd much rather create and build than kill and destroy. Conquest and battle games didn't appeal to him in the slightest way. The only reason a man should ever pick up a sword was to protect those he loved, not to willfully take the life of someone else's beloved.

Still sputtering in fury, Galenus stormed off.

"One day, Galen," Aricles called after him, "you're going to learn to love farming. I promise you!"

"Should that day ever come, I hope Misos spears my idiot head to the wall!" he shouted back as he went to wash, and change clothes.

"It never ceases to amaze me how the two of you can look so much alike and be so different in disposition and manner. It's as if you're night and day to each other."

That's because Aricles had purposely shouldered responsibility very early in his life so that Galen wouldn't have to.

Aricles straightened as his father joined him and offered him a cup of water. Grateful, he drank it down in one gulp. "Galen's not so bad, Father. He's a good man, with a great heart."

"He needs that wildness inside him tamed before it leads to his utter destruction. Out of my three sons, he is the one who keeps me up at night with worry. As well as the fact that Perseus idolizes him so. I fear one day, he will follow his older brother to war and I'll lose the two of them."

"I wouldn't have that fear. Perseus would never leave his beloved Julia for war."

His father smiled and patted him on his bare shoulder. "I never thought of that, and you're right. He'd sooner die than leave her. Thank you for setting my mind at ease." His father took the cup from him. "Now if I could only get my eldest son interested in a woman. . . ."

Aricles didn't comment as he went back to fertilizing the plants. Though his father didn't know it, he'd been in love, too, at Perseus's age. And his heart had been crushed when he'd stumbled upon her in the woods, having sex with another man. Even though the two of them had been privately courting for several months, he hadn't stolen so much as a single kiss for fear of dishonoring her. He'd thought her perfection, and she'd laughed in his face at his courtesy.

I need a man's love, not a fool's.

Since then, he hadn't gone near another woman. He left them to his twin, who held as much regard for their hearts and feelings as Claudia had held for his. If he wanted to be mocked and ridiculed, he had brothers for that. He didn't need a woman to do it, too.

"Akri!"

He looked up at Gideon's alarmed cry to see a band of seven demons flying toward the servant and his father. Ari's heart pounding, he glanced about for Galen. But his brother was still off washing and had no clue they were under attack.

Damn it!

Aricles dashed to the fence to grab a long wooden stake and his brother's xiphos. Using the stake as a javelin, he threw it at the demon closest to reaching his father who was running back toward him while the demon flapped its massive wings and licked its black lips. The stake struck the demon in the center of its chest. The demon fell to the ground with an echoing shriek as it died.

As fast as he could, he crossed the field to fight back the remaining six. By the looks of them, they were Charonte—one of the fiercest of the demon breeds. And unfortunately, humans and Atlanteans were their food of choice.

Aricles dodged their foul claws and managed to avoid their fangs as he fought them with everything he had. Sad for the demons that he shared his brother's fighting prowess. He might not enjoy swordplay and killing, but he was damn good at it. Within a handful of minutes, he had the demons lying in pieces on the ground.

The sight of their remains sickened him, as did the blood on his hands and body.

His father embraced him. "Thank the gods you were here."

"Thank Galen for leaving his xiphos behind while he went to wash." Aricles grimaced in distaste. "And speaking of, I'll be back to help with their carcasses as soon as I clean up."

Repulsed by the needless waste, he headed for the stream that ran through the middle of their property.

He'd just begun washing himself when a bright light flashed in front of him. Grabbing Galen's sword, he hesitated as he saw a beautiful woman in a long white peplos, and a man dressed in black.

"Rest easy." The man held his hands out to show that he wasn't here to battle. "We just wanted to talk to you for a few minutes."

Aricles lowered the sword, but kept it in his hand. "About?"

"I would like to recruit you." The woman's voice was soft and melodic. Soothing. A perfect match for her tall, ethereal beauty.

"For?"

The man laughed. "You're not one to waste words, are you?"

"Malphas," the woman chided. "You're not helping."

"Forgive me, goddess."

Goddess . . .

Now her beauty made total sense. But what would one of them want with a simple farmer? He couldn't fathom it.

Bathymaas studied the man in the stream. Tall and well muscled, he looked as fierce washing as he had fighting Malphas's demons. His reddish-brown hair was cropped short in back and longer in front. And while he was very handsome, it was his intelligent blue eyes that were searing. "Are you aware of the war that has broken out, Atlantean?"

He frowned. "What war?"

Malphas crossed his arms over his chest. "Are you familiar with the term 'Chthonian'?"

Aricles shook his head.

It was the goddess who explained. "They are a handful of humans, Atlanteans, or Apollites who are born with the powers of a god so that they can protect their people from the gods who would abuse or take advantage of them. Each is endowed with the ability to slay a god and not upset the order of the universe or destroy it. But for every god they kill, they lose a degree of their own power. If they slay too many gods, they die."

"And unfortunately, they got crossed up and have been going at each other's throats for almost a year now."

The goddess nodded. "There is no one who can protect their peoples while they war, and certain groups are taking advantage of their lax attention to prey on innocents. That is why I'm assembling a team that can temporarily take over their protection duties until the Chthonians come to their senses."

Aricles narrowed his eyes as he understood why they were here. "You want me to fight for you?"

"Yes."

Aricles laughed at the very idea. "No, thank you. I'm not a soldier. I'm a farmer."

Malphas snorted. "Then why were you in an arena fight two days ago?"

"I wasn't. You saw my brother."

"That was your brother?" Malphas asked suspiciously.

"Yes. Galenus. I am Aricles."

Malphas looked even more confused. "But you're the one who fought off the demons just now."

He shrugged. "Galen and I learned and practiced together. But he's the one who loves the xiphos, not me."

Malphas smiled at the goddess. "I think we found our last two."

Aricles shook his head. "No, you haven't."

Malphas stepped forward, but the goddess stopped him.

"Go find this Galenus and ask him to join us. I want to speak to Aricles alone."

"Yes, my goddess." Malphas vanished without question.

Aricles left the stream and dried himself with the towel he'd left on the bank. "If you think you can change my mind, my lady . . . you can't. I want nothing to do with war."

"Do you know who I am?"

"Diafonia, Apollymi, Symfora . . ." He named all the warring goddesses of the Atlantean pantheon. "None of it matters to me."

"I am Bathymaas, the embodiment of all justice. My role in this world is simple—to maintain the balance between right and wrong. To hold it sacred and make sure that neither side squashes the other. I'm sure you can respect that."

"I can."

"Then fight for me."

Shaking his head, he started past her.

She placed a gentle hand on his arm to stop him. "Please, Aricles. The gods have given you an amazing gift and skill. Who better to wield a xiphos for me than a man who takes no love or glory of war? Unlike others, you won't fight for the sake of it, but for the right reasons."

He wanted to say no to her. But as he looked into those green-tinged, golden eyes and felt the warmth of her hand on his flesh, he lost himself to her wiles. The saddest part? She wasn't even using them on him.

And still he wanted to bury his face against her hair and inhale the sweet scent of her. He'd never been so drawn to any woman. Not even Claudia.

She's not a woman.

No, she was a goddess.

And he was nothing more than a simple, backwoods farmer.

"So what say you, good Aricles? Will you represent your people and be a champion for me for the good of all?"

He wanted to say no. Desperately. But his heart locked down his common sense as a desire to make the goddess smile answered for him. "Who am I to fight the will of the gods?"

"Aricles! You'll never guess what . . ." Galen's words faded as he broke through the trees to see Bathymaas with him. He arched a curious brow.

Bathymaas turned toward Galen, but didn't react physically. "You're twins."

Aricles gave her a wry grin. "Since birth."

Malphas laughed, but Bathymaas's expression didn't change at all. "You'll have to forgive the goddess. She doesn't understand humor, or any emotion, for that matter."

Those words shocked him. "Truly?"

Bathymaas nodded. "Now, if you'll collect your things, we will take you to your new home."

Galen let out a jubilant shout while Aricles cringed. His father wouldn't be happy with this, he knew it, and when they returned to the small stone cottage where they'd been born, he was proven right.

"I won't have it!" their father snarled while they packed their meager belongings. "I need at least one of you here."

"Father," Galen breathed. "You don't understand what an honor this is. We were hand-selected by the goddess herself. We have to honor the gods and their will, is that not what you've always taught us?"

Their father turned tormented blue eyes to Aricles, imploring him to stay.

"I can keep Galen safe so long as I'm with him. I'll make sure he comes home to you in one piece."

His father cradled the back of Aricles's head in his hand and pulled him into his embrace. "My sons are all I have in this world. I could not bear to live if I lost one of you."

"We will be careful. Even if I have to hogtie Galen."

His father kissed each of his cheeks then moved to do the same with his brother. "I always knew I'd lose you to Misos, but I'd hoped to have more years with you before you left for war. A score of years just isn't enough. Take care of your brother, Galen. Let no harm befall him or you."

"I will, *Papsi*." His eyes gleaming with joy and eagerness, Galen grabbed his sword and pack, and headed for the door.

Aricles sighed as he swept his gaze around the room he'd shared with Galen and Perseus, who was off with his Julia. At ten-and-six, his baby brother was as much a slave to his heart as Galen was to his libido. He hated that he wouldn't have a chance to say good-bye to him. "Tell Perseus I will miss him and to not dawdle with his lessons."

His father smiled. "Take care, *m'gios*."

"And you, *Papsi*." Aricles hugged him one last time before he followed Galen to where the goddess and her servant waited for them.

"You look like you haven't had a bowel movement in a month," Malphas said as soon as he saw him.

Scowling, Aricles wasn't sure what to make of the man who would be their trainer and commander.

Galen snorted. "He always looks that way. He was born constipated." His brother reached for him. "Come, Ari, be young for once in your life."

"I tried your recklessness once and found it exhausting. Melancholy suits me just fine."

Malphas laughed. "So where's *your* xiphos?"

"I don't have one."

"He always uses a piece of wood to spar with me."

Grunting his displeasure, Malphas inclined his head to his goddess. "I guess we're ready."

One moment they were out in the woods, and in the next, they were inside a temple the likes of which Aricles had never seen. Made of solid gold, it glistened all around him. Bright-colored images and geometric designs were painted all over the gold.

"Where are we?" he asked.

The goddess folded her hands in front of her. "Thebes, in Egypt. This is my main temple. My father's is next door."

"Your father?"

"Set."

Aricles's eyes widened. While he knew few gods outside of his native Atlantean pantheon, Set was one everyone knew. Said to be the most ferocious god in existence, the god of chaos even terrified his own family. "I didn't think he could have children."

"I wasn't born to him. I was created for him."

"I don't understand."

Malphas snorted. "After Set had a little emotional breakdown that cost several gods their body parts and lives, the primal Source decided that they needed to give him something else to focus on and make him happy." He gestured to Bathymaas. "What better than a beautiful, emotionless daughter to watch over?"

Galen flashed a grin to Aricles. "What better, indeed?"

Malphas passed a look of warning to Galen. "Put it back in your loincloth, punkin'. Our goddess is a virgin and is to remain so. She wouldn't even know what to do with a kiss so don't try for one unless you want to meet the bad end of my sword and her father's fury."

Galen grimaced. "Pity, and noted."

Malphas led them to a room where four other men were lounging about. "Welcome to the Ēperon. We have two warriors from each mortal race." He jerked his chin to the two men who were dicing. One was a mountainous beast who made a mockery of the brothers' six-foot-six stature. For that matter, one of his beefy arms was easily the same diameter as Bathymaas's waist. He wore his long golden-blond hair braided down his back. The other was well muscled, too, and probably stood two to three inches taller than the brothers. His white-blond hair was cropped short and he had a full beard. "Representing the Apollite race we have Haides." He was the larger of the two. "And Hector."

They exchanged pleasantries as Malphas indicated the man on his bed, who was reading a scroll. He had black hair and eyes and a full shaggy beard that was the same length as his hair. "Our humans are the philosophical Monokles, and," he gestured to the one who was sharpening his sword, "Phelix." He had bright red hair that fell just past his ears.

Malphas clapped Galen on his shoulder. "Warriors, meet our Atlanteans. Galen and Aricles."

Haides narrowed his eyes on them. "How do we tell them apart?"

Galen grinned. "I'm the one who's actually alive and likes to partake of fun activities. Aricles seldom smiles and will most likely be discussing philosophy with Monokles."

Aricles kept his features blank. "And I'll be the one spanking Galen's ass during training."

Hector laughed wholeheartedly. "I like them already." He indicated a vacant chair to his right. "Stow your gear and join us."

Aricles took Galen's things. "Go on. I'll take care of it."

As always, Galen didn't hesitate to accept his offer.

While he went to game, Aricles looked at Malphas. "Which beds are ours?"

"The two under the window. Your training will begin an hour after dawn. Have a good night and remember, no bloodshed in the goddess's temple. Save it for the battlefield." Malphas left them to get acquainted.

Aricles went to put their personal effects in the chest between their beds. Listening to his brother jest with his two new friends, he pulled out his small knife and the piece of wood he'd started carving four days ago. It was a vague feminine figure. He hadn't seen the carving's face clearly.

Until today.

He'd started it as an offering for one of the goddesses of his homeland, but now . . . Bathymaas would be perfect for it. Seeing her regal grace in the wood, he began reworking the piece.

After a few minutes, Monokles came over to watch him. "You make that look easy. How long have you been a carver?"

"Since the summer I first stayed with my grandfather in Ena. It was something he would do every night, after chores were finished. I was four or five, and he'd hold me in his lap and patiently instruct me."

"I never knew my grandfathers. One was a Greek hero who died in battle when my father was a boy, and the other was a cavalry officer who perished at war while my mother carried me. What of yours? Was he a retired officer?"

Aricles shook his head. "He was a simple farmer, as his father was before him. By nature, Atlanteans are peaceful . . . with the peculiar exception of my brother, who was corrupted in his youth by a friend who told him too many Greek tales."

Monokles went rigid. "Is that a swipe at me?"

"Not at all, good Monokles. You have every right to be very proud of your soldier family. As I am of mine who toiled their farms. My insult was directed to my twin, solely. He thinks the rest of his family members are backwoods rubes because we would rather till the soil than make war with our neighbors."

Those words seemed to puzzle him. "Yet you're here. Why?"

Aricles shrugged. "Our place is not to question the will of the gods. But rather to do our best to honor them, our ancestors, and ourselves."

Monokles scowled. "How old *are* you?"

"Twenty, and you?"

"A decade older, and yet you speak like a sage ancient."

Galen snorted. "That's because my brother was born an old man. He came from our mother's womb spouting wisdom, and with more patience than any mortal man should ever possess. He should have been a priest."

"Is that true?" Monokles asked. "Would you have preferred priesthood?"

"Probably, but at the time to take vows, I had other obligations." He'd been in love with Claudia and had planned on marrying her. To pay her father's bridal price, he'd been working three jobs in addition to his home chores.

But a farmer was the last thing she'd wanted to be tied to.

Now, it was too late to become a priest.

Perhaps it was bitter irony that he'd ended up in the service of a goddess, after all.

W*hat are you* doing?"

Bathymaas looked up from her sfora at Malphas's question. The small orange ball allowed her to spy on their recruits. "I wanted to make sure that our two newest additions didn't meet with resistance from the others."

"Are they mixing well?"

"They seem to be." She studied Aricles as he continued to masterfully whittle while his brother diced with the others. "Do you think we made a mistake forcing Aricles to leave his farm?"

Caleb gaped at her question. "Is that doubt I hear?"

"I don't know," she answered honestly. "Mortal feelings are beyond me. But I know how complicated sensory beings are. I don't want him to be in pain because of our decision."

Caleb arched a brow at that. In all the centuries he'd served his goddess, he'd never heard her question a decision before. Stunning, really.

Nor had she ever cared about someone's feelings. He wasn't sure what to make of that. Or what it was about Aricles that would cause her to doubt her decisions now.

Weird.

"Sentient beings adjust . . . in time."

She met his gaze. "You've never adjusted to being without Lilliana."

He winced at a bitter truth that stung him hard. "I'm a demon and very different from them. Besides, Lil changed me from what I was, and then was violently taken from me. It's not the same as leaving home to serve a goddess and defend my people."

Bathymaas pulled back from saying anything else. She knew how much it hurt Caleb to talk about his wife. And for the first time, she felt a strange ache in her chest for him over his loss. She wasn't sure why.

Yet there was no denying it was there.

If only she knew why she felt this now.

October 28, 12,252 BC

Bathymaas watched Aricles sitting alone on the bank of a small stream. Since they had moved the Ēperon from her Theban temple to the Atlantean island that was centrally located in the Aegean, she'd kept a close eye on her men. They were targets now. Not just from the Chthonians, but from the gods as well. And the last thing she wanted was for them to be attacked before they stood ready to defend themselves. While they were all valiant warriors, it was harder to fight against demons and gods than mortals.

And while the other five were eager to take their places as elite warriors, Aricles stood alone with his reticence for battle. As with now—while the others were off to seek fleshly comforts—he sat on his grassy bank with no other company than his shadow.

Frowning at him, she had no idea what it was he did there, or why he appeared so content with it. Nor did she understand why he wasn't with his brethren. . . .

Aricles cocked his head as he felt Bathymaas's presence behind him. Strange how he was so attuned to her. Even before the scent of sweet lilies reached his senses, he'd known she was here with him. "Am I needed, my goddess?"

"No." She paused by his side to touch the handmade pole he held in his hands. "What is it you do?"

He pulled at the line. "I'm fishing."

"For what?"

"Fish."

Her frown deepened. "Is this how it's done?"

"It is. Would you like to try?"

"I'm not sure. What does one do to fish?"

Aricles smiled at her innocent question. While the other members of his band lost patience with her inability to understand human activities and emotions, he found her quite beguiling and endearing. "Come and sit with me, my lady, and I'll show you." He removed his cloak and laid it down on the ground to protect her clothing and to give her some padding from the damp grass.

In the daintiest and most graceful manner he'd ever seen, she sank down by his side.

He carefully showed her the metal hook he'd made. "You bait the hook." He picked up a worm from the small clay pot where he'd gathered them a short time ago and showed her how.

"Does that hurt them?"

"I try not to think about that."

"Oh, sorry."

He wiped his hands. "Once it's anchored to the hook, you place it into the water and wait for a fish to take the bait. Then you pull the fish to shore and capture it."

She watched as he tossed the line in. "How long does it take?"

"It could be right away or hours from now, or even not at all."

That seemed to confuse her even more. "Does this not bore you?"

He shook his head as he heard his brother's insults in his mind over his favorite pastime. "Not really. I find it relaxing to sit with my thoughts and listen to the wind whispering to me through the trees."

"You do have a serenity about you that others lack."

That was a polite term for what Galen called his boorishness. "I'm a simple man, with simple needs."

She ran her hand over the carvings he'd made on the pole. They were for the god of water, Ydor, who was said to favor fishermen. "And what are those needs you speak of?"

Aricles scratched at his chin. "Good company. No conflict. And a full belly is always nice."

Bathymaas was amazed at his short list. "No love or shelter?"

"Shelter can be found anywhere. A cave or tent. As for love . . . I'm quite happy without it."

How very strange to her. "I thought all men wanted to be loved."

"Personally, I'd rather not have the pain of it."

"Is that why you're not wenching with the others?"

Aricles laughed. "What they're about today has nothing to do with love, my lady. That is a physical act that doesn't involve their hearts."

That made even less sense to her. "Then why aren't you with them?"

"What can I say? My brother wenches enough for both of us." Aricles paused as he saw her trying to understand his flippant explanation. She was so intelligent about most things, but when it came to human emotions, she was as childlike and innocent as Malphas had warned them. "The honest truth, my lady . . . when I was a boy and staying with my grandfather, my aunt came in late one night. She was hysterical and in tears to find herself pregnant from a man she thought loved her. She'd given her body to him and when she conceived his child, he'd confessed that he'd only been dallying with her and had no interest in making her his wife. My grandfather told me that women, unlike men, quite often confuse sex with love, and that many women attach great significance to the physical act. I loved and adored my aunt, and when she killed herself days later, after she'd gone to her lover and he'd again insulted and denied her, it tore a hole in my heart. I vowed that I would never hurt a woman like that, and that I would take no lover except for my wife."

"But you're not married."

"And that is why I'm fishing instead of wenching."

"Oh," she breathed then hesitated as she digested his explanation. "So you've never had a woman?"

Cringing internally from that question, Aricles blushed. "And I would deeply appreciate it if you didn't tell anyone that, my lady. Men can be quite insulting over such things."

"Why?"

"Honestly, I've never been quite sure. It seems to me they would be grateful that it's one less competitor in the market, and yet that's not how they see it at all. Rather they think it makes a man weak and effeminate to not tup every female he meets."

Bathymaas tried to make sense of that as something began to tug at the pole in her hands. "Is this a nibble?"

"It is, indeed." He moved to sit behind her and wrap his arms around her so that he could show her how to pull the fish in. The warmth of his body and rich, manly scent of his skin made her head reel in a way it never had before. For some reason, she wanted to bury her nose against his skin and revel in it. . . .

How very peculiar.

His rock-hard muscles flexed around her as he lifted the pole to show her a wiggling fish. "There it is." He moved away so as not to get the water on her dress.

He carefully placed the fish in a small wicker basket then wrapped the line and hook around the pole.

"Is that it?"

Aricles nodded. "I only need one for a meal. Some people fish for sport and release the fish after they catch it, but I only do that when it's too small or young to be eaten."

He was ever kind and compassionate to all things. In spite of the fact that he was a lethal warrior, Aricles was a very gentle man.

"May I watch you prepare it? I've never seen anyone do that before, either."

"Of course, my goddess."

He moved farther up the bank to where a small firepit had been prepared. Pulling out a knife, he sat down to remove the fish's scales.

She studied the graceful way he set about his task. "You move with such expertise. . . ."

"I've been doing this a while."

It showed.

And that made her curious about him. "Aricles? Would you mind if I joined you again to fish another day?"

"I would be honored."

Bathymaas sat back and continued to watch him prepare his meal. Most likely, she shouldn't spend time with just him, and yet it wasn't right in her mind that he was alone when she knew people, as a rule, didn't like solitude. It only seemed fair and right that he should have someone to talk to on his days off, too, while the others sought other forms of companionship. Not to mention, she liked being able to ask him questions and have them answered. Unlike the others she knew, he didn't lose patience with her. And it helped her to better understand sentient mortals.

Perhaps these excursions would benefit them both.

March 3, 12,251 BC

"They're incredible, aren't they?"

Bathymaas wasn't sure what Caleb meant. "How so?"

"Sorry, goddess. I forgot you can't understand nuances. . . . The way the brothers move. As if they are one mind. Back to back. Perfect synchronicity. I don't know if it's from being brothers or twins. But I've never seen anything like it. If we had an army of them, we'd need no others."

She agreed. They *were* incredible fighters. While the other four were the best of their breeds, they weren't able to defeat Galen and Aricles.

"Are they ready to fight?"

Caleb screwed his face up. "I don't know. Battle brings out either the worst or the best in everyone. Sometimes both. Hard to predict until they're in it, how they'll react."

"They will stand united."

"Spoken by a woman who has no feelings and who has never had to fight for her life against a harrowing number of vicious enemies."

Bathymaas touched the scar on the demon's neck from a battle wound that had almost taken his head. Even before her birth, he'd been a warrior. "Were you ever afraid?"

"For myself? No. I never cared if I lived or died. I just fought."

"Does it help if you care?"

"Again, goddess, depends on the person. Everyone is different."

She watched as Aricles swung at Haides's head and then countered an attack from Phelix. "He is our best, isn't he?"

Caleb nodded. "He's the one I'd want at my back."

That was the highest testament Caleb could give. "How ironic that our best is the one who least wants to fight."

Caleb snorted. "No, goddess. The real irony is, the demon who was born to end their kind is the one training them to hold back his own."

"You were never evil, Malphas. You were born of equal parts."

"And suckled on venom and hatred, solely. I completely disagree with you, my lady. The only good in me died a violent death. Vengeance is all that sustains me now."

But she didn't believe that. She suspected Caleb denied his decency to protect himself from more harm. Otherwise he wouldn't be here with her, helping to train her soldiers. He would have joined his mother and sought to end the world they were trying desperately to save. . . .

Just as Aricles had denied himself any real pleasure or frivolity. To protect his brothers and father from the demons that often preyed on their small farm while his father was deep in his cups, Aricles had learned to fight like their attackers. To stay sober and vigilant at all times. She'd seen the scars on his flesh from the battles he'd had as a boy. A boy who should have been protected from harm, not left as the sole protector of his family. Battles his father knew nothing about. It was what had led Galen to learn to fight, too, and was a large part of why Galen hated their farm so much.

If I'm to fight and die, it's going to be for glory and money. Not to save pigs and cattle.

But Aricles fought only for his family.

His quiet nobility was what she respected, and his intellect fascinated her. For a man who lived on a farm, he knew a great deal about philosophy and politics. And even more about nature and science.

Had Aricles been born noble, he would have been a brilliant statesman.

"Shit!"

She arched a brow at Caleb's unexpected profanity. He started forward to where Monokles and Hector were about to kill each other, but before he could reach them, Aricles disarmed both men.

"Here now! Is that really what you intend?" Aricles asked Monokles. "You want Hector's head?"

"He didn't pull back." Monokles gestured to the wound on his arm. "I'm bleeding! And I want his ass for it!" He lunged, but Aricles caught him again and pushed him back.

With the patience of an ancient priest, Aricles patted Monokles's shoulder. "And when the pigs dance, the cows feast."

Monokles scowled. "What language are you speaking?"

"It's an Atlantean saying. Don't give in to your temper. Angry eyes are blind, especially in battle. The best way to lose your life is to be so focused on the sword that dealt you the wound on your arm that you miss the knife coming for your heart." He glanced over to Hector.

"Never forget that one hand washes the other, and both wash the same face."

That finally curbed Monokles's temper. "You should have been a philosopher, Ari." He held his hand out to Hector. "Brothers?"

Nodding, Hector took it and smiled. "Always . . . Come, let's get that injury tended. I'm sorry I didn't check the length of my attack. It won't happen again."

Bathymaas watched as Caleb led them off while Aricles waited for her approach.

"My lady." The rich, deep timbre of his voice never failed to raise strange chills on her skin.

"When the pigs dance, the cows feast? Another of your grandfather's sayings?"

He grinned sheepishly. "It is."

"You should write them down."

His laugh added more chills to her. "If for no other reason than to make Galen insane."

"How so?"

"He hates those sayings. It's why he withdrew so quickly when I spoke it. He thinks they're as hokey as I am."

"*I* don't think you're hokey, Aricles."

"Because beauty sees only beauty . . . and you are the most beautiful of all." With a crisp salute that heightened the definition of his well-sculpted muscles, he followed after the others.

Bathymaas bit her lip as she watched after him. She shouldn't feel anything at all, yet . . .

Aricles fascinated her.

And she couldn't wait to talk to him again when they were alone.

May 30, 12,251 BC

Bathymaas sat within the circle of Aricles's arms, holding the pole, while they fished and he read her a letter from his father about his brother Perseus's upcoming wedding. Over the last few months, she'd begun to look forward to their quiet afternoons and she didn't know why. Other than the sound of his voice did very strange things to her breathing and skin. She had no understanding of it at all.

And as she leaned back against his hard, muscular shoulder and chest, and watched him read to her, she became curious about his lips. Before she could stop herself, she reached up and touched them.

He paused to look down at her with an arched brow.

"Are all men's lips as soft as yours, Ari?"

A sweet smile spread across his face. "I suppose, goddess. But I don't make it a habit to feel the lips of other men so I don't know for certain." There was a hint of amusement in his voice.

She loved the fact that he didn't comment whenever she said something inappropriate or ignorant. Unlike others, even Caleb, he never grew annoyed with her.

And his lips intrigued her greatly. As did the line of his strong, sculpted jaw and the dusting of prickly whiskers that teased the flesh of her fingers. "Why do people kiss mouth-to-mouth?"

"It's said to be quite pleasurable."

"And have you ever kissed someone?"

"Not on the mouth, my lady."

All of a sudden, a part of him began swelling against her hip. Frowning, she sat up to look down at it. "Did you get injured just now?"

His face turned bright red as he shifted and moved back from her a bit. "No, my lady."

She was only more confused by his answer and actions. "Is that not why body parts swell?"

He visibly cringed. "Most of the time."

"But not all?"

"No." He hesitated and cleared his throat before he spoke again. "That part of a man swells whenever he's . . . aroused."

There was something she'd never considered or known. "I arouse you?"

He turned even redder. "Forgive me if it insults you, my lady. I have no control over it. But don't worry, I respect your status and birthright, and I will never touch you inappropriately. I swear it."

A peculiar sensation struck her chest like a blow. Was it pain?

She wasn't sure.

And she was fascinated by the bulge beneath his chiton. "Have you done this before?"

His deep blue gaze burned into hers. "Every time you're near me, goddess. Or anytime I smell your scent."

Her eyes widened. "But I've never felt you . . . not until now."

He averted his gaze and shifted uncomfortably again. "I normally bind myself so that you won't."

"Does that not hurt you, too?"

By his expression, she knew he felt awkward and embarrassed. Yet, as always, he was patiently trying to explain the matter to her so that she could understand it. "A great deal. Yet I'd rather be in pain than insult you."

"But you can't insult me. I don't have feelings for you to hurt."

A tiny smile played at the edges of his lips. "I forget that, my lady."

"How can you?"

"Because you don't seem to be without them all the time. Like now . . . your brow is creased as if you're puzzled or confused, and those are emotions. You seem to be very caring and extremely inquisitive. All of those are emotions, too."

Were they?

"I have emotion?"

"You seem to, yes."

Could it be that she'd had emotion all along and never knew it? Her body did react to things, but she'd written them off as automatic responses she couldn't control.

Like his bulge.

Was it possible that those physical reactions were emotions she'd disregarded?

"Ari? What do feelings feel like?"

He set the pole aside and turned her to face him while they talked. "They're hard to define. But I shall try for you." His handsome brow furrowed as he considered it. "Well . . . sometimes I have an ache in my chest when my brother appears sad or is hurt about something. That's sympathy pain because I want him to be happy and healthy."

"What does love feel like?"

Aricles fell silent as he looked at the childlike wonder on her face. The way the sunlight made those incredible hazel eyes glow with her fire and beauty. In his heart, he knew he was already in love with her, had been for weeks now. Ever since she'd started joining him for his peaceful afternoons.

But how could he explain what he felt?

"There are different kinds of love." That seemed like the best starting point.

"Such as?"

"Well, I love my father, but that's more obligatory. He cared for me when I was a boy and I care for him now that he's older."

"But you said he didn't care for you when you were young."

Aricles licked his lips as he tried to explain a very complicated relationship that often left him as confused as she was. While he did love his father and would die for him, a part of him hated and resented his father, too. "He took care of us until the death of our mother. He was a great father when we were small. Then the loss of the woman he loved, crippled him until he could no longer support us emotionally." Or even financially. Rather, his father had given up on life for a long time. "Without my mother, he didn't want to live either, and so he crawled into his cups and stayed there. So someone had to take care of him and the farm." Aricles tried not to remember those first years after his mother's death. They'd been hard and harsh as he struggled with his own grief while trying to care for his brothers and father, as well as their farm.

"So love is obligatory?"

"Not exactly. I mean . . . yes, it is, but it's not."

She rubbed at her forehead. "I don't comprehend this."

Aricles pondered it for a moment. "Love obligates you because you want to take care of the person who holds your heart. Their happiness and well-being mean much more to you than your own. So yes, but it's not truly obligatory, because you don't really *have* to take care of them. It's your own desire that makes you feel such."

"Ah . . . that makes sense."

"And," he continued, "when they're gone from you, it's a harsh loss that haunts and saddens you. All you want is to see them smile. To watch joy light up their face, and to be with them."

Bathymaas nodded. "I think I understand now." It was how she felt about him. She didn't like to see him struck in practice, and when he bled, it caused pain to her chest. Like now . . . she was still concerned with the fact that he was bulging when she'd never known him to do that before.

And the thought of him hurting . . .

It, too, gave her a pain in her chest.

She lowered her gaze to his groin. "Why are you not bound today?"

The color returned to mottle his cheeks. It was so adorable and sweet that it somehow made her want to touch them and ease his embarrassment. "I was injured in practice and didn't want to risk reopening the wound with the binding."

She gasped. "Where were you hurt?"

"Across my hip."

Aricles caught her hand as she reached to see it. His breathing ragged, he stared at her with a pain-filled expression. "Please, goddess. I'm hard enough already. If you touch me there . . . it'll only be worse for me."

"My touch hurts you?"

He nodded.

"Then why do you spend time with me?"

He smiled at her as he let go of her wrist. "Because the pleasure of your company is worth the pain it causes me."

That made no sense to her whatsoever. "I cannot comprehend mortal emotions. How can any pleasure be worth pain?"

"It just is."

The fact that he was willing to suffer to be in her presence brought a strange sensation to her stomach. She wasn't sure what it was, but it compelled her to lift her hand and lightly brush her fingers against his lips again. "Will you kiss me, Aricles, so that I can see why people do it?"

He expelled a long breath and the light faded from his eyes. "I would love to, my lady. But I fear I've never kissed anyone like that. I'm sure I would bungle it."

"I wouldn't know if you did since I've never had a kiss either. And even though you might bungle it, I still think I'd like to see what the fuss is about. Are you not curious, Ari?"

Aricles felt his heart pound at her question. He was more than curious about how her lips would taste. But he was also a bit scared.

Who are you to question a goddess?

He was her servant and her warrior. . . .

Still unsure, he gently laid his hand against her cheek and stroked her lips with his thumb. "Are you certain you want me to do this?"

She nodded.

Ever so slowly, he lowered his lips to hers. The moment he tasted her, his entire body erupted with a heat so high that it made his past attractions to other women seem mild and insignificant. He shook all over as images of making love to Bathymaas tormented him. He would give anything to hold her like that, but he knew it could never be and he was lucky she'd allowed him this much.

Bathymaas wasn't sure what to expect, but as his tongue swept across hers and his scent filled her head, something inside her splintered. Her breathing intensified even more . . . as did his. She felt his heart pounding against her hand. Strong and powerful.

Like him.

He was so hard and fierce, except for his lips that were soft and gentle. And in spite of his inexperience, his kiss was wonderful and it did the oddest things to her body. Made her throb and ache.

Aricles's head spun at the taste of Bathymaas. In all his fantasies, he'd never dreamed a kiss could be so sweet. His body roared to life, making demands on him the likes of which he'd never felt before. It took every ounce of self-control he had to placate himself with just this tiny part of her.

Pulling back, he stared down at her beautiful face.

She opened her eyes and for the first time, he saw real emotion in those golden depths. Her eyes flared before she cupped his head in her hands and pulled him back for another sizzling kiss.

Bathymaas knew she should release him. It would be the smart thing to do, and yet . . .

She wanted to possess him in a way she couldn't comprehend. More than that, she wanted to push him back and straddle him. To run her hands all over his body, and she had no idea why. While she'd occasionally seen animals have sex, she'd never really thought about it. It was what they did to have offspring.

But right now, she wanted him inside her. It was as if her body starved for him the way her stomach craved food.

And she had no idea why.

Did he feel that, too?

Forcing herself to withdraw, she tried to steady her breathing as she looked up at him from beneath her lashes. "Is this emotion, Aricles?"

"It is for me, goddess."

"What do you feel?"

"Hunger, my lady. Possessiveness. Tenderness." Love. But he didn't dare say that out loud. He'd already made that mistake with a woman. "Most of all, protective and caring."

Bathymaas looked down at her arms and the strange bumps that always came to her whenever he was near. "What are these?"

"Chills."

She ran her hand over his biceps. "You have them, too. Do you also want to touch me?"

"I do, my lady."

"And yet you don't."

"I told you I wouldn't dishonor you. I would sooner die than cause you any harm."

Her vision clouded and her throat tightened as he spoke. She blinked several times, but instead of getting clearer, her vision worsened and something wet fell down her cheeks. "What is this? Am I going blind?"

With a tender expression, he lifted his hand and gently brushed his thumb against her face. "They're called tears."

"Why do I have them?"

He tenderly dried her cheeks. "Whenever something hurts inside you or something touches your heart they can manifest unexpectedly."

Frowning, she looked down and lifted the Egyptian amulet from between her breasts. "But my heart is here. Nothing has touched it."

Biting back a smile at her innocence, Aricles placed a single finger between her breasts. "No, my lady, your heart is in here." But as he spoke the words, he realized she didn't have a heartbeat. He scowled.

She held her amulet out to him. "I'm not like you, Ari. When I was a child, I discovered that those who are born to mothers have hearts and heartbeats and that I do not. I asked my father about it and he gave me this amulet and said that it contains his heart that he lost to me the moment I was created. He said it holds his love for me and that even though I'd never understand what love is, that so long as I wore my amulet, I'd have a piece of him with me to keep me safe in his absence. *This* is my heart." Her frown deepened at the happy expression that brightened his face. "Why do you smile like that?"

"Because you now have two hearts, my lady. Your father's and mine."

She still didn't understand what he meant. Placing her hand to his chest, she felt his heart beating. "Yours is like my father's. Strong."

"Even so, hearts are fragile and easily broken."

"How?"

"It doesn't take much. When you love someone, a single tear," he wiped away another of hers, "or frown can shatter a heart. And if something happens to the one you've given your heart to, their loss can break it into so many pieces that it never heals again."

Her jaw went slack. "Then it's a good thing you gave yours to me to keep. For I can never die or be harmed."

His smile widened. "I am lucky, indeed."

"And this physical side of love . . . is it important?"

"No. Love can endure without it."

"Are you sure?"

Aricles nodded as he brushed back a piece of hair from her face. He knew that they would never be physically intimate, and while a part of him craved that experience, he loved her enough to not ask for something he knew he couldn't have. Something he wasn't worthy of. But at the same time, the thought of not sharing these quiet afternoons alone with her, of not having her drill him with random odd and embarrassing questions, hurt more than he could bear. "I am."

Suddenly, she pulled her amulet off and placed it around his neck. The stone amulet was still warm from her body temperature. "What are you doing?"

She placed her hand over it. "You gave me your heart. It's only fair that I give you mine."

He smiled at her precious and innocent sweetness that touched him all the way to his soul. "It doesn't work like that, my lady. Love isn't about fairness. It's about emotion."

"You are about emotion. I'm about fairness." She patted her necklace. "This is fair. I don't need two hearts and you can't live without one. So I have yours and you have mine."

And he would never treasure anything more. He placed his hand over hers and reveled in the inner beauty that was his goddess. "Thank you, my lady."

Bathymaas inclined her head to him as she stared at their joined hands. For the first time, she was beginning to understand why people did the strange things they did.

Not for themselves, but for others.

As she'd told Ari, she couldn't be hurt or killed. But that wasn't true of him. And the more she thought about something happening to him, the more her chest tightened. The harder it was to breathe. Even without asking, she knew this was physical pain. Something she should be completely ignorant of.

Yet that was no longer true.

Somehow, they had exchanged hearts, and if anything ever happened to Ari . . .

She honestly feared what she might do. When her father had given her a heart, he'd never said what would happen should it break or shatter. All her life, she'd kept it safe. But now that Ari had it, she could no longer keep it from getting hurt.

Most of all, she couldn't keep *him* from harm.

"Be careful for me, Ari."

"Always, my goddess. You are the very air I breathe."

Warmth spread through her at those words. For some reason, they were important to her.

Just like him.

August 23, 12,251 BC

As soon as they dismounted in the small town nearest the cottage where they'd been born, Galen pulled Aricles to the side so that he could whisper while Bathymaas looked about at the people who called Didimosia home. "Why is the goddess with us?"

"She wanted to see a wedding."

Glancing back to where she waited with their horses, Galen grimaced. "She makes me nervous."

Aricles smiled at his brother. "Relax. She won't harm you." He clapped his hand against Galen's shoulder then returned to the woman he loved and adored.

Dressed in the finest white silk, she was beauty incarnate and looked extremely out of place in the mortal realm. For his brother's wedding, he and Galen were dressed in their best chitons and chlamyses. But compared to her, they looked like the rubes Galen accused them of being.

Her ethereal gaze swept his body, making him even harder than he'd been. "Ari . . . It is so strange to see you in clothing."

Aricles blushed as several people turned to stare at them with great curiosity.

Bathymaas frowned as she noted their reactions. "Did I say something inappropriate?"

"No, my lady. They thought something inappropriate."

To his shock, her cheeks darkened. "Is this embarrassment?" she whispered to him.

"Do you want to fall into a hole where no one can see you, and take back your words?"

She nodded vigorously.

"Then yes, my lady. That is embarrassment."

The most adorable scowl contorted her beautiful features. She leaned closer to whisper in his ear. "I don't like this emotion, Ari."

"Most people don't."

"How does one cope with it?"

"We keep our chins up and carry on with as much pride as we can manage." He took her hand and placed it in the crook of his elbow so that he could lead her toward the local gathering hall his father had rented out for Perseus's wedding feast.

Running ahead of them, Galen went in first, with his arms raised. "The party may commence! The most important person is now in attendance." He grabbed Walla, one of the girls they'd grown up with, and carried her to a corner where the wine was kept.

Bathymaas arched a brow at Aricles over Galen's words and actions. "Should I ask?"

"Mental defect from when I threw him out of our crib for stealing my rattle. We usually overlook it."

Bathymaas laughed then froze . . . as did Aricles. Eyes wide, she swallowed audibly. "I found that funny."

He smiled at her. "You have a most beautiful laugh."

And that made her smile.

Realizing what she'd done, she quickly squelched it. Panic gripped her and that, too, made her panic all the more. As Lilliana had done with Caleb, Aricles had changed her. Greatly. He was so unlike anyone she'd ever known. So sweet and gentle.

Kind.

And the more he explained emotions to her, the more she knew she felt them. Especially whenever he was around.

But she would have to be more careful lest someone else realize that she was no longer without emotion. As the goddess of justice, she should never have experienced them. Ever. How could she be impartial or just with emotions clouding her judgment?

And yet, she liked what Aricles made her feel.

All of it.

Steeling her expressions, she allowed him to lead her to his father and introduce them. A much older and thinner version of the twins, he wasn't quite as tall, but still she could tell where Aricles and Galen had inherited their good looks.

He offered her a kind smile. "So you're the goddess who stole my boys from me. I can see now why they didn't hesitate to follow you." He gave her a quick wink. "Were I a hundred years younger, I'd have gladly followed you, too."

She inclined her head to him. "Thank you, Master Praxis."

"You made it!"

She turned at the happy male voice to see a shorter, younger version of Aricles and Galen. All the men in their family seemed to be virtual copies of each other. Same rabidly blue eyes and reddish-brown hair . . .

Same handsome smiles.

Aricles hugged his younger brother then introduced them.

Perseus bowed proudly. "My wife and I are honored by your attendance, goddess. Thank you for allowing my brothers to come. I can't tell you how much I appreciate it."

She glanced to Aricles, who was more like a father to Perseus than Praxis was. "I don't think I could have kept them away . . . even with my powers. They are terribly devoted to you and your father."

Blushing, Perseus ran back to his petite blond bride, who was as obviously in love with him as he was with her. Bathymaas watched as they embraced and he kissed her with the same amount of passion she'd felt when she kissed Aricles.

Suddenly breathless, she glanced at Ari and felt the peculiar wave of heat surge through her body that always hit her whenever she looked his way. In her mind, she imagined being the bride and Aricles running up to her with the same exuberance.

"Are you all right, my goddess?"

The concern in his voice made her weak in the knees. "I'm fine, Ari."

He handed her a kylix of watered-down wine.

While Aricles spoke to his father, she wandered about the room, listening to people and watching how they acted and interacted. People had always fascinated her. They were so incongruous and unpredictable.

So very odd.

The music was lovely, and those who danced did so with carefree, happy abandon. It was only then that she realized Aricles never partook of such frivolous behavior. Unlike Galen, who hoisted a woman over his shoulder and twirled about with her while drinking from a silver kylix, Aricles was forever rigid and dignified. Controlled.

Circumspect.

He'd told her that it stemmed from the year his mother had died, when he was eight. Perseus had been just a toddler, and their father had been so distraught that he'd been unable to function without his wife. For two months straight, his father had lain in bed with drink, rising only to attend the most basic of bodily functions. All the upkeep for their farm, servants, and family had fallen to Ari's young shoulders. His father had given him no chance to grieve himself for his mother while he took care of his brothers, but rather had thrown him into adulthood far too soon. And then when his grandfather had taken ill two years later, he'd been sent to care for him and his farm until his grandfather had died.

Barely twelve years old, Aricles had been alone with his grandfather when the man had taken his last breath. And all the funeral preparations had fallen to him, too.

It wasn't until now that she fully understood what the loss of his childhood had meant for him. Other men his age were laughing and groping at the women around them. Dancing and singing with unfettered joy. They leaned up against others without thought or concern.

Like Galen.

Meanwhile, Ari stood sober and somber.

Except for when they were alone. Then he could be giddy and sweet. His eyes would light up with life and he'd jest with her as he helped her to understand humor and human ways.

As if sensing her saddened mood, Aricles started for her then was diverted by a small girl who was trying to reach for bread on the table. With a kind smile, he picked her up and helped her to get it then returned her to her feet.

The girl's mother joined them and thanked him before she led her daughter away. Bathymaas stared at the woman's distended belly. It was obvious she was about to have another child, maybe even tonight. She'd never paid attention to pregnant women before.

Now . . .

She placed her hand on her flat stomach and tried to conceive what it would feel like to have a baby growing there. Biting her lip, she met Ari's gaze and a strange chill ran over her as she imagined what his baby might look like. Surely it would be as beautiful as its father.

"Are you all right, goddess?"

She frowned at his question. "Why do you never call me by name, Ari?"

Clearing his throat, he glanced away. "It's not my place to use it."

But she suspected there was more to it than that. It was as if he used her title to remind himself that he wasn't divinely born. And while he might not have the genetics, he certainly had the character.

Not to mention the immortal heart she'd given him.

"I should like to hear it from your lips. Just once. Would you humor me?"

There was no missing the devotion in those beautiful blue eyes as he looked down at her. "I will always humor you . . . Bathymaas."

She savored the richness of his accent as he finally spoke her name. "Do you ever dance, Aricles?"

He laughed nervously. "I tried it once and quickly learned, as you mentioned earlier, that embarrassment is a highly unpleasant emotion."

She so loved how he explained things. "I don't suppose you'd want to try it again. . . ."

"For your pleasure alone, my goddess, I would gladly make a fool of myself."

He set her cup aside and offered his hand to her. Without hesitation, she took it and allowed him to pull her to the floor with the others. As they danced, she saw no reason for him to be embarrassed. Indeed, he was quite adept at this. But more than that, every time she felt his arms around her and his hard muscles flexing, she became even weaker in the knees.

Aricles forgot about everyone else in the room as he watched the happy glint in Bathymaas's eyes and the smile that played at the edges of her lips. For a woman who'd never danced before, she was more than accomplished.

Because she's a goddess.

It scared him how easily he forgot that whenever he was with her. He'd long ago ceased seeing her as anything other than his heart.

Even now, all he wanted to do was pull her close and hold her like he did whenever they met at the stream to fish. And when she stepped into his arms and placed her head against his shoulder, he melted. Closing his eyes, he inhaled her precious scent and wished they could be like this forever.

All too soon, the song ended and he was forced to release her from his embrace.

He opened his eyes and caught Galen's glower of consternation, which he knew he deserved. He had no right to lust after a goddess. No right to be so familiar with the one they served.

Yet his brain was as deaf as his heart. Neither listened to common sense. His entire body betrayed him with wants, needs, and dreams he knew he shouldn't feel.

Bathymaas stood up on her tiptoes and placed a chaste kiss to his cheek. "Thank you for humoring me."

He inclined his head to her and did his best to ignore his brother as Galen continued to glare at him.

Hours later, after they'd returned to their island barracks, Galen cornered him in the back hallway.

"What is going on with you and the goddess?"

Aricles kept his tone level and his expression blank. "I don't know what you mean."

"Yes, you do. You *love* her."

"Of course, I do. I love all the gods."

"Yes, but not like you do her. I'm not stupid, Ari. And I know what I saw."

He shrugged Galen's anger away. "I am nothing more than her soldier. The same as you and the others."

"And if I don't believe you?"

"You're a fool."

Galen cursed him under his breath. "Fine, but if I'm right, brother, be careful. Love never works out between mortals and gods. If something were to happen to you . . ." Tears welled in his eyes before he quickly blinked them away. "I'd have to grow up and that's the last thing I want to do."

Smiling, Aricles hugged him close then kissed his head. "Fear not, little brother. I shall be here for quite some time to annoy you."

"You better be. Otherwise, I'll have to follow you to Kalosis and beat the shit out of you."

February 8, 12,250 BC

Tomorrow Bathymaas would have to send her Ēperon out to battle. The Greek gods had been overstepping their bounds for weeks now, and their forces would have to be quelled. This was what her team had been trained for.

Yet . . .

Over and over, she tried to think of some reason to keep Aricles out of the fight.

Unfortunately, there wasn't a logical one.

She shouldn't care. She shouldn't. It wasn't her place to have feelings for anyone. But as she contemplated the thought of his being injured, she couldn't breathe for the ferocious pain inside her. No wonder he'd told her he could do without love.

It *was* agony.

And it was something she couldn't tell anyone that she felt.

Not even Aricles.

To do so would only cause him to be harmed. She was never to know emotion and yet he'd managed to make her feel when nothing and no one else ever had.

Her gaze went to Malphas who was formulating their battlefield strategy over a map table. He'd lost his love a long time ago. There was a permanent darkness in his eyes from it and she'd seen him break down into tears from time to time when he thought he was alone . . . all the times when he'd reach for the locket he wore that contained a bit of hair from his love.

She'd never understood that until now.

"Perhaps we should let the Greeks fight this out for themselves."

Malphas looked up at her with a stern frown. "Who *are* you?"

"Bathymaas."

He laughed. "There's the goddess I know. The one a second ago . . . never met her before."

Ah, now she understood why he'd asked that question.

Sighing, she closed the distance between them so that she could look over his plans. "Are you sure they're ready?"

"I wouldn't send them into battle if I wasn't. They've learned to be a team and have bonded well. They no longer see themselves as humans, Apollites, and Atlanteans, but rather your Ēperon. You have their loyalty over their homelands."

Still, she couldn't bear the thought of someone striking Aricles. Of them bruising his flawless body.

But she had no choice. She had to send him out and appear to all that she couldn't care less.

How she was going to do that, she had no idea.

Please, Ari . . . don't get hurt.

And yet she had an awful sense of foreboding that said the fight would not go well for any of them.

February 9, 12,250 BC

Standing on the edge of a cliff so that she could watch the fight, Bathymaas chewed her thumbnail as her men battled a Greek phalanx. Malphas was at the head of them, but it was Aricles who held her attention. True to Malphas's words, her entire team was incredible. Yet it was obvious which of them was the strongest and most skilled.

Not even Malphas with his demon powers could equal Aricles's abilities. He fought as if he heard his enemy's thoughts. As if he knew every move they'd make before they did.

With little effort, her men broke through the shield wall and had the Greeks on the defensive.

Still, it was hours before they finally emerged victorious.

Breathing with relief, she headed down for them as the air stirred around her. She turned to find the Greek god Apollo behind her. Dressed in full armor, he glared his furious displeasure.

"So it's true. You *are* replacing the Chthonians." His tone was accusatory.

She made sure there was no such emotion in her response. "Not permanently. But yes, until they stop their war, my team will fill in for them, to make sure the mortal races are safe from those who would harm or subjugate them."

From heartless gods like you . . .

He growled low in the back of his throat. "I am not happy, Bathymaas. My mother is even less so."

Bathymaas had to stop herself from curling her lip at the mention of Leto. She was a selfish bitch who'd always coveted Bathymaas's powers. But more than that, Leto wanted revenge on her. When the Greek goddess had been pregnant with Apollo and Artemis by Zeus, and his wife Hera had been out for her blood over it, Leto had demanded Bathymaas do something to Hera as punishment.

Unfortunately for Leto, justice was on the side of Hera, the wife who'd been wronged. Leto had no business seducing Zeus. It wasn't like she hadn't been forewarned. Everyone knew of Hera's jealous paybacks against those who trespassed on her husband's groin.

Furious, Leto had promised her that one day she would get even with Bathymaas for not helping her with Hera. But that day wasn't today.

"I cannot help your feelings or your mother's, Apollo. Justice is met."

Apollo vanished then reappeared at her back. Wrapping an arm around her waist, he pulled her up against him so that he could whisper in her ear. "Are you really as frigid as you appear?" He splayed his hand against her stomach and rubbed himself against her so that she could feel his bulge. But unlike Ari's, his left her cold and repulsed. "I'm an accomplished lover, Bathymaas. And with you, I'd be on my very best behavior. I promise, you wouldn't be emotionless in my bed."

She shrugged herself out of his embrace and turned to face him. "You know better. I have no interest in you, Apollo." He did this whenever they were together.

And she hated it.

He glared at her. "You owe me *something* for tearing my men apart today."

"I'm allowing you to live. Is that not enough?"

A furious tic worked in his jaw. "One day, Bathymaas . . . I *will* have you."

Over her dead body. But she didn't dare say that out loud. "Should I summon my father?"

Apollo left her instantly.

Relieved beyond belief, she flashed herself to her men's camp. She'd expected them to be celebrating. Instead, it was so quiet, she heard the light breeze whispering around her.

Where were they?

Curious, she headed to Malphas's tent. But what she found there made the breath leave her chest and her panic rise. Aricles lay on Malphas's cot with four arrows embedded deeply in his chest.

It took everything she had not to scream and run to him. "What happened?" she asked with a calmness she definitely didn't feel.

"Apollo . . . god of archery," Malphas snarled. "The battle was over when that bastard appeared in front of us and said this was his reward for our best fighter. Before we.even realized he was armed, he shot four arrows into Aricles and vanished."

Her blood boiled as she ached to feel Apollo's heart in her fist. How dare he!

But her vengeance could wait. Aricles was all that mattered. He lay with his eyes half open as he panted in pain.

She closed the distance between them and took his hand into hers. "Aricles?"

Smiling in spite of his obvious agony, he met her gaze. "Sorry I failed you, goddess."

Her throat tightened as he made reference to his promise not get hurt during battle. Technically, he'd kept it.

No one said anything about after it was over.

"You didn't fail me." Knowing she was about to lose her fight to hold back her tears and emotions, she glanced around at her men. "I need all of you to leave us."

Bowing, they obeyed.

Except for Galen. His blue eyes swam with tears. "Will he live?" His voice broke on the words.

"I promise you. Now go and let me heal him."

Nodding, he quickly made his exit.

Alone with Aricles, she sank to her knees as tears fell from her eyes. Her hands trembling, she went to pull the arrows out, but he stopped her.

"You can't, my lady. Their tips are barbed and you'll only harm me more. They have to be pushed all the way through my body to be extracted."

She sobbed aloud at the thought. "I will kill that bastard for this!" she snarled.

He cupped her cheek in his hand and smiled. "You're showing emotion, my goddess."

She covered his hand with hers as she struggled to stop her tears. But it was a lost cause. She wasn't the warrior he was. "There has to be another way to take them out and not hurt you." Closing her eyes, she summoned her aunt Menyara to her.

Petite and gorgeous, with caramel skin and black hair, her aunt was also the Egyptian goddess Ma'at . . . another goddess of justice.

And one of healing.

Best of all, Menyara was the only person, besides her father, Bathymaas trusted.

Menyara gasped as soon as she saw her tears. "Child, what has happened to you?"

Sobbing, she gestured toward Aricles. "Please heal him, Aunt Mennie. Please."

Her eyes widening, Menyara nodded without hesitation. She

placed her hand to Aricles's chest and then on the arrow that had narrowly missed his heart. "Take a deep breath."

Kneeling beside him, Bathymaas held his hand as he braced himself.

Aricles nodded to let the new goddess know he was ready.

She dissolved the arrow, but her actions burned him inside and out.

Aricles choked on the misery of it all. Agony made his vision turn dull as his heart pounded even more pain through his body.

Bathymaas bent her head down and pressed her cheek to his while she placed her left hand on the other side of his face. Closing his eyes, he let her scent and warmth ease him.

Until her aunt dissolved the next one.

He roared with the force of it.

Bathymaas tightened her hold on him. "Breathe, love. Just breathe."

Love . . .

She'd never used that word with him before. Smiling in spite of his agony, he placed his left hand over hers.

By the time the last arrow was dissolved, he was barely conscious from the agony of it all. Still Bathymaas held him as her tears fell against his skin.

Panting and weak, he met the gaze of her aunt, who appeared less than pleased by their relationship.

"He needs to rest easy tonight, May," she said to Bathymaas. "By morning, he'll be sore, but functional."

Bathymaas squeezed his hand before she stood up. Still, she held on to it. "Thank you, Mennie."

Her aunt wiped at the tears on her face. "Oh, girl . . ." She pressed her lips together and shook her head. "Do not tell your father about this . . . or anyone else. Ever."

"I know."

Menyara placed her hand on Aricles's shoulder. "If you had any other heart, boy, I'd see you dead for what you've done to my baby." She cupped their entwined hands in hers. "You both have my blessings for this fiasco, and I will never breathe a word to anyone about you. But be careful. This secret could destroy you both." She kissed Bathymaas's cheek then vanished.

Before she could stop herself, Bathymaas lay down by his side and held him to her. "You are not allowed to be hurt again, Ari. Do you understand?"

He smiled at her stern command. "I shall try."

"No, you will succeed." She brushed her hand over his now scarred chest. "I am going to create armor the likes of which no one has seen to protect you when you fight. None of this bare skin showing anymore. It leaves you too vulnerable."

"But this is how our people fight."

"It's stupid."

"All war is, my goddess."

He was right about that, and she hated that she'd ever conceived this idea. Yet if she hadn't, she'd have never met him. Never known his warmth and heart.

Out of mud comes the bloom. And he was *her* bloom.

Rising up, she placed a tender kiss to his lips. "Get better for me, Ari."

He brushed the hair back from her face and offered her another smile through his pain. "I will. I promise."

And he never intentionally broke his promises. Rubbing her nose playfully against his, she gave him a quick kiss then reluctantly withdrew from him so that he could rest and heal. She covered him with the blanket.

When she started away, he caught her wrist in a gentle grip. "I love you, Bathymaas."

More tears filled her eyes at his tender words. "I love you, too, Ari."

And yet they dare not show it. Not to a soul. The injustice of that made her want to scream. It wasn't fair that they had to keep this a secret when others got to shout their joy from the highest mountaintops.

She lifted his hand to her lips and kissed his scarred knuckles. And as she did so, she felt a peculiar stirring.

Eyes wide, she gaped at him.

"What, my lady?"

Unable to believe it, she pressed her hand to her chest and felt . . .

Her heart.

It was beating!

Biting her lip, she took his hand and pressed it between her breasts. "Do you feel it?"

He was every bit as aghast as she was. "You have a heart."

"No," she said breathlessly. "It's not mine. You gave me yours. It's your heart that beats inside me, Ari."

Aricles was stunned as he felt the warmth of her skin and the strong beat beneath his fingertips. And while he rejoiced, he was also terrified over it.

What had they done?

It couldn't be a good thing to change a goddess.

Ever.

Suddenly, a knock sounded against the tent post.

Bathymaas jumped away from him at the same time Malphas spoke. "May we enter, my goddess? I have a nervous old woman out here who is about to wet himself with worry that his brother is dead."

She wiped her face and drew a ragged breath before she fell into her emotionless role. "Come in."

Galen ran to the bed and pulled the blanket back so that he could inspect his brother's chest. All that was left there were four scars from where Menyara had sealed the wounds closed. "How is this possible?"

Bathymaas cleared her throat. "I summoned my aunt for him. He must rest tonight, but will be better by morning."

Aricles grunted as Galen hugged him with a crushing hold. "By morning, dullard," he choked out. "Tonight, I still feel like I've been shot by four arrows."

Laughing, Galen released him. "Remember your promise to me, brother. You are not to make me a responsible adult yet."

Aricles snorted. "Go and drink yourself stupid. Celebrate with the others and I'll see you in the morning."

"But not too early." Galen winked at him before he rose and kissed his cheek. "Sleep well."

"And you . . . make sure you sleep at some point before morning."

Caleb let out an irritable sigh. "Guess I'll be bunking with the others tonight. Don't get used to this, Aricles. I don't give up my bed or tent easily." Malphas bowed to her then followed after Galen. "Save some wine for me, you gluttonous bastard!"

Bathymaas moved to ask Aricles if she could get something for him, but he was already asleep. Relieved, she ran her finger down the line of his perfectly sculpted jaw and savored the sensation of his whiskers tugging at her skin.

She'd known him for almost two years now. In some ways it seemed like they'd just met, and in others, it was as if she'd known him forever. She picked up her amulet and stared at the stone heart her father had given her. This trinket was no longer the warmth inside her body. Her heart now belonged with Aricles. He was what sustained her and she would be lost without his quiet, gentle nature.

Even though she should be horrified by what he'd done to her, she wasn't. Instead, she climbed back into bed to lie beside him so that she could hold him while he slept. But as she closed her eyes, she couldn't help the fear that stalked her. He was mortal. She was not. What hope could their love possibly have? Was there any way for this to end, other than very badly for them both?

April 4, 12,250 BC

"Run away with me, Ari."

Aricles tightened his arms around Bathymaas as they fished in their spot. "I can't, my love. And neither can you. We have too many responsibilities for that."

"I don't care, anymore. Injustice will continue. It's the nature of mortals. No matter what I do, they still hurt each other. Ergo, I cede and give up this useless fight. All I want now is to be with you."

Closing his eyes, he inhaled her sweet lily scent, wishing that he could forget everything and leave with her. But he couldn't. And neither could she. If they did, he had no doubt that in time, she'd learn to hate him for changing her. "We must do what we can to help others."

She sighed heavily. "And that's why I love you, even though I hate you." She kissed his cheek.

He smiled at her contradictory words. That was the only downfall to her emotions. They were now mercurial at times.

Bathymaas stroked the arm he had across her stomach as she felt his erection against her back. He no longer bound himself, but neither did he ever make a move to touch her more intimately than a kiss. "Ari? Do you ever think about having children?"

"I used to."

"And now?"

"I will never love anyone but you, my goddess. So I no longer think about it."

He was willing to die virgin rather than dishonor her. It was one of many reasons why she loved him. He'd already made the vow publicly that he would hold himself chaste in her honor.

But such a precious heart didn't deserve to suffer.

"Would you make love to me if I asked it of you, Ari?" She felt his cock jerk at her question.

"Bathia," he chided gently, "you know better."

Bathia was an Atlantean endearment for her name that he only used when she tugged at his heart. Most of the time, he still referred to her as "goddess" or "my lady"—so as to remind himself that she was born of the Source and not mortal like him. It was why she treasured any time he used her name.

"But I want to know what it's like to be with you fully. To have you inside me. And I can think of no better gift than to carry your child for you. My own little Aricles."

Aricles clenched his teeth as he savored those words. They meant more to him than any others. Yet . . .

"You are to remain virginal. You know that. Who am I to defile a goddess so pure?"

"You're the man I love above all others. Even myself."

"Bath—"

She placed her fingers over his lips to keep him from protesting. "Tell me you haven't thought about it. Honestly."

A smile quirked at the edges of his lips. "Every waking moment, as you have felt whenever you lean against me. I can't get near the scent of a lily without growing hard."

She took his hand into hers and led it to her breast. "Then ease your pain with me."

His heart pounded at the sensation of her breast against his palm. There was nothing more in the world he wanted than to taste her taut peak, but . . .

"I am nothing but a weak mortal, Bathia. You are a goddess. I have no right to touch or claim any part of you."

She turned around in his arms to kneel in front of him. "Have I the right to touch you?"

"I am ever your servant, my lady. Of course." He spoke without thinking. And he was completely unprepared when she lifted his chiton so that she could cup his erection in her delicate hand. His breath rushed out as her fingers gently stroked and teased him. "Bathia . . ."

"Shh," she whispered against his lips while she caressed his body. After a second, she pulled back with a light squeak. "Did I break you?"

He frowned at her alarm. "What makes you think that?"

She held her hand up to show him. "Why do you leak so?"

His frown melted into a smile. "I don't know. It just does that sometimes."

Frowning, she studied her hand. "Is it the same as when I grow moist between my legs whenever you're near?"

Aricles gaped at her question. For a full minute, he couldn't think of how to respond. She was so unabashed about taboo subjects that it often caught him off guard. "I-I suppose it is."

She brushed his chiton aside so that she could stare at his erection. "Your body is so different from mine. Are all men like you?"

"I would assume, but I don't make it a habit of being with naked men, especially when they're aroused."

She smiled at that then lifted her hand so that she could taste what she'd milked from him. The sight of her doing that made his mouth go dry. She had no idea how difficult it was to be with her open innocence. For all the centuries she'd lived, she knew so little about mortals and even less about the relationships of men and women.

"It's very salty."

"I wouldn't know."

She dropped her hand to him again to stroke the length of his cock. He gasped as unmitigated pleasure ripped through him.

"You do like it when I do this to you, don't you?"

More than she would ever know. "Goddess . . . please . . . you're torturing me."

"Then make love to me, Ari." She unpinned her peplos and let it fall open, baring herself completely to his hungry gaze.

He couldn't breathe at the sight of her perfect naked body. Of her full, lush breasts and the dark hair at the juncture of her thighs.

Before he could stop her, she placed his hand back on her bare breast. The sight of his tanned skin against hers and the feel of her taut nipple against his palm . . .

He was undone.

Rising to his own knees, he kissed her deeply while she cupped him again in her hand. He reached down between their bodies to hold her hand to his cock while he rocked himself against the sweet pressure she provided.

Bathymaas smiled at the pleasure she saw on his face. And when he moved his hand from hers to touch her where she physically ached, she gasped at the most exquisite bliss she'd ever felt.

"You're so wet," he breathed against her ear.

"I told you, I'm always that way whenever you're near, but I'm not sure why."

He gently laid her back against the ground with one arm pressed against her spine. The strength of him never ceased to amaze her. He was so ferocious and at the same time gentle.

The dark hunger in his eyes as he stared down at her set her on fire. His hand continued to stroke and delve deep inside her, making her even more breathless as he teased her skin with his tongue.

Then, slowly, methodically, he kissed and nibbled his way to her ear and throat then her breasts. Her entire body felt electrified by his touch. And when he replaced his hand with his mouth, she cried out in total ecstasy.

Aricles could barely catch his breath as his heart pounded furiously in his chest. Never in all his life had he tasted anything sweeter than her body. She sank her hands into his hair, pressing him closer to her while he slowly pleasured her. Over the years, he'd tried to imagine what it would feel like to have a woman, but none of those fantasies could compare to this reality. And it wasn't just because she was a goddess. It was because he loved her with every part of his being.

There was nothing he enjoyed more than sitting quietly with her, answering her myriad of questions. Even when they were embarrassing and horrifying. She was the only person he'd ever truly enjoyed conversing with. The only one he could sit with for hours and not become bored or irritated.

All of a sudden, her grip tightened in his hair. She threw her head back and cried out as her entire body shook. Closing his eyes and smiling, he savored her even more.

When she finally stopped, she looked down at him. "What did you do to me?"

"It's called an orgasm, my lady."

Still breathing heavily, she frowned. "Have you ever had one?"

"No. I've only heard my brother and other men speak of them."

"You need to have one. They're rather remarkable."

Laughing, he nibbled his way back up her body to kiss her then he moved away to retrieve her peplos for her.

She scowled at him. "What are you doing?"

"I'm withdrawing while your maidenhead is still intact."

She sat up to pull him closer to her. "My Ari never withdraws from anything."

He cupped her precious face in his hand as he tried to make her understand why he retreated now. "I don't want to cause you any harm."

"How can loving me cause me harm?"

Still, he had no right to do this. "You deserve better than a backwoods farm boy, my goddess."

"My Phoenix is a hero and a champion, and while in his heart he's a farmer, he is not backwoods. And I will not have you insult him."

He grinned at her words. She always chided him whenever he insulted himself, and then used the battle name the others had dubbed him to remind him that he was more than what he felt in his heart. He didn't know what it was about her, but she could always make him feel like a king with nothing more than a single glance or a few words.

Leaning back, she pulled him with her. "Now come inside, my lord, and find your pleasure."

And when she bent her knees and spread her legs for him, he no longer had the ability to deny her request. Cursing himself for his own weakness, he laid his body over hers then gently slid inside.

Bathymaas gasped at the thick fullness of Aricles filling her body. For several heartbeats, neither moved as they stared at each other. She smiled up at him. "I love you, Ari."

The intensity of those blue eyes scorched her. "I love you, too. With every part of me." Slow and easy, he began to rock himself against her hips.

Gasping, she moaned at how good he felt. He dipped down to give her a kiss that stole her breath.

She savored the warmth of his body in and around hers as she brushed her hand against the sharp, hard ridges of his abdomen. He was all strength and power.

And best of all, he was hers.

He'd never touched another woman like this. Never shared this part of himself with anyone else. It made her love him all the more.

Suddenly, he quickened his strokes and ground his teeth. An instant later, he growled and shuddered against her.

Her smile widened. "See, I told you."

He laughed quietly. "And you were very right. It was amazing. I finally understand why my brother is so fascinated by women." His breathing ragged, he lifted himself up on his arms to stare down at her while they were still joined. "I love you, my goddess, and I swear to you that I will *never* willingly touch any woman save you."

She cupped his face in her hands. "You've made me whole."

Aricles held his breath as raw panic filled him. He was thrilled that she was happy, but deep inside he couldn't stop thinking that this wasn't right and that somehow the gods would punish them both for daring to love each other.

June 2, 12,249 BC

Bathymaas withheld her smile as she listened to the crowd cheering for her beloved Ēperon as they rode through the gates of Corinth while she stood on a palace balcony. They were resplendent in the gleaming bronze body armor she'd created for them. When they held their shields and stood side by side, it covered every inch of them and kept them safe.

Over the last year, they had earned a name for themselves in battle that guaranteed all seven of them would go down in the annals of history as some of the greatest champions who ever lived.

They had more than proven themselves worthy successors to the Chthonians who continued to war against one another. Most of the pantheons had now learned to behave, but still the Greeks warred on with reckless abandon and disregard. It infuriated her that Apollo, Ares, Zeus, Poseidon, and Leto couldn't stop preying on the humans.

Or worse, they would raid the Atlanteans as if they wanted war between the two pantheons so that there would be countless mortal lives lost.

It was something she couldn't allow.

So she kept her vigil over her men as they returned from battle. Ever since Apollo's vicious attack on Aricles, she knew to watch for more treachery from him.

And speaking of, she felt Apollo's presence behind her.

"Well, well . . . I was hoping you'd come."

Turning away from the procession below, she faced the young Greek god. "Why do you continue to tip the scales of justice?"

"Don't you know?"

"Not at all."

He reached out to touch her face. "It's to get your attention."

She scowled at him. "I beg your pardon?"

"Don't beg. It's unbecoming of a goddess so beautiful." He put his hands on each side of her waist and pulled her against him. "Is it really true you have no feelings?"

She pushed against him, but couldn't loosen his grip. Stamping down her irritation, she knew better than to show it. "It is."

"So if we were to have sex, you would be ambivalent to it?"

"I would assume."

"Should we test it and see?"

She blasted him away from her. "No. We shall not."

Apollo caught himself against the wall and glared furiously. "You shouldn't deny me, Bathymaas. I don't take rejection well."

"You should learn."

That only angered him more. He flashed himself to stand in front of her then backhanded her so hard, she fell to the floor. Blood suffused her mouth as a most foul pain exploded through her head, stunning her. She'd never dreamed how much a blow hurt, and it gave her an all new respect for her Ēperon and what they went through in battle.

"Did you feel *that*?" Apollo growled as he seized her again. He reached for the top of her gown.

Suddenly, he went flying past her as an enraged bellow sounded.

A blur followed after him and slammed him into the wall. It took her several seconds before she realized it was Aricles beating on the god.

"Aricles!" she breathed, rushing toward him before Apollo recovered enough to return the attack.

As soon as she touched his arm, he stopped pounding on Apollo and stepped back. "Are you all right, my goddess?"

She cupped his cheek and nodded then she turned to face Apollo.

He pushed himself up from the floor, glaring at them. "I demand retribution for his hubris."

She bit back her furious disbelief. "Hubris? How so?"

"He attacked a god."

"To protect a god. His actions were justified and you should be grateful I don't unleash him on you for what you dared. You know better."

Apollo spat the blood in his mouth onto the ground, where it made a bright red splatter. "I will have my revenge on him for this."

"Touch him and I will have your heart in my fist. Now get out of here while you're able."

Aricles didn't dare move for fear of what he'd do to Apollo until the god was gone. But as soon as they were alone, he cupped Bathymaas's cheek in his hand to study the bruise that was forming on her delicate skin. "You should have allowed me to kill him."

"And risk his mother or father calling out for your head? Never."

He pulled her gently against him and held her in the safety of his arms. "I should have been here for you."

"You were."

A tic worked furiously in his jaw. "What if he attacks you again?"

"I will be careful."

"Bathia . . ."

She kissed him lightly to silence his protest. "Nothing's going to happen to me. You're the one I worry over. How did you know I needed you?"

"I don't know. I had a bad feeling and I couldn't breathe until I got here."

Rising up on her tiptoes, she hugged him close. "I'm glad you came to investigate it."

A*pollo cursed as* he saw his face in the mirror. That human bastard had ravaged his beauty. Fury made his hand tremble as he washed the blood from his lips, nose, and cheek.

"What happened to you?"

He met his mother's shocked gaze in the mirror. Like him, she had golden-blond hair, but her eyes were the same color green as his twin sister, Artemis. "One of Bathymaas's Ēperon attacked me."

"On the battlefield?"

"No. I was just teasing her and the bastard started pounding on me."

His mother gaped. "Did she not punish him for it?"

"Of course not. They're her pets."

Leto lifted her chin as fury darkened her eyes. "And you are *my* son. How dare a mortal lay hand to you!" She closed the distance between them to gently inspect his face. "I will take this up with her immediately."

"She won't listen. I already demanded restitution and she said it was justified."

Leto curled her lip. "She's no business being the final say on our kind. She's too capricious with her laws of fairness. I'm still seething over how you and Artemis were forced to be born, and the curse Hera gave you both with no repercussions. No matter what that bitch says, it was *not* justified."

"Believe me, *Matisera*, I know. I should rip the throat out of her Ēperon guard with my fangs and let her see for herself how fair that curse is."

"I would agree, but she'd only kill you for it and claim that as justice, too. No . . . we need something to take to the other gods. Something that shows she's not impartial."

"Like what?"

Leto let out a heavy sigh. "We have to catch her breaking the rules."

"And how do we do that?"

"We follow her, dear boy. Sooner or later, she's bound to screw up something."

October 22, 12,249 BC

"Is it just me or does it seem like the gods have a vendetta against us?"

Aricles looked up from his carving to meet Hector's gaze. "They want us dead."

"Ah, good. I'm not the only one who's noticed. And here I thought it was just me."

Grimacing, Galen moved to sit on the foot of Aricles's bed. "It is disconcerting, isn't it? And battle isn't all I thought it'd be."

Aricles arched his brow at his brother's somber tone. "Is that remorse I hear?"

"It's remorse. I keep going back to that day on the farm when they came to recruit us. Do you remember what you said to me while we packed?"

"Not to forget your cloak?"

Galen laughed and shook his head. "You told me that battle wouldn't be the same as the war games I'd played. That the day would come when I'd grow tired of walking through blood-saturated fields."

"And has that day come, brother?"

He nodded. "I never gave thought to how young some soldiers would be. Or how wroth the gods would become with us."

Hector let out a heavy sigh. "I think we are all feeling that. I swear one of the soldiers I killed today couldn't have been any older than fifteen . . . if that."

Haides moved to sit on Galen's bed next to them. "It'll soon be four years since I was last at home. My sister has married and had two children since I left. . . . I miss my family."

Galen sat back. "Our brother had a baby . . . a son almost a year ago and we've seen nothing of him. And for some reason, I keep thinking of Talia." He met Aricles's gaze. "Do you remember her?"

"She was beautiful and thought you hung the very moon in the sky."

Galen smiled sadly. "Aye, she did. But she was too circumspect for me. I always thought she'd be a better match for you."

Aricles bit back the reminder that Galen's other problem with her was that she'd refused to bed him. "And now?"

"I should like a wife with such morals and convictions, and sweet nature. One I can trust to remain faithful to me should I ever be away. Do you think she might still be available?"

"I know not, little brother."

Haides jerked his chin toward Phelix who was asleep on his bed across the room. "Ever notice even he has stopped sharpening his sword?"

Monokles nodded as he joined them. "I keep thinking of something my father used to say to me—Fight on, my son. Not only with sword and spear, but with everything you have." Sighing, he shook his head. "But now, it's the words of an Athenian priestess that haunt me—you should reach the limits of virtue before you take up your sword and cross the border of death."

"We're all homesick." Aricles glanced at each one in turn. "But we have taken a vow to fight for our goddess and for the people of our homelands. As the old saying goes, only the dead have seen the end of war. We cannot forget that well begun is only half done. People have learned to watch for our red cloaks and black armor. They turn to us for protection now. How can we abandon them?"

Galen sighed wearily. "Interesting words considering the fact that you're the only one of us who didn't want to be here."

Aricles paused his carving. "I still have no desire to make war. But I am not a coward and I won't have the gods or anyone else making that allegation toward me."

"He's right," Haides agreed. "They would mock us if we withdrew."

Aricles offered them a sad smile. "I think we could all use a furlough. I'll talk to Malphas and the goddess to see if we can have a week to ourselves so that we can see our families and make peace in our hearts."

Monokles clapped him on the shoulder. "You're always looking after us. Thank you, brother."

Aricles inclined his head to them. "Anything for you, you know that." He set his carving aside and left their barracks to head to the small temple they'd erected for their goddess. Every time they came home from battle, they'd leave an offering to her for her favor and honor. Not that it was needed. She always watched over them.

And while she seldom stayed in the temple, she would come any time Aricles called for her.

"Bathia?" he said gently.

She appeared instantly with a bright smile before she pulled him against her. "I hadn't realized you'd returned from battle."

For fear of betraying themselves, they tried not to be together too much during war and training. She was finding it harder and harder to not react whenever he was injured, and his fear for her safety was extremely distracting while he had people trying to kill him.

"We came in this morning." He kissed her lightly on the lips and savored the taste and scent of her. "I've missed you."

"And I, you." Closing her eyes, she sank her hand in his hair and took a deep breath against his neck that left him covered with chills.

He wanted inside her so badly, his body felt as if it were on fire. But this was neither the time nor the place. "May I ask a favor of you?"

"Anything."

"The men are weary. Is there any way to arrange a small reprieve so that they can visit their families?"

"You ask for them and not yourself?"

"You *are* my family, goddess. I am more than content to be here, even in your absence."

She fingered his lips before she kissed him. "I wish we never had to be apart, for any reason."

As did he, but it couldn't be helped. "You are always in my heart, no matter where I am."

She pulled him close and held him tight. "Tell the men that they may take three weeks to ride home and see their families, so long as another war doesn't break out. I might have to recall them, and they should be ready to return at any time. But hopefully, they won't be needed."

When he started to pull away, she stopped him. "However, I'm hoping you won't go with them."

He pressed her hand against his lips and kissed her palm. "I will stay."

With one last kiss, he returned to the barracks to let the others know. Everyone was thrilled, except Galen who frowned at him. "Why can't you come with me?"

"Should something come up, one of us is needed to stay behind. I volunteered."

"It's not fair!"

"Fair has nothing to do with life or war, little brother. It just is. And we get through both as best we can. Now, pack. Take your furlough and send my love to Father, Perseus and Julia, and their son. Tell them that I think of them often."

"All right. But I shall miss you."

"I will miss you, too. However, I will enjoy a night's sleep without your snoring."

Laughing, Galen shoved at him. "I'm not the bear in the room. That would be Hector."

Hector grinned as he packed up his gear. "I would say I'm insulted by that, but it's true."

Aricles went to his chest and pulled out the small carved horse and soldier he'd made for his nephew. He handed them to Galen. "Take these to Theodorus and tell him that his uncle will hopefully see him soon."

"I will."

"And give Talia my best, too."

Galen blushed, yet didn't speak as he continued to pack.

Within an hour, even though it was almost nightfall, the men were gone and Aricles was alone in the room that seemed suddenly too quiet. Since he'd been born a twin and had shared a room at home with both his brothers for as long as he could remember, he'd never spent a night alone before. It was strangely unsettling.

That was his thought until he felt a warm presence behind him. His heart lightened instantly.

He turned, expecting Bathymaas.

Instead, it was the Greek god Apollo.

Aricles shot to his feet to confront him. "What are you doing here?"

An evil grin spread across his face. "Time for payback, Atlantean. And this time, there's no one here to interrupt us."

October 23, 12,249 BC

Frowning, Bathymaas materialized in the Ēperon barracks. She'd expected Aricles to call out to her once the others had left, but it was long after nightfall, and she was certain they'd gone home by now.

Her frown deepened as she saw him in bed with no light whatsoever. Scared he was ill, she quickly closed the distance between them. "Ari?"

Horror filled her as she saw his battered face. Bruises covered him all over. There was one fierce mark in the shape of a handprint on his throat, as if someone had held him down and choked him.

With a light groan, he pushed himself up.

"What happened?"

Shame and torment darkened his gaze. "It's fine, my goddess. I'll heal."

"Who did this to you?"

"It doesn't matter."

"It matters to me! Was it one of the Ēperon?"

He swallowed hard before he answered. "No. They went home in high spirits."

"Then who?"

He refused to meet her gaze. "Bathia, please . . . I've no wish to discuss it."

Tears clouded her vision as she saw how badly he'd been beaten. How she wished she had the power to heal him. But unfortunately, she didn't have the ability. "I'll call my aunt. She'll—"

"Please, Bathia . . . I'd rather no one else know about this."

"Why?"

A single tear fell down his cheek. "Please, let it go."

"You're scaring me, Ari. I've never seen you like this before. I don't understand."

Aricles fought the tears that choked him over what Apollo had done. He'd give the god credit—the bastard knew how to punish some-one and ensure they'd rather die than tell another soul about it.

Bathymaas sat down by his side and brushed the hair back from his face. "Is there anything I can do?"

He still couldn't bring himself to look her in the eyes. He wasn't sure if he'd ever be able to do that again. "Just stay with me for a little while . . . I don't want to be alone right now."

She took his hand into hers and held it to her heart. "I have no intention of leaving you, precious. . . . Have you eaten?"

He shook his head.

Using her powers, she summoned him a platter of meat, cheese, and fruit. Then to his complete shock, she hand-fed it to him. That went a long way in easing his horror, shame, and pain. But it still wasn't really enough.

Right now, all he wanted was to die.

Bathymaas felt her own tears sting her eyes at the way Ari contin-ued to act. How she wished she had the powers to read his mind or turn back time to see what had been done. She hadn't been joking when she said he scared her. Something inside him had been broken.

Wanting only to fix it, she conjured a bowl of water and gently cleaned his injuries. As she brushed her cloth over his neck, she paused at the sight of a bite wound.

Apollo.

It had to be. As part of her curse against Leto, Hera had con-demned the twins to live on blood. Unlike the other gods, Apollo and Artemis had to drink from others in order to live. It'd been a harsh sentence, but Bathymaas had had no way to undo it. Not without killing the twins.

"This was done because of me, wasn't it?" she breathed.

For the first time since her arrival, he met her gaze. "Nay, my lady. Never think that."

He could deny it all he wanted, but she knew the truth. This had been his punishment for stopping Apollo's rape.

In that moment, a darkness came over her. One that was bitter and violent.

Terrifying.

She'd never felt anything like it before. All she wanted was to ex-act revenge on Apollo for hurting him.

And one way or another, she would make Apollo pay for this. . . .

October 30, 12,249 BC

Bathymaas ached at the sight of the tormented shadow that had yet to leave Aricles's eyes since his fight with Apollo. A fight he still refused to talk about. It pained her that she couldn't ease his anguish, no matter what she tried. Aricles had told her that she helped just by being with him, but she knew better.

Apollo had left a lasting scar on his soul, and for that, she wanted the Olympian's heart in her fist.

Trying not to think about it, she sat in the circle of Ari's muscular arms while they fished at their spot. Leaning against him, she could feel the deep beats of his heart against her shoulder blade. "I'm glad you stayed with me. I would have missed you terribly had you gone."

He kissed the top of her head. "I would have missed you, too."

"Are you homesick for your father and brother?"

"A little, but I'd be more homesick for you had I gone with Galen to see them."

Those words thrilled her. "Are you just saying that to make me feel better for my selfishness in keeping you here?"

"No, Bathia. Promise."

Rising up onto her knees, she turned to face him and pushed him back to rest on his elbows. "I want to take the sadness from your eyes, Ari. Tell me what to do to make you happy."

Aricles smiled at those precious words. "I'm happy just being with you."

She pressed the backs of her fingers against his whiskered cheeks. "Your smile is tinged with sadness and it makes me hurt to see it so."

Aricles closed his eyes and savored the warmth of her hand against his skin. He hadn't touched her since Apollo's attack. The shame had been too much for him and he hadn't wanted to taint her with it.

But now . . .

He needed her to hold him. Leaning forward, he kissed her and let

59

the scent of her skin and her soft touch erase all the pain inside his heart. She was all he really needed. "You are the air I breathe, Bathia."

"Then marry me, Aricles."

He pulled back with a gasp. "Goddess—"

She placed her fingertip to his lips to keep him from speaking. "I know your arguments, Ari. But I don't care about anything else. I've spent eternity protecting others, and thinking only of their needs. I want to be selfish now. Every time I close my eyes, I dream of me and you and our baby in a small cottage. Just the three of us. Tell me honestly that you haven't thought of it, too."

"Oh, Thia, of course I have."

"Then run with me."

"I can't leave my brother and the others. Who would fight with them if I were gone?"

"Then I shall end this war between the Chthonians. Would you marry me if I did so?"

Aricles bit his lip at the sweetness of her request. "You already own my heart, body, and soul, Bathia. I willingly gave them to you long ago."

"Then you are my husband?"

He smiled and brushed back a strand of hair from her cheek. "I can think of no greater honor than to have you as my wife."

Lifting the hem of her peplos, she straddled his hips and kissed him soundly. "You are mine, Aricles of Didimosia. Proud warrior and gentle farmer—so named the Phoenix by your brethren. I will have no other to love, and you are, and will always be, my husband."

"And you, Bathymaas, goddess of justice and owner of my heart, are the only woman I'll ever love. You are everything in my world and all I'll ever live for." He kissed her hand. "You are forever my wife."

Bathymaas removed the pins from her peplos, baring herself to him. She trembled at the beauty of his eyes as all the sadness faded from them and was replaced by love. That was what she was used to seeing whenever he looked at her. She'd missed it terribly.

Pulling up his chiton, she removed it to leave him bare before her. She brushed her hand over the chills on his arms as she smiled at him and toyed with the necklace she'd given him. He never took it off.

She bit her lip as he gently slid her peplos down her hips and off. They both shivered when the center of her body brushed against the hard, rippled muscles of his abdomen.

Aricles arched his back as she leaned forward and brushed her breasts against his chest before she laved his nipple. Gone was any thought of anything other than the woman in his arms. And when she slid herself onto him, he growled as ecstasy pierced him. He lifted his hips to drive himself even deeper into her body as she rode him slowly. For once, they didn't have to fear Malphas or one of the others stumbling upon them. They were alone and had a full fortnight still to enjoy each other's company.

He cupped her breasts in his hands while she smiled down at him. "This settles it, love. I'm not moving from here for the rest of my life."

She laughed at his teasing. "I believe I was the one who begged *you* to run away."

He hissed as she reached behind her back to cup him. "I must have been out of my mind to refuse."

"Well . . . since you're so compliant . . ."

Lifting his hand to her face, he stared deep into her eyes. "Right now, Bathia, you could ask me for the moon and I'd find some way to get it for you."

Bathymaas savored those words, just as she savored the sensation of having him deep inside her. Wrapping herself around him, she rolled until he was on top. Without a word, he took the lead and thrust against her hips until she couldn't take it anymore. Crying out, she raked her hands against his spine and clutched him against her.

Aricles ground his teeth at how good it felt whenever she held him like this. There was nothing he loved more than the sight of her face when she came for him. She was the earth and heaven to his Kalosis. Completely lost to her, he buried his face against her neck so that he could inhale her lily scent as he found his own release.

Shaking and breathless, he laid himself against her, taking care not to crush her with his much larger frame.

She ran her finger down the line of his jaw as she stared into his eyes. "My precious husband."

"My beautiful wife."

Leto *turned toward* her son with an arched brow as Apollo manifested next to her to see the slut-whore with her bastard human. "Told you, didn't I?"

He gaped at the sight of Aricles rutting with Bathymaas. Fury mottled his cheeks. "When did this happen?"

"From the way they went at it, without hesitation, I'd say it's been happening."

"And the bitch dared to deny me while whoring herself for a fucking mortal!"

Leto rubbed his back sympathetically. "She's not worthy of you, my son. Rather she craves the cock of a mongrel dog. The last thing you want is to touch something so fouled."

But that wasn't what he felt. He wanted vengeance on both of them for this betrayal.

And by Zeus, he would have it.

Leto smiled at him. "We now have the way to break them both."

Apollo caught his mother's arm as she started to leave to tell the others that Bathymaas wasn't as impartial as they thought. "Wait . . . let's think about this for a minute. If we tell the other gods, Bathymaas still has her band of warriors to fight us and interfere with our plans. But if we hold off, we can use this to destroy the Ēperon for once and for all, from the inside out. We can make them turn on each other."

She laughed. "I knew I raised you right, boy. And once those bastards are dead, we'll destroy both Bathymaas and her human tsoulus."

November 1, 12,249 BC

Aricles froze on his way to the stable as he felt a now familiar presence that made him sick to his stomach.

Apollo.

Ready to battle, he turned on the Olympian and glared at him.

"What do *you* want?"

With a sinister smile, Apollo ran a hungry gaze over Aricles's body. "What I want is not the same reason as to why I'm here. . . . It seems my mother learned something quite fascinating about you and the goddess you serve."

His blood ran even colder as he steeled himself to show no emotion whatsoever. "I don't know what you're talking about." He tried to step around the Greek god, but Apollo cut off his path.

"Oh, I think you do. And I have a little proposition for you." Apollo raked him with a smirk. "You will either get a cold and be unable to fight in the next couple of battles we intend to initiate, or I'll tell every god in existence that our little justice queen is doing the forbidden dance with her champion. In fact, for all I know, she's having sex with her entire Ēperon."

Growling, Aricles started for Apollo, but the god blasted him back so hard, he rebounded off the wall.

"Don't push your luck, Atlantean. You're not *that* good, either in bed or out of it." Apollo closed the distance between them and seized him by the throat. Using his powers, he held Aricles completely immobile. "Will you cooperate, or do I ruin her forever? Have you any idea of the mockery she'll endure? Or what the other gods will do to her for violating her sacred duties as an impartial judge?"

Bile rose in his throat at the prospect, but what choice did he have? No one could ever learn about him and Bathymaas. It would destroy her. "I'll do it."

"Good, boy." Apollo ran his finger down the side of Aricles's face.

"Pity I don't have more time for you today. But I have a battle to plan. Next time, however . . ."

Aricles jerked away from him, wanting to plant his xiphos straight through the god's stomach.

If only he could, but their weapons only worked against the gods when Bathymaas charged them.

Apollo stepped back and raked a sneer over him. "By the way, I'm not the only one who knows about you two. There's another god, so if you're thinking you can spear me during battle and protect Bathymaas . . . think again. So long as I live, my mother will remain quiet. Should I expire too soon, everyone will know about your transgressions. Both with Bathymaas and with me. So much for your vow of chastity, right?" His smile turned even more mocking. "And tell me how much your goddess would love you if she ever found out that I had a piece of your ass, too? And if you breathe a word of this to her, I will see her powers stripped and kill her myself."

Aricles looked away as shame and fear filled him. A tic started in his jaw as he gripped his sword and forced himself not to attack. "I will never understand how the Greek people stomach you."

And he was going to find a way to kill this bastard. Sooner rather than later.

January 20, 12,248 BC

Dressed in his armor, Aricles stood on the edge of the battlefield as the rest of the Ēperon readied for the coming battle. He'd started to fight with them, until he'd seen Apollo. The god had given him a look that let him know Aricles wouldn't be a part of this skirmish either.

The moment Aricles stepped back from his horse, Hector glared angrily at him. "You are going to fight this time, aren't you? Or are you sick again?"

When Aricles didn't respond, Haides slammed his fist into his cuirass, forcing Aricles to take another step back. "He has no intention of fighting this day either. Look at him . . . he's not even armed with his spear."

Galen frowned. "What's wrong with you, brother? What changed with you while we were away? This is our fifth battle that you've refused to fight in."

When Haides went to attack him, Malphas came between them. "Ēperon, down. Save it for battle."

Haides spat on Aricles. "I'm not battling with a coward I can't trust at my back. He's as likely to stab it as my enemy is."

Malphas turned to Aricles. "Are you still ill?"

Wiping away the saliva from his face, Aricles nodded.

Monokles curled his lip. "There's nothing wrong with him. He's as fit to fight as any of us."

Phelix shoved him from behind. "Get him out of our sight, Malphas. None of us want him here. Send the bastard home with the rest of the women."

Before Aricles could move, Haides ripped his helm off his head and threw it to the ground. "Go!"

His hand trembling, Aricles retrieved his helm and headed back to camp, leaving the others to fight without him. But with every step he took, he hated himself more.

I can't do this anymore.

But what choice did he have? Either way, he'd be shamed. At least this way, he was the only one who suffered. Bathymaas was protected. So long as the bloody backlash didn't spray onto her, he could manage to deal with it.

He clenched his sword in his angry fist, wanting to cut off Apollo's head. If he took up his xiphos again in war, Apollo would tell everyone that he'd slept with Bathymaas. It wouldn't matter that they were married. Bathymaas was a virgin goddess whose impartiality must always be above reproach.

Her love for him would make all of her judgments suspect. And the gods would band together to punish her for it.

It would ruin her.

"Ari?"

He froze at the sound of Bathymaas's voice. "Yes, my goddess?"

"What's wrong?"

He shook his head, unable to tell her.

She placed a gentle hand to his arm between the mail of his shirt and his vambrace. "Tell me."

"I can't."

"I know something happened with you. Why won't you talk to me about it?"

Wanting only to pull her into his arms and hold her until the pain inside him stopped bleeding out his heart, Aricles stared at her. More than anything, he ached to tell her the truth about why he couldn't fight with the others. It'd never been in his nature to lie or withhold. But how could he? How would she look at him if she knew how badly he, her chosen warrior—her husband—had been overpowered and used by another man? The last thing he could bear was to see her look at him with the same disgust he felt for himself.

"I should leave and return home."

"Aricles . . ."

"Please, Bathymaas. I'm a distraction for the others. They no longer trust me or consider me one of them. It would be best for all."

Tears glistened in those golden eyes that had carved a permanent place in his heart. "It wouldn't be best for me."

He cupped her cheek in his hand as his emotions shredded him. "You deserve better, my goddess. I'm not worthy of you."

"How can you say that?"

"Because it's true."

A single tear fell down her flawless cheek. "Malphas is summoning me. I have to go."

Wiping the tear away with the back of his fingers, he nodded an instant before she faded away. Heartsick, Aricles returned to the tent the Ēperon had been sharing as they fought the Greek gods in this latest war.

Yesterday's harsh defeat after he'd refused to fight hadn't set well with his friends or his brother. Not that he blamed them. He'd be angry at him, too.

I have no choice.

As much as he loved the others, he loved Bathymaas more. Let the rest of the world burn to the ground. She was the only thing that mattered to him.

For her alone, he would die.

Angry, hurt, and aching, he started packing his gear. *I never desired any of this.* All he'd ever wanted was to be a simple farmer. To have a quiet life far away from the horrors of battle.

To work hard in a field all day and hold his wife at night, and watch their children grow.

He kicked at the trunk that held his battle gear, hating it with every part of himself.

If not for Bathymaas, he'd be gone already. But he couldn't leave her. Especially not now.

Sick to his stomach, he sat down on his cot and hung his head in his hands.

Hours *later, Aricles* had just begun to pack up for the others when he heard a furious bellow. He turned as Haides came running into the tent to pound him to pieces. He kicked the larger man back. "What is wrong with you?"

"Hector's dead because of you, you bastard!"

Those words hit him like hammer. "What?"

"You heard me. You left us to die!"

Aricles knocked him back and ran from the tent to verify his claim. He didn't have to go far.

Covered in blood, Hector lay just outside, his features pale and his eyes glazed. The other members of the Ēperon stood over his body.

Aricles fell to his knees by Hector's side. Grief and guilt tore him apart. And it wasn't helped as all of them turned to glare their mutual hatred and contempt at him.

Even Galen.

Tears filled his eyes and choked his throat. "Who killed him?"

Malphas sighed. "Apollo."

Aricles roared with the weight of his fury. He reached to touch Hector, but Phelix kicked him away.

"You're not worthy to touch a hero, coward!"

His vision turned dark and for a moment, Aricles almost attacked him. However, his anger wasn't for Phelix. It was for the bastard Apollo, and Aricles wasn't about to shed the blood of an innocent.

Galen spat on the ground by his side. "Go on and leave us, Aricles. It's what you're best at."

Then, as a single unit, they turned their backs to him to let him know that their brotherhood was severed. None of them wanted anything more to do with him.

Not even his own twin.

B*athymaas?"*

She paused at the unfamiliar voice. Turning, she was stunned to see the Greek goddess of war and wisdom, Athena, approaching her. Tall and dark-haired, the goddess was dressed in a bloodred peplos. "Athena? What are you doing here?"

"Something I shouldn't, but I despise treachery in all its forms."

Bathymaas frowned. "And what treachery do you speak of?"

She hesitated before she answered. "I overheard Apollo and his mother plotting . . . against you."

Foreboding choked her, but she knew better than to let Athena see it. "Me?"

Athena nodded. "Apollo is extorting one of your men . . . Aricles. My brother has some kind of leverage over him and he is forcing Aricles out of battle so that we can win."

Bracing herself for the worst, she made herself appear nonchalant. "What kind of leverage does he have?"

"No idea. But knowing my brother, I'm sure it's foul."

Bathymaas inclined her head to the goddess. "Thank you for letting me know. I won't forget your kindness."

Nodding, Athena left Bathymaas to her thoughts.

Bathymaas teleported instantly to the camp where she found her men attempting to tear Aricles apart. They had him bound naked on the ground while they took turns lashing, kicking, and stomping him.

While Caleb didn't participate in the abuse, he didn't stop them, either.

"What is this?" she demanded as she moved to protect Aricles from them.

They stood down immediately and backed away.

Her hands trembling, she cut the ropes that bound her husband. The pain in his eyes wrung her heart.

Aricles wiped the blood away from his lips. "It's just a mild disagreement, goddess."

She was aghast that he'd dare defend them after the cruelty she'd just witnessed. Enraged, she touched one of the horrid whip marks on his back. It was a full quarter inch deep and left his skin bleeding and ravaged. "If this is mild, I'd hate to see severe." She covered him with her cloak. Rising to her feet, she passed a chiding stare over all of them.

None of them appeared the least bit contrite. If anything, their eyes held a light that said they'd be back on him as soon as she was gone.

Bathymaas ground her teeth before she stepped away. "Aricles, walk with me."

Each of the men spat at him as he approached her.

Even his own brother.

And that broke her heart and ignited her fury.

Bathymaas scowled at them. "You are a team."

"Were," Haides snarled. "Now we're two men down. None of us want Aricles with us after this."

She saw the unity inside their hearts and it sickened her. "Galenus? Are you in agreement?"

He glared at his brother before he nodded.

Aching for Aricles, she led him away from the camp while the others started the preparations for Hector's funeral. She felt for his loss and bled over the needless sacrifice. Hector had been a good man.

But right now, her thoughts were preoccupied with her husband.

She sighed heavily. "Tell me what Apollo is using to keep you from fighting."

"Bathia—"

She stopped and turned to face him. "I want the truth, Ari. Tell me."

Anguish darkened his eyes as he glanced back to the Ēperon. "He knows about us, and if he finds out that I've told you, he'll kill you."

She scoffed at the ludicrous threat. "He doesn't have those powers."

"But he has the power to tell the other gods that you're no longer virgin."

"So what if he does?"

His blue eyes singed her. "You will be shamed."

"There are worst things in this world."

He shook his head. "I can't allow that to happen to you because of me. I can't."

"And I can't allow you to be called a coward by your brother and friends for protecting me. How can you ask that of me, your wife?"

"Bathia, please."

She glanced down at his ravaged body and shook her head. "I won't allow this. *I won't.*"

Before he could stop her or she could reconsider, she took his hand and returned them to where the others were preparing Hector's body.

Aricles started away, but she grabbed his arm and pulled him back to her. When he opened his mouth to protest, she gave him the hottest kiss of his life.

Utter silence descended. Aricles felt the heat creep over his face as he realized they were the center of everyone's attention. Pulling back, he swept his gaze across five pairs of widened, shocked eyes.

Bathymaas turned to face them. Stepping back against his chest, she pulled his arm around her waist and held it there. "Aricles and I are married. The Greek god Apollo found out and he threatened to discredit and shame me before the other gods unless Aricles refused to fight. To protect my honor and name, he has allowed all of you to insult and attack him, and I will not stand for him to be hurt again. By anyone."

Aricles wouldn't have thought they could have been more shocked.

He was wrong. For several minutes no one moved or spoke.

They didn't even blink.

Not until Galen stepped forward and punched him. Hard. "You bastard! You married and didn't tell me?"

Bathymaas moved to blast him, but Aricles caught her hand before she could damage his brother.

"It's all right, my lady. That's his normal reaction."

Her eyes flashed red. "He needs to find another."

Galen shook his head. "How could you have not told me? I'm your brother! Your twin! When did you marry?"

"While you were all gone," she answered for him.

Malphas cursed as he glared at Aricles. "Have you any idea the shit storm you're about to unleash?"

A tic started in Aricles's cheek before he nodded. "It's why I backed down from the fighting." He glanced over to Hector's body as tears blinded him. "I didn't want anyone hurt. Least of all Bathymaas."

Malphas growled. "Now *I* want to punch you. . . . But I understand." He rubbed his hand against the gold necklace that never left him. "The heart wants what it wants, and nothing will deny it. But damn . . ." He turned his glare to Bathymaas. "Damn."

Monokles scowled. "So what does this mean?"

Malphas gestured to Bathymaas. "The gods will attack her for this. Openly. Those who hate her will say that she can no longer perform her duties because she's been corrupted by the touch of a mortal. And they will be after Aricles with everything they have."

Phelix narrowed his eyes on Aricles. "I still don't trust him. He bowed out when we needed him most."

"To protect his wife," Haides reminded Phelix. "Right or wrong, I doubt there's a one of us who wouldn't do whatever he had to to keep his woman safe."

Monokles nodded. "He's right. There's nothing I wouldn't do to protect my wife and her honor."

Galen hugged Bathymaas and then his brother. "I hate you."

"I hate you, too."

Bathymaas scowled at Aricles who smiled at her then explained their contradictory words. "We don't mean it, my lady. Rather, it's our way of saying that we're still mad, but are willing to forgive."

"Mortals are so strange. . . ."

Caleb nodded in agreement. "And we have a man to bury and mourn. Let us attend to that and then we'll deal with this next disaster."

Bathymaas teleported Aricles into his tent so that she could clean him up and dress him. "I can't believe you allowed them to do this to you."

He shrugged. "I would gladly suffer this and more to keep you safe."

And that was why she loved him so. Brushing his hair back from his eyes, she sighed. "Apollo will be coming for us."

Aricles swallowed hard as a wave of pain went through him. He started to tell her what Apollo had done to him, but the words froze on his tongue. No matter how hard he tried, he couldn't bring himself to say out loud the horror of that day.

Please don't hate me, Bathia, when he tells you what he did to me.

But in his heart, he knew that she would never look at him the same way once she learned of it. And that made him every bit as sad as the loss of Hector.

It's all my fault.

He should have been strong enough to fight Apollo off.

And now. . . .

Kissing her on the brow, he knew that he had to do something to stop Apollo. And what he intended was as stupid as it was brave.

January 23, 12,248 BC

Aricles frowned as he heard a fierce fight going on in Bathymaas's temple. Grabbing his hoplon and xiphos, he ran toward it as fast as he could to find Apollo blasting Bathymaas.

Without hesitation, he went for the god and attacked him with everything he had.

Apollo cursed as Aricles knocked him away from her. The Greek god blasted him, but Aricles didn't care. He ignored the pain and continued on, beating the god until Apollo was pressed against the wall.

Unprepared for Aricles's ferocity and skill, Apollo staggered back then fell to his knees. "Everyone is going to know about the two of you! Everyone!" Then the coward vanished.

Releasing his battle cry, Aricles still wanted the bastard's blood for attacking his wife. He dropped his weapons and ran to where she sat on the floor. Her left cheek was bruised and swollen. Her nose bloodied.

"Bathia?" he breathed, terrified for what Apollo had done to her.

Tears welled in her eyes as she laid her hand against his cheek. "My poor Ari."

Confused, he scowled at her words. "Did he rape you?"

"No. I attacked him."

Relief flooded him, until she spoke again.

"Why didn't you tell me he raped you, Ari?"

Unable to meet her gaze, Aricles withdrew from her. He didn't want to see disdain or hatred in her eyes. Or worse . . .

Disappointment.

He was the one who was supposed to protect her. But how could he when he lacked the strength to protect himself?

She closed the distance between them and placed her hand on his arm. "Ari, talk to me."

73

"What can I say, goddess?

Bathymaas ached at the anguish she heard in his voice. At the shame she saw in his eyes as he refused to look at her. "Sweetie . . . it wasn't your fault."

He finally met her gaze and the raw fury there scared her. "You think that makes it right? I'm a man, Bathia. A warrior."

"You're mortal and he's a god."

"And I'm supposed to keep *you* safe."

She shook her head. "He came at you from the shadows. It was a coward's attack because he knew he couldn't defeat you if he attacked you as a warrior."

"Still not helping."

Cupping his face in her hands, she forced him to look at her. "I love you, Ari, and I never meant for my love to hurt you."

"It doesn't hurt me, goddess, it strengthens me."

"No. It's made you vulnerable and for that, I'm so sorry."

He frowned at her words. "Why do you apologize to me?"

Bathymaas couldn't speak as her new emotions ravaged her. Guilt, horror, pain . . . She didn't like these feelings at all. But beneath all the ones that hurt was the fierce adoration she had for the strength and inner beauty of her husband. "I should have left you on your farm when you asked me to."

"Then I wouldn't have had you."

The love in his gaze brought tears to her eyes. "Ari—"

He stopped her words with a kiss. "I would brave anything for you, my lady."

"And I, you."

Finally, he drew her into his arms and held her close. "I'm sorry I embarrassed you."

She frowned at his words. "Embarrassed me how?"

"By not being the man you deserve."

Tears flowed down her cheeks. "Don't you *ever* say that! In all my life, I have never known a better, more noble man than you. God or mortal." She pulled his head down and held him close.

Aricles trembled at the sensation of her arms wrapped around him. In that moment, he hated Apollo with everything he had. No doubt the bastard was already spreading news of their relationship, far and wide.

I'm going to kill him. . . .

. . .

Apollymi, *goddess of* destruction and creation, I humbly summon you. Please do your most earnest and humble servant the honor of appearing," Aricles whispered the words as he poured scented oil over the hot coals at the base of Apollymi's statue on Didimosia. He hadn't been to this temple since his grandfather had brought him here on a sacred pilgrimage when he was a boy.

Looking up at the statue, he was as struck by the goddess's beauty today as he'd been then. But it was the cruelty in her stone eyes that was still terrifying.

That cruelty that he was now imploring.

Unaware of his intentions, her priests were all in their corner, and he was alone in the main temple hall to make his blood offering to the most dangerous god in their pantheon.

At first, he thought she'd ignore him. But just as he was ready to leave, he felt the same stirring in the air that came anytime Bathymaas materialized before a mortal.

There in front of him stood a vision of feminine beauty. Almost as tall as he was, she had long wavy blond hair and swirling silver eyes. "You have some nerve, mortal. You swear allegiance to an Egyptian goddess I loathe, take up sword for her, and now you *dare* summon me? Really?"

He went down on one knee before her. "For that, I beg your indulgence, goddess. But I'm here because I've been told that you and I have something in common."

"And that is?"

"Hatred for the Greek god Apollo."

Her eyes flashed red. "I despise all things Greek."

"And that is why I offer up my soul and my sword to you."

She scowled at him. "I don't understand."

Swallowing hard, he forced himself to make a bargain he hoped he didn't live to regret. "The god threatens what I love, and I plan to challenge him, and while I know what a capable warrior I am, I also know that I lack the abilities to destroy a god on my own."

A slow smile curved her lips. "You are a ballsy bastard . . . and that I respect." She paused to consider his words. "What will you give me for this favor should I grant it?"

"Name it, my goddess, and I'll pay it."

Apollymi approached him slowly. She jerked his chlamys away from his left shoulder blade to show where Bathymaas had placed her mark on him after he swore himself to her alone. "What have you done, mortal? Rezar will kill you for daring to touch his beloved daughter."

"Have you never been in love, goddess?"

She growled low in her throat. "Love makes fools of us all, eventually. Even the great Bathymaas." She pulled his chlamys back over the mark. "I still should kill you."

Aricles didn't flinch or react to her words at all.

"Have you nothing to say to that?" she asked him.

"I'd rather you not."

She laughed. "You are lucky you're so brave. That alone has saved your life today." She stepped back and narrowed her gaze on him. "And unfortunately, you can't kill Apollo . . . as much as I'd love for you to."

Aricles felt his spirits crash at her words.

"But . . . you can defeat him, and when you do, bring him to me, bound and gagged, and that will be my fee." She manifested a bronze xiphos and held it out to him. "Use this to level the field and once you have him defeated, bring him here to me."

He frowned at the weapon in his hand that didn't look any different than the one he normally carried into battle. "What is special about this sword?"

"It was dipped in the River Styx. It will allow Apollo to bleed as any mortal."

"Thank you, goddess."

She inclined her head to him. "Good luck, Aricles, and beware of treachery."

"Always." After saluting her with the sword, he strapped it on as she vanished.

He placed his hand on the hilt and he left her temple. Now he had an appointment to keep, and Apollo was definitely going to bleed.

January 24, 12,248 BC

Aricles sighed contentedly as he held Bathymaas in the quiet morning hours. Now that the others knew the truth, they'd laughed at him when he'd gone to bed in their barracks.

"You have a beautiful goddess for wife and you'd sleep here with us, alone? Are you insane?"

He smiled at the memory of Galen's indignant tone. Brushing the hair back from her cheek, he placed a kiss there at the same time a bright flash lit up the room.

Aricles barely had time to blink before he was blasted out of the bed and pinned to the floor. Every bone in his body felt shattered. Unable to move, he was forced to lie there as a huge man stalked him with murder in his gold eyes. Well built and stout, he was obviously someone's god of war.

Bathymaas came awake with a gasp. *"Papas, no!"* She leapt from the bed, dragging the sheet with her so that she could wrap it around her naked body. She grabbed the god's huge biceps. "Don't hurt him!"

"I don't want to hurt him. I want to kill the rancid bastard dog!"

She planted herself between them. "I love him, *Papas*. If you kill him, you will destroy my heart."

His eyes tormented, Set pulled her into his arms and held her tight. He pressed his lips to her head as he glared at Aricles. "You have a heartbeat?"

She nodded.

Set cursed. "When Apollo said he'd seen you with a man, I went to gut that Greek bastard, but Ma'at stopped me. Have you any idea what you've set into motion, daughter?"

Tears fell down her cheeks. "I don't care. He is all to me."

Brushing her tears aside, Set sighed heavily then released whatever invisible hold he had on Aricles. "I wish you'd told me first."

"I knew you wouldn't approve and I didn't want you to hurt Ari."

Completely embarrassed, Aricles quickly dressed.

Set growled deep in his throat as he stepped away from Bathymaas. "Leto is calling for your removal and punishment. She says that the war you've been waging against the Greeks isn't one of justice, but rather a favor for your Atlantean husband."

She was aghast at the ludicrous accusation. "Ari wants nothing to do with war."

Set scowled at him. "But he's your best fighter."

"Who wants nothing to do with war," Aricles repeated. "I was a farmer before all this, and I preferred that to fighting."

Set laughed angrily. "None of that matters. They're still demanding blood from us."

"And I've demanded Apollo's."

Bathymaas gasped as she stepped away from her father to face her husband. "What have you done, Ari?"

"I issued a challenge to Apollo. We are settling this the only way the Greeks understand. With violence."

"No," she breathed. "You can't!"

"He's right."

She glared at her father. "No, he's not."

"Yes, daughter, he is. If he beats Apollo, it would end the bloodlust and intimidate the others. They'll back down."

"And if they don't?"

Set brushed his hand against her chin. "You are new to emotions, Bathy. And I doubt you understand the power of fear." He looked past her to Aricles. "When are you to fight him?"

"Two days from now."

"Make sure you don't lose, boy."

Aricles glanced to his wife. "I promise, I won't."

But even as he said that, Bathymaas had a terrible feeling in her gut. Something bad was going to happen. She had no doubt.

January 25, 12,248 BC

Bathymaas trembled as she watched Aricles sparring with Galen. Terrified over the upcoming fight, she glanced to Caleb. "Do you think he can win against Apollo?"

"Honestly?"

She nodded.

"I do."

"Are you saying that to comfort me?"

Caleb laughed. "I keep forgetting that you have emotions. So, no. I don't think about comforting you, even now."

How she wished she could forget she had them.

Over and over, her mind conjured images of Aricles dying horribly. No matter how hard she tried, she couldn't banish them. They kept returning to torture her.

Unable to stand it, she left the others and went to Mount Olympus where Apollo lived with the majority of the Greek gods. As much as she hated it, she had to make a deal with her enemy. It was the only way to ensure Aricles's safety and life. While she believed Malphas's words that Ari could defeat the god, she couldn't risk Apollo cheating.

And Apollo was definitely *not* above that.

Apollo dropped the lyre he was playing as she manifested before his chaise inside his private temple. "Has the equator frozen over?"

She rolled her eyes at him. "I'm here to issue you a challenge."

He scoffed. "I'm tired of these challenges from you and your boy-toy. Not to mention, I already have a fight tomorrow."

Shrugging with a nonchalance she didn't feel, Bathymaas arched a brow. "I'm impressed. I had no idea that you craved humiliation so much."

"How do you mean?"

"We both know you can't beat Aricles. He's the best fighter who *ever* picked up a hoplon and sword. And as of tomorrow, everyone else will know it, too. I merely came to try and save some of your dignity. But since you're so desperate for public degradation, who am I to deprive you?" She started to leave, but he stopped her.

"What did you have in mind?"

"A contest between gods. You and I. That way, if you lose, no one will mock you for it."

"And if I win?"

As if *that* could ever happen. But she needed to give him some kind of hope, otherwise he'd never agree to this. "What do you want, Apollo?"

"You to stand down and allow my mother to be the supreme goddess of justice."

She was aghast at his request. "Truly? That's what you want?"

He nodded.

Leto would never be a decent goddess of justice. The bitch had no understanding of it. But that didn't matter. Apollo would *never* defeat her.

"Fine then . . . I challenge you to a contest of bowmanship. We are both gods of archery. Grab your bow and meet me outside my temple."

"Now?" he asked in shock.

She glanced about his empty temple. "You have something better to do?"

He narrowed his gaze on her. "I want witnesses to this."

Gaping, Bathymaas was astonished by his request. "What? You think I would cheat *you*?"

"Who knows what you might do? You have emotions now. I wouldn't put anything above you."

She lifted her chin as anger ripped through her. "Never have I been more offended, but since I know you're far more likely to cheat than I am, I, too, will bring a witness. I'll see you there in an hour."

He inclined his head to her. "One hour."

A*re you sure* about this, daughter?"

Bathymaas reached up to touch her father's cheek. "I am. I can't take a chance on Apollo harming my husband. Ari is everything to me."

Set held the bow he'd given to her when she was a child. Only Bathymaas could draw the string to it, and she never missed whatever she was aiming for. With the exception of Ari and her father, it was the one thing she treasured most in the universe.

The air behind her stirred.

Turning, she found Apollo and his twin sister, Artemis. With long, curly red hair, Artemis was one of the more beautiful goddesses.

Even so, a chill of foreboding went down Bathymaas's spine at Apollo's chosen second. "You asked your sister?" It was known by all that the god had little use or love for his twin.

"You didn't give me much time to prepare." Apollo eyed her father as if Set made him extremely nervous.

And well he should. A primal god, her father was known to rip the fun body parts off men he didn't like. Which was why she'd asked him to come. With her father present, she was hoping Apollo would be on his best behavior.

Bathymaas took her bow and jerked her chin toward their targets at the end of the field. "Three shots."

Apollo made no move to conjure his weapon. Instead, he pursed his lips. "Perhaps we should make this more interesting."

She narrowed her eyes on him suspiciously. "How so?"

"As you said, we're both gods of archery. How about we shoot at my sister's golden hinds?"

Artemis gasped. "Apollo, you can't! They were gifts to me and I need them to pull my chariot."

Apollo gave her a withering glare. "You only need four of them and you have five. I say we take one and release it in a herd of other deer and let them run. Whoever shoots the golden hind in the heart wins."

Artemis curled her lip. "I vote I challenge Bathymaas and we shoot at you, brother dearest."

Set and Bathymaas laughed.

Apollo not so much.

Turning his back to his sister, he faced Bathymaas. "Are you up to the challenge?"

"Where are these hinds?"

"In Artemis's meadow."

Bathymaas frowned at the obvious trick. Should her father step one foot on Olympus, the other Greek gods would call out for a supreme war. "You'd allow us to venture to Olympus?"

"I can have one of the hinds put here if you'd rather."

"Of course, I'd rather."

Without reacting to her tone, he glanced over to Artemis. "Go fetch the first hind you see and mix it with a herd here. Then let us know when you release them."

"I hate you," Artemis snarled under her breath before she went to comply.

Bathymaas lowered her bow as Artemis vanished. While they waited for Artemis's return, she couldn't shake the uneasy feeling in her stomach.

Something awful was going to happen. She could feel it.

But before she had time to fully examine that sensation, Artemis returned. "I have a buck mixed in with the others. Say the word and they're released."

Apollo finally manifested his bow. He glanced to Bathymaas. "Ready?"

"Whenever you are."

"Release the deer!" Apollo called out.

Bathymaas nocked her arrow and waited.

After a few seconds, the deer herd ran through the trees in front of them.

Apollo shot a heartbeat before she did. His arrow went into the flanks of the hind. Hers went straight to its heart.

Relieved it was over and she'd won, Bathymaas started to smirk, until the hind began to change form. Her breath caught in her throat.

No!

Dropping her bow, she teleported to Aricles. Naked, he lay on the grass with Apollo's arrow embedded in his thigh.

And hers in his heart.

"Ari," she sobbed, sinking to her knees. She pulled him into her arms. "How?"

Blood trickled from the corner of his mouth. His breathing came in short, ragged breaths. "I was . . . with Galen . . ."

Bathymaas screamed out for her aunt to come help her.

Ma'at appeared instantly then froze. "What is this?"

"Apollo . . . he transformed Ari into a hind and I shot him."

Her eyes filled with tears, Ma'at knelt by her side. "Child, you know I can't heal your arrow wounds. No one can."

Utter despair claimed her as she stared into the pain-filled eyes of her husband. "Ari . . . I didn't know it was you."

"Shh," he breathed, reaching up to cup her cheek. "Don't cry, Bathia. You are my heart and I will always be with you. If it takes me ten thousand lifetimes, I will find my way back to you, I promise." As he went to smile, he expelled a single breath and his hand fell from her face.

The light faded from his eyes and as it did so her amulet that he wore around his neck broke into two halves.

Screaming in utter anguish, she cradled him to her chest and rocked his body as grief tore her apart. Someone, she assumed Ma'at, placed a comforting hand to her shoulder.

"Rezar! Stop it!"

She looked up at Ma'at's cry to realize that it was Artemis by her side, and her aunt was trying to keep her father from killing Apollo and Leto.

Tears glittered in the Greek goddess's green eyes. "I didn't know, Bathymaas. I'm so sorry. He was grazing outside my temple. I just assumed he was one of mine. I had no idea my mother had done this to him and to you. I swear it." The agony in her voice attested to the truth of her words.

But it changed nothing.

Aricles was dead.

By her own hand, and by Apollo's and Leto's treachery. And as she sat there with his body in her arms, a frightening cold filled her. It chilled every part of her being and stilled her beating heart.

She'd been conceived as a goddess of justice. But this wasn't just.

It wasn't right.

And her husband's wrongful death would not go unavenged.

Kissing his cold lips, Bathymaas laid him on the ground and covered his body with her cloak.

Artemis gasped and shrank away from her as she rose to her feet and turned toward Apollo and his mother.

For this, there would be hell to pay.

And hers would be the hand that gathered the payment.

Epilogue

January 3, 12,247 BC

Set held his infant daughter in his hands as his heart broke all over again. With tears streaming down his cheeks, he met Ma'at's gaze and saw his own sorrow mirrored in her eyes. After the death of her husband, Bathymaas had gone on a bloodthirsty rampage that had almost cost the Olympian pantheon all their lives. But since Apollo's life was tied to the sun, they couldn't allow her to kill him, or else the entire world would have ended. But her rage had been such that no amount of logic could keep her from her vengeance.

Uniting for the first time in history, the gods and Chthonians had all gathered to lay a death sentence on her. Something Set couldn't allow. Desperate, he'd gone to his sister, who'd conceived the plan to have Bathymaas reborn with half a heart and with no memory of her precious Aricles.

Now she slept again in his arms, tiny and defenseless.

"Will you ever let me hold my daughter?"

He glanced up at Symfora's request. She lay on the bed where she'd delivered his daughter to him just a few minutes ago. The Atlantean goddess of sorrow and woe, she'd been the perfect mother for his child. If anyone would understand his daughter's pain, it was Symfora.

Kissing his daughter on the brow, he carried her back to Symfora and placed her in her mother's arms. "She is beauty incarnate."

"As is her father." Symfora cradled her with the love he wanted his girl to know. "So what are we to call her?"

"Bet'anya."

Symfora arched a brow at that. "House of Misery?"

"She is to be your goddess of misery and wrath, is she not?"

"Indeed." She glanced down at her daughter and offered a rare smile. "But I shall call you Bethany, little one."

84

Set cringed at the name that was almost identical to Aricles's nickname for her. Symfora could use it if she chose to, but he would never call her by the name her husband had given her. She would always be his precious Bet.

He took her small, fragile hand into his. *I hope I haven't harmed you, daughter.* Because of the Source powers they'd used for her birth, Bet only had half her heart.

The other half lay with her Aricles and wouldn't return to her until he did.

You better find her, you bastard.

Otherwise, Set would rain a wrath down on this world that would make Bathymaas's seem merciful. But in his heart, he knew true love when he saw it.

Come what may, Aricles would find and reunite with his Bathymaas. And no matter what powers sought to divide them, Set held no doubt that they would one day be together again. . . .

———

*R*ead *more about Bathymaas and Aricles in* Styxx.

Phantom Lover

1

"Men are the scourge of the universe. I say we line them all up along the highway and then mow them down with big trucks." Chrissy paused as her light blue eyes widened with a new thought. "No, wait. Steamrollers! Yeah, let's steamroll them all until they're nothing more than slimy wet spots on the road."

Arching a brow at the rancor, Erin McDaniels looked up from her desk to see her co-worker Chrissy Phelps gripping the edge of Erin's tan cubicle wall. The large brunette's eyes were flashing mad and Chrissy had the look of a woman one step away from the edge.

"Having trouble with the boyfriend again, eh, Chrissy?"

"Actually, it's my younger brother who has me ticked, but since you brought up the boyfriend thing, take my advice: Be the black widow. Find a guy, have fun with him, then eviscerate him in the morning before he can brag about it to his friends."

"Okay," Erin said stretching the word out. "I think someone needs a time-out."

"Someone needs a two-month vacation in the Bahamas without her boyfriend along." Chrissy's eyes brightened. "Oooh, hey, sex camp. Yeah. That's the ticket. We need to start a sex camp where women can tell their hubbies they're going to a fat farm and instead of the boot camp diet with Nazi dieticians, they go to the beach and have hot men treat them like goddesses!"

Erin laughed.

"No, I'm serious. We'd be rich."

Erin laughed even harder. "You'd better get back to work before Lord King Bad Mood catches you over here again."

"Yeah, I know. See, proves my point. All men should be shot."

Erin was still laughing as Chrissy returned to her desk. Two seconds later, Chrissy was back, peeking over the cube wall again. "Hey, are you still having those nightmares?"

Erin's humor fled as she remembered the horrendous nightmare she'd had last night where she'd been cornered in a dark cave by an unseen force that seemed to want to feed off her terror. For the last three weeks she'd barely slept a wink. Her exhaustion was getting so bad that she was even having dizzy spells.

"Yes," Erin said.

"Did that medicine the doctor gave you help?"

"No. If anything, I think it made the dreams worse."

"Oh, man, I'm sorry."

Erin was, too. She'd hoped for at least one good night's sleep. But that no longer seemed possible.

Their boss's door opened.

Chrissy dodged off as their rotund, militant boss left his office in a huff and headed toward the coffeepot with his extra large coffee mug in hand. Oh, yeah, like that man needed any more caffeine to add to his jittery crankiness.

Erin sighed as John filled his mug to the brim and her thoughts turned back to her nightmares.

Honestly, she no longer knew what to do about them. They were just so bizarre, and every night the dreams seemed to worsen. At the rate she was going, she figured she'd be a raving lunatic by the end of the month.

Rubbing her eyes, she focused on her computer screen. She had to get her marketing report in by Friday, but all she really wanted to do was sleep.

In the back of her mind she kept seeing that huge, snarling monster that came for her. Hearing him call her name as he reached his taloned hand out, trying to claim her. Like some bad horror movie, the scenes kept haunting her, whispering through her thoughts during any unguarded moment.

Shaking her head, she dispelled the images and focused on her computer screen. But as she read, Erin felt her eyelids getting heavy again. She blinked fast and widened her eyes in an effort to stay awake.

Marketing report, marketing report . . .

Oh, yeah, like that was a good way to stay awake. Why not down a couple of sleeping pills and drink a glass of warm milk while she was at it?

What she needed was more caffeine, and since she couldn't stand coffee, she'd have to go to the Coke machine. Maybe the walk down the hall would help revive her, too.

She slid her chair back and opened her desk drawer to get her change, then rose to her feet.

As soon as she was upright, a strange buzzing began in her head. The world tilted.

And in one heartbeat everything went black and her body froze. . . .

Erin felt herself falling down a deep, dark hole. All around her, winds rushed and howled in her ears, sounding like huge, frightening beasts trying to shred her.

They were hungry. They were desperate, and they wanted *her*.

They whispered her name on breaths of fire. Told her they waited only for her.

Not again! She couldn't take any more of this horrible nightmare. *Wake up, wake up!*

But she couldn't.

Erin reached out to grab anything in the darkness to stop herself from falling. There was nothing to hold on to. Nothing to save her.

"Help!" she screamed, knowing it was futile but needing to try.

Still, she fell.

She didn't stop falling until she reached the cavern she knew all too well. Dark and dank, it smelled of rotting decay. She heard the hissing and screams, the absolute agony of souls in torment.

Run away!

Her heart pounded as she stumbled in the dark, over the rough floor that seemed to grab on to her feet with rocky fingers as she tried to find an exit. She struggled to see, but the oppressive darkness wouldn't let her. All it did was stab at her eyes like tiny needles.

She reached out with her hands and touched a slimy wall that slithered and moved under her fingers. Disgusting though it was, at least it gave her some support, something tangible that might lead her home.

And she had to find a way home. The frightened voice in her head told her that if she didn't get out of this now, she'd never be able to escape it.

Panicked, she saw a dim light flickering up ahead. She ran toward it as fast as her legs would carry her.

The light. It would save her. She was sure of it.

She ran into a large cave where the light was shining over the veined and broken walls that oozed some kind of gelatinous muck. The smell of sulphur burned her nose and the screams grew louder.

Erin skidded to a halt. If she had been terrified before, it was nothing compared to what she felt now.

The dragonlike monster, with shimmery blood red scales and jet-black wings, rose up in front of her, snarling. His long teeth snapped as he eyed her hungrily.

He moved closer to her, lulling her with his eerie silver-blue eyes. Eyes that seemed to see more than just her physical self. It was as if they saw all the way into her mind, her soul.

And she knew the beast wanted her. That he longed to possess her with a fevered madness.

Oh God, this was it. The beast was here to take her. To consume her.

There was no escape.

Erin stumbled back, toward the entrance. She wouldn't just lie down and die. It wasn't in her. She was a fighter. And she would fight until the last breath left her body.

Turning around, she ran to the opening, but before she could escape, it closed up, sealing her in.

"You're not going to leave me so soon, Erin," the scaly dragon lisped, his talons scraping the floor as he drew closer. "I need the light inside you. Your thoughts. Your feelings. Your goodness. Come to me, and let me feel the warmth of you wash over me."

He lunged for her.

Erin closed her eyes and imagined a sword in her hands to fight him.

She got a tree limb. Not her weapon of choice, but it was better than nothing. She swung it at him, catching him hard across the face.

Laughing, he shook his scaly head as if he didn't feel the blow at all. "Such spirit. Such intelligence and ingenuity. And you wonder why I want you so. Show me more, Erin. Show me what else you can come up with."

She forced him to step back while she wielded her tree limb. It was a stupid weapon, but it was all she had for the moment.

As if growing bored, the dragon jerked the limb from her hands. "I want your mind, Erin. I want to feel your fear of me."

He moved even closer.

Before the beast could reach her, a bright light flashed between them, stinging her eyes even more. It grew in intensity until it appeared brighter than the sun. When it finally faded, it revealed another monster.

Erin swallowed in terror. Why couldn't she control this dream? Ever since she'd been a child, she'd been able to wish herself out of bad dreams. But for some reason, she had no control in these nightmares.

It was as if something other than her was directing them. As if she were nothing more than a marionette whose strings were being pulled by the monster.

The newest monster appeared in the form of a giant snake. Only in place of a head, she had a woman's upper body. Her scaly green complexion looked craggy, and her bluish eyes glowed.

The she-snake slithered toward her, smiling a fanged smile as she raked her eerie gaze over Erin's body. "What a tasty little morsel she is."

"She is mine!" the dragon roared. "I will not share her."

The she-snake licked her lips as her long tail slithered across the floor. "She is strong enough for us both." Then she turned toward the dragon, her hideous face a mask of rage. "Besides, I saw her first and well you know it. You found her through me and I won't let you have her."

The dragon attacked the snake.

Terrified beyond belief, Erin took advantage of their combat to pick up a rock and pound at the cave's opening. "Let me out," she demanded between clenched teeth.

She closed her eyes and tried to imagine the wall opening and her running through it.

It got her nowhere. Not until the tail of the dragon whipped around trying to sting the snake. The snake ducked, as did Erin, and in one resounding crash, the tail splintered the wall.

Trembling, Erin ran out into the darkness again. The screaming howls intensified.

"Please," she begged out loud, "please wake up! C'mon, Erin, you can do it." She pinched herself and slapped her own face as she ran, and did everything she could think of to make herself come out of this nightmare.

Nothing worked. It was as if the monsters wouldn't let her go.

She rounded a corner and found herself sliding down a small slope. At the bottom was a boiling pit where the snake-woman waited. The heat of the pit burned Erin as golden-red lava percolated.

The snake rose up before her, smiling. Those demonic eyes with their diamond-shaped pupils watched her eerily. "That's it, little prize. Come to me. It's my turn to feed off you."

Erin turned to run again, but her feet were locked to the ground. They wouldn't move at all.

The snake drew closer.

Closer.

So close Erin could feel the flick of the snake's tongue. Smell the greasy slime of her body and hear the rasping of her scales moving against the rock floor.

Defenseless, Erin closed her eyes and called out with her mind for help. She tried to summon a protector. Tried to imagine a champion who could come and defeat her monsters.

Just as the snake reached her, the cavern shook.

The snake pulled back an instant before a man appeared between Erin and the beast.

And he wasn't just any man. Clad in a suit of black armor, he had incredibly broad shoulders and long jet hair. Erin couldn't see his face, but she could feel the power of his presence. Feel the warrior essence of him as he prepared to fight the demon.

The snake shrieked in outrage, "Stand down, V'Aidan. Or perish from your stupidity!"

Erin's summoned champion laughed out loud at the she-snake's anger. "I'd perish from your breath long before my stupidity killed me, Krysti'Ana."

Screaming in outrage, the she-snake increased to ten times her size. Her massive jowls snapped and she hissed as the cavern walls around them shook even harder than before. Loud crashes sounded as pieces of stone broke free of the cavern and formed into stone men.

Erin's savior turned to her, and her breath caught at the sight of his face. More handsome than anything imaginable, he held eyes that were so clear and blue, they seemed to glow. A shock of jet-black hair fell over his forehead and contrasted sharply with his tawny skin.

Before she could move, he wrapped his lean, muscular body around hers in a protective cloak, shielding her as the monsters attacked en masse.

Erin could feel the blows he took as they vibrated from his body into hers. She didn't know how he stood the pain of it. How he maintained his hold on her.

All she knew was, she was grateful for it. Grateful for the power and strength of his presence. Grateful that he cradled her so gently and that she was no longer alone to face her nightmare.

The warm, spicy scent of his skin soothed her. Instinctively she wrapped her arms around his lean armored waist and held on to him, afraid of letting him go. "Thank you," she breathed, shaking. "Thank you for coming."

She saw the confusion in his gaze as he frowned down at her. Then his face hardened, his eyes turned icy.

"I have you, *akribos,*" he whispered quietly, and yet his deep, accented voice rolled over her senses like a powerful tidal wave. Soothing, warming. "I won't let the snake Skotos take you."

She believed that, until one of the new monsters seized her about the waist with a stone tentacle. She screamed as it tore her from her savior's grasp.

The dark knight created a sword out of air and pursued them through the dark cavern. She watched as he dodged the other stone monsters, as he literally ran down the walls themselves to get to her. He jumped over the thing carrying her, to land before them and cut off the monster's escape.

The creature caught him about the waist with a hard kick and sent him slamming high into the wall.

V'Aidan didn't seem to feel the pain at all as he slid down the wall to the floor. More monsters swarmed over him, but he fought them down. His face was a mask of determination until he stood strong and victorious over their broken bodies.

He narrowed his eyes on the thing holding her, then held his hand out, and a red glow blasted the monster, splintering it.

The knight grabbed Erin then, scooped her up in his arms, and ran with her through the darkness.

Erin wrapped her arms around his neck and held on for dear life. She could still hear the snake calling out.

"I will have her, V'Aidan. I will have both of you!"

"Don't listen," V'Aidan said. "Close your eyes. Think of something soothing. Think of a happy memory."

She did and, oddly enough, the most comforting thing she could imagine was the sound of his heart pounding under her cheek. The deep accent of his voice.

"V'Aidan!" the she-snake's voice echoed in the cavern. "Return her to me or I will make you wish you had never been born."

He laughed bitterly. "When have I ever wished otherwise?" he mumbled under his breath.

Suddenly the wall before them burst open, spilling more monsters into their path.

"Hand her over to us, V'Aidan," a large gray lizard-man demanded. "Or we will see you pay with the flesh off your back."

Still holding her close, V'Aidan spun around to flee but couldn't.

They were surrounded.

"Give her to us," an old dragon croaked, reaching out its claws. "She can feed us all."

Erin held her breath as she saw the indecision in her dark knight's eyes.

Dear Lord, he was going to hand her over.

Her heart pounding, she touched his face, her fingers brushing against his hard, sculpted jaw. Erin didn't want the monsters to have her, but inside she understood his reluctance to help her any further. He didn't know her at all. There was no reason for him to endanger himself.

He's not real.

It's a dream.

The words whispered through her mind. But like so many dreams, this one felt so real. *He* felt real.

And she had an unnatural desire to protect him.

"It's okay," she breathed. "I don't want you hurt. I can fight them on my own."

Her words seemed to confuse and surprise him.

The monsters moved in.

"Release her or die, V'Aidan," the lizard-man hissed.

Erin felt the knight's tender touch as his fingers brushed the side of her neck, sending chills all over her.

The look in his eyes was needful and tormented.

"They will not have you," he whispered. "I will take you some place where they can't reach you." He bent his head and captured her lips.

The heated passion of his kiss stole her breath.

The dream monsters faded away into vaporous clouds until nothing was left.

Not the cave, not the screams.

Nothing.

Nothing except the two of them and the sudden need she had inside her to taste more of him.

Closing her eyes, Erin inhaled the warm, manly scent of V'Aidan's skin. He ravished her mouth with passion as his tongue swept against hers and his teeth gently nipped her lips.

Now this was a dream.

He was a dream.

A perfect, blissful moment worth savoring.

She heard him growling like a wild beast as he trailed his lips down her jaw and buried them against her throat. Licking. Teasing. Inciting her desire.

Every nerve ending in her body fired at his touch. She burned for him. Her breasts swelled, wanting to feel the strokes of his tongue across the taut peaks while his hands held her. Her core throbbed with an aching, demanding need.

He lifted his head to gaze down at her and it was then that the rest of the scene filled itself in. The two of them stood outside on a bright, moonlit knoll.

The peace of the moment comforted her. She smelled the damp pine around them, heard the bubbling of a nearby waterfall.

Their clothes melted from their bodies as he laid her down on the ground, which, oddly, wasn't hard. The moss under her was softer than a cloud, and it contrasted sharply with his hard muscles pressing down on her.

She liked this dream much, much better.

"You are gorgeous," she whispered, staring at his sleek long dark hair falling around his face. His body was lean, meticulously defined, and flawless. Never had she seen a better-looking man.

She reached up and traced the sharp arch of his dark brows over those silvery-blue eyes. The color of them was so intense, it took her breath.

Then she trailed her fingers down the stubble of his cheeks to his hard, sculpted jaw. She was so grateful to him. So happy to have him hold her after the terror the monsters had put her through.

For the first time in weeks, she felt safe. Protected.

And she owed it all to him.

V'Aidan captured her hand in his and studied her fingers as if he'd never seen anything like them. There was such a tender light in his gaze that she couldn't understand what caused it.

Moaning so deep in his throat that it vibrated through her, he led her hand to his mouth and ran his tongue over the lines on her palm. His tongue stroked her flesh with featherlike caresses while his teeth gently nipped her fingers and palm. His eyes shuttered, he seemed to savor the very essence of her skin, her touch. Her taste.

Erin shivered at the hot look on his face as he kissed her again. His hands roamed her body, stroking and delving, seeking out every part of her, and stoking her inner fire until she worried it might completely consume her.

He slid his mouth from her lips, down her body to her breast. Erin hissed in pleasure. His hand gently cupped her breast, holding the peak up so that he could take his time tasting it, rolling it over his tongue as he growled again. She'd never seen a man take such pleasure from simply tasting a woman before.

V'Aidan was heaven. Pure and simple heaven. The perfect, attentive lover. It was as if he could read her mind and know exactly where and how she wanted to be touched.

His erection pressed against her hip as his hand sought out the fire between her legs. Spreading her legs wider for him, Erin trailed her hands over the muscles of his back, muscles that rippled and flexed with every exquisite sensual move he made.

She buried her lips against his throat, tasting the salt of his skin. Chills spread over his body, making her smile that she was giving him pleasure in turn.

Never before in her dreams had she been this at ease with a man. It was the first time she'd made love without worrying if her lover would find fault with her body. If somehow she wasn't good enough for him.

Her dream lover made her feel special. Made her feel womanly and sexy. Hot. Desirable.

She held her breath as he slid his fingers through her moist curls at the juncture of her thighs, separating the tender folds of her body until he could slide his long, tapered fingers deep inside her. Hot fire stabbed her middle.

Groaning at the exquisiteness of his touch, she ran her hands through his silken hair and held him close.

He stroked and teased her body with his fingers as his mouth worked magic on her breasts. The power of his touch, the feel of those hard, defined muscles pressing down on her . . .

It was more than she could stand.

Leaning her head back, she cried out as ribbons of ecstasy tore through her. Still he kept giving her pleasure. He didn't slow down until the last deep shudder had been wrung from her.

Breathless and weak, she wanted to please him the way he had pleased her. She wanted to look into his eyes and watch him climax, too.

Rolling him over onto his back, Erin ran her hand down the perfect tawny muscles of his shoulders, his chest, his abdomen and hips and raked her fingers slowly through the dark curls between his legs. V'Aidan sucked his breath in sharply between his teeth as she trailed her lips over the hard muscles of his chest to his rock-hard abdomen.

And as she laved his tawny flesh, she cupped his hard shaft in her hand. V'Aidan shuddered in her arms. The look of pleasure on his face thrilled her as he slowly rocked himself against her palm.

She sheathed him with her hands, delighting in the velvety feel of him pulsing between her palms. He ran his fingers through her hair. The muscles in his jaw flexed as he gazed into her eyes while she tenderly milked his body.

"I love your hands on me," he breathed, his voice deep and ragged. "I love the way you smell. The way you feel."

He took her chin into his hand and stared at her with a look that told her he wanted her even more than the dragon had. It was primitive and hot, and it stole her breath.

In that moment, she knew he was going to take her. Take her in a way she'd never been taken before.

Burying her hands in his hair, she couldn't wait for it. She wanted him to possess her.

His eyes flashing and wild, he growled before seizing her lips with his. He kissed her so passionately that she came again as he rolled over with her in his arms and pressed her back once more against the cloudlike moss.

He brought his knee up, between her thighs, and spread her legs wide as he placed his body over hers. She shivered in anticipation.

"Yes, V'Aidan," she breathed, arching her hips in invitation. "Please fill me."

His eyes feral and possessive, he drove himself into her.

Erin moaned at his hardness inside her. She'd never felt anything better than all his strength and power surrounding her, filling her totally. As he moved against her, she feared she would pass out from the bliss of it.

He touched her in ways no man had ever touched her before. As if he truly treasured her. As if she was the only woman who existed for him.

His moves were untamed as he thrust into her. Slow. Deep. Hard.

She wrapped her legs around his, sliding them up and down to feel his leg hairs caress her.

He dipped his head and captured her breast in his mouth, teasing it mercilessly as he stroked her with his body. She moaned deep in her throat, cupping his head to her.

Then, he leaned back on his legs so that he could stare down at her. Erin swallowed at the sight of him above her as she looked into his eerie silvery-blue eyes. He held her legs in his hands as he continued to drive himself even deeper into her.

His sublime strokes were primitive and hot and tantalizing. And they tore through her, spiking pleasure so intense it went all the way up her back and down to her toes.

V'Aidan licked his lips as he watched her watching him. Erin couldn't move. His eyes held her paralyzed. All she could do was stare at him. Feel him, deep and hard inside her.

She saw his pleasure mirrored in his eyes, saw him savoring her. And when he looked down to where they were joined, she shivered.

"You are mine, Erin," he said between clenched teeth, thrusting himself even harder and deeper into her to emphasize the words.

He took her into his arms and cradled her to his chest as if she was unspeakably precious.

Erin clung to him while she felt her pleasure building even higher. In white-hot sparks she came again in his arms. He buried his face into the crook of her neck and cried out as he joined her.

She lay perfectly still while he shuddered around and in her. His breathing heavy, he didn't move for several minutes.

Pulling back, he looked down at her. "I am with you, *akribos,*" he whispered. "I will always be with you."

A strange wave of heaviness came over her. She closed her eyes. Even so, she could still feel and understand what was going on.

V'Aidan draped her over his chest as he lay on his back. She could feel his hands gliding over her while she inhaled the warm, manly scent of his skin.

Even asleep, she felt him near and knew he watched over her, protecting her from the others. And for the first time in weeks, she rested in total peace and comfort.

"Sleep, Erin," he said quietly. "The Skoti can't reach you here. I won't let them."

Erin smiled in her sleep. But as the darkness came for her again, an odd voice rang out in her head.

Now who poses the greater threat to you, Erin? Krysti'Ana or V'Aidan?

2

Erin came awake slowly to find herself flat on her back, outside her cube. For a second she couldn't move at all, then her body slowly began to function again.

The first thing she saw was Chrissy's worried frown.

The second was the two EMTs sitting next to her. Her boss, along with several other co-workers, stood off to one side frowning down at her. John's face told her the only thought in his mind was how much paperwork he'd have to fill out over this.

"What happened?" Erin asked.

"You passed out," Chrissy said. "It was like you were frozen or something."

Erin covered her face with her hands as embarrassment filled her. Just her luck to have the most erotic dream of her life witnessed by half her office.

Oh God, shoot her now!

"How do you feel?" the paramedic on her right asked as he helped her sit up.

"I feel . . ." Her voice trailed off. She felt incredible, actually. Better than she had ever felt before.

"Ma'am?" the paramedic insisted. "Are you okay?"

Erin nodded, trying desperately to hold on to the image of V'Aidan, but it faded and left her feeling oddly lonely. "I'm fine, really."

"I don't know," Chrissy said. "She's been acting weird a lot lately. Hasn't been sleeping. Maybe a short hospital stay where she can sleep—"

"Chrissy!" Erin snapped. "What are you trying to do?"

"Get you some help. Maybe they have something that can make you sleep through the night."

"I don't need to sleep," she said, amazed at the truth of those words. "I feel completely rested."

The paramedic looked at Chrissy. "Her vitals are normal. If she says she's fine, she's fine." He handed Erin a release form. "Sign that and you're on your own, but if I were you, I would go to my doctor just to be safe."

Chrissy gave her a doubtful look.

"I'm fine, Chrissy," Erin insisted, signing the release.

Even so, John told her to go home and take the rest of the week off.

Completely embarrassed, Erin didn't argue as the EMTs left. She merely gathered her things then headed out of the building, to the parking lot.

Chrissy followed her to the car. "Listen, what I was going to say before John went for coffee and you hit the floor is that my boyfriend is a psychologist who specializes in sleep disorders."

Erin paused at her green Escort. Strange that Chrissy hadn't mentioned that before, but it explained why she had been so interested in Erin's dreams since all this started. "Really?"

"Yeah. His name is Rick Sword and I was telling him about you. He says he thinks he can help." Chrissy handed her a crisp dark gray business card. "I really think you should give him a call."

Erin studied the card. At the moment, she'd never felt better in her life, but maybe she should give him a call just in case the nightmares returned.

"Thanks," Erin said, getting into her car. "I just might do that."

Chrissy stared at her from outside the car and mouthed the words, *Call him.*

Erin waved to her then headed home, but as she drove through downtown traffic she really didn't feel like going back to her apartment alone.

In all honesty, she felt rather strange. She could almost sense V'Aidan's presence. She swore she could still smell the masculine scent of sandalwood that had clung to his skin, sense him in her thoughts.

"It was just a dream," she said out loud.

Still, it had been an incredible dream. So real. So vivid and erotic. So incredibly satisfying.

She stopped at a red light and glanced down at the card on her passenger seat. Before she could talk herself out of it, she grabbed her cell phone and called Dr. Sword.

His receptionist immediately put her through to him as she headed her car toward the expressway.

"Ms. McDaniels," he said eagerly. "Chrissy has told me so much about you. I would really like to speak to you if you have time."

Something compelled her to accept. "Okay, sure. When?"

"What are you doing for lunch?"

Erin gave a nervous laugh. "I guess 'meeting you' would be the correct answer."

His own laughter answered her. "Tell you what. Why don't we meet out in public for the first time? I find it puts people more at ease. Do you like Thompson's Restaurant at Five Points?"

"Okay. What time?"

"How about right now? It should be just opening up for the day."

"Sounds like a plan. I'll be there in about half an hour."

"Good. I'll be waiting."

Erin pulled onto the expressway and headed toward their rendezvous.

Once she reached the mall, she parked her car outside the quaint restaurant that specialized in jazz music and Bohemian food then headed inside.

There were only a handful of people in the dark interior, all of whom were seated at tables. It was only then she realized she'd forgotten to ask the doctor what he looked like.

"Erin?"

She turned to see a tall, distinguished-looking man in his early forties entering through the door behind her.

"Yes?"

"Rick Sword," he said, extending his hand out to her.

She shook it. "Nice to meet you."

"Yes," he said with a cool smile. "Yes, it is."

He got them a table in the back of the restaurant, and once they were seated and had placed their orders, he listened as she explained her nightmares to him.

Erin felt a little nervous at first, but as she explained it to him and he didn't appear to judge her, she went into more details.

"And then this guy, V'Aidan, was there and he called the snake monster a Skotos." She paused as she trailed her straw around her Coke. "You probably think I'm nuts by now."

"Hardly," he said, his blue eyes sincere. "In truth, I find you fascinating. Tell me, have you ever heard of the Skoti before?"

"No, never."

"Hmmm, interesting."

She frowned as he made a few notes on the pad he'd carried inside with him. "Why?"

"Well, they're part of history. Tell me, did you ever take an ancient Greek civilization or mythology course in college?"

"No, not really. I mean, we covered the basic Greek pantheon in high school and I had to read the *Odyssey* and *Oedipus Rex* in college, but that was it."

"Hmmm," he said as if he found that interesting, too.

"Why do you ask?"

"I was just wondering how the idea of the Skoti got implanted into your subconscious."

There was a peculiar note in his voice that made her extremely apprehensive. "What are you saying, they're real?"

He laughed. "That depends on whether or not you believe in the ancient Greek gods. But they were part of that culture. They were, for lack of a better term, nightmare demons. They were said to infiltrate the dreams of humans so they could suck emotions and creativity. It made them high, if you will."

"Like energy vampires?"

"Something like that. Anyway, the legend goes that they would visit a soul a few times during its lifetime and move on. It's how the ancients explained away their nightmares. Supposedly, every so often a Skotos would latch on to a particular victim and go back over and over until the person became insane from the visits."

"Insane how?"

He took a sip of his drink. "The scientific theory behind the legend would be that the visitations, whatever they really were, disrupted normal sleep patterns, causing the victim to never really rest or rejuvenate during the night, thereby causing mental duress. If it continued long enough, it would lead to mental instability."

A shiver went down her spine. This sounded just a little too much like what had been happening to her. "So, how does someone get rid of a Skotos?"

"According to legend, you can't."

"Can I fight them?"

He shook his head. "No, but the ancient Greeks believed in perfect balance. As you have the evil Skotos, likewise you have the benevolent Oneroi who fight them for you."

"Oneroi?"

"They were believed to be the children of the dream god Morpheus. They were champions of humans and gods alike. Incapable of feeling emotions, they spend eternity protecting humans in their sleep. Whenever the Skoti latch on to a human and begin to drain too much from that person, the Oneroi come in and save the human from their clutches."

"Like V'Aidan did me."

"So it would seem."

"And the Skoti, where do they come from?"

"They were the children of Phobetor, the god of animal shapes. His name means 'frightening,' hence their dominion over nightmares."

"So the Skoti and Oneroi are related?"

He nodded.

"Fascinating," she said, mulling over her new knowledge while thinking about her dreams.

Vaguely she recalled the threats the Skoti had made against V'Aidan. Was it possible that somehow these demons had really infiltrated her sleep? Could V'Aidan and the others possibly be real?

It was ludicrous and yet . . .

Her face flamed. If they were real then she'd just had a one-night stand with a perfect stranger.

"Dr. Sword," she asked seriously, "do you believe they exist?"

His light blue gaze bored into her. "Young lady, I have seen things in my life that would make anyone prematurely gray. I learned a long time ago not to discount any possibility. But personally, I find the idea of Greek gods infiltrating my dreams highly disturbing."

Her face burned even more. "I assure you, you don't find them half as disturbing as I do."

He smiled. "I suppose not." He reached to the small leather case on his belt and pulled out a Palm Pilot. "Tell you what. Why don't you and I schedule an appointment next week to have your dreams monitored? We can hook you up to our machines, put you under a long sleep, and watch your brain waves. Maybe that will give us a scientific clue about what's going on."

She nodded gratefully. "Now that sounds a whole lot better than Greek gods and demons running loose in my dreams."

V'*Aidan sat high* above the ocean, perched on a small ledge that barely accommodated his long frame. He'd come to this place as far back as he could remember. Ever since he'd been a young child back at the dawn of time.

It was here he'd come after his ritual beatings that had been designed to strip his feelings and compassion away. Here he'd rested, waiting for the pain of his existence to lessen until he could again find the numbness he was sworn to live by.

Here on his perch he could hear the roar of the waves and stare out at the vastness of the water and feel oddly at peace.

Only now that peace was gone. Shattered.

Something strange had happened to him when he had made love to Erin. It was as if he'd left a piece of himself with her.

Even now, he could sense her. If he closed his eyes, he could even tell what she was feeling.

Worse, he craved her in a way that was all-consuming. He wanted to be with her again, to feel her soothing touch on his skin. He'd never once known such gentleness existed, and now that he did . . .

"You broke a rule, didn't you?"

He clenched his teeth at Wink's voice above him. Looking up, he met two large inquisitive silver eyes that were fastened on him with interest.

Wink was the last god he wanted to see at the moment. The son of Nyx, the night goddess, and Erebus, the embodiment of primordial darkness, Wink was technically V'Aidan's great-uncle and one of the oldest of the gods. However, he acted more like some prepubescent human. His youthful face was always beaming and bright and he wore his long brown hair braided down his back.

The most annoying thing about Wink was that he loved practical jokes and was forever making fun of the children of Myst.

"I did nothing."

"Oh, come on, 'fess up, V. I heard your siblings talking about you. They said you took a human from them and vanished. Now, give me the dirt."

"Go away."

Wink smiled at that. "Then you did do something. Oooh, and it must be good, for you to be so secretive."

V'Aidan stared at the swirling ocean below. "Don't you have something better to do? Like torment gods who can actually get irritated at you?"

Wink grinned even wider. "Sarcasm. Hmm, someone's been around humans a long time."

V'Aidan didn't respond.

He didn't have to. Wink moved toward his shoulder and sniffed like a puppy with a pair of dirty socks. Wink's eyes widened as he pulled back. "You *are* irritated at me, aren't you?"

"I can't feel irritation and well you know it."

It didn't work. Wink came around to float by V'Aidan's side, his eyes larger than saucers. He took V'Aidan's chin in his hand and studied his eyes. "I can see *emotions* in there, swirling, mixing. You're scared."

V'Aidan jerked his chin out of Wink's grasp and pushed him away. "I most certainly am not. I fear nothing. I never have and I never will."

Wink arched a brow. "Such vehement denial. Your kind never feels such passion when they speak, and yet you do."

V'Aidan looked away, his heart pounding. He felt the strangeness of panic in his chest. And he remembered a time once, aeons ago, when he'd been a child and he had dared ask the wrong question.

"Aphrodite, why can't I have love?"

The goddess had laughed at him. "You are the child of Myst, V'Aidan. She is formless, shapeless. Vacuous. The best you can hope for is to feel fleeting, muted emotions, but love . . . love is solid, eternal, and beyond your understanding or abilities."

"Then why can I feel such pain?"

"Because it, like you, is a fleeting phantom. Like the great ocean it ebbs and flows, swelling to titanic proportions, then sweeping down into nothingness. It never lasts for long."

Over the centuries, he had learned the goddess was wrong about pain. It, too, was eternal. It never went away.

Not until he had held Erin.

Closing his eyes, he didn't understand it. What had she done to him?

Wink poked him on the shoulder. "Come on, V, tell me why you are in such a state."

He looked up at his great-uncle. Trust of any kind was as alien to V'Aidan as love. Still, he needed Wink's experience. Wink had been around longer and knew more than he did. Perhaps Wink could give him an insight. "If I tell you what happened, you must swear by the River Styx to tell no one. No one."

Wink nodded. "May Hades chain me in Tartarus, I swear by Styx to never utter a single word of what you tell me."

V'Aidan took a deep breath and braced himself for betrayal. "I had sex with a mortal."

Wink arched a proud brow and smiled. "Nice, isn't it?"

"Wink!"

"Well, it is. I highly recommend it." Wink paused speculatively. "Was it a man or woman?"

"A woman, of course. What kind of question is that?"

"A very nosy one and in keeping with my charming personality."

V'Aidan rolled his eyes. Now he understood what the other gods meant when they said Wink could be a major pain in the ass.

"So," Wink continued, "was she any good?"

A wave of desire tore through V'Aidan, piercing his groin with heat at the very mention of her. Still, he refused to answer that question. It was personal and none of Wink's business.

"Judging by the look on your face, I'll take that as a yes."

V'Aidan growled at his great-uncle and sought to change the subject. "Anyway, something happened."

"Something?"

"It changed me somehow."

Wink snorted. "That's just stupid. If sleeping with a mortal changed a god, there's no telling what I'd be now. As for Zeus . . . perish the thought."

V'Aidan ignored his words. The worst part of all was this incessant need he felt to see Erin again. To feel her hands on him.

He craved her tenderness.

Craved her warmth.

He had to have her.

"V'Aidan!"

Wink paled at the sound of Hypnos's voice. Hypnos was the one god who held dominion over all the gods of sleep. Sooner or later, all of them answered to him.

"Uh-oh," Wink whispered. "He looks mad." Wink vanished, leaving V'Aidan alone to face the old god's wrath.

V'Aidan looked up over his head to see the old man's angry scowl. But since he'd never seen any other look on Hypnos's face, he couldn't judge it. "He looks the same to me."

"V'Aidan," Hypnos growled. "Don't make me come down there to get you."

V'Aidan snorted in response. If Hypnos thought to scare him, he'd have to try something new. V'Aidan had learned a long time ago not to care.

Rising up to the cliffs above, he went to meet the god who made Skoti and Oneroi alike quiver in fear. He alone could give them real emotion.

V'Aidan felt nothing as he approached the old man.

"You seduced a mortal in her sleep."

The accusation hung between them as V'Aidan stared at him.

"What have you to say for yourself?"

V'Aidan said nothing. What could he say? He had committed a forbidden act. Other gods could take humans as they wanted, but not his kind.

He wasn't the first one of his kindred to violate that mandate. However, he wasn't foolish enough to think for one minute Hypnos would be merciful toward him.

He wasn't a favored son.

"You know our code," Hypnos said. "Why did you break it?"

Because I wanted to be held. Just once.

For one moment in eternity, I wanted to pretend someone cared.

The truth tore through him. Regardless of what Hypnos did to him as punishment, it had been worth it.

He would never forget that one precious moment when he'd held Erin in his arms and she had slept peacefully on top of him. Her breath tickling his chest, she had done something no one had ever done before. She had trusted him.

Her warmth had seeped into him, and for the first time since he'd been born, if not love, he had known tenderness. And it had been enough.

Hypnos looked at him as if he were disgusting. Vile. But then, V'Aidan was used to that, too.

"Take him," the old god said, shoving him into the hands of his punishers. "Strip the human taint from his flesh and make sure that he will never forget the pain of it."

3

It was after midnight before Erin finally found the courage to go to sleep. She was terrified of what her dreams might bring and yet she wanted to see V'Aidan again.

How stupid was that?

He wasn't real and there was no guarantee she'd ever have another dream with him in it.

Still, she wanted a small miracle.

Surrendering herself to the domain of Morpheus, she let her exhaustion take her.

Instead of the falling sensation she'd learned to expect from her dreams, she felt as if she were flying high above the world. For the first time in weeks, she had normal, happy dreams.

No one chased her. No one scared her.

It was heaven, except for the absence of one particular phantom lover.

Sighing in her sleep, Erin saw herself dressed in jeans and a tank top, sitting outside on the porch swing that used to hang on the patio at her Aunt Mae's house. The day was perfect, bright and pleasantly warm with fragrant air laced with honeysuckle and pine. She'd spent so many youthful summers here on this farm in the California mountains.

How she had missed it.

"What is this place?"

She started at the deep, accented voice behind her.

Turning around, she saw V'Aidan leaning against the white porch railing, his hands braced on each side of him, watching her. His long black hair was tied back into a ponytail and those clear silver eyes were guarded. His black button-down shirt only emphasized the perfect muscles of his body, and his jeans had holes in the knees.

For some reason she couldn't fathom, he looked a bit pale and tired, his features pinched. Even so, she was glad he was here.

She smiled at him. "It's one of my favorite places from childhood."

"What did you do here?"

She stood up and approached him, but he quickly moved away. "Is something wrong?"

V'Aidan shook his head. He shouldn't be here. He should have stayed far away from her, and yet . . .

He couldn't.

As soon as she'd fallen asleep, he had felt her soothing presence calling out to him.

Determined, he had fought it as long as he could.

But in the end, it had been futile.

He'd come here against his will. Against his common sense. His body, even though it healed a hundred times faster than a human's, was still sore and aching from his punishment. It reminded him of the high cost he would have to pay again should anyone learn where he was.

She placed her hand on his arm. V'Aidan closed his eyes as pain swept through him. His arms were so incredibly sore, but not even the agony of his wounds could conceal the hot, intense shiver he felt at her touch.

"Come." She slid her hand down his arm to capture his hand in hers. He stared in amazement at their fingers laced together. And he tried not to feel just how soothing her touch was against his skin. How much he wanted to strip her clothes from her and make love to her for the rest of eternity.

"Let me show you," she said.

He allowed her to lead him down the porch steps and across the yard to an old barn. As they walked hand in hand, her imagination stunned him. Her dream was so vivid and vibrant. He'd never visited anyone who had created something so wonderfully detailed.

She released his hand to open the well-oiled doors of the barn and show him where three horses rested inside stalls.

V'Aidan watched her toss a horse blanket over the back of a pinto, then lead it to him. It amazed him that the horse didn't shriek at his scent. Never before had an animal tolerated his presence in a dream. But the brown-and-white pinto seemed completely at ease with him. That spoke volumes about how much power her mind held.

"Have you ever ridden?" she asked.

"No."

She showed him how to mount the horse then she climbed up to ride in front of him. V'Aidan held on to her waist as she kicked the horse into a gallop and they rode through the fields.

The feel of the animal under him, with her in his arms as they rode, washed over him. He felt so strangely free and almost human.

She rode him out to a lake where they dismounted and the horse vanished into a brown cloud of smoke.

Erin sat on the grass and started picking wildflowers to weave into a crown. Enchanted, he watched her hands blend the stems together into an intricate piece that bore little resemblance to a simple headdress.

While she worked, he drew her back against his chest so that he could hold her.

Just for a little while.

"You are so incredibly creative," he said. "This place is so . . . you," he finished. And it was. Bright, friendly, welcoming. It was everything good.

Everything Erin.

She laughed happily and the sound of it brought a foreign comfort to his chest. "Not really."

"Yes, you are." It was what had made him seek her out originally. "Why do you suppress your creativity?"

She shrugged.

V'Aidan leaned his cheek against her brown hair and traced circles on her stomach with his hand. "Tell me."

Erin had never been the kind of person to confide in others, and yet she found herself telling V'Aidan things she'd never told another soul. "I always wanted to be creative, but I was never any good at it."

"You are."

"No. I tried to play the flute as a girl, and I remember when they were holding auditions for junior high school I went to play my scales and couldn't hit any of the lower notes."

"You were nervous."

"I was untalented."

She felt V'Aidan's breath on her neck as he nuzzled her gently. Heat coursed through her, tightening her breasts.

What was it about his touch that set her on fire? And the more she felt of his touch, the more she wanted him.

"I'll bet you would make a great artist."

Erin smiled at him and the confidence he had in her abilities. It was a nice change of pace. "I can't draw a straight line with a ruler."

He kissed her then. Deep and passionately. His tongue brushed against her lips, sending waves of desire spiraling through her. She moaned against his mouth, cupping his head as needful desire coursed through her.

He nipped her lips. "Maybe you should be a writer."

"That I most certainly can't do."

"Why?"

"I get sick at the thought of it."

He frowned. "Why?"

Erin glanced away as she remembered that horrible day. "I was in college and I wanted to be a writer so badly that I could taste it. In order to major in creative writing, we had to submit our best piece of fiction. So I came up with a short story idea that I thought was great and really different. I worked and reworked it until I was sure it was perfect. I submitted the whole packet to the head of the department and then waited to hear back."

She swallowed as she remembered how she'd learned of the professor's decision. "The *Literary Journal* came out a few weeks later, and in it were all the short stories from the students who were being admitted."

"You weren't in it?"

Her stomach tightened. "I was in it, all right. She had chosen my story to highlight what not to do if you ever wanted to be taken seriously as a writer. She ridiculed every aspect of my story."

His arms tightened around her.

"You can't imagine how humiliated I was. I swore I would never again do anything creative. That I would never put that much of myself into anything to be mocked for it."

Tears stung her eyes and she would have cried had V'Aidan not leaned her head back and run his tongue under her chin to her throat. His body soothed the pain away and she moaned at how good he felt. How safe he made her dreams.

"Why is this so important to you, that I be creative?" she asked.

He pulled back and gave her a hard stare. "Because it's your repressed creativity that is drawing out the Skoti. If you will release it, they will have no fodder for your nightmares."

That sounded wonderful until she thought about it. "And what about you?"

"What about me?"

"If the Skoti are gone, will you be gone, too?"

He looked away and she saw the truth of it. Her heart ached at the thought of him never coming to her again. Even though they had just met, she needed him. Liked the way he protected her. Touched her.

As a shy only child she'd lived her life with only a few friends and even fewer boyfriends. She'd never really been close to anyone. Yet she felt bonded somehow to V'Aidan. Felt a connection, a need to be with him.

"I don't want you to leave me."

V'Aidan's heart lurched at the words no one had ever uttered to him before. He was only used to people trying to drive him away.

She leaned back against his shoulder so that she could look up at him and touch his face.

She was so beautiful there. "Why do you desire my company?" he asked.

"Because you're a champion."

"No, I'm not."

"Yes, you are. You saved me from the Skoti."

He swallowed at that. "If you ever saw the real me, you would hate me."

"How could I?"

He closed his eyes as memories surged through him. This dream with her, it was an illusion. There was no truth to it. What he heard, what they felt . . . all formless delusions.

And yet he wanted it to be real. For the first time in his life, he wanted something true.

He wanted Erin.

"You don't even know what I am," he whispered.

"Yes, I do. You're an Oneroi. You defend people from their nightmares."

V'Aidan frowned. It had been a long time since anyone knew of that term. "How do you know about the Oneroi?"

"Someone told me about them earlier today and I did some research after I got home. I know lots of things about you now."

"Such as?"

"That you can't feel any emotions whatsoever. But I don't believe that one."

"You don't?"

"No. You're too gentle."

V'Aidan was stunned by her words. Gentleness was something he had never thought to hear applied to him. Hypnos would laugh himself into a hernia at the thought.

"Hey," she said suddenly. "Let's do something I have always wanted to do but never had the guts."

"What?"

She looked over at the lake in front of them. "Let's skinny-dip." Before he could answer, she shot to her feet and pulled her top off.

His breath caught in his throat as he stared at her bared breasts. Her nipples were hard and he swore he could already taste them. His body on fire, he took a step toward her and halted only as he felt the pain of his wounds lance up his back. If he undressed, she would see the wounds. See what they had done to him. And he never wanted her to know of it.

"You go," he said. "I want to watch you."

Erin didn't know where she found the courage to undress while he watched. She'd never been so bold in real life. Yet in her dream she didn't mind. In truth she liked the hot, lustful look on his face as she stripped her jeans and panties off and headed for the water.

V'Aidan watched her swim. Watched the water lapping against her bare skin. Her breasts glistened in the light as she floated on her back, and he could see the moist tangle of curls between her legs.

He ached to go to her and spread her legs until he could . . .

He turned away then.

"V'Aidan?"

The concern in her voice tore through him. He had to leave her.

Unable to stand it, he ran through the forest, ignoring the agony of his body. It was nothing compared to what lay in his heart.

Suddenly he felt himself changing. He saw his hands losing their human form. Felt the burning sensation of his skin as his flesh transformed . . .

"V'Aidan?"

His heart pounding, he knew he couldn't stay. Not without her finding out the truth.

Closing his eyes, he teleported out of her dream.

4

Erin woke up to the sound of her phone ringing. Groaning out loud, she rolled over to answer it.

It was Chrissy. "Hiyas, chick. How are you enjoying your morning off?"

She would be enjoying it a whole lot more if someone hadn't interrupted her dream while she was trying to find V'Aidan so that she could strip him naked and drag him into the water with her.

"It's okay," Erin said, stifling her agitation.

"Did I wake you?"

"Yes, you did."

"Oh, I'm sorry. Were you having another nightmare?"

Erin smiled at the memory. "No, not a nightmare."

"Really?" Chrissy asked in disbelief. "Not a single second of one?"

"Nope. Now if you'll excuse me, I'd really like to go back to sleep."

"Yeah, sure," Chrissy said with an odd note in her voice. "Why don't you do that?"

Erin lay in bed for a solid hour, trying to go back to sleep to find V'Aidan, but it didn't work.

She felt so good from their time together that she had no choice but to get up.

Aggravated at herself for not having more control over her ability to go back to sleep, she piddled around the house.

By late morning, she found herself at her computer, staring at her marketing report.

As she worked, V'Aidan's kind, encouraging words drifted through her mind. And before she knew what she was doing, she closed out her spreadsheet and was opening up her word processor.

Erin sat there for hours, typing furiously. It wasn't until late afternoon that she stopped.

Completely happy for the first time in years, Erin stared at what she'd done. Proud of her accomplishment, she wanted to share it with someone.

No, she corrected herself. She wanted to share it with V'Aidan.

She printed off her pages, then took them to the couch. Lying down, she clutched the papers to her chest and willed herself to sleep in hopes of seeing him again.

She found him standing in a meadow. He was dressed all in black right down to his leather biker boots. His jeans hugged his hard thighs, and his black T-shirt looked yummy as it stretched over a chest so lean and toned that it could only be real in her dreams.

The cool breeze tugged at his loose hair, and his silvery eyes shimmered in the daylight.

"I came looking for you," she said happily.

He appeared puzzled by her words. "Really?"

"Yes."

She sat down in the middle of her summer meadow with beautiful jewel-toned butterflies all around her. After their discussion last night, Erin had been trying to let her inner artist out. She wore a light peasant blouse and a loose skirt that rode up on her thighs when she sat.

Best of all, she conjured up a box of Nutter Butter Bites.

V'Aidan moved closer. "What are you eating?"

"Nutter Butters. Want some?"

He dropped to his knees by her side. "What are they?"

She ran her hand through the red box and scooped out a handful to show him the tan-colored circles. "Peanut butter cookies. They're really good, and the best part of all—in dreams, they have no calories."

He laughed at that. "Would you feed me one?"

More nervous than she could fathom, she held a cookie up for him. He licked her finger as he took the cookie into his mouth. "It's delicious. Your finger, I mean."

She smiled at him and kissed his cheek.

He looked so stunned that it was almost laughable.

"Hey," she said, putting the box aside and grabbing up the papers she'd brought with her. "You'll be proud of me."

He arched a brow.

"I wrote today. For the first time since college."

"Really?"

She nodded. "I actually finished ten pages. Want to see?"

"Of course I do." He took the pages from her hands and sat down in front of her to read them.

Erin watched his gaze sweeping over the page. She ached to reach out and run her hands over his glorious body. He was as toned as an athlete. Better still, his taste was more addictive than chocolate.

When he finished, he glanced up at her and the proud, encouraging look on his face stole her breath. He was so devastatingly handsome, so warm, that it made her weak.

"Vampires?" he asked.

She grinned. "I know it's a weird topic, but I just sort of channeled them. What I like is that they're so different from other vampire stories."

"They remind me of some people I know."

Erin gaped in disbelief. "Get out! You know vampires?"

"I know lots of them."

"Are you teasing me?" she asked suspiciously, still not sure if he was serious or not. "There really is such a thing?"

He didn't answer. Instead he flipped back through the pages. "You're very talented, Erin. You shouldn't let this go to waste."

Hearing it from him, she could almost believe it. "You think so?"

"Yes, I do."

He set the pages aside and stared at her.

Erin's blouse began unlacing itself. She shivered at the dark, hungry look on V'Aidan's face as he watched it. Slowly, bit by bit, the laces came out of the holes. Her nipples hardened in expectation. Then, the opening widened, baring a single breast.

"Hey!" she teased.

He smiled unrepentantly. "My favorite part of dreams. Clothing is optional."

Erin hissed as he cupped her breast in his hand; then she gave him a whammy of her own.

He looked down at his new clothes with a frown. "What is this?"

She bit her lip at his costume. "You look *good* as a pirate."

He laughed. "Ahoy, matey," he said, laying her back against the grass. "Me cap'n's ship needs a port."

She moaned as he kissed her. "Me cap'n's port needs a ship."

They made love for an eternity. Erin had V'Aidan every way a woman could have a man. She took him under her, over her, and from behind her.

She spent hours running her hands and mouth over all that glorious tawny skin until she knew his body even better than she knew her own. In the end they soared into the sky, where they made love while the stars twinkled all around them.

Erin lay quietly in his arms, just listening to his heart beating under her cheek.

"V'Aidan?" she asked, sitting up to watch him. "Where do you go when you're not in my dreams? Do you visit other women?"

His hot look scorched her. "No. I don't want any other woman."

"Really?"

"I swear it."

She picked his hand up and kissed his palm. "Then what do you do?"

His eyes glowed. "I think up ways to make love to you."

She laughed out loud at the thought. "You know what I want to do?"

"After the night we've had, I honestly can't imagine."

"I want to show you a carnival. Have you ever been to one?"

"No."

Closing her eyes, Erin wished them to a state fair.

V'Aidan was aghast at her world. The bright lights and music . . .

Used to only visiting people in their nightmares, he'd never heard music before. The sound was wonderful and warm.

There were only a handful of people around and he let her take his hand and feed him cotton candy, candy apples, funnel cake, and corn dogs.

In between the food, they rode all kinds of rides that made his head spin. But not nearly as much as the woman herself did.

"Hey!" she said as they approached another booth. "Let's get our picture made. I've always wanted to have an old-timey photo done. What do you say?"

"Whatever makes you happy."

V'Aidan allowed her to dress him up in an Old West outfit while she dressed as a saloon girl, but his favorite part was when she sat in his lap where he could hold her. Better still, the dress she wore fell over them so that her bare thighs rested against his loins. It amazed him how fast his body leaped to life.

How could he want to make love to her when he'd already spent hours lost in her body? Yet there was no denying the fire he felt. The urge he had to free himself from his pants and press her hot, wet body down on him.

"You okay?" she asked, looking at him over her shoulder.

He nodded, even though his groin burned like an inferno.

In the first picture, they were cheek to cheek. The second was with her cradled in his arms, and for the last one she leaned over and kissed his cheek at the very last minute.

Erin took the pictures from the photographer and frowned. "Oh, good Lord," she breathed. "I look like the boobie prize."

"Excuse me?"

Her eyes sad, she handed him the pictures. "You're so incredibly handsome and I'm just a plump, round, average-looking nothing."

V'Aidan felt as though she'd slapped him. "Erin," he said, his voice thick. "You are not nothing. You are the most beautiful person I have ever known."

She smiled weakly. "You're sweet."

V'Aidan stopped her and turned her to face him. "No, I'm not. Do you want to know what I see when I look at you?"

Erin swallowed, her gaze searching his face. "Sure."

V'Aidan handed her the pictures again.

Looking at them, Erin gasped at what she saw. Her mouse-brown hair glowed with golden highlights. Her face had a perfect peachy complexion and her dark brown eyes were bright and shiny. She looked breathtaking.

And it was so *not* her.

"This is what you see?" she asked V'Aidan.

He nodded, his face grim. "That is what you are to me."

Erin reached to hug him, but before she could, a weird buzzing sounded.

V'Aidan vanished instantly.

"No!" she groaned as she woke up to the sound of someone ringing her doorbell.

Disappointed to the point of violence, she got up and answered the door.

She blinked in disbelief. Chrissy stood on the other side.

"Hey," Chrissy said brightly. "Sorry to disturb you, but John wanted me to drop off more data for the report."

Trying really hard not to be snappish, Erin opened the door and took the disks from Chrissy's hand. "Thanks. Sorry you had to come all the way out here."

"No prob." Chrissy frowned at her. "Were you asleep again?"

Erin blushed. "Yes, I was."

"Are you sure you're okay?"

"Positive."

"Nightmares?"

"Completely gone."

"Oh," Chrissy said, her voice strangely flat. "Glad to hear it. So then, normal dreams?"

Erin frowned at how choppy and odd their conversation was. "Wonderful dreams, anyway."

Chrissy nodded. "Ah, well, that's good. I'll see you later, okay?"

"Thanks again," Erin said as she closed the door.

She leaned her head against the door and cursed. Who or what did she have to kill to have an uninterrupted day with V'Aidan?

Over the next few days, Erin began to fear even more for her sanity. Not because of her nightmares anymore but because she no longer wanted to be awake.

Every night V'Aidan would come to her. She took him dancing and showed him all kinds of places and things he'd never seen before.

Worse, she learned that he had some degree of control over when she fell asleep. He'd told her he could borrow mist from his Uncle Wink and, much like the Sandman, Wink's mist could induce sleep.

On Friday afternoon when she felt a severe wave of tiredness come over her, she knew what V'Aidan had done.

He was becoming more and more impatient with waiting for her to fall asleep, and in the back of her mind she wondered if one day he would pull her into his realm and not let her go.

When she opened her eyes, she found him lying beside her, his eyes burning her with their intensity.

"Are you angry with me?" he asked, tracing her cheek with his hand.

"I should be. I really wanted to watch that movie."

"I'm sorry," he said, but his face told her he didn't have a smidgen of remorse.

"No, you're not."

He smiled down at her. "No, I'm not, but I don't want you to be angry with me for it."

She laughed at him. "You're evil."

His playfulness died instantly. "Why do you say that?"

She frowned at the hurt look she didn't understand. "I was joking, V'Aidan."

His jaw ticced angrily under her hand. "I never want you to think I'm truly evil."

"How could I?"

V'Aidan dipped his lips to hers, tasting her, wanting to devour her. He needed her and the more he was with her, the worse it became. He'd never known anything sweeter than those lips. Nothing more precious than her small, heart-shaped face.

Erin was overwhelmed by the passion in his kisses. Each one seemed to be even more possessive than the last.

Then he moved his lips lower, over her breasts, where he paused to take his time savoring each mound. As he teased her, white rose petals fell from the sky, covering her.

Erin laughed. "What is this?"

"My gift to you," V'Aidan said. "I want to bathe you in roses."

"Why white?"

"Because, like you, they are pure and beautiful."

Then he kissed her lower, across her stomach, her hip, down her leg, and then up her inner thigh until he kissed her where she ached.

Erin moaned at the feel of his mouth against her, his tongue sweeping across her nub, then down to where she throbbed. He growled, the sound vibrating through her.

He seemed to delight in giving her pleasure first. He never took his own until she'd climaxed at least twice before him.

She shook in the throes of her first release. When she was finished, V'Aidan pulled back with a devilish grin that made him appear boyish. "I love the way you taste. The way you smell."

She smiled warmly at him. "I love being with you. I don't even want to wake up anymore. I just live moment to moment, wishing I were asleep and waiting until I can see you again."

A dark look crossed his features.

Had those words hurt him? She couldn't imagine how or why they would, and yet . . . "V'Aidan?"

He moved away from her and his black clothes immediately returned to cover his body.

"V'Aidan, what is it?"

V'Aidan didn't answer.

What he was doing was wrong, and not just because it was forbidden. He didn't care about rules.

What he cared about was Erin.

And every time he pulled her into his realm he was robbing her of the pleasures of her own world. Of her life.

This was wrong, and for the first time he understood exactly how wrong it was.

"V'Aidan!" the howling shout echoed through the trees surrounding them.

He knew that angry bellow. "You must leave," he said, sweeping a quick kiss across her lips.

"But—"

He gave her no time to argue before he sent her back to her world and rolled over onto his back to appear nonchalant.

She had barely vanished before M'Ordant appeared to stand over him. Dressed in the same black clothes, M'Ordant looked very similar to V'Aidan. Same black hair, same silvery-blue eyes. The only thing they differed in was height. V'Aidan stood a good four inches taller and he wore the look of a deadly predator.

M'Ordant looked like a person the humans called a Boy Scout.

"What are you doing?" M'Ordant asked.

"I am lying in the sun," V'Aidan said, placing his hands behind his head. "You?"

"Is that an attempt at humor?"

V'Aidan shrugged as he looked up at his brother. M'Ordant was one of the oldest of the Oneroi and was one of Morpheus's most favored sons. "If it were an attempt, it would be wasted on you, now wouldn't it?"

"More humor?"

V'Aidan sighed. "Why are you here?"

"I have heard distressing news about you."

"And to think I thought all news about me was distressing."

That was lost on his brother as well as M'Ordant stared down at him. "Did you learn nothing from your punishment?"

Yes, he'd learned to be more careful seeking out Erin. To tell no one of the precious time they spent together.

"You're boring me, M'Ordant. Go away."

"You can't be bored."

"And a good thing, too, since I'd no doubt perish from it while in your company."

M'Ordant stared at him blankly. "I am merely here as a courtesy. As of this moment, the woman is tagged. Summon her again, and you will deal with me."

"Well, it certainly wouldn't be the first time you and I have crossed."

"True, but I have permission from Hypnos to make it the last time if you interfere with her again."

Erin *went to* sleep that night and waited for V'Aidan to show himself.

He didn't.

When she woke up in the morning, she trembled with loss and worry. Had something happened to him?

He'd acted so strangely yesterday. And that shout . . .

What could have happened? Could the Skoti have found him? Hurt him because he protected her?

"V'Aidan," she whispered. "Where are you?"

V'*Aidan ached as* he heard the plea in Erin's voice. He stood at her side, so close all he had to do was shift slightly and he would touch her. "I'm here, Erin," he whispered. "I've been here all night."

She didn't hear him.

He'd stayed by her bed the entire time she slept, watching her. Making sure none of the Skoti found her. He was sure Krysti'Ana was behind M'Ordant's appearance.

V'Aidan was all that stood between Erin and Krysti'Ana. So long as he visited her dreams and they were together, his sister would never be able to claim Erin.

Erin's mind was ripe with happiness and creativity. Her dreams were vivid and warm and bubbling over with emotions. Any Skotos would be attracted to her.

And now he could neither protect her nor . . .

His thoughts scattered as she wept.

Pain lacerated his chest at the sight of her grief. She sobbed as if her heart were broken.

Why?

But worse was the helplessness he felt. He hurt for her. "Please don't cry, *akribos*," he whispered, trying to gather her into his arms.

It didn't work.

He wasn't of her world. He could never be part of her world. Grinding his teeth, he cursed his formless existence.

Erin wept until her eyes grew heavy. Until she was spent and so tired, she couldn't move.

And as she slipped back into sleep, she thought for an instant that she caught a glimpse of V'Aidan in her room.

The next thing she knew, she found herself high on a mountaintop, looking out on the ocean.

The grass caressed her bare feet as the waves crashed on the surf far below. Wind whipped through her hair, plastering her white sundress to her body.

She breathed in the crisp, clean air and listened to the gulls cawing. How peaceful.

Just when she thought her dream couldn't improve, she felt two strong arms wrap around her. "Do you like it here?"

She shivered at the deep accent of V'Aidan's voice in her ear. "Yes, I do."

She turned in his arms to see his hot gaze staring down at her. She trembled at his concerned look, at the handsome lines of his face.

"Tell me why you were crying," he demanded.

"I was afraid something had happened to you."

"And it made you sad?"

She nodded.

V'Aidan shook with the knowledge. He leaned down and rested his chin against her shoulder and inhaled the sweet scent of her skin. She felt so incredible in his arms.

She had worried over him. It was unbelievable.

"Where were you?"

"I was with you," he breathed. "I just thought you'd want a night off."

She laughed at that. "You say that as if being around you is a trial."

"Isn't it?"

She looked aghast at the very idea. "No. Never."

"Why do you like being around me?"

"You make me happy."

He frowned. "I made you cry."

"Only a little."

"And still you want to be with me?"

"Of course I do."

The woman was the greatest fool in history.

He knew he didn't have long before M'Ordant would find them. He'd brought her to his land to help mask what he'd done, but it wouldn't shield the tag permanently.

But before he returned her, he wanted to share one last piece of himself with her before he said good-bye to her forever.

V'Aidan moved away and pointed out to the horizon that his special perch looked out onto. "Did you know you can see the edge of the world from here?"

"Excuse me?"

He smiled. "It's true. See that gold glinting in the sunlight? That's where the human world begins."

"Where are we?"

"This is the Vanishing Isle. Greek sailors used to believe they would come here when they died so that they could always be near the ocean."

"And why do they call it the Vanishing Isle?" she asked.

"Because you can only see it for a few minutes at sunup and sundown. Much like the pot of gold at the end of a rainbow, you can try to reach it, but you never will."

She looked up at him. "Are you really a Greek god?"

"Would it scare you if I were?"

"Do you want me to fear you?"

V'Aidan hesitated at her question. It was the answer that truly surprised him. "No, I don't."

She smiled a smile that shook him all the way to his heart. "Is this where you live?"

"Sometimes."

"Why only sometimes?"

"There are certain times of the year when I am banned from here."

Her brows drew together into a concerned frown. "Why?"

"The other gods don't like my kind. I am a pariah to all."

"Why would they feel that way? You are a champion."

"Not really. I'm a dream master and not what you see. I'm nothing more than the image you have made for me, but in reality I have no substance. No feelings."

"I don't believe that. A man without feelings would never have helped me the way you have."

He fingered her cheek. "You are so naive. Are all women like you?"

"No," she said with a devilish gleam in her eyes. "I've been told many times that I am highly unusual."

V'Aidan dipped his head down and took possession of her mouth. Erin sighed as she fisted her hands in the folds of his black shirt. "You taste like heaven," she breathed.

He needed to let her go. It was time.

But . . .

He couldn't do it.

Zeus have mercy on him, he couldn't send her back. Not when all he really wanted to do was hold on to her for the rest of eternity.

The air around them sizzled with electricity as the sky above turned dark. Erin trembled in his arms.

"What is that?" she whispered.

It was his death.

"Don't worry, *akribos*," he said, "I will protect you." The emotion behind the words stunned him most of all. He meant them, and for the first time ever he understood them.

Suddenly one of Zeus's lightning bolts hit the ground, driving them apart.

Erin fell several yards from V'Aidan.

V'Aidan tried to reach her, but before he could, ten demon Skoti appeared and surrounded her.

In her snake form, Krysti'Ana laughed, the sound cackling louder than thunder. "Tell me, human," she lisped. "What do you fear more? Dying yourself or seeing him die in your place?"

"Let her go," V'Aidan said, rising to his feet. He summoned his black armor to shield him and he pulled his sword from the air around them.

"Never," Krysti'Ana said with a laugh. "I need her ideas. I need her mind. Look at you. Look at me. See what she has done to us? You didn't make her weaker by releasing her creativity. You made her stronger. I have never been so powerful."

It was true. Erin's mind, her depth of spirit, was a treasure. One he had sworn to himself that he would protect at any cost. "Release her, or I will kill you." He pierced each of the Skoti with a murderous glance. "*All* of you."

Krysti'Ana laughed even harder at that. "You are forbidden to take my life."

"Forbidden or not, I will kill you before I see her harmed."

Erin watched in terror as the Skoti attacked V'Aidan. He fought them with his sword and arms, but he was outnumbered. It was futile. They flew at him, tearing his skin with their claws, shredding his armor.

The she-snake caught him with her tail and slammed him into a tree.

V'Aidan's entire body throbbed as he tried to push himself to his feet. In his human form, he didn't stand a chance against so many of them. He couldn't teleport out and leave Erin behind, and without touching her he couldn't teleport out with her.

"What's the matter, little brother?" Krysti'Ana taunted. "Why do you not change to fight me?"

V'Aidan glanced to Erin and he knew why. He didn't want to frighten her. He only wanted . . .

He only wanted her love.

The thought tore through him. He was to never know such. Was beyond it. But still the need was there. Aching. Yearning.

V'Aidan struggled to breathe. He could live and lose the possibility of her love forever or he could be what she thought he was and die in this human form.

If he died, she would have no one to protect her. . . .

Lost and unsure, he did what he'd never done before.

He called for help. "Hypnos!"

The god's reply came in the form of M'Ordant.

The Skoti backed down, circling back to Erin and Krysti'Ana in a protective circle.

M'Ordant approached him slowly, his face completely void of any emotion. "What would you have Hypnos do, V'Aidan? Would you have him offer you mercy for your crimes? Tell me, is there any rule made which you have not broken?"

"I . . ." He looked to Erin as she struggled against the Skotos holding her. Deep in his heart he had known what Hypnos's answer would be. He was nothing to the gods. Nothing to anyone.

But at least this way, Erin would be returned to her world and she would be free of the Skoti forever. "Protect her for me."

M'Ordant arched a brow at that. "For you? My job is to protect her *from* you." M'Ordant turned to face the Skoti. "He is yours to do with as you please. The woman, however, belongs to me."

V'Aidan felt the foreign sensation of tears in his eyes as he looked at Erin.

She was safe.

As for him . . .

He didn't want to live without her anyway.

Sinking to his knees, he dropped his sword and waited for the Skoti to carry out his sentence.

Erin screamed as she realized the monsters intended to kill V'Aidan. They circled around him like hungry lions stalking prey.

"Come," the unknown man said, taking her by the arm.

"They're going to kill him."

"If they don't kill him, I will."

"Why?"

He didn't answer. Erin felt the familiar pull of the Oneroi trying to send her home.

But she wouldn't go. She wouldn't leave V'Aidan alone to face the monsters.

Twisting out of M'Ordant's hold, she ran toward the Skoti and shoved her way through them.

She found V'Aidan on the ground, covered in blood. His armor in pieces around him, he lay helpless.

V'*Aidan felt someone* tugging at him. The desperate, grasping hands hurt him even more as they rolled him to his back. He looked up, expecting to see Krysti'Ana poised to end his life, but instead he met the dark brown eyes of heaven.

Erin wrapped herself around him, shielded him with her body as she willed herself to wake up. He heard her loud thoughts screaming in his head.

He wanted to tell her to go but couldn't.

His strength gone, V'Aidan could do nothing more than wrap his arms around her and cradle her gently. Her tears stung his wounds and he wanted to tell her not to cry for him. He wasn't worth it.

He'd never been worth anything until she had taught him kindness.

He heard M'Ordant trying to get through the Skoti to pull Erin back, but the Skoti refused.

"I'll have them both," Krysti'Ana snarled. "His life and her mind."

Closing his eyes, V'Aidan summoned the last of his powers. He kissed Erin on the lips, then sent her home.

As she shimmered out of his world, V'Aidan felt himself slipping, sliding down a deep hole. The world shifted and spun. Too weak to fight it, he allowed himself to go wherever it took him, and he was sure that place would be Tartarus.

Not that it mattered. Any day without Erin in his life was hell.

Erin woke up from her nightmare with a jerk and a scream lodged in her throat. She couldn't be back, not without V'Aidan. She had reached down deep inside her and had fastened on to him with all she possessed.

Her eyes were clenched shut. She didn't want to open them yet.

Didn't want to know that she had left him behind to die.

There had to be some way back to him. Some way to save him.

Her heart pounding, she felt something shift beneath her.

Opening her eyes, she realized she was back in her bed . . . and lying draped over a naked and bleeding V'Aidan.

5

"Ow," V'Aidan said as he lay in stunned disbelief. His entire being ached from his wounds, but then he'd suffered a lot worse beatings than this.

Still, in this "real" physical body it hurt so much that he could do nothing more than shake from the weight of the pain.

The only thing that made it bearable was Erin's presence. The softness of her body on his.

And quick on the heels of that thought came the one that if she had managed to bring him here, the others would follow to reclaim him.

V'Aidan had no fear for himself, only that they would come while he was too weak to protect her.

"Oh my gosh, it's you. It's *really* you!"

Erin reached up and touched his swollen jaw where one of the creatures had struck him hard. She brushed his hair back from his forehead and caught the panicked look in his eyes before he shielded it.

Even though bruises and cuts marred his face, she'd never seen anything more spectacular than V'Aidan alive and in her bed.

He was human.

She didn't know how she had managed it. Maybe it was her determination combined with his powers that had been forcing her away from him. Maybe it was a lot of things.

But all that mattered right now was that he was here with her. He wasn't a dream.

V'Aidan was a real-life man.

"I have to get out of here," he said, trying to get up. "I don't belong here."

No, he belonged to her dreams, and yet . . .

He was actually here. With her.

"I'm bleeding?" he asked, looking at his arm in disbelief. "Is this blood? This is blood. I'm bleeding."

She nodded, torn between the desire to cry for his wounds and to laugh out loud that she had somehow managed to bring him back with her.

"I need to get you to a doctor."

"No!" He winced. "I'm not supposed to be here. I'm not . . ."

V'Aidan paused. "I'm not human." He closed his eyes to teleport himself home. It didn't work.

Over and over he tried, and over and over he failed.

His heart pounded. It had been untold millennia since he had walked the mortal realm.

He'd forgotten the vividness of this world. The brightness of the colors and sharpness of sounds and smells.

Erin slid off the bed and disappeared while he tried to sort through it. How could he be here where she could see him?

How could he bleed real blood?

It had to be the fact that his demigod essence had been drained out of him during his beating.

The only way to kill a god was to remove all powers from him, which was what the Skoti had been doing. Erin's mind must have found some way to bring him over the threshold in that last moment before he died.

He should be in Tartarus by now, paying for his crimes for the rest of eternity. But somehow she had saved him. Somehow she had brought him here. There was no other explanation.

The power of her mind and spirit was phenomenal.

Erin returned with a damp washcloth. Carefully she wiped the blood from his face and body.

V'Aidan trembled at the softness of her hand and the way the cloth felt gliding over his flesh. She was always so kind. Until her, he had never understood that concept. Never known what it was to help someone else.

Before he realized what he was doing, he captured her lips, then winced as pain swept along his swollen jaw.

"Ow," he said again, pulling back.

Erin slid her hands over his chest as she inspected his wounds. In dreams, her touch had been muted, now it possessed a tender heat unimaginable. It left him breathless and raw.

V'Aidan reached out and cupped her face so that he could study her beautiful features. "Why are you helping me?"

"Because you need it."

He couldn't fathom such an unselfish reason. Such things didn't exist in his realm.

"You need to rest."

"I need clothes," he said.

"I will have to buy you some."

"Buy?"

"Purchase. You don't just walk into a store and have them give you what you need."

V'Aidan listened to the patience in her voice. Patience he wasn't used to. He knew so little about her human world. He'd been relegated to viewing it through the distortions of dreams and nightmares.

The pain inside him, he did know. It was the only emotion left to his kind. It was why they invaded human sleep. There they could feel other things. Even muted emotions were better than none at all.

"Would you . . . please," he forced the foreign word out, "get me some clothes?"

"Yes."

Incredible. She was so willing to help him. He was baffled by it. Slowly, carefully, he left the bed and walked around her room.

Erin's entire body shook as she left him to fetch a tape measure. How could this be real?

Was she still dreaming? There was a surrealness to this that made it seem like fantasy, and yet . . .

She cursed as she stubbed her toe against the plant stand in her living room.

No, that pain was real.

This wasn't a dream. V'Aidan was really in her world, and if she had pulled him here, maybe, just maybe, she could keep him here.

Erin! What are you thinking? A man like V'Aidan doesn't belong here. He's not even human.

And yet he was more human, more man, than anyone else she'd ever known.

She didn't want him to leave. And that thought frightened her most of all.

V'*Aidan looked up* as Erin returned a few minutes later with a strange cloth coil. "What is that?" he asked as she approached him while unwinding it.

"It's a tape measure. I need to know your size to buy your pants."

She wrapped a portion of it around his waist, her hands raising chills on his body, her touch raising another part of him as well.

"Thirty-three waist," she said, her breath falling on his chest.

She sank to her knees before him.

V'Aidan shivered at the sight of her brown hair between his knees as she bent to place one edge of the tape on the floor by his foot. She ran it up the inside of his leg.

Erin swallowed at the strength of his body. And when she reached his groin, her heart pounded. He was rigid and hard, and when her hand lightly brushed his sac, he hissed sharply.

"Thirty-six," she said absently, her gaze catching his.

The heat there was intense, and for the first time, she was actually afraid of him. He was a living man now, one who could possess who knew what strengths and powers in this world.

And they were alone in her house.

V'Aidan took her hand in his and led it to his erection. "I need you to touch me, Erin," he whispered, trailing her hand down the length of his shaft. He shivered from her softness. "I need to know that this is real and not . . . not a dream."

Because deep in his heart he was afraid this was nothing more than Hades tormenting him already. Perhaps he was dead and this was the way they intended to torture him.

Erin quivered at the sensation of his hard, hot manhood in her palm, and his strong, tapered hand leading her strokes. In her dreams, she'd always been uninhibited with him. Her phantom lover had never been real, only a figment of her imagination.

But it was a living, warm body she touched now. One of flesh and blood. A beautiful, masculine body that made her quiver and burn with something more than lust.

The look in his eyes scorched her. And she knew what he wanted. He wanted comfort. He needed to know that she still cared for him. Even in this world that was alien to him.

Was he as afraid of all this as she was?

How long could they be together before their respective worlds tore them apart?

V'Aidan knew he should release her, yet he couldn't bring himself to do it. He needed her. Needed her touch in a way that defied explanation.

She rose up on her knees and, to his utter shock, placed her mouth on him. He moaned at the feeling of her lips against the tip of his shaft, of her hot tongue stroking him. She cupped him gently with one hand, stroking his sac in time with the flicks of her tongue against him.

Never had anyone touched him like this. He felt weak before her. Powerless against her.

And in that moment, he knew he would never again be able to let her go.

Dear Zeus, what was he to do?

She was mortal and he . . .

He was cursed.

Erin stroked and soothed him, and when he released himself she didn't pull away.

Only when he was drained and weak did she pull back and look up at him. Then slowly, meticulously, she kissed her way up his body until she stood before him.

"It'll all be okay, V'Aidan," she whispered. "I promise."

No, it wouldn't. He knew better. There was no way to hide from the others. Sooner or later, they would come.

But he didn't want to scare her. Someway, he would protect her. No matter the cost to him.

He gathered her into his arms and held her close. If he could, he would fly her away from here. Take her back to the Vanishing Isle and keep her forever.

And then he felt it. Felt the evil presence of his sister. The hairs on the back of his neck rose. In this condition he would never be able to stop Krysti'Ana.

The phone rang.

"I'll be right back."

He released her; all the while he looked around trying to find Krysti'Ana. Her malevolence washed over him. Somehow she knew he was here.

He reached out with his thoughts, but in his weakened, wounded state he couldn't contact her.

It didn't matter.

He knew his sister's unspoken promise. She would be coming soon and he would have to find some way to protect Erin from her clutches.

Erin returned. "Sorry about that. It was a friend from work." She headed toward her bathroom. "I'm going to take a quick shower, then buy your clothes, okay?"

He nodded but didn't speak. He couldn't. Not when thoughts of his siblings occupied his mind.

He walked around Erin's small apartment, trying to find where his sister could be hiding. He found nothing, and as the minutes went by, his sense of her grew weaker, though whether from her leaving or from his own diminishing powers, he wasn't sure.

Erin left the bathroom, her face bright and rosy. "I can't believe I have you here." She threw herself into his arms and held him tight. "Oh, V'Aidan, tell me they can't get you now."

He opened his mouth to answer her honestly, then stopped himself. He didn't want to steal the happiness from her bright brown eyes.

"We're safe," he said, the word sticking in his throat.

She kissed him then, hot and passionately, then left him alone while she went for his clothing.

V'Aidan returned to lie on the bed and rest himself. If he could sleep, he could replenish his strength a lot faster, but he didn't dare close his eyes. Didn't dare fall asleep where he could reenter his world.

They would be waiting for him. With Erin's help, he had escaped them before. But he was sure there wouldn't be a second escape.

Sooner or later, they would take him; then Erin would be alone.

A *little while later,* V'Aidan heard Erin enter the apartment. Her shoes made the lightest of noises on the carpet. Even so, he knew her distinctive walk. Knew her scent, her sound. Knew things about her he'd never known about anyone else.

He turned over in the bed as she entered the room with a bag in her hands.

"I didn't mean to wake you," she said.

"I wasn't sleeping."

She moved forward and set the bag on the foot of the bed, then came to rest beside him. She placed her hand against his brow, then frowned.

"How do you feel?" she asked gently.

"Like I've been beaten."

She rolled her eyes at his blasé tone. "You have a pretty bad fever there. Maybe I should—"

"You can't call a doctor, Erin. Just because I appear human, it doesn't make me one of you."

"I know." She sat by his side and brushed his hair back from his damp brow. "So what are we going to do?"

He took her hand in his and ran the backs of her knuckles along his jaw, which had already begun to heal. Her touch was sublime. He'd never known such a thing existed. "I don't know."

"I was thinking while I was out that maybe we could find a ceremony or something to make you human. Some kind of ritual."

He smiled at the idea. "It's a good thought, love, but there's no such thing."

V'Aidan watched her then, and it was on the tip of his tongue to explain to her exactly what he was. But he couldn't bring himself to do it. Not after they had been through so much.

All he wanted was to enjoy what little time they had, and with that thought, he forced himself to get up.

Erin protested his movements as he dressed. "You're still hurt."

"I'll be fine," he said dismissively. "My kind heals fast."

Erin growled low in her throat as she watched him dress. The man wouldn't listen.

Insufferably male, he refused to relax for the rest of the day. He wouldn't even stay behind and rest while she went to the grocery store.

But she had to admit she really did like having him along. She'd lived alone for so long that she hadn't realized just how much fun someone could have in the produce department.

"So," V'Aidan said as she thumped a cantaloupe, "what are you listening for?"

She held it up to his ear and thumped. "This one is too ripe." Then she held up another one and let him hear the difference. "This one isn't."

She put the good cantaloupe in the cart, then turned around to catch him thumping bananas. Erin quickly grabbed them away from him. "We don't thump those."

"Why?"

"It'll bruise them."

"Oh." He looked around, then paused. "What about those?"

She turned to see the grapes. "Only thump if you want to turn them into wine."

He pulled her into his arms. "What about if I thump you?"

She smiled. "I'd probably make all kinds of interesting noises."

He grinned at that and gave her a quick, scorching kiss that sent heat throughout her entire body.

As they walked through the store, Erin couldn't help noticing the stares V'Aidan collected. She became aware again of just how different the two of them were. He was tall, sexy, and gorgeous and she was plain and simple.

She'd only had a few boyfriends and most of them had been as average-looking as she was. But V'Aidan . . .

He deserved a beautiful woman.

"Hey?" he asked as they reached the dairy section. "Are you all right?"

"I'm fine."

"You look sad."

"Just tired."

She saw the concern in his celestial eyes. "How tired?"

It was then she caught his meaning. "They'll be after us again when we sleep, won't they?"

He looked away and she had her answer.

"If they don't kill him, I will." M'Ordant's words echoed in her head.

"I won't let them have you," she said, taking V'Aidan's arm. "There has to be some way we can fight them."

He draped his arm over her shoulders and held her close. "You would fight for me?"

"Yes."

"Then I am the luckiest being in the universe."

V'Aidan gave her a tight squeeze as he inhaled the scent of her hair. And he wondered morbidly if she would feel that way if she knew the truth of his past.

If she ever knew the truth of him . . .

He wanted to tell her. But he didn't dare.

V'Aidan clenched his teeth. She would never know, any more than he would let her be harmed because of him. He would fight this battle, all right. Fight until either he won or they killed him. But he would do it the way he had lived since the dawn of time.

Alone.

He and Erin finished shopping and were putting their items in the car when V'Aidan heard a woman shrieking in the dark parking lot.

He saw a man running away.

"Oh, no," Erin breathed. "He stole her purse."

Without thinking, V'Aidan took off after the man. He caught up to him at the alley beside the grocery store.

The man turned on him with a gun and aimed it straight at his heart. "Don't mess with me, man. I'm your worst friggin' nightmare."

V'Aidan couldn't help laughing at his words. "You have no idea."

The man fired the gun. V'Aidan ignored the bullet that entered his chest without pain or blood. He took the purse from the man, then caught the thief by his throat and held him against the wall.

It was then V'Aidan felt himself slipping. He felt his true form welling up. His hand went from that of a human to—

"V'Aidan?"

Erin's voice brought him back. He recovered himself and stared at the thief, who was now ghostly pale from having witnessed the changes on V'Aidan's face.

"The next time you want to steal from someone, think of me waiting for you every time you close your eyes."

The thief quietly wet himself.

Erin ran up behind him with a security officer in tow. V'Aidan released the thief into the officer's custody then handed him the woman's purse.

"Are you all right?" Erin asked, her eyes falling to the hole in V'Aidan's shirt where the bullet had entered his flesh. Mortal weapons couldn't harm an immortal being.

V'Aidan nodded. His powers were returning.

"Take me home, Erin," he said, his heart tugging at the word. He'd never had a home before. Never really understood the meaning of the word and what it entailed.

Until now.

He followed her to her car and they drove back to her apartment in silence.

In fact, they spoke very little as Erin made their dinner and they ate it.

Afterward, he helped her clean up and watched her closely. What would it be like to stay here, like this? To have this woman by his side every night? If he had such, he would never make her hurt. Never let her want. He would do anything in his power to shelter and comfort her.

But all the wishing in the world couldn't make it real.

It was only a dream. . . .

Once they were finished cleaning up their dinner, they lay entwined on the couch while she watched television.

V'Aidan watched her. He held her cradled to his chest, feeling her breath fall on his skin.

Love me, Erin.

The words hung in his heart, unspoken as he ran his hand through her hair. He had no right to ask for her love. Had no right to ask anything of her.

"You are a scourge, boy. Despicable. Unsightly and cold. No one will ever welcome something like you. It's why you have to creep into their dreams. It's the only way anyone will ever have anything to do with you."

All too well he knew the truth of Hypnos's words.

Over the centuries, he had hardened his heart to the world. To everything. He'd shut himself off completely until the night when a pair of fear-filled brown eyes had looked up at him with kindness and hope.

Now, he just wanted a way to live out his life staring into those eyes. Feeling her tiny hands on his skin.

Erin listened to V'Aidan's heart beating under her cheek. He smelled of warm sandalwood and spice. She ran her hand over where the thief had shot him, still amazed that no scar or wound remained. It was an awful reminder of the fact that her entire day with V'Aidan had been an illusion.

He wasn't born of her world. And no doubt tonight they would be parted for eternity.

The thought broke her heart. She couldn't stand the thought of not seeing him again.

If this was her last night with him, then she wanted it to last.

Crawling up his body, she met his gaze and saw the hunger in the crystal silver gaze. She cupped his cheek in her hand and kissed him.

V'Aidan growled at the taste of her as his body roared to life. He tore the shirt from her as he rolled to press her down into the couch.

Erin heard the cotton fabric tear but didn't care. She wanted him with the same desperation. She pulled his shirt over his head and feasted on the sight of his bare chest. Only scars remained of the wounds he'd suffered, and he'd told her that, by tomorrow, if he survived tonight, even those would be gone.

He removed their clothes so fast that she could barely follow his moves. He leaned her up against the back of the sofa arm and drove himself deep into her.

They moaned in unison.

She wished she could keep him inside her forever. She never wanted another day without him in it.

V'Aidan made love to her feverishly, savoring every deep stroke. He caressed her breasts as he kissed her, felt her from the top of his head all the way to his toes.

Her warm body surrounded his, fit him to perfection. And the feel of her hands on his back . . .

It was bliss. Pure bliss. He closed his eyes and delighted in the feel of her breasts on his chest, her tongue on his throat. Oh, yes, he wanted to stay here with her.

Forever.

Erin ran her hand through his long hair, her fingers clenched as pleasure ripped through her, each thrust deeper and harder than the last. She wrapped her legs around his waist, bucking her hips in time to him. Drawing him into her body even deeper. She clung to him as she came, crying out his name.

He kissed her lips and quickened his pace until he released himself inside her.

Erin lay still, feeling his essence fill her. She didn't want to move, didn't want to feel him leave her.

"I love you, V'Aidan," she said before she could stop herself.

V'Aidan froze at the words. Pulling back, he stared at her in disbelief. "What?"

Her cheeks turned pink as her brown gaze shredded what was left of his heart. "I love you."

"You can't. It's not possible."

"Possible or not, I do."

V'Aidan gathered her into his arms and held on to her desperately. He shook from the force of what he felt for her. So powerful, so overwhelming.

Sated to a depth he'd never known before, he pulled her on top of him and listened to her even breaths as her sleep took her.

He wanted to wake her up but knew better. Unlike him, she had to have her sleep.

"Erin," he whispered softly as he stroked her hair. "I promise you, I'll always be what you think I am."

Resigned to the inevitable, he closed his eyes and waited for M'Ordant and Krysti'Ana to come for them.

6

V'Aidan woke up to a piercing screech that felt as if it would shatter his eardrums.

He groaned at the awful sound as Erin stirred on top of him.

"What is that?" he asked.

"My alarm clock," she said, rising from him to rush to her bedroom.

It wasn't until her return that they both realized what had happened.

Nothing.

"Did you have any dreams?" he asked.

She shook her head. "You?"

"No," he said, smiling.

"Do you think . . ."

His smile faded. "No. They can find us. Sooner or later, they will."

Erin closed her eyes and cursed the thought of it. "Maybe they won't bother." She saw the doubt in V'Aidan's eyes.

Wanting to cheer his dour mood, she pulled him up by his arm. "C'mon. Let's take a shower and then I'll call in sick to work."

"You can't. What if you get fired?"

She shrugged. "I'll find another job."

He shook his head at her. "You are amazing."

She smiled at him.

Erin called into work only to be reminded of the marketing report that had been due on Friday, which she had forgotten to drop off.

"The meeting is at noon," John told her.

"Okay, I'm on my way up there with it."

"Is something wrong?" V'Aidan asked as she hung up the phone.

She shook her head. "I just have to take something to the office. Want to come with me?"

"Sure."

They didn't speak much as she drove across town. V'Aidan held her hand the entire time and Erin had to admit she liked the strength of his hand wrapped around hers.

Once they reached her building, Erin led V'Aidan into the maze where her cubicle was. He watched the hustle and bustle of corporate life with a dispassionate stare.

Erin went to John's office, only to find it empty.

With V'Aidan directly behind her, she dropped the report in John's in-box, then turned to leave.

Chrissy stood in the doorway with Rick Sword behind her. The two of them stepped into the office and closed the door.

Erin heard V'Aidan curse.

What the devil was going on?

"What are you doing here?" V'Aidan asked, his voice laced with anger.

"Waiting for you." Chrissy stepped around them and pulled the blinds closed. "You won't dare fight us in her workplace, will you, V'Aidan? All we have to do is make ourselves invisible to the humans and they won't see or hear anything but her. And *her* they'll lock up in an asylum as soon as we're gone."

Erin still didn't understand what was going on. But she had a sick feeling that she had been duped from the very beginning by all of this.

If V'Aidan could be real then so could they.

"What is this?" Erin demanded.

Chrissy's eyes flashed to yellow and it was then Erin knew the truth.

Chrissy was the she-snake from her nightmares.

"Stay out of it, human," Rick said. "We will deal with you after we finish with him."

V'Aidan pulled Erin behind him.

"How very sweet." Chrissy's tone was mocking. "One would think you were Oneroi the way you coddle her."

"He *is* Oneroi," Erin shot back, her entire body shaking from panic. How could she and V'Aidan fight them here? Like this?

Rick laughed at her words. "Is that the lie you told her?"

V'Aidan held his breath. He didn't want her to find out like this. "Erin, I . . ." His words faltered as he turned to see the confused look on her face.

He didn't want to tell her the truth. He didn't want to be what he was anymore. She had shown him something better and he didn't want to go back to the way he'd been.

"What does she mean?" Erin asked.

"He's your dragon," Krysti'Ana said mercilessly. "The thing I fought the first night we met in your dreams."

"No." Erin shook her head. "It's a lie. V'Aidan, tell me it's a lie."

He wanted to, but he couldn't. He'd lied so many times that it shouldn't have mattered to him. Yet it did.

"I'm a Skotos, Erin."

Her eyes filled with tears. "It was you! You who made me so terrified I couldn't sleep? You who chased me and . . . and . . ." She couldn't even begin to recount the torture he had put her through during those first few weeks. She had thought she was losing her mind. "Why did you trick me into thinking you were Oneroi? Was it just so you could feed from me?"

"At first, I only wanted to get you away from Krysti'Ana. I knew you wouldn't go with the dragon, so I appeared to you as a man. And then later . . ." His voice trailed off as his eyes went dead.

"You lied to me."

"I know."

She backed away from him. The agony in her eyes sliced him.

V'Aidan clenched his teeth as grief washed over him. "I needed you, Erin. And I didn't know how else to keep you with me." He reached for her.

She cringed and the gesture tore through him. She no longer wanted his touch.

Like all the others, she, too, rejected him.

The hurt betrayal on her face made him feel lower than any of the insults the others had ever dealt him.

"I should have known," she whispered, "someone like you pretended to be could never really want someone like me."

V'Aidan winced at the pain in her voice. "Erin, don't say that. You are the most wonderful person who has ever been born."

"Is that another of your lies?"

V'Aidan closed his eyes. There was nothing he could say to make this right. He'd been wrong from the very beginning.

All he could do now was make sure no other of his kind hurt her.

"M'Ordant!" he called, summoning his brother to him.

The Oneroi appeared between Krysti'Ana and Rec'Sord.

V'Aidan took a deep breath. "I will go with them peacefully if you will keep them from her."

"It is my job, is it not?"

V'Aidan nodded. It was the job of the Oneroi to help. It was the job of a Skotos to use and destroy.

He turned to look at Erin, but she refused to meet his gaze. Judging by the tears she fought, he would say he'd done his job very well this time.

His last view of her was when M'Ordant wrapped his arm around her the way he yearned to.

Krysti'Ana and Rec'Sord grabbed him to take him home.

"I'm sorry, Erin," V'Aidan whispered as they shimmered from her realm into his. "I'm so very sorry."

Erin didn't move. She knew V'Aidan was gone. She'd heard the sincerity of his apology as he vanished. But inside she was all raw emotions. Raw betrayal. She kept seeing the horrible dragon in the cave. Feeling the scaly talons on her.

How could that be the same man who had made love to her? The same man who had made her love *him*?

The betrayal of it lacerated her heart. Why? Why had he made her believe in him?

"I don't understand any of this," she said to M'Ordant.

"Sh," he said, brushing her hair back from her face. "Krysti'Ana and Rec'Sord wanted you for their own, but V'Aidan got to you first. When she found out he'd beat her to you, she was livid."

"But how did he find me?"

"Something in your subconscious called out to him. He was only supposed to give you a single nightmare and move on, but he didn't."

"And Chrissy?"

"When she couldn't take you from him, she called in her mate, Rec'Sord. I was alerted shortly thereafter to protect you. I told V'Aidan to leave you. He refused."

Her head swam from M'Ordant's information and from the pain and hurt inside her. "Why did he refuse to leave me?"

"I don't know. I guess it's just what he is. The Skoti suck the hopes and dreams out of others. I suppose he got a kick out of playing the hero with you. Building you up so he could hurt you more."

Erin felt so foolish. So betrayed. How could she have been so blind?

The eyes, she thought with a start. She should have realized the eyes were the same color.

Was she really that desperate for a hero that she would accept a demon in disguise?

Suddenly, she felt ill.

Heartbroken, she headed home, wanting to forget she had ever heard of V'Aidan.

E*rin sat alone* for the rest of the day, thinking, remembering.

"You should be a writer." V'Aidan's kind voice echoed through her head.

It wasn't the demon she remembered as she sat on her couch, clutching a pillow to her middle. It was the man. And as she sat alone in her apartment, she realized she would never again see him.

Never be able to share her day or her thoughts.

Most of all, she couldn't tell him her dreams. V'Aidan might have started off by feeding from her, but in the end he had given her so much more.

He had been her friend as much as he had been her lover.

The loss tore through her.

But what could she do? He was back in his world and she was in hers. It was over.

There was nothing left.

In the end, the Skotos had won after all. V'Aidan had drained all her happiness, all her hopes, all her dreams. What was left was an aching, empty shell that wanted nothing more of this world or the other.

A*s the days* went by, the pain of betrayal began to lessen and Erin remembered more of her dreams.

The more she remembered, the more she wanted to see V'Aidan one last time. Could she have been so stupid as to let him completely fool her?

She didn't think so.

V'Aidan wasn't that cruel. She'd seen things in him that defied what she knew him to be. His words came back to her. Words of protection. He had taught her to release her creativity to keep the Skoti away.

And there at the end . . .

"I will go with them peacefully if you will keep them from her."

No, those weren't the words of a monster. Those were the words of a man who cared more for her safety than for his own. Such a man, regardless of what M'Ordant had told her, was not all evil.

Desperate, Erin went to sleep, trying to find V'Aidan again. It didn't work.

Erin woke up in the middle of the night, terrified. Where was V'Aidan and why wouldn't he come to her?

For more than a week she tried everything she could think of to reach V'Aidan. Nothing worked. And as every day passed, she hurt more.

There had to be some way to contact him.

Discouraged and heartbroken, Erin sat at her desk, dazed. She'd barely slept in days and she was so weary.

"V'Aidan," she whispered. "Why won't you talk to me?"

"Erin," John said from his doorway. "In my office. Now."

By the tone of his voice she figured she was in serious trouble. No doubt he was going to fire her for missing so much work.

What did she care anyway? At this point, she was only going through the motions of life. Nothing was important to her now. She'd lost the only thing that gave her life meaning. The only one who had ever believed in her.

Soul-sick, she got up and walked the short distance to John's office.

"Close the door. Sit down."

She did as he commanded.

He sat there for several minutes, sipping his coffee, reading his E-mail.

She wondered if he had forgotten her. Then he turned, pulled his glasses down the bridge of his nose, and stared at her. "It's awful, isn't it?"

"What?"

"Loving an immortal."

Erin had a sudden urge to clean out her ear. "Excuse me?"

"Oh, come on, don't play innocent with me. Why do you think Chrissy was working here?" He pointed to the dolphin tattoo on his left forearm. "I'm an oracle for the Greek gods. Which is why I'm so damned tired and cranky all the time. They have the most annoying habit of bursting in when you least expect it." He sighed disgustedly. "The least they could do is pay me, but oh no, I was lucky enough to be born into this. And benefits . . ." He snorted. "No sleep, no pay, no peace. Got to love it."

She disregarded his tirade. "So, you're like the Oracle of Delphi? I thought they were all women."

"Those particular oracles are, but not all of us are female. Obviously. We are merely human channels to the various gods."

Totally baffled, she stared at him, wondering if maybe this was a dream, too, or if the Big Guy had lost *his* mind. Something wasn't right, at any rate.

"Okay, so you're an oracle. Want to tell me why you hired Chrissy if you knew she was a dream-sucking monster?"

He shrugged. "She is a god and I have no choice except to serve her. She wanted a chance to scope out human targets. I merely provided her a safe cover."

"You sold me out?"

"No," he said, his stern look turning gentle. "They weren't supposed to drain you the way V'Aidan did. Trust me. What he did was wrong. And you can rest assured he is being adequately punished for it."

Her heart stopped at the forbidding note in his voice. "Punished how?"

"What do you care?" he asked, pushing the glasses back up on his nose. "You're rid of him. Right? No more Skoti in your dreams. You have your life back to yourself."

"I want to know." No, she *needed* to know what had happened to him.

John took a drink of coffee. "Why they sent him to Tartarus, of course."

Erin didn't understand the term, and at the moment she wished she'd paid more attention in school. "Is that like jail?"

"Oh, no, hon. It's hell. They killed him the minute they took him back to his realm."

Erin couldn't breathe as tears welled up in her eyes. The weight in her chest was excruciating. It wasn't true. It couldn't be true. "They killed him?"

"Didn't you know?" he asked simply. "Didn't he tell you what they were going to do to him? V'Aidan was never one who played by the rules. He'd already been banned centuries ago from taking human form and banished from this realm."

"Why?"

"Because he would pretend to be human. Skoti are not supposed to have any creativity of their own. They're not supposed to want love. Not supposed to want anything except a single night of dream surfing, hopping from one person to the next. He'd behaved for centuries, until he found you. Even after they stripped all his skin from his immortal body, he couldn't stay away from you."

John sighed. "Hypnos had already banned his transformation

powers, so he decided there was nothing more to be done with him. Since V'Aidan wouldn't obey him, they sent him to Tartarus for the rest of eternity."

"But he didn't hurt me. Not really."

"Didn't he? You look awful from here. Like you've been crying for months. And I swear you've lost at least ten pounds since all this started."

"That's not his fault."

"No?"

"No. I don't want him to suffer because of me."

His gaze searching hers, John pulled an envelope out of his desk drawer and handed it to her.

"What's this?"

"Open it."

Frowning, Erin did as he said and saw the three pictures of her and V'Aidan at the carnival. Her hand shook as grief and agony swirled in her heart. "Where did you get these?"

"M'Ordant sent them to you. He thought you might like them as a souvenir."

She stared at V'Aidan's handsome face. At the love in his eyes.

"I have to see him," she insisted.

John shook his head and sighed again. "Well, I'm afraid it's too late now."

"It can't be. Please. I need to see him again. Please, tell me there's some way I can reach him.

John narrowed an intense gaze on her. "That depends on whether or not you really love him."

Erin *still couldn't* believe what she was doing. She'd allowed John to teleport her into the Underworld, where he'd told her M'Ordant would be waiting to guide her to V'Aidan.

Not that she really believed in the Underworld, but at this point . . .

M'Ordant materialized in front of her. "Are you sure about this?"

"Yes."

Nodding, he led her through a deep, dark cavern that reminded her much of the one V'Aidan had used to torment her. They walked for what seemed like miles before they came to a small cave.

A light was shining inside and she could hear a man's voice speaking. "You're thinking of her again, aren't you?"

She looked inside and saw the once-proud dragon lying weakly on the floor with his back to her. Someone had chained his neck to a large boulder. His shoulders were slumped, his wings lying broken and useless on the earthen floor. His reddish skin had an ashen, dehydrated look and every inch of his body was covered with bleeding welts.

Erin swallowed at the sight. Could that monster really be the man she loved?

"What's her name?" the man asked. "Elise? Erika?"

"Erin," the dragon rasped, his voice both familiar and yet foreign to her. "Her name is Erin."

"Ah, yes, Erin." The man shook his head. "Tell me what kind of worthless fool gives up immortality for a woman? Especially a woman who threw him so quickly to his death?"

"She was worth it."

"Was she? M'Ordant told me she was dreaming of a man last night. Some golden-haired type. Got to figure that if she's dreaming of someone so soon, she's probably already got him picked out and is ready to sleep with him. Bet she's giving him the high hard one even as we speak."

The dragon let out an anguished cry that tore through her.

The man didn't seem to care. He dumped food and water into two containers and moved them away from the dragon. "You'd better hurry. I don't think you've made it yet before your food evaporated." Then he vanished.

Erin watched as the dragon struggled to reach the food and water. His wounds bled anew as he limped, straining against the boulder that would only barely budge. He held one to his heart, and when she saw what it clutched, her own heart splintered apart in pain.

It was that stupid wreath of wildflowers she'd made.

V'Aidan collapsed just before the water, his claw reaching out desperately for it.

Tears streaming down her face, Erin ran to where he lay. She grabbed the water, noting half of it was already gone, and as she touched the container, she knew why. It was red-hot. It burned her hands, but she didn't care.

V'Aidan needed the water.

Kneeling down, she helped him sit up enough so he could drink.

V'Aidan gasped at the liquid as it soothed his parched throat. His eyes were so swollen from his beatings that he couldn't see who helped him. All he knew was that at last he had a moment of peace from his burning thirst.

"Thank you," he breathed, laying his head back down.

"You're welcome."

He froze at the voice that had stayed with him all these weeks. The voice that both soothed and tortured him.

It was then he felt her gentle touch against his scaly flesh.

Erin cried over what they'd done to him. She ran her hand along his rocky flesh, unable to believe they had reduced him to such a state.

He tried to push himself away from her. "Go. I don't want you to see me in this hideous form."

She laid her cheek against his and held him close. She now understood what he'd meant that night at the carnival. "I don't care what you look like, V'Aidan. I love you as you are."

Those words tore through him. "You're not real," he said, his voice ragged. "My precious Erin can't love a monster. No one can. She is goodness and light, and I . . . I am nothing."

He looked up and roared at the ceiling, "Damn you, Hades! How dare you mock me like this, you bastard! Isn't it enough for you that I ache every minute of every hour for her? Just leave me to suffer in peace."

Erin refused to let go of him. "It's not an illusion, V'Aidan. I want us to go home. Together."

Tears welled in his swollen eyes, stinging them unmercifully. It was a cruel lie. He'd never had a home. Never had love.

He pulled against the chain that choked him, wishing for one moment that he could be with Erin again in her dreams. It had been the only time in eternity he had ever known happiness. "I am damned here, Erin. I have no powers. Nothing to offer you at all. You must go. If you stay here too long, they won't let you leave."

Erin looked around his cold, dark prison that smelled and slithered. She'd never seen a more inhospitable place. Her worst fear had been being stuck in this cave with the dragon.

But if that was what it took to have V'Aidan, then she was willing to do it. "I'm not going to leave you again."

He lifted his head and she could tell he was trying to see her. "What are you saying?"

"I'm saying that if you can't go home with me, then I will stay here with you. Forever."

V'Aidan gaped at her. "You don't know what you're doing." He pushed at her with his talon. "Go!"

She didn't move. "I will not leave you."

He gathered her into his arms and held her close. "If you really love me, Erin, you won't stay. I could never stand the thought of knowing you were here because of me. Please, love, please go and never look back."

Erin sat in indecision, holding his talon in her hand. How could she leave him here, like this, knowing no one else would help him? Comfort him?

M'Ordant moved forward and pulled her away from V'Aidan, then walked her to the opening, where he kept her still.

For several minutes, V'Aidan didn't move at all. Then he lifted his head and tried to look around.

"Erin?" he asked quietly. "Are you still here?"

M'Ordant motioned for her silence. "She's gone now."

V'Aidan's lip quivered with sadness. "You sent her home?"

"Yes."

"Thank you." He lay down as if all his strength had been stripped from him.

"Tell me," M'Ordant said. "Why didn't you want her to stay with you?"

"You wouldn't understand."

"Understand what?"

"Love."

M'Ordant snorted. "What does a Skotos know of love?"

"Absolutely nothing . . ." He took a deep breath. "And everything. I couldn't ask her to stay here when I know how much this place scares her."

"But you wanted her to stay?"

V'Aidan nodded weakly. "More than I want my freedom. Now, leave me, brother."

Erin wiped the tears from her face as she stared at M'Ordant. She gave him a hopeful look.

"Can I stay?" she whispered so that V'Aidan wouldn't hear her.

His face impassive, M'Ordant shook his head and led her from the room. "It's not up to me."

"Then who?"

He refused to answer. "You have to leave."

"I won't leave him," she said, her voice firm. "And no one is going to make me."

Erin found out those were famous last words as she came awake back in her office. When dealing with Greek gods, human will didn't amount to much.

Heartbroken, she wept, thinking about V'Aidan in his hell and the fact that she was the cause of it.

Worst of all, there was absolutely nothing she could do to help him. Nothing.

V'*Aidan.*"

V'Aidan clenched his teeth at Hypnos's voice. He tucked Erin's wreath under a nearby rock to keep the god from seeing it and taking it from him as he had done the pictures.

It was all V'Aidan had of her and he couldn't bear the thought of losing it.

He forced himself upright and cleared his throat of the grief that choked him. "I didn't realize it was time for more punishment."

Hypnos snorted. "I can't break you, can I?"

He sensed the god moving around him.

"You know," Hypnos said irritably, "I have tried since the dawn of time to make you fear me. And you never have. Why is that?"

"I can't feel emotion, remember?"

"No. What you are is disrespectful, irreverent, and sarcastic. You have never fit in with us. And the thing that has always made me maddest with you is that you never even tried to."

V'Aidan gave a weak laugh. "A Skotos who is evil to the bone, imagine that."

"Well, therein is your problem. Unlike the others, you never were. I never could kill that last tiny bit of goodness in you. That last bit that was capable of honor. Capable of sacrifice."

V'Aidan frowned.

"M'Ordant told me what you did for Erin. Both on earth and here. As a result, Hades has informed me that he can't keep you in Tartarus. Only souls who are completely incapable of love can stay here."

A burning sensation started in V'Aidan's body, and with every heartbeat that passed, he felt himself growing stronger.

"It seems to me, boy, you have a decision to make."

E*rin opened the* door to her apartment. The familiar hole in her heart burned as she imagined what it would be like to come home, just once, and have V'Aidan here.

She'd been doing that a lot lately. Daydreaming. She'd never really daydreamed before. And she'd been writing. But there was no one to share it with.

That hurt most of all.

Toeing her shoes off, she set her keys down on the mantel and happened to see a white rose petal on the carpet. She frowned as she noticed several more.

They seemed to form a trail leading to her bedroom. She followed them.

When she got to the doorway, her heart stopped.

V'Aidan was asleep in her bed. His sleek black hair was spread out over the pillows, the covers tangled in his long, tawny limbs.

He was the most gorgeous thing she'd ever seen in her life.

Erin laughed as tears welled in her eyes. How? How could he be here?

Rushing to her bed, she dropped to her knees and tried to wake him.

He didn't budge.

No matter what she tried, he wouldn't wake.

"V'Aidan?" she said, swallowing in fear. "Please, look at me."

Nothing.

Terrified, she saw a small note card on the nightstand.

Picking it up, she read it:

It is through true love that all miracles are performed. If you really love me, Erin, kiss my lips and I will be born into your world as a mortal man. Otherwise, I shall be waiting for you only in your dreams.

You have until midnight to decide.

V

She didn't need until midnight to decide. Cupping his face in her hands, she kissed him with all the love in her heart.

His chest rose sharply as his arms wrapped around her and held her tight.

Erin laughed happily as V'Aidan deepened their kiss. Her head swam from his warmth, his passion, and she never wanted to let him go.

Nipping her lips, he pulled back to smile at her. The love in his silvery-blue eyes scorched her. "I take it you want to keep me?"

"Buddy, you try and leave me and I'll follow you to the ends of the earth and beyond to find you and bring you home."

V'Aidan laughed. She'd already proven that to him.

Erin shivered as he unbuttoned her shirt. "I think I know what you want to do first as a mortal man."

He ran his tongue over her throat, up to her ear, where his breath sent chills through her. "Believe me, love, you won't be sleeping tonight."

Epilogue

Two years later

V'Aidan lay on the sofa with his infant daughter asleep on his chest. He stared at her mop of chestnut curls, curious about what she was dreaming.

He felt his wife standing over them.

Looking up, he caught Erin's gorgeous smile. "Hi," he said, wondering what she was up to. There was a gleam in her eye much like the one she'd had the day she'd told him she was pregnant.

"Guess what?" she asked, her voice rife with excitement.

"You're pregnant again?"

She rolled her eyes at him. "It's only been three months since we had Emma."

"It happens."

She blew him a raspberry, then brought her arm from around her back and shoved a book into his hands.

V'Aidan stared at it blankly until the name on the cover registered. "Oh my God," he breathed, "it's your novel."

"I know," she said, jumping up and down. "My editor sent me the first copy of it! They'll be shipped to the stores next week."

Careful not to wake the baby, V'Aidan shot off the couch to grab Erin into his arms.

Erin sighed at the feel of his lips on hers. Even now, those lips could incinerate her. And his smell . . . Goodness, how she loved the scent of his skin.

"Thank you, V'Aidan," she said, pulling back to stare into those hauntingly silver eyes. "I would never have written it without you."

"And I would never have lived without you."

Erin held him close, delighting in the feel of him and her daughter. The two of them were the greatest gift Erin had ever known.

And it was then she realized that even out of the darkest nightmare, something good could come. It had taken strength and courage, but in the end, it had been worth the battle.

"I love you, Erin," he whispered against her hair.

"I love you, V'Aidan, and I always will."

Winter Born

Prologue

It was hard to find an all-powerful, mythical being in a crowd of thirty thousand.

Or at least it was in theory.

At the yearly Dragon*Con science fiction convention in Atlanta, Georgia, however, it was another story entirely. There were two Yodas and a Dragon Rider from Pern checking in at the hotel's front desk while a full regiment of Storm Troopers walked by. There were gods and goddesses, all manner of aliens, warriors, and ladies gathered there. Pandora had even seen the Wicked Witch of the West cruise by on her motorized broomstick.

Since she'd sat down ten minutes ago, Pandora had counted nine Gandalfs, and if she didn't miss her guess, there were at least two dozen elves, fairies, orcs, goblins, and assorted others gathered around, talking on cell phones, or smoking just outside the hotel doors.

And one mustn't forget the entire cabal of vampires and demons walking around handing out fliers for people to come to their room for a "blood party" and Buffy film fest.

Not to mention she'd already been invited twice to the Klingon Homeworld in Room 316 at the Hyatt Regency across the street. Meanwhile a group of supposedly androgynous Borg men had tried to "assimilate" her as soon as she entered the lobby of the Marriott Marquis.

This had to be the strangest gathering she'd ever seen, and when given the fact that she was a Were-Panther who up until three days ago had lived solely among her own preternatural kind, that said something.

"I'm never going to find him," she murmured to herself as an extremely tall, gorgeous Goth man stopped in front of her.

Good glory, the man was sinfully delectable!

And he was the last thing she needed to be staring at, yet she couldn't seem to help herself. He was utterly compelling.

He wore a pair of dark sunglasses even inside the hotel while he scanned the motley crowd as if looking for someone. Something about the man commanded attention and respect. Of course, it didn't help that her hormones were currently elevated by the change going on inside her as she came into full womanhood. Her entire body was humming from hormonal overload which, up until his appearance, she'd been keeping under very careful control.

Now she sizzled for a taste of him and it was all she could do to stay seated.

He had to be at least seven feet tall, augmented by the flame biker boots that added at least three inches to his height. He had long black hair that flowed around his broad shoulders, and wore an old, faded motorcycle jacket with a skull and crossbones painted on the back. The worst part was that he wore *nothing* underneath that jacket and every time he moved, she glimpsed more of his tanned, ripped body.

His black leather pants hugged a perfect bottom that would rival any of her Were brethren. Every part of her wanted to stand up, cross the small distance between them, and pull his tall, lean body against hers until the vicious, needful hunger in her blood was fully sated. But even as she felt that primal sexual hunger, the animal part of herself sensed an air of lethal danger from him.

He wasn't the kind of man a woman approached without an invitation.

"Akri!"

The man turned as a woman around his age came running up to him. Cute as she could be, she was dressed like a demon, complete with a set of black wings that looked spookily real as they twitched and flapped. Her skin was red and black, and her hair matched his. She even sported a pair of glowing red horns on her head. Her short purple skirt was flared and she wore a black leather bustier with three large silver buckles on the front. Black and purple striped leggings and a pair of six-inch platform combat boots completed her odd outfit.

The tall "demon" handed the man a credit card. "It's broke again, *akri*," she said, pouting around a pair of vampirelike fangs. "The man downstairs done said that the Simi can't charge nothing else until I'm not over my limit no more. I don't know what that means, but I don't like it. Fix it, *akri*, or else I might eat him. The Simi gots needs and I needs my plastic to work."

The man laughed as he took it from her and pulled out his wallet. He handed her three more credit cards.

The "demon" squealed in delight and pulled him into a hug. She put the credit cards into her coffin-shaped purse, then handed him a small shiny red nylon bag. "By the way, I boughts those for you before I broke my plastic. Since you don't got your real hornays, these are some fake ones to tide you over until we go home."

"Thanks, Sim," he said in an incredibly deep, evocative voice as he took the bag from her.

She smiled, kissed his cheek, then dashed off into the crowd with her wings flapping behind her.

The man looked at Pandora then and gave her a half-grin that could only be called wicked, and yet it seemed somehow knowing. He inclined his head to her, then headed off after the woman who'd just left him.

Every instinct in her body told her to follow him, but she didn't listen.

She was here to find the legendary Acheron Parthenopaeus—an ancient, immortal Atlantean her sister had hoped would help hide Pandora from those who were hunting her. Not chase after some hot, young human who looked stunning in leather.

Acheron was her last hope.

Unfortunately, neither she nor her sister had any idea what he looked like. All they knew was that he came to Dragon*Con every year with his daughter.

He was older than time and more powerful than any other of his kind. She scanned the older men in the crowd who were dressed as wizards, warriors, or other creatures, but none of them seemed to be particularly wise or powerful, nor were they with a daughter.

Just what would an eleven-thousand-year-old man look like anyway?

Sighing, Pandora stood up and went to the bannister so that she could look down to the lower levels of the hotel and scan the crowd.

He had to be here.

But where? How could she find anyone in this thronging mass of people . . . er, aliens.

Chewing her lip, she debated where to go look for him. Suddenly, a tall man in an elegant black suit caught her eye. He wasn't particularly old, probably in his mid-thirties, but she sensed an unmistakable air of power from him.

Maybe he was the mysterious Acheron. And he was heading for the bank of elevators.

Pandora rushed after him, and barely made it before the door closed them inside the small compartment with a Renaissance drummer, a green-fleshed alien, and Darth Vader.

But that wasn't what made her heart stop. As she glanced out through the glass wall of the elevator, she saw four things that terrified her.

It was a group of devastatingly gorgeous men. The two shortest of the group were identical in looks and they had to be at least six feet four. They all had jet-black hair and were dressed in black Goth clothes.

The four men stood in a specific formation that she knew all too well, with their backs to each other as they scanned the crowd hungrily, intently, as if seeking something in particular. They were fierce. Animalistic.

It was as if they had literally caught wind of something, and in one heartbeat she knew what that something was.

Her.

"Oh no," she said under her breath. By their build and beauty and actions, she would know their breed anywhere. No group of humans could be that handsome or that intense. Nor would any other species be so alerted by her scent.

They, like her, were Were-Panthers, and by the look of them, they were young and virile.

And she was in heat . . .

1

Dante Pontis wasn't the most patient of creatures. And his patience was quickly running out.

He'd been trapped in a limo from Hartsfield Airport to the hotel with his brothers, Mike and Leo, as they bitched and moaned over the fact that Dante had forced the two young panthers to fly coach from Minnesota to Atlanta while he and Romeo had simply "flashed" themselves here.

And all because the last time he and Romeo had psychically transported the twins somewhere, they had caused such a scene on arrival that they'd almost gotten busted by the humans.

Dragon*Con was far too crowded to take a chance on the four of them "appearing" before so many witnesses.

The key to Were-Hunter survival was to blend in with the humans, not scare the shit out of them.

"You know," Romeo said to them, "you're both lucky I wouldn't let Dante trank you and send you over in a cage. It's what he wanted to do."

"You dick," Leo snarled at Dante as he raked him with a repugnant glare. At six feet four, the panther was still growing and would probably equal Dante's height of six feet six in the next decade or so.

Leo and Mike were identical twins whom Dante had raised after their mother had abandoned them on their father's doorstep. It was typical Were-Panther behavior. The women would mate with the men, get pregnant, then leave the cubs for the men to raise while the women prowled around unfettered.

If the cubs were daughters, they would remain in the male-dominated pack until puberty, which struck them around the age of twenty-four. Then all the "seasoning" female cubs would form their own group and leave to search for mates.

In the last two hundred years, Dante and Romeo had raised a

large number of cubs, since their father was famous for dumping his litters on them and heading for the hills.

Like Dante, the twins had wavy black hair and tawny Italian skin when in human form.

Unlike him, they were only sixty years old, which in their life span made them practically children.

And they acted it.

It was time to either kill them or get away from them. Since Romeo was still rather bent over the fact that Dante had killed off their brother Salvatore for betraying them, Dante decided it would be best to get to his room before Leo and Mike joined Salvatore as skins on the wall at his club.

"I don't understand why I have to share a room with Leo," Mike snarled. "He snores."

"I do not. Besides, you whistle when you sleep."

"No, I don't."

Dante passed an irritated look at Romeo. "Why are they here?"

"To get women," Mike said.

Romeo ignored him. "You were afraid to leave them alone at the Inferno without me. The last time you did that, they damn near burned the place down."

Dante expelled a disgusted breath. "And why can't I kill them again?"

"You would miss them."

Yeah, right. Dante snorted at that as he handed off the card key to Leo and Mike.

"Wait, wait, wait, wait," Leo said as he examined it. "These aren't concierge level."

Dante gave him a bored stare.

"Are you concierge?" Leo asked Romeo.

"Yes."

"Why aren't we concierge?" Mike asked Dante.

Dante crossed his arms over his chest. "Because you're unworthy."

Mike opened his mouth to speak, but before he could, a trace of a scent washed over all three of them instantaneously.

Dante went rigid as every hormone in his body suddenly became activated and sizzled. Against his will, he found himself turning around and scanning the crowd in the hotel lobby.

He smelled a virgin pantheress in heat.

They all did.

The scent was unmistakable. It was warm and sweet. Feminine and innocent. Succulent. Inviting. And it made him salivate for a taste of her. His panther sight dimmed as it scanned the females present and detected none of his kind.

"Where is she?" Leo said, his voice ragged as if he were having a hard time holding himself back.

"Too many humans here to tell," Mike said as he tilted his head back to sniff the air. "They have her scent moving in multiple directions."

Dante passed a look to Romeo, who was staring up at the elevator. He turned to stare as well, and saw no one but Darth Vader.

"Did you see her?" he asked.

Romeo shook his head. "Sorry. I was mesmerized by the naked green alien."

"Arrr," Mike snarled. "You're worthless, Romeo. What kind of panther gets fixed on an alien when there's a virgin pantheress in heat?"

"A mated one," Romeo shot back. "Unlike you losers, my hormones are contained."

Dante sniffed and shook his head to clear it of her scent before his animal hormones relegated him to the same childish antics as his twin brothers. "Yeah, and I want to keep mine that way. Frick and Frack, you're on panther patrol. Find her and keep her far away from me."

Mike and Leo exchanged evil grins before they bolted into the crowd.

Dante rolled his eyes at their haste. There were times when they really were losers.

"Aren't you the least bit interested?" Romeo asked as they headed for the elevators. "It's not every day we run across a virgin panther."

"Hell, no. I'll stick to humans. The last thing I want is a mate who'll cruise into my life once a year, screw my brains out for two days, then run off until she delivers my litter to me to raise without her. No offense, being you and Dad sucks and I've raised enough siblings to never want to raise my own young without the benefit of a mate."

Romeo laughed. "Yeah, but for the record, it's one helluva two days."

Dante shook his head at him. "You can have it. I'd rather take my pleasure where and when I find it."

He entered the elevator, then paused as he realized Romeo wasn't joining him.

"I'll catch you later," he said.

"You sure?"

Romeo nodded.

"All right." Dante got in and pushed the button for his floor. He stepped back against the glass and did his best to bring his body back under control.

But it was hard.

Every animal instinct he possessed demanded that he stalk this hotel until he located the female.

Since he was a Katagari Were-Hunter, the need to copulate with her was almost overwhelming. Katagaria were animals who could take human form, but at the end of the day, they were animals and not humans. Their animal half ran roughshod over their human sensibilities and it was the animal heart inside them that ruled them and their actions.

What he needed was some time in his room where he could take his animal form and put the female out of his mind.

He was old enough to be able to curtail his nature. To control it. He wasn't about to let any woman have control over him.

Especially not a pantheress.

Pandora *fumbled with* her key card as she struggled to open her door.

What was she going to do? The man in her elevator wasn't Acheron. And those had been panther males down there. If they caught another whiff of her . . .

She was doomed. There was no way the animal inside her would refuse a virile male. She was in heat and the need to mate reigned supreme inside her. If any male came near her who her animal self sensed could possibly impregnate her, she would throw herself at him.

Around humans, that impulse was controllable. The chances of a human male being her mate were almost impossible. So the animal inside her might be curious and enticed, but it would stand down to her human rationale.

Around a Were-Panther, that animal need wouldn't listen to reason. It would pounce for a taste of the male.

She would have no control.

A shadow fell over her.

Pandora squeaked and jumped back as she looked up and saw one of the men from downstairs. This close to him, she couldn't mistake his Panthiras attributes.

His scent was undeniable.

He was lean and powerful in human form. Deadly. His handsomeness would guarantee him any female who caught his interest . . .

even her own feminine senses reacted to him, but not so much that she couldn't fight him.

Even more frightening than his innate feral masculinity, his scent was Katagaria—the animal branch of their species—while she was Arcadian, the human branch.

Letting go of her room card, she crouched to attack and was amazed that the animal inside her wasn't leaping out to mate with him.

"It's okay," he said quickly. "I've got good news and bad news for you."

"And that is?"

He held his hand up so that she could see the geometric mark on his palm. At least that explained why she could resist the urge to copulate with him. "I'm mated so you're completely safe from me."

Pandora still wasn't ready to trust him, but at least as a mated panther, he wouldn't be able to have sex with her. Once a Were-Panther male was mated, he was impotent around any female other than his "wife." "I take it that's the good news?"

He nodded.

"And the bad?"

"I'm here with three brothers who aren't."

She started to bolt.

"No, no," he said, reaching out to take her hand. He pulled back before he did. "Don't be afraid of me. I really mean you no harm, okay? I have ten daughters myself and I understand your fear."

She still wasn't ready to trust that he wouldn't take her to his brothers for their enjoyment. That was what the ones seeking her would do and she had no intention of becoming a community toy for every unmated male in their pack. "What do you want?"

"Believe it or not, I'm going to help you."

She chose not to believe that. At least not yet. "Why would you do that?"

"*Because* of my daughters," he said sincerely. "You're just a baby and I don't trust Leo or Mike not to hurt you. They wouldn't do it on purpose, but they're young too and not real good at holding back. No doubt they'd both pounce on you at once and who knows what they might inadvertently do."

And that was exactly what she was afraid of. "That's only two brothers. What of the third?"

"Dante's different. Honestly, you'd be lucky to find someone like him for your first. He's a selfish bastard who doesn't like to share much of anything with anyone and he'd make sure no one else touched you while you were with him."

But his brother was still an animal and she had no interest in taking a Katagari lover.

"Is that supposed to comfort me?" she asked.

He shook his head. "No, but don't worry. Dante's a lot older than they are and, lucky for you, he doesn't want a mate. He plans to stay far away from you so I can keep him off you by simply telling him where you are."

Pandora calmed a degree. He was telling her the truth, she could sense it. One of the good things about being part animal was that she knew whenever someone was lying to her.

"Okay," she said slowly. "Thank you for your offer to help. I don't want a Katagari to touch me."

His nostrils flared at that.

She stiffened. "You said it yourself. You get carried away and you hurt us. My older sister was killed by a pack of Katagaria males who snapped her neck while attempting to mate with her when she was my age. I'm barely twenty-four. I don't want to die. Not like that."

That seemed to calm him down. He bent over and retrieved her card from the floor. "Get me something with your scent on it so I can spread it around and keep Leo and Mike away from you."

Pandora nodded, then opened the door to her room. She went to her suitcase and pulled out the T-shirt she slept in.

"Do you know Acheron Parthenopaeus?" she asked as she handed it to him.

"Yes, why?"

"I was told to find him. My surviving sister said that he could help me get home again."

The panther frowned at her. "I don't understand. Why didn't you go home on your own?"

She sighed as frustration filled her. How she wished it were that simple. If she were an older pantheress, she could easily find her own way home, but her kind didn't get all their psychic abilities until after their first mating.

Even then her powers would have to be trained and honed so that she could wield them. That was something that could take decades, if not centuries, to master.

"I was kidnapped from the future by a group of Katagaria panthers and brought to this time period against my will. Unfortunately, my powers are just starting and I have no control over them or any way home on my own until I master them. The last thing I want is to overshoot my time period or end up with the dinosaurs."

He looked at her suspiciously. "I still don't understand why they took *you*. Why go to the future for a mate when there are plenty of packs here?"

She clenched her fists at that. "It's some stupid pact my pack made with theirs. Since we seem to have an abundance of females, my pack agreed to sacrifice a number of females every generation from certain families so that the Katagaria panthers would leave the rest of the pack alone. Every time one of the winter born females in the chosen families starts to season, the same pack comes to our home and brings us to their time period to mate with them. They don't want Katagaria females since they won't stay and raise their young. They keep us instead and use us as slaves. My one surviving sister helped me to escape after they brought me here before they could induct me into their pack. She sent me to Atlanta to find Acheron. She said he could return me to my time period."

"How does she know Acheron?"

Pandora ached at the thought that she would benefit from her sister's misery. "Before she was mated to one of their males and had her own children, she was trying to escape their pack. One night, she overheard some of the Katagaria talking about a Dark-Hunter named Acheron, and after they went to sleep, she searched for him online. By the time she found out enough information to locate him, she was pregnant and couldn't leave her children behind, so she gave her information to me once they brought me over."

"Hell of a sister you have there."

"Yes," Pandora agreed. "She's the best sister in the world and I would give anything if I could help her, too."

The panther stepped back with a sigh, then started for the door.

She took his arm to keep him from leaving as another thought occurred to her. "Could *you* help me get home?"

He shook his head. "My powers aren't quite that strong. If I wanted to take anyone other than myself across time, I would have to wait for the full moon. The only one in my pack who could do it without waiting is Dante and if you get near him—"

"I'll attack him for sex."

He nodded.

Damn.

At least all wasn't lost though. "But you do know Acheron, right? Will he help me?"

"I don't know. He's strange sometimes and no one ever knows how he's going to react or what he's going to do or say. But you can always ask. The best thing is for you to stay here in your room where Mike and Leo hopefully can't find you—like I said, they're young and aren't as experienced at tracking prey. I'll spread your scent around to keep them off you. Once I've got them occupied, I'll bring Ash to you. Okay?"

It was more than okay. It was great. She'd never thought to find a Katagari male who could be so kind.

"Thank you." As he moved away, Pandora stopped him again. "Really, thank you."

He offered her a kind, fatherly smile and patted her hand. "Animals protect their own. I'm doing this to help my brothers as much as I'm doing it to help you. If they were to hurt you, they'd never forgive themselves, and I'd have to listen to them lament for eternity."

Releasing her, he moved to the door and left the room.

Pandora took a deep breath, and for the first time since she'd been stolen from her people, she began to relax a little.

Now all she had to do was stay put until he returned.

But that wasn't as easy as it would normally be. The female in her that was just entering womanhood was all too aware of the fact that there were three unmated panthers in this hotel.

That alien and new part of her wanted with a vengeance the mating ritual that would induct her into adulthood.

It craved it.

For an Arcadian, the ritual was simple. Had she stayed at home, she would have chosen an elder panther from her pack to gently introduce her to the animal side of herself. Once he unlocked her full powers by copulating with her, he would have taught her how to shift from human to panther and how to protect herself and use her newborn powers.

The Katagaria were completely different. She'd heard the horror stories directly from her sister Sefia. They took their *nearas*—virgin females who were cresting—and allowed every unmated male of the pack to have sex with her to see if she was the mate to one of them.

They would use her without mercy until all their males were fully sated.

Her sister Sefia had been one of the lucky ones. On the night they had deflowered her, Sefia had been mated to a Katagari panther who had then decided to keep her more as a pet than a mate.

Katagaria females left their mates once they were out of heat, and only returned whenever they were in season. If a male tried to mate with a Katagari female when she wasn't in heat, she would attack and possibly kill him.

Once their season passed, the Katagaria females left their males and stayed with their sisters to travel about until their next fertile cycle. If the female became pregnant, she'd birth her young among her sisters, and as soon as the cubs were weaned, she would take them to the father to raise.

Arcadian pantheresses were much more coveted since they were ruled by human hearts that wouldn't allow them to abandon their children until adulthood. Unlike their Katagaria cousins, the Arcadians stayed with their young and their mates. The male panthers didn't have to wait for an Arcadian female to go into heat. She would be receptive to her mate at any time.

The worst part was that a panther male couldn't rape a panther female when she was in heat. All he had to do was come near her and she would willingly accept him. It was nature and a pantheress had no control over her body at such times. It wouldn't listen to any reason or rationale.

She would beg him to fill her.

The shame of that would come later, after the mating was done. Then, the Arcadian pantheress would feel embarrassed that she had acted like an animal and not a human.

Pandora moaned low in her throat as her desire sparked again and coiled through her. Her breasts were heavy, her body hot and alive with need.

Go . . .

The command was overwhelming, but she refused to heed it. She was a human, not an animal.

The Katagari male would return with Acheron and she would be among her own kind again.

Then everything would be normal.

D*ante couldn't get* the fire out of his blood. The animal in him was awake and craving.

Needing.

One whiff should not have affected him this much, and yet as he drifted through the dense crowd of people pretending to be aliens and paranormal entities, he couldn't stop himself from trying to find her scent again.

It was all he could do to stay in human form and not revert to his true animal body.

The hunter wasn't listening to him.

Damn it!

He caught a glimpse of Acheron Parthenopaeus across the vendor booths. Oblivious to the humans who paused to gawk at his seven feet of height, the Atlantean Dark-Hunter was reading a Dark Horse *Grendel* comic book.

Seeking the distraction of talking with a friend, Dante headed toward him.

"Ash," he said as he drew near. "You seem remarkably relaxed." Which was true. In all the centuries he'd known the man, Dante had never seen him so at ease.

Acheron looked up from his comic and inclined his head in greeting. "What can I say? This is one of the few places I can take Simi where she doesn't stand out. Hell, she actually looks normal here."

Dante laughed at that. Ash's pixielike demon seldom blended in anywhere. "Where is she?"

"Shopping like a demon."

Dante shook his head at the bad pun. Knowing Simi, he figured it was probably quite true. "I tried to call your cell phone when we got in to see if you made it."

Ash immediately tensed as he put his comic down and pulled out another issue. "I turned it off on the day I got here."

"Really?" Dante asked, stunned by Ash's confession. It wasn't like him to be out of touch with his Dark-Hunter charges. "What if one of the Dark-Hunters needed you?"

Ash shrugged. "If they can't survive alone for four days once a year, they deserve to die."

Dante frowned. "That's harsh, for you."

He looked at him dryly. "Harsh? Tell you what, you take my phone and skim through the three thousand phone calls I get every day and night and see how harsh I am. I truly hate modern technology and phones in particular. I haven't had a full four hours of sleep in over fifty years. 'Ash, I broke a toenail, help me. Ash, my head hurts, what should I do?'"

Ash curled his lip in repugnance. "You know, I've never understood it. They make a deal with the devil herself and then expect me to bail them out of every minor scrape. Then when I show up to help them, they cop an attitude and tell me to blow. So if I'm selfish for wanting four days a year to be left alone, then I'm just a selfish bastard. Sue me."

Wow, someone was cranky.

Dante took a step away from the Atlantean. "Well then, I'll make sure I don't bug you."

Ash pulled out another plastic-covered comic from the long white box on the table. "You're not bothering me, Dante. Really. I'm just trying to zen myself out of a bad mood. I made the mistake of turning on my phone ten minutes ago and I had four hundred and eighty-two messages waiting on voice mail. I had it on all of three seconds before it started ringing again. All I want is a little break and no damn phone for a few days." He let out an aggravated breath. "Besides, I'm the one who told you to come."

"Yeah, thanks. This is . . ."—he hesitated as a centaur pranced by on what appeared to be modified ski boots that looked eerily like hooves—"interesting."

Ash smiled. "Yeah, just wait until you see the Ms. Klingon Beauty Pageant. It's something else."

Dante laughed. "I'll bet. So what good bands should I check out for my club?"

Ash grabbed three Dark Horse *Tales of the Vampires* comics and added them to his growing pile. "Last Dance is really good. They're playing tonight, and Ghoultown, too. But the one band you have to see is the Cruxshadows. They're right up your alley and rule the Dark-wave scene. The lead singer Rogue'll be over in the Hyatt later signing autographs at their booth. If you want, I can introduce you."

"That'd be great." The only reason Dante had come to Atlanta was because Acheron had assured him Dragon*Con was one of the best places to see several alternative bands so that he could hire them for gigs at his club in Minnesota.

Simi came running up to them with two male "Klingons" trailing behind her. "*Akri?* Can I go to the Klingon homeworld?"

Ash smiled at his demon. "Sure, just don't eat any of them."

The demon pouted. "But why not?"

"Because, Simi, they're not really Klingons. They're people pretending to be Klingons."

"Well, pooh, fine then. No eats. But I'm going to go now. Bye bye." She dashed off with the two young men.

Ash handed the comics to the vendor, then pulled out his wallet.

"Shouldn't you go do a head count on the homeworld population?" Dante asked.

"Nah. She'll do what I said . . ." Ash paused as if something occurred to him. "Then again, I didn't tell her not to eat a Bajoran or

Romulan. Damn." He paid for the comics. "You're right, I better go count."

Ash took a step away, then stopped. "By the way, you might want to head upstairs right now and check out your room."

"Why?"

He shrugged. "Make sure it meets with your needs."

Dante frowned. "I've already been there."

"Go there again."

The animal in Dante picked up a weird scent from Acheron, but he wasn't sure what it was.

But as the Atlantean headed off, he felt an inexplicable pull to do what Acheron had suggested.

Dante headed out of the vendors' area, toward the escalator. He'd barely reached it when he smelled the pantheress again. He turned sharply to the left, expecting to see her.

She wasn't there.

Still, he was hard for her. Ready. The animal inside was growling for a taste of her body.

He headed up the escalator to escape the scent.

It seemed to grow stronger.

His head low, he scanned the crowd intently, but none of his people was there.

Closing his eyes, he sniffed the air. Her fragrance was subtle now. And it was . . .

He whirled around.

There was no woman there, only Romeo, and he reeked of the pantheress. Dante couldn't stop himself from sniffing Romeo, who immediately shoved him away.

"Man, you skeeve me when you do that. And don't do it in public. Someone might get the wrong idea about us."

He ignored his brother's reprimanding tone. "Where is she?" Dante demanded.

"Out of reach."

Her scent washed over him, even stronger than before. His body was raw. Needful. Every part of him craved her.

And it wasn't taking no for an answer.

"Where?" he growled.

Romeo shook his head.

But he didn't have to be told. Every hormone in his body sensed her. Against his will, Dante took off at a run as he cut through the crowd toward the elevator.

Without thought, he flashed himself from the lobby to the sixteenth floor.

The scent was even stronger here.

More desirable.

More intense.

Dante stalked his way down the hall until he found her door. He couldn't breathe as her scent filled his entire being. Leaning his head against the wood, he closed his eyes and fought the sudden urge to kick the door in.

That would probably scare her, and besides, he didn't want to have an audience for what he intended to do with her.

He knocked on the door with a clenched fist and waited until a small, petite brunette opened it. She had large, lavender eyes and long hair that curled around an oval face.

His breathing ragged, he stared at her, wanting her with every piece of him.

But for all his sexual hunger, he knew that it was now her move . . .

2

Pandora couldn't breathe as she stared at the tall, sexy panther in her doorway. He embodied everything that was primal and male. His hands were braced on each side of the frame as he looked at her with an intensity so raw, it shook her. Masculine power and lethal grace bled from every pore of his magnificent body.

He had long black hair pulled back into a queue. His eyes were a clear blue that appeared almost colorless against his tanned skin and long midnight lashes. His face was elegantly carved and yet had a rugged quality that kept him from being pretty.

He was dressed in black jeans and a black poet's shirt. There was something timeless and old about him. Something that reached out to her and set her entire body on fire.

Without her invitation, he stepped into the room and bent his head so that he could rub his face against her hair.

Pandora gasped as that simple action sent chills all through her. His breath scorched her extra-sensitive skin, which wanted only to be touched by him. Her nipples hardened in expectation of what was to come.

"*Gataki.*" He murmured the Greek word for "kitten" as he took a deep breath in her hair.

The human half of her wanted to shove him away from her. The animal part refused. It wanted only to cuddle with him. To rip his clothes off and know once and for all what it would be like to have sex with a male.

The door to her room slammed shut of its own volition.

Pandora circled around him, rubbing her body against his as she fought the urge to cry out in pleasure.

"Do you accept me?" he asked rhetorically. It was technically the woman who chose her lover, but when a female was this sexually aware of the male, there was really no way out.

All Pandora could do was nod. Her body would never allow her to deny him. He was too virile. Too consuming.

Too much of what she needed.

He turned on her with a fierce growl as he seized her for a scintillating kiss. Pandora moaned at the taste of him. No one had ever kissed her before. It was forbidden until her first cycle for any male to touch a female not related to him.

Ever since she'd been a teenager, she and her girlfriends had whispered about what they wanted for their first matings and who they would choose.

Pandora had expected Lucas to be her first. Almost four hundred years old, he was legendary among her people for his prowess and ability to teach a young pantheress her passion.

But his handsomeness paled in comparison to the dark stranger before her. This male tasted of wine and decadence. Of mystical, exotic power and knowledge.

His tongue swept against hers as her body heated to a fever pitch.

"Are you Dante?" she asked him as she nibbled his firm lips.

"Yes."

Good. At least he wouldn't share her. It was a small relief to know that.

"What is your name, *gataki?*"

"Pandora Kouti."

He pulled back to smile at her.

"Pandora," he purred as he buried his hands in her hair before inhaling the sensitive flesh of her neck, then licking it slowly. Teasingly. "And what surprises are you hiding from the world in your box, Pandora?"

She couldn't answer as he continued to lick her skin. Her knees buckled. Only the strength of his arms around her kept her from falling.

Dante knew he should leave. He should flash himself into a cold shower somewhere.

But he couldn't.

She was too hypnotic. Too tempting. The animal in him refused to leave until he'd tasted her.

And he would be her first. He could smell her innocent state.

That knowledge alone was enough to make him roar. He'd never taken a virgin before. For that matter, he'd rarely taken any woman of his own species. A pantheress was violent by nature. She had to be held down, and if a male wasn't fast enough, he could be maimed or killed during mating.

Once an orgasm seized a pantheress, the ferocity of it would make her feral. She would turn on her lover with claws and teeth bared. In the case of a Katagari female, she'd turn immediately to her animal form and attack her lover.

The male had to be ready to pull back and flash to his animal form or he wouldn't be able to defend himself from her surging hormonal and psychic overload.

It was a sobering thought.

Dante had never cared much for violent mating. He preferred to take his time pleasing his lover. To sample every single inch of her body at his leisure.

He'd always loved the taste of a woman. The scent of her. The feel of her soft limbs rubbing against his rougher ones. Always liked to hear the sounds of her ecstasy echoing in his ears as he brought her to climax over and over again.

And Pandora . . .

She would be unlike any lover he'd ever known. His first Arcadian.

His first virgin.

Kissing her deeply, he dissolved the clothes from their bodies so that there was nothing between his hands and her sweet, succulent flesh.

She shivered in his arms.

"It's okay, *gataki*," he said as he skimmed his hand down her supple back. "I won't hurt you."

His words seemed to make her panic. "You're a Katagari male."

He nibbled her shoulder, reveling in the taste of her soft, salty-sweet skin. She was truly decadent. A mouthwatering treat to sate the beast inside him.

"And I won't hurt you," he reiterated as he nibbled his way around her shoulder blade, down her back, and then around front so that he could taste her breast.

Pandora cried out the instant his mouth closed around her hard, sensitive nipple. Her body jerked and sizzled.

What was this? All she could think of was having him inside her. Of having all that hard, tawny skin lying over her as he showed her exactly what it meant to be loved by a man.

He was all sinewy muscle.

All strength. Power.

Wickedness.

And for the moment, he was *all* hers . . .

He pulled back from her with a growl before he scooped her up in his arms and carried her to the bed. She felt so dainty in his arms, so coveted.

The covers pulled themselves back so that he could set her in the center of it. Pandora's nervousness returned as the chill of the covers brushed her fevered skin.

She'd waited a lifetime for this moment. What would happen to her? Would she be changed?

Would he?

Dante gave her a fierce, ragged kiss as he spread her arms out above her head. Two seconds later, something wrapped itself around her wrists and held them there.

"What are you doing?" she asked, even more nervous than before.

His gentle touch soothed her as he massaged her tense shoulders. "I want to make sure neither of us is hurt, *gataki*. You've never had an orgasm before and you have no idea what it's going to do to you."

"Will it hurt?"

He laughed at that as his large, masculine hand cupped her breast. "No, it won't hurt at all."

She wanted to believe him. The animal in her didn't detect a lie so she relaxed. Dante might not be the man she would have chosen first, but he was proving to be gentle enough to soothe the human part of her.

He laid himself beside her so that he could study her body. He skimmed a callused hand over her breasts, then moved it lower so that he could toy with the short, crisp hairs at the juncture of her thighs.

She clenched her teeth as fire consumed her body. She ached for that hand to move lower. For it to caress the burning ache between her legs until she could think straight again.

"Tell me what you dream of, Pandora," he said quietly as his thumb teased her sensitive nub.

She licked her lips as pleasure tore through her. But it did nothing to ebb the vicious bittersweet pain inside her.

Dante blew a fiery breath across her erect nipple. "How does an Arcadian take a male inside her body?"

"Don't you know?"

He moved so that he was draped on top of her. She moaned at the delicious feel of his naked body pressing down on hers. In that moment, she wanted to see his hair unbound.

"Untie your hair," she said.

The tie came loose immediately.

It was rare among the Arcadians to find a male so at ease with his psychic abilities. They were taught to hide them unless they were fighting their animal cousins.

Dante didn't appear to have such hang-ups and she wondered if all Katagaria were like him.

"You are powerful, aren't you?" she asked.

He nodded as he stared at her in a way that reminded her so much of a panther that it was almost scary.

Pandora watched his light eyes carefully, seeking any sign that he would turn feral on her and hurt her. "Are you going to devour me?"

His smile was wicked. "Until you beg me to stop."

Dante leaned forward so that he could press his cheek to hers and savor the feel of her delicate skin. She was totally enjoyable.

With humans, he had to hide what he was from them. But Pandora knew exactly what he was and, unlike a Katagari female, she wasn't fighting him. She responded to his caresses just as a human would. With delight and innocent trust.

It was refreshing and touched a foreign part of him deeply.

He wanted to please her in a way he'd never wanted to please anyone else.

Reaching down between them, he gently separated the tender folds of her body so that he could touch her intimately.

She cried out in ecstasy.

Her response delighted him. Dante used his powers to shield the sounds from escaping the room as he kissed his way down her body to where his hand played.

Pandora could barely think as she felt Dante spread her legs wide. It was as if every part of her was burning. Her head spun with pleasure.

And then she felt the most incredible thing of all. Dante's mouth teasing her. Hissing, she threw her head back and arched her spine as his tongue worked incredible magic on her. He sank one long, lean finger deep inside her as his tongue continued to explore every tender fold with a thoroughness that was blinding in its intensity.

Dante couldn't take his eyes off her as he watched her head rolling back and forth on the pillow. There was nothing a male of his species valued more than the taste of a virgin's climax.

His kind was known to kill for the privilege of taking a virgin, and for the first time in his life, he understood that primal desire.

The revelation shocked him. He'd always told himself that a female wasn't worth another panther's life. But as he watched her innocent, unabashed reaction to his touch, he was no longer so sure.

There was no artifice in her response. She was reacting honestly to him. Openly. And he loved it.

When she came, crying out his name, he felt something deep inside him shatter with pride and satisfaction.

Dante held her hips still, expecting to have to pull away from her.

He didn't. She lacked the violent tendencies of his kind. Instead of attacking him, she stayed on the bed, panting and purring as she continued to let her climax flow.

Pandora wasn't sure what had just happened to her. But it had been incredible. Wonderful. And it left her wanting even more from him. She still felt her body spasming as Dante continued to stroke and tease until she was weak from it.

Her hands suddenly free, she reached down and sank her hand into his long, silken hair as he gently rolled her onto her stomach.

He lightly nipped her buttocks.

"What are you doing?" she asked as he placed a pillow underneath her stomach.

"I'm going to show you what it feels like to have a male inside you, Pandora."

She shivered at the erotic image that played through her mind of Dante thrusting against her. "Please don't break my neck."

He brushed her hair aside and placed a gentle kiss on her nape. "I would never hurt you, *gataki*."

She shivered at his whispered words.

He lifted one of her legs up, then drove himself deep inside her. Pandora cried out as he filled her to capacity. He was long and hard, and so deep that she couldn't draw a breath.

Never had she felt anything like his fullness inside her. Or the intimacy of him touching her in a place no one ever had before.

More than that, she felt something breaking as electrical energy surged through her. Every inch of her body sizzled and hummed.

Dante ground his teeth as pleasure tore through him. He'd never felt anything better than her tight, wet heat around him. It was all he could do not to thrust himself into her hard and furiously until he was fully sated.

But he didn't want to scare or hurt her in any way.

Holding himself up on one arm, he ran his tongue over the sensitive skin of her ear and breathed lightly into it. She shivered under him.

He smiled at that as he trailed his hand over her skin so that he could again sink his fingers down her swollen clit.

Pandora groaned at the sensation of his hand moving in time to his long, gentle strokes. No man, Arcadian or otherwise, could be more tender. She would never have believed this was possible from an animal.

Only this wasn't an animal who was holding her. He was more human than anyone she'd ever known.

And kind. There was no pain and she wondered if he were using his powers to heighten the pleasure his touch delivered. She only wished she knew enough about her new powers to return the favor to him.

He began moving slowly against her, then faster. Faster. And faster still.

Pandora gasped at the speed of his thrusts as they continued to crescendo. Growling from the pleasure of it, she rocked her hips against his, driving him in even deeper until it was all she could do not to scream.

Dante ground his teeth as she moved in sync with him. She was exquisitely demanding. And when she came again, he laughed until the sensation of her body gripping his sent him over the edge and he too climaxed.

He roared out loud as ecstasy tore through him with waves and waves of pleasure.

She collapsed under him an instant before she rolled over onto her back.

Expecting her to attack, Dante almost leaped from the bed. But she reached one tender arm up and wrapped it around his shoulders to hold him close to her.

The smile on her face warmed his heart. "Thank you," she breathed. "It's the first time in days that my body feels like it belongs to me again."

He inclined his head to her, then reached down to take her small hand into his so that he could plant a kiss on her knuckles. No wonder Katagaria males took Arcadian females. It was so nice to lie like this with her.

If she were Katagaria, he'd most likely be bleeding in the aftermath of their encounter. Instead, she toyed with his hair and stroked him.

At least until she groaned.

Dante smiled in anticipation. It was her cycle heating up again.

She purred as her hand tightened in his hair and she eagerly rubbed herself against him.

His body hardened again instantly.

He was as ready for her as she was for him. The animal in him could smell her need and it answered accordingly.

This was going to be a long afternoon and he was going to relish every part of it.

And every part of her . . .

Pandora *lay quietly* in bed while Dante showered in her bathroom. She should be horrified by how many hours they had spent in her bed. He had bent her in more positions than she would have thought possible.

And she had loved every one of them.

He was incredible . . . and extremely limber.

She was sated to a level that defied her imagination. Normally, a pantheress would need days for a male to satiate her.

But Dante had been so thorough, so exhausting, that she felt an incredible sense of peace.

Who would have thought it possible?

She heard the water turn off. A few seconds later, Dante returned to the bed with his hair damp and curling around his shoulders.

He was completely naked and unabashed about it. She stared in awe at that tawny body liberally dusted with short, black hairs.

"Feeling better?" she asked.

He gifted her with a smile that made her stomach flutter. "I would have felt better had you joined me for a bath."

She blushed at that. He'd made the offer and she had declined, though why she couldn't imagine. It wasn't like he hadn't caressed and studied every inch of her in the last few hours. But somehow the thought of showering with him had seemed too personal.

Too strange.

He lay down beside her and pulled her into his arms.

Pandora sighed contentedly. It was so nice to be held by him.

One minute he had a long, masculine arm draped over her waist, and in the next, it was the limb of a panther.

She bolted out of the bed with a shriek.

Dante flashed instantly back into human form. "What's wrong?" he asked.

"Don't do the panther thing around me, okay? It really creeps me."

He frowned at her. "Why?"

"I . . . I just can't stand the sight of them."

He gave her a harsh, condemning stare that set her ire off. "You're one of us, baby. Get used to it."

She cringed at the thought. She was not in the same category as a Katagari female. They were crude and mean, and had no care whatsoever for anyone other than themselves.

"Oh, no I'm not," she said, growling the words at him. "I'm a human being, not an animal like you."

Dante narrowed his eyes at words that shouldn't hurt him and yet for some unfathomable reason did. He'd gone out of his way to be tender with her.

And what had it accomplished?

Not a damn thing except to have her disdain him over something he couldn't help any more than she could help being human.

There was nothing wrong with being a Katagari. He took a lot of pride in his heritage.

His kind was definitely superior to hers. At least they didn't lie, cheat, and steal for no reason.

Curling his lip, he climbed out of bed and flashed his clothes back on.

"Fine. Have a nice life."

Pandora jumped as he slammed out of her room.

"You too!" she called childishly, knowing he couldn't hear her.

What did she care anyway?

He was an animal. But as she headed for the bathroom, she missed the warm feeling she'd had when he held her. The sweet sound of her name on his lips as he carefully made love to her.

The way his tongue had stroked and soothed her.

Grinding her teeth, she forced the image away and went to shower. And as the water came on, she thought of Dante's brother who had yet to bring Acheron to her. He must have sent Dante to her instead.

How dare he!

She should have known better than to trust an animal. Why would one of them help her anyway?

Angry at both of them, and at herself for being so stupid as to trust them, Pandora regulated the water and started scrubbing with a vengeance.

Suddenly, the bathroom curtain was whisked open.

Pandora gasped as she spun about to find Dante standing there, blue eyes glaring at her.

"You never answered my question."

She sputtered at him. "Excuse me, I'm in the middle of a bath here."

"Yeah, I know, and I'll let you get back to it once you tell me why panthers bother you."

That was none of his business!

Tears burned in her eyes as her ordeal over the last two weeks overwhelmed her. Her unbalanced hormones didn't help matters any and neither did the fact that all she really wanted to do was go home.

Before she could stop herself, the truth came pouring out in wrenching sobs. "Because every time I see one of your people, you steal someone away from me whom I love and I hate all of you for it. Now your kind has taken me away from my home and my family so that I can either be a whore to the entire pack or a slave to one of you."

Dante felt an odd sensation in his chest as she started weeping. Not once in almost three hundred years had he felt such a sense of helplessness.

Such a desire to help someone.

"And what's worse," she said, her voice cracking, "I know I can't really go home because they'll just send me back here to the Katagaria pack that stole me. Panthers have taken everything from me. Even my virginity."

Dante turned the water off with his thoughts and pulled a towel off the rack before wrapping it around her.

"I don't know what I was thinking when I ran away," she sobbed. "Acheron won't help me. Why should he? And even if he wanted to, what could he really do? Dark-Hunters can't interfere in our business. I just wanted some hope. Something other than what is meant for me. I don't want to be a panther whore. I just want to have my own life where no one hurts or uses me. Is that so wrong?"

"No, Pandora," Dante said as he pulled her sodden body into his arms and held her tight. "It's not wrong."

He kissed the top of her head as he pulled another towel down to dry her hair.

Pandora hated herself for falling apart like this. She was normally calm and collected. But it was beyond her ability to cope now.

All she wanted was her life back. One day where she was again in charge of her body and her destiny.

One day of clarity.

What her people had done was wrong and she knew it. She hated all of them, Arcadian and Katagaria, for forcing this on her.

No woman should ever have her choice taken away from her.

She tried to stop crying as Dante rocked her gently in his arms. He was being much kinder than she deserved. Not even her own father would be so understanding of this breakdown. He'd never been the kind of man to tolerate emotional outbursts well and he'd trained all his daughters to suffer in silence.

Yet Dante didn't say anything. He just held her quietly while she cried.

"I don't know what to do," she said, stunned when the words came out of her mouth. It wasn't like her to confide in someone and to admit that she was in over her head . . .

She couldn't believe what she was doing.

Maybe it was because she didn't know where else to turn.

Or maybe it was just after the time they had shared where he hadn't hurt her that she was willing to almost trust him with the truth of her situation and feelings.

"We'll figure something out for you," Dante said as he rubbed her back. "Don't worry."

"Why would you help me? Your brother said you were a selfish bastard."

He gave half a laugh at that. "I am selfish. I'm cold and vicious. I don't have any friends and I spend all my time looking for Arcadians who bother me so I can pick a fight and hurt them. Hell, I even killed my own brother when he sold my pack out to the Daimons. Truly, I am every bad thing you think of when you hear the term 'Katagaria.'"

And still he hadn't hurt her.

He gently laid his hand against her cold cheek to wipe away her tears. "Yet I don't want to see you cry."

She shivered at his hypnotic words.

"Get dressed, Pandora, and we'll go find something to eat and talk about what we can do to help you."

"Really?"

"Really."

She pulled him down so that she could give him a scorching kiss. "I'm sorry I called you an animal, Dante."

"It's okay. I am one."

No, he wasn't. In that moment, he was her hero. Her champion. She would never insult anyone so kind.

As soon as she pulled on her jeans and a red shirt, he led her from the room, downstairs to the lobby that was packed with even more people than earlier.

"This is some party, huh?" she asked as she saw a group of four women dressed only in warning tape wrapped around their bodies surrounded by a group of Storm Troopers, cross the lobby.

"It's definitely something," he said, holding her hand as they passed a woman who was leading a man around on a leash.

"Do you come here often?"

He shook his head. "First time."

Before she could speak again, Pandora felt a vicious pain sear across her palm. Hissing, she jerked her hand back at the same time Dante started shaking his own hand as if he'd burned it.

Pandora frowned as a bad sense of foreboding went through her.

She looked at her hand and watched as an attractive geometrical design formed over her palm, confirming her worst fear.

She was mated.

And there was only one male it could be . . .

3

Dante stared in horror at the sight of his mating mark. No. This couldn't be real and it damn sure couldn't be happening. Not to him.

He took Pandora's hand and held it up against his so that he could compare their palms.

There was no denying it. The marks were identical.

She was his.

Damn.

"You bastard!" she snarled angrily. "How could you be the one meant for me?"

"Excuse me?" Dante asked, baffled by her rage. If anyone had a right to be angry, it was him. After all, he'd been minding his own business when she traipsed into his sensory circle. Had she just stayed put, neither one of them would be in this situation.

"In case you didn't notice, sweetheart, I'm not exactly thrilled by this either."

She glared at him for two seconds before she whirled on her heel and headed off into the crowd.

Part of him was tempted to let her go, but that wouldn't accomplish anything. Neither Katagaria nor Arcadian had any say in who the Fates chose as their mates. Any more than they knew when or where they'd find the one person who was designated for them.

The only way to find a mate was to sleep with him or her and to wait for the mark to appear.

Whenever it did, they only had three weeks to perform their mating ritual or they would spend the rest of their lives sterile. For a female, it wasn't such a bad thing since she could continue to have sex with any man who caught her attention. She just couldn't have children with any male other than her designated mate. But for a male . . .

It was worse than death. The male was left completely impotent until the day his mate died.

Dante shivered at the thought. Him, impotent? Those were two words that would never be said together.

He would die first.

He headed through the lobby in hot pursuit of his "mate."

Pandora *was seething* as she headed blindly through the crowd. All she wanted was to put some significant distance between her and Dante.

This was awful.

Terrible!

Wasn't it?

Most Arcadians dreamed of finding their mate as their first lover. That way, they wouldn't have to fear their prowling instinct, which would debase them as they hopped from male to male, trying to find the one who could breed with them.

It was a dream come true to find a mate so early and so easily. Most of her kind spent centuries looking. And many died without ever being mated at all.

Technically, she'd been lucky, and yet she was angry because she was bound to a *Katagari* male. Talk about jumping from the frying pan into the fire! This morning her worst fear was being enslaved to a Katagaria pack.

Now she was captured even more fully than before. If she left Dante, she would never be able to have children. He was the only one who could give her that.

"Damn these hormones," she snarled as more tears gathered in her eyes. It was hard to think straight.

Someone grabbed her from behind.

"Gotcha," a deep, masculine voice said in her ear.

It wasn't Dante.

The panther inside her roared to life, rejecting any male not her mate. She whirled about and struck without thought, making contact with the stranger's groin.

Doubling over, he hissed in pain. But before she could escape, another male took her arm.

She froze as she realized he was an exact, equally handsome copy of the man she had just racked.

"Leo." The lethal growl cut across the tense air and shivered down her spine. Dante's voice threatened violence and death. "Let go my mate, boy."

The panther holding her let go instantly and cursed. "You've got to be kidding me."

Dante shook his head as he joined them. "I wish I were." He scowled at the other male, who was still cupping himself. "You okay, Mikey?"

"Yeah," he said, grimacing as he forced himself to straighten. His face was still an awful shade of red and he was panting. "Just my luck that you would find a mate who is as pissy as you are."

"I take offense to that," Pandora said.

Mike gave her a menacing scowl. "And I take offense to my sudden need for testicle retrieval. You know, I would have liked to have fathered some children one day."

Leo laughed at his twin brother's discomfort. "I'm just glad you got to her first."

Mike curled his lip. "Shut up."

Dante rolled his eyes before introducing his brothers. "Pandora, meet my brothers, Leonardo and Michelangelo."

"Like the Teenage Mutant Ninja Turtles?" she couldn't resist asking.

"Like the Renaissance painters," Leo snapped. He exchanged a snarl with his twin brother. "I seriously hate those damned turtles."

As if on cue, four people dressed as said turtles walked by and frowned at them.

"I swear the gods are mocking us," Mike said as he saw the green-foam-covered humans.

"I know the feeling," Pandora said, sighing. There were no better words to describe her present predicament.

She had no idea what kind of . . . creature the Fates had joined her to.

Then again, Dante wasn't the one acting so bizarrely. She was the one with hormonal overload poisoning. She honestly couldn't blame Dante if he started choking her.

She just wished she could be herself for a few hours so that she could sort through all this better.

"Well, I see all of you found her."

Pandora looked past Leo to see the first one of the brothers she'd met. Ironically, he was the only one whose name she didn't know.

"Shut up, Romeo," Leo said irritably. "Don't think we don't know it was you who spread her scent around this hotel to drive us crazy. You almost got me killed when I grabbed Simi by mistake and she pulled out a bottle of barbecue sauce to sprinkle on me. If Ash hadn't come up when he did, that damn demon would have gladly eaten me."

Romeo laughed for only an instant before he sobered. He sniffed the air.

"Oh shit," he breathed as he looked from her to Dante. "You're mated?"

"Yeah," Dante said. "Thanks, Romeo. Had you not had her scent all over *you*, I wouldn't have been able to pinpoint her so easily. I really appreciate the road map."

Pandora stiffened at Dante's sarcasm. "Thank you for making me feel really bad. You know, you could try and be a little more positive about this."

"True," Romeo said. "She is Arcadian and not nearly as likely to roam."

It was Pandora's turn to be "thrilled." "Just think, now all of you have a babysitter for your litters and someone a lot weaker to knock around whenever you get angry at your enemies."

All four of the panthers scowled at her.

"What are you talking about?" Dante asked.

"It's all you want me for, right?"

He looked at her aghast. "You're my mate, Pandora, not my servant. Anyone in my pack, including my brothers, who disrespects you disrespects me. And believe me, that's one thing no one will *ever* do."

The sincerity of that tore through her.

He really meant it.

Gratitude and happiness welled inside her, and for the first time since her father had handed her over to their enemies, she had some real, true hope. "Really?"

"You may be Arcadian," Romeo said, "but you're a member of our pack now and we'll treat you as such."

"But what of the children you told me about?" Pandora asked Romeo. "Won't you make me watch them?"

"They're *my* offspring," Romeo said. "I've been raising cubs and siblings for more than three hundred years, even Dante. Why would that change now?"

But she had assumed . . .

"Who watches them while you're gone?" she asked.

It was Mike who answered. "Our brother Gabriel and our cousin Angel."

"Yeah," Dante said. "They do fine with cubs. It's Frick and Frack here who screw them up and get all of them into trouble."

Mike gave him a droll stare. "I really wish you'd stop calling us that."

"When you grow out of your awkward pubescent stage, I will." Dante checked his watch. "That should be, what? Another fifty, sixty years?"

"We're older than her," Leo said, pointing to Pandora.

"Yeah, but she's got something neither of you do."

"And that is?"

Dante rubbed his eyes as if his head were beginning to hurt. "If you can't see what she has that neither of you do, you need even more help than I thought."

Leo made a disgusted noise at him. "I'm not going to stand here and be insulted. Since I can't touch your pantheress without losing a limb or my balls, I'm going to pursue something a little less dangerous."

Dante and Romeo exchanged an amused look that was completely mischievous.

"Why don't you try one of the filking rooms?" Dante asked. "I heard from Acheron that a lot of wild things go on in there. Women taking off their clothes. Wine being passed around to anyone who wants some."

Both of the twins' faces lighted up.

"That sounds good and dirty to me," Mike said. "Perfect. Later."

Pandora laughed as the twins bolted away from them. "You do realize that filking is just science fiction folk singing, right?"

Dante gave an evil laugh. "I know. I just wish I could be there when they realize it, too."

Romeo shook his head. "You are so mean to them. It's a wonder they don't kill you while you sleep."

Dante scoffed. "Yeah, right. Those goofs are lucky I tolerate them."

"And yet you do," Pandora said, smiling at the knowledge. "Why is that, Dante?"

Romeo returned her smile. "Because my brother has a heart that he hates to own up to."

"Shut up, Romeo."

"She's your mate, Dante. Be honest with her. Don't let the past sour you for eternity. She's not Bonita, you know?"

Dante growled and lunged for Romeo, who stepped back lightning fast.

"Later," Romeo said before he left them.

"Bonita?" Pandora asked as soon as they were alone . . . or at least as alone as a couple in a crowd of thousands could be.

Dante didn't answer. From his expression she could tell he was thinking of something very painful.

Her heart wrenched at the thought. Was she an old lover? "Who was she?"

He let out a long, tired breath before he answered. "She was the bonded mate to one of my older brothers, Donatello. He was the pack leader before me and he loved his mate more than his life."

Pandora felt for the panther. "Let me guess. She betrayed him."

"No," he said to her surprise. "They were bonded together, and one night while she was home from her journeys, she lashed out at him while they were having sex and ripped into his jugular. They both died before he could get help."

Pandora covered her mouth as she envisioned the horror. Once Were-Panthers bonded their life forces together, neither of them could live without the other. If one died, they both died.

How terrible that Bonita had killed them in one act of thoughtless passion.

"I'm so sorry," she whispered.

"Thanks," he said quietly. "It was a damn waste of two decent panthers." His gaze penetrated her. "It's why I never wanted a pantheress for a mate or even a lover. I don't want my cubs orphaned because I let my guard drop and left myself open to a female's attack."

"I would never rip at you."

"How do you know?"

"Well," she said as they started moving through the lobby, "right now I don't even know how to turn into a panther. So that alone makes you safe. I tried to do it a couple of days ago and all I got was a tail that was very hard to hide until I went to sleep and it left me."

Dante laughed, and though she ought to be offended that he was laughing at her misfortune, she wasn't. There was something about him that was truly charming.

"I've never heard of that happening before," he said.

"Stick around. All kinds of weird things have been happening to me lately."

He brushed the hair back from her face. "I think I might like to do that. If you don't mind."

For some reason, the thought warmed her. Dante was a lot of fun to be with.

When they weren't fighting.

"What do you expect of your mate, Dante?"

He shrugged, then put his arm around her as they cruised by the banquet tables that were lined with fliers and giveaway items. "Nothing more than any other panther, I guess. I expect you to come home when you're in season and leave when you're not."

It was too good to be true.

"You would let me leave if I wanted to?"

He frowned. "It's the nature of our species, Pandora. Why would I stop you?"

"But the other pack—"

"Ain't right in the head," he said, interrupting her. "There's something profoundly wrong with anyone who would try to get a panther to act against his or her nature. That's something I'd expect an Arcadian to do, not a Katagari."

She smiled up at him as she felt another hormonal surge go through her.

By the sudden feral look on Dante's face she could tell he sensed it, too.

His arm tightened around her.

"Can we wait?" she asked quickly. "I don't want to rush mating with you again until we get a few things straight between us."

Even though sex with him would clear her head, her human heart wanted more between them than just a physical relationship. She wanted to know the human part of her mate.

"Such as?" Dante asked.

"I don't know," she answered honestly. "I know in my heart that committing myself to you is the best thing for both of us. It's probably the only thing since I no longer have a pack to shelter me. But the human in me wants to know you better before I take such a permanent step."

To her relief, he didn't try to balk or force her.

"What do you need from me?"

"Just be with me as a human for a little while and let me get to know you, okay?"

Dante nodded even though what he really wanted to do was take her back upstairs and give her what both their bodies craved.

But she was young and scared. This was a momentous step for both of them. Bonding was eternal and it wasn't something to be taken lightly.

True kindness to someone else was all but alien to him. He understood loyalty. Obligation.

But love and tenderness . . .

Panthers didn't dream of such things. They only understood immediate needs. The ones for food, shelter, sex.

Offspring.

And yet he wanted something more from her. Something deeper.

He wanted her acceptance.

Her touch.

It was stupid. What did he need with such things? He had money. Power. Magic.

He could force her to do anything he wanted her to. But it still wouldn't give him what he wanted.

Her heart.

Damn him for his human half.

Sighing, he led her toward the Marquis Steakhouse where they could get something to eat.

The night went by quickly as Pandora followed Dante around to various booths and concerts where alternative bands were displaying their wares and talents. Dante seemed to have a knack for finding really good performers who were excited about being offered money to play in his club in Minnesota.

"How long have you had your club?" she asked as he bought three CDs from a band called Emerald Rose who had been playing earlier outside the conference rooms at the Hyatt.

"Almost thirty years now."

Wow, that was a long time. Dante looked good for a man who was more than two hundred years old.

Really good.

"And the humans don't realize that you're always there and that you never age?"

He shook his head. "When they leave the Inferno, we tamper with their minds a bit. Even if they come in every night, they never remember those of us who don't age or change."

"That must be nice. In my . . ." She hesitated to say "pack" since they had thrown her out. "In my world, we stay away from the humans as much as possible."

"So what's the future like where you live, anyway?"

"Not that much different from this. Haven't you ever been?"

"Not since I was a cub. When I first got control of my time-travel powers, I hopped around quite a bit. But after a while, it got boring. Things and places changed, but the people didn't. So I decided to stay with my pack in Minnesota and not worry about the past or the future."

She would love to be able to time-jump like that. It was true freedom and that was one thing she'd never known.

"Can you teach me how to use my powers like that?" she asked.

"Of course."

She smiled. None of her sisters who had been sent into this time period had been taught anything. The Katagaria hadn't allowed them to develop their powers for fear they would leave. Some of them had even been forced by the Katagaria to wear *metriazo* collars to ensure that none of them would ever be able to use their magic.

It was harsh and cruel.

"Is it hard to time-travel?" she asked.

"Not now, it's not for me. But I've had centuries to perfect my powers. When you first start it can be . . . surprising. Last time I left Leo and Mike at home, they time-jumped from Minnesota 2002 to the Aleutian Islands 1432 instead of New York 2065. It was a bitch trying to find them and get them home again."

"I'm surprised you went after them."

"Yeah, well, they annoy me, but I understand they're just cubs who will eventually grow up . . . probably to annoy me even more."

She laughed at his offbeat humor as they drifted through the strangely garbed crowd. She had to admit that Dante was a lot of fun once he got used to you and stopped being so feral and snarling.

"You do have a heart, don't you?"

"No, Pandora," he said, his blue eyes scorching her with their intensity. "I don't. I only have responsibility. And I have a shitload of it."

Maybe, but she wasn't quite so sure. For one thing the arm he had draped around her shoulders didn't say "burden," it said "protective."

And she wanted to pretend it said something even more. Something like friendship.

Maybe even love.

Dante paused at a dealer's display case. A tiny smile hovered at the edges of his lips as something caught his eye. He motioned for the dealer to come over.

"Can I help you?" the older woman asked as she approached them.

Dante pointed to something under the glass. "I'd like to see that."

Pandora didn't know what it was until the woman handed it to Dante and he turned toward her. She couldn't help laughing at the gold pendant in the form of a panther wrapped around a sapphire as he fastened it around her neck.

Pandora held the pendant in her hand so that she could examine it. "How unusual."

"Yes, it is," the woman said. "That's a shaman designer I met out West. He takes vision quests and then makes a necklace based on what animal guides him. That one there he said was a panther that led him through a nightmare and saved him."

How oddly apropos.

She looked up at Dante and smiled.

"I'll take it," Dante said, pulling out his wallet.

Pandora stared down at the exquisitely crafted piece while he paid. She was so warmed by the gesture, especially since Romeo had told her how selfish Dante was.

"Thank you," she said when he returned to her side.

"My pleasure."

Smiling even more, she lifted herself up on tiptoe and placed a chaste kiss to his cheek.

"You keep doing that," he whispered in her ear, "and I'll have you upstairs and naked in a heartbeat."

An overwhelming wave of desire tore through her body. It was the pantheress in her that needed to feel him inside her. They'd done enough talking and the wild part of her personality now wanted appeasement, too.

"I wouldn't mind it one bit," she whispered back.

That was all it took. One second they were in the crowd and the next, he'd pulled them off into an alcove where no one could see them and poofed them into a suite.

"Is this your room?" she asked as she glanced around the elegant accommodations.

"It's *our* room," he said as he stalked her like the hungry predator he was.

She stiffened at his tone. "Is that an order?"

"No, Pandora. But so long as we are mates, what is mine is yours."

"You're being strangely accommodating for a selfish panther Romeo said held no interest in a mate."

Dante paused at that. It was true. He'd never wanted to be bound by anything, especially not a mate. Yet for some reason, he didn't mind Pandora in the least.

"The Fates didn't ask me who or what I wanted for my own." He held her marked palm up for both of them to see. "But they have chosen you as mine and I take care of what belongs to me."

"And if I don't want to belong to you?"

"I can't force you to mate with me, Pandora, you know that. You are free to leave my protection at any time and go wherever you want."

Pandora swallowed at the thought. Yes, she could. But where would she go? The journey to Atlanta had been scary and fraught with the fear of having a pack find her and abuse her or the humans learning that she was a Were-Panther and locking her up.

Many ordinary things had baffled her.

How to buy a bus ticket. How to order food. Those things were all different in her time period. Everything there was done with universal credits. There was no money in her world. No fuel-burning vehicles.

The transports in her century were more akin to monorails and you paid your way with your palm print. Everything at home was automated and clinical.

She didn't know how to survive in the current human world. Didn't know how to use her powers.

It was terrifying here.

Except for Dante. He offered her more than anyone ever had. Protection and education.

He was her safety.

And he was her designated mate. Mating with a male was a physical act. It was the bonding ceremony that was emotional. She could easily mate and then have his protection.

Her heart would still belong solely to herself.

But if she refused to mate with Dante, he would have no reason to protect or educate her. And why would he? Her refusal would leave him impotent. Something she was sure wouldn't endear her to him.

"You will give me total freedom without any limitations on it?" she asked.

"I know no other way."

In that moment, she realized that she could learn to love this panther standing in front of her. He didn't have to give her anything. He could theoretically take anything from her that he wanted. The other panthers did.

If a woman wasn't mated to one of the Katagaria pack, they kept her anyway and used her as a whore for all of them.

But Dante offered her the world and asked for nothing in return. Nothing except a few words that would unite their physical bodies.

"And our children?" she asked him.

"We have a large nursery for them in Minnesota."

She cocked her head. "You realize they'll most likely be human and not cubs."

He looked perplexed by that. "Then I'll read Mr. Spock."

Pandora laughed. "He's the character from *Star Trek*, not the child expert. No wonder you're here."

He brushed the hair back from her face and gave her a sincere, heated look that melted her. "I will do whatever I have to to take care of them. I promise you. Human or cub, they will be protected as my offspring and they will have whatever they need to grow strong and healthy."

She pressed her marked palm against his. "Then I will mate with you, Dante Pontis."

Dante couldn't breathe as he stared down at her and those blessed words rang in his ears. He should be running for the door. But if he did that, he'd never have sex again.

Sex with only one woman. He was really paying the piper for all the years he'd been tormenting Romeo about being mated.

And yet he couldn't quite muster up true fear. Some hidden part of him liked the idea of Pandora being his.

Lacing his fingers with hers, he walked backward toward the bed, pulling her with him.

He used his powers to turn down the bed and strip their clothes from them before he lay on his back and pulled her over him.

The mating ritual was older than time. It was instinctive to their species and it would bind them for the rest of their lives. The only way to break it would be for one of them to die. Whoever survived the union would then be free to try and find another mate . . . if there was another one out there.

It was extremely rare for any Were-Hunter, Katagaria or Arcadian, to find a second mate.

Pandora bit her lip in nervous trepidation. All her life, her thoughts and energy had been spent on worrying about the actual act of sex. Since she was promised to a Katagaria pack, she'd never really thought much about ritual mating.

Now she was almost scared as she tried to take Dante into her body. This was a lot more difficult than she would have guessed. Every time she tried to straddle him, his cock went astray.

Dante smiled gently. "Can I help?"

She nodded.

He shifted his hips, then guided her onto him. They both moaned in pleasure as her body took him in all the way to his hilt.

This was it. A man who ought to terrify and repulse her was about to become her mate.

She would have children with him and somehow they would bridge the differences between their cultures and personalities and become the sole physical comfort for each other.

If she had to have a Katagari lover, she couldn't imagine a better panther to have as her own than Dante.

Pandora could barely think as she felt heat coming from their joined hands that held the mating mark. She moved against him slowly, then spoke the words that would unite them. "I accept you as you are, and I will always hold you close in my heart. I will walk beside you forever."

Dante watched her intently as he felt every inch of her body with his. He'd never thought to have a mate at all and had relegated himself to a future bereft of children. Now the thought of having his own cubs warmed him.

She was his.

A hot, demanding possessiveness unlike anything he'd ever known before tore through him as he watched her ride him slow and easy. Not feral like a pantheress.

Human and yet not. Who would have thought that Dante Pontis could be tamed by such a small creature? And yet her tender touch seared him with a humanity he wouldn't have thought possible.

The beast inside him was calm. No longer searching, it lay at peace as if she fit some part of him he'd never known was missing.

Smiling up at her, he cupped her face with his free hand and repeated the vow back to her.

Pandora moaned at the deepness of his voice until an unexpected pain sliced through her as her canine teeth started to grow.

Pandora hissed. This was the *thirio*, a need inside both their races that wanted them to bite each other and combine their life forces so that if one died, they both did.

Like the mating ritual itself, the choice of bonding was hers alone to make. Dante could never force it on her.

Nor did he ask it of her now.

True to his words, he left it entirely up to her and only watched her as she rode him.

Pandora kissed the hand that held his mark, then led it to her breast as her orgasm pierced her.

Dante couldn't breathe as his own climax blazed. He roared in satisfaction as his teeth finally began to recede.

It was done now. There was no going back.

They were joined, but not bonded.

Still, she was his.

He reached up to touch the necklace he'd bought for her. She looked beautiful naked in his arms. Her spent body was still wrapped around his.

"Pandora Pontis," he breathed. "Welcome to my pack." With that thought in mind, he pulled the small signet ring off his little finger, wished a spell onto it, then handed it to her.

Pandora studied the antique piece. It was beautiful, with gold filigree surrounding a large sapphire stone where an ornate *"DP"* was engraved. "What is this?"

"A homing beacon so that wherever you find yourself, you can always come back to me simply by thinking of me."

She scowled at his words. "I don't have those powers."

"I know. It's why I'm giving you the ring. The spell works from my powers and it's unbreakable."

Her lips trembled at his kindness. He'd really meant it when he said she had her freedom. Swallowing against the lump in her throat, she slid the ring onto her left hand. It was a perfect fit. "Thank you."

He inclined his head to her, then pulled her lips to his so that he could give her a passionate kiss.

A bright flash filled the room.

Pandora pulled back with a cry as someone grabbed her from behind.

Two seconds later, all hell broke loose.

4

Pandora cried out as she realized that eight panthers from the pack that had originally snatched her from her time period had suddenly appeared in Dante's suite.

"How dare you run from us!" their *tessera* leader snarled as he slung her away from the bed and Dante, into the arms of two of his cronies.

Pandora fought their hold as Dante threw his hand out and blasted the man who had grabbed her. The leader recoiled into the wall, but came right back on his feet.

Dante crouched low, ready to pounce on them. "Don't you dare touch her."

The leader straightened to give Dante a murderous glare. "Stay out of this, *panthiras*. She belongs to us."

Dante came off the bed with a snarl. "The hell you say." He turned to panther form as he attacked.

With the exception of the two holding her, all the men in the room transformed into panthers to fight. Pandora cringed at the growls and roars as the animals slashed and clawed each other in a primal battle.

Terrified that they might hurt Dante, she bit the man to her right, then stomped the foot of the one to her left. They let go of her, then reached for her again.

She spun away from them. Clothes appeared instantly on her body.

"*Run,* gataki," Dante said in her mind. "*They won't be able to find you in the crowd.*"

The next thing she knew, she was downstairs in a women's bathroom stall.

"Dammit, Dante!" she snarled as she left the stall and almost ran into a human woman dressed in an ornate burgundy and gold Renaissance gown who appeared to have just left the stall before her.

The woman gave her a fierce scowl that Pandora ignored as she brushed past her.

She had to get back upstairs with some reinforcements.

Dante couldn't fight that many panthers on his own. They'd kill him.

Her heart hammering, she ran out of the bathroom to find herself inside a roomful of dealers. She scanned the booths hoping to find one of Dante's brothers.

Instead her gaze landed on a medieval weapons booth that was lined with every kind of weapon imaginable.

Pandora headed for it. She skimmed through the weapons. They had poleaxes and swords, which would be too awkward for her. She had no idea how to skillfully wield one, and the daggers would force her to get too close to the panthers.

But the double-sided handaxe . . .

She seized it without hesitation, then closed her eyes, conjured up an image of Dante, and prayed his spell actually worked. Her head swam as she was whirled back into the room in the middle of the fight.

Pandora tightened her grip on the axe, then realized she wasn't sure which panther was Dante.

Not until one attacked her. Assuming her mate wouldn't do such a thing, she swung the axe with every ounce of strength she possessed.

It made contact with the beast's shoulder.

The panther howled as he limped away.

"*Pandora!*" Dante snapped in her mind. "*What are you doing?*"

"I'm saving my mate," she said between clenched teeth as she went after another panther. "You're not Dante, are you?"

"*I'm behind you.*"

"Good." She swung at the panther in front of her who dodged her first blow but was caught by her second one.

Before she could swing again, she found herself back in the handicapped bathroom stall, this time with two women who were trying to unlace a female Klingon costume.

They both gaped at her as they stared at her bloodied axe.

Too worried over her mate, Pandora paid them no attention.

"I'm getting tired of this!" she growled, then wished herself back to Dante.

Dante cursed in her head as she reappeared in his room. "*I'm going to take that damned ring from you.*"

A panther leaped at her.

Pandora started to swing, but caught herself as the panther flashed to Dante's naked, human form. He wrapped his arms around her and flashed her into her hotel room.

"Dante?" she breathed, her voice shaking as she realized he was covered in blood from the fighting. He looked terrible. There were bite wounds and scratches all over him.

Dante wanted to speak, but in truth it was taking way too much of his powers to assume human form while injured. His human body ached and throbbed.

He had to protect Pandora.

Closing his eyes, he summoned Romeo.

But no sooner had he sent out the call, than his human legs buckled.

"Dante?" Pandora asked as she pulled him into her arms.

He had no choice except to return to his panther's body.

To his surprise, she didn't release him or flee in fear of his animal form. She held him tight and stroked his fur.

He licked her chin, but couldn't muster any more strength. He was in way too much pain.

Pandora's heart stilled at the way Dante was acting. He had to be hurt badly to not even move.

A flash of light startled her. She reached for her axe, then hesitated as she saw Romeo in human form by the bed.

His gaze narrowed on her as he saw his brother's limp form and the bloody axe. "What did you do to him?"

"Nothing. The other panthers came for me and I tried to help Dante fight them off."

Something hit the door, then flashed into the room. Romeo whirled as a panther rushed them.

Dante leaped out of her arms so fast that she shrieked. He went straight for the panther's throat as Romeo changed form.

Pandora grabbed the axe from the floor and scrambled to a corner.

One by one, four more panthers appeared in the room. There was no way to tell them apart as they fought with Romeo and Dante. Roars and growls echoed in her ears and the scent of blood filled her nostrils.

Two more panthers appeared.

How she wished she knew if they were friend or foe. All she could do was grip her axe and pray.

The one panther she thought was Dante appeared to maim the one he was fighting by snapping the hind leg of his opponent. A baleful whine filled the air as the panther evaporated from the room.

The victorious panther turned to another that was fighting with the two new panthers. With his powerful jaws, he grabbed it by the neck and slung it away from the two.

He charged the downed panther, using his shoulder to drive it farther away from her and from the other two who snapped behind him.

His enemy tried to claw at his head, but the panther ducked his head and bit into his opponent's throat.

The opponent became wild, thrashing before she heard something break. It went limp.

Two more panthers vanished instantly.

The remaining four turned on the one panther that had been left behind and cornered it. It roared fiercely, then poofed out as well.

Terrified of what that meant, Pandora tensed as the four panthers turned to face her.

She watched them, determined to fight to the bitter end as they stalked nearer.

Three of them fell back while the fourth approached her.

"Dante?" she asked hesitantly, hoping it was him.

He collapsed at her feet before he placed one large paw on her foot and licked her ankle.

She sobbed in relief as she slid down the wall to pull his head into her lap.

The other three flashed into Romeo, Leo, and Mike.

"How badly are you hurt?" Romeo asked the twins.

They were a bit scuffed up, with bruises and bloodied lips and noses, but weren't hurt nearly as badly as Dante had been.

"We're okay, thanks to Dante."

Romeo approached her slowly.

"He's unconscious," she said quietly as she kept her hand on Dante's ribs to make sure he was still breathing. "There were eight of them in the beginning. He fought them alone."

"Dammit, Dante," Romeo snarled as he picked the panther up in his arms. "Why didn't you call us sooner?"

"Put him in my bed," Pandora said, moving to pull back the covers.

"Are you sure?"

She nodded.

Romeo set him down, then ordered Leo to keep watch at the door in case the others came back.

"Mike," he said to the other twin. "Go grab Acheron and tell him I need a favor."

Pandora crawled into the bed beside Dante. Part of her was terrified to be so close to him in his animal state and yet the other part of her wanted only to comfort her mate.

She'd never been this close to a panther before. It was scary and yet not.

Somehow it seemed right to be here.

His black fur was so dark, it reminded her of midnight velvet. She carefully brushed the whiskers of his muzzle back, then sank her hand in the soft fur of his neck.

Even though she knew it was true, it was hard to believe this was the same gorgeous man who had made the tenderest love to her.

And he had risked his life to protect her.

Her heart swelled with joy and with something she thought might be the first stirrings of love. No one had ever protected her. Not like this.

Pandora placed her hand near one of the vicious bite wounds above Dante's shoulder. "Will he be okay?" she asked Romeo.

If she didn't know better, she'd swear she saw pride in his eyes as he watched her.

"He's had worse."

"Really?"

"Really."

Romeo reached out and took her left hand so that he could see Dante's ring. His grip tightened on her hand. "That belonged to our brother Donatello," he said quietly. "I've never known Dante to take it off."

"He put a spell on it so that I could come back to him any time I wanted to."

Romeo smiled at that. "You have no idea just what a completely unbelievable feat that was for him."

"No, I think I do know." It ranked right up there with her lying beside him right now when she was terrified of panthers. This wasn't something she would have done even a few hours ago—and now . . .

Now she accepted the fact that this was her eternal mate. And for the first time in her life, she was beginning to understand exactly what that really meant.

Someone knocked on the door.

Pandora jumped.

"Relax," Romeo said as he moved to answer it while Mike stood aside. "The bad guys don't knock."

Pandora frowned as Romeo let in Leo and the gorgeous Goth man she'd seen downstairs. Leo went to stand beside Mike while the Goth came toward the bed.

"Pandora," Romeo said, "meet Acheron Parthenopaeus."

Acheron inclined his head to her.

She gaped. "You're the ancient Dark-Hunter?"

Acheron gave her that same wicked grin he had given her earlier. "The one and only."

A weird ripple went through her. "You knew me downstairs when our gazes met, didn't you?"

He nodded.

"If you knew I was looking for you, why didn't you say something?"

His gaze went to Dante. "Because it wasn't time for you to meet me yet." He glanced to Romeo. "And it's not time for you to lose another brother."

Pandora watched as the wounds on Dante healed instantly.

Romeo smiled in relief. "What do we owe you for that, Ash?"

Acheron shrugged. "Don't worry about it. I'll call the favor in at a later date."

Dante flashed into human form. He looked up at her with a tender expression that melted her.

"Ash," he said, without looking at the Dark-Hunter. "Could I trade another favor for you to watch my mate for me while my brothers and I take care of something?"

"Absolutely."

Dante placed one large, warm hand against her cheek, then chastely kissed the side of her face. He got up and gathered his brothers to him.

"We'll be back in a minute."

Before she could ask him where he was going, they vanished.

"What is he doing?" she asked Ash.

"Knowing Dante, I'm confident he's going to guarantee that your 'friends' never return to threaten you or anyone from your pack again."

It *didn't take* Dante long to find the rogue pack of Katagaria panthers. They were camped in a small, isolated commune just outside of Charleston.

Ironically, they even had a sign up declaring the area a wildlife preserve.

With his three brothers behind him, he walked through the wooded area until he found the first panther he'd fought. The panther was lying wounded with a human woman tending him.

"Who leads this pack?" he asked the pair.

The panther didn't answer, but when the petite, blond woman did, Dante recognized a voice that was almost identical in tone, accent, and cadence to Pandora's. "Aristotle is the *regis*. He's sleeping over there." She pointed to a tree.

Dante inclined his head respectfully to her, then went to the tree to call down their leader.

Aristotle responded by only opening one bored eye. "*Who are you?*"

"Take human form when you address me, you bastard," Dante said harshly. "Or there won't be enough left of your pack to even start a new one."

The panther flashed into human form, then moved to stand before Dante in a stance that said he was ready to fight. He was four inches shorter than Dante and had short black hair that matched his black soulless eyes.

"Who the hell are you?" he snarled.

"Dante Pontis."

Aristotle's eyes widened as he took an immediate step back.

Dante's brutal, take-no-prisoners reputation was known far and wide, and it was respected or feared by all their kind.

"To what do I owe this honor?" Aristotle asked.

"A group of your *strati* tried to take my mate from me. Now I'm here for blood."

Aristotle sputtered. "There was some misunderstanding. My men went after an Arcadian whor—"

Dante slugged him before he could finish the insult. "Pandora Kouti-Pontis is my mate. If you speak of her with anything other than extreme reverence in your tone, you piss me off."

Aristotle turned pale. "I had no idea she belonged to you. Believe me."

"Now you do, and if I ever see any of you near her again, I'll end all your problems. Permanently."

P*andora was sitting* in the Grandstand Lounge with Acheron, his daughter demon Simi, and two gods while they waited for Dante's return.

This had to be the oddest moment of her life. The demon was busy eating an extremely rare hamburger drenched in barbecue sauce while the gods and Acheron were telling Pandora stories about how they'd all met Dante.

Apparently her mate had quite a rambunctious club that catered to all manner of bizarre clientele. The gods and Acheron made routine visits there.

Zurvan, who went by the name Cas, was the ancient Persian god of time and space. He was the elegantly dressed man she had followed earlier toward the elevators, thinking he was Acheron.

Ariman—not to be confused with the Persian god Ariman—had been an ancient Phoenician god who had had the misfortune of visiting Atlantis at the time the continent was destroyed. He'd been in human form, trying to seduce a young woman, and as a result, he was now trapped in human form with no god powers except immortality.

He wasn't happy about it either.

"I really wish one of you would take mercy on me and fix me or kill me," Ariman said for the fifth time since he had joined them at their table.

Cas rolled his eyes, then turned toward Acheron. "I think we ought to banish him from our presence so we can't hear him bitch anymore."

Ash laughed.

"You're such—" Ariman's words broke off as he spotted the women who weren't wearing anything except warning tape. "Later." He bolted after the women.

Cas shook his head. "He is never going to learn, is he?"

Ash took a drink of beer before he responded. "Be grateful he doesn't. It gives us endless hours of amusement watching him screw his life up."

Cas snorted. "Considering how screwed up yours is, that says something."

"Let's not go there," Ash said, his eyes flashing red before they returned to their spooky swirling silver shade.

Sometimes it was very scary to hang out with supernatural beings.

"Pandora?"

She froze at the sound of a voice she never thought to hear again. Afraid she was hearing things, she turned to see her sister Sefia running up to her.

Pandora shot to her feet to throw her arms around her sister. Oh, it was too good to be real! "What are you doing here, Sef?"

"Your mate brought me," she said as tears poured down her

cheeks. "He made them let us all go. Now it's up to us if we want to return to our mates or not."

Pandora was stunned as she looked past her sister to see Dante and his brothers approaching at a much more sedate pace.

"Dante?" she asked as he stopped by her side.

He shrugged nonchalantly as if he hadn't just given her the impossible. "It wasn't right what they were doing to their females and I figured you'd rather travel with your own female kind than with mine."

She still couldn't believe he'd done this. He had formed a new pack of female panthers for her to roam with. "What about the pact they made with our pack?"

"It's dissolved," Dante said. "If they pull any more of your kin out of their time period, I'm going to send them a special welcoming committee."

"Damn, Dante," Cas said from behind her. "That's harsh. Last time you turned your brothers loose on a pack, they left no male standing."

"I know." Dante looked back to her. "And so do they. Your sister and her friends are all safe now."

Pandora threw her arms around his shoulders and held him close. "Thank you!"

He hugged her back, then kissed her gently.

Pandora turned back to Sefia as another thought occurred to her. "What about your children?"

"Their father is raising them, per Dante's orders." Sefia looked at Dante with glowing eyes. "Your mate took all of the women to La Costa and is paying for us to stay and be pampered there for as long as we like."

"And we volunteered to guard them," Mike said, indicating himself and Leo.

"Is that a good idea?" Pandora asked Dante. After all he and Romeo had said about the twins, she wasn't sure whether having them as guards would be a help or a hindrance.

Dante's face mirrored her skepticism. "I personally don't think so, but Romeo talked me into it. There's a large number of the females who aren't mated."

"And Dante owes us big after the filking fiasco," Leo said irritably. "There weren't any naked women there, just some guy singing about *Star Trek* and Romulan brew. It really pissed us off."

Pandora had to stifle her laughter.

"Are you coming with us?" Sefia asked.

Pandora felt a lot more torn than she should have. Spending time with her sister at a resort or staying with a Katagari panther at Dragon*Con . . .

There shouldn't be a choice.

So why did she feel this way?

"It's entirely up to you," Dante said quietly. "I told you I wouldn't interfere with your freedom."

"C'mon, Dora," Sefia said, taking her hand. "We're going to have a lot of fun."

Dante's face was completely stoic and yet she sensed his sadness.

"I'll be back soon," Pandora promised him.

He nodded.

"I'll take them upstairs to my room to flash them to the resort," Romeo said.

Dante didn't speak as he watched his brothers disappear into the crowd with Pandora and Sefia.

He'd done a good deed and now he knew why he hated doing good deeds.

They were painful.

What did he get out of it? Not a damn thing except a pain so profound that he felt as if something were shredding his heart.

"Here," Ash said, handing him a beer. "Have a seat."

Sighing, Dante took the beer and grabbed the chair where Pandora had been sitting on his arrival. "I did the right thing, right?"

"No," Simi said as she wiped barbecue sauce off her chin. "The panther woman didn't want you to leave her and now you made her go away. That was just stupid if you ask the Simi. Not that anyone ever does, 'cause if they did, then they would be smart. Some people are smart. But many, like you, are too stupid to ask me what I think. See?"

"It's not that simple, Simi," Dante said, wondering why he was trying to explain himself to a demon who had no understanding of human emotions or animal relationships. "She doesn't want me to own her."

"Well, the Simi doesn't understand that. Owning's not so bad. I own *akri* and he kind of fun."

Dante arched a brow at Ash who didn't bother to correct his demon.

Whatever. Those two were far beyond his understanding anyway.

"I'm telling you, Faith," a woman said as she and a friend walked by them. "There's a portal in the handicap stall downstairs that allows people to drop in from alternate universes. I was in there with Amanda helping her with her costume when this woman popped in, holding an axe. She immediately popped back out."

Dante laughed at that, even though a fierce pain cut through him at the memory.

Only his pantheress would be so bold as to defy his orders.

"I better go pay for that axe before someone puts out an APB on my mate," he said to Ash, Cas, and Simi.

But as he got up and headed down to the dealers' room, he couldn't squelch the need he felt to find Pandora and bring her back.

He wouldn't do that to her.

Dante was nothing if not a panther of his word.

5

Pandora spent two days in La Costa with her sister and the other females while Leo and Mike tutored them well on how to use their
powers. They also tutored some of the unmated females on things she
didn't even want to think about.

But none of her newfound freedom made her happy.

In fact, the longer she stayed here, the more her heart ached. Every
time her gaze fell to her marked hand, she thought about the panther
she'd left behind.

No, she thought about the man. The one who had given her so
much.

"How's Dante doing?"

She paused outside the sliding glass door that led to Mike and
Leo's room. The two panthers were in there alone and she wasn't sure
which one was which. One of them was resting in a blue recliner,
while the other appeared to have just ended a phone call.

That one tossed a cell phone to the dresser before he shrugged.
"Romeo said he's still screwed up."

The one in the chair sighed heavily. "Yeah. I can't believe he didn't
tell Pandora about his phobia."

"What phobia?" Pandora asked as she came through the door to
confront them.

The twins looked at her sheepishly.

"It's not nice to eavesdrop," the one in front of the dresser said in
a reprimanding tone.

She was in no mood to take that from him. "And it's not nice to
talk about people either, but since you're talking about my mate, I'd
like to know what you mean."

The twins exchanged a pained look.

"What do you think, Mike?" Leo was the one who'd had the cell
phone.

Mike leaned back in his recliner as he silently debated for a few seconds more. "Might as well tell her, I guess. I don't see what it would hurt."

Leo let out a loud breath before he spoke again.

He looked at her. "When Dante was a cub, he and his litter and a group of our cousins escaped their babysitter and went out prowling on their own. After a few hours, they got lost and one of the females with them got really scared because it was getting dark. She didn't want to try and find her way back until morning so Dante agreed to stay with her and keep her safe. Our brother Sal told Dante he'd be back with help and then led the others off."

Pandora frowned at his story. "Why would that make him phobic?"

"Because it was a cruel prank," Mike said bitterly. "As soon as Dante went to sleep, Tyla snuck out and they all headed back home without him. Dante woke up alone and had no idea what had happened to her or how to get home. He was terrified."

Pandora was appalled at how mean his siblings and cousins had been to leave him behind. A cub on its own could be picked up by humans and put in a zoo or, worse, killed by any adult wild animal that came across it.

"They left him there by himself for a solid week," Leo continued with the story. "Every time someone asked about Dante, they made up some lie about where he was. When Donatello found out what they'd done, he went back to the woods to get him. He found Dante practically starved to death. He'd been living off scraps and having to keep predators away with no help. He was weak from exposure, but still he'd kept searching for Tyla, afraid something had happened to her."

His face sad, Mike shook his head. "Romeo has always said that that was what made Dante so damned selfish. After they returned, Dante was freaky about ever running out of food or trying to help someone. He started hoarding things and turning on anyone who threatened him."

Her heart ached for her mate. It must have been horrible for him to be afraid for his life while trying to find Tyla. And all because of a joke.

"I hope Donatello punished them for what they did."

Mike sighed. "He did, but the damage had already been done. Like Acheron so often says, there are a lot of things in life that 'sorry' doesn't fix and that was one of them."

"Ever since then," Leo said, "Dante can't stand for anyone to leave him. He practically climbs the walls if he can't account for his family."

"That's why he went to find you two when you were lost, isn't it?" she asked.

Leo nodded. "His worst fear is to have someone he loves not be able to find their way home again."

Tears filled her eyes as she looked down at the ring Dante had given her when they mated.

Now it all made perfect sense.

Why he didn't want a wandering Katagari female for a mate . . .

Why he tolerated his brothers even when they drove him insane . . .

Why he had freed her sister and the other women to travel with her . . .

And why he had given her Donatello's ring.

Closing her eyes, Pandora conjured up an image of Dante.

D*ante was watching* the acid metal band on a TV monitor. But his mind wasn't really on the act or the handouts and CDs on the table in front of him.

It was on the fact that he should never have let Pandora go.

You can't keep her . . .

He should have at least tried.

But at least she wasn't out there alone. He'd made sure that she would have her sister with her.

A warm hand touched his arm.

Grinding his teeth, Dante turned, ready to rebuff yet another woman coming on to him. He was really getting tired of telling them he wasn't interested.

But as he opened his mouth and his eyes focused on the beautiful face of his latest admirer, all thoughts scattered.

It couldn't be.

Not this soon.

"Pandora?"

"Hi," she said with a smile that made him feel sucker-punched. "I missed you."

This had to be a dream. His pantheress couldn't be back.

He wanted to tell her that he'd missed her, too, but the words wouldn't come. All he could do was react.

He pulled her into his arms and kissed her fiercely, letting her feel that every part of him wanted her never to leave him again.

Pandora laughed at his heated welcome. "I think you missed me, too."

Dante left her lips to take a deep whiff of her hair so that he could memorize and savor it. "You have no idea."

Actually, she did. She hadn't doubted the twins before, but this thoroughly confirmed their story.

She nuzzled his neck, inhaling the warm spicy scent of his masculine skin. "Want to get naked?"

He laughed. "Yeah, but not here."

Pulling back from her, he took her hand and led her to a secluded corner so that he could flash them into his room.

They were both naked and in his bed three blinks later.

Dante couldn't breathe as he felt the impossible softness of Pandora lying beneath him.

Nothing felt better than her caresses. The fact that she was warm and welcoming. He slid himself inside her, and groaned at just how good she felt.

Pandora savored his hardness inside her and now more than ever she was glad she was human and not a real panther. Her Katagaria cousins only sought sex when they were in heat.

She could seek it anytime she wanted and she wanted Dante right now. Needed to feel his strong, powerful thrusts.

But the human in her wanted even more.

It wanted him with her forever.

"Will you bond with me, Dante?"

Dante froze as her whispered words went through him. "What?"

She held her marked palm up. "I don't ever want to leave you and I don't want to live without you. Not for one minute. Bond with me, Dante, so that neither one of us is ever abandoned again."

He took her hand into his and kissed her as love for her overwhelmed him.

He thrust against her hard and furiously as she repeated her vows to him and he returned them to her.

This time when his teeth grew, he pulled back to stare down at her an instant before he sank his fangs into her neck.

Pandora arched her back as the pain of his bite quickly turned to pleasure. Her head spinning, she sank her own teeth into his shoulder.

For that one instant in time, every thought and emotion Dante felt coursed through her.

Any doubt she'd ever had about him fled as she felt his love for her, and it ignited her own.

This was what was meant to be.

He was hers and she was his.

She cried out as she came in a fierce wave of pleasure. Dante's own growl of pleasure filled her ears.

Joined together, they drifted through the ribbons of ecstasy until they were fully drained and spent.

Dante collapsed on top of her and she cuddled him in her arms. "I love you, Dante," she breathed. "And I promise I'll never again leave you."

He smiled languidly as he stared at her. "I love you, too, Pandora, and anytime you want to leave, I'll gladly go with you."

Epilogue

In the Marriott's lobby, Dante stood off to the side with Acheron while everyone at the hotel was packing up to leave. All the Klingons, Storm Troopers, fairies, and so on were now in normal dress with only scattered parts of their costumes evident as, one by one, they returned to real life.

Dragon*Con was over.

Just like Ash had promised him a year ago when he told him to come to Atlanta, it had been a remarkable weekend that would stay with him forever.

"You knew Pandora would be here when you told me to come, didn't you?" he asked the Atlantean.

Ash shrugged. "There's always room for error, but yeah. I did."

"You're a scary SOB."

Ash laughed.

Dante felt Pandora's presence behind him.

Turning, he saw her and Simi coming over to them.

Simi was beaming as she carried a wide collection of bags. "I gots my last bit of shopping done," she announced proudly. "You should be glad, Dante, your panther-woman don't buy much."

"You know you could have spent whatever you wanted," he said to Pandora.

"I know, but all I wanted was this."

He frowned as she handed him a small wooden box. "What is it?"

"Open it and see. I bought it just for you."

Dante opened it to find what appeared to be a bell-shaped necklace. "I don't get it," he said.

Pandora took the necklace out and placed it around his neck. "This is just in case you ever again have to fight someone else. Next time, I'll know which panther you are and I won't accidentally cut your head off. I plan on living a long, long life with you, Mr. Pontis. And no one, not even you, is going to stop me."

A Dark-Hunter
Christmas

Prologue

Born to impoverished Irish immigrant parents at the turn of the century, James Cameron Patrick Gallagher entered this world with a large chip on his shoulder.

It didn't help any that he was birthed in the backroom of a sweatshop that should have been condemned, to a timid, fretful woman who'd been forced to return to work just hours after she had delivered him into the hands of his nervous, alcoholic father. A father who was indifferent to the boy at best and violent at worst.

From the moment of that first wail forward, Jamie spent his life fighting for respect. Fighting his way out of the poverty that haunted him as he grew up in the Irish slums of New York.

At age fifteen, he found his way out.

The year was 1916 and two important events happened to him. His father died after he slipped and fell into the river on his way home from a three-day drinking binge. Two weeks later, Jamie went to work for the renowned gangster Ally Malone so that he could support his mother and eight younger siblings. A thug and a bully, Ally had shown him a way to make money that had made Jamie's poor mother's knees ache from the untold novenas she had prayed for her son.

But that was okay as far as Jamie was concerned. His new lifestyle afforded him the ability to buy his mother silk pillows to cushion her work-worn knees, and instead of praying with a cheap wooden rosary, she now had one made of gold and ivory.

It was a rosary she'd thrown in his face the day she had learned the real truth about her son: Jamie wasn't a poor innocent lad being led astray by those out to take advantage of him. By the time he was twenty, he was a fierce gangster to be reckoned with.

Disowned by his mother, he'd given his younger brother a reputable job so that Ryan could care for the family without their mother knowing it was Jamie's ill-gotten gains that kept them all fed.

Jamie had learned to harden his heart and to care for no one or nothing. He became Gallagher. A man who had no other name. One who let no one near him, let no one know him. He was ice-cold and rock-solid.

Until the day Rosalie had come into his life and chiseled away his granite casing. The daughter of Portuguese immigrants, she had been walking home from an all-day Mass.

Jamie had stumbled over her in his haste to catch up with a "business" associate he needed to take care of.

It had been a cold winter evening with snow falling down on the city. February 11, 1924—a date that was branded into his heart and mind for all eternity. The minute Rosalie had turned her dark brown eyes on him, his entire body had been consumed by fire. For the first time in years, he felt something more than cold, blind hatred.

"I'm so sorry," she had whispered in her exotic accent, brushing at his expensive, handmade suit. "I didn't see you for the snow."

"It was my fault," he hastened to assure her. No doubt any other man in his position would have hit her or yelled at her. That thought sent a wave of unreasonable fury through him.

She was a complete stranger and yet he felt possessive toward her. Respectful. Two emotions he'd never accorded any woman not related to him.

"Rosalie!" her mother had snapped as she came back for her daughter. "You do not talk to such men. How many times must I say that to you." She took Rosalie by the arm and offered him a pleading, servile glance. "Forgive my daughter, *senhor*. She is young and foolish."

"It's fine, *senhora*," he said quickly. Then he met Rosalie's wide-eyed stare. She was truly beautiful. Her black hair was braided and coiled around her head, exposed to him when her church veil had fallen off after they collided. Her dark brown eyes were pure. Innocent. Completely unspoiled by the bloody violence that made up his life. Most of all, her eyes were kind.

He didn't want anything to sully that gaze. To make it hard and cold. Bitter.

Like his.

"May I have permission to court your daughter?" The question was out of his mouth before he could stop it. Her mother's expression was one of pure horror. White Irishmen didn't court Portuguese women. Society would never tolerate such a thing.

"No," she said sharply, hauling her daughter away from him.

Jamie might have taken no for an answer.

Gallagher didn't.

It had cost him well over one hundred dollars in bribes to locate Rosalie, but she had been worth every cent of it. Regardless of her parents, his associates, and society as a whole, he had made her his wife on June 17, 1925.

Rosalie alone had known Jamie. And he had died trying to get to her side while she struggled to bring his one and only child, his son, into the world.

It had been a cold snowy night then, too. Just days before his thirty-third birthday. He'd known the authorities were after him, had known he had a mole in his company even though he had been trying to go straight.

None of that had mattered.

Rosalie had needed him, and he had refused to let her down.

It was a decision that had cost him his life and his soul.

1

Seventy years later
New Orleans

Gallagher frowned as he felt something tickling his lower back. It was a sensation that he'd learned years ago signaled a Daimon was nearby. He turned his one-of-a-kind 1932 Bugatti Atlantic Aerolithe down a side street and parked it.

Oh yeah, the feeling was there, even stronger than before. He left the car and paused as he got his bearings. In the last seventy years, he'd only been to New Orleans a handful of times, and though the city didn't change much, it still took him a couple of minutes to remember the lay of the French Quarter.

The moonlight filtered down past the wrought-iron railings and hanging plants to illuminate the old brick of the buildings. Faint laughter and music could be heard as well as cars passing by. He cocked his head to listen, hoping for a sign of where the Daimons were.

A scream rang out.

Rushing off after it, he tore through the back alleys until he found the young woman near a garbage pile, surrounded by four male Daimons while a fifth Daimon had already sunk his fangs into her neck.

Infuriated, Gallagher rushed them. They charged him in unison, not that it did them any good. A couple of well-placed blows and one quick stab to their chests, and they were history.

Gallagher ran to the woman and knelt down by her side. Gently, he turned her over to find a girl no older than twenty. He cursed at the fate that had brought her into the path of the Daimons.

Luckily she was still alive, even though she was struggling to breathe. He pulled his monogrammed handkerchief out of his coat pocket and used it as a makeshift tourniquet over her vicious neck wound.

Moving quickly, he carried her back to his car, then rushed her to the nearest emergency room where he learned that the hospital staff wasn't big into admitting unknown women who were carried in by strangers in bloodstained clothes.

Once he had Nick Gautier on the hospital phone with the clerk and he was sure the unknown girl would be cared for, Gallagher took a deep breath.

He hung around the hospital, wanting to make sure she would live. Anxious and unable to just sit while the staff tended her, he found himself wandering around the corridors. The place was really decked out for the holidays. The green and red garlands and poinsettia cut-outs added a warmer feel to the antiseptic white. A couple of nurses and young female visitors smiled invitingly at him as he passed by. But then, women always had. At six-foot-four with black hair and eyes, he was well-muscled and hard-edged. The kind of guy that dames tended to notice.

He'd never been vain about it. It was just a fact of life that women liked to look at him and often propositioned him. And though he'd been tempted a time or two over the decades, he had never touched another woman.

Not so long as his wife had lived. Gallagher might have broken every law on the books, but he had never broken a single vow. Especially not one made to someone he loved. Even after Rosalie's death, he still hadn't felt the inclination to touch another woman. So Gallagher just nodded kindly to them and kept walking.

Before long, he found himself on the pediatric ward. His stomach knotted as he realized where he was. There had been a time once when he'd hoped to come to a hospital to see his son.

He'd never made it.

Hurried and not thinking, he'd left his office building at a dead run and had been trying to get into his car when he'd found himself surrounded by cops.

Gallagher, who had never backed down from a fight, had held his hands up. For Rosalie's sake, he'd been willing to surrender to them.

They had shot him dead in the street like a rabid animal.

Unable to deal with the memory, Gallagher was just about to turn around and leave when something odd caught his eye . . .

He saw a strange-looking elf dressed in a red Santa shirt with a very short red skirt, and red-and-white thigh-high stockings that vanished into a pair of scuffed-up black combat boots. She sang to a group of kids with a voice that would rival a heavenly choir for its melodic beauty. The woman was tall and in a freakish way extremely attractive, with eerie, reddish-brown eyes that must have been some kind of contact lenses, pointed ears, and hair that was jet black and streaked with red.

But what floored him most was the man with her.

Acheron Parthenopaeus. The glorified leader of the Dark-Hunters sat on the floor, surrounded by children while he played a black guitar and sang chorus to the woman's lead.

Gallagher was stunned by the sight. In all the years he'd known Ash, he had never seen the man relaxed. Normally, Acheron had a presence about him that was decidedly lethal and cool. One that warned people to keep their distance if they wanted to live.

But that wasn't the Ash he saw now. The man on the floor looked more like a kid himself. Approachable and kind. Ash's deep voice mingled with the elf's as they sang Jackie Deshan's "Put a Little Love in Your Heart."

"Now there's a sight you don't see every day, huh? Two punked-out Goths throwing a Christmas party for sick children."

Gallagher turned to find a middle-aged African-American doctor beside him. She looked tired, but amused, as she watched Ash and his elfin helper with the children.

"You've no idea," he said to her.

The doctor smiled. "I have to admit it took me some getting used to when I started working here a few years ago. I thought they were joking when they first told me about the Goth Guardian Angel and his children's fund."

Gallagher arched a brow at the nickname. "So he comes here a lot?"

"Every few months or so. He always brings gifts for the children and staff, and then plays with the kids for awhile."

Gallagher couldn't have been more stunned had she told him Ash routinely burned the hospital to the ground. "Really?"

"Oh, yeah. We figure he must be some rich kid with a need to do some good. The darnedest thing is, whenever he comes, the kids become perfectly calm and serene. Their blood pressure goes down and we never have to give them any painkillers while he's here. After he leaves, they sleep comfortably for hours. And best of all, the cancer patients go into remission for several weeks afterward. I don't know what it is about that young man, but he really makes a difference in their lives."

Gallagher could understand that. Even though Ash could be terrifying, there was something oddly comforting about the Atlantean.

The instant Ash realized he was there, he saw the veil come down over the man's face. The humor faded, and Ash stiffened noticeably. Ash became the grim, take-no-prisoners leader that Gallagher was well-versed with.

As soon as the song was finished, Ash handed his guitar off to one of the older children and excused himself. He stood up and left the room with a loose long-limbed, predatorial gait. Ash's face was impassable as he crossed his arms over his chest and approached Gallagher.

"St. Ash—who knew?"

Ash ignored his comment. "What are you doing here?"

Gallagher shrugged. "I was just passing through."

He cocked his head. "Passing through? Last time I checked, Chicago was north of Baton Rouge, not south."

"I know. But since I was so close, I just wanted to stop in at Sanctuary and wish everyone a Merry Christmas."

Ash listened to Gallagher's thoughts and let the man's emotions wash through him. Jamie's wife had died of old age this past summer, and her death had hit the Irishman hard.

As soon as he'd "heard" about her death, Ash had gone to Jamie immediately only to find out that Jamie had broken his Code of Conduct and visited her while she'd been in the hospital. Ash had chosen to overlook the breach. He might not have ever known the love of a human being, but he did understand those who were lucky enough to have it.

"Tell you what, since you're here, why don't you just stay on until after the New Year?"

Jamie scoffed at that. "I don't need your pity."

"It's not pity. It's an order. Since Kyrian is retired, Talon could use an extra hand. Things get rather rowdy this time of year. Lots of Daimons head down south where it's warmer and people are out for New Year's."

"Are you full of crap or what?"

Before Ash could answer, the elf woman came out of the room holding a young toddler to her hip.

"*Akri?*" she said to Ash in a strange sing-song kind of voice. "Can I keep him?" She patted the plump leg that was exposed from beneath the hospital gown. "See, he good eating. Lots of fat on this one."

The dark-headed toddler laughed.

"No, Simi," Ash said sternly. "You can't keep the baby. His mother would miss him."

She pouted. "But he want to go home with the Simi. He said so."

"No, Simi," Ash repeated.

She huffed at him. "No Simi, no food. Nag, nag, nag. Does your daddy nag you, too?" she asked the boy.

"Nope," he said as he pulled at one of the black and red horns on top of her head.

Ash sighed. "Simi, take the baby back inside."

She moved to stand before Ash. "Okay, gimme a kiss and I'll go."

Ash looked extremely uncomfortable as he glanced at Gallagher, then back at her. "Not in front of the Hunter, Simi."

She made a strange animal-like noise as she looked at Gallagher. "The Simi wants a kiss, *akri*. I'll wait all century. You know I will."

To say Ash looked peeved was an understatement. He leaned over and kissed her quickly on the brow.

She beamed proudly, then trotted off with the child.

"Who is that?" Gallagher asked. "Or should I say, *what* is that?"

"In short, she's not your concern." Ash rubbed his hand over his forehead as if he were in pain. "Where were we?"

"I asked why you were giving me temporary duty in New Orleans."

"Because Talon could use a hand."

"I wonder what Talon would say?"

"He would tell you not to piss me off."

Gallagher gave a half laugh at that. "All right then. I'll take it under advisement."

Ash watched the woman in the room with the kids. "You can camp with the Peltiers at Sanctuary. Right now I better go before one of those kids ends up on a milk carton."

Gallagher watched as Ash rushed into the room to take a little girl from the elf and then set the child aside. The elf danced away and moved on to another child.

Shaking his head at the oddity, Gallagher headed for the elevator to go back below and check on his patient. The nurse told him she would be fine. Gallagher let out a relieved breath.

The nurse stood up and patted his arm. "Come on," the woman said, inclining her head toward the back. "She wants to thank you."

"I don't need any thanks."

"Sug, we all need thanks. C'mon."

Before he could stop himself, he let the nurse lead him back to a small emergency room that had curtained walls. The petite brunette sat up on her stretcher with an oversized bandage on her neck. Her large green eyes were a bit dazed, but they brightened as soon as she looked up to see him. The nurse left them alone.

"Are you the man who saved me?" she asked.

Feeling awkward, he nodded.

The girl fidgeted with the blanket that covered her. "Thank you. Really."

"My pleasure. I'm just glad I found you when I did."

"Yeah, me too."

Gallagher turned to leave. "Well, I need . . ."

His voice trailed off as a lovely young woman came through the curtains. She was tall, probably around five-ten or so with jet-black hair and deep blue eyes. "Jenna!" she cried as she saw her friend on the stretcher. "Oh thank God, you're okay. The lady on the phone said you'd been attacked."

Jenna's eyes teared up. "I don't know what happened. I was just going out to my car, and I don't remember anything after that. If not for him, I'd probably be dead."

The girl turned around and froze. She looked at him as if she'd just seen a ghost.

Gallagher stared back defiantly. "Something wrong?" he asked.

She frowned. "No." She waved her hand around as if feeling silly. "I'm sorry, you just remind me of someone."

"Old boyfriend?"

"No, my great-grandfather."

"That's not particularly flattering. I thought I looked rather good for my age."

She laughed at that. "No, I mean . . . oh, never mind."

Jenna cocked her head as she looked at him. "He does look like him, Rose. You're right."

Rose. The name hit him like a blow.

Before he could move, the girl named Rose approached him. She pulled out an engraved gold locket from underneath her brown sweater. It was a locket he knew intimately. Right down to the garnet and diamonds that formed a circle on the front of it, to the inscription on the back.

For my Rose.
Happy Anniversary 1930.

She opened the locket to show him the two pictures inside. One was the photograph Rosalie had requested he have made just months before he died and the other was of his son at age two. "See," the girl said, showing him the photograph. "You look just like my Grandpa Jamie."

His heart aching, Gallagher swallowed. He wanted to reach out to touch it, but his hands shook so badly, he didn't dare. "Where did you get that?"

"My great-grandmother gave it to me last spring. Since I was named after her, she wanted me to have it." She smiled sadly and then closed the locket and returned it to rest under her sweater. "My father said Grandpa Jamie was a gangster, but I don't believe it. Gram Rose would never have married someone like that. She was a saint."

It was all he could do to breathe. To not crush her into his arms and weep. His great-granddaughter.

Rosalie.

This vibrant young woman was his living tie to his wife. When he spoke, his voice was thick and deep. "She must have loved you a great deal to give you that."

"I know. She wore it every day of her life until she gave it to me. It's just weird, you know? You looking so much like him and all."

Gallagher cleared his throat. "Yeah. Weird." He couldn't take his eyes off her. He didn't see much of himself or Rosalie in the girl, but he felt the bond of kinship deep in his heart.

She was his family. And he could never tell her. Just as he had never been able to tell her father or her grandfather.

Gallagher had bartered his soul for vengeance and then been forced to step back into the shadows and surrender the care of his family over to strangers. But at least the Squire Council had been there. After Gallagher had become a Dark-Hunter, they had sent in people to make sure his family survived.

The government had taken everything from Rosalie. Confiscated even his legitimate assets and left her destitute. The Squires had given her a job, and after a few years, they had sent in suitable beaux to date his wife and one of them had finally married her.

While Harris had lived, he had sent Gallagher updated photos and news about Gallagher's son and grandchildren. The Squire's Council had ensured the safety and well-being of his family while he had gone about his business of hunting and killing Daimons.

Ash had warned him how hard it would be.

"So long as you have direct descendants still living, it will haunt you. But it does get easier . . . in time."

Other Hunters had told him the same thing, but right now with his great-granddaughter standing before him, he didn't believe it. God, it was so unfair.

Or maybe this was his atonement for living the violent life he had chosen.

Always an outsider. A part of the world, but not in it. He winced at the truth.

Weary and hurt, he excused himself from the girls and made his way out of the hospital. The street outside was virtually empty. The late hour had sent everyone home seeking warmth. Comfort.

He doubted if he would ever feel either again.

When he pulled into the private garage that was across the street from Sanctuary, Elizar Peltier came out of the back door and stopped. The man's long, curly blond hair was pulled back from his face. He wore a pair of black chinos and a baggy black sweater.

"Jamie Gallagher," he said slowly. "I'll be damned." He turned and called into the open door, "Kyle, go tell *Maman* to put on a plate of corned beef and cabbage. We have a Dark-Hunter in need of food."

Gallagher nodded his thanks. "Hi Zar, it's been awhile."

"About thirty or so years, I think, since we last had the pleasure of your company."

Time was truly fleeting to an immortal. "Yet you still remember my favorite food."

Zar shrugged. "I never forget a friend."

Neither did Gallagher. They were too few and far between.

Zar led him to the building next door to the Sanctuary bar. Built at the turn of the century, Peltier House was the home of the Katagaria family and their hodgepodge group of refugees. The house connected to the bar through a downstairs door that was guarded at all times by one of the eleven Peltier sons.

In the Hunter world, they were legendary because they greeted everyone as friends: Were-Hunters, Dream-Hunters, Dark-Hunters or others. It mattered not. So long as you minded your manners and kept your weapons concealed, they let you enter and leave in peace. Those who broke the one house rule of "No Spill Blood" quickly found themselves leaving in pieces.

The elegant Victorian mansion was quiet now except for the muffled sound of the Howlers playing on the stage next door in the bar. It was furnished in expensive turn-of-the-century antiques that had been in the house since they were new. The bear clan didn't like change. Gallagher was glad for that. It felt strangely like coming home again.

"How long are you staying?" Zar asked as he led him up the hand-carved mahogany stairs.

"Until the New Year."

Zar nodded. "*Maman* will be glad to hear that." He showed Gallagher to a room at the end of the hallway.

Gallagher stepped inside and found a warm, cozy bedroom. The windows were well-shuttered and covered by heavy drapes that would keep the daylight from reaching him.

"Here's a cable modem for your laptop if you brought one."

The corner of Gallagher's mouth lifted. "All the comforts of home."

"We try. I remember well the days of running and hiding, and never having a single comfort. Take a few minutes to get settled in and join us when you're ready."

Gallagher watched Zar leave while feelings and memories went through him. He appreciated the bears' courtesy, but he would trade all his money and immortality for one single night spent with his wife and son.

One single Christmas with them, watching Rosalie's face light up as she opened a gift.

The pain of his loss racked him. He didn't want to hurt and wish for things he could no longer have. He sat on the bed and stared at the wall. He saw his great-granddaughter's face and wondered if she would go home at Christmas to be with her family.

For that matter, he wondered if he should go home himself. At least Chicago was familiar to him. Weary and heartsick, he lay down on the bed to just rest for a second. He only wanted to escape for an instant into memories of a time when he had been human.

Gallagher *woke up* to find that three days had passed while he slept. He didn't remember anything about his dreams.

"Why did you let me sleep so long?" he asked Mama Peltier as soon as he left his room and found her in the downstairs parlor on the right.

In human form, she was an elegant, tall blonde woman who most often wore a stylish suit. Though she looked no older than forty, she was in fact close to eight hundred years in age. "Acheron said you needed to rest and I agreed."

"But three days?"

She shrugged. "Do you feel better?"

Strangely, he did. At least physically.

It was just after dark on Christmas Eve. The bear clan was slowly filing down the stairs and gathering into the two main parlors where dual twelve-foot-tall pines were decorated.

Gallagher stood back, watching the whole crew of Katagaria and Arcadians who made Peltier House their home, gather around for the coming celebration. The tiny bear cubs climbed over presents and tried to eat and climb up the trees while their fathers and mothers, in human form to make Gallagher feel more at home, pulled them back. Justin Portakalian came down in his panther form and picked up one of the smaller cubs by the scruff of his neck and rolled him playfully across the floor.

It was the most bizarre Christmas gathering Gallagher had ever seen in his one-hundred-plus years of living. He felt even more out of place than he had felt three days ago when he arrived. As members from The Howlers came in to join the party, Gallagher decided he needed a breath of fresh air and a moment of quiet to clear his head. He headed out into the cold dark night and drifted aimlessly through the French Quarter. Before he realized it, he was outside the St. Louis Cathedral.

It had been a long time since he'd last been in church. There were only a few people headed inside. No doubt most of the parishioners would wait until the Midnight Mass. He started to turn away, but instead found himself heading inside with the others.

The foyer was dark, but his Dark-Hunter sight saw the interior clearly and he moved toward the small font of holy water that rested on the wall to his left, just beside the church store. He blessed himself, then opened the dark wood doors that led into the cathedral. The beauty of the stained glass and statuary immediately took him back to the days of his youth.

Gallagher genuflected, then sat down on the last row. Here, he felt his Rosalie. Devout, she had never missed a Holy Day of Obligation or Feast Day. He had dutifully gone with her even though he'd hemmed and hawed about it. Ever patient, she would sit by his side, patting his arm and smiling to herself over the fact that she had gotten him to do the impossible.

"I miss you, Rose," he breathed, his chest tight with the pain of her loss.

He wanted to stay here where he felt her, but he couldn't. No Dark-Hunter could remain in any old church for very long before the ghosts of the past came out to possess them.

And he was too weak at this moment to fight them.

Getting up, he made his way silently out back to the font, then out to the street.

It was cool out, but nowhere near the coldness he felt inside himself. Gallagher headed down Chartres Street. He didn't know where to go. He didn't feel like going back to Sanctuary and there was no real need to hunt on Christmas Eve. Since most humans were at home with their families, the Daimons tended to stay in as well.

"Hel-lo!"

He paused at the familiar sing-song voice. Turning around, he found "Simi" behind him.

"Hi," he said, half-expecting to see Ash with her.

But apparently she was out alone. Simi bounced up to him. "What'cha doing out here all alone?" she asked. "Did you forget how to find Sanctuary?"

"No. I want to be alone for a bit."

She cocked her head and frowned. "Why? Were the bears mean to you? Mama can get a bit cranky whenever I play with the cubs. She thinks I'm going to eat one, but bleh! They're way too hairy. Now if she'd let me skin one, I might be interested."

He laughed in spite of himself. "Are you joking?"

"Oh no. I never joke about hairy food. It's disgusting." She looked up at him. "If they weren't mean to you, then why did you leave?"

"I don't know. I guess I didn't feel right being there."

"Why?"

He shrugged. "What are you doing out here?"

"Not much. *Akri* is off with that red-headed demon so he said I could go play just so long as I don't eat nothing not cooked by a human. But all my favorite places are closed so I thought I'd go find the bears myself and see if Jose, since he's human, would make me up something good that wouldn't make *akri* mad if I ate it."

"*Akri* is Ash?"

"Yes."

"And the red-headed demon?"

"Artemis the bitch goddess. You know her. She's the one who stole your soul."

"She didn't steal it."

Simi blew him a raspberry. "Of course she did. She steals everything." She stood up on her tiptoes and stared into his eyes. "Hey," she said, taking his chin in her hand so that she could move his head back and forth while she examined him. "You're hurting in there. That would make *akri* very sad. He doesn't like for his Dark-Hunters to hurt and the Simi don't like it when *akri* is sad. Why are you hurt?"

"I miss my family."

Releasing him, she nodded sympathetically. "I miss mine, too. My mama was good people. 'Simi,' she would say, 'I love you.' *Akri* loves me, too."

She tilted her head down so that he could see her horns which were now covered by what appeared to be very small knitted hats. "See, *akri* even gave me hornay warmers so my horns wouldn't get cold. You want some hornay warmers, too?"

This had to be the oddest conversation of his life. He didn't know why he stayed here talking to her. Maybe it was her childlike manner. There was something very charming about her.

"I don't have horns."

"You want some?" she asked hopefully. "I could give you some real colorful ones. *Akri* has some black ones, but he doesn't let other people see them."

"Ash has horns?"

"Oh my, yes. They are quite lovely. Not as lovely as mine, but they are still very nice. The Simi would say she hopes you see them, but if you ever did, you'd be dead and I think the Simi would miss you. You seem very nice, too."

Gallagher frowned as she rummaged around in her giant over-sized, beaded purse. After a few seconds, she pulled out an oven mitt that looked like a fish. She handed it to him.

"That is quality. From QVC. My favorite place. Do you watch QVC?"

"No."

"Well, you should. *Akri* says I watch it too much, but he never complains when I shop there. They like me, too. Put me on television and call me Miss Simi. I like that."

He handed her the fish back.

"Oh no, that's for you. Presents make people happy. The Simi wants you to be happy."

Oh yeah, this was without a doubt the strangest moment of his life. Both mortal and immortal. "Thank you, Simi."

She waved his words aside with her hand. "No need to thank me. See, that's what families do. They take care of each other."

His stomach tightened at her words. "I no longer have a family. I had to give them up."

She looked at him curiously. "Of course you have a family. Everyone has family. I'm your family. *Akri* your family. Even that smelly old goddess is your family. She's that creepy old aunt who comes around but nobody likes her so they make fun of her when she's gone."

He laughed again. "Does she know you say that about her?"

"Of course. I say it to her face all the time. That's why *akri* told me to come play while he's with her. He don't like it when we fight."

She took his hand into hers. "Listen and I'll tell you what *akri* once told me. We have three kinds of family. Those we are born to, those who are born to us, and those we let into our hearts. I have let you into my heart so the Simi is your family and she won't give you up. If you are sad right now, then I'm thinking your family is still in your heart, too, and they are taking up so much room that you have no room for anyone else."

"I can't give them up."

"And you shouldn't. Ever. No one should ever forget those they love. But it's like with QVC—whenever I fill up my room with too much stuff, *akri* builds me another room. Somehow there's always space for more. Your heart can always expand to take in as many people as you need it to. The people who live there, they don't go away. You just make room for one more person and then another and another and another."

With her arm in his, Simi walked him down the street. "Don't you want Simi to be your family?"

He thought about her words and strange analogy.

She leaned forward and whispered. "This is the part where you say, 'Yes, Simi, I would like to be your family.' 'Cause if you don't, then I'll have to take my mitt back and barbecue you. *Akri* is still upset about the last Dark-Hunter I barbecued and that was . . . oh, a thousand or so years ago. He part elephant when it comes to remembering things. So tell me, do you want Simi to be your family?"

He smiled in spite of himself. "Yes, Simi, I would like to be your family."

She beamed. "Good. You're such a smart Dark-Hunter."

Before Gallagher realized it, Simi had led him back to Sanctuary. She opened the door and stood back, waiting for him to enter. The earlier loudness was nothing like what was happening now. There were four hawks lined up on one curtain rod, dancing in time to the rocking Christmas carols. The Howlers (all in human form) were singing while Dev Peltier played the piano. A white tiger was lying on its back on the sofa while Marvin the monkey jumped up and down on its belly.

A large black bear he assumed was Aimee Peltier was feeding two baby cubs peanut butter sandwiches. A red-headed human woman with a scar on her face came up to them and grabbed Simi into a hug. "Hey little demon, where's boss man?"

Simi shrugged. "He off attending to Lord Queen Pain-In-My-Butt. How are you, Tabitha? Is your sister and Kyrian coming?"

"No, they'll be here tomorrow. Morning sickness hit Amanda as they were leaving, but Talon said he'd be here just as soon as he could." The two of them drifted off into the crowd.

Gallagher stood back, watching the revelry. There were Arcadians here, Katagaria, Dark-Hunters, demons, humans, and who knew what else. By all rights none of them should get along and yet they were together tonight.

Bound by something other than blood. They were bound together by their hearts.

Colt came up to him. An Arcadian Sentinel, his job was technically to hunt and slay the Katagaria. But years ago the Peltiers had rescued and protected Colt's mother and then raised him after her death. He was as loyal to the bear clan as any of their natural sons.

Smiling, he pulled a pineapple mitt out of his back pocket. "Man, Gallagher, you must really rate. You got one of the good fish. All I got was a lousy pineapple."

"What, does everyone she meet get one?"

"Nope. Only family."

Gallagher looked around at that and saw something he hadn't noticed earlier.

Everyone there had a mitt.

Until Death We Do Part

Prologue

Romania, 1476

He was coming for her. She knew it. Esperetta of the house of Dracul could hear him out in the cold darkness. Unseen. Fearsome. Threatening.

And he was getting closer.

Closer.

So close, she could feel his breath on her skin. See his evil eyes as he relentlessly stalked her through the night while she ran from him, hoping to find some way to escape.

He wanted her dead.

"Esperetta . . ."

There was magic in that deep, sultry voice. It'd always had a way of making her weak. Of lulling her into a stupor. But she couldn't afford that now. Not after she knew him for the monster he really was.

She stumbled through the darkness as the fog seemed to wrap itself around her, slowing her down, pulling her back toward where he waited to devour her. The cry of wolves echoed on the wind that sliced through her dirt-stained gown and cloak as if she were naked in the woods.

Her breathing labored and painful, she tripped and fell against a wall of solid black steel. No, not steel.

It was *him*.

Her hand was splayed over the frightening gold emblem on his armor of a coiled serpent that mocked her with its venom. Terrified, she looked up with a gasp into those deep, dark eyes that seemed to penetrate her. But that wasn't what scared her. It was the fact that she was in her white burial gown. The fact that she'd clawed her way out of her own grave under the weight of the full moon to find herself alone in the church cemetery. She'd stared down at the tombstone that had held her name and death date for almost an hour before she'd found the courage to leave that place.

No longer in Moldavia as she'd been when she went to sleep, she was in a small village outside of Bucharest. In the churchyard by her father's castle, where she'd been born. Needing to understand what had happened to her, she'd made her way toward her father's home, only to find an even worse horror than waking in her own grave.

She'd seen her husband kill her father before her very eyes. Seen him gleefully hand her father's head off to his Turkish enemies. Screaming, she'd run from them, out into the night.

And had run without stopping until now. Now she was in the arms of a man whose black armor was covered in her father's blood. A man she'd sworn to love for all eternity.

But it wasn't this man she'd loved. This was a coldhearted monster. A liar. He might bear the same imposing height. The same long black wavy hair and sharp, aristocratic features, but it wasn't Velkan Danesti who held her now.

It was the devil incarnate.

"Let me go!" she snarled, wrenching herself away from him.

"Esperetta, listen to me!"

"No!" she shouted, moving away as he tried to touch her again. "You killed me. You killed my father!"

He scowled at her and if she hadn't seen his darker side for herself, she might even believe the sincerity he feigned. "It's not what you think."

"I. Saw. You. Kill. Him."

"Because he killed *you.*"

She shook her head. "You lie! You're the one who gave me the poison. You! Not my father. He loved me. He would never have hurt me."

"Your father stabbed you through the heart when he saw you dead to make sure you weren't feigning."

Still, she didn't believe him. He was lying and she knew it. Her father would never have done such a thing. When Velkan had given her the sleeping balm he'd told her that it would make her sleep so soundly that no one would know she was alive. He'd promised that no one would bury her, since that had always been her fear. Side by side, they were supposed to awaken from their sleep so that they would be free to stay together forever.

But she hadn't awakened in her bed. She'd awakened in her grave.

Now, she knew what he'd planned all along. To kill her and her father so that he could avenge his own father and take their lands for his family. Velkan didn't love her. He'd used her and like a fool, she'd played into his hands and cost her father his life.

She ran for the woods again only to have Velkan overtake her.

She tried to pull away, but he held her arm in a fierce grip.

"Listen to me, Esperetta. You and I are *both* dead."

She frowned at him. "Are you insane? I'm not dead. I only slept as you said I would. What madness are you trying to convince me of?"

"No madness," he said, his eyes burning into her. "When we wed, I bound our souls together with my mother's sorcery. I told you that night that I didn't want to exist without you and I meant it. When your father killed you, I swore vengeance against him, and after he killed me, a goddess came and offered me a bargain. I sold my soul to her so that I could avenge you by killing him. *For you.* I didn't understand when I made the bargain with Artemis that it would involve you, too. Because I live, you live. We are joined together. Forever." Then he did the most unbelievable thing of all. He opened his mouth to show her a set of long, sharp fangs.

He was an upyri!

Her heart pounded in terror. It couldn't be! This wasn't her beloved husband, he was an unholy demon. "You're in league with Lucifer. My father was right. All of the Danestis are an evil who must be purged from this earth."

"Not evil, Esperetta. My love for you is pure and good. I swear it."

She curled her lip at him as she pried his grip from her arm. "And my love for you is as dead as my father," she spat before she ran through the fog once more.

Velkan forced himself to stand still and not follow her again. His bride was young and she'd been through a shock tonight.

She would return to him. He was certain of it. In all the violence and horror of his life, she'd been the only thing he'd ever had that was good and gentle. She alone had touched his long dead heart and caused it to live again. Surely, she wouldn't stay angry at him. Not when all he'd done was protect her.

She would see the truth and she would return to him.

"Come back to me soon, my Esperetta." And then he uttered the one word that had never left his lips before. "Please."

1

Chicago, 2006

"Just out of curiosity, can an immortal choke to death on a baby?"

Retta Danesti cut a vicious glare to her best friend as she tried to swallow the bite that was lodged painfully in her throat. As a shape-shifter who'd befriended her over five hundred years ago, Francesca was well aware of the fact that Retta's husband had sold their souls to the goddess Artemis and by default made Retta immortal.

And Francesca's latest news had stunned her so badly, she'd sucked a piece of bagel down her windpipe, where it burned like fire.

Francesca pounded her gently between the shoulder blades. "C'mon, babe, I knew it would piss you off, but I didn't mean for it to kill you."

Retta reached for her bottled water and finally cleared her throat even though her eyes were tearing up unmercifully. "Now what did you just tell me?"

Francesca put her hands in her lap and gave her a level stare. "Your husband is opening the Dracula Theme Park in Transylvania next summer and the key attraction is the mummified remains of Vlad Tepes—Dracula himself. Apparently Velkan's going to release the body to scientists so that they can verify the remains through tests and prove that it really is The Impaler of medieval legend."

Every part of Retta seethed. "That rank bastard!" She cringed as she realized several heads in the deli turned toward her.

Francesca lowered her voice and spoke behind her hand. "He doesn't really have your father's remains, does he?"

Retta recapped her water as she wished a thousand vile things on Velkan's head. Including pestilence and plagues that would cause a certain part of his anatomy to shrivel up and rot off. "It's possible. After all, Velkan killed him and was probably the one who buried him. Although I doubt he has the head since he gave *that* to my father's enemies."

She clenched her bottle even tighter. "Damn him! First he gives Stoker that ridiculous book, then he starts the tours, then the Dracula restaurant and hotel, and now this. I swear, God as my witness, I'm going to get an axe and kill him once and for all."

Francesca's light blue eyes were warm with concern. Even though she was a wolf in animal form, those eyes were very catlike when she was human. The only thing the human Francesca shared with her wolf counterpart was her thick, dark chestnut hair. And speedy reflexes. "Calm down, Retta. You know he's only doing this to get under your skin."

"And it's working."

"C'mon, he wouldn't really do this."

"To get back at me? Yes, he would." She ground her teeth in frustration as she continued to call down the wrath of hell on his head. For centuries, Velkan had done nothing but strike at her and her family. "I hate that man with every fiber of my being."

"Why did you marry him then?"

That was something she didn't want to think about. Even five hundred years later, she could still see the night they'd met clearly in her mind. She'd been on her way home from the convent, for a visit with her father when her party had been attacked by Turks. They'd killed everyone but her and were well on their way to raping her when all of a sudden her assailants had been beheaded.

Too scared to scream, she'd lain on the ground, covered in their blood, waiting for her own death as she looked up at the men in armor who were routing the few attackers who'd managed to run.

Dressed in his dull black armor that held a gold serpent emblem, the knight who'd killed her would-be rapists had quickly wrapped her in his fur-lined cloak and picked her up from the ground. Without a word to her, Velkan had carried her on the back of his destrier to his home, where he'd made sure she was well tended and fed.

She could still remember the sight of his fierceness, the raw power that had bled from every part of him. He'd worn a black basinet helm that'd been fashioned to look like a bird of prey so that it inspired fear in his enemies. And it had definitely scared her to the core of her soul.

She'd had no idea of his features until later that night when he'd come to check on her. But it wasn't his handsomeness or his strength that had captivated her, it'd been his uncertainty around her. The fact that this man who'd been so intrepid and strong before the Turks had actually trembled when he reached out to touch her.

It'd been love at first sight.

Or so she thought.

Her heart aching from the memory, Retta curled her lip as she banished that memory and reminded herself that in the end Velkan had betrayed her and murdered her father. "I was young and stupid, and had no idea what I was letting myself in for. I thought he was a noble prince. I had no idea he was barely one step up from a monkey." She grabbed the printed-out page that Francesca had brought to lunch from Yahoo! News. "I take that back and I deeply apologize to all the primates of the earth for insulting them. He's not worthy of monkeydom. He's a slimy slug trail."

Francesca dipped her french fry into ketchup. "I don't know, I think it's kind of sweet that he keeps doing these stunts to get you to come see him."

Yeah, right. "That's not why he's doing this. He's trying to torture me and get back at my father. This isn't about tender feelings. It's about a man who's ruthless. A man who, even after five hundred years, can't let my family rest in peace. He's an animal." Sighing, Retta tossed the paper back to the table and reached into her purse for her Treo phone.

"What are you doing?"

"I'm booking a flight to Transylvania so that I can kill him in person. Then I'm going to stop these antics once and for all."

Francesca snorted. "No, you're not."

"Yes, I am."

"Then make it two."

Retta would have questioned that, since shape-shifting Were-Hunters could teleport from one location to another, but for some reason Francesca had always liked to travel with her. Of course, if Retta were smart, she'd make Francesca teleport her, too, but she hated to travel that way, even though it was virtually instantaneous. She might be immortal, but Retta liked to pretend she was as normal as possible. Besides, if Were-Hunters didn't know the area and shifted to it, they could hit a tree or manifest right in front of someone. Both experiences had nasty repercussions.

She paused in her dialing to watch Francesca pour more ketchup. "Why are you coming?"

"After all these years of listening to you rant about Prince Dickhead, I want to meet him for myself."

"Fine, but remember to avert your gaze from his. He'll suck the goodness right out of the marrow of your bones and leave you as morally bankrupt as he is."

Francesca let out a low whistle. "Dang, remind me not to make you mad. I mean, really, how bad can he be?"

"Trust me. They don't come any worse than him. And you're about to see just how right I am."

2

Retta had forgotten the beauty of her homeland. But as they made their way up the narrow mountain pass toward the hotel where she and Francesca would stay, old memories slammed into her. Even with her eyes wide open, Retta could still see this land as it had been when there were no power lines or modern buildings to mar it. No roads except for dirt paths worn by horses as they traversed the Wallachian landscape on their way to villages and Bucharest.

God, how she missed the mountains of her childhood. As a young woman, she'd spent countless hours staring out at them from the windows of her convent. No matter the season, they'd always been breathtaking—like a piece of heaven that had fallen to earth. It had never failed to capture her imagination and make her wonder what it would be like to fly over the mountains and explore distant countries.

Of course in her human lifetime that had been an impossible dream. Since her death, she'd traversed the entire globe trying to escape Velkan's cruelty.

As they rode in the taxi, they passed many thatched cottages that seemed lost in time. Some she could have sworn were here five hundred years ago when she'd fled this land to escape her husband.

She'd vowed that night to never return.

Yet here she was. And she was every bit as uncertain now as she'd been then. Her future every bit as unclear. The only thing that had kept her going back then had been Francesca's friendship. Francesca had joined her in Germany as Retta had been making her way from Wallachia to Paris. They'd met in a small inn where Retta had stopped for food.

There had been an awful rainstorm that had come up suddenly while she dined. It was so bad that her driver had refused to go onward until it stopped. Because of that, there weren't any rooms left for rent. Francesca had been kind enough to share her room with Retta.

Since that fateful night, they'd been virtually inseparable. There was nothing she'd treasured more over the centuries than Francesca's loyalty and wit.

"You okay?" Francesca asked.

"Just thinking."

Francesca nodded as she looked out the window. "Is it the way you remembered it?"

She didn't comment as she realized the driver was looking at them in the rearview mirror.

"Goat!" Retta shouted in Romanian as the animal darted into the road in front of them.

The driver slammed on the brakes, causing her and Francesca to tumble forward in their seats. They both let out "umphs" as they hit the back of the front seat and had the breath knocked out of them. Exchanging looks of aggravation, they resettled themselves back into place.

Francesca fastened her seat belt.

The driver smiled at them from the rearview mirror. "You are one of us, eh?" he said in Romanian. "I thought you looked like a natural daughter."

Retta didn't respond. How could she? He'd die to know just how natural a daughter she was. After all, it was her infamous father who had made this little corner of the world such a tourist spot.

That thought made her ache as she remembered the turbulent time of her mortal years. This land had been covered in blood as battle after battle was fought between the Romanian people and the Turks. Between her family and her husband's as they vied for political power. She'd foolishly thought that by marrying Velkan she could ease the war and hostility between their families so that they could focus on the land's invaders.

That mistake and the well-known tragedy of their lives during the fifteenth century was what would lead a man called William Shakespeare to write *Romeo and Juliet* roughly a hundred years later. And just like his couple, their secret marriage had led to both their deaths.

But it'd been her husband's black sorcery that had led to their resurrections and immortality. Damn him! Even after all these centuries she couldn't forgive him. Besides, what few times she'd weakened, he'd always done something to renew her anger.

She pushed that thought aside as they reached the hotel. She got out first while the driver went to pull their suitcases from the trunk. Retta looked up at the quaint hotel with its highly arched roof and stylized black trim. Dusk was upon them as she took her suitcase from the older man and paid him his fee.

"Thank you," he said.

Retta inclined her head as she and Francesca made their way toward the hotel's black wood stairs.

Francesca frowned at a flyer that was on a bulletin board at the base of them. It was identical to several others except for the fact that it was written in English. "Did you see this? Dracula's tour begins in an hour at the old church."

Retta seethed. "A pox on both his testicles."

Francesca laughed at that. "That's harsh."

"Yes, it is. But he deserves a lot worse. Bastard."

"May I help you with your bags?"

Retta jumped at the deep, thickly accented voice that appeared suddenly. Where the hell had he come from? Turning around, she met the gaze of a handsome man in his late twenties who stood just in front of her. A man who looked enough like Francesca to be her brother—right down to the dark chestnut hair and strikingly blue eyes. "Are you with the hotel?"

"Yes, my lady. My name is Andrei and I will be here to serve you in any manner you wish."

Francesca laughed, but Retta had a sneaking suspicion that his double entendre wasn't from trying to speak a different language. He knew what he was offering. "Thank you, Andrei," she said coldly as she handed him her bag. "We just need to check in."

"As you wish . . . madame?"

"She's a madame, I'm a miss," Francesca said, handing him her suitcase as well.

"I knew I should have left you in Chicago," Retta mumbled as Francesca winked at the handsome Romanian. Yet she wasn't flirting with him, which for Francesca was a first.

"I am sure you will both enjoy your stays here at Hotel . . ."—he paused for effect before he rolled the next word with true Romanian flare—"Dracula. We are having a special tonight. Staked steak with a tart raspberry sauce and minced-garlic mashed potatoes for keeping away those evil vampires." There was a devilish gleam in his eyes that Retta didn't find charming or amusing.

Rather, it just pissed her off.

"I imagine the garlic will keep away much more than vampires, eh, Andrei?" she asked sarcastically.

He didn't speak as he led them up the stairs to the hotel's doors.

There was a stereotypical winged vampire head on each door that opened into the blood-red lobby. There were pictures of different Hollywood depictions of Dracula everywhere, along with sketchings and paintings of Retta's father.

And her "favorite" was the golden cup in a case with the plaque that declared it to be the cup her father had set out in the central square of Tîrgovişte. He'd proclaimed his lands so free of crime that he'd put it there to tempt thieves. Terrified of him, none had ever dared to touch it. It'd stayed in the square all throughout his reign.

Right next to that was what appeared to be a stake with dried blood on it and a plaque that said it was the one her father had used to skewer a monk for lying to him. Bile rose in her throat.

"Ever feel like you've walked into a nightmare?" Retta asked Francesca.

"Oh, c'mon. Enjoy it."

Yeah, right. The only thing she would enjoy was kicking Velkan's balls so hard that they came out of his nostrils. Hmmm . . . maybe she was her father's daughter after all. For once she understood her father's deep need to torture his enemies.

Andrei led them across the lobby. "Would you like tickets for tonight's tour?"

Retta spoke without thinking. "Like another hole in my head."

He frowned at her.

"That's American slang for 'no thank you,'" Francesca said quickly.

"Strange. When I was in New York it was slang for 'no fucking way.'"

"You were in New York? When?" Francesca asked in a stunned tone.

"A year ago. It was . . . interesting."

Something strange passed between them.

Retta shook her head. "It must have been quite the culture shock for you."

"It took a little getting used to, but I enjoyed it there."

"What made you come back?" Retta asked.

His gaze bored into hers as if he knew who and what she was. "Once Transylvania is in your blood, it never leaves you."

Retta disregarded that. "Tell me, Andrei. Do you know a Viktor Petcu?"

He arched one handsome brow. "And why would you wish to speak to him?"

"I'm an old friend."

"I somehow doubt that, since I know all of his old friends and I would have remembered a woman so beautiful in his past."

Someone tsked.

Retta turned toward the counter to find a woman moving to stand before the old-fashioned ledger that was there. Appearing around the age of forty, she was dressed in the traditional Romanian peasant blouse and loose skirt. Tall and quite striking, she was someone Retta hadn't seen in over five hundred years.

Surely it couldn't be . . .

"It is not Viktor she wants, Andrei," the woman said, indicating Retta with a tilt of her chin. "She is here for Prince Velkan."

"Raluca?" Retta breathed as she stared in shock at the woman.

She bowed to her. "It is good to have you home again, Princess. Welcome."

Her jaw slack, Retta approached the woman slowly so that she could study her features. She looked only slightly older than she'd been when Retta had last seen her. Only then Raluca had been a servant in Retta's father's castle.

"How is this possible?"

The woman glanced to Andrei before she answered. "I am a Were-Hunter, Princess."

Were-Hunter. They were akin to the vampires or Daimons her husband had been created to kill. The Daimons had once been mortals who'd run afoul of the Greek god Apollo. A group of them had assassinated the god's mistress and child. As a result, Apollo had cursed them all to having to drink blood to live and for all of them to die at the tender age of twenty-seven. The only way for them to live longer was to steal human souls. Dark-Hunters had been created by Apollo's sister Artemis to kill the Daimons and free the human souls before they died.

Several thousand years after that, an ancient king had unknowingly married one of their cursed race. When his wife had decayed on her twenty-seventh birthday, he'd realized that his beloved sons would meet their mother's fate. To save them, he'd magically merged the souls of animals with their race until he'd found a way to save them. Thus, the Were-Hunters had been created. Able to bend the laws of physics and with highly developed psychic sense, the shapeshifters lived for centuries.

But it was rare for a Were-Hunter to be near a Dark-Hunter, never mind serve one. Since Dark-Hunters were created to kill their Daimon cousins, most Were-Hunters avoided them at all costs.

Most.

Retta looked over her shoulder to Francesca, who was now squirming uncomfortably. A bad feeling went through Retta as she realized that Francesca had befriended her just weeks after she'd fled Romania. They'd known each other almost fifteen years before Francesca had confided the truth of her existence to Retta.

Now she had a suspicion that sickened her.

"Lykos?" Retta asked Raluca. That was the Were-Hunter term for their wolf branch.

"Raluca is my mother," Francesca said quietly. "Andrei and Viktor are my brothers—it's why I never used a surname. I didn't want you to realize I was one of the family."

Retta couldn't breathe as she stood there with her emotions in turmoil. Anger, hurt, betrayal. They were all there and they each wanted a turn at Raluca and Francesca, but most of all, they wanted Retta to beat her husband. "I see."

"Please, Princess," Raluca said, her bright blue eyes burning with intensity. "We're only here to help you."

"Then call me another cab and get me back to the airport ASAP."

Francesca shook her head. "We can't do that."

Retta glared at her. "Fine then. I'll do it myself." As she moved toward the phone on the desk, Raluca pulled it away.

Retta saw the sympathy in Raluca's eyes as she cradled the phone to her chest. "I'm truly sorry, but you can't leave here, Princess."

"Oh yes, hell I can and I am." Retta started for the door, only to have Andrei block her path.

"You are in danger, Princess."

She narrowed her eyes on him. "Not me, buddy. But you are if you don't move out of my way."

Francesca took a step toward her. "Listen to him, Retta, please."

She turned on Francesca with a hiss. "Don't you dare start on me. I thought you were my friend."

"I *am* your friend."

"Bullshit! You lied to me. Deceived me. You knew how I felt about Velkan and yet you never once told me that you serve him."

Francesca glared at her. "Yes, Retta. Prince Velkan sent me to watch over you because he was afraid for you to be alone. As you've said repeatedly over the centuries, you were young and naive. You spent the whole of your life behind a convent wall. The last thing he wanted was for you to be hurt again, so I was charged with your care. Is that really a crime after all we've been through together?"

"I didn't need a babysitter. How could you play both sides of the fence when you knew how much I hated him?"

Those blue eyes singed her with sincerity. "I never played you. Okay, so I didn't mention that he'd sent me to stay with you originally. So what? We *are* friends."

"Uh-huh. Friends don't lie to each other."

"What lie?"

"You said you never *met* him."

"She has never met him," Raluca said quietly. "I am the one who sent my daughter after you at the prince's request. She was the one closest to your area when you left here. But Francesca has never met His Highness. Not once."

That made Retta feel better than she wanted to admit, but still it didn't rectify any of this. They'd all deceived her and she was too tired to play this game anymore. "It doesn't matter. I'm going home."

Andrei blocked her way again. "You *are* home, Princess."

"Like hell." She feinted to the right, then rushed left, past him.

He caught her in his arms before she could make it to the door.

"I don't want to hurt you, Andrei, but so help me, I will."

Before he complied, Francesca went to the door and locked it with a key. "You're not leaving."

"Damn you!"

"Look, spew at me all you want, but you need to be aware of why I brought you here."

Retta crossed her arms over her chest. "Let me guess. Velkan wants to see me?"

"No," Raluca said, joining them. "The only thing His Highness would like to see in regards to you, Princess, is your disembowelment."

Now that surprised her. "Since when?"

It was Andrei who answered. "Since about halfway through the sixteenth century when it became obvious that you had no intention of returning. He's been cursing your name ever since. Loudly, too, I might add."

Raluca nodded eagerly.

For some reason Retta didn't want to think about, that actually hurt her feelings. She'd assumed that all of his attempts to besmirch her father's name and reputation had been his way of getting her to contact him. Of course, she'd had no intention of ever doing that since she still wasn't convinced he hadn't intended to kill her the night he'd given her his sleeping potion.

"Then why am I here?"

Andrei took a deep breath before he answered. "Because of Stephen Corwin."

She was baffled by the name. How in the world could *he* fit into this madness? "The investment broker?"

"Among other things," Francesca said. "Remember when I told you I had a weird feeling about him?"

"You have weird feelings all the time. Nine times out of ten, they're attributable to either pizza or spoiled beer."

Francesca gave her an unamused stare. "Yeah, right. Remember when I told you that his scent bothered me? That I couldn't place it? Well, I did some checking and it turns out he's a member of the Order of the Dragon. Sound familiar?"

Retta rolled her eyes. Both her father and grandfather had been members. Their epitaphs of Dracul and Dracula had stemmed from their membership. "That order ceased to exist not long after Velkan killed my father."

Raluca shook her head. "No, Princess, it didn't. They merely went underground and wanted the rest of the world to think that. It was a cousin to Mathhias Corvinus who lost his wife to a Daimon. Horrified by the demon who claimed her life and soul, he reestablished the order to purge the world of the undead. They went on a killing spree of Daimons, and he called for his brethren to help him. But they didn't stop there. They killed our people and countless Dark-Hunters as well. They don't distinguish between us. To them, one preternatural being is the same as the other and all of us should be exterminated. Even now, centuries later, they hunt us without discrimination, brutally slaughtering all they find."

Retta felt terrible about that, but it still didn't explain why they wanted her to stay here. "What has this to do with me?"

Francesca took a deep breath before she answered. "I think Stephen was sent to *kill* you."

Retta scowled at her friend. "Are you insane? There's no way."

"Remember the tattoo on his arm you told me about? The one of a dragon coiled around the cross? It's their emblem. He's one of them, Ret, trust me."

"Trust you? After all these centuries when you were lying to me? Think again. Stephen wouldn't hurt me. He's had ample time to try."

Francesca gave her a deep, meaningful stare. "Are you sure?"

Retta hesitated, then hated herself for it. Stephen had never once given her an indication that he was anything more than an acquaintance who wanted to be more significant in her life. But since she was still technically married and an immortal, she'd kept him at bay. "Of course I'm sure."

"Then why has he been sniffing around you?" Francesca asked coldly.

"Because maybe he likes me?"

"Or he was trying to use you to get to Prince Velkan," Raluca said. "That has been my theory. It is why the prince made sure that all mentions of you and your mother were purged from historical records. He didn't want anyone to learn that Vlad Dracula had a daughter, and most especially he didn't want them to know that you had married him. He knew that The Order would pursue you to the ends of the earth if they ever learned of your existence."

"It makes sense," Andrei added. "The Corvinuses and the Danestis have a long history of bad blood between them."

Still Retta discounted their argument. "This is not the Middle Ages, people. In case you haven't noticed, the wars are over."

"No," Andrei said, glancing past her, toward the door. "I think the war is only beginning."

Frowning at his dire tone, she turned her head to see what had his attention.

Her heart stopped beating as she saw the tall figure dressed in black armor, complete with helm and heraldry.

It was Velkan's.

And he was heading straight for her.

3

Retta couldn't so much as draw a breath as Raluca opened the door and Velkan swaggered in. At six foot four, he'd seemed like a giant to her when she'd been human. And again, she remembered the first time she'd seen him. Blood had coated that black armor. The blood of those out to rape and kill her. She could still recall the sound of steel scraping steel as he moved. The sight of his dexterity even though every inch of his body had been covered by armor.

More than that, she remembered the beauty of his face . . . the tenderness of his callused hands as they caressed her bare skin. The way he'd held her as if she were unspeakably precious, as if he feared she would shatter in his arms and leave him alone again.

Those memories surged and buried all the anger and hatred she'd nursed against him. There for a moment, she wanted to go back to the beginning of their marriage. Back to the days when she had lived and died for this man. When she had trusted him without question.

He had been her entire world.

She'd known this moment would come, and in her mind she'd practiced a thousand things to say to him.

A thousand and then some.

But every one of them fled her memory as he approached her and some foreign part wanted to embrace him after all these centuries. She wanted to rush into his arms and just feel him hold her again.

She'd expected him to curse her or kiss her. To stare at her as if he couldn't believe she was here. To try to strangle her. Something. Anything. But in all her imagined scenarios nothing had come close to what he did next.

He walked right past her as if he didn't know her and seized Francesca in a fierce hug before he danced around the room with her.

Baffled, Retta put her hands on her hips as a wave of rage whipped through her body. How dare he grab another woman and not even acknowledge her! She opened her mouth to speak only to be hushed as the knight started laughing in a tone that was nothing like Velkan's. It was light and almost boyish.

"Oh, my little sister! It's been far too long since I last saw you. How have you been?"

"Viktor," Raluca said with a laugh. "Put Francesca down before you bruise her."

Francesca pulled the bird-shaped helm from his head, exposing his laughing features, as opposed to Velkan's serious countenance. With brown hair and teasing blue eyes, Viktor quickly complied with his mother's orders and set Francesca back on her feet. Laughing, she hugged him close while Retta let out a long breath.

That had been close. Too close in fact and it made her realize that she didn't want to meet Velkan on *his* terms. She needed to make sure that she had control of their first meeting. That her emotions and body didn't betray her again.

"It's so good to see you," Francesca laughed at her brother. "I've missed you so much."

And those words tugged at Retta's heart as she saw the affection her best friend shared with her family. Retta's own brothers had died hundreds of years ago, as had their entire lineage. There was no joyous homecoming for her. No parents.

No husband.

Nothing.

That hurt most of all.

Viktor paused as he realized that they weren't alone. "Princess Esperetta?"

"Yes," Raluca answered for her.

Panic flickered in his blue eyes. "We must get her out of here before the prince sees her."

Finally someone who actually saw reason.

Raluca waved his words away. "He won't come here this early."

Viktor shook his head in denial. "She can stay the night, but come the morrow, she needs to leave before he learns that she is here."

Francesca argued with him, "I brought her here for protection. She must stay."

"No," Retta said, growing tired of the way they spoke about her like she was a lost puppy who was out in the garage. "I came here because Velkan is planning on putting my father's remains on display."

They exchanged a puzzled frown as Francesca turned a bit sheepish.

Absolute rage tore through Retta's entire being. "Don't tell me you lied."

Francesca cringed. "Only a little. I knew if I told you that, that it was the one thing that would get you to leave Chicago."

In all her life, Retta had never been more livid. "Unbelievable! Un-friggin'-believable. How could you do such a thing?"

Francesca was completely unrepentant. "I did it to protect you."

Retta held her hand up as pure disgust filled her. "Thanks, Frankie. It's not like I have a life as well as clients who need me."

"You can't have clients if you're dead. Besides, Trish is handling them. They won't even miss you."

"Save me the bullshit." She looked at Viktor. "Get me a cab and I'm out of here. Right now."

He started for the counter.

"Viktor," Raluca said in a thick, drawn-out accent. "Touch that phone and you will regret it for the rest of your existence."

He arched both brows as he froze in place. "But Mother . . . the prince will—"

"I will deal with the prince. You need to prepare yourself for the tour. Now go."

Retta could tell he wanted to argue but didn't dare. Instead, he cast a sullen look her way before he complied with his mother's orders.

"Where is Velkan?" Retta asked Raluca.

"Not to be flippant, Princess, but he is wherever it is he wishes to be."

"You won't tell me?"

Raluca hesitated before she answered. "I will not allow you to blindside him in his home after all he has suffered for you, Princess. I know of your feelings toward him from my daughter."

"And still you side with him?"

Raluca's gaze went toward the blunted spike tip on the wall. "I will protect His Highness with every breath I hold in my body. But for him, I would have been impaled, too." And with those words spoken, she turned around and left Retta alone with Francesca and Andrei.

Retta gave Andrei an expectant look.

"He will be in the Bloody Dungeon later."

"The what?"

"It's a club," Francesca explained. "One where Daimons tend to pick off tourists who want to meet real vampires."

Well, didn't that make perfect sense? "What time does he go there?"

Andrei shrugged. "Any time between now and dawn."

"You are just so helpful, Andrei."

"I try to be, Princess."

"And you fail with such panache."

He ignored her sarcasm.

Sighing, Retta looked at Francesca. "I don't suppose I could talk you into just poofing me home again, could I?"

"You don't like to teleport. It makes you queasy. Besides, I thought you didn't like me anymore."

"I'm bordering on it. But you are the only family I have. Good or bad, and right now it's definitely bad. Let me go home and I will forgive you."

"I can't do that, Retta. Sorry. But trust me, this is for your own good."

Fine then. Come morning, she'd slip away from them one way or another. She looked back at Andrei. "We are one hundred percent sure Velkan won't come to this hotel, right?"

"Oh, I can absolutely guarantee it. He wants nothing to do with your family. He only ventures here once in a blue moon."

That just made her all warm and toasty inside. "Then why do you run this place?"

He grinned at her. "The money. We make a killing on it."

Great, just great. "Whatever. I'm going to bed now. Give me a key and let me put this whole nightmare behind me."

Francesca frowned. "Aren't you hungry?"

"No. I just need to sleep and forget this whole day has happened."

Andrei went behind the counter to sign her in. "Would you like Dracula's Suite?"

Retta narrowed her eyes at him. "Keep pushing, Andrei, and you and I are going to play a game."

"And what game is that, Princess?"

"Find the Ball in My Hand."

He frowned. "I don't see a ball, Princess."

"Oh, you will, just as soon as I snap it off your body."

He flinched.

Francesca laughed. "She's teasing, Andrei. Her bark is always worse than her bite."

Wishing she'd left her friend at home, Retta took the key card from his hand. "Where's the room?"

"Top floor."

Without a word, Retta grabbed her suitcase and headed for the elevator. She got in and turned around to see Francesca and Andrei teasing each other as the doors closed. Pain sliced her heart. How she wished she could have her family back again. She'd adored her two little brothers. They had been one of the greatest joys of her human life. And a twinge of guilt went through her that she'd deprived Francesca of hers. She hated they'd been apart all these centuries.

But that had been Francesca's decision, not hers.

Sighing, she rode the elevator up to the room, and as soon as she pushed open the door she felt the need to go downstairs and hurt Andrei and Raluca. To say the place was tacky would be an insult to tackiness. The suite was large and airy, with blood-red walls that were decorated with every kind of woodcutting imaginable that depicted impalements.

She rolled her eyes as she headed for the bedroom, then stopped dead in her tracks. Unlike the sitting room, this one was done in black, white, and gray and was identical to the bedroom from Bela Lugosi's *Dracula*, where he'd bitten his fair maiden.

"You people are sick," Retta said, grateful that at least in here there were no reminders of her father.

Setting her suitcase down, she peeled her coat away from her body as she toed off her shoes, then headed for the bed. She'd take a little nap to get the edge off her exhaustion and then she'd see about finding a rental car to get back to the airport. One way or another, she was going to get out of this place and go home.

She pulled the covers back and tucked herself into the large bed that cushioned her like a cloud, and before she knew it, she was sound asleep.

But her sleep was far from peaceful. In her dreams, she could hear her father's voice calling out to her. She could see Velkan delivering the death blow that had ended her father's life as his serpent emblem drifted through her mind, over all the images.

You are the daughter of the dragon. . . . Death to the Danestis.

She came awake with a start. Retta lay silent as she listened to a fierce wind whipping against her windows. But that wasn't what had disturbed her.

She sensed a foreign presence in the room. It was powerful and frightening.

Reacting on pure instinct, she quickly rolled to her feet and struck out at where she sensed the presence. There was nothing there but air.

Now the presence was behind her.

She whirled about to confront the intruder only to find herself face-to-face with the last person she expected.

Velkan.

He stared at her with eyes so black she couldn't even tell where the iris stopped and the pupil began. Dressed in a pair of jeans and a tight black shirt, he wore his long, wavy black hair pulled back into a ponytail. He still had the same sharply chiseled features. The same feral look that announced to the world this was a man who not only could take your life but one who would relish the killing.

God, he was unbelievably sexy. Tall and commanding, he made every part of her warm and breathless. And as she stood toe-to-toe with him, she was tormented by images of being held between those muscular arms while he made love to her. Of being kissed by that perfect mouth. Of fingering the long scar that ran from the outer corner of his left eye to his chin. A scar that in no way detracted from the beauty of that masculine face. If anything it added to it.

She couldn't even think as a wave of pent-up emotions seared her to the spot.

Velkan couldn't breathe as he stared into eyes so blue they reminded him of the summer sky he'd not seen in over five hundred years. The scent of her hung heavy in his nostrils, reminding him of a time when that scent had clung to his body. Her skin was still as pale as a snowy field. Her hair the deep auburn red of a fox.

Not once in all these centuries had he forgotten her beauty. Her scent. The sound of her voice calling out to him.

The sound of her voice cursing him to death.

It was a mistake to be here. He knew it.

Still he was here, staring at a woman he wanted desperately to kiss.

A woman he wanted to kill. He'd given her everything he had and more, and in return she'd spat at him. He hated her for that even as a buried part of him loved her still. He'd lived and died for her. Had died a death no human being should ever have to suffer. And for what? So that she could run from him and deny they'd ever loved each other.

His father had been right. Women were useless outside of the bedroom and only a fool would ever give his heart to one.

"What are you doing in my room?" she breathed, finally breaking the taut silence that was rife with their bitter emotions.

His gut tightened at the sound of her cadent voice that was so similar to what he remembered and at the same time alien. She no longer bore her native accent. Now she sounded like the women in the American TV shows that Viktor watched.

Velkan ached to reach out and touch her, but honestly he didn't trust himself not to choke her if he tried. Anger, lust, and tenderness were at war inside him and he had no idea which of them would ultimately win. But none of it boded well for the woman in front of him.

"I wanted to verify your presence with my own eyes."

She held her arms up in a sarcastic gesture. "Obviously, I'm here."

"Obviously."

She stepped back, her eyes guarded. "Well then, you can leave." She gestured toward the door.

It was hard to stand here when all he wanted to do was pull her into his arms and taste those mocking lips. The air between them was filled with their mutual hatred. Their mutual desire. He still didn't know how it had come to this. How a man could love a woman so desperately and still want to kill her.

It didn't make sense.

A million thoughts clashed inside his head. He wanted to tell her that he'd missed her. He wanted to tell her that he wished she were dead. That he'd never laid eyes on her.

Most of all, he just wanted to stay here and soak in the beauty of her features until he was drunk on them. *You are one sick bastard.* This was a woman who'd abandoned him five hundred years ago.

He might not have much in his life, but he did have his dignity. Be damned again if he'd allow her to take that from him. With a curt nod to her, he stepped back and turned toward the window to leave.

"I want a divorce."

Those words stopped him cold. "What?"

"You heard me. I want a divorce."

He laughed bitterly as he looked at her over his shoulder. "As you wish, Princess. But make certain that you take a camcorder to the courthouse, as I would like to see the look on their faces when you present them with our marriage scroll and they note the date of it."

"That's not what I mean," she said coldly. "I want to be free of you. Forever."

Those words tore through him like a hot lance and did twice the damage. Grinding his teeth, he looked out the window, into the black night that had been his only solace all these centuries past. "Then take your freedom and leave. I never want to see your face again."

Retta didn't know why his words shredded her heart, but they did.

They even succeeded in bringing tears to her eyes as she watched him turn himself into a bat before he flew through her open windows.

In spite of everything, she wanted to call him back, but her pride wouldn't let her. It was best this way. They would both be free now. . . .

Free for what?

She was still immortal. And no matter how much she hated it, she was still in love with her husband. Tears flowed down her cheeks as she realized the truth. She should never have come back here. Never.

But now it was too late. After all this time, she knew the truth. She loved Velkan. Even with all the lies and the betrayal. He still held her heart captive.

How could she be so stupid?

Closing her eyes, she saw him as he'd been on the day they'd married. It'd been a small monastery in the mountains. For the first time since childhood and in order to honor her, Velkan had laid aside his armor and wore a simple doublet of black velvet. Still unrefined even though he was a prince, he'd left his long hair loose to trail over his shoulders. She'd been dressed in a gown of dark green samite and velvet, trimmed in sable that matched her fur mantle.

It'd been the only time she'd seen him clean-shaven. His dark eyes had scorched her as he stared at her and uttered the words that would bind them together before God.

What she hadn't known then was that Velkan's mother had been a sorceress who'd taught her son well. And while he and Retta had taken holy vows, he'd bound her to him with the darkest of arts.

Without telling her.

What he'd done was unforgivable. So why then did a part of her ache to forgive him?

Retta tilted her head as she heard a light scratching at her door.

"Velkan?" she whispered. Her heart leaped at the prospect of it being him again.

Before she could stop herself, she rushed to the door and opened it. Her jaw dropped at the sight of the last person she'd expected to be there.

Tall and blond, he was a far cry from her darkly sinister husband. And for the first time, she realized he was pale in comparison to the man she'd left behind.

"Stephen? What are you doing here?"

His light blue eyes were filled with sympathy. "My name is not Stephen, Retta. It's Stefan."

Before she could ask him what he meant by that, he blew something into her face.

Retta staggered back as her senses dulled. Everything shifted around her. Reacting on instinct, she kicked her foot out, catching him right between the legs. He doubled over immediately. But as she tried to close her door, her sight went black and she fell to the floor.

4

Velkan landed on the balcony of his mansion that overlooked the quiet valley, and shifted back into human form. Five hundred years ago, this place had been accessible by a dirt road that led up the mountainside to his courtyard. It was a road he'd closed and let be overgrown two hundred years ago when he realized how often he watched it, waiting for Esperetta to return.

Now that road was completely covered by brambles and vines as the forest had reclaimed it. The only way to venture here was by flight or teleportation. Two things that helped to keep away anyone who had no business here.

Velkan paused on the carved-stone balcony to look back toward town. He'd already cleared out the Daimons who'd come to town to prey on the tourists and he still had hours before dawn. His house was completely dark and silent in the night. Viktor had chosen to stay at the hotel with his family—no doubt in fear of Velkan's mood.

And the man had every right to be afraid. Velkan didn't like surprises and Esperetta's arrival had definitely qualified as that. The Weres should have told him to expect her. What they'd done was unforgivable to him.

The gilded French doors to his room opened silently at his approach, then slammed shut behind him. Long ago, his wife had been terrified of his supernatural powers. What he had now made a mockery of the ones he'd borne as a mortal man. Back then, he'd been limited to simple premonitions, curses, potions, and spells that had to be worked with blood and ritual.

Now his powers were truly fierce. Telekinesis, shape-shifting, and pyrokinetics. Over the centuries, he'd become the monster Esperetta had feared. He held his hand out and the bottle of bourbon flew to him. Uncorking it, he drank the bourbon straight from the bottle as he walked past a mirror that didn't cast his reflection.

He laughed at that. Until he neared the fireplace where Esperetta's painting hung. The look on her face froze him to the spot. And as always, it took his breath.

He'd commissioned it right before their wedding. He'd hired Gentile Bellini and had practically been forced to abduct the man out of Venice for the work. But Velkan had known that no one other than that artist would have ever been able to capture her youth and innocence.

Bellini hadn't disappointed. If anything, he'd excelled past all of Velkan's expectations.

Esperetta had been so nervous that day. With bright summer flowers in her dark auburn hair and dressed in a light gold gown, she'd been an absolute vision. Bellini had placed her in the garden outside of Velkan's residence—a garden that was now a gnarled, unsightly mess from lack of care. She'd been fidgeting unmercifully until she'd spied Velkan sitting on the wall, watching her.

Their eyes had met and had held, and the shyest, most beautiful smile that ever graced a woman's face had been captured by the artist. It was a look that could still bring Velkan to his knees.

Snarling at the picture, he forced himself to walk onward, away from it. He should have burned it centuries ago. He still wasn't sure why he hadn't.

In fact, he could send a blast to it even now and burst it into flames. . . .

His hand heated up in expectation. But he balled it into a fist as he left his room, then descended the stairs to the first floor, where Bram and Stoker waited for his return. Calling out to his Tibetan Mastiffs, he made his way to his study, where his fire had all but gone out.

He shot a blast of fire into it, making it roar to life. It bathed the room in a dull orange light and caused the shadows to dance eerily along the cold stone walls. He petted his dogs as they welcomed him home with joyful barks and licks. Then they bounded off to retake their seats beside his padded chair. Sighing, Velkan took his seat so that he could stare into the fire that did nothing to warm him. The light was painful for his eyes, but honestly he didn't care.

He glanced over at the dogs on each side of him. "Be glad that you're both neutered. Would that I had been so fortunate." Because right then, his body was hard and aching for the one woman who would never again submit to his touch.

His anger mounting, he took another swig only to curse over the fact that the alcohol couldn't do anything to him. As a Dark-Hunter he could never get drunk. There was no escape from this pain.

Growling, he threw the bottle into the hearth, where it shattered into a thousand pieces. The flames sparked in greedy consumption of the alcohol. The dogs lifted their heads in curiosity while Velkan raked his hand through his hair.

As bad as it had been before, it was so much worse now knowing that she was only a short distance away. Her scent still hung in his nostrils, making him even more feral than he'd been before.

You should go to her and force her to take you back.

That was what the Moldavian warlord Velkan Danesti would have done. He'd have never allowed a slip of a woman to lead him about.

But that man had died the night an innocent young woman had looked up at him with eyes so blue, so trusting, they had instantly stolen his heart. Perhaps this was his punishment for having lived such a brutal human life. To want the one thing he couldn't have. Esperetta's peaceful, soft touch.

Restless with his thoughts, he rose to his feet. Bram rose as well until he realized that Velkan was only going to pace the room. The dog settled back down while Velkan did his best to banish his memories.

But unfortunately, there was no way to cleave his heart from his chest and until he did that he knew he would never escape the prison his wife had condemned him to.

R*etta came awake* to a stinging headache and found herself tied to an iron chair. The room, which was industrial, like an old warehouse or something, was dark and damp, with an awful stench that was similar to that of a pair of old gym socks mixed with the smell of rotten eggs. It was all she could do to breathe past the stench as she tried to wrest her wrists free of the ropes that held her down.

She could hear faint voices from an adjoining room. . . .

She strained to hear them, but all she caught was a faint whisper until a loud roar rang out.

"Death to the Danestis!"

Great chant, especially since she was technically one of them. Granted, she didn't want to claim kinship, but on paper . . .

"She's awake."

Retta turned her head to see a tall, gaunt man in the doorway. Dressed in black slacks and a turtleneck, he reminded her of a slick city drug dealer, complete with a gold-capped tooth. And he eyed her as if she were the lowest life-form on the planet.

"Thank you, George," an older man dressed in black slacks and a blue button-down shirt and sweater said as he moved past him. There was something innately evil about the older man. He was definitely the kind of guy who'd like to pull the wings off butterflies as a kid. Just for fun.

And pulling up the rear was her "good" friend Stephen, tall and blond. She'd originally liked him because he was the complete antithesis of her husband. Whereas Velkan's features were sullen and intense, Stephen's were wholesome and sweet. He'd reminded her of a very young Robert Redford.

If only she'd known that Stephen wasn't the boy next door. At least not unless you happened to live next door to the Munsters.

She glared at him with every ounce of hatred she felt. "Where am I and what am I doing here?"

It was the older man who answered. "You are our hostage and you are in our . . . place."

Gee, he was ever so helpful. "Hostage for what?"

It was Stephen who answered. "To get your husband to come to us."

She burst out laughing at the absurdity of that statement. "Is this a joke?"

"No joke," the older man said. Since she didn't know his name, she dubbed him Slim in her mind. "For centuries my family has been hunting him, trying to kill the unholy, unnatural creature he has become."

"And we've been hunting you," Slim said as he stepped forward from the doorway.

The old man nodded. "But always you and he escaped us."

"Wow, that doesn't say much about your skills, since I didn't even know I was being chased."

He rushed forward as if to strike her, but Stephen caught him. "Don't, Dieter. She's only trying to provoke you."

"She's doing a good job."

Retta cleared her throat to draw their attention back to her. "Just out of curiosity, why have you been hunting me?"

Stephen stepped closer to her and offered her a cocky smile. "Because you are the one thing we know that will draw Velkan out into the open. He's never responded to any lure we've cast at him . . . yet."

"Yeah, well, bad news for you, pal. He won't come for me, either."

Dieter scoffed at her. "Of course he will."

She shook her head. "Hardly. News flash, guys. All of you have committed a felony for no good reason. I saw Hubby earlier tonight and he made it plain that he never wants to see me again."

The men exchanged puzzled stares.

"Is she lying?" the old man asked Stephen in German.

Retta had to force herself not to roll her eyes. Surely they weren't so stupid as to think she couldn't speak German?

"She has to be," Stephen answered abruptly. "Good God, the man was impaled for her. In all the centuries while our kind have watched him, he's never been with another woman or we would have used her to get to him. There's not even a record of a one-night stand, and he keeps tabs on Esperetta constantly. Face it, the werewolves would never have sacrificed a daughter to stay with her if he wasn't absolutely adamant that she be protected. Those aren't the actions of a man who hates her."

Slim concurred. "The werewolf I tortured and killed said that he keeps her room just as she left it five hundred years ago. It even has the gown she wore when they married. There's a painting of her when she was human in his bedroom and photographs that have been sent to him to prove that she lives and is happy. He stares at the photographs every night. There's no chance that he doesn't hold her sacred. If he hated her, he would have destroyed all traces of her centuries ago."

"Likewise," Stephen said with a hint of rancor in his voice, "she lives as a nun. I couldn't even get a kiss from her the whole time I've known her. She's only trying to protect him. I'm sure of it."

Retta couldn't breathe as she heard those words. It was true. She'd never touched another man. Had never even been interested in one. Of course, she'd told herself that once burned, a thousand times shy. And she couldn't very well date, let alone marry, a human man who would begin to wonder why she didn't age. After all, there were only so many ways to lie about plastic surgery before it became obvious she was immortal.

And in all this time, she'd convinced herself that Velkan hadn't been as faithful to her. During their lifetime, no woman would have ever expected fidelity from her husband. It was absurd. Even her father, who was adamant about his Christianity and who demanded absolute faithfulness from his subjects, had been known to have mistresses.

So she'd convinced herself that Velkan had never really missed her. That he'd taken what he wanted and used her to kill her father.

Could it be that Velkan really did love her? That he missed her?

If it were true, then she deserved to die at their hands. Because if it were true, then she'd been punishing a man for centuries for no other crime than loving her.

No one should be hurt because of that.

Surely she hadn't been that stupid. Had she?

I am such a rabid bitch. No wonder Velkan had told her to get lost. She was lucky he hadn't choked her. Clenching her teeth to stanch the pain that ached inside her, she tried her best to remember what he'd said the night she'd left Romania. She could see the moonlight on his face, the blood on his armor.

They'd argued, but now she couldn't remember anything other than her confusion and fear of him. She'd been absolutely convinced that he'd tried to kill her by burying her in the ground. That he'd lied about the tonic he'd given her.

But had he?

Please don't let me be wrong. Please. "He won't come for me," Retta said from between clenched teeth. "I know he won't."

Dieter narrowed those rodent eyes on her. "We shall see. Not that it matters. Either way, we kill *you.*"

I*t was almost* five in the morning when Velkan found himself alone in his bedroom. Then again, he was always alone in his bedroom. God, he was such a fool. Any man worth his salt would just find a willing female and sate the ache in his loins for a woman's body.

But Velkan refused to forsake the oath he'd taken to Esperetta. He'd vowed before his father's God to honor her and to keep himself for her only, and he'd stood by that oath.

Even though he hated himself for it.

There was only one woman who held his attention and it was why he despised her so much. She'd left him with nothing. Not even his manhood.

Damn her.

Suddenly there was a knock on his door. "I told you to leave me alone, Viktor," he snarled, thinking it was his Squire.

"It's not Viktor," Raluca said from the other side of the doorway.

How unlike her to venture here so close to the dawn. Not that the dawn held any sway for her, but normally Velkan would be preparing for bed.

Frowning, he opened the door with his thoughts to find her there, wringing her hands. Her sons and Francesca were behind her and all of them echoed their mother's worry. His stomach shrank. "What has happened?"

Raluca swallowed. "They have taken her."

He knew instantly that Esperetta was the her. "Who has?"

"The Order of the Dragon," Andrei said, his voice tinged by anger. "Once they notified us that they held her, we tried to get her free, but . . ."

"But?" Velkan prompted.

Francesca stepped forward. "They have her tied inside a cage. An electric one. There's no way for us to get to her without it immobilizing us."

Velkan gave them a droll stare. "Fine, let her stew there, thinking about how much she's betrayed me. When the sun sets, I'll go get her."

The Weres exchanged a nervous glance before Raluca spoke. "It's not that simple, my prince. They've put her on a small stool with no rungs. And that stool is on an electrified floor. If she puts her legs down at all or slips from the stool, it'll kill her instantly."

Francesca nodded. "They have enough juice on that floor to light up New York City."

He wanted to tell her that he didn't care, but the fear in his heart told him exactly how much of a lie that was.

But before he could move, Raluca was by his side, with her hand on his arm. "You know you can't go, either."

He narrowed his eyes on her. "I'm not afraid of them."

"It's too close to dawn," Raluca insisted. "You'll end up like Illie if you go. They know our weaknesses."

Velkan took her hand in his and squeezed it gently. Illie had been her mate who'd died at the hands of the Order. Five years ago, he'd been captured when one of their Order had used a Taser on him. The electricity had shot through his cells, turning him from man to wolf and back again. It was one of the few things that could completely incapacitate a Were-Hunter. Enough electricity would ultimately kill them.

And if the Order had Esperetta, then they already knew Velkan's weakness.

"Would you have her die?" he asked Raluca.

He saw the pity in Raluca's face. She'd been Esperetta's nurse before his wife had been oblated to the convent.

"Not by choice. But better her than you."

"Mom!" Francesca snapped. "No offense, but I choose Retta in this. She's an innocent victim."

Her mother turned on her with a snarl. "And the prince has guarded us for centuries. But for him, I would be dead now and so would your brothers."

"We're wasting time," Velkan said, cutting them off. "I need you to take me to her so that I can free her before the sun rises." He saw the reservation in Raluca's eyes. "It's why you came, is it not?"

She shook her head. "I came only because I knew you would be angry if I failed to tell you what had happened."

She was right about that. He would never stand by and see Esperetta harmed—even if he did hate her. "Don't fear. You can teleport me there and I can turn off the electricity, then you can teleport both of us out, long before the sun rises."

Francesca screwed up her face. "It's not that easy. The switch is inside the cage. You'll be electrocuted trying to switch it off."

He sighed at the prospect, but it changed nothing. He just wished he could use his telekinesis on it. But electricity was the one thing he couldn't move with his mind. Its living nature made it highly unpredictable, and he could accidentally hurt or kill someone by trying to manipulate it mentally. He would have to manually shut it off. "Fine. It won't kill me." It would just hurt like hell.

"There's more," Viktor said quietly.

This he couldn't wait to hear. "That is?"

"They have a generator rigged and another switch that is also inside another electric cage. If you turn it off, it won't give us enough time to reach her before they fry us, and unlike you, we're not immune."

Raluca nodded. "And they have her out in a courtyard. The wall of which is surrounded by mirrors to reflect the rising sun directly onto you should you go to her. Their intent is for none of us to survive this."

And they'd done a good job setting this trap.

Velkan let out a tired breath as he considered what was about to happen. But it didn't matter.

"My wife is in danger. Take me to her."

Retta ground her teeth as every muscle in her legs ached from the strain of keeping them off the floor. The effort showed itself in small tears in her eyes. This had to be the most excruciating pain she'd ever experienced. Honestly, she didn't know how much longer she could stand it and not rest her legs.

The dry hum of electricity was a cold reminder of what would happen to her if she didn't keep them lifted. . . .

"You can do it," she whispered.

But what good would it do? They were determined to kill her regardless. Why was she even fighting the inevitable? She should just put her feet down and get it over with. Put herself out of her misery.

Velkan wouldn't come for her. Francesca couldn't. It was over. There was no need to delay the inevitable, and yet Retta couldn't make herself give up. It just wasn't in her.

"What is it about you and this country that you are ever finding yourself in peril whenever you're here?"

She jerked her head up as she heard that deep, resonant voice that went down her spine like a gentle caress. "Velkan?"

He stepped out of the shadows and neared the edge of the electrified floor that separated the two of them. His face was awash with shadows and yet he'd never looked more handsome to her. "Is there anyone else stupid enough to be here?"

She glanced up at the sky that was growing lighter by the second. "You can't stay. You have to go."

He didn't say anything as he turned into a bat and flew toward her. Her heart pounding, she watched as he neared the cage, but the wire was too tight for him to fly into the cage with her.

She could swear she heard him curse before he turned back into a man. And as soon as he did, the force of the electrical current threw him back ten feet, onto the grass. This time there was no mistaking his fierce curse.

"Forget it!" she said, looking up at the sky again. It was too close to dawn. "There's no need in both of us dying."

Shaking his head, he ran at the cage and grabbed the wire. Retta cringed at the sound of his skin frying as he seized it. His entire body shook from the force of the electricity. It had to be unbearable. And still he held on, pulling at the wire until he'd torn through it. Amazed by his strength and courage, she was crying by the time he threw the switch and turned the electricity off.

"There's another—" Before she could say more the electricity returned. She jerked her feet up as a thousand curses came to her mind for the people who'd rigged this damned place.

Velkan grabbed ahold of the cage and snarled an instant before he punched straight through the metal floor. Two seconds later, he pulled a thick wire up from underneath and tore it in half.

The humming ceased as the electricity vanished again.

Too scared to put her faith in that, she waited for it to return. And as each second ticked by while she watched Velkan's frayed appearance, relief coursed through her.

He'd done it. Her tears coursed down her cheeks as gratitude swelled in her heart. In spite of the fact that she wasn't worth it, he'd come for her. And in that moment, she remembered exactly why she loved this man. She remembered all the reasons that she'd wanted to spend her life by his side.

Velkan reached for her.

Until sunlight cut across his body. Hissing, he jerked back, instinctively covering his face. Then he took another step toward her only to have more mirrors turned to him.

Even so, he crawled toward her, while Stephen and the others kept the mirrors on him, so that he could loosen her hands. She quickly freed herself.

Her rage mounting, Retta tried to wrap herself around her husband, but she wasn't large enough to cover him from the deadly rays that made his skin blister and boil. His entire body was smoldering as he tried to make it toward the wall where there were still shadows.

He staggered at the same time Stephen and the others left the house. They were coming to finish Velkan off, but she'd be damned if they'd get to him without fighting her.

Retta stood her ground, ready to battle until she felt someone grab her from behind. She turned to strike but caught herself as she saw a friendly face.

"It's me," Francesca said as she flashed them from the garden.

One second Retta was a hair from death, and in the next she was in a room she hadn't seen in centuries . . .

Velkan's bedroom.

Retta's heart pounded in fear. "We can't leave him."

"We didn't."

She looked around her as Viktor flashed into the room with Velkan in tow before he sank to the floor between Andrei and Viktor. Horror filled her as she stared at what remained of him. He was bloodied and scorched. The scent of burnt hair and flesh invaded her senses, making her queasy.

But she didn't care. Terrified that he was dying, she rushed to Velkan's side and rolled him over. Tears gathered to choke her as she saw the damage done to him. "Velkan?"

He didn't speak. He merely stared at her and blinked.

Pushing her aside, Viktor and Andrei picked Velkan up from the floor and moved him to the bed.

Retta followed, wanting to help.

"You should go," Viktor said coldly as Andrei struggled to peel Velkan's shirt from the flesh that seemed to be melted to it. "You've done enough damage."

"He's my husband."

Viktor narrowed his cold blue eyes at her. "And you walked out on him five hundred years ago. Remember? Do him a favor and let history repeat itself."

"Viktor!" Francesca snarled. "How dare you."

"It's all right," Retta said, calming down her friend. "He's only doing his job."

Then Retta moved to stand beside Viktor. This time when she spoke, she lowered her voice and let her raw emotions show in every syllable. "Get in my way again, boy, and you're going to learn that Velkan isn't the only one in this family who has fangs." That said, she pushed her way past him to reach the bed where Velkan lay.

She wasn't sure if he was still conscious until she paused by his side. Her stomach shrank at the sight of his blistered and charred skin.

But it was the pain in his eyes that took her breath. In spite of the part of her that wanted to run from the horrible sight of him, she reached out and placed her hand to an undamaged part of his cheek.

He closed his eyes as if he savored her touch.

"Thank you, Velkan," she breathed.

He took a breath as if he would respond, but before he could, he passed out on the bed.

Viktor moved to stand next to her. "Are you going to just stare at him or are you going to actually help us tend him?"

She looked to Viktor, whose face bore all the rancor of his voice. "You're such an asshole, Viktor."

He opened his mouth to respond, but Francesca covered his mouth with her hand. "Lay off, little brother. They've both been through a lot today."

Curling his lip, he moved to the other side of the bed, where Andrei was still trying to get the shirt off. Retta helped him undress Velkan, but as she saw a fierce scar in the center of Velkan's chest, just over his heart, she paused. That hadn't been there when he'd been mortal. It literally looked as if someone had staked him through the heart.

"What on earth?" she said, fingering it. It was at least six inches wide and four deep. "How did this happen?"

Viktor gave her a droll stare. "Can't you handle the sight of your father's handiwork?"

She frowned at Viktor. "What are you talking about?"

"The scar," Andrei said quietly. "It's where the lance left his body after your father ordered him impaled."

Retta jerked her hand back, not wanting to believe it. "I don't find your humor funny."

"I'm not joking."

Nausea filled her as she looked back to Velkan's blistered face. Then she looked to Raluca, who nodded grimly.

"I don't understand," Retta whispered.

Raluca's eyes were kind as she explained. "After your father killed you, Princess, he viciously turned on Velkan. He tortured him for weeks until he finally had him impaled in the square at Tîrgovişte. That's how he died and was able to become a Dark-Hunter."

Still, she had a hard time believing it. Her father had loved her so much. Would he really, even in anger, have killed her? He may have hated the world, but to him, his children had always been sacred. "Why didn't Velkan tell me?"

Viktor snorted. "Oh, I don't know. Maybe because you ran from him when he tried and didn't stop running."

"Viktor!" Raluca snapped.

"Everyone stop 'Viktoring' me. I speak the truth that all of you are too scared to say. She ought to understand what he's gone through to keep her safe. What he suffered as a human. For. Her." Viktor turned back toward Retta. "He didn't mind his own death—he'd planned on that. It was yours that destroyed him. He'd surrendered himself to your father, knowing the bastard was going to impale him. He thought that by having you drink the sleeping potion your father would see you dressed for burial and leave you be. His plan was for my mother to take you to Germany, where Francesca was living, and to keep you safe while your father tortured him. He never dreamed your father was going to stab you in the heart while you lay dead."

That hadn't been the plan Velkan had given her. They were to lie side by side as if dead and then awaken once her father was safely gone and convinced of their deaths. Velkan was then supposed to take her to Paris, where they could be together without fear of her father's reprisal against Velkan. Free of the war that was waged between their families.

She looked to Francesca for the truth, but for once her friend was speechless. "Velkan surrendered to my father?"

"What did you think he was going to do?" Viktor asked angrily.

"He told me we would both drink the potion and that my father would see us dead, then leave us in peace."

Viktor nodded. "And you drank it first."

"Of course, and then I saw him drink it right after me."

Viktor shook his head. "He never swallowed it. Once you were unconscious, he spat it out and placed you in state for viewing. He was afraid that if you were both unconscious your father would behead both of you. So he remained conscious and told your father that you'd died of disease. Your father promised him that once he saw you, he would be content to take Velkan and leave. Velkan submitted to him and had to watch him kill you."

And she had run out on him. . . .

Again, her gaze went to Francesca for verification. "Why didn't you tell me?"

Her gaze sad, Francesca sighed. "You didn't want to hear it. If I ever tried to take his side, you yelled at me, so I learned to drop the subject."

It was true and Retta knew it. She had no one to blame but herself.

Retta's heart ached as she thought about how many years . . . no, centuries she'd deprived herself and Velkan of because she'd been stupid and unforgiving. No wonder Viktor hated her. She deserved it.

Clenching her teeth, she looked up at the picture over the fireplace—the one that had been her wedding portrait. Tears gathered in her eyes as she recalled the day it'd been sketched. The sight of Velkan on the wall, watching her with nothing but adoration on his face. He'd looked like a woodland sprite come to life to stand guard over her.

She blinked away her tears before glancing back at the bed where her husband lay. "We have to get him healed."

"Why?" Viktor asked.

"So that I can apologize."

But getting Velkan healed proved to be easier said than done. The sun damage was hard for even an immortal to overcome. Not to mention they still had the threat of The Order out there wanting them dead. At least here in Velkan's home The Order couldn't get to them.

"You should go rest."

Retta looked up at Raluca's voice. The older woman stood in the doorway with a chiding look on her face.

Retta stretched in her chair to ease her sore and cramped muscles. She'd been by Velkan's side for the last four days while he slept. At first his continued sleep had seriously concerned her, but Raluca and Viktor had assured her that it was natural for a Dark-Hunter to sleep like that whenever he was injured. It was what enabled his body to heal.

True to their words, every day Velkan's skin did seem better than the day before. Now he merely looked as if he had a serious sunburn and the bruises were all but gone.

"I don't feel like resting," Retta said quietly.

"You have barely eaten or slept."

"It's not like I can get sick or die."

Raluca tsked at her as she turned around muttering. "Fine. I'll bring your food here, but trust me. If the prince awakens he will be grateful *he* doesn't have a heightened sense of smell."

Highly offended, Retta daintily sniffed at herself to make sure she didn't stink.

"Relax. She was only teasing."

Her heart stopped beating as she heard that deep voice. "Velkan?" She shot from her chair to the bed to see his eyes open.

"I thought you'd be gone by now."

She swallowed against the tight knot in her throat. "Hardly. I have much to do."

"Such as?"

Retta swallowed against the lump in her throat before she answered. "Apologize to you."

"Why would you do that?"

"Because I'm stupid and pigheaded. Judgmental. Unforgiving. Mistrustful—you can stop me at any time, you know?"

One corner of his mouth lifted to taunt her. "Why should I? You're on quite a roll. Besides, you missed the worst flaw."

"And that is?"

"Hotheaded."

"I learned that one from you."

"How so?"

"Remember that time when you threw your boots into the fire because you had trouble getting them off?"

Velkan frowned at her words. "I never did that."

"Yes, you did. You also gave your favorite saddle to the stable master because it scratched your leg as you dismounted and told him he could have it but, personally, you'd burn it, too."

That one he remembered well. He still bore the scar from it. But what surprised him was the fact that she remembered the incidents. "I thought you banished all traces of me from your memory."

She looked away sheepishly. "God knows I tried, but you're a hard man to forget." When she looked back at him, their gazes met and locked. "I've been so stupid, Velkan. I really am sorry."

He lay there completely stunned by the heartfelt emotion in her voice. There had a been a time when he prayed to hear those words from her lips. A time when he'd pictured this moment.

"Can you ever forgive me?" she asked.

"I could forgive you anything, Esperetta, but I could never trust you again."

Retta scowled at his words. "What do you mean?"

"When you left and didn't return, you proved to me that you had no faith in me as a man or a husband. You were so suspicious of me that you honestly thought I could kill you. Obviously, we had a lot of problems in our marriage that I didn't know about."

"That's not true."

"Then why didn't you come home?"

Because she thought he'd kill her. She really had. "I was young. We lived in turbulent times. Our families had spent generations killing each other—"

"And you thought that the only reason I married you was to kill you." He shook his head. "You know as well as I do that I was disowned by my family when they learned we'd wed."

It was true. His family had turned them out. His father had sent an army to seal this house and make sure that Velkan would never enter it again.

But the worst had been his father burning everything that had held Velkan's symbol or name. Even the family crest book that bore the Danesti lineage had been burned and a new one created that left no trace of Velkan's birth.

"I thought that you'd had enough of running from our families. And we both know that had you returned home after killing me and my father, your father would have welcomed you back."

Those black eyes burned her. "I made my decision as to who held my loyalty on the day I bound myself to you, Esperetta. I knew the cost and the pain our union would cause my family and still I thought you were worth it. You spat on me and you spat on the love I wanted to give you."

"I know I hurt you."

"No," he whispered. "You didn't hurt me. You destroyed me."

Tears welled in her eyes. "I'm so sorry."

"'Sorry' doesn't even begin to fix five hundred years."

He was right and she knew it. "Why did you tie our souls together without telling me?"

His eyes burned her with sadness. "I didn't want to live without you . . . in either this life or the next. I had intended to tell you what I'd done, but your father ran us to ground before I had the chance. Little did I know that when I sold my soul to Artemis for vengeance your soul would go with mine."

What he didn't say was that she'd caused him to suffer the very thing he'd wanted most to avoid . . . a lifetime spent without her.

In that moment, she hated herself for what she'd done. And she didn't blame him for not forgiving her.

He'd given her the world and she'd spurned him. Unable to stand the mistake she'd made, she got up. "Are you hungry?"

"Yes."

"I'll get you something to eat. Hang tight." Retta paused at the door to look back to where he lay on the large bed. It was the bed she'd lost her virginity in. She could still see that night so clearly. She'd been terrified and excited. Velkan for all his ruthlessness had left her untouched and in a room down the hallway.

He'd promised to take her the next day to her father's agents and release her. It'd been the last thing she'd wanted. Her father would have sent her back to the convent to live out a life of prayer and hard work—not that anything had been wrong with either of those. But she'd already fallen in love with her dark warlord and she didn't want to go back without a small token.

Her intent had been nothing more than an innocent kiss. But the moment their lips had touched, Velkan had swept her up in his arms and she had submitted to him willingly—even more eager to taste him than he was to have her.

Closing her eyes, she could still remember the feel of him inside her as he clutched her leg to his hip and thrust against her. "I will never let you go, Esperetta," he'd whispered fiercely in her ear.

And then he'd given her a kiss so hot that her lips still tingled from it.

How had she ever turned her back on that? A tear slid down her cheek before she brushed it away and headed downstairs to the kitchen. She scratched Bram on the head as she passed the giant animal that reminded her more of a cow than a dog.

"Good to see you out of that room," Raluca said as she set her tray down that was filled with food.

"I'm only here because Velkan is awake and hungry."

Francesca snorted as she entered the kitchen behind her. "And you're here getting food? What kind of stupid are you? I'd be in bed with him."

"Frankie!" Raluca snapped. "Please. I am your mother."

"Sorry," she said, but her tone was less than apologetic.

Retta sighed as she straightened up the flower in the vase Raluca had put on the tray. "It doesn't matter what I want. I blew it with him a long time ago."

Francesca shook her head. "You can't blow it with someone who loves you that much."

"I daresay you're wrong. I just wish you guys would let me go home."

"The Order would be all over you now that they know for a fact you're real. You can never go home again."

And she couldn't stay here. How perfect was this?

Raluca gave her a sympathetic smile. "He loves you, Princess. He's hurt, but underneath that is the man who went through a fate far worse than death trying to save you. He won't let something as cold as pride keep you from him."

"It's not pride, Raluca. It's broken trust. How do you repair that?"

"That's up to you, Princess. You have to show him that you want to stay with him."

"And how do I do that?"

"You close your office and have Andrei and Viktor bring all of your belongings here."

"What if he won't let me?"

"How can he stop you? You're the Lady Danesti. This home is half yours."

Retta smiled as she considered that. But in order to stay here, she'd have to give up everything.

No, not give up. So she couldn't be a divorce lawyer in Romania. She wouldn't be able to keep up her practice too much longer anyway. Some people were already getting a bit suspicious because she hadn't aged.

She looked around the stone walls that somehow managed to be warm and inviting. *Stay with Velkan . . .*

Somehow that wasn't nearly as frightening as it had been. But in order to stay, she'd have to reclaim the heart her husband had closed to her. *C'mon, Ret, you're made of sterner stuff than this.* And she was, too. She wasn't going to walk out on him again.

But as Raluca said, she'd have to find some way to show her husband just how serious she was.

5

Velkan ached with a pain that was second only to impalement. His Dark-Hunter powers should have healed him by now . . . it told him just how severe his injuries had been that he was still hurting from them.

He turned as he heard the door open.

It was Esperetta, and there for a second he was back five hundred years ago when they'd shared this room together, when she had willingly joined him here every night.

Once he'd reclaimed this house after his death, he'd taken great pains in making her room down the hall look just as it had when she'd lived here. But though her personal items were there, she'd never really used it for anything other than dressing. In contradiction to the customs of their time, she'd shared this room with him for sleeping . . . and for other things the memory of which warmed him completely.

Wincing, he could still imagine the way her scent had clung to his sheets and pillows . . .

The way it had clung to his skin.

Be strong, Velkan. He had to be. The last thing he wanted was to let her hurt him any more than she already had.

She came forward a bit hesitantly before she set the tray down on the table by his bed. Her long hair was pulled back into a ponytail and she looked extremely tired. And yet she managed to be the most beautiful woman he'd ever seen. "Do you still prefer your steak served with onions and stewed apples?"

Her question surprised him. He couldn't believe that she'd remembered that. Nodding, he watched as she pulled the silver top off the platter and then uncovered the onions.

"Are you not eating?" he asked as she handed him the plate.

"I'll just take some of the bread. I'm not really hungry."

He shook his head at her. "Bring the bread plate and split this with me."

"You need it."

"I will live and I can send for more. Now bring me the plate."

She arched a brow at his sharp tone.

"Please," he added, softening his voice.

Retta paused at that. This was a man who was used to issuing commands. To her knowledge, he'd never even uttered "please" before. Her heart softening, she picked up the plate and did as he asked.

"Thank you," she said as he halved his food with her. "By the way, I have a bone to pick with you."

"Only one?"

She smiled in spite of herself. "At the moment."

"Then I can't wait to hear it," he said before tasting his steak.

"'Bram' and 'Stoker'?"

He laughed, a deep, resonant sound. "It was fitting, I thought."

Retta growled at him. But she didn't mention her room, which she'd seen the night of her arrival. It had been an eerie reminder of their past and it had brought home to her just how much Velkan loved her. Even if he denied it, she knew the truth. Everything had been laid out as if he'd expected her to return at any moment.

When she'd seen it, she'd actually sat down on the floor and wept over her own stupidity.

Forcing that thought away, she cleared her throat. "Did you have to give that man that awful book about my father?"

He shrugged those broad shoulders before he wiped his mouth. "I was stationed in London at the time and bored. He'd been working on the book and had been calling the lead character Radu—which, no offense to your uncle, isn't nearly as compelling as Vlad Dracula. Besides, it's not my fault the book took off. It would have been forgotten completely if not for the movie decades later."

She narrowed her eyes on him suspiciously. "I heard you had a hand in that, too."

"That is a rumor of which I'm quite innocent."

"Uh-huh." Even so, she wasn't really angry at him. At least not now. A century ago, she'd wanted to cleave his head from his shoulders, but strangely, now that she was here, she felt an odd kind of peace. It was so bizarre.

He set his plate aside.

"You're not through, are you?"

"I'm not really hungry."

The only problem was that she was starving . . . and it wasn't for food. What she really wanted a taste of was that delectable mouth of his. He was sinful and decadent. He'd always been that way, and it had been so long since she'd last had a kiss.

Velkan could barely focus as his body burned for a taste of his wife. How cruel to be this close to her and to not be allowed to sate the need that burned so furiously inside him.

She finished her food, then moved to retrieve his plate. As she did so, she turned to look at him. It was a mistake.

Unable to stand it, he buried his hand in her soft auburn hair and pulled her closer to him. He expected her to push him away.

She didn't.

Instead, she met his lips with remarkable passion. It was as if she wanted to devour him.

Velkan growled at her enthusiasm. It'd been the last thing he'd expected from her. But God, how good she tasted. It was the most incredible moment of his life and all he could think of was pulling her naked body flush to his.

Retta couldn't get enough of him as she folded herself into his arms. At least not until she eagerly brushed her hands against his ribs and felt him cringe from the pain of his injuries. "I'm sorry," she breathed, pulling back.

But he didn't let her go far. He pulled her back to him and gave her a kiss so sizzling that it melted her completely. With a teasing laugh, she nibbled his lips. "You're still hurt."

"You're worth a little pain," he whispered before he buried his lips against her throat.

Retta groaned as chills spread over her, and her body heated up immediately. It'd been way too long since they'd been together. She'd all but forgotten how good this felt. How good Velkan felt. Leaning back, she pulled him with her until his weight was pressing her into the bed. Still his lips didn't leave her neck as he unbuttoned her shirt. His eyes were dark with hunger as he cupped her breast while his thumb slipped beneath the lace to touch her skin. She shivered at his hot touch as she pulled his shirt from over his head.

His skin was still burnt and angry looking, but even so, she'd never seen anything more exquisite. He was so ripped that she could see the outline of every muscle on his chest. And she remembered the first time she'd seen him naked. He'd been hesitant, afraid of hurting her. And she'd been stunned by the size of him. By the contrast of his masculine body to hers. Where she was soft, he was hard. Where her skin was smooth, his was chafed by battle scars and calluses. And his scent . . .

It was warm and masculine, all-consuming.

Shivering, she reached around and undid her bra, then let it fall to the floor.

Velkan could barely breathe. He still couldn't believe she was allowing him to touch her. Not after all the anger she'd spewed. All the insults that had gotten back to him over the centuries. If he were smart, he'd send her packing. But how could he? No matter the anger, he knew the truth.

He still loved her. He still wanted her.

She was everything to him.

And she might change her mind. . . .

That would be too cruel for words. Cruel even for the daughter of Vlad Tepes.

Her eyes dark with longing and passion, she moved from the bed to divest herself of her pants. Velkan thought he was going to die as she reached for her panties. His breath came in short, sharp bursts as she licked her lips, teasing him, exciting him. The tips of her fingers went beneath the black satin fabric.

"Do you want me to leave?" she asked as she hesitated while he waited for her to lower that damned skimpy piece of fabric.

What, was she insane? Or just plain cold?

"Hell, no," he growled.

Smiling, she slowly pulled the panties down her legs until she could step out of them. In that moment, it was a struggle not to come from the sheer pleasure of seeing her naked alone. Damn, but she had the hottest body the gods had ever gifted to a woman. Granted her breasts weren't very large and her hips were a bit wide, it didn't matter to him. There was no woman more perfect.

Retta loved the power she felt as he watched her with hooded eyes. Even so, she could tell how eager he was. But that was nothing compared to how badly she wanted a taste of him.

She pulled the covers away from Velkan's body, then crawled back onto the bed between his legs while never breaking eye contact with him. Her mouth dry, she finally dropped her gaze down the bulge in his pajama bottoms. She could have sworn she heard him whimper.

But still he didn't move while she moved her hand so that she could cup him through the flannel. He hissed as if it were sheer torture, and yet she knew by the look of relief on his face that he was enjoying it immensely. It still wasn't enough. Her heart hammering as her entire body burned for him, she dipped her hand into the slit of his pants to seek him out. His skin was so hot and smooth as she touched his cock. He was already wet and leaking. She brushed against the tip of him, making him arch his back as if he were being tortured on the rack.

Laughing in delight at his response, she pulled her hand away so that she could taste the salty sweetness of him.

Velkan was absolutely on fire as he watched her lick the tip of her finger. But that was nothing compared to how he felt as she reached for his waistband to pull his pants off. He lifted his hips to accommodate her even though her slowness was starting to piss him off. He wanted to savor this, and at the same time he wanted inside her so badly that he could barely contain himself. It was all he could do not to seize her and whip her under him.

But his patience paid off as she tossed his pants over her shoulder, then dipped her head down to take him into her mouth.

The sight of her hair fanning out over his lap while she tasted him was almost more than he could suffer. She looked up at him and met his eyes with nothing but raw hunger in her gaze. . . . He had to grind his teeth to keep himself from his orgasm. But it was hard and he didn't want this over so quickly.

He had to lean back and stare at the ceiling just to control himself, and even so he still felt the moist heat of her mouth as she tongued him from hilt to tip.

Retta groaned deep in her throat as she saw Velkan clutching the sheet in his fists. He lifted his leg between hers, and when his thigh touched her core she almost came from the sheer pleasure of it.

But that wasn't what she wanted. She wanted to make amends to him for all the centuries she'd allowed her unfounded fears and stupidity to keep them apart. She owed him so much and she wasn't going to leave him until he knew just how sorry she was for what she'd done to both of them.

Her body throbbing, she slowly kissed her way from his cock to his navel. Then she moved to his nipple so that she could lave it while he sank his fingers deep inside her. Closing her eyes, she savored his touch as she moved herself so that she straddled his hips.

He moved his hand and cupped her face before he kissed her, and in that moment every bad thought she'd ever carried for him melted and she couldn't remember what about him had ever made her flee. Closing her eyes, she savored his tongue and mouth. Savored the feeling of his hands on her face before she lowered herself onto him.

Velkan shivered as she took him in all the way to his hilt. He'd dreamed of this moment for the last five hundred years. And all those dreams paled in comparison to this one moment in time. He inhaled the sweet fragrance of her skin as she rode him slow and easy.

This was all he'd ever wanted in his entire life. Esperetta in his bed. His body inside hers. He growled deep in his throat as she continued to ride him, driving both their pleasure onward. She nipped and licked the pad of his finger as he gently traced the curve of her lips.

Needing to touch her, he dropped his hand down so that he could cup her breast in his hand and let her hardened nipple tease his palm. He lifted his hips to drive himself even deeper into her.

Retta smiled and took Velkan's hand into hers while she gave them both what they needed. The look of pleasure on his face only added to her own. It felt so good to be back with him. So natural. For the first time in centuries, she honestly felt like she was home.

And she was never going to leave it again.

That thought swept through her an instant before her body shuddered and spasmed. In a glorious flood of ecstasy, her body splintered. Crying out, she leaned forward over Velkan as he quickened his strokes, heightening her pleasure even more.

And when he came, he whispered her name like a breathless prayer. That gave her more hope than anything else that he'd forgive her.

Her heart pounding, she laid herself on his chest while he held her close in the firelight. There was no sound in the room except their breathing and the sound of his heart thumping under her cheek. Closing her eyes, she inhaled the scent of them and caressed the muscles of his arm.

Velkan lay quietly as he felt every inch of her body pressed against his. He loved the sensation of her flesh on his. Of her hand gliding over his arm. But he knew this couldn't last.

He knew he couldn't trust her.

No matter what he felt right now, the past stood strong in his mind. And it was a past he didn't want to relive. Learning to get through each day while that pathetic part of him had kept watching the road, thinking, no, praying, she would come back to him.

She might be with him now, but she didn't trust him. She never would. And that burned through him like a stringent poison.

"What are you thinking?" she whispered.

"I'm wondering when you'll be on the next flight out of here."

"I'm not leaving, Velkan."

"I don't believe you. You have a business to run. A life to get back to."

Retta grew quiet at that. He was right . . . and he was wrong. "I've had other businesses in the past that I had to walk away from. I can leave this one as well. I belong here, with you."

He didn't say anything, but the doubt in his eyes tore through her.

"Will you at least give me another chance?"

"At what?"

"Being your wife."

"Do you think that could make you happy? I'm stationed here in Romania. In the backwoods of the world that you've embraced. You wouldn't be happy without all the conveniences you're used to. Besides, Dark-Hunters aren't married. They're not supposed to have any kind of emotional ties whatsoever."

"Then we'll get our souls back and be free."

"And if I don't want that?"

She was taken aback by his question. "You'd rather stay in Artemis's service?"

"I'm immortal, and I'm an animal, remember? I live for war."

"You would choose that over me?"

His black eyes burned her. "You chose much less than that over me."

Retta looked away, ashamed. He was absolutely right. Her heart heavy, she slid herself off him. Her gaze fell to the areas of his body where his skin was still blistered from his rescue of her. "Then I guess there's no future for us."

He let out a tired sigh. "We were never meant to be, Esperetta."

She ground her teeth in frustration. "Then do we divorce?"

"Why bother? Death has already separated us."

Not true. Stupidity had separated them, not death.

Retta scooted from the bed and gathered her clothes before she dressed without another word to him. She didn't know what to say. "So that's it then?"

"That's it."

She nodded as she opened the door to the hallway. She hesitated. "I have to say I'm surprised."

"By what?"

"Your cowardice. I always thought you had more guts than this."

He turned in the bed to give her his back. "Then we're even."

"How so?"

"I misjudged you, too. I once thought you were worth dying for."

The door slammed shut in her face.

Retta stood there staring at the wood, her mouth agape, his words ringing in her ears. She glared at the door, half-tempted to kick it in and beat him. But she wouldn't give him the satisfaction of it.

Fine. If he wanted to play it that way, so be it. Far be it from her to argue. As he'd pointed out, she had a life in America. Lifting her chin, she turned and walked toward her room down at the end of the hallway.

And with every step she took, more tears gathered in her eyes as pain filled her. Her heart broken, she opened the door to find Raluca in her room, shaking her head at her.

Retta cleared her throat. "Don't give me that look. You don't understand."

"I do understand." Raluca crossed the small distance between them and held her hand out to her.

Needing to feel comfort, Retta took Raluca's hand and then gasped as a spike of hotness tore through her. It ripped her from this room out into a lightless void that was searing and frightening. She heard winds howling in her ears as something whipped against her body. She held her hand up to protect her eyes as a sudden light pierced the darkness.

No longer in the manor, she found herself in the small cottage where she'd taken refuge with Velkan after their families had learned of their marriage. His family had disowned him and her father had vowed to see Velkan dead. And it'd been her father who'd found them first.

Completely disembodied, she stood in the corner where she could watch Velkan, who was kneeling beside her comatose body. Because they were in hiding, he didn't wear the armor of a warrior. He was dressed in a simple tunic and hose. To her utter shock, there were tears in his eyes as he held her hand in his and kissed her fingertips. She'd never seen him look so vulnerable.

"I won't let anyone hurt you," he whispered, lowering her hand from his face. "Raluca will see you safe for me. Please don't be angry that I'm leaving you. It's the only way I know to free you to live the life you deserve." He rose up so that his lips were only an inch above her own. "I love you, Esperetta. Always." And then he pressed his lips to hers before he tore away with a growl.

Still, she saw the lone tear that slid from the corner of his eye, down his whiskered cheek. He brushed it away before he turned and opened the door to their cottage.

There before him was her father with his army. Dressed in armor, her father wore no helm to cover his stern, chiseled features. His long black hair brushed his shoulders as he narrowed his black eyes on her husband. She winced at the rage that contorted her father's face. Never once had she seen this side of him. To her, her father had only been loving and indulgent. Kind. Velkan drew his sword and stood there as if to take all of them on.

"You're outnumbered, boy," her father snarled. "Is this how you would die?"

"In battle, aye. It's what I prefer." Velkan glanced back over his shoulder. "But you promised me that you'd allow my servants to take Esperetta home for a proper burial. Do you still swear it?"

Her father's lip curled before he nodded.

Velkan planted the blade of his sword into the ground beside his foot. "Then I surrender to your . . ." he paused before he said, "mercy," from between gritted teeth.

Two of her father's men dismounted before they came to take Velkan. As soon as they held him, her father slid from his horse. He came forward with an angry swagger.

"She's dead," Velkan spat, trying to free himself. "Leave her in peace."

Her father scoffed as he entered the cottage and moved to stand beside her. Retta held her breath as she saw the pain that darkened his brow. His lips quivered ever so slightly as he looked down on her body. He lifted his hand to press it against her mouth and nose so that he could hold them closed.

"I told you," Velkan said, his voice rife with anger. "She's dead."

Her father jerked the dagger from his waist as he turned on Velkan with a fierce curse. "She's nothing but a Danesti whore." And then her father plunged the dagger straight into her heart.

Velkan let loose a cry so anguished that it made every hair on her body stand up as he shook off the men who held him and grabbed his sword. Before he could pull it free, two arrows were shot into his back—one striking his shoulder, the other to the left of his spine. Velkan stumbled to the side, and when he failed to go down, another arrow was shot into his leg. He cried out, reaching for the fallen sword. Until another arrow was embedded into his forearm.

"Don't kill him!" her father roared. "Not yet!" He kicked Velkan's sword out of reach before he shoved the arrow at the small of Velkan's back deeper into his body. Velkan growled, trying to move, but there was nothing he could do.

Instead, he looked to where she lay inside. "Esperetta," he breathed in a tone that was filled with tragedy and loss.

Her father seized Velkan by the hair and pulled him back. "She's the least of your concerns, you bastard."

Velkan tried to fight, but he was too wounded to have much effect on the knights who were better armed.

Unable to bear it, Retta turned away. "Take me out of here, Raluca. Now."

She did, but still she didn't take Retta back to the manor. Instead, Raluca took her to where her father was torturing her husband. Retta's breath caught in her throat as she saw him bleeding and bruised as they laid hot pokers over his skin.

"Stop!" she screamed, closing her eyes and covering her ears. "Take me home. Now!"

To her instant relief, Raluca obeyed her.

Retta glared at her in anger. "What was the point of that?"

"Understanding."

"I got it, okay? I was willing to—"

"No, not for you. I know you were ready to start over. But now you know why Prince Velkan isn't. You couldn't even look at what your father did to him and you didn't even see the worst of it." Raluca's eyes blazed in anger as she glared at her. "What do you think he'd have given if he could have simply closed his eyes and told me to take him home?"

Retta swallowed against the knot in her throat. Raluca was right. He'd endured hell for her.

"I can't undo what I did and he won't forgive me. If you have some magic trick in your bag that will give us common ground, then by all means pull it out. But at this point, I'm not the one being stubborn here. And I'm not the one who has to forgive. I've apologized. There's nothing more I can do."

Raluca let go her hand before she gave a curt nod. "You are absolutely correct, Princess. Forgive me."

And before she could even blink, Raluca vanished from the room.

Velkan *tensed as* he felt a presence behind him. He turned quickly in bed to find Raluca staring at him with a gimlet look that was unsettling.

"Is something wrong?"

"Yes." She reached out and touched his arm.

Velkan sucked his breath in sharply between his teeth as his vision dimmed. Suddenly he wasn't in his room. He was in complete darkness with an awful weight pushing down on his chest. It was hot and stifling. Oppressive. Something smelled like rotten earth. Damp and cold. It choked him. He couldn't breathe as a putrid terror coursed through his body. Desperate, he pushed against the darkness.

It wouldn't budge.

More desperate than before, he shoved even harder. Only this time, it caused something to rush in on him. He coughed and choked as his entire face was covered with heavy black dirt. The weight of it was excruciating. The thick, grainy taste filled his mouth and nostrils as he kept pushing and digging, trying to free himself of it.

He'd never felt anything like this. Every movement only made it worse. Every second ticked by with an excruciating slowness as he fought against his prison. Eternity seemed to have passed before he finally broke free of it. Wheezing and vomiting earth, he found himself climbing out of a grave that bore a single name and date.

ESPERETTA D. 1476

Confused, he looked down at his hands, only they weren't his. They were feminine and they were torn and ravaged from the digging. They were Esperetta's.

Still coughing, he tried to move free of the grave, but the weight of his dress pulled him back toward the coffin. Afraid of falling, he kicked his feet, tearing the hem, and used his trembling arms to get his weight out of the grave.

And as he lay on the ground, trying to remove the taste of dirt from his mouth, his thoughts whirled.

What had happened?

We'll be together, Esperetta. Trust me. When you awaken, I'll be there by your side. We shall go to Paris, just the two of us, and start our lives over. No one will ever know who we are.

Only they weren't together. There was no sign of Velkan now. Panic set in as Esperetta looked about the cold, desolate cemetery. Where could he be?

A wave of terror went through her as she feared for him. Surely he wasn't dead. Not her Velkan. He'd always been so strong. So fierce.

"Please," she begged as tears gathered in her eyes. She had to find him. The last thing she wanted was to live without him. He meant everything to her.

Unsure of where to go, she headed through the cold darkness toward the town lights, desperate for him. It wasn't until she'd reached the street that she realized she wasn't far from her father's home.

Why was she here? She'd taken her serum far away from this place.

With Velkan.

With nowhere else to go, she headed for her father's palace. But she never reached the doors. Before she could do more than slip inside the gate, she'd heard the sound of swords clashing.

And then she'd heard her father cry out.

Without a clear thought, she'd run toward the sound only to skid to a stop as she saw her father lying dead at Velkan's feet. Her mouth worked a soundless scream as she watched her husband kick at her father's body and curse him. But that wasn't the worst of it. The worst came from the single sword stroke that separated her father's head from his body.

The cold satisfaction on Velkan's face burned her eyes as he gripped her father's head by the hair and pulled it up from the ground. "Death to the house of Dracul. May you all burn in hell." Those words rang in her head.

Velkan was a monster!

This time her scream came from deep within her soul.

Velkan jerked as that scream resonated through his memory. He tried to free himself of Raluca's tight grip, but she refused to let him go.

"Enough!" he roared. "I don't want to see any more."

She finally released him.

Velkan's breathing was ragged as he stared at the Were-Hunter. "How can you do that?"

She folded her arms over her chest. "My father was a Dream-Hunter. I inherited a few of his abilities, such as manipulating reality so that you could experience that night as Esperetta."

"Why would you do this?"

"Because I lost my mate to the hatred of an Order that should have never existed. There's nothing I can do about that, but you two have lost each other because you're both too prideful and stubborn to admit you're wrong."

"How could I ever tru—"

"Velkan!" Raluca snapped in a tone he'd never heard before as she called him by his name. "You have seen that night through her eyes. It wasn't her fault. You kept the truth of her father from her. You never once let her know as a mortal how demented Vlad was. No one did. To her, he was a decent and caring father. She never saw his brutality. But you . . . you she saw. On the night you met, you beheaded a man on top of her. She was just a young woman who'd been sequestered in a convent. Can you imagine the horror of that?"

He looked away as he remembered just how scared Esperetta had been. Her entire body had quaked in his arms the whole way home and she'd been racked with nightmares for months on end. He'd held her in the darkness and sworn to her that he'd never allow anyone else to ever hurt her again.

Until her father had killed her.

But that changed nothing. Esperetta didn't love him and he would never expose himself to that kind of pain again. "You ask more than I can give."

"Very well, but know this. The princess hasn't left your side since you were brought here. She could have tried to escape us, but she hasn't. She's stood watch over you like a lioness guarding her pride. And for five hundred years I have sacrificed my daughter and her happiness to watch over Esperetta for you. I've had enough of that. If the princess leaves, she leaves alone."

"I forbid it."

"I am your servant, my lord. My daughter isn't. If you want the princess guarded, then I suggest you do it yourself."

Velkan gaped at her words. She'd never spoken to him like this. Never once. "You're not serious."

"Oh, but I am. Francesca isn't getting any younger and I want grandchildren. It's time she was free to find her mate. You threw yours away by choice. Francesca should at least have the chance to be so stupid, no?"

He honestly had no response to that. What could he say? He was a fool. But how could he put aside the centuries?

How could you not?

"You lie there, Prince, in your bed alone. I'm going to book a flight out for the princess. She's a big girl. We'll let her find her own way in the world." And with that Raluca left him alone.

"Good riddance," he said sullenly under his breath, but even as the words left him, he knew better. He couldn't allow Esperetta to leave here. Not while the Order was out there. She wasn't strong enough to protect herself from them.

They were a cunning bunch.

He would simply go to her and . . .

Beg her to stay.

He flinched at the voice in his head. He'd never begged for anything—not even mercy while her father had tortured him. He would order her to stay. And she would . . . laugh in his face most likely.

You'll have to beg.

"Then she can leave." But he knew better than that. In fact, he was already stepping out of his bed. His emotions torn, he quickly dressed in a pair of pants and a loose-fitting button-down shirt.

As he started for the door, it swung open and almost hit him. Aghast, he watched as Andrei and Viktor entered with a large trunk between them. Esperetta followed them into the room.

He was baffled as they placed the trunk at the foot of his bed. "What is this?"

The men didn't answer. In fact, they refused to meet his gaze as they hastened from his room.

"There's another trunk that needs to be moved, too," Esperetta told them.

Viktor cringed as he looked at Velkan, then nodded. "Yes, Princess."

"What trunk?" Velkan asked, stepping closer to his wife.

"My trunk. I'm moving in."

"In where?"

"My room. Here."

Completely stunned and flabbergasted, he opened and closed his mouth, unable to speak.

Esperetta walked over to him and placed her finger on his chin before she closed his mouth. "I know you don't trust me, but tough shit."

He would have gaped again at her profanity had her hand not prevented it.

"This is my home and you're my husband. I made a mistake and for that I'm sorry, but I'm through being an idiot."

He pulled back from her. "Dark-Hunters can't be married."

"Well then, someone should have told Artemis before she made her bargain with you and brought me back to life, huh? You were created as a married Dark-Hunter. I hardly think they can complain now."

She did have a point about that.

"But—"

She ended his words with a kiss.

Velkan growled as she explored every inch of his mouth and buried one hand in his hair. "Esperetta—"

"No," she said, tightening her grip in his hair. "I won't hear any protests from you."

He laughed at that. "I wasn't protesting. I only wanted to say welcome home."

Retta drew her breath in sharply at his words. "Really?"

He nodded, but even so she could tell that he didn't truly believe her. But at least he was allowing her to stay. It was a start, and it was one that gave her hope.

The door opened again as Viktor and Andrei brought in the next trunk. They paused in the doorway.

"Should we come back later?" Andrei asked.

"Yes," Velkan said, his voice thick. "And take your time about it."

The men reversed course.

Retta laughed until Velkan kissed her again. Yeah, this was what she needed, at least until he pulled back and glanced at the trunk. "You didn't arrive here with trunks."

She bit her lip sheepishly. "It's symbolic," she confessed. "They're actually empty." Then she frowned as she realized he was dressed. "Where were you going?"

"No place."

She arched a brow at that as a sneaking suspicion went through her. "No?"

She saw him hesitate before he spoke in a deep, emotionally charged voice. "I was going to find you and ask you to stay."

"Really?"

He nodded. "I don't want you to leave, Esperetta."

"You're willing to trust me then?"

He hedged. "Well . . ."

"Velkan!"

He kissed her lips, melting her anger. "I will trust you, but only if you swear to never leave here again."

She wrapped her arms around his shoulders and met that dark gaze levelly. "I will only leave if you're with me. Promise." Then she rubbed the tip of her nose against his before she met his lips and sealed that promise with a scorching kiss.

Epilogue

In all the centuries, Velkan had never bothered with The Order. He'd left them alone to run amok without his interference. But all that was about to end.

They'd threatened Esperetta and had almost killed her. Now that he had his wife back, he wasn't about to let anyone take her from him again.

Without preamble, he used his powers to open the door to Dieter's home. Velkan strode through the doorway as if he owned it. Dieter and Stephen looked up with a gasp, as did five other men.

And before Velkan could move, an arrow was shot at his chest. He caught it in his fist and tossed it to the floor. "Don't even try that again," he snarled.

"W-what are you doing here?" Dieter said as a fine sheet of sweat appeared on his forehead.

Velkan pinned each member there with a hostile glare that should adequately cow them. "I'm here to bury the proverbial axe. Where exactly I bury it is entirely up to you. Either we can bury it in the ground and let bygones be bygones or I can bury it in the heart and head of every one of you here. Either way, the persecution of my wife and her friend stops now."

Dieter stiffened. "You don't come in here and order us about."

Velkan shot a blast that knocked him off his feet. "Be smart. Take the out I'm offering you. I promised Esperetta that I wouldn't be a barbarian anymore. So I'm trying to be civilized about this and let you live even though the warlord inside me would rather I bathe in all your entrails."

"We are sworn—"

"Save it," Velkan snapped, cutting Dieter off. "I was one of the members of this Order five hundred years ago and I know the oath you've all taken. And I've taken a new one. The next man or beast who threatens my wife or my servants will not live to regret that stupidity. Is that understood?"

He waited until each man had nodded.

Velkan took a deep breath. "Good. Now that we have an accord, I'll leave you in peace."

Turning toward the door, Velkan caught sight of something from the corner of his eye. Before he could react, a single gunshot rang out.

He snapped his head toward a corner of the room where Esperetta stood with Raluca, Francesca, Viktor, and Andrei.

Esperetta was holding the gun in her hands. Her eyes were narrowed on the men in the room. "Anyone else want to try and go for my husband's back?"

Velkan looked to see Dieter lying on the floor with a single gunshot in his chest. Stunned, Velkan met Esperetta's gaze.

She didn't speak as she moved forward to take his hand while the wolves stood their ground. "Gentlemen," she said quietly. "I think most of you have met Illie's family and I believe they'd like a word with you. Alone."

Stephen came to his feet. "Retta . . ."

"Save it, Stephen. You already told me what I needed to know."

Velkan wasn't sure what he should do, but as Esperetta pulled him from the house, he followed. And as soon as the door was closed behind him, he heard the screams of the men.

He stared in stunned awe of his wife. "I thought you wanted them spared."

"I'm not the girl you married, Velkan. I'm a woman who now understands the way the world works. They wouldn't have stopped coming for us. Ever. Frankie and her family owed a blood debt for what the Order did to her father. I say *bon appétit.*" She stepped into his arms and placed a chaste kiss to his cheek. "Thank you."

"For what?"

"For trying to be a gentleman when I know it goes against every part of your nature."

He took the gun from her hand and threw it into the woods before he cupped her face in his hands. "For you, Esperetta, anything."

She gave him a speculative look. "Anything?"

"Yes."

"Then come and get naked with me. Right now."

Velkan laughed before he kissed her lightly on the lips. And for the first time in his life, he gladly submitted to someone else's orders. "As you wish, Princess."

A Hard Day's Night Searcher

1

"Isn't it great?"

Rafael Santiago wasn't a religious man in any sense of the word, but as he read the short story Jeff Brinks had published in the SF magazine in his hands, he felt a deep need to cross himself. . . .

Or at the very least, club the college student over the head until he lost all consciousness.

Keeping his expression carefully blank, Rafael slowly closed the magazine and met his Squire's eager look. At twenty-three, Jeff was tall and lean, with dark brown hair and brown eyes. He'd only been a Squire to Rafael for the last couple of months, since Jeff's father had retired. An eager young man, Jeff had been good enough at remembering to pay bills on time, run Rafael's business, and help to protect his immortal status from the unknowing humans. But the one thing Jeff had wanted more than anything else was to publish one of the stories he was always scribbling on.

Now he had. . . .

Rafael tried to remember a time when he'd had dreams of grandeur, too. A time when he'd been human and had wanted to leave his mark on the world.

And just like him, Jeff's dreams were about to get the boy killed. "Have you shown this to anyone else?"

Damn, but Jeff reminded Rafael of a cocker spaniel puppy wanting someone to pet his head even though he'd just unknowingly pissed all over his owner's best shoes. "Not yet, why?"

"Oh, I don't know," Rafael said, stretching the words out and trying to mitigate some of the sarcasm in his tone. "I'm thinking the Night-Searcher series you're starting might be a really bad idea."

Jeff's face fell instantly. "You didn't like the story?"

"Not a question of liking it really. More a question of getting your ass kicked for spilling our secrets."

Jeff furrowed his brow, and by his baffled look it was obvious the boy had no idea what Rafael was talking about. "How do you mean?"

This time there was no way to keep the venom out of his voice. "I know they say to write what you know, but damn, Jeff . . . Ralph St. James? Night-Searchers? You've written the whole Dark-Hunter/ Apollite vampire legend, and I really resent your making me a Taye Diggs clone. Nothing against the man, but other than the occasional bald head, the color of our skin, and a diamond stud in the left ear, we have nothing in common."

Jeff took the magazine from Raphael's hands, flipped to his story, and skimmed a few lines. "I don't understand what you're talking about, Rafael. This isn't about you or the Dark-Hunters. The only thing they have in common is that the Night-Searchers hunt down cursed vampires like the Dark-Hunters do. That's it."

Uh-huh. Rafael looked back at the story again, and even with the magazine upside down his eyes fell straight to the scene. "What about this, where the Taye Diggs look-alike Dark-Hunter is confronting a Daimon who's just stolen a human soul to elongate his life?"

Jeff made a sound of disgust. "That's a Night-Searcher who found a vampire to kill. It has nothing to do with the Dark-Hunters."

Yeah, right. "A vampire who just happens to steal human souls to elongate his life as opposed to the normal Hollywood variety where they live forever on blood?"

"Well, that's just cliché. It's so much better to have vampires who have really short lives and are then compelled, against their wills, and by a hatred fired by envy, to lash out at the human race. Makes it so much more interesting, don't you think?"

Not really. Especially since he was one of the people caught up in that battle. "That is also the reality we live in, Jeff. What you just described is a Daimon, not a vampire."

"Well maybe I borrowed from the Daimons a little, but the rest is all mine."

Rafael flipped to the next page. "Let's see. What about the cursed Tyber race that pissed off the Norse god Odin and is now damned to live only twenty-seven years unless they turn vampire and steal human souls. Substitute 'Apollite' for 'Tyber' and 'Apollo' for 'Odin' and again you have the story of the Apollite race who turn Daimon."

Sighing, Jeff crossed his arms over his chest. He shook his head in denial.

"And what about this part here where the Night-Searchers sell their souls to the Norse goddess Freya, who is a vibrant redheaded femme fatale dressed all in white, to get revenge on whoever caused them to die?"

"No one is going to figure out that Artemis is Freya."

Rafael growled at him. "For the record, unlike Artemis, Freya happens to be a strawberry blonde. But you were right about one thing. She is gorgeous and highly seductive. Definitely hard to say no to her."

"Oh." Deepening his scowl, Jeff looked up. "How do you know all that?"

Rafael grew quiet as he remembered the night he'd met the Norse goddess and she had tempted him well. That had definitely been one hell of a day. . . . "Freya's the goddess who hand selects warriors for Valhalla. Or in the case of myself, she wanted to take me off with her to her own hall and add me to her harem."

Jeff gaped. "And you chose to fight for Artemis instead, what kind of stupid are you?"

There were times when the kid could be eerily astute. "Yeah, well, in retrospect it was a bad bargain on my part. But at the time, Artemis was offering me vengeance on my enemies it seemed so much more appealing than being Freya's love slave . . . which gets back to Freya being Artemis in your story."

"But you just said she's not Artemis and she comes after warriors, too. So it could happen. She could make a bargain like the one I wrote about in my story."

And icicles could grow on the sun. Freya collected warriors, she didn't send them back to the mortal plane to fight Daimons/vampires. Artemis did that. But not willing to argue the point anymore when it was obvious Jeff didn't see it, Rafael moved on to the next similarity. "And what about this? Ralph—Jesus, boy, couldn't you come up with something better than a bodily function to name me—was a Caribbean pirate, son of an Ethiopian slave and Brazilian merchant. . . ." He glanced down to read the description. "At six six, Ralph was one to intimidate anyone who saw him. With his shaved head that was tattooed with African tribal symbols given to him by a shaman he'd met in his travels, he walked the earth as if he owned it. But more than that, the black tattoos blended at times with his dark brown flesh, making the two of them seem indistinguishable from each other as if he bore some kind of alien skin."

Unable to read another word of the description that was so eerily close to himself that it made him want to choke his Squire, Rafael let out a disgusted breath. "While I'm both flattered and highly offended, I can assure you, this won't win you a Hugo or Nebula nomination."

Jeff pulled the magazine out of his hands again in a high-handed manner. "I resent that. It's a great story. And you don't exactly have those tattoos, either, now do you?"

Rafael's right eye started twitching from the aggravation. "I have intricate scroll work tattooed up my neck to the base of my skull and like *Ralph*"—he growled the word—"I have them on both arms. They're close enough to what you describe. No matter how you disguise this trite bullshit, it's my life, Jeff. Penned in an awkward manner. It's things I didn't want to see in black-and-white print. You're lucky after three hundred years that I've mellowed. In my human days, I'd have slit your throat, pulled your tongue through the opening, and left you tied to a tree for the wolves to eat."

"Ew!"

"Yes," he said, taking a step toward the overgrown adolescent, "and effective. Trust me, no one betrayed me twice."

"What about the guy who killed you?"

Rafael's eyes flared as he fought his urge to kill the boy. It was a damn good thing that he liked Jeff's father and the man had served him well for over twenty years. Otherwise Jeff would be meeting with an "accident" right about . . . oh, now.

Taking a deep breath, Rafael asked in a tone that belied his anger, "I only have one more question. What's the circulation on this rag?"

Jeff shrugged. "I don't know. About one hundred and fifty thousand worldwide, I think."

"You are so dead."

"Oh, come on," Jeff said, dismissing the very real danger he was facing. "You're overreacting. No one is going to care." The best place to hide is out in the open. Haven't you ever heard that? Step out of the Dark Ages, Rafe. Everywhere you look there are vampires and a whole counterculture dedicated to them. Open your mouth to a woman, show her your fangs, and she'll beg you to bite her. Trust me. I have a fake set I wear to parties and use frequently. Nowadays being undead doesn't get you killed. It just makes it easier to get laid."

Rafael shook his head. "Your argument has reached a whole new level of lame."

"Please, spare me that, old wise one. There's a whole new school of thought going around about how best to protect and hide you guys. If we start telling people about the Dark-Hunters, but make them think it's a book series or some urban fantasy thing, when they actually meet one of you, they'll just think you're either actors or roleplayers. Or at the very worst, they'll think you're insane, but never will they believe you're real."

He was seriously considering getting Jeff a CAT scan to make sure the kid still had a brain. "What Einstein came up with this?"

"Well . . . originally it was Nick Gautier."

"And the poor man is now dead. Shouldn't you guys be following someone else's ideas?"

"No. It makes perfect sense. Get out of the basement, Rafe, and hang with the new generation. We know the 911."

Rafael snorted. "It's 411, Jeff, and you don't know shit. But you are going to need 911 once the Council learns about this."

"I'll be fine, trust me. Nick and I aren't the only ones who think like this these days."

Those words had no sooner left his mouth than Rafael's cell phone started ringing. He checked the ID to see "Ephani." An ancient Amazon who'd crossed over almost three thousand years ago, she was definitely an acquired taste. But even so, he liked her a great deal. Pulling the phone off his belt, he answered it.

"What's up, Amazon?" he asked, stepping away from Jeff while his Squire continued to admire his story in the magazine.

The kid had no sense of self-preservation.

"Hey, Rafe. I . . . um . . . I'm not sure how to break this to you, but do you know what your Squire's been up to lately?"

Deciding to play it cool, Rafael cut a glare at Jeff. "Writing the great American novel, what else?"

"Uh-huh. Have you ever read one of those novels he's been working on?"

"Not until today. Why?"

She let out a long sigh. "I'm assuming you have a copy of the *Escape Velocity* magazine with his story in it, right?"

"I do."

"Good, then it won't come as a shock to you to know that my Squire just left and she's heading over to your house to have a *talk* with Jeff. If I were you—"

"Say no more. He's leaving the country even as we speak. Thanks for the call, Eph."

"No problem, *amigo*."

Hanging up the phone, he narrowed his eyes on Jeff. "That was Ephani warning me that you're about twenty minutes from dying."

Jeff's face turned stone white. "What?"

He nodded. "Her Squire, Celena, Ms. Blood Rite, I-kill-anything-that-breaks-formation, is on her way over here to have a word with you. Since Celena isn't real big on conversation, I'm taking that as a euphemism for 'kick your ass.'"

Rafael paused as those words conjured one hell of an image in his mind—Celena kicking *his* ass in that pair of stiletto corset boots she often wore. And in his mind she was wearing nothing but a thong. . . . Yeah . . . that was something he definitely wouldn't mind.

A native of Trinidad, Celena had the most perfect mocha complexion he'd ever seen. It was so smooth and inviting that it begged a man to taste it.

And her lips . . .

Angelina Jolie had nothing on her. She moved slow and seductive like a cat and he'd spent more than his fair share of time wanting her to rub that lean, curvy body of hers up against his.

But unfortunately, she was a Squire and he was a Dark-Hunter. By the rules of their world, she was off limits to him, and though Rafael didn't give two shits about most rules, Celena lived for them.

It was a crime against nature in his opinion that a woman that fine couldn't be corrupted.

"What do I do?" Jeff asked.

"Well, not to insult a man who looks like a rocket scientist in comparison to you, but . . . *run, Forrest, run.*"

"But I didn't do anything wrong. It's a new era where—"

"Do you really want to argue that point while someone, who is only a few minutes away, is speeding over here to most likely kill you?"

Jeff paused for a single heartbeat before common sense finally seized him. "Where should I hide?"

If it wasn't for the fact that as a Dark-Hunter Rafael was impervious to illness, he'd swear a migraine was starting right behind his left eye. "Get to the basement and hide there. Don't make a peep and don't leave until I tell you it's safe."

Jeff nodded before he ran for the door. Two seconds later he was back. Rafael watched him with a frown as he searched around the room until he located the baseball bat he'd used yesterday at the batting cages. He picked it up and cradled it to his chest before he headed back toward the basement.

"What are you doing?" Rafael asked.

"Protection."

Yeah, right. Celena was highly trained and deadly. A whack with the bat would only piss her off an instant before she jerked it out of Jeff's hands and beat him with it, but far be it from him to tell Gomer that.

"Hide well," Rafael said, exaggerating his voice.

Jeff nodded again before he dashed down to where Rafael's bedroom and living area were.

Pressing the heel of his hand against his brow where the imagined pain seemed to be located, Rafael glanced around the parlor of his Victorian house to make sure that Jeff hadn't left anything like his underwear lying about. The boy was a good Squire in that he kept up the appearance that someone lived in the house who actually aged but seriously sucked when it came to general housekeeping.

At least for once the place was decent. Except for the Xbox that Jeff had left stretched from the plasma TV to the leather sofa. Rafael had just turned the game off and put it away when he heard a fierce knock on his front door.

Rafael straightened his shirt before he sauntered over to answer it. He could already see Celena's curvy outline though the frosting on the glass. The porch light highlighted her medium brown hair that she wore pulled back from her face to trail in a ponytail of small braids from the crown of her head.

Her lips were perfect and outlined in dark red glossy lipstick. She had catlike almond-shaped eyes and an attractive mole right above the left arch of those lips.

Damn, she was the finest-looking woman he'd ever seen. Opening the door, he gave her the sexiest smile he could. "Hi, Celena."

But she was all business. Her dark brown eyes didn't even glance his way. They went straight past him, into the house.

"Where's Jeff?"

"Don't know."

That finally succeeded in getting her to look at him, but then she quickly glanced away and continued to search the house with her gaze. "What do you mean, you don't know? After dark, a Dark-Hunter is always supposed to know the whereabouts of his or her Squire."

"Ah, c'mon," he teased. "You don't really tell Ephani every place you go after dark, do you?"

"Of course I do."

She tried to step past him, but he quickly blocked her way and kept her outside on the porch.

"So what do you want with Jeff?" he asked in a nonchalant tone.

"That's Squires' business."

"Really? I thought anything that concerned a Hunter's Squire also concerned the Hunter, since he's my partner, in a purely platonic sense."

The edges of her lips twitched as if she found something funny about his words.

He couldn't explain it, but he really wanted to see a full-blown smile from this woman. "What?"

One corner of her mouth lifted into an attractive grin, but it still wasn't the smile he wanted to see from her. The kind that would light up her eyes and make her laugh. "I was just thinking about Rum, Sodomy, and the Lash—the pirate's credo."

He laughed at that even though he should have been offended. "Jeff is too hairy for my tastes. I much prefer a woman's smooth skin . . . the softness of a female body. I never was one to cuddle a porcupine."

Celena swallowed at the seductive tone in Rafael's deep voice. The sound of it had always reminded her of James Earl Jones, except Rafael's was marked by a heavy Brazilian accent. One that sent a chill down her spine.

She knew she had no business even looking at him with anything remotely similar to lust, and yet the man set her hormones on fire. Especially that wicked scent of masculine power tinged with Brut aftershave. It was a deadly combination.

Not to mention the fact that he was wearing a tight black V-neck sweater that only emphasized how perfectly formed he was. It clung to every dip and bulge of the muscles on his body. How was a woman supposed to keep her mind straight when a man like this was in front of her?

Clearing her throat, she forced her thoughts back to business. "Where is he?"

A devilish glint taunted her from the midnight depths of his eyes. "Tell me what you want with him and I might tell you where he is."

Narrowing her gaze, she found it difficult to maintain her outraged anger while he looked at her with that playful air. And that seriously annoyed her. "I'm here to take him into custody and deliver him to the Council."

"Well, that sucks." Even though his tone was sincere, she could tell he was mocking the Council and their orders. "Bank robbery, handing out the passwords for the Dark-Hunter Web site, carjacking, mugging, cats mixing with dogs, and now this . . . writing a short story. High crimes all. You get the rope and we'll hang him for it. God forbid the whole twelve subscribers of that magazine should actually read a fictional story and think it real."

She glared at him. How dare he make light of this. "It has a *substantial* readership."

"And Jeff used a pseudonym for not only us but himself as well. As the kid says, what better place to hide than under people's noses?" Even as he said that, he couldn't believe he was backing Jeff's story. But then that was what friends should do for each other. "It's nothing to worry over."

"Nothing?" Celena was aghast at his light tone. How could he write this off as if it were nothing more than a simple hangnail that bothered them? "He's exposed us."

"No, Talon getting filmed in the middle of a hissy fit in New Orleans exposed us. Zarek getting caught on tape exposed us. This is minor. I mean, damn, Acheron was able to cover up all the others with little incidence. This, too, shall pass."

Not bloody likely. "This is entirely different."

"I agree. Jeff is mortal and only has a handful of years left to him, whereas Talon and Zarek have an eternity to continue being stupid. Let's not shorten the kid's life any more than we have to, shall we?"

He did have a point, but she hated to admit that. Besides, that didn't matter. She was here to do her job. Rafael didn't control her. She was a representative of the Council. "What happens to him isn't my decision. It's the Council's. I'm merely here to collect him."

"He's just a kid."

"He's only two years younger than I am and he's certainly old enough to know to keep his mouth shut."

"Haven't you ever done something you knew you shouldn't and then regretted it?"

She didn't hesitate with her answer. "No."

"No?" he asked incredulously. "You've never once broken a rule, lied, or got away with anything?"

"Only once in junior high when my sister came home late, because I didn't want to get her into trouble. Then one week later, she did it again and was injured in a car wreck, trying to get home before dawn, which taught me the value of lying to help someone. Since then I've never told another one and I don't intend to start now. I have integrity."

"Wow. You have one boring life."

"I resent that."

Those dark eyes teased and tormented her with a mixture of

amusement and pity. "Resent all you want, but it's true. How have you managed to live such a perfect life?"

And that she resented even more. "It's not perfect. It has moments of . . ." She paused as she realized what she'd almost let slip. There were times when she really hated how uptight she was. But every time she'd ever tried to do something that was even remotely fun or even the least bit dishonest, she'd paid for it in the worst sort of way.

Like the time in high school when her sister had talked her into skipping school. They'd no more than driven down the street when her sister had plowed into the side of a Mercedes. Or the one time Celena had cut a man off in traffic only to get a flat tire immediately.

She had bad karma, which kept her perpetually toeing the line. If she'd been Jeff, the moment they published that story she'd have probably died of ink poisoning or something equally as bizarre.

But this wasn't about her. It was about a man who'd broken his Squire's oath, and he needed to be reprimanded.

Rafael tilted his head as he waited for her to finish her sentence. She was thinking of something, and from the darkness of her eyes and the furrow of her brow he could tell it was painful for her. "Of?"

Her expression turned blank. "Nothing."

Rafael gave her his best smile as he considered a way to save Jeff and to get him the one thing he wanted most . . . more time with a woman who tempted him.

"C'mon, Celena. Learn to live a little."

"I have rules to follow and a job to do. Surely even you can appreciate that."

"But don't you want to break free and have some fun just once in your life?"

She didn't answer, but by the look on her face he could tell that he was getting to her.

"Look," he said, trying to weaken her even more, "let's make a deal. Give me a week and if I can't get you to break one single Squire's rule, I'll hand Jeff over and let you hang him. . . . Hell, I'll even buy the rope. But if I do get you to break a rule . . . one teensy little rule, you'll let him go."

She shook her head. "It'll never work. The Council won't wait a week."

"Sure they will. Tell them you can't find him and that you're looking for him."

Her face hardened. "I can't do that. It's a lie."

She was a tough one. He'd never met anyone with so much resolve to do the right thing before. But then again, he'd been a pirate in his mortal life and high moral fiber wasn't exactly something they had a plethora of. In fact, those possessed of that madness usually found themselves killed off fairly quickly.

It was part of what he found so fascinating about her. How could someone live her life as she did? He didn't understand it, and a strange part of himself wanted to.

It was the same part of himself that wanted to know more about this woman other than the fact that she looked edible in those black jeans and crop top.

"You know," he said playfully, "it's not a lie. You really don't know where he is, and I can make sure that he runs from you for eternity."

She let out a tired breath as if she were suddenly tired of fighting him. "Why are you doing this?"

For once, Rafael was honest. "Because as stupid as he is, Jeff is a friend of mine, and I'm not going to hang him out to dry."

Celena had to admire that. Many Dark-Hunters could care less what happened to their Squires. To them a Squire was a servant, plain and simple.

"C'mon, Celena." He gave her a wink. "It's the only shot you have at getting him."

"And if I don't break a rule in a week's time?"

"I'll hand him over."

She cocked her head as she considered that. Rafael wasn't exactly known for keeping his word. "You swear?"

"Every day."

She hissed at him. "That's not what I mean and you know it."

For the first time, his handsome face turned completely serious. "On my word as a pirate who died defending his crew, absolutely."

He said it with such conviction that she found herself actually believing it. Besides, he was right. If he wanted to hide Jeff, there wasn't much they could do to reclaim him. And knowing the two of them, Jeff and Rafael would probably rub all their noses in it, too.

"Okay. I'm going to trust you. In seven days, I'll be back to collect him. Have him here and waiting."

She turned to leave only to find Rafael's hand on her arm, pulling her to a stop.

"Whoa, wait a sec, love. You don't think it's that easy, do you?"

"How do you mean?"

That devilish gleam returned to his midnight eyes. "There can be no faith without doubt. No strength without temptation. In order for this bargain to stand, you have to be *here* so that I can oversee your behavior myself."

She stiffened at his implication. "My word is gold."

"And usually mine is pyrite. At the moment, though, to see this through, I want you here to serve me. It's only fair anyway, since you're the reason I'm being deprived of Jeff's service, such as it is."

"Who will look after Ephani?"

"Call in a substitute. That's what you would've had to do to find him anyway, right?"

Celena was beginning to hate this man. "You can't be serious."

"Quite. Now is it a deal, or not? Think quickly before I change the terms again."

And he probably would, too, just to annoy her. "Fine, it's a deal." And yet even as she said those words, she had the sneaking suspicion that she'd just signed her soul away to the devil.

2

As soon as Rafael had Celena out of his house, he rushed to the basement only to find Jeff lying back on his black leather sofa, feet up on the coffee table, playing his PSP as if he didn't have a care in the world. It was so unbelievable that Rafael stood in the doorway for a full minute, staring with a slackened jaw.

Jeff was the kind of man that as pirates they'd have buried alive in the sand and left to rot. Why? Because people like him really were too stupid to live. It was a public service to speed them to their graves.

Honestly, the temptation to kill him was there and it was strong. Damn strong.

Yet again, Jeff was lucky Rafael had mellowed tremendously over the centuries. Not to mention the small fact that Rafael wanted an opportunity to break at least one more major rule before one of them died.

Jeff had no idea that he owed his life right now to the fact that Celena had the most tempting lips this side of paradise and if Rafael wanted a taste of them, he had to get Jeff out of here before she returned.

Rafael grabbed the tiny remote from the table to his left and turned the PSP off.

"Hey!" Jeff snapped, looking up. "I was on level four and I didn't save it."

"Screw level four. I need you to get out of here, pronto."

"And go where?"

"My boat in the marina."

Jeff curled his lip in distaste. "And do what?"

"Live through the night, which is more than you're going to get to do if you don't stop lipping off. Now get up and get started. I've bought you some time, kid, but it's finite. You have to go lie low for a week."

While Jeff made juvenile noises of discontent, Rafael's attention fell to his laptop, which was on the table at Jeff's feet—that should do to keep him occupied and out of trouble.

At least until the poor bastard published something again.

Picking the laptop up, Rafael handed it off to Jeff. "Go write your great American novel, but for God's sake, do what everyone else does and make the whole story up."

Jeff grimaced at him. "You know I get seasick."

"You'll survive seasickness. Lead poisoning's another matter. There's enough staples and such on board that you should be fine. Keep your ass below deck and if you so much as look at the helm, I'll cut your head off myself. You're not to go joyriding or anything else on my boat—it really is worth more to me than your life. Do not leave the lower deck under any circumstances barring fire, and whatever you do, keep a bucket nearby and don't puke on anything."

Jeff screwed his face up as if that were the most sickening thought he'd ever had. "But I want to stay here."

"And people in hell want ice water and if you don't go to the boat, you'll probably be able to take it to them in person in about twenty minutes. Get out, Jeff. Now."

Jeff started to grumble as he got up, then caught himself. "Can I take the PSP?"

"If it will speed you on your way."

"You got any more games for it?"

Raphael growled low in his throat as he picked the small black game case off the coffee table and chucked it at him. "Anything else?"

"A hooker would be nice."

"Jeff . . ."

"I'm going. I'm going."

The pain in Rafael's skull returned as Jeff made his way back upstairs at a pace that would make a slug proud. Oh yeah, they'd have sacrificed him on the main deck ten seconds after boarding.

"Could you pick up the pace, Jeff? We only have another eight or nine hours until daybreak."

He cast a grimace at Rafaél over his shoulder. "You're such a bossy asshole."

"Comes with being a pirate captain . . . which my father was, too, by the way. He wasn't a merchant like you have in your story. He ate those for breakfast."

Jeff actually stopped on the stairs. "Really?"

"Jeff!" he snapped. "Up. The. Stairs."

Mocking his words, Jeff finally managed to make it up to the door. It took about fifteen minutes to get him packed and out of the house, along with more warnings about what Rafael would do if Jeff so much as scuffed a board on his boat.

Jeff had only been gone at most five minutes before Celena returned. Rafael had to force himself not to glance down the street after Jeff, since it was obvious the two of them must have passed each other on the road. But unlike Jeff, Celena was quick on the uptake and would realize why Rafael was looking north.

No doubt she'd catch the snail and salt him well.

"Welcome back, my lady," Rafael said as Celena adjusted the black backpack on her shoulder as she neared his door.

She only grumbled in response as she stepped past him and entered his house. "I can't believe I have to do this," she said under her breath.

He was a bit stung by her words until he realized she still wasn't looking at him. In fact, she avoided it with such determination that it made him smile. No woman did that unless she was interested and was trying to fight it.

"Let me show you where to bunk."

Celena stepped back so that Raphael could lead her toward the mahogany stairs in the middle of the house. She really did hate being here. How could she serve a man who distracted her so much? And as he headed up the stairs and she had an unobstructed view of that tight, perfectly formed butt, it was all she could do not to reach out and grope it.

This was wrong on so many levels. How had she allowed him to talk her into this?

It's the only way to get Jeff. Or was that just an excuse so that she could be here with him? Not wanting to even consider that thought, she forced herself back to business. She'd have to keep her thoughts on her work and not on how good Rafael looked while dressed all in black. . . .

Or more to the point, wonder what he'd look like without those clothes on.

He took her to the first room on the left. "This is the guest room, not that I ever have guests, except for . . ." He glanced at her and winked. "We won't go into that, but it's clean and well kept."

"Thanks," she said, stepping inside to find a room that was decorated in Victorian antiques. It was actually quite lovely, with heavy burgundy drapes and gold brocade Chippendale chairs. The Victorian tester bed held a matching burgundy and gold bedspread that looked lush and inviting.

Not half as inviting as it would be with a naked Rafael in it, but what could she do?

Ask him to join you?

Yeah. Shaking her head at her errant thoughts, she set her backpack on the mattress, then turned to look at Rafael, who cut a tempting pose in the doorway. With him dressed in black pleated pants and a black sweater that clung to his body, it was hard to think straight. Which meant she needed to get him out of here before she lost all sense of her duties and succumbed to the idea of stripping him bare.

"Shouldn't you be out patrolling?" she asked.

"Still too early. Besides, there hasn't been much Daimon activity lately." He crossed himself. "Since Danger died, it's been unnaturally quiet."

"Yeah, that's what Ephani says, too. It's like they've moved on, which is weird. You'd think killing a Dark-Hunter would have invigorated them."

Without commenting, he moved closer to her . . . so close that the scent of him invaded her senses. More than that, it warmed her completely. There was something calming about that scent of Brut and man. Something tempting and sinful.

It kept her spellbound as he paused right beside her and lifted his hand to brush a stray braid from her shoulder. Her heart racing, she couldn't move. All she wanted was to feel him touching her.

A small smile hovered on the edges of his lips as he dipped his head toward hers. She knew he was going to kiss her and still she couldn't move.

Not until his lips parted and she glimpsed his fangs.

He's a Dark-Hunter.

That jolted her enough that she could take three steps back. "We should reorganize your house while I'm here so that it's more efficient."

Rafael bit back a foul curse. One more second and he would have had her. "House is fine."

"No. No, it's not. Do you even have an evacuation plan for what to do if it were to catch fire during the daylight? You know you could roast and die quite easily, then you'd be a soulless Shade and screwed for eternity."

That went over him like a cold shower. Now there was something he'd never thought about before, and he was pretty good at putting together disaster plans.

"It happens a lot with these older homes," she continued. "What with their faulty wiring and all. I heard of one Dark-Hunter who died like that just last year."

"Who?"

"I can't remember the name, but it was one of the Dark-Hunters in England. Total barbecue. You can check it on the Web site."

He'd really rather not. No Dark-Hunter liked to read about the death of another one. It brought home that even though they were technically immortal, there were still things out there that could kill them. And having died already, it wasn't something Rafael wanted to experience again.

Still, she didn't relent. "You should contact a friend of mine. He specializes in fireproofing underground bunkers for Dark-Hunters. He can put in a sprinkler system and—"

"You're rambling."

"No, I'm not. Dark-Hunter safety is a Squire's number one priority. In fact, I'll call Leonard first thing in the morning and see when he can come out for an estimate. We should also make sure that you have a roll bar in your car in case you flip over in a wreck. Oh, and a steel bar shield on the driver's side in the event you run up under something, so that you can't be decapitated."

Without conscious thought, Rafael's hand went to his throat. Damn, the woman gave paranoia a whole new meaning.

"We should also look into the history of this house and make sure that it was never used as a bed-and-breakfast."

"Why?"

"If property has ever been used as a community place such as a boardinghouse, restaurant, or anything open to the public, then the Daimons can enter without an invitation. You don't want them barging in on you and killing you, now do you?"

"Not really."

"Then we need to do a property search. Unless your last Squire did that."

"No."

She tsked. "I need a piece of paper. This is going to take a while."

And by the time she fished that paper out of her backpack and started making a list, Rafael felt ill. The woman should work as a Codes Inspector. Jeez. She thought of dangers that had never occurred to him.

She even went outside and inspected the grade of his basement, which wasn't high enough, in her estimation. After all, according to her, a foundation shift could cause a crack that could theoretically expose him to daylight.

Not bloody likely, but she seemed determined to ferret out any possible—heavy emphasis on the "possible"—threat.

By the time ten o'clock rolled around, he was more than ready to begin his patrol. He came up from the basement to find an arsenal on the table.

Two daggers, three stakes because two could break in a fight, a Daimon tracker that he'd always profaned using, a Kevlar jacket, his cell phone, and a watch were all laid out for him.

When she lifted the Kevlar to help him into it, he merely stared at her. "Bullets can't kill me."

"No, but they do hurt. The Daimons could, in theory, shoot you until you're too weakened to fight them and then behead you."

He shook his head at her as he again declined to put on the jacket. She was perturbed as she set it aside while he hid the daggers in his boots.

"Want to put a cone around my head like a dog to make sure that they can't decapitate me while we're at it?" he asked sarcastically.

"I would," she said to his instant incredulous dismay, "but Ephani got really angry when I tried that with her, so I learned that it's more important for you to blend in than protect the neck. But I do have this." She pulled a thick black steel collar from her pocket. "If you wear it under a turtleneck, it's not so obvious. Kind of medievally looking."

He had no response to that. It was the most ludicrous thing he'd ever heard. In fact, as he tucked the stakes away, he had to force himself not to use them, on his latest menace. . . .

Her.

She handed him the watch. "I double-checked the sunrise on weather .com and cross-checked it with the meteorological society and my friend who's an astronomer to be sure it was accurate. It's at six fifty-nine A.M. sharp. I've already set the alarm to give you a twenty-minute warning." Next, she held out a piece of paper. "Here's a list of how long it will take you from various parts of the tri-city area to get back here. I'll keep an eye on your tracers to make sure that you have adequate time to make it back home without threat or harm."

Then she handed him a folded-up black body bag. "And in the event you can't make it back, zip yourself up in this and press the panic alarm I added to your key chain. Then I can come get you home before the daylight makes you burst into flames."

Again, he was speechless.

She picked up his cell phone. "I preprogrammed my number in on the speed dial under one and Acheron under two. Did you know you didn't have any numbers listed as 'ICE'? You should always have an In Case of Emergency contact number. So I put mine in for that, too."

"What about Jeff?"

"Since he won't be with us much longer, I didn't bother."

This was madness. No wonder Ephani hadn't fought him on having Celena replaced for a week. Jesus, Mary, and Joseph, the woman was insane.

"Anything else, Mom?" he asked.

"Yes. Play nice with the other kids and don't let the Daimons get the drop on you. Use the tracer so that you know where they are at all times."

Raphael couldn't get out of his house fast enough. So much for his thoughts about trying to seduce her. He'd rather face the Daimon horde blindfolded and with both hands tied behind his back.

More than that, he'd rather go babysit Jeff. If anyone had ever told him that he'd prefer the lazy, lackadaisical boy to the hot Caribbean sex goddess, he'd have laughed in their face.

Now he could appreciate Jeff's laid-back nature.

Maybe it's just a ploy of hers. . . .

He paused at that thought. Maybe she was just doing this to drive him away. It was possible.

Very possible.

Oh yeah, he was on to her now. It made total sense.

Fine then. Two could play this game.

Getting into his car, he smiled. *"En garde, ma petite."* They were about to go to war, and at the end of this, he was going to win.

3

Rafael wasn't winning his war. He was losing it miserably and not even with style. No matter what he tried, Celena circumvented his best efforts. The woman was a machine, and after forty-eight hours of having her in his house, he'd had enough.

Sitting on his couch in the basement an hour after sunset—because, quite frankly, if he went upstairs, he might kill her—he called Ephani, who answered on the third ring.

"Come get your Squire," he said without preamble.

Her tone was dry and snide. "Hi to you, too, Rafael. Nice to hear from you."

"Cut the crap, Eph, and come get her before I kill her."

"She's making you crazy?" He could hear the humor in her voice.

"You think? How do you stand it night in and night out, and not lose your mind?"

"She's a little obsessive, but—"

"A *little*?" he asked incredulously. "The woman makes a serial stalker look like a Boy Scout."

Ephani snorted. "She's not *that* bad."

"Oh yes, she is. Trust me. I almost lost my head to a Daimon the first night she was here."

"How so?"

He clenched his teeth at the memory. "Picture this. There I am in the alleyway, sneaking up on a group of Daimons who have this college kid trapped between them. Just as I go to make my move to save the kid, the phone rings with Ms. I-have-no-purpose-save-to-make-you-crazy calling to tell me that according to the tracer she has on me it's time for me to head home so that I won't get caught out in daylight."

Ephani was laughing so hard that he wanted to reach through the phone and choke her.

"It's not funny."

She kept laughing.

Rafael let out a disgusted sigh. "Did she reorganize your kitchen and fill it up with wheat germ and shit? I tried to explain the whole I'm-immortal-I-live-forever to her, but she doesn't get it. She said that even immortals need to eat healthy foods."

Still Ephani was laughing.

And still Rafael wanted to kill the Amazon as well as Celena. "This really isn't funny, Eph."

"Oh yeah, it is. Gah, Rafe. You're such a man."

"And I'm going to take that as a compliment."

Clearing her throat, Ephani finally sobered. "There's a few things you need to understand about Celena."

"You mean something other than she's nuts?"

Ephani tsked at him over the phone. "She's not nuts."

He glanced up to the ceiling. No doubt Celena was up there right now doing something extremely odd in order to protect *him*, the immortal warrior. "I think I'll reserve my opinion."

"Trust me, Blackbeard. She's not nuts."

"Then what is she?"

"Scared." The word surprised him. Celena certainly didn't act that way. "Have you tried to ask her anything about her family?"

"A couple of times, but she won't talk about them."

"That's right and do you know why?"

"She's nuts?" This time he said it with a little less enthusiasm.

"No . . . she's scared."

But that didn't make sense to him. "Of what?"

"Of losing the people she loves, so she tries to keep up walls to protect herself. If she doesn't talk about people, then they can't be close to her. But it's a crock. I know this because when her father died a year ago, it almost killed her. She still cries about him in the middle of the day when she thinks I'm sleeping."

The news floored him. That was so opposite of the hard-nosed woman upstairs. There was nothing vulnerable about her, and honestly, he couldn't imagine her crying about anything. "Celena?"

"Yes, Celena. And do you know why she's so anal about her duties?"

"She's nuts?" He was back to being convinced. Anyone who executed their duties to such an nth degree wasn't normal.

"No," Ephani said in an irritated tone. "Like Jeff, she's from a Squire family. The Dark-Hunter she grew up with was killed eight

years ago because he was cornered by a group of Daimons and executed. If that wasn't bad enough, the first Dark-Hunter she was as-
signed to died because she couldn't make it back before sunup. Celena
tried to get to her in time, but there was no place for her to hide, so
she turned into toast minutes before Celena got there. The Council
warned me when they sent her over that she was a bit . . . traumatized
by the event. Hell, if you think she's bad now, you should have seen
her when she first came to work for me."

If she was worse, then he was grateful he hadn't met her then. But
all that actually explained a great deal about her psychosis.

"And she must really like you to be so paranoid that she's calling you all the time to make sure you get back home in time. She's
not that bad even with me." Then she added under her breath,
"Then again, I always follow her patrol plans and get back before she
freaks."

Rafael was quiet for a second as he considered Ephani's words.
"That puts a lot of perspective on her, doesn't it?"

"Yeah."

"Okay," he said with a sigh, "I won't kill her tonight."

"Please don't. All in all, I'm rather fond of her, and I have to say I
much prefer her to the one I'm dealing with right now. This one's kind
of lazy. She even balked at making my scrambled eggs with cheese
and onions in them."

Rafael laughed at that. "I guess it's what you're used to."

"I guess. But send Celena home soon. I miss her."

He shook his head. "By the way, thanks, Eph."

"No prob. Just take care of my girl."

"Will do." Rafael hung up the phone and tucked it back in his
pants pocket. His mind whirling with what he'd learned, he headed
upstairs to find his "breakfast" waiting.

Grabbing a piece of bacon, he had to admit that this was the one
thing he liked about having Celena around. Unlike Jeff, she was up all
night with him and made sure that he had plenty of food prepared.
She even packed him a snack bag to take with him. Of course it was
full of wholesome foods that he poked at like an alien life-form, but it
was a nice thought.

"Hi."

He swallowed his bacon as she brought him a glass of orange
juice. "Hi."

After he took the glass, she lifted a notebook up from the table.
"I've made notes on your patrolling patterns. I've noticed that you

tend to stay here in Columbus around campus until about midnight and then you head over to Starkville. I was thinking that—"

He took the pad from her hand and set it aside. "I like *my* pattern, Celena."

"But it would be safer for you to patrol Starkville first and then head back this way."

"And I was a pirate who laughed as he died and spat in the face of my killer. Safety's not my concern."

"It should be," she insisted.

"Why?"

Her brow creased by worry, her face held a very faint hysterical note in it. "Because you could die and become a Shade, wandering the earth with no body and no soul, in constant pain and misery. Wanting food. Wanting someone to hear you. Wanting someone to just touch you and having no one able to see you. To—"

He stopped her words by laying his fingers on her lips. Personally, he didn't like the gruesome image she painted with her words. "It's okay, Celena. I'm not going to die."

But he could see the pain and fear in her eyes. "That's why you should rethink your pattern."

Moving his fingers from her soft lips, Rafael dipped his head down to capture her mouth only to have her retreat from him again.

He let out a tired breath. "Don't you ever date?"

"Not anymore. To bring an outsider in could threaten the safety of Ephani. What if I were on a date and she needed me?"

"What if a meteorite fell through the house right now and flattened us both?"

She actually glanced up at the ceiling.

If it wasn't so serious, he'd laugh. "Celena, you can't go through your entire life worrying about what *might* happen." He closed the distance between them. "Any more than you can go through life alone. Trust me on this one. It's lonely as hell."

"You live that way."

"Not always. I do reach out to someone from time to time."

Instead of comforting her, those words brought out her anger. "And I'm not your one-night stand. We both have duties to attend to. Oaths to uphold."

"I would kiss you anyway, but I have a feeling that if I tried—"

"I'd kick you in the nuts and tear your ear off." There was no mistaking the sincerity of her angry tone.

"That would hurt."

"That's the idea."

Rafael shook his head at her. She was saucy, and as she walked away from him he couldn't help the heat that flooded his body. Everything about her appealed to him on a primal level.

Honestly, he was losing his mind being this close to something that tempted him while unable to touch it. No wonder the Council preferred to assign only Squires who were the opposite sex of what a Dark-Hunter lusted for.

I can't take it. He needed some distance from her.

"I'm going to kill Daimons now."

"But it's early."

"I know. But I have a feeling they're out already and I need to patrol." Or stay here with the hard-on from hell until he lost what little sanity he had left. As Oscar Wilde once said, he could resist anything except temptation.

Before Rafael could make it to the door, his phone rang. Without looking at the ID, he answered it.

"Rafe?" It was Jeff whispering in a panicked tone.

"Yeah?"

"There's a group of Daimons here at the marina."

"It's too early for them to be out."

"Tell *them* that!"

"Calm down and tell me what's going on."

"It's spooky as hell. There's some kind of party going on at the houseboat next door that started at sundown and I just saw six of them heading for it."

"All right. Lie low and I'll be there in a few minutes."

Celena frowned at the concern in Rafael's voice. "Is there a problem?"

"Major Daimon alert."

Before she could ask anything else, he was gone, but his words rang in her ears. Major Daimon alert . . .

This could be bad.

You're a Squire. Her place was at home, especially after dark. And then she saw Eamon's face in her mind. His smiling face as he teased her about not eating peas.

"Did ya do yer homework, lass?"

God, how she'd loved that man. He was like an older brother, a best friend, and a father all rolled into one. And in one heartbeat, the Daimons had killed him.

Let's face it, with the exception of Ephani, you've had a bad run with Dark-Hunters. The more she cared for them, the more horrible their deaths.

And she loved Rafael. She'd loved him since the first moment she'd met him after she moved to West Point, Mississippi. He was intelligent, smart, and he had a wicked sense of humor.

Now he was going to fight the Daimons. Alone.

A thousand scenarios went through her head, with all of them coming to one single conclusion.

Rafael dead. Panic set her heart to beating furiously as she looked about his home. She couldn't pack up another Dark-Hunter's home. She couldn't hold another vigil service to pay respect to someone she loved.

She couldn't.

And before she could stop herself, she grabbed the tracer off the table and her keys.

4

When Jeff had said that there was a group of Daimons heading for a party, Rafael had taken that to mean that there were only six Daimons at a *human* party. You know—a regular party with teenaged or college-aged humans groping each other while drinking heavily. The kind of party that he normally crashed so that he could protect the humans from the Daimons who wanted to feast on their souls.

What the rocket scientist had failed to mention to Rafael was the small fact that the Daimons were headed into an *Apollite* wedding reception. Something he, himself, hadn't realized until he'd walked onto the boat that was filled with tall, gorgeous pale *blond* preternatural people.

Oh yeah, the six-foot-six bald black man dressed all in black leather really didn't blend into the overdressed crowd of Nordic vampires. And Rafael had to admit that right now, looking at the Apollites and Daimons who were staring angrily at him, made him feel like the last steak in the Kennel Club.

It was so silent, the only sound he could hear, even with heightened hearing, was his own heart beating. Though there was blood in their goblets—he could smell it—there didn't appear to be any humans around who needed saving.

Except for, maybe, him.

One of the Apollites closest to him arched a brow before he spoke. "Bride's side or groom's?"

"I'm with catering," Rafael said in a flat tone.

A Daimon stepped forward to give him a cold, feral once-over. "Yeah, you look like food to me."

The Daimon female beside him smiled, showing off her fangs. "We can't really eat him, since his blood is poisonous to us, but killing him should have some entertainment value. What do you think?"

Yeah, he'd walked right into the lion's den. There were at least twelve Daimons that he could sense. Add another twenty Apollites. Normally Apollites didn't fight against Dark-Hunters, since Dark-Hunters were forbidden to touch them until they stopped feasting on fellow Apollites and began feasting on human souls, thereby becoming Daimons. Then it was open warfare between them.

However, this group didn't seem too concerned with keeping the unspoken truce between Dark-Hunters and Apollites. They truly were bloodthirsty.

And now they were attacking.

Reaching under his coat, Rafael grabbed his steel stake and plunged it into the heart of the first Daimon to reach him. With an anguished cry, the Daimon exploded into dust. Two more came at him. He caught the first one a quick hit that sent him flying backward, into the arms of another Daimon, while he flipped the second one over and stabbed him straight in the chest.

Before he could straighten up from the kill, the Daimons overran him like ants over a sugar cube. He hit the ground face-first as they clawed at him. He could feel something biting into his back that felt like a knife wound, but it was hard to tell as he struggled to get them off him.

Celena knew she was breaking the rules, but Rafael didn't have to know it. All she was going to do was make sure he was okay, then head back to his house. No one would ever know what she'd done. No one.

She parked her car as close to the docks as she could before she took off running toward where the tracer in her hand said Rafael was. A thousand fears shredded her as she relived the night Sara had died. Celena had been trying to get to her. They'd been on the cell phone together as she raced to make it in time.

The last sound she'd heard had been Sara screaming as she burst into flames.

Grief threatened to overwhelm Celena. She couldn't lose another Dark-Hunter. And especially not Rafael. She'd loved him far too long to let him die.

With no clear thought of what she had in mind to do to help him if he was in trouble, she ran onto the boat, then skidded to a stop.

It was total chaos.

But more than that, there was no sign of Rafael anywhere. He appeared to be buried by the large stack of Daimons and Apollites in the center of the boat.

Her eyes welling with tears, she met the gaze of a woman in a wedding dress for only an instant before she pulled a stake out of her coat.

"Rafael?" Celena cried, heading for the fray.

A Daimon turned on her then. Celena kicked him back and kept going toward the largest group of them. She knew that was where Rafael had to be.

She couldn't see anything as she pushed, kicked, and fought until she finally saw what she'd come for. Rafael knocked a Daimon off him while another was trying to pin him to the ground. But what made her panic swell most was the Daimon coming toward them with an axe.

If they managed to cut off Rafael's head, it was over.

The Daimons pulled back as someone grabbed her from behind. Reacting on pure instinct, Celena head-butted her assailant with the back of her head and launched herself at Rafael who still lay on the ground. From the corner of her eye, she saw the axe falling.

She curled herself around Rafael's head and waited for the pain of the axe slicing through her.

It never came.

There was a sudden silence that rang out as everything seemed to freeze into place. Her heart racing, Celena opened her eyes to see the Apollites and Daimons staring above her. She rolled over to find the Daimon who'd held the axe. Only now the axe was gone.

It was in the hands of the groom who stared not at them but at the others with a stern glare. "Enough!" he roared. "This is supposed to be my wedding!" He looked over at the bride, whose face was pale, her delicate lips trembling. "And you're upsetting Chloe. I've only got five more years with her before I die and the last thing I want is to have what few memories I have left ruined by a bunch of blood-thirsty assholes." He picked out with his gaze the ones who must be Daimons. "No more bloodshed!"

The Daimon next to Celena curled his lip. "He killed my brother."

The groom snarled. "Your brother was a dickhead and he's lucky I didn't kill him. I told all of you that you weren't to cause any problems tonight, didn't I?"

The Daimon turned sheepish.

The groom tossed the axe overboard before he approached them. To Celena's complete shock, he held his hand out to her.

She exchanged an uncertain look with Rafael before she reached out, clasped the groom's hand, and allowed him to pull her to her feet.

"You can't let him go," another Daimon sneered.

"It's my wedding. I can do what I please. This is supposed to be a night of celebration—"

"Then let's celebrate by killing a Dark-Hunter."

The groom looked disgusted. "Someone stake that bastard, please, and for the sake of the gods, dust Benny off the table by the fountain. That powder's disgusting and it's getting into the blood." He helped Rafael up. "Don't worry. It's not human blood. It's ours."

Rafael wasn't sure what to think as he faced the Apollite in front of him. They could have killed him and Celena both. He was having a hard time believing that they would just let him go.

"Why are you doing this?" Rafael asked.

The groom looked back at his bride. "Because life's too short to spend it fighting when you could be holding the one you love. And love's too rare to squander it with petty concerns." He took his wife's hand in his and held it tight. "I'm lucky I have Chloe and I have no intention of letting a war I didn't start rob me of one second of my time with her. Go in peace, Dark-Hunter."

Rafael was surprised by his words, but even more so by his charity. "You're a good man."

The Apollite scoffed. "I guess we'll see in about five years, huh? If I die peacefully, then I'm good. If not, then we'll face each other again as predators." He indicated the ramp with a jerk of his chin. "Now go before I change my mind."

Deciding not to press his luck, Rafael draped his arm around Celena and held her close to him to protect her as they made their way off the boat. He didn't stop walking until they'd made their way over to the dock by his boat. He paused at the prow to turn back and see the Apollites and Daimons resuming their party.

"That was flipping amazing!" He looked up to see Jeff in the shadows.

He reminded Rafael of a kid who'd just got away with something. "I thought you were dead. Man, I was in the process of calling Acheron for help when I saw the two of you leaving. How did you manage it?"

Instead of removing his arm from around Celena, Rafael leaned his head against hers. "Luck . . . which I'll take over skill any day."

Jeff's face sobered as he realized Celena was there. He actually gulped. "I'm dead, aren't I?"

Rafael held his breath as he met Celena's speculative gaze. He expected her to shove him away from her and go after Jeff.

Instead, she wrapped her arm around Rafael's hips. "I made a deal with Rafael, and it seems you're safe from me."

A small smile hovered at the edges of Rafael's lips as he stared at her in the moonlight. "Go home, Jeff."

"Okay, let me pack and—"

"No," he said sternly. "Go home right now and don't stop until you're safe in your room. You can get your stuff later."

He could tell Jeff wanted to argue, but luckily for his Squire, the man caught the tone of his voice and immediately left. And as soon as he did, Rafael did what he'd been dying to do. He finally kissed Celena.

Celena moaned at the taste of Rafael as his tongue swept against hers. He cupped her face in his hands as she inhaled the sharp scent of his skin and aftershave. It was a breathtaking combination, and all she wanted to do was peel his clothes off him and lick every inch of his body.

She knew she had no business with him, and for once she didn't care about rules. The Apollite had been right. There were some things more important than something so trivial.

Rafael pulled back from the kiss. "Why did you come for me?"

"I was afraid you were in danger."

He shook his head at her. "You know that was amazingly stupid of you. I'm rancid meat to them, but you . . . you're a buffet. You're damn lucky they let you go."

She smiled up at him before she repeated her earlier words. "Yeah, well, I'll take luck over skill any day."

He laughed before he kissed her again. "And that still doesn't tell me why you came after me. You broke a dozen rules by following me tonight."

And for some reason that didn't bother her. Nothing had mattered to her except seeing him safe. "I know, but I couldn't let you die."

"Why?"

She bit her lip as the reasonable side of her brain begged her not to say anything else. But all the years of her hiding her emotions for this man rushed to the forefront, and after being with him for this last week, she couldn't hide it anymore. "Because I love you."

Rafael couldn't have been more stunned had she stabbed him. He stood there in complete shock as he watched her eyes dilate ever so slightly. In all the centuries he'd lived, only one other woman had ever said those words to him . . .

And she had died in his arms on their wedding night under the assault of his enemies.

He'd never had the chance to taste her. Never had a chance to show her just how much he loved her.

He wasn't going to take that chance with Celena. His body burning, he scooped her up in his arms and carried her on board his boat.

"What are you doing?" she asked as she wrapped her arms around his neck.

"*Carpe noctem.* I'm seizing the night. But most of all, I'm seizing the woman in my arms."

Celena didn't say another word as he took her below the deck. As soon as they were out of the sight of any passersby, she literally ripped the shirt from his back so that she could finally touch the body that had haunted her dreams for the last few years.

Her career as a Squire was over, but she didn't care. The only thing that mattered right then was being with Rafael. She shivered as he pulled her shirt over her head and cupped her breast through her bra.

Closing her eyes, she savored the heat of his hand as he pushed the satin aside to touch her flesh. She captured his lips with hers as she feverishly opened his fly, then dipped her hand down to touch him. He hissed in response, making her soar in satisfaction.

"Boy," he whispered against her lips, "When you break the rules, you seriously break the rules."

Celena didn't respond as he pulled her pants down her legs. She sucked her breath in sharply between her teeth as she saw him kneeling on the ground at her feet. Lifting her foot, she let him remove her shoes, which he tossed over his shoulder before he undressed her.

His dark eyes flashed an instant before he reached up to remove her panties. Her entire body burned as he bared her to his hungry gaze. Reaching down, she traced the outline of his lips as he gently tongued her fingertips. She'd dreamed of this moment a thousand times.

He was the main reason she'd never really dated. After she'd met him, other men never seemed to compare. They weren't as handsome. Weren't as dangerous.

Weren't as forbidden.

And now she was finally going to know what it felt like to hold him. . . .

Rafael couldn't breathe as he slowly rose to his feet. He still couldn't believe that Celena was here with him. That she who lived for rules and regulations was willing to sacrifice her Squire's oath.

His heart pounding, he reached down to brush his hand against the softness of her abdomen, then lower to the short, crisp hairs until he found what he sought. He groaned at the sensation of her wet heat against his fingers while she stroked him with her hand.

Unable to stand it anymore, he pinned her back against the wall and kissed her passionately.

Celena clung to him as she lifted one leg to wrap it around his hips. Taking the invitation, he drove himself deep inside her.

Rafael's head spun as an unimagined ecstasy tore through him. Celena had almost died to protect him. No woman had ever done such a thing for him before. Her strength, her courage . . .

It was unlike anything he'd ever known.

And now she met him stroke for stroke as they made love furiously. He smiled as each thrust was punctuated by the sound of the beads on the ends of her braids scraping against the wall.

Celena buried her lips against Rafael's throat as she forced herself not to think about what was going to happen tomorrow. She couldn't stay with him. She knew it. He was a Dark-Hunter. But here for the moment, he was hers, and that was all that mattered.

Arching her back, she cried out with every powerful thrust of him inside her as she clutched him to her. He dipped his head down to capture her breast and tongue it in time to his strokes. She cradled his head to her as her body was overwhelmed by pleasure. With every stroke it increased until she finally couldn't stand it anymore. Her body burst into a thousand tendrils of ecstasy.

Rafael growled as he felt Celena climaxing. Wanting to give her even more, he quickened his strokes and watched as she threw her head back and moaned.

His smile faded as he lost himself to his own orgasm. Burying himself deep inside her, he shook with the force of it. Her breathing ragged in his ear, she gently stroked his back as he slowly drifted back into himself. This was one of the most amazing moments in his life. Not because of the sex, but because he was being held by a woman who was willing to sacrifice herself for him. A woman who was willing to break the rules. . . .

Most of all, a woman who loved him.

He kissed her tenderly on the lips. "Don't leave, Celena."

"I'll be here until morning."

"No," he said, his voice thick with the emotions that were churning inside him. "I mean don't leave. Ever."

Her mouth opened ever so slightly. "What are you saying, Rafael?"

"I love you."

She couldn't believe her ears. It was more than she'd ever hoped for. "You don't have to say that."

"It's not that I'm saying it. It's that I'm feeling it."

Thrilled by his words, she squeezed him tight. "So what's to become of us now?"

"Looks like I'll be joining the human race again."

"Are you sure?"

Rafael grew quiet as he considered it. If he continued being a Dark-Hunter, he'd have to let her go.

The Apollite's words rang in Rafael's head. He'd been alone for all these centuries. Not once in all this time had any woman ever made him feel his emotions more strongly than Celena. She made him crazy, angry, happy. . . .

But most of all, she made him feel like he could fly.

He didn't want to live without this. Without her.

"Yeah, I'm sure. That is, if you're willing to take Artemis's test."

"For you, my pirate, I'd walk through the fires of hell."

Epilogue

Celena stared at Acheron, the Dark-Hunter leader, as he explained that in order to free Rafael from Artemis's service she would have to kill him. "You've got to be kidding me."

"Do I look like I'm joking?"

She raked her gaze from the top of Acheron's long black hair to the tips of his custom-made Goth biker boots with bat buckles. And at six foot eight there was a lot of him to rake, too, but every bit of his long, lean frame was deadly sincere, which made her sick to her stomach.

How could she kill the man she loved? What kind of psycho had instituted that policy?

Then she looked to Rafael, who was standing behind Acheron, in the hallway. His handsome face betrayed nothing but trust. His black eyes were kind and gentle, encouraging, and that made the love she felt for him swell.

"I can't kill him."

Acheron let out a patient breath. "He won't be dead long. You simply stop his heart from beating, then you hold the stone against his bow and arrow tattoo. His soul will leave the stone and return to his body."

"You can do it, baby," Rafael said with that decadent accent of his. "You told me just last night that you wanted to choke the life out of me."

Instead of smiling, she grimaced at him. "That was for hogging the remote, and I wasn't serious. This is entirely different."

Acheron shrugged. "Fine then, he continues being a Dark-Hunter, and the Council will reassign you away from him."

Her heart stopped at the mere thought of not seeing him anymore. "You can't let them do that."

"I control the Dark-Hunters. The Squires are their concern, not mine. I have no jurisdiction there, which is why Jeff is now cooling his heels in Squire jail for writing that story. I personally thought it was funny, but the Council doesn't really have a sense of humor, do they?"

Frustrated, Celena wanted to argue, but she knew better. If she and Rafael were to ever have a normal life, he would have to be human again.

Right now, the Council knew nothing about their relationship, but sooner or later they were bound to find out and then there would be hell for her to pay.

Unless she and Rafael were already married. Then there was nothing the Council could do. There was no law prohibiting her from marrying a human male. It was the only loophole they could hope for.

"Okay," she said with a determined sigh. "I can do this."

This time it was Acheron who hesitated. "There's one more thing you need to know."

She gave Acheron a peeved stare. "And that would be?"

"The stone with his soul in it will burn your skin the minute you touch it, and it won't stop until his soul has returned to his body. If you drop the stone before that time, he'll be a Shade."

Oh, that was a pleasant thought. In freeing him, she could very well be damning him to an eternity of hell. Shades couldn't eat, couldn't be seen or heard. It was a fate far worse than death.

And she could be the one to gift him with that oh, so not pleasant existence.

Still Rafael's gaze burned into her. "I want to be with you, Celena. As a man."

How could she argue with that? What's more, she wanted it, too. So long as he remained a Dark-Hunter, they couldn't have children. But if she freed him . . .

They could have a family. They could be married and grow old together. It was all she wanted.

"Okay," she breathed. "Tell me what to do."

Acheron pulled a long, evil-looking dagger from his boot and handed it to her. "Pierce his heart and leave the dagger in until he goes limp." He shrugged his black backpack off his shoulder and took out a black box that was about the size of a softball. He opened the lid to show her a vibrant blue stone that was chiseled with intricate markings. It was a strange, compelling object that seemed to hum with life.

She reached for it only to have Acheron move it away.

"Remember, it burns. I'll hand it to you and then you press it to Artemis's mark."

She gulped as she stared at the stone. It was hard to fathom that was Rafael's human soul in there. "Are you sure this works?"

"Kyrian, Talon, Valerius—"

"Okay," she said as Acheron listed off the Dark-Hunters she knew had gone free. "Let's do it."

Rafael pulled his shirt off so that she could see the double bow and arrow mark on his left shoulder.

Her heart pounding, she gripped the dagger tight in her hand and met his obsidian gaze. The love there scorched her.

"You can do it," he whispered. "Just pretend I'm Jeff."

She wanted to laugh at his joke, but she couldn't even muster it. Instead, she ground her teeth and did the hardest thing she'd ever done in her life.

She tried to stab him, but the dagger didn't so much as pierce his skin. Stunned, she tried harder, but still it wouldn't budge. "What's wrong?" she asked.

Acheron grimaced. "Damn. We forgot to drain his Dark-Hunter powers out of him. You can't kill him while he's immortal . . . at least not and leave his body whole."

"Then what do we do?"

Acheron scratched the back of his neck. "I'm not supposed to interfere, but what the hell? For you two, I'll make an exception."

He took the dagger from her hand and plunged it into Rafael's heart, up to its hilt.

Rafael staggered back before he slid slowly to the floor.

"Oh God," she cried, horrified by what Acheron had done, as she knelt down beside him.

Rafael's face was contorted by pain as a small trickle of blood left the corner of his mouth.

Instinctively, she reached for the dagger to pull it out.

"Not yet," Acheron said, pulling her back. "He has to die or he can't go free."

Tears filled her eyes as she panted along with Rafael. He cupped her cheek in his palm as he offered her a small smile. "It's okay, Celena."

She only hoped he was right.

Covering his hand with hers, she held it tight as she watched the light fade from his eyes. And she gave a small cry as the last breath was expelled from his body.

Acheron took the stone from the box and held it out to her. His swirling silver eyes bore into hers. "Don't drop it."

Nodding, she took it from him only to scream out as a furious pain seared her skin. It burned worse than any imaginable fire and it was all she could do to maintain her hold. The only thing that kept her from releasing it was the knowledge that Rafael would die if she did.

She ground her teeth as Acheron helped her place the stone over the mark. Tears flowed down her cheeks from the pain and fear as she waited for Rafael to open his eyes.

It seemed an eternity had passed before Acheron pulled the dagger out of his chest.

An instant later, Rafael took a deep breath and blinked his eyes open to look at her.

Celena laughed in giddiness as she saw eyes that were no longer black. Now his eyes were a light amber brown that sparkled with human life. He was even more handsome than he'd been before.

Biting her lip, she pulled him into her arms and held him close.

Acheron moved away and returned the dagger to his boot.

"Thanks, boss," Rafael said as he pushed himself to his feet.

Acheron gave him a kind grin. "I'm not your boss anymore, Rafael. *She* is."

Rafael laughed. "That doesn't bother me."

Acheron snorted. "Yeah, be glad you're human now. Nothing like answering to one single woman for eleven thousand years to make you wish for the end of time."

Celena laughed again. "Thank you, Acheron."

He inclined his head to them. "You kids have fun."

Rafael looked down at the woman in his arms and tightened his hold on her. "Trust me, we will."

And as soon as Acheron was gone, Celena pulled him down for a fierce kiss. Rafael's head swam at the taste of her. It was a taste he would now spend the rest of his life savoring.

Shadow of
the Moon

1

New Orleans

Fury Kattalakis was about to walk straight into the dragon's lair. Well, not exactly. There *was* a dragon in the attic of the building he was headed toward, but that dragon wasn't nearly as dangerous to Fury as the bear guarding the door.

That nasty sonofabitch hated his guts.

Not that he cared. Most people and animals hated his guts which was fine by him. He didn't have much use for the world anyway.

"The things you do for family," Fury said under his breath. Though to be honest, this whole family concept was still new to him. He was more used to being screwed over by everyone around him. It wasn't until his brother Vane had taken him in during the summer of '04 that he'd realized not everyone in the universe was out to kill him.

The bear, however, still was . . .

Dev Peltier tensed as soon as he saw Fury step out of the shadows near the door of Sanctuary—a rough biker bar and dance club that stood at 688 Ursulines. Like that address hadn't been chosen intentionally by the bear clan who owned it. They were nothing if not ironic.

Dressed in a black Sanctuary staff t-shirt and jeans, the bear looked human at present, complete with long curly blond hair, black biker boots, and a pair of sharp eyes that missed no detail or weakness, not that Fury had a weakness. But for all of Dev's human appearance, to those lycanthropes such as Fury, Dev's alternate form was like a thrumming beacon that warned all otherworldly types that Dev was ferocious.

Then again, so was Fury. What he lacked in magick abilities, he more than made up for in sheer strength . . .

And FU attitude and anger.

No one got the better of him. Ever.

"What are *you* doing here?" Dev growled.

Fury shrugged nonchalantly and decided that a fight wouldn't get him inside—which was what he'd promised to do. Him . . . keeping a promise to someone other than himself . . . yeah. Right. Hell was freezing over. He still wasn't really sure how he'd allowed his brother Fang to talk him into this act of blatant suicide.

The bastard owed him.

Big time.

"Peace, brother." Fury held his hands up in mock surrender. "I'm just here to see Sasha."

Dev bared his teeth threateningly as he raked a glare over Fury's body that normally would have caused Fury to slug him for the insult. Damn, his brother Vane was rubbing off on him. "The Kattalakis patria isn't welcome here and you know it."

Fury arched a brow as he looked up at the sign over Dev's head. Flat black with electric blue and brown, it held a motorcycle on a hill that was silhouetted by a full moon. It also proclaimed Sanctuary to be the home of the Howlers, the house band. To the unobservant, it looked like any other club sign. But to those born cursed, like them, the shadows in the moon formed the outline of a dragon rising—a hidden symbol to the preternatural beings the world over.

This club wasn't just named Sanctuary, it was one. And all paranormal entities were allowed inside where no one could harm them. At least so long as they obeyed the first rule of a limani. No spill blood.

Fury tsked at Dev. "You know the laws of our people. You can't pick and choose who enters. All are welcomed equally."

"Fuck you," Dev snarled.

Fury shook his head as he bit back his natural caustic retort. Instead, he decided to handle it with biting sarcasm. "Thank you so much for the offer, but while you do have a certain feminine quality in your demeanor and a remarkable head of hair that any woman would envy, you're far too hairy for my tastes. No offense."

Dev curled his lip. "Since when does a dog care about what it humps?"

Fury sucked his breath in sharply. "I could go so low with that that even the gutter would envy us, but . . . I know what you're trying to do. You're trying to provoke a fight with me so that you can legally turn me away."

He clenched his fists, and he made a show of struggling with what he wanted to do and what he'd promised to do. "I really, really want to give you that fight, too, but I have to see Sasha and it can't wait. Sorry. We'll have to hump and fight later."

Dev growled threateningly, a pure grizzly sound. "You're on thin ice, Wolf."

Fury sobered and narrowed his gaze to that of his wolf form. When he spoke, his voice was low and feral and filled with the promise of whup-ass that was waiting if Dev wanted to continue this game. "Shut up, sod off, and let me in."

Dev took a step toward him.

Faster than Fury could even tense in expectation of the hit Dev was about to deliver, Colt was there. A head taller than both of them, Colt had short, jet-black hair and lethal eyes. He put one large paw of a tattooed hand on Dev's chest and held him back.

"Don't do it, Dev," Colt said in a low, even tone. "He's not worth it."

Fury should probably have been insulted, but the truth had never bothered him. "He's right. I'm a worthless bastard fathered by a bastard even more worthless than I am. You definitely don't want to have your sanctuary license pulled over the likes of me."

Dev shrugged away Colt's touch, which caused the sleeve of his shirt to pull up and expose the double bow and arrow tattoo on his arm. "Whatever. But we're watching you, Wolf."

Fury gave him a one-finger salute. "Then I'll try not to piss on the floor or hump the furniture . . ." He glanced down at Dev's black, silver-studded boot. "Your leg, though, might be another matter."

Dev growled again while Colt laughed and tightened his hold.

Colt indicated the door with a jerk of his chin. "Get your ass inside, Fury, before I decide to feed you to him."

"I'm seriously not worth the indigestion." With an antagonistic wink at Dev, Fury sauntered past them to enter the bar where the music was loud and pumping, something that made the wolf in him want to whine in protest as it assaulted his heightened hearing.

Since Colt was one of the Howlers, they weren't on stage yet. But there was already a good-sized crowd gathered. Tourists and regulars were dancing or milling about on the first level of the three-story bar. No doubt it was just as crowded on the second floor, too. The third floor, however, was reserved for their kind only.

Fury tucked his hands into his back pockets as he moved through the people. It was easy to spot the bikers from the others since many of them were old school and covered in leather. The younger, hipper crowd wore nylon or Aerostitch suits like his while the tourists and college kids wore everything from short skirts to khaki pants to jeans.

As Fury passed the tables where customers could sit down and eat, he caught the gaze of the beautiful blond waitress who just happened to be the sister of the asshole outside.

Aimee Peltier.

Like her brother Dev, her long hair was blond, and she was tall and thin. Lithe. All in all, very attractive except for the fact that when she went to bed at night, she turned into a bear. He shuddered at the thought. His brother's taste in women left a lot to be desired.

Aimee froze the moment she saw him.

He subtly indicated the bar with his eyes to let her know he had a message for her. She was the real reason he was here, but if any of her numerous brothers found that out, they'd both be dead.

So he continued on his way to the bar where three bartenders were making drinks. Since Dev was one of a set of identical quads, Fury felt like he was seeing double as another werebear came over to him. The only reason he could pick out Dev from his other three identical brothers was from the tattoo on his arm. With the other three, well, he really didn't give a rat's ass about who it was.

The quad narrowed his eyes threateningly. "What you want, Wolf?"

Nonchalant, Fury sat down. "Tell Sasha I need to see him."

"Why you need to see him?"

Fury gave him a droll stare. "Wolf business, and the last time I sniffed, which I'm trying real hard not to do 'cause the stench of you assholes is rough on my heightened sense of smell, you're a bear. Grab his hide and send it over."

"Do you have to piss off everyone you meet?" That soft voice went down his spine like a caress.

He turned to find Margarite Neely standing beside him. Tiny and human, Margery had one of the finest posteriors he'd ever seen on a woman. But therein was the problem. She was human, and he had a hard time relating to that breed, or any breed for that matter. Social skills were so not his forte. Like Margery had pointed out, he tended to piss off anyone dumb enough to come near him. Even when he didn't mean to.

"It's a congenital habit that serves me well most days."

Laughing, she held a bottle of beer out toward him.

Fury shook his head, declining the offer. That stuff on his taste-buds . . . nasty. He frowned at her. "I'm surprised to see you down here." She was the nurse for the Peltiers, and he normally only saw her when he was injured and in need of care. As a rule, she avoided the bar area and stayed in the hidden hospital that was attached to it.

She took a swig of beer. "Yeah, but there's some bad mojo going down. I had to have a drink to steady my nerves."

Since he'd never known her to drink, that intrigued him. "What kind of bad mojo?"

Sasha joined them and answered for her. "There's a Litarian in Carson's office."

Fury scowled at Sasha, whose face was pale. If he didn't know better, he'd think the wolf was shaken. "Yeah, so? There's a lot of shit in his office most days." Carson was the resident doctor and veterinarian that all the Were-Hunters in New Orleans went to when they were in need of medical services. The fact that he had a lion in his hospital shouldn't even cause an eyebrow to raise.

Margery shook her head at him. "Not like this, Fury. He can't turn human or use his magick."

Now *that* was shocking. "What did you say?"

"The Arcadians hit him with something," she said in a low tone as if afraid of being overheard. "We don't know what. But it drained his powers instantly. He can't even project his thoughts to his mate."

Fury couldn't breathe at the thought of that happening. Even though his base and primary form was that of a wolf and he lacked a lot of magick control, he still couldn't imagine what it would be like to live entirely as an animal. "And you're sure he's not a regular lion?" It was a stupid question, but one that had to be stated.

They both gave him a "duh" stare.

Fury held his hands up in surrender. "Just checking. You guys could have had an aneurysm or something."

Margery took a deep draught of her beer. "It's been a bad day."

"Yeah," Sasha agreed, taking the bottle from her and duplicating the gesture. "We're all rattled by it. Imagine minding your own business and having a tessera come out of nowhere, pop your ass with something we can't identify, and then losing yourself forever."

Fury let out a long breath. "I saw that movie once. It sucked."

Sasha bowed his head sheepishly as he remembered Fury's past. "Sorry, man. I didn't mean anything by it."

No one ever did. Yet it stung regardless of intent.

"You needed to see me?" Sasha asked, changing the subject.

Fury checked his peripheral vision to make sure none of the bear clan were nearby. Then he gave a pointed look at Margery. "We have a bit of Wolf business, if you don't mind."

"It's all right. I need to get back upstairs anyway. The Litarian's mate had to be tranqed earlier and she should be coming out of it any moment." She stepped past him to slap the bar to get the Bear's attention. "Remi, give me one more bottle and I'm back to work."

Fury choked at her words. "Glad I'm not the patient."

Margery gave him a chiding glare. "It's for Carson."

He snorted. "And I repeat what I said. Just what I need, a bunch of drunk fucks working on me." He met Sasha's amused expression. "Remind me not to do anything stupid tonight. Oh wait, I'm here. Too late for that warning, huh?"

Sasha ignored that question as he crossed his arms over his chest and shifted his weight to one leg. "What do you need, Fury? We're not exactly friendly."

Fury led him a few feet away from where Remi was handing off another bottle of beer to Margery. "I know, but you're the only wolf the Peltiers aren't suspicious of and the only one I could trust to get this to Aimee." He palmed the small note into Sasha's hand. "Make sure you wipe your ass with it or something to get the stench of Fang off it. I did what I could, but he's pretty fragrant."

Sasha looked less than pleased by the request. "You know the last time I involved myself in subterfuge, I was mortally wounded and branded, and saw my entire clan put down over it. Take my advice and don't let your brother drag you down with him."

"Yeah, but I'm not stepping in between two gods." Which was what had almost gotten Sasha killed. "I'm just doing a favor for my brother."

"That's what I told myself, too. But the problem with family, they get you into shit and then abandon you to it. Or worse, get themselves killed off."

It was true, and he knew it. But he owed Vane and Fang for welcoming him in when no one else ever had.

For his brothers alone, he was willing to die.

"So will you give her the note?"

Sasha ground his teeth. "I'll do it. But you owe me."

Actually Fang owed him, but . . . they were brothers, and for the first time in his life, he understood what that meant. "I know and I really appreciate it."

Sasha slid the paper into his back pocket. "You know what really kills me over this is that I've never seen two animals act more human. What kind of Romeo-Juliet bullshit are they playing anyway?"

Fury shrugged. "Hell if I know. He says she's the only one who understands him. Given the girly way he's been acting lately, I actually agree with that 'cause I definitely don't get any of it. If he starts wearing lipstick and pink, I vote we take him out and shoot him. Put his whiny ass out of *my* misery."

The corner of Sasha's lips curled up as if he were trying not to smile.

"What are *you* doing here?"

Fury tensed at the sound of Nicolette "Mama" Peltier's deep French accent. Since his brother was making time with Mama's only daughter, Aimee, he more than understood her hostility toward their entire clan, but it didn't mean that he appreciated the tone.

He started to tell her what she could do with it, but before he could draw breath to answer, Sasha spoke up. "I asked him to come. I wanted to warn him about what happened to the Litarian."

Mama relaxed a degree, but her expression was still deeply troubled, "That's bad business there." She cast her gaze around the room as if looking for someone suspicious. "May the gods take mercy on us all if we don't stop the ones behind this. I shudder at the thought of what else they might be capable of."

So did Fury. "Are the bears doing anything to find out who's responsible?"

She shook her head. "*Non*, the laws of sanctuary prohibit it."

"Then I'll do some digging."

Sasha snorted. "You just can't help this kamikaze streak you have, can you?"

Fury grinned. "Not really. I find it easiest if I just go with it rather than fight it. Besides, if someone is screwing with us, I want to know who and how. Most of all, I want their throat for it."

Respect glowed in Nicolette's eyes. She looked at Sasha. "Take him upstairs before too many scents contaminate the lion so that he can track the ones who did this."

Sasha inclined his head to Nicolette before he motioned for Fury to follow after him.

Fury didn't speak as they left the bar and headed through the kitchen and into Peltier House. Once they were out of sight of any humans, Sasha used his powers to vanish and pop into the doctor's office on the second floor. Fury was a little more cautious.

Because no one had mentored him on how to use his magick when he hit puberty, his control of it was less than desirable. More to the point, he refused to let anyone know just how little control he had. No one knew his shortcomings and lived to tell them.

So he walked up the stairs to the rooms that were set aside for medical aid.

As soon as he entered the small office area, he saw Margery, Carson, and Sasha waiting for him.

"Why didn't you follow me?" Sasha snapped.

"I did."

"Yeah but—"

Fury interrupted him. "I'm not leaving a power trail for one of you assholes to use against me. Walking works for me. So where's this lion?"

Carson stepped to the back of the office where another door led into the hospital area. "I have him in here."

Fury followed him. As soon as he entered the sterile room, he froze. There was a woman leaning over the lion on the gurney, weeping. She had one hand buried deep in his mane while the other was lying palm-up on the table. In the center of her palm was the elaborate design that marked her as someone's mate. The affection she showed toward the lion made it a safe bet that he was hers.

"Anita?" Carson said gently. "This is Fury Kattalakis. He's here to help find the ones who did this."

Sniffing, she lifted her head to give him a look that said she wasn't impressed with his offer. "My pride is after the ones who caused it."

"Yeah," Carson said gently, "but the more trackers we have, the more chances to find them and hopefully get a cure."

"We are lions—"

"And I'm a wolf," Fury said, cutting her off. "If I need raw brutality and force, I'll call you. But if you're looking for someone who did you wrong, nothing tracks better than one of us."

Carson put his hand on the woman's arm. "He's right, Anita. Let him see if he can help us find the culprits before they prey on someone else."

She tightened her hand in the lion's mane before she got up and stepped away.

Fury approached the table slowly. "Is he fully animal or does he retain any human rationale?"

Carson sighed. "We're not sure."

Those words wrung a deep sob from the woman.

Fury ignored her and approached the table. The lion growled low as Fury neared him. It was an animal warning. The wolf inside Fury rose to the forefront, but he tamped it down. While the wolf might want to fight, the man knew a lion would tear him up. Sometimes it was good to have human abilities, even if those sometimes went to war with his wolf's heart.

"Easy," he said in a level tone as he balled his hand into a fist to protect his fingers. If there was nothing inside the lion but animal, it would respond to any hostile or fear pheromones it smelled. He held his hand out slowly so the lion could catch his scent and intent.

The lion swatted at him but didn't hurt him. Good. Fury put his hand on the lion's back. Leaning closer, he felt the muscles shifting, but they weren't bunching to attack. He breathed in and smelled the scent of Carson, Margery, the female lion, and others. But it was the lightest smell that sent him reeling . . .

A wolfswan.

Fury looked at the lioness. "Have you been around any other Lykos?"

Anita indicated the wolf by Carson. "Sasha."

"No," Fury said slowly. "Female."

Anita scoffed. "We don't mix with other breeds. We are purists."

Maybe . . . but there were other scents he picked up on, too. Jackal, panther, and wolf. "When were you around a jackal?"

"Never!" she spat, indignant at the mere suggestion. The jackals weren't exactly anyone's favorite breed. In the land of outcasts, they were the omega animals. The ones everyone avoided and picked on.

Sasha moved closer. "I smell it, too."

Carson exchanged a worried look with Margery. "Anita, tell us everything you can remember about the ones who attacked your mate."

"I didn't see them. Jake was out with his brother, in natural form, just running to run. They were harming no one. His brother said that a tessera of Arcadians flashed in and came at them. They fought, and the Arcadians shot Jake with something, and he went down hard. Peter ran for help."

"Where's Peter now?" Fury asked.

A tear slid from the corner of her eye. "Dead. Whatever they shot hit him in the head. He only lived long enough to tell us what happened."

Carson handed her off to Margery before he led Sasha and Fury out of the room. "I've dug through Peter's head and couldn't find anything. There's no entry wound, no exit wound, no blood. Nothing. I don't know what killed him."

That didn't bode well. "Magick?" Fury asked.

Carson shook his head. "But what would be that powerful?"

Sasha shifted his weight. "The gods."

Fury disagreed with that. "I didn't smell a god. I smelled us."

Sasha let out a long sigh. "You know how many Lykos patrias exist?"

"Since I'm the Regis for the Katagaria, yeah, I do. There are thousands of us and that's just in this time period." What he didn't tell them was that the scent was one he was more than familiar with. One from a past he'd done his damnedest to forget. "I'm going to do some digging around and see what I can come up with."

"Thank you," Carson said.

Fury disregarded his gratitude. "No offense, I'm not doing this for you. I'm worried about my people. We need to know what's causing him to hold onto his form."

"And if it's reversible," Sasha added.

Fury nodded. "I'll be in touch."

"Hey, Fury?"

He turned to Sasha who hit his chest three times with his fist, then swept his hand down. A silent gesture to let him know Sasha wouldn't forget to give the letter to Aimee. He inclined his head respectfully before he left the room and headed downstairs.

But with every step he took, his long-buried memories burned through him. He went back in time to a woman who had once been his entire world. Not his lover or relative, she'd been his best friend.

Angelia.

And in one heartbeat, when his brother had told his clan what he really was, she'd not only betrayed her sacred promise to him, she'd tried to kill him. He could still feel the bite of her knife as she drove it in to the hilt—the scar was still jagged on his chest just inches from his heart. The truth was, she hadn't really missed that organ. Her words to him had done more damage than any weapon ever could.

If she was behind this, he'd make sure it was the last mistake that bitch ever made.

2

Angelia hesitated inside the infamous Sanctuary bar. They'd popped into the third level of the limani—the area that had been designated for those teleporting in so that no one would see them—and were now trying to get the lay of the foreign landscape. Dimly lit, the club's ceiling was painted black, and the walls were made of dark red brick. Black railings and trim added to the cave-like feeling of the place.

She'd spent most of her life in medieval England, preferring the open countryside and untainted air to the chaos of twenty-first-century life. Now she knew why. Buildings like this were claustrophobic. She was used to thirty-foot arched ceilings. The flat one above her head couldn't be more than ten feet, if that.

Skittish, she eyed the electric lights around her. As a Were-Hunter, she was susceptible to electrical currents. One tiny jolt and she could lose control of not only her magick, but her human appearance as well.

How did her people live in these horribly crowded and overly electrified places? She'd never understand the appeal. Not to mention the clothes . . .

She wore a pair of blue coarse pants and a white top that, while it was soft, was very strange.

"Are you sure this is a good idea?" she whispered to her companion Dare.

He stood a full head and shoulders above her. At first glance his hair looked dark brown, but in reality it was made up of all colors: ash, auburn, brown, black, mahogany, even some blond. Long and wavy, that hair was more beautiful than any male's should be. She, herself, would kill for it. Yet he thought nothing about it or the fact he was unbelievably sexy and hot. Not that she'd ever sleep with him. He was practically Katagaria with the way he went through women, and as an Arcadian female, she found that animalistic behavior repugnant.

Still, he was one of the fiercest wolfswains in her patria, and the women of her clan had been fighting over him for centuries.

Tonight he was out for blood.

Luckily it wasn't hers.

He turned those smug hazel-green eyes on her. "If you're scared, little girl, go home."

She barely stamped down the urge to shove him in anger. His arrogance had always rubbed her the wrong way. "I fear nothing."

"Then follow and remain silent."

She made an obscene gesture behind his back as he headed for the stairs. That was the one drawback to living in the past. Male egos. Here she was, an Aristos, one of the most powerful of their breed, and he still treated her like she was his inferior waste.

Gods, how she wanted to beat him down.

But he was the grandson of their former leader and the head of her tessera, so she was honor-bound to follow him. Even if she wanted to kill him.

Remember your duty, she reminded herself. She and Dare were born of the Arcadian branch of Were-Hunters. Humans who had the ability to shift into animals. Their job was to police the Katagaria. The Were-Hunters who were animals able to shift into humans. Just because the Katagaria sometimes wore the skin of mankind didn't make the beasts one of them. They had no understanding of human rationale, complex emotions, or decorum. At the end of the day, the Katagaria were still animals. Primal. Brutal. Unpredictable. Dangerous.

They preyed on people and each other like the animals they were. None could be trusted. Ever.

Yet how ironic that it was a group of Katagaria who owned this bar and who maintained its laws of peace. In theory no one here could harm anyone else.

Yeah, right. She didn't believe that for a minute. They were probably just better at hiding the bodies.

Or eating them.

Harsh and judgmental, perhaps, but there was a sixth sense inside her that said they should leave before they finished their mission.

That feeling worsened as they descended past the second level where a bear bared his teeth at them in warning as he looked up from the card game he was playing against a group of humans. Frowning, she waited for Dare to react, but he merely continued on his way to the bottom floor. She assumed he must have missed the bear's reaction, though that wasn't like the man who normally caught every nuance of hostility around him.

Suddenly a loud electrical shriek pierced the air, making her flinch as it assaulted her wolf's hearing. She covered one ear with her hand as she prayed it wasn't bleeding. "What is that?"

Dare pointed to the stage where a group of Weres were tuning instruments. A loud guitar wailed before they started a song and the crowd cheered them.

She grimaced at the sight and sounds. "What terrible music," she groused, wishing they were back home and not in the midst of this dive.

Once they were on the ground floor, Dare was only able to take two steps before he was surrounded by five of the meanest-looking were-bears she'd ever seen. The eldest of them, who looked to be their father since he bore an uncanny resemblance to the younger ones, stood over seven feet tall. He looked down at Dare as if he were about to tear him into pieces.

"What the fuck are you doing here, Wolf?"

Dare's nostrils flared, but he knew the same thing she did. They were outnumbered and in hostile territory, surrounded by animals.

Angelia cleared her throat before she spoke to the eldest bear. "Isn't this Sanctuary?"

One of the younger blond bears shoved at Dare. "Not for him, it's not. It's more like cemetery."

Dare caught himself and held the look of hell wrath on his face. Luckily, he held his temper and didn't fight back.

Yet.

A tall blond woman, who resembled the men closely enough to be another relative, stopped beside them. She gave Dare an insulting once-over before she raked the werebears with a scathing glare.

The bearswan laughed at them. "He's not Fang, guys. Congratulations, you're about to skin an innocent wolf." Tucking her tray under her arm, she stepped away only to have the eldest bear stop her.

"He looks and smells like Fang."

She snorted. "Trust me, Papa, he's nothing like Fang. I know my wolf when I see him and that boy there is seriously lacking."

The youngest bear in the group snatched at Dare's hair. "He has the mark of a Kattalakis."

The waitress rolled her eyes. "Fine, Serre. Kill the bastard. Not like I care one way or another." She walked off without looking back.

Serre let go of Dare's hair and made a sound of disgust. "Who the hell are you?"

"Dare Kattalakis."

Angelia froze at the deep, resonant voice that went over her like ice. It was a voice she hadn't heard in centuries, and it was one that belonged to someone she'd assumed was long dead.

Fury Kattalakis.

Her heart pounding, she watched as the bears parted to let him approach. Tall and lean, Fury held the kind of toned body that most men had to work out for. But not him. Even in his younger years, he'd possessed defined muscles that had made the other males in their patria green with jealousy and the women swoon with heat.

If anything, these past centuries had honed him even more. Gone was the insecurity of his youth. The wolf before her was sharp and lethal. One who knew exactly what he was capable of.

Merciless bloodshed.

The last time she'd seen him, his blond hair had been long. It was much shorter now, falling just to his collar. But his eyes were still that unique color that was one shade darker than turquoise.

And the hatred in them sent a chill over her.

His black leather Aerostitch-styled jacket had red and yellow flames on the sleeves, and on the back was a white skull and crossbones that peeked out threateningly from behind the flames. Unzipped in the front, it showed off a plain black t-shirt underneath. The Kevlar padding on the jacket added to the width of his already wide shoulders. Black Aerostitch pants were tucked into a pair of black biker boots that held silver buckles up the sides.

She swallowed at the incredibly sexy sight he made as he stood there, ready to take them all on. And against her will, her heartbeat sped up. Whereas Dare was hot, Fury was incredible.

Mesmerizing.

And that werewolf had a butt so tight and fine, it had to be illegal even in this day and age. It was all she could do not to stare at it. Or more to the point, stare at him.

Ignoring her obvious ogling, Fury glared at Dare. "Long time no see, brother."

"Not long enough," Dare said between his clenched teeth.

"You know him?" the father bear asked.

Fury shrugged. "I used to. But if you guys want to chop him up and make hamburgers out of him, I wouldn't mind in the least. Hell, I'll even go get the grinder."

Dare moved toward him.

Serre grabbed him and held him back. "Hitting him here would be a very big mistake on your part. Even if we don't like him."

Fury winked sarcastically at the bear. "Love you, too, Serre. You guys always make me feel so welcome here. Appreciate it."

"Our pleasure." Serre let go of Dare.

The father bear sighed. "Since it appears we've made a mistake, let's leave the wolves to their business." He cast a warning look to Dare. "Remember. No spill blood."

None of them spoke until the bears were completely out of earshot.

Fury watched the two before him warily. Dare and he, along with Vane, Fang, and their two sisters, Anya and Star, were litter mates. All born at the same time to their Arcadian mother. Their mother had kept him, Dare, and Star, and then sent the others to live with their Katagari father.

That was when they'd assumed Fury had been human. Yeah. And the moment his family had found out he wasn't, they'd turned on him and tried to kill him.

So much for human compassion.

As for Angelia . . . he hated her even more than he hated his brother. At least Dare he understood. The punk had always been jealous of him. From the earliest memory of his childhood, Dare had been there, trying to push him out their mother's affections.

But Lia had been his best friend. Closer than siblings or even lovers. She'd blood-promised to stand at his back for eternity.

Then the very moment Dare had exposed his secret, she had turned on him, too. For that alone he could kill her.

Even so, he had to admit she still dazzled him. Her long black hair was shiny and soft. The kind of hair that begged a man to brush his hand through and bury his face in until he was drunk from her feminine scent. Her large dark eyes held a sleepy quality to them that was as seductive as it was pretty. And her lips . . .

Large and plump, they begged for kisses. They were also the kind of lips a man couldn't help but imagine wrapped around a part of his anatomy while she looked up at him with those dark bedroom eyes.

Damn, the very thought made him hot and hard.

Clenching his teeth, he narrowed his eyes at the scrolling marks that covered half her face. Those marked her as the worst sort of sanctimonious Arcadian.

A Sentinel.

They were the ones who thought themselves so much better than the Katagaria. Even worse, they were sworn to hunt them down and cage them like the animals the Arcadians accused them of being.

It was hard to believe he'd ever thought he cared about her. He must have been insane.

"I saw your work on the Litarian," Fury said, his tone guttural. "Want to tell me how you did it?"

Dare, whose eyes looked so much like Vane's that it was spooky as hell, glared at him. "I don't know what you're talking about."

Fury sneered at him. "Yeah, right. And I assume the two of you are here for drinks because those kind of screwed-up coincidences happen all the time." He sniffed the air. "Oh wait, what is that? Bullshit? Yes, I smell lots of bullshit."

"As if," Dare spat. "You can't smell shite in this cesspit of cheap alcohol, oversprayed perfume, and animal stench."

"Oh see, there you're wrong. I live in this cesspit. Picking out the scent of shit is my specialty, and, Brother, you reek of it. So if I were you, I'd tell me what you did, or I'm going to turn you in to the Peltier bears."

Dare scoffed. "What are they going to do? They have to maintain the laws of No Spill Blood."

"True, but there are three Omegrion reps under this roof and two more live just a howl away. We call a vote and . . . Basically, brother, you're fucked."

"No, *brother*," Dare mocked the word. "You are."

Before Fury could blink, Dare lifted a gun and aimed it at Fury's head. Fury caught Dare's wrist at the same instant it fired. Ducking and twisting, he fell to his knees, pulling Dare's arm with him.

Screams rang out around them.

"Gun!" someone shouted, causing the human patrons to panic as they ran for the door.

Angelia caught Fury by his throat.

"Hold him down!" Dare snapped as he tried to wring his hand out of Fury's.

Fury refused to let go of Dare's hand. If he did, the bastard would shoot him with whatever he'd used on the lions.

Angelia wrapped her arm around his throat, choking him. "Let him go, Fury."

Before he could answer, all three of them were thrown apart. Fury tried to get up, but someone had them pinned down with one hell of a forcefield. Growling, he struck out with his powers in anger. Instead of breaking the hold, it turned him into a wolf.

He barked at Mama Peltier, who moved to stand between them. But he knew from experience that it wasn't her powers he felt. The trouble was, he didn't know who they belonged to.

"No one comes into my house and does this," she snarled. "All three of you are banned from here, and if I ever catch you inside Sanctuary again, you won't live long enough to regret it."

"He attacked us," Dare said. "Why should we be banned?"

Dev hauled him up from the floor. "Anyone who participates in a fight is thrown out. Those are the laws."

Colt was far more gentle picking Angelia up.

"There was no bloodshed," Angelia argued.

Mama curled her lip. "Doesn't matter. You almost exposed us to the humans. Lucky for you, they evacuated quickly. Now get out."

Fury tried to turn human again to tell them what was going on, but his magick wasn't cooperating. Not even his mental powers were working. It most likely had to do with the fact that someone else's powers were holding him down.

Damn it!

Dare glared at him and made a gesture to let him know it wasn't over. Then, he and Angelia left.

"That means you, too, Wolf," Dev growled. "Max, let him go."

The forcefield dropped.

Finally he was able to turn back into a human. Though he could have done without the public nudity. Unlike other Were-Hunters, he couldn't manifest clothes at the same time as he shapeshifted. *I really hate my powers . . .*

As he reached to scoop up his clothes, they were put on his body. Confused, he looked around and caught Aimee's gaze. She inclined her head to let him know that she was the one who'd helped him. No doubt Fang had told her about his weakness.

Dev stepped forward.

"I'm going," Fury said. "But before I do, let me congratulate all of you on your stupidity. Those two assholes who just left were the ones who screwed the lions upstairs. I was trying to get the information out of them."

Dev cursed. "Why didn't you tell us?"

"I was trying. Next time you forcefield someone to the ground, you might not want to stifle their ability to talk, too."

The dragon, Max, shook his head. "I thought you were just going to insult me for holding you down. It's what you normally do whenever you speak to me."

"I probably would have had I not had something more important to tell you."

Dev cleared his throat to get their attention. "Are they from this time period?"

"No."

Mama nodded. "Then they have to be in town somewhere. There's no full moon for them to use to time jump."

Fury wished, but there was another truth about his old friend. "The woman was Aristos. She's not bound by the moon. They could be anywhere, in any time."

Dev sighed. "Well, at least we got the humans out before they saw anything unnatural happen."

"Bully that." Fury zipped his jacket up. "Now if you'll excuse me—"

"Hey."

He looked at Dev.

"You're still banned from here."

"Like I care." He'd been banned from much nicer places than this, and at least there he'd had people who'd actually cared for him . . . at least for a few years.

Without a backward glance, he left them and headed back to Ursulines. The street was strangely quiet, especially given the fact that a large number of humans had gone screaming into the night only a few minutes before. The threat of violence must have really gotten under their skin.

But that didn't change the fact that he still had a wolf to track. Two of them to be precise. Common sense told him to return to his pack and tell Vane what was happening.

Fury scoffed. "Lived my whole life without any sense. Why should I start having some now?"

As he reached his bike, a strange fissure of power went down his spine.

He turned in expectation of a fight, but before he could even move, he was hit with a fierce shock. Cursing, he hit the ground hard. Pain exploded through him as he changed into his wolf form, then human, then wolf again. He was completely immobilized as his body struggled to hold onto one form and was incapable of it.

Dare walked up to him slowly, then kicked him hard in the ribs. "You should have died, Fury. Now you're going to wish you had."

Fury lunged at him, but his muscles wouldn't cooperate. If he could lay hand or paw on the bastard, he'd rip his throat out.

He looked up at Angelia to see sympathy on her face an instant before Dare shot him again. Unbelievable pain ripped through him as he struggled to stay conscious.

It was a losing battle. In one heartbeat, everything went black.

"What are you doing?" Angelia asked Dare.

"We need to know what he knows about our experiment. More to the point, we need to know who he's been talking to. We can't afford for our secret to get out."

She cringed as she watched Fury's body continue to shift from human to white wolf and back again. At least until Dare wrapped the collar around his throat that kept him as human. Since Fury's natural form was a wolf, keeping him as a human, especially in daylight, would weaken him.

And it would hurt.

She shook her head at his actions. "You know he's not going to tell us anything."

"I wouldn't be so sure."

The Fury she remembered would never tell secrets. He'd die before he did, and he could take a lot of pain. Even as a child, he'd been stronger than any other. "How can you be so certain?"

"Because I'm going to turn him over to our Jackal."

Angelia sucked her breath in sharply at the threat. Oscar was a jackal whose heart was so black, he was more animal than man. "He's your brother, Dare."

"I have no brother. You know what the Katagaria did to my family. To *our* patria."

It was true. She'd been there the night Dare's Katagari father had led the attack on their Arcadian camp. Just a child, she'd been hidden as the attacks began. Her mother had smeared her with earth to mask her scent before she'd placed her in the cellar.

Even now, she could see the wolves as they attacked her mother and killed her while she'd watched in horror through the slats in the floor.

Dare was right. They had to protect their people. The animals needed to be stripped of their powers and put down like the rabid creatures they were.

Even Fury.

"Are you with me?" he asked.

She nodded. "I won't see another child suffer my fate. We have to protect ourselves. Whatever it takes."

3

Angelia paced the small camp they'd made as she listened to Fury insulting Oscar while he and Dare tortured Fury for information. Honestly, she didn't have the stomach for it. She never had.

Maybe Dare was right. Maybe she shouldn't be on a tessera after all.

Then again, she was a warrior of unparalleled skill. In battle, she didn't hesitate to kill or to wound. It was just the idea of beating someone who couldn't fight back that sickened her.

He's an animal.

No doubt he'd kill her in a heartbeat. She knew that with every part of herself and yet . . .

She cringed as Fury howled in pain.

An instant later, Oscar came outside toward her and the fire they'd made. Without a word, he walked past her and manifested an iron pole.

Frowning, she watched as he placed it in the fire. "What are you doing?"

"I thought a little branding might loosen his tongue."

A wave of nausea went through her.

Dare came outside the tent with the same look of disgust on his face. "I say you should ram it up his ass until he talks."

Oscar laughed.

Horrified, she didn't move until they started back with the poker in hand. "No!" she said sternly.

Oscar angled it at her. "Get out of the way."

"No," she repeated. "This is wrong. You're acting like one of *them.*"

Dare's expression was stern and cruel. "We're protecting our people."

But this wasn't protection. This was all-out cruelty. Unable to bear it, she tried another tactic. "Let me question him."

Dare frowned. "Why? Like you said, he won't say anything."

She gestured toward the tent as she tried to keep her anger under control. "You've been beating on him for hours, and it's gotten us nowhere. Let me try another approach. What will it hurt?"

Oscar put the poker back into the fire. "I need to eat anyway. You have until I finish, and then I'm going to try my way again."

Repulsed by them both, Angelia turned around and headed into the tent. The sight of Fury on the floor stopped her dead in her tracks. Still in human form, he was naked with his hands tied at an awkward angle behind his back. Another rope held his legs tied together. He was covered with bruises and cuts to the point that she could barely recognize him.

The fact that he was this wounded and in human form had to be excruciating for him. Anytime they were wounded, they reverted to their natural form. For her it was human. For Fury . . .

He was a wolf.

Trying to keep that in mind, she knelt by his side.

He growled threateningly until he looked up and met her gaze. The pain and torment in those dark turquoise eyes made her wince. And as she dropped her gaze, she saw the scar on his chest. The wound where she'd stabbed him.

Guilt tore through her over what she should never have done.

"Why don't you just finish the job," he said, his tone hostile and deadly.

"We don't want to hurt you."

He laughed bitterly. "My wounds and the glee they had in their eyes when they gave them to me tells me a different story."

She brushed the hair back from his forehead to see a vicious cut that ran along his brow. Blood poured from his nose and lips. "I'm sorry."

"We're all sorry for something. Why don't you be an animal for once and just kill me?" He glared at her. "You might as well. I'm not going to tell you shit."

"We need to know what happened to the lion."

"Go to hell."

"Fury—"

"Don't you fucking dare use my name. I'm nothing but an animal to all of you. Believe me, all of you made it more than clear to me four hundred years ago when you beat me close to death and then dumped me out to die."

"Fury—"

He barked at her like a wolf.

"Would you stop?"

He continued making wolf noises.

Sighing, Angelia shook her head. "No wonder they beat you."

Baring his teeth in true canine fashion, he growled, then woofed. There was nothing human in the sound or his demeanor.

Angelia stepped back.

The moment she was away from him, Fury slumped on the ground and stopped making any sounds at all. He lay completely still.

Was he dead?

No, his chest was still moving. She could also hear his faint breathing. As she watched him, her thoughts turned to the past. To the young man she'd once been friends with. Even though he was younger than her by four years, there had been something about him that had touched her.

Where Dare had always been arrogant and bossy, Fury had held a vulnerability that had made her protective of him. More than that, he'd never treated her as inferior. He'd seen her as a partner and confidant.

"*I'll be your family, Lia.*" Those words haunted her. It had been Fury's vow to her once he'd learned that her family had been killed by the Katagaria—by his own father's pack. "*I won't ever let the wolves hurt you. I swear it.*"

Yet she'd stood by this morning while they'd tortured him relentlessly.

It's nothing compared to what you did the last time you saw him.

It was true. She hadn't stood by him then either, and he'd been beaten a lot worse than this.

"Fury," she tried again. "Tell me what we need to know, and I promise you this will stop."

He lifted his head up to pin her with a furious glare. "I don't betray *my* friends."

"Don't you dare say that to me. I was protecting my people when I attacked you."

He let out a disbelieving snort. "From *me*? They were my people, too."

She shook her head in denial. "You don't have people. You're an animal."

He twisted his lips into a vicious snarl. "Baby, you untie me, and I'll show you just how much of an animal the man in me really is. Trust me. He's a lot cruder than the wolf is."

"Told you," Oscar said as he joined them in the tent. He angled the red-hot poker toward the flap. "You should leave. The stench of burning flesh is going to be hard on your nose."

She saw the panic in Fury's eyes as he tried to scoot away from them.

Oscar grabbed him by the hair and rolled him over. Fury kicked at him, but there wasn't much he could do given how tied up he was. Still he fought with a courage that was admirable.

"Get out," Dare said as he entered the tent.

As she started for the flap, Fury let out a howl so fierce and pain-filled that it shattered her soul. Turning, she saw that Oscar had dropped the poker across his left hip where it burned in a foul stench.

Right or wrong, she couldn't let them do this to him anymore.

She shoved Dare out of her way, then kicked Oscar back from Fury. Before they could recover themselves, she knelt by Fury's side and placed her hand on his shoulder. Using her powers, she took them out of the tent and moved them farther into the marsh where they'd been camped. Since she didn't know the area all that well, it was the safest place she could take him.

When he met her gaze, there was no gratitude there. Only rage and a hatred so sharp it was piercing. "What are you going to do now? Leave me here for the gators to eat?"

"I should." Instead, she manifested a knife to cut through the ropes that held his hands.

Fury was stunned by her actions. "Why are you helping me?"

"I don't know. Apparently I'm having a moment of extreme stupidity."

He wiped at the blood on his face as she cut the ropes on his feet. "I wish your stupidity had kicked in sooner."

She paused at the sight of the raw blister on his hip where the jackal had laid the poker. It had to be killing him. "I'm so sorry."

Fury snatched at the collar on his throat and jerked it free.

Angelia gasped at the action. No one should be able to remove their collar.

No one.

"How did you do that?"

He curled his lip at her. "I can do a lot of things when I'm not being shocked."

She started to leave, but before she could, he snapped the collar around her throat. Shrieking, she tried to use her powers to either attack him or remove it.

It was useless.

"I saved you!"

"Fuck you," he snarled. "I wouldn't have been there had the two of you not jumped me last night. You're lucky I don't return the favor you did for me."

Raw panic tore through her as she realized he could do anything to her and she'd be powerless to stop him. "What are you going to do?"

There was no mercy in his expression. No reprieve. "I ought to rip your throat out. But lucky for you, I'm just a dumb animal and killing for revenge isn't in my nature." He tightened his grip on her arm. "Killing to protect myself and those in my pack is another story. You'd do well to remember that."

As she opened her mouth to respond, Fury flashed them out of the marsh and into his brother Vane's large Victorian house.

Vane's mate was in the living room, standing by the couch where their son was napping. Tall and curvaceous with short, dark auburn hair, Bride was one of the few people Fury actually trusted. She let out an almost wolf-sounding yelp before she spun about and gave them her back. "Good grief, Fury, warn me if you're going to jump in here naked."

"Sorry, Bride," he said, trying to keep his focus. But it was getting hard given his wounds.

"What happened to you?"

He looked over his shoulder to find Vane standing in the doorway. He wanted to answer, but the drain on his powers combined with the wounds was more than he could take. His ears were buzzing. The next thing he knew, he was a wolf again and exhaustion was overtaking him.

"*Don't let her escape and don't take that collar off,*" he projected to Vane before he let the darkness take him under again.

Angelia jumped away from Fury in his wolf form. Realizing he was unconscious, she started for the door only to find a man there who bore a scary resemblance to Dare. This guy, however, was a lot more intimidating and even more handsome. "I need to leave."

He looked past her to the woman by the couch. "Bride, take the baby and get upstairs." Though his tone was commanding, it was also gentle and protective.

She heard the woman leave without questioning him.

As soon as she was gone, he narrowed those eerie hazel eyes on her that were more wolf than human. "What are you doing here and what happened to my brother?"

She tilted her head at his question. His scent . . . it was unmistakable. "You're Arcadian. A Sentinel like me." But unlike her, he chose to hide the marks on his face that designated him as one of their rare and sacred breed.

He curled his lips. "I'm nothing like you. My allegiance is to the Katagaria and it's to my brother. He told me to keep you here and so I shall."

Anger ripped through her. She had no intention of staying here. "I have to get back to my patria."

He shook his head, his face set by determination. "You're part of my mother's patria which makes you my mortal enemy. You're not leaving here until Fury allows it." He stepped past her to where Fury lay.

She was aghast at his actions. "You're kidnapping me?"

Effortlessly, he picked Fury up from the floor. No small feat given the size of the wolf. "My mother kidnapped my mate and took her back to medieval England where the male members of your patria then attempted to rape her. Be grateful I don't return that favor to you."

Those words were so eerily similar to Fury's that it sent a chill over her. "I just want to go home."

"You're safe here. No one's going to hurt you . . . unless you try to leave." He turned and carried Fury up the same stairs the woman had taken just a few minutes before.

Angelia watched him until he was out of sight. Then she ran for the front door. She'd only made it three steps before four wolves appeared in front of her. Baring their teeth and snapping, they blocked her way.

Katagaria.

She could tell from the smell of them. That scent of wolf mingled with human and magick. It was daylight which meant it was hard for them to appear human. Not impossible, but difficult, especially if they were young or inexperienced.

She tried to press forward, but the animals prevented it.

"Do what Vane told you."

She turned and froze in shock. In human form, this werewolf looked similar enough to Dare to be his twin. "Who are you?"

"Fang Kattalakis, and you better pray to whatever god you worship that nothing happens to Fury. My brother dies and I will have your throat." He looked at the wolves around her. "Keep her guarded." Then he returned to a wolf's form and ran up the stairs.

Angelia backed slowly into the living room. Catching the sight of another door to the outside, she started for it only to find more wolves in front of her.

Fear sliced through her as she remembered being a helpless child as the wolves ravaged her mother. Over and over she heard the screams and relived the nightmare of them tearing her parents into shreds. She tried to blast the wolves before her, but the collar rendered all her powers useless.

She was at their mercy.

"Get back," she snarled, throwing a lamp at one of them.

The others snarled and woofed, circling her.

She couldn't breathe, as panic set in. They were going to kill her!

Vane *wanted blood* as he saw the deep wounds on Fury's body.

"What happened?"

He turned to find Fang standing in the doorway. "It looks like the Arcadians grabbed him and had some fun with him."

Fang's nostrils flared. "I saw one of their bitches downstairs. Want me to kill her?"

No.

Vane frowned as he heard Fury's voice in his head. Fury opened his eyes to look at him.

Where is she?

"Downstairs. I have the pack guarding her."

Fury turned human instantly. "You can't do that."

"Why?"

"Her parents were killed by our pack. Ripped apart in front of her when she was only three years old. She'll be terrified."

Before Vane could respond, Fury vanished.

Angelia *kept swinging* at the wolves with her broken lamp as they closed in on her. Terrified, she wanted to scream, but the sound was lodged in her throat. All she could really see was blood, and feel the same horror she had the night her parents' screams had echoed in her head.

She couldn't breathe or think.

The next thing she knew, someone was grabbing her from behind.

She turned, trying to hit her new attacker, then froze as she saw Fury there in human form.

His touch gentle, he took the lamp from her hand and set it on the floor. His expression stoic, his eyes were every bit as blank, "I won't let them hurt you," he said, his tone soothing. "I haven't forgotten my promise."

A sob came out from deep inside her as he pulled her against him.

Fury cursed at the way she trembled in his arms. He'd never seen anyone more shaken and it pissed him off. "Back off," he barked at the others. "You're acting like fucking humans." Angry at their cruelty, he led her toward the stairs.

"I didn't need your help," she snarled at him.

But he noticed that she didn't pull away. "Believe me, I'm well acquainted with your willingness to stab and kill in cold blood."

Angelia stumbled at those harsh words that were tinged with a well-deserved hostility. It was true. He'd been unarmed when they attacked him and she'd left him to his family and their brutality.

Shame and horror filled her. "Why did you save me just now?"

"I'm a dog, remember? We're loyal even when it's stupid."

She shook her head in contradiction. "You're a wolf."

"Same difference to most people." He stopped before a door and knocked.

A gentle voice told them to enter.

Fury pushed it open and nudged her inside. "It's me, Bride. I'm still naked so I'm hanging out here. This is Angelia. She's not real fond of wolves so I thought she might want to stay with you . . . if that's okay with you?"

Bride rose from her rocking chair as she cuddled a sleeping toddler in her arms. "Are you all right, Fury?"

Angelia saw the fatigue on his face and could only imagine how much he must be hurting. Still, he'd come for her . . .

It was amazing.

"Yeah," he said in a strained tone, "but I really need to lie down and rest for awhile."

"Go sleep, sweetie."

Fury paused and met Angelia's gaze with a feral hostility so potent, it chilled her all the way to her soul. "You hurt her, you even give her a bad look that hurts her feelings and so help me, I will slaughter you like yesterday's meal and no power, yours or otherwise, will save you. Do you understand me?"

She nodded.

"I'm not kidding," he warned again.

"I know you're not."

He inclined his head to her before he shut the door.

Angelia turned to find Bride closing the distance on her. Without a word and still holding the toddler, Bride stepped past her and opened the door. Fury was back in wolf form, lying in the hallway where he must have collapsed as soon as he closed the door.

Her expression sympathetic, Bride knelt on the floor and sank one hand in his white fur. "Vane?"

He manifested in the hallway beside her. "What the hell's he doing here? I was looking for him downstairs."

"He wanted me to watch Angelia."

Vane looked at Angelia and gave her a nasty glare. "Why?"

"He said she was scared and wanted me to stay with her. What's going on?"

Vane's face softened as he looked at his mate. The love he felt for her was more than obvious and it touched Angelia's heart. No man had ever looked at her with that kind of tenderness.

He brushed a strand of hair back from her face before he dropped his hand down to the dark hair of the sleeping toddler. "I'm not sure myself, baby. Fury always talks more to you than he does me." He returned his gaze to Angelia and it turned lethal and cold. "I warn you now. Anything happens to my mate or my son, we will hunt you down and rip you into so many pieces they'll never find all of you."

Angelia stiffened. "I'm not an animal. I don't prey on people's families to get back at them."

Vane scoffed. "Oh, girl, trust me. Animals don't revenge-kill or attack without cause. That's *purely* human. So in this case, you better act like an animal and guard her with your life. 'Cause that's what I'm going to take if she so much as gets a paper cut in your presence."

Angelia returned his lethal stare with one of her own. If he thought to attack her, he was going to learn that she wasn't a weakling. She was a trained warrior and she wouldn't go down without a brutal fight. "You know, I'm really getting tired of being threatened by everyone."

"No threats. Just a stated hard-core fact."

Angelia glared at him, wanting to go for his throat. If only she wasn't wearing her collar.

"All right, people," Bride said. "Enough. You," she said to Vane, "get Fury in bed and take care of him." She stood up and walked to Angelia. "You, follow me and I promise I won't threaten you unless you do something to deserve it."

Vane laughed low in his throat. "And keep in mind that even

though she's human, she took out my mother and caged her. Don't let her humanity fool you. She can be as vicious as they come."

Bride made an air kiss at him while she cradled her son's head with one hand. "Only when I'm protecting you and Baby Boo, sweetie. Now get Fuzzhead in bed. We'll be fine."

Angelia stepped back to allow Bride to lead the way back into the nursery. The walls were a pale baby blue decorated with teddy bears and stars. She put the toddler in his matching white-and-blue crib before she lifted the side into place.

Feeling awkward, Angelia folded her arms across her chest. "How old's your son?"

"Two years. I know I should take him out of the crib, but he's a kinetic sleeper and I'm not ready for him to accidentally fall out of bed yet. Silly, huh?"

She bit back a smile at Bride's concern. "Protecting your family is never silly."

"No, it isn't." Bride sighed as she brushed a hand through the baby's dark hair. Turning, she faced Angelia. "So you want to tell me what's going on?"

Angelia debated on the sanity of that. Telling her that she'd helped kidnap Fury and then stood back while two of her tessera ruthlessly tortured him didn't seem like an award-winning act of intelligence.

More like suicide given the nature of these "people."

"I'm not sure how to answer that."

Bride's gaze narrowed. "Then you must be one of the ones who hurt him."

"No," she said indignantly. "I didn't torture him. I wouldn't do that to anyone."

Bride cocked her head suspiciously. "But you let it happen."

She was smarter than Angelia wanted. "I *did* stop them."

"After how long? Fury was in pretty bad shape and I know how much damage he can take and still stand and fight. To pass out like he did . . . someone beat on him for a while."

Angelia looked away, ashamed. It actually hurt her on a deeper level than she would have thought possible that she hadn't intervened sooner. What kind of person stood by while someone was brutalized? Especially someone she'd once called friend.

Yet twice now in her life, she'd allowed Fury to almost be killed and done nothing to protect him.

She wasn't any better than the animals she hated, and that part of herself she despised even more.

"I'm not proud of it, all right. I should have done something sooner and I know it. But I did keep them from doing anything more to him."

"You're rationalizing your cruelty."

Angelia clenched her teeth. "I'm not rationalizing anything. Honestly, I just want to go home. I don't like this time period and I don't like being here with my enemies."

Bride gave her no reprieve. "And I don't like what was done to Fury, but until I know more about it, we're not enemies. The hostility at this point is only coming from you. I told Fury I'd keep you company and that's what I'm doing. No enmity here."

Angelia cut a vicious glare toward the woman and her patronizing tone. "You have no idea what this feels like."

"Oh wait . . ." Bride said with a sarcastic laugh. "I was minding my own business when Bryani sent in a demon to kidnap me here in my time period and take me to her village in medieval England—this back when I didn't even know such things were possible. Once there, everyone I came into contact with threatened me when I'd done absolutely nothing to any of them, ever. And that included Dare Kattalakis. Then the males of their patria tried to rape me for no other reason than I was mated to Vane . . . Oh, wait, what am I saying? We hadn't gone through the mating ritual yet. They were willing to attack me for nothing more than bearing his mark. So, I think I do have a little clue about what you're feeling here. And in our defense, you're not being manhandled."

Angelia put more distance between them. What Bride described had been four years ago. And though she hadn't participated in it, she knew from the others how much damage they'd intended to do to the woman before her, and that sickened her, too. "I wasn't there when they did that to you. I was out on patrol. I only heard about it afterward."

"Well, bully for you. It was still extremely traumatic for me. And unlike *your* people, I can assure you that not a single wolf in this house will attack you unless you provoke it by something *you* do against them."

Angelia scoffed at her arrogance and naivete. "You're human. How can you entrust your life to animals? Don't you understand how savage they are?"

Bride shrugged. "My father's a veterinarian. I was raised around all kinds of animals, wild and tame, feathered, furred, scaled, and other. And honestly, I find them much more predictable than any human. They don't backstab and they don't lie or betray. In all my life, I've never had an animal hurt my feelings or make me cry because of something they did."

"Count yourself lucky," Angelia sneered. "I watched my entire family as they were eaten alive by the very pack of animals you have downstairs in your house with your child. The blood of my parents flowed from their bodies through the floorboards and drenched me while I lay in terror of being torn apart by them."

She looked to the crib where Bride's son slumbered, peacefully unaware of how much danger he was in because of his mother's stupidity. "I was only a year older than your child when it happened. My parents gave their lives for mine and I watched as they gave them. So you'll have to excuse me if I have a hard time thinking good of any animal except those who are dead or caged."

"It really makes you wonder what was done to the animals to be so provoked, doesn't it?"

Angelia turned at the sound of the low, deep voice that rumbled like thunder and sent chills over her. Standing head and shoulders above her, this man had a bad attitude so fierce it bled from every pore of his skin.

Dressed all in black, he wore jeans, Harley biker boots, and a short-sleeved t-shirt that showed off a perfect male body. He had a long silver sword earring in his left lobe with a hilt made of a skull and crossbones.

As he scanned her body, his lips were twisted into a sneer made even more ominous by his black goatee. Straight black hair that reached to his shoulders was brushed back from a pair of startlingly blue eyes.

His demeanor tough and lethal, he reminded her of a cold-blooded killer. And when he looked at her she had the feeling he was measuring her for a coffin.

Her heart pounding, she glanced down to his left hand. Each finger, including his thumb, was covered with a long, articulated silver claw and tipped with a point so sharp that it was obviously his weapon of choice. This man liked to get down and dirty with his kills.

To call him psychotic would be a step up for him.

Instinctively, she took three steps back.

Bride laughed a happy sound as she saw him and disregarded the fact that he obviously wasn't right in the head and that he was most likely an even bigger threat to them than the wolves downstairs. "Z . . . what on earth are you doing here?"

He cut those cold eyes away from her and focused on Bride. "Astrid wanted me to check on Sasha. Apparently something bad went down at Sanctuary last night and she's worried about his safety."

Bride's eyes widened. "So what do you know?"

He cut a suspicious glance toward Angelia that made her blood run cold. "Some Arcadians have found a way to trap Katagaria in their animal forms and strip out their magick. Sasha said the ones responsible attacked Fury and no one had seen him since. Hence my unannounced presence here without Trace's playmate. If Sasha's threatened, Astrid's upset. If Astrid's upset, I'm going to kill whatever's upsetting her until she's happy again. So where's Fury?"

From any other man, that would have come across as a joke, but Angelia didn't doubt for one instant that Z fully intended to carry out his threat. Especially not the way he was flexing those claws on his hand.

"Wow, Zarek," Bride said slowly, her eyes shining with amusement. "I think that may be the most words you've ever spoken to me during any single visit. Maybe even all of them combined. I'm impressed. As for Fury, I think I should state that he's not the one who upset Sasha, so please don't kill him. I'd miss him if he was gone. He was badly wounded and passed out as soon as he got home."

He let out an expletive so foul, Angelia actually blushed from it.

Zarek narrowed his gaze in her direction. "What about her? Does she know anything?" The tone of it wasn't a question. It was an undeniable threat.

Angelia straightened and tensed, ready to fight if need be. "I'm an Aristos. I don't think you want to tangle with me."

He scoffed at her bravado. "Like I give a shit. I'm a god, baby, so in the grand scheme of things, if I wanted to rip your head off and use it for a bowling ball, there's not many who could stop me and most of those who could would be too afraid of me to even try."

She had a feeling he wasn't boasting.

"Zarek," Bride said in a chiding tone. "I don't think torturing her will get you the information you want."

A slow, sinister smile curved his handsome lips. "Yeah, but it could be fun. I say let's try it and see." He stepped forward.

Bride planted herself in front of him. "I know you want to please your wife, and I can seriously appreciate that. But I told Fury that she'd be safe. Please don't make me a liar, Z."

He growled deep in his throat and for the first time Angelia respected Bride, who didn't flinch under his cutthroat scrutiny.

"Fine, Bride. But I want to know what's going on, and if I have to stay here without my wife and child for too long . . . let's just say it won't go well for any of you. Where's Vane?"

"With Fury. First door on your right."

He flexed his claws before he turned and left. He started to slam the door, then glanced back at the sleeping toddler and changed his mind.

He closed it quietly.

"Thank you," Angelia said as soon as they were alone.

"You're welcome."

She rubbed her hands up and down her arms in an effort to dispel the chills his presence had left behind. "Is he always like that?"

Bride covered her baby with a small blue blanket. "Actually, I'm told he's a lot mellower now than he used to be. When Vane first met him, he really was suicidal and psychotic."

"And you think that's changed . . . how?"

Bride smiled. "Good point, but believe it or not, when he brings his son over to play with mine, he's actually very gentle with the two of them."

That she would pay money to see. She couldn't imagine someone that insane being paternal or tender.

Pushing Zarek out of her thoughts, Angelia walked to the window to look out on the street below. It was so unlike her home. But she knew that Dare and Oscar would be looking for her. Dare was one of the best trackers in their patria. He shouldn't have any trouble finding her and bringing help.

May the gods have mercy on this pack when they arrived . . .

"So . . ." Bride said, letting her voice trail off a bit. "Care to tell me what this weapon is that you guys have invented?"

Angelia didn't speak. The weapon was ingenious, and it was one they would die to protect. With it, they had proven that mankind was at the top of the food chain. None of the animals in the Katagaria would have ever been able to design it.

It was the one thing that could protect her people from them forever.

"It really makes you wonder what was done to the animals to be so provoked, doesn't it?" Z's words haunted her. Honestly, she'd never really thought about that before. All she'd ever heard was that the attack had been unprovoked and undeserved.

She had no reason to doubt that.

But what if it hadn't been?

"Why did Bryani attack you?" she asked Bride.

"She claimed she was trying to save me from being mated to her monster of a son. Personally, I think she was just a little whacko."

That was an undisputed fact. Bryani had been the daughter of their leader. As such, her story was known by everyone. It was a story the mothers in their patria used to frighten misbehaving children. Given what the Katagaria had done to the poor woman, it was amazing she had what little sanity she did. "They kept her in their den and repeatedly raped her. Did you know that?"

Bride's expression turned sad and sympathetic. It was obvious the tragedy of that event wasn't lost on her. "Only Vane's father did that, but yes. Vane has told me everything about his family."

"And did he ever say why they attacked us that night?"

Bride frowned. "Don't you know?"

"We have theories. Everything from the wolves must have been hungry and smelled our food to they were rabid Slayers bent on drinking our blood. But no, no one knows why we were attacked."

Bride looked stunned by her words. Her expression turned from disbelief to disgust. "Oh, they know exactly what they did. They just don't want anyone else to know. Those lying dogs . . ."

Now it was Angelia's turn to be baffled. "What are you talking about?"

When Bride answered, her tone was rife with anger and disdain. "Not *one* male in your pack has ever confessed to what they did?"

"We were innocent victims."

"Yeah, and I'm the tooth fairy. Trust me. The attack was provoked." Bride shook her head. "You know, I will say this, the Katagaria at least admit what they do. They don't lie to cover it up."

"Well, if you know so much, then please enlighten me about what happened."

"Fine. The Katagaria had a group of females who were pregnant and unable to travel." That was common to both the Arcadian and Katagaria. Once a female was pregnant, she couldn't shapeshift or use her power to teleport until after the children or pups were born.

Bride folded her arms over her chest. "Since they were in medieval England at the time the females conceived, the males took their females deep into the woods away from any people or their villages to make their den in safety. They'd been there for several weeks with no problems. Then one night, the males went out to hunt for food. They found deer and were chasing them when two of the wolves ended up in snares.

"Vane's father, Markus, turned human to free the two who were trapped and while he was at it, he was approached by a group of Arcadian males—the ones who'd set those traps. Markus tried to explain that they meant no harm to them, but before he could, the Arcadians executed the two wolves in the traps, then shot arrows at the others. Outnumbered, the pack returned to their den where they found most of their women and children missing."

Angelia swallowed as a bad premonition went through her.

"The wolves tracked their scent back to Bryani's camp, where they found the remains of most of their women. They'd been butchered and their hides strung up to tan. There were a handful of pups still alive, but caged. So the wolves waited until nightfall . . . At dusk, a group of the Katagaria led the Arcadian males out of camp so that the others could go in and free their remaining women and children. Bryani's father and others attacked them and the brutal fighting you remember happened."

Angelia shook her head in denial. "You lie! They attacked us unprovoked. There was no reason for what they did. None."

"Sweetie," Bride said in a gentle tone, "you don't know the real truth any more than I do. I can only tell you what Vane's pack has told me about that event. Honestly, I believe them for several reasons. One, they don't have any females that old. Something happened to kill them off. And now every male over four hundred years old in their pack is insanely protective of any female brought in. I've been with the wolves for the last four years and not once have I seen them be aggressive to anyone unless they or their pack was threatened. Nor have I ever known one of them to lie. If anything, they're honest to the point of brutality."

Angelia still refused to believe it. "My people wouldn't have attacked women and children."

"They tried to attack me."

"In retaliation!"

"For what? Vane hadn't hurt them and I most certainly hadn't. Not one male in your entire patria, including your leader, Vane's own grandfather, would come to my defense. None. But I tell you what. If anyone or anything came into this house and threatened me, there's not a wolf downstairs who wouldn't give his life to keep me safe. And that goes for any female in their pack, too."

The baby woke up and started crying for his mother.

Bride left her to pick him up. "It's okay, Trace. Mommy's here."

He laid his head on her shoulder and rubbed his eyes. "Where's Daddy?"

"He's with Uncle Fury and Uncle Z."

The boy perked up instantly. "Bob play with Trace?"

She smiled indulgently. "No, honey. Bob didn't come with Uncle Z this time. Sorry."

He pouted until he saw Angelia. Then he turned bashful and buried his head against Bride's shoulder.

Bride kissed his cheek. "This is Angelia, Trace. Can you say hi?"

He waved at her without looking up.

In spite of it, Angelia was strangely charmed by the small boy. She'd always loved children and had hoped to one day have a litter of her own. "Hi, Trace."

He peeped at her over the safety of his mother's shoulder. Then he whispered in Bride's ear while his mother rubbed his back affectionately.

In that moment, a repressed memory came flooding back to her. It was something she hadn't thought about in centuries. Fury and several boys had been injured while climbing a tree. The boys who'd skinned their hands and knees had run to their mothers for comfort. Fury had broken his arm. Crying, he'd gone to his mother, too. Only when he reached Bryani, she'd angrily shoved him away.

Angelia's uncle had started to comfort Fury.

Bryani had stopped him with a sharp growl. "Don't you dare comfort that boy."

"He's hurt."

"Life *is* pain and there is no comfort for it. The sooner Fury accepts that, the better off he'll be. Let him know early on that the only one he can depend on is himself. He broke his arm by being stupid. He must tend to it."

Her uncle had been aghast. "He's just a child."

"No. He's my vengeance and one day I'm going to unleash him on his own father."

Angelia flinched at that memory. How could she have forgotten it? Then again, Bryani had never been an overly doting parent, so why should it stand out in her memory any more than all the other times Bryani had failed to comfort her sons? It was why Dare was so cold to everyone around him. He'd spent his entire life trying to earn his mother's acceptance.

And it was the last thing she'd ever give her children.

"Does it feel good to be hugged?"

She could still hear Fury's baffled tone as he'd asked her that. It'd been her fourteenth birthday and her uncle had hugged her before he allowed her to go outside and play with Fury. "You've been hugged, Fury."

He'd shaken his head. "No, I haven't. At least not that I remember."

She'd tried to think of a time when someone had held him, but true to his words, she couldn't recall a single time. Heartbroken, she'd put her arms around him and given him his very first hug.

Instead of hugging her back, he'd stood there with his arms at his side. Stiff. Unmoving. Not even breathing. It'd been as if he was afraid to move for fear of her hurting or abandoning him.

"Well?" she'd asked after she released him.

"You smell nice."

She'd smiled. "But did you like the hug?"

He'd walked into her then, rubbing his head against her shoulder in a very wolflike manner until she'd wrapped her arms around him again. Only then did he stop moving. "I like your hugs, Lia." Then he'd run away and hidden from her for three days.

He'd never allowed her to hug or touch him again.

Even with all the secrets they'd shared. Even when she cried. He'd never touched her. He would merely hand her a cloth to wipe her eyes with and listen until she felt better. But never had he come close to touching her again.

Until today, when he'd gone to protect her from the other wolves. Why would he have done that?

It made no sense. He was an animal. Disgusting. Brutal. Violent. There was nothing redeeming about them. And yet she couldn't shake the images of her past. The times when Fury, an animal, had been closer to her than anyone else.

"I'm a Sentinel, Fury!" She'd awakened to find her marks and had snuck out of their cottage at dawn to find Fury by the stream where he'd gone to sleep. It'd been a strange custom that she hadn't understood at the time. Only later would she learn that he slept there because he was a wolf and he'd been afraid of his family learning that secret.

He'd smiled an honest smile. Unlike the other males of their patria who'd been jealous when they learned she'd been chosen, Fury had been genuinely happy for her. "Have you told your uncle?"

"Not yet. I wanted you to be the first to know." She'd tilted her head to show him the faint markings that had yet to be fully formed. "Do you think I'll be pretty once the lines fill in?"

"You're the most beautiful wolfswan here. How could your marks ever make you anything else?"

She'd gone to hug him, but he'd run off before she could.

Even though she'd told herself he was nothing but an animal, the truth was, she'd loved him. And she'd missed him horribly.

Now he was back.

And nothing had changed. He was still an animal, and she was here to kill or maim him so that he would never be able to hurt another human being again.

4

Fury came awake slowly, his body aching. For a moment, he thought he was still trapped in human form. But as he blinked his eyes open, he breathed a sigh of relief. He was a wolf and he was home.

He rubbed his snout against the lilac-scented sheets. Bride always sprayed them with her spring water stuff whenever she made the bed. Normally he hated the smell. But today it was heaven.

"How you feel?"

He lifted his head to find Vane propped against the wall, watching him. Flashing into human form, he was grateful Vane had put him under the covers. "I'm okay."

"You look like shit."

"Yeah, well, I wouldn't date you either, asshole."

Vane gave a short laugh. "You must be feeling better. You're back to your usual surliness. And speaking of surly, Zarek was here. He wants to talk to you when you're up and about."

Why would an ex–Dark-Hunter-turned-god want to talk to him? "What does he want?"

"He filled me in on what's been happening at Sanctuary. They cancelled their celebration and have the whole place locked down until they get to the bottom of this new attack. No one can come or go."

"Good. Where's Angelia?"

"She's in the nursery and refuses to come out. I think she's hoping her patria can track her here and release her from us animals."

Fury snorted at the idea. "Nah, she's probably plotting my dismemberment." Sitting up, he took a breath before he stood and went to pull his clothes out of the chest of drawers.

"You know I can dress you."

Fury scoffed at his brother's offer. "I don't need your help."

"Then on that note, I'm going downstairs to eat dinner."

Fury's ears perked up at that. "What did Bride make?"

"Leftover turkey and ham."

"Mashed potatoes?"

"Of course. She knows how much you love them."

That made his stomach rumble greedily. Fury debated on whether he should eat or see Angelia.

He was really hungry . . .

But . . .

"Save me some."

Vane inclined his head to him. "Wouldn't think otherwise. Oh, and Fang has been dying to know if Aimee got his note."

He pulled on his pants. "I gave it to Sasha to hand to her. So I assume she has it by now unless Dare happened to eat Sasha before he could complete his mission."

"Doubtful. Z would have been a lot surlier had that happened. I'll let him know." Vane exited the room.

Fury finished dressing, then left to see Angelia. He knocked on the door before he pushed it open to find her sitting in the rocker with her back against the wall. She jerked up as if she'd been napping.

Damn, she was the sexiest thing he'd ever seen. Especially the way her lips were swollen from sleep.

She almost smiled until her face froze as if she remembered that she wasn't supposed to be nice to him. "What do you want?"

"I wanted to make sure you were all right."

She tightened her grip on the chair's arms. "No, I'm not all right. I'm stuck here with animals whom we both know I hate. How can I be all right with that?"

He gave her a droll stare. "Yeah, well, no one's beating on you. From where I stand that looks pretty damn good."

Angelia looked away from that gimlet stare of his and tried not to focus on how handsome he was. On how beautiful those turquoise eyes could be . . .

But the longer he stood there, the harder it was to remember he was nothing but an animal just like the ones who'd threatened her downstairs.

He stepped into the room.

She shot to her feet to keep distance between them. "Stay away."

"I'm not going to hurt . . ." His voice trailed off as his eyes dilated dangerously.

Angelia swallowed as she recognized her worst fear had manifested.

He'd caught her scent. Terrified, she backed into the wall and prepared to fight him until one of them was dead.

Fury couldn't move as raw lust burned through him. His body instantly hard, it was all he could do not to attack her. No wonder she'd blockaded herself in this room. "You're in heat."

She picked up Trace's brass piggy bank as if she was about to throw it at him. "Stay away from me."

That was a lot easier said than done since every male particle of him was attuned to her in a way that was virtually irresistible. The wolf in him salivated at the scent of her and it wanted nothing more than to throw her down and mount her.

Lucky for her, he wasn't the animal she thought him to be.

He approached her slowly. "I'm not going to touch you."

She threw the bank at his head.

He caught it in one hand before he returned it to its spot on the dresser.

"I'm not kidding, Fury," she growled at him.

"And neither am I. I told you I wouldn't hurt you and I have no intention of going back on my word."

Her gaze dropped down to the bulge in his pants. "I won't mate with you willingly. Ever."

Those words cut him more than they should have. "Trust me, baby, you wouldn't be worth the scratches. Unlike the Arcadian bastards you're used to, I don't have to force a woman into my bed. Sit up here and rot for all I care." He walked out and slammed the door behind him.

Angelia didn't move for several fearful heartbeats as she waited for his return.

He was gone and she was safe again . . . she hoped.

Over and over, she heard the stories in her head about how the Katagaria treated their females when they were in heat. If unmated, the woman was handed off to the unmated males of the pack, who passed her around until they'd had their fill of her. The female had no say whatsoever.

"You're all animals," she snarled, cursing the fact that it was her fertile time of the month and she was trapped here with them. "Where are you, Dare?"

As if in answer, a flash startled her.

She tensed as she realized it wasn't Dare coming to her rescue.

It was Fury. His eyes brittle with anger, he stalked toward her. A true predator bent on the gods only knew what.

"Don't touch me!" She struck out at him.

He caught her hand in his and held it. "You know what? I'm going to teach you a valuable lesson."

Before she could ask him what it was, he teleported them out of the nursery and into a dining room.

Angelia panicked as she realized the room was filled with eight male wolves in human form. By their scents, she knew they were as unmated as Fury was.

Her heart hammering, she tried to run, but Fury wouldn't let her. Blocking her escape, he quickly pulled his clothes on.

"You will sit and you will eat," he growled low in his throat. "Like a civil human," he spat the word as if it were the lowest thing imaginable.

How she wished she had her powers to blast him and make him pay for this. No doubt she'd be the first course and he'd probably hold her down while the others raped her.

Fury walked her toward the table, to the right hand of Bride where a young, handsome wolfswain sat. His eyes darkened as he caught a whiff of her scent.

Angelia braced herself for his attack.

His eyes black and dilated, he stood up slowly. This was it . . .

He was going to throw her down for all of them.

Just as she was sure he would, he inclined his head respectfully to Fury, picked up his plate and glass and moved away to sit at the other end of the table.

Fury sat her in the vacated chair.

Bride, who'd been watching curiously, let out a sigh. "I take it the two of you will be joining us."

Fury nodded. "We will."

A younger wolfswain who was sitting across the table from her stood up immediately, making Angelia flinch. "I'll get plates for them."

Bride smiled kindly. "Thank you, Keegan."

Thin and blond, he practically ran into the other room only to return with china and silverware. He handed one setting to Fury, then turned to Angelia. "Would you like me to serve you?"

"Sit, Keegan," Fury barked.

He immediately put the place setting in front of her and returned to his seat.

There was so much tension in the room that Angelia could almost taste it. Ignoring it, Fury put food on their plates and then set one in front of her.

"Uncle Furry!"

She looked up to see Trace entering the room with Fang. He ran from Fang to Fury, who scooped him up into a tight hug.

"Hey, whelp." He squeezed him even harder while the boy laughed in happiness.

"Trace hit his target!"

Fury laughed, his face softening to the expression she'd known so well in their younger years . . . before they were enemies. "Glad I wasn't here for the potty training. Good job, Fang."

Trace squirmed out of Fury's arms to run to his mom. "Trace hit three ducks, Mommy."

"That's wonderful, baby. Good job." She pulled him up to sit in her lap.

Fang's eyes widened as he neared them and he, too, caught her scent. He sucked his breath in sharply, before he sat down on the other side of Fury. "Sorry you missed Thanksgiving this afternoon."

Fury put more mashed potatoes on his plate. "Yeah, me, too."

Angelia didn't understand why that would make him sad. "Thanksgiving?"

Fury looked at her as he cut a piece of turkey on his plate. "It's an American holiday. Every year they come together with their families to give thanks for their lives and company."

"It's why all the wolves are here," Bride said. "The mated ones went home with their wives earlier. Traditionally, the unmated males stay here for dinner and marathon gaming tournaments."

Again, she had no idea what they were talking about. "Gaming tournaments?"

"Video games," Keegan said.

Fury scoffed at the young wolf's eagerness. "She's from medieval England, whelp. She has no idea what you're talking about."

"I can show you."

Fang rolled his eyes. "Down, boy. Arcadian females equate being with us to bestiality."

His face stricken, Keegan returned to his food and didn't bother to look at her anymore.

One of the older males at the table pushed his plate back. "I've lost my appetite. Thank you, Bride, for the food." He looked at Vane. "You need me to stay and help protect your house?"

"I'd appreciate it if you would. We still don't know how many are able to wield whatever took down the lion."

He inclined his head before he headed toward the living room.

Two of the others joined him.

Fang handed a bowl of bread to Fury. "So, Keeg, you been practicing Soul Calibur?"

Keegan grinned. "I'm going to pwn you so bad, buddy. No ring-outs this time."

Vane laughed. "Careful, Keegan, he's setting you up. Fang knows all the special moves for half the characters."

That set up a whole conversation about a subject Angelia had no understanding of. But as they chatted and joked with each other, she relaxed.

Strange how they didn't seem so animalistic like this . . .

They seemed almost human.

Trace slowly moved from his mother's lap around the table to all the men who took turns holding him for a bit. When he got to Fury, he stood on his legs and reached over to her.

"You got drawing face like my daddy sometimes."

Her cheeks heated up as that brought her back to the full scrutiny of the wolves.

The wolf on the other side of Keegan sighed heavily. "Damn, woman, stop panicking every time we look at you. We're not going to throw you down and . . ." He stopped as he looked at Trace. "Do what you think we're going to do. Yes, we know what's going on with you. And no, we don't do that to women."

Bride took Trace back from Fury. She handed him a roll to eat while she directed her attention to Angelia. "I know you don't know Katagaria customs. When a woman is . . ." She paused and looked at the baby before she continued, "in *your* condition, she selects the male she wants. If she can't decide, they fight and she usually picks the winner, and if he doesn't satisfy her, she picks another. But it's always the woman's choice. The males give their lives and their loyalty to their women. Since their survival hinges on their ability to procreate, that is hardwired into their beings."

As Bride started to rise, Keegan took Trace from her arms to hold. "Do you need something?" he asked her.

"Just going to the restroom, sweetie." She patted him on his arm as she walked past him.

Angelia looked at Fury as he ignored her presence.

Was that why he'd never touched her? Thinking back, she remembered how he'd always been more respectful to his mother, sister, and her than Dare had been. Always worried about them and their well-being. If they'd ever needed anything, he'd been there for them.

"Why did you bring me here?" she asked him.

He swallowed his food before he answered. "I want to know what that weapon is."

Everyone's attention focused on her and every hair on her body stood on full alert. They were poised to attack and she had a hard time controlling her panic.

"We've already had this discussion," she said between clenched teeth. "You can torture me all you want, but I will tell you nothing."

Vane laughed. "Katagaria don't torture . . . they kill."

Two of the older wolves stood up. "So we kill her?" they asked in unison without even a hint of emotion in their voices.

"No," Fury said. "I've given her my protection."

"Oh." The younger one who'd spoken picked up his plate and carried it into the kitchen.

Bride returned to the table and retook her chair.

One by one, all the men left except for Vane, Fury, Fang, and Trace.

"What happened to Zarek?" Fury asked.

Fang swirled his wine in his glass, something that struck her as very human. "He and Sasha are hunting down Dare."

"I hope they don't kill him before I do."

"He's your brother," Angelia reminded him.

Fury cut a harsh glare at her. "Let me explain something to you, babe. When Fang and Anya found out Vane was human, they protected him from our father. If he was wounded or sleeping, they'd take turns guarding his human form to make sure no one learned his secret. The instant Dare found out I was a wolf, he called out the patria to kill me. I think I should return that favor to him tenfold. At least he's a grown man, not an adolescent who had no real way to protect himself from the stronger, older warriors."

"He also has an unfair weapon. I think we should take it and . . ." Fang paused as he looked at Trace. "Put it someplace really uncomfortable."

Fury's gaze didn't leave hers. "I'd like to put it in the same place he wanted to drive that hot poker."

Angelia shook her head at his brutality. "All of you do realize that holding me here is an act of war."

Fury arched one brow. "How so?"

"You are wolves holding a patria member."

Vane snorted. "And I'm the Regis of your patria. Absent, true, but I am the head of the Kattalakis Arcadian Lykos. As such, you fall under my governance. To declare war on Fury and his Katagaria pack would require my edict, which I'd never give."

"So you condone his behavior?"

"For the first time in our relationship, and as scary as that thought is . . . yes. And as the Regis, I want to know what that weapon is that you used on the lion. Failure to give it to me will result in a trial and I think you know what the Katagaria council members will demand as punishment."

Her life. But not before she was brutalized. Whenever a Regis, especially one who ruled your particular patria requested something of you, you were compelled to give it.

Never had she hated that law more than at this moment. "We call it the Pulse."

Fury scowled. "What the hell is that?"

"It sends out small electrical charges. Not so much that it causes us to change back and forth, but rather it keeps us locked in our base form."

Bride sighed. "Like that collar you wear."

She nodded. "Only the pulse is permanent."

Fang shook his head. "It can't be. If it works on electrical impulses, it has to have a battery."

"It uses body chemicals to keep it charged."

Vane looked ill at the thought of it. "Can it be pulled out?"

"It's too small to be seen. There's no entry wound and no way to find it once it's inside a body."

Fang nodded. "That's what Carson said, too."

Bride grimaced in distaste. "Who would invent such a thing?"

"A Panther in the year 3062," Angelia said with a sigh. "He's now selling them to the highest bidders."

"Why?" Vane asked. "We don't need money like that."

Fury pinned him with an angry glare. "You're thinking like one of us, Vane. The Panther's Arcadian. Think human for a minute. Greed is their god."

Angelia was beginning to understand the differences herself.

Vane looked at Fury. "You should take her to the Lion at Sanctuary. Let her meet his mate who can no longer communicate with him. Or better yet, let her meet his children who will never know how much their father loves them. Never hear the sound of his voice as he tells them how proud he is. Or warns them of danger. Good job, really. I couldn't be prouder of your brutality."

Angelia refused to be intimidated by him. She knew better. "Animals don't do that."

Fury choked on his food before he pinned her with a vicious glare. "Yeah. I *never* said anything like that to you, did I?" He stood up and wiped his mouth. "You know what? I'm sick of looking at you. I remember a girl who used to be capable of caring about others. One who gave people the benefit of the doubt before she attacked them. But obviously she died. I want you out of here before you finish destroying what few good memories I have of that girl." He jerked the collar off her neck, then left the room.

Stunned, Angelia sat there, unable to believe what had just happened.

She was free . . .

"Uncle Furry?" Trace looked up at his mother. "Why is Furry mad, Mommy?"

"His feelings were hurt, baby. He'll be all right."

Vane met Angelia's baffled gaze. "You're free to leave. And I should warn you, the lions are out for blood. The guy you nailed . . . his brother is Paris Sabastienne, and you killed their youngest brother. While as a rule animals aren't big on vengeance, they are big on protecting their family. You've attacked them without provocation and they intend to slaughter all of you when they find you to keep you from doing this to any more members of their pride. You are their prey. Good luck."

Angelia swallowed in panic. "But I didn't shoot him."

Fang shrugged nonchalantly. "They're animals. They don't care who pulled the trigger. They're hunting by scent, and yours was all over Jake. Have a good life, cupcake, at least for the next few hours."

Angelia drew a shaky breath at his morbid forecast. As much as she hated it, she knew he was right. She wouldn't get far and there really was nothing she could do. She'd been a part of this. Willingly.

There was no way to change the past. Any more than she could keep the lions from killing her. They wouldn't listen to reason and honestly, if that had been done to someone she loved, she wouldn't be forgiving, either.

This was what she deserved for her part in Dare's brilliant plan. She would fight, but she wouldn't run. It wasn't in her. If this was her fate, then she would meet it with dignity.

Yet she didn't want to die without at least saying she was sorry to one person.

Excusing herself, she flashed from the table, up to Fury's room.

What she found there stunned her most of all.

Fury stood in front of the dresser holding the small medallion she'd given him when he'd reached puberty at twenty-seven.

"*What's this for?*" he'd asked her when she'd handed it over to him.

"You're a man now, Fury. You should have something to mark the occasion."

It hadn't been expensive or even particularly nice. Just a small circle with an X on it. Yet he'd kept it all these centuries.

Even after she'd betrayed him.

Balling it in his fist, he looked at her. "Why are you here?"

She wasn't sure really. No, that wasn't true, she knew exactly why she'd come. "I couldn't leave without telling you something."

He rolled off his retort in a dry, brittle tone. "You hate me. I suck. I'm an animal unfit to breathe the same air." He dropped the necklace back into the top drawer and closed it. "I know the tirade. I've heard it my entire life. So go away."

"No," she said, her voice cracking from the weight of her fear and guilt. "That's not what I wanted to tell you." Uncertain of her reception, she approached him slowly, like she would any wounded animal. She placed her hand over the one he had balled into a fist. "I'm sorry, Fury. You gave me your friendship and loyalty, and when I should have treasured it, I turned on you. I have no excuse for it. I could say I was afraid, but I shouldn't have been afraid of you."

Fury stared at her hand on his. All his life he'd been rejected. After he'd left his mother's patria, he hadn't reached out to anyone for fear of being hurt again. Because of his untrained powers, he'd always felt awkward around everyone.

The only person who'd ever made him feel like the man he wanted to be was . . .

Her.

"You stabbed me."

"No," she said, tightening her grip on his hand. "I stabbed at a painful memory. You know me, Fury, but what you don't know is that I have never in my life turned into a wolf. Even though it's part of me, it's a part that I have never been able to accept. I've lived my entire life trying to silence a nightmare that has never relented. We were friends, you and I. And not once since you left have I ever found anyone who made me feel like you did. In your eyes, I was always beautiful."

He met her gaze and the pain inside him scorched her. "And in your eyes, I'm a monster."

"A monster named Furry?"

He snatched his hand away from hers. "He can't pronounce my name yet."

"No, but you answer to it and you protected a woman who twice wounded you."

"So what? I'm a stupid asshole."

She reached up and touched his face. "You were never stupid."

He turned his face away. "Don't touch me. It's hard enough to fight your scent. After all, I'm just an animal and you're in heat."

Yes, she was, and the closer she was to him, the more that basic part of herself wanted to be with him. Every hormone in her body was on fire and it was weakening her will.

Or was she just using that as an excuse? The truth was, even without this she'd spent hours at night remembering him. Remembering his scent and his kindness. Wondering what it would have been like had he been Arcadian and still with her.

In all these centuries, he'd been her only real friend and she'd missed him terribly.

Swallowing her fear, she forced herself to say what she really wanted to. "Sate me, Fury."

He blinked at her words. "What?"

"I want you."

He shook his head and cast her a scathing glare. "That's your hormones talking. You don't want me. You just need to get laid."

"There's a house full of men downstairs I could pick from. Or I could go home and find one. But I don't want them."

He moved away from her.

She followed him and wrapped her arms around his waist. "Your brother told me that the lions are hunting us. I have no doubt they'll find me and kill me. But before I die, I want to do the one thing that I used to dream about."

"And that is?"

"Be with you. Why do you think while you were in the patria that I never chose a male to sleep with after I reached my prime?"

"I figured you thought they were limp."

She smiled at his insult. It was so classic Fury. "No. I was waiting for you. I wanted you to be my first." She trailed her hand down to cup him in her hand.

Fury sucked his breath in sharply. It was so hard to think while she fondled him. Hard to remember why he wanted her to leave.

"Be with me this one time." She nipped at his earlobe.

Chills ran the length of his body as the wolf in him howled in pleasure. In all honesty, he'd never taken many lovers. Mostly because of the woman whose hand was squeezing his cock through his jeans. How could he trust another one after the way she'd betrayed him?

He'd always held himself back from the other wolfswans. When they'd been in heat, he'd withdrawn until the woman had claimed another wolf.

It was easier that way. He didn't like human emotions, and he didn't like any kind of intimacy. It left him too vulnerable. Left him open to hurt, and he didn't like being hurt.

He should shove her away and forget how good it felt to be held. He was just about to do that very thing when she wrapped her arms around him and gave him the one thing he hadn't had from anyone other than his nephew.

A hug.

"Do you have anyone who holds you?"

That one question shattered his last resistance. "No."

She walked around him and lifted herself up on her toes to reach his lips. Fury hesitated. Wolves didn't kiss when they mated. It was a human action and it was one he'd never experienced.

But as her lips touched his, he realized why it meant so much to the humans. The tenderness of her breath tickling his skin. Of their breathing mingling while her tongue parted his lips to taste him. That was something the wolf in him understood.

Growling, he pulled her into his arms, tasted her fully.

Angelia moaned at the gentle ferocity of his kiss. He cupped her face in his hands as he explored every inch of her mouth. Part of her couldn't believe she was touching a wolf.

But it's Fury . . .

Her Fury.

Even though they didn't pick their mates, he was the one man she'd given her heart to, even when she'd only been a child. *"You'll always be my best friend, Fury, and one day when we're grown we'll be warriors together. You protect my back and I'll protect yours."* How innocent that promise had been.

And how hard to keep.

Fury pulled back from the kiss to look down at her with those eyes that seared her with his pain and uncertainty. She was afraid. He could smell it. He just didn't know what she was afraid of. "You know what I am, Lia. You're about to den down with an animal. Are you ready for that?"

Den down . . . it was Katagaria slang and repugnant to the Arcadians.

Angelia traced the outline of his lips. "If this is my last night to live, I want it to be with you, Fury. Had the Fates not been cruel to us and turned you into an animal when you hit puberty, we would have done this centuries ago. I know exactly what you are and I love you in spite of it." She smoothed the angry frown on his brow. "Most of all, I love you because of what you are."

Fury couldn't breathe as he heard words he'd never thought to hear from anyone's lips.

Love.

But did she mean it?

"Would you die for me, Lia?"

It was her turn to scowl. "Why do you ask me that?"

"Because I would die to keep you safe. That to me is what love is. I want to make sure that this time we both understand the terms. 'Cause if love to you is stabbing me and leaving me to die, then you can keep it."

She choked on a sob at his heartfelt words. "No, baby. That wasn't love. That was me being stupid, and I swear to you if I could go back and change that moment, I would stand there and fight for you . . . like I promised you I would."

Closing his eyes, he nuzzled his face against her cheek, stroking her skin with his whiskers. Angelia smiled at the purely wolf action. He was marking her as his. Mingling their scents together.

And honestly, she wanted his scent on her skin. It was warm and masculine. Pure Fury.

He stepped back and pulled her shirt over her head. His eyes flashing, he ran his hands over her bra, gently massaging her. She smiled at his hesitancy. "They won't bite you."

A slow smile curled his lips. "No, but their owner might."

Laughing, she nipped at his chin as she reached around to unfasten her bra.

Fury sucked his breath in sharply as she dropped the bra to the floor. On the small side, her breasts were still the most beautiful things he'd ever seen. His blood thrumming in his ears, he dipped his head down to taste her.

Angelia shuddered at the way his tongue teased her nipple. He nuzzled and suckled her in such a way that she actually came from it a few moments later. Crying out, she felt her knees give way from the ferocity of her orgasm.

Fury scooped her up in his arms and held her close as he carried her to the bed.

"How did you do that?" she asked breathlessly. "I didn't even know that could cause that."

He made a rumbling sound deep in his throat that was purely

animalistic as he laid her back on the mattress. He bent his head down to sweep his hair against her breasts while he unfastened her jeans. "I'm a wolf, Lia. Licking and tasting is our foreplay." He slid her pants and panties down her legs before he removed them and her shoes.

Her heart hammering, she waited for him to return to her.

He jerked his shirt off over his head, showing her a body that was perfect in spite of the scars and bruises that marred the deep tawny skin. Cocking his head, he watched her. "Why are you hesitating?"

"I'm not hesitating."

"Yes, you are. I might be a wolf, but I know what Arcadian wolf-swans do when they take a lover for the first time. Are you rejecting me?"

"Never," she said emphatically.

"Then why aren't you welcoming me?"

"I was afraid it would insult you. I don't know what Katagaria do. Should I turn over?"

Anger darkened his eyes. "Do you want to be screwed by an animal, or loved by a man?"

She sighed in frustration. No matter what she did, she made him angry. "I want to be with Fury as *his* lover."

Fury savored those words. "Then show me like you would any lover."

Her smile warmed him completely as she spread her legs wide. Her gaze never wavered from his as she reached down to carefully spread the folds of her body and hold herself open to him so that he could see exactly how wet she was for him. How ready and willing she was.

Arcadian custom dictated that he enter her while she was like that. They would mate face-to-face with very little tasting.

But that wasn't what he wanted. Removing his pants, he crawled up the bed between her legs.

Angelia trembled, waiting for him to enter her with one forceful thrust. Instead, he nipped her fingers, licking her moisture from them. His gaze on hers, he held her hand in his before he took her into his mouth.

Arching her back, she groaned at how good he felt there. His tongue swirled around her, delving deep inside her body. Her head swam from the intense pleasure that kept increasing more and more until she feared she'd explode from it. Unable to stand it, she buried her hand in his hair while he continued to please her.

And when she came again, he stayed there, wringing every single spasm out of her until she thought she would weep from the sweet ecstasy.

Fury was panting from the pain in his cock as he ached to take her. Among his kind, the female must be fully sated. If not, she'd take another lover after him. It was a mark of shame to have a female call for another male to satisfy her, and though he hadn't taken many lovers, he'd never had one call in for a second.

There was no way he was going to allow Angelia to be his first.

Sitting back on his haunches, he held his hand out to her.

She took it and frowned. "Is something wrong?"

He pulled her up slowly until she was sitting on the bed. "No. You wanted to know how a wolf takes his woman . . ." He moved her to the foot of the bed where he put her hands on the brass poles.

Angelia wasn't sure about this. "What are you doing?"

He kissed her passionately before he indicated the dresser with a tilt of his head. "Look in the mirror."

She did and watched as he moved around to her back. The moment he was there, he lifted her up so that they were kneeling on the bed with his chest pressed against her back. He brushed the hair away from her neck so that he could nip her skin. Wrapping her in his arms, he nuzzled her and breathed in her ear.

His muscles flexed around her as he cupped her breasts in his hands. He nudged her legs wider apart, then dipped his hand down to tease the tender folds.

Angelia watched his play, entranced by it. How could someone so fierce and dangerous be so gentle?

When she was wet and aching again, he lifted his head to meet her gaze in the mirror. With their gazes locked, he slid himself deep inside her.

She gasped at the girth and length of him there. Biting his lip, he thrust against her hips, sinking in even deeper while his hand continued to tease her. She felt her powers surging. Sex had always made her kind more powerful. Stronger. But never had she felt like this.

It was as if he were feeding her from a primal power source.

Fury buried his face against her nape as his senses swirled over how good she felt. There was nothing sweeter than the feel of her body around his. If she were a wolf, she'd be clawing at him by now, demanding he ride her harder and faster.

Instead, she let him take his time and savor her softness. Savor the beauty of intimacy. This was a side of himself that he'd seldom shared with any female.

And deep in his heart he knew why that was.

Because they'd never been his Lia. How many times had he closed his eyes and pretended it was Lia he held? Pretended it was her he smelled.

Now there was no pretending. She was here and she was his.

"Say my name, Lia," he whispered in her ear.

She frowned at him. "What?"

He thrust deep inside her and paused to look at her in the mirror. "I want to hear my name on your lips while I'm inside you. Look at me like this and tell me again that you love me."

Angelia cried out in pleasure as he thrust against her again. "I love you, Fury."

She could feel him growing larger inside her. It was something all the males of their species did. The more pleasure they felt, the more they expanded. The thick fullness caused her powers to soar even more. Arching her back, she reached over her head to cup his cheek.

He quickened his strokes while his hand continued to tease her cleft. There was a ferocity to his strokes now. One that was both commanding and possessive. She'd always heard the term of being taken by a lover, but this was the first time she'd experienced it.

And this time when she came, she actually howled from the sheer ecstasy of it.

Fury ground his teeth at the sound of her orgasm. At the sensation of her body spasming against his. It ignited his powers, arcing them until they caused the lamp on the nightstand to shatter. Still he pleased her, wanting to wring every last sigh and murmur from her.

It was only after she collapsed back against him that he allowed himself to come, too. He growled at the sudden burst as his release exploded and he finally felt his own relief.

Angelia smiled at the sight of Fury in the mirror as he buried his head against her shoulder and shuddered. His panting mixed with hers while he held her in his arms and kept her there. Unlike regular humans, they would be locked together like this until his orgasm finished—which would take several minutes. Normally, an Arcadian male would fall against her and wait for it to end.

Instead, Fury took the brunt of her weight while he nuzzled her neck and held her tight.

"Did I hurt you?" he asked.

"No."

He laid his cheek against hers and rocked her gently. Angelia smiled, placing her hand to his cheek. In all her life she'd never experienced a more tender moment.

And to think it was in the arms of an animal that she'd found it. It was inconceivable.

They stayed there like that until he finally was soft enough to pull out without hurting her. Angelia fell back on the bed.

Fury lay down beside her so that he could stare at her naked body. "You are so beautiful." He traced the Sentinel markings on her face.

"I'll bet you never thought you'd mate with an Arcadian."

"I did until I turned out to be a wolf."

She looked away at his blunt truth. "Why did you keep that secret from me?"

He laughed bitterly. "Oh gee, I can't imagine. Maybe because I was afraid you'd freak out and hate me. What a ridiculous thought that was, huh?"

Blushing, she looked away, ashamed of the fact that he'd been right about her and he shouldn't have been. "I'm sorry for that."

"It's all right. You weren't the only one who tried to kill me."

No, his entire patria, including his mother, siblings, and grandfather had tried to kill him. And still he'd managed to survive.

"Did your father welcome you in?"

"I never gave him the chance to reject me. I found his pack and when I saw how little respect he had for Vane and Fang, I decided to lay low and not tell him I was his son. I figured one near-death experience at the hands of a parent was enough for anyone." He traced circles around her breasts. "You've really never shapeshifted?"

"Why would I?"

He stopped to stare at her. "I think you should."

"Why?"

"It's part of who and what you are."

So what? "It's a part I don't have to accept or like."

"Yes, you do."

She tensed at his tone. "What are you saying?"

"I'm saying either you shift into a wolf, or I'm going to shock you and make you."

She gasped at his threat. "You wouldn't dare."

"Try me."

Horrified, she sat up. "This isn't funny, Fury. I don't want to be a wolf."

His turquoise eyes were relentless. "For one minute, humor me. You need to know what it is you hunt, and what it is you hate."

"Why?"

"Because it's what I am and I want you to understand me."

She wanted to tell him to shove that. She did understand him, but before she could say that, she stopped.

He was right. How could she understand what he was when she'd never experienced it herself? If it was important to him, then she would do this.

"For you only, and only for one minute."

He inclined his head and waited.

And waited.

When a full three minutes had gone by and she was still human, he arched a brow at her. "Well?"

"Okay. I'm doing it." Glaring at him, she flashed into her wolf's form.

Fury smiled at the sight of her on his bed. Dark brown with black and red strands running through the wolf's coat, she was as beautiful in this form as she was in her human one. He ran his hand through her fur. "See, it's not so bad, is it?"

Can you understand me?

"Of course I can. Just like you can understand me. Now look around the room. See how different things look. How much sharper sounds and scents are."

She looked up at him.

"You're still human, Lia. Even as a wolf. You retain all of yourself in this form."

She flashed back to herself. "Do you—"

"Yes. What we are in one form, we are in the other. Nothing changes."

Angelia sat there thinking that over. She'd assumed as a wolf that they became animals with no rational thought at all . . . but that hadn't been true. She'd kept all her cognizance. The only difference had been heightened senses.

Gratitude swept through her, and as she went to kiss him, a searing pain tore through her hand. Gasping, she sat back, shaking it to help alleviate the pain.

Fury cursed before he lifted his hand and blew air across it. As he did so, the geometric pattern of his pack appeared on his palm.

It was identical to the one on hers.

Holy shit . . .

"We're mates?" Angelia gasped.

Fury looked at her in disbelief. "How?"

She continued staring at her palm. In their world, the Fates determined who they would mate with at their births. The only way to find the mate was to sleep with them and if it was meant to be, they would have matching marks.

Those marks would only appear for three weeks, and if the woman failed to accept her mate within that time, she would be free to live out her life free of him. But she would never be able to have children with anyone else.

The male was left celibate until the day she died. Once mated, he could only sleep with his wife. He would never be able to have an erection for anyone else.

"We were chosen." She placed her palm to his and smiled. "You are my mate."

Fury was having a hard time with this. He'd always wondered what it would feel like to be mated. The Dark-Hunter Acheron had told him that he'd already met his mate, but he hadn't really believed him.

To have it be the one woman he'd always loved . . .

It just didn't happen like this.

He looked at Angelia, his heart pounding. "Will you accept me?"

She rolled her eyes. "No. I'm here naked with you because all my clothes fell off by accident and I can't find them."

"You're a sarcastic little critter, aren't you?"

"I learned it from you."

Laughing, Fury leaned forward to kiss her, but before he could make contact with her lips, a bright flash exploded. He pulled back and scowled as four lions appeared in his room.

Their expressions were furious as they threw something at him.

Fury caught it and then grimaced before he dropped the jackal's gruesome head to the floor. "What the hell is this?"

"I'm Paris Sabastienne," the tallest lion said, "and I'm here to kill the bitch who killed and ruined my brothers."

5

Angelia used her powers to clothe them as she braced herself for Fury to hand her over to the Litarians for their dinner.

Instead, he rose from the bed with an aura so deadly it gave her chills. "I don't know what you think you're doing here, tree-humper, but you don't come into my brother's house with that attitude and tone." He looked down to the severed head on the floor. "And you damn sure don't bring filth into the presence of my mate."

"We've tracked her scent here."

Fury gave him a sinister smirk. "And do you smell it in my room?"

One of the lions moved to grab Fury. Faster than she could blink, he twirled away from the lion and then pinned him against the wall. Hard.

"You really don't want to test me," Fury snarled, banging the lion's head into the wall. "I'm not a gazelle on the savannah, punk. I'll have your throat faster than you took the jackal's head."

Paris stepped forward. "There are four of us and one of you."

"Two of us," Angelia corrected, cutting him off from Fury. "And the only thing deadlier than a wolf is his mate when he's threatened."

Paris approached her. He sniffed the air around her as he eyed her warily.

"Is it her?" one of the other lions asked him.

"No," he said disgustedly. "We've lost the scent." He turned toward Fury. "This isn't over, Wolf. We won't stop until we're satisfied. If I find the bitch responsible, I will feast on her entrails."

Fury shoved the lion he held at Paris. "You're not welcome here. Really. Get out."

Paris made a feral growl before they vanished.

"And take your nasty trophy head with you," Fury snarled as he slung it into the portal with them so that it went wherever it was they were going.

Angelia let out a slow breath in relief. "What just happened? How did they not smell me?"

Fury shrugged. "The one power I did develop was the ability to mask my scent. Since it's now part of yours, I was able to mask yours, too."

"That's why you don't smell like a Katagari!"

He inclined his head to her in a sarcastic salute.

But that raised another question in her mind. "So how is it Dare found out about your base form if he couldn't smell it?"

Fury looked away as pain swept through him. To this day, the betrayal of it shredded his soul.

Angelia placed her hand on his cheek where he had his teeth clenched tight. "Tell me."

He didn't know why he confided in her when it went against his nature. But before he could stop himself, the truth came pouring out. "We were attacked by a group of outlaw humans in the forest. They shot an arrow. Dare didn't see it, but I did. I shoved him out of the way and took it for him."

She winced as she understood what had happened. "The pain made you change forms."

Fury nodded. "He knew as soon as I fell down. I tried to stop him before he reached the village, but by the time I got there, my mother had already been told."

The rest she remembered with crystal clarity. She'd heard the shouting and had gone to the main hall where they'd all gathered. Fury had been bleeding, but he was still in human form.

Dare had shoved him at their mother. "He's a fucking wolf, Mum. I saw it."

Bryani had grabbed Fury by the hair. "Tell me the truth. Are you a Katagari?"

Fury's gaze had gone to Angelia's. Pain, shame, and torment had shone deep in his eyes. But it was the pleading look there that had taken her breath. He'd silently begged her to stand with him.

"Answer me!" His mother had demanded.

"I'm a wolf."

They'd set on him with a vengeance so fierce that she found it hard to believe that she'd ever taken part in it. But there, in that moment . . .

She was such a fool.

"Will you ever trust me again?" she asked him.

He took her marked palm into his hand. "Do I have a choice?"

"Yes, you do. This only means I can bear your children. It has nothing to do with our hearts."

Fury sighed. No, it didn't. His parents hated one another. Even now all they did was plot each other's murders.

"If you can lay aside your hatred of my kind, I'm willing to forget the past."

Angelia looked around the room. "I will have to live here in your time, won't I?"

"Do you really think you can go home wearing the mark of a Katagari?"

He was right. They'd destroy her.

Fury stepped away to give her space. "You have three weeks to decide if you can live with me."

"I don't need three weeks, Fury. I agreed to den down with you, and so I have. I will even bond with you."

Anger sparked in his eyes at her suggestion. "No, you won't. I have too many enemies who want me dead. I won't bond your life force to mine. It's too dangerous."

She laughed. "*You* have enemies? What was that lion tessera that just left? Who were they after?" She cupped his face in her hands. "You and I should have had a lifetime together already. I allowed my stupidity to rob us of four hundred years. I don't want to lose another minute of being with you."

"You didn't feel that way twenty-four hours ago."

"You're right. But you've opened my eyes. What Dare is trying to do is wrong. I can't believe I've ruined that poor lion's life. God, how I wish I could go back and shove Dare when he fired the gun so that he'd miss."

Fury's face went stark white. "Dare killed an unarmed lion?"

"No, that was the jackal. Dare shot the one who lived."

"And your part in all this?"

"Stupid onlooker who thought she was going to make the world safe for other little girls so that they wouldn't have to watch their family get eaten. I didn't realize that I was fighting for the monsters and not against them."

Fury sighed. "Dare's not a monster. He's just an insecure asshole who wanted his mother to love him."

"And what about you?"

"I was an insecure asshole who knew he could never get too close to his mother for fear she'd smell the wolf on him and kill him."

She pulled him into her arms to kiss his lips. "Mate with me, Fury."

"You're a bossy thing, aren't you?"

"Only when there's something I want." She looked at the bed. "Shouldn't we get naked?"

He put his hands on her arms and held her back. "We have to settle this first. I want to make sure that you're mating with me out of choice and not out of fear."

"Don't you think I'm smart enough to know the difference?"

"I'm the one who has to be sure of your motivation."

Because he still didn't trust her. The sad thing was, she couldn't blame him. "Very well then. How do we end this?"

"I think I have an idea."

Angelia *sat downstairs* with Fang sniffing at her hand.

"No wonder he was acting so weird. The bastard's mated."

"Fang!" Bride snapped at him. "Leave the poor woman alone, or at least congratulate her."

"On what? Being mated to Fury seems like a nightmare to me."

There was a time Angelia would have agreed. Strange how she no longer did. "Your brother is a wonderful wolf."

Bride smiled approvingly.

"So where is lover-wolf, anyway?"

"He said he was going to see a friend about getting the lions off my trail."

Fang's face blanched.

"What?" Angelia asked, immediately scared by his reaction.

"Fury doesn't have any friends."

Why would he have lied to her? Dear gods, what was he doing? "Then where is he?"

The question had barely left her lips before Vane appeared. He glared at her before he turned to Fang. "I need you at the Omegrion. Now."

Fang frowned. "What's going on?"

"Fury has turned himself in as the one who maimed the lion."

Angelia shot to her feet. "What?!"

"You heard me! Stupid idiot. I've been summoned by Savitar who asked me to bring any witnesses who can testify to his innocence."

Fang cursed. "Where was he when it happened?"

"I don't know."

Fang shot to his feet. "I'm going."

They started to leave.

"Don't forget me." Angelia moved to stand in front of Vane.

Vane hesitated.

Fang gave him a stern look. "She's his mate, V. Let her come."

Nodding, he took her with them to Savitar's island and into the chamber room where the Omegrion met and decided the laws that governed all shapeshifters. Her entire life, Angelia had heard stories about this place. Never had she thought to see it.

Here the Regis, one representative for each branch of the Katagaria and Arcadians, met. It was amazing to her that they didn't fight. But then that was why Savitar was here.

More like a referee, Savitar held the final fate of all of them in his hands. The only problem was no one really knew what Savitar was. Or even where he came from.

"Where's Fury?" she asked Vane.

"I don't know."

"Are all the members here?"

He scanned the group. "All but Fury."

Before she could ask another question, she felt a ripple of power behind her. Turning, she found an unbelievably gorgeous man there. At least six-feet-eight, he had long dark hair and a goatee. Dressed in surf clothes, he eyed her suspiciously.

"You have your witnesses, Wolf?" he asked Vane.

"I do."

"Then let's proceed." He walked past the round table where the Omegrion members sat and took a seat on a throne that was set apart.

"Savitar?" she asked Vane.

He nodded.

Damn. He *was* scary.

Savitar let out a long, exaggerated sigh. "I know everyone here wants to be somewhere else. Trust me. So do I. But for those who haven't heard and you'd have to live under a rock . . ." He looked over to the Arcadian Hawk Regis and hesitated. "Okay, so some of you do, which is why I have to explain this. It appears some of our good Arcadians have created and now used a weapon that can take away your preternatural abilities and lock you into your base form."

Several members sucked their breaths in sharply.

Savitar nodded. "Yeah, it sucks. Two days ago, a couple of bastards decided to go hunting. I have the head of two of the four people responsible." He indicated the lions to his left. "The family of the victim wants the other two. Dead. But tortured first. I can respect that."

"Do we hunt?" Nicolette Peltier asked.

"No. It seems one of those responsible has come forward to turn himself in. He claims he killed the fourth member and doesn't want to run."

"Where is he?" Paris's brother demanded.

"Wait your turn, Lion, or I'll be wearing your eyeballs as jewelry."

The lion backed down immediately.

Savitar snapped his fingers, and Fury appeared before his throne in chains.

Angelia started for him, only to have Vane stop her.

Fury did a doubletake as he saw her. "Dammit, Vane, I told you not to—" A muzzle appeared on his face.

Savitar glared at him. "Next person or animal who interrupts me is going to get gutted."

Fury's gaze was locked on hers. *Don't speak*, he projected to her. *It's better this way. Trust me. You can go home and have your life back.*

Was he out of his mind?

That thought died as she saw Dare appear next to Fury.

Savitar eyed Dare with contempt. "We have a witness who swears he saw Fury in the act. Since that corroborates what Fury has said, I suppose your vote on his fate will be an easy one. Unless someone in the room has something more to add."

Sasha stepped forward. "Fury didn't do it. He's protecting someone. I know him. I might not like his ass, but I know he's innocent. I was there at Sanctuary when he saw the lion and he knew nothing about it."

"It's true," Nicolette Peltier said. "I, too, saw him. He told me he would find the one responsible and make them pay."

Savitar stroked his chin. "Interesting, isn't it? What do you have to say about that, Fury?"

The muzzle vanished. "They're on crack."

Savitar shook his head. "Anyone else on crack?"

Tears stung Angelia's eyes at the sacrifice Fury was willing to make. But she couldn't let him do this. Looking down, she traced his symbol on her palm.

It would have been her greatest honor to be his mate and have his children.

If only it could have been.

"Fury's innocent," she said, stepping forward. "He confessed to save—"

"Me."

Angelia froze in shock as Dare cleared his throat.

"What was that?" Savitar asked.

Dare glanced to her, then looked at Fury. "I'm the one who fired the shot that maimed the lion. The one who killed the other is already dead."

"And the others?"

"Also dead."

Fury shook his head at Dare. "Why are you doing this?"

"Because it was my wrongdoing, and I refuse to have an animal show me up by being noble. Fuck you."

"We had a bargain," Fury said under his breath.

"I'm altering it." Dare looked back at Angelia. "It's time for once that I did the right thing for the right reasons."

Savitar folded his arms over his chest. "We have another confession from Dare Kattalakis. Going once, going twice . . . are there any more confessions in the room? Anyone else want to admit to shooting a lion?" He paused. "Didn't think so."

The lions moved forward. "Then he's ours."

Savitar shook his head. "Actually, he's mine. Sorry. You've already taken the heads of two Arcadians. Be glad I don't demand justice for their families. We're going to assume they were guilty, but without a trial . . ."

The lions looked less than pleased, but no one dared to question him.

"As for this little toy they used, don't worry. I've already made sure the inventor doesn't invent anything else. I have my people tracking down the handful he sold and we should have them destroyed soon. In the meantime . . ."

Dare vanished, and Fury's shackles melted.

"Omegrion is adjourned."

The council members flashed out.

Except for the wolves and Nicolette. Fury walked over to where they were standing. He held his hand out to Sasha. "Thanks."

"No problem. And we're still not friendly."

Fury's eyes danced with humor. "Yeah, you prick, I hate your guts." He looked at Nicolette. "It was decent of you, too, to speak up."

"You are still banned from my house . . . unless you're wounded." She teleported out.

Fury shook his head, then looked at Lia. All humor died. "You were going to turn yourself in to save me."

"I told you, Fury. I will always stand at your back."

He took her hands into his and then kissed each one in turn. "My back isn't where I want you."

She arched a brow. "No? Where would you prefer me, then?" She expected him to say under him—it was what an Arcadian male would say.

But he didn't.

"I want you at my side. Always."

"Ugh," Fang groused. "Wolves, get a room."

Angelia smiled. "Sounds like a great idea."

The next thing she knew, they were home.

Savitar *didn't move* as he watched the last of the wolves clear the room. The moment it was empty, he felt a power surge next to him.

It was Zarek.

"Sasha went home, Z."

"Yeah, I know. I was checking with you about our earlier discussion."

"My demons got most of the weapons."

"But . . ."

"There are still a few out there."

Zarek cursed. "If Sasha gets nailed with one, Astrid will lose her mind."

"Believe me, Z, I know." Savitar looked out toward the clear horizon, but inside, he knew the same thing that Zarek did. There was a storm brewing. Fierce and violent.

They'd stopped this minor bout. But it was nothing compared to the one that was coming.

Fury *lay in* bed, naked, with Angelia on top of him. Their palms were still pressed together from their mating ritual.

"I still can't believe you would have died so that I could go home."

"I can't believe you were going to call me a liar and take my place under the guillotine. Next time I try to save you, woman, you better stay saved."

She laughed, then nipped at his chin. "I shall promise to behave, on only one condition."

"And that is?"

"That you bond your life force to mine."

He scowled at her. "Why is that so important to you?"

She swallowed against the lump in her throat. "Don't you know?"

"No."

"Because I love you, Wolf, and I don't ever want to spend another day in this life without you. Where you den, I den, and when you die, I die, too."

Fury looked up at her in disbelief. In all his life, he'd only ever wanted one thing.

And Lia had just given it to him. A woman he could love and depend on.

"For you, my lady wolf, I would do anything."

Anglia smiled as she felt him growing hard again. Kissing his hand, she knew that this time they wouldn't just have sex. This time they would be joined throughout all eternity.

Fear the
Darkness

New Orleans, 2007

Nick Gautier was finally home.

And he was pissed. As the taxi wended its way from the airport in the midmorning traffic toward his Bourbon Street home and he saw the scars that were still left by the hurricane Katrina, his blood literally boiled.

How could this have happened? Closing his eyes, he tried to blot out the boarded-up windows and fallen signs. The white FEMA trailers. The malls and stores that were in shambles. But those images were replaced by the news feeds he'd seen of victims stranded on rooftops, of fires burning, of rioting in the streets. . . .

Nick couldn't breathe. New Orleans was his home. His touchstone. This city had birthed him. She was his lifeblood and the soul he'd sold to be reborn. And in one heartbeat, she'd been torn asunder. Crippled.

Never in his life had he seen anything like *this*.

Growing up here, he'd lived through numerous hurricanes over the years. They hadn't had the money to evacuate like most people for the worst storms so he and his mom would get into her broken-down red Yugo or Mennie's Taurus and drive up to Hattiesburg, Mississippi, where they would camp out in a grocery store parking lot, eating Deviled Ham sandwiches on stale bread with mustard packets, until it was safe to return. Somehow his mother had always made those days fun and adventurous, even when they were hunkered down in the car during tornado warnings.

After the storms cleared, they'd come home to a sight similar to what he saw now, only on a lesser scale, but within a few weeks' time, everything would be back to normal.

It was now going on two years after the hurricane and still there were closed businesses—businesses that had been here for years, and in some cases, centuries. There were entire areas of the city that looked as if the hurricane had just blown through.

Most of his friends were either dead or relocated. People he'd known for decades.

In one heartbeat, everything had changed.

Nick gave a bitter laugh at the thought. He, personally, had changed more than anything else. No longer human, he wasn't even sure what he was anymore.

The only thing that kept him going was his furious need for vengeance on the ones he blamed for this catastrophe.

He moved his hand to scratch his neck then froze as he felt the bite mark there. By taking a blood exchange, Stryker had made him his agent. If Nick obeyed the Daimon lord then Stryker would give him the means to destroy the man who'd ruined Nick's life . . . and his town.

Acheron Parthenopaeus. At one time, they had been best friends. Brothers to the bitter end. Then Nick had made the mistake of sleeping with a woman he hadn't known was Ash's daughter.

Ash had torn him apart over it.

That he could handle. What had made them enemies was the night Nick's mother had died right after that, and Ash had allowed it. Unlike the other immortal beings who made New Orleans home, Nick knew the secrets that Ash carried. He wasn't just the leader of a group of immortal warriors who served the goddess Artemis, and protected mankind from the vampiric Daimons who ate their souls.

No . . . Ash was a god in addition to leading the Dark-Hunter army for Artemis. He had the power to do *anything* he wanted. He could have saved Nick's mom or at least brought her back from the dead the way he'd saved Kyrian Hunter and his wife Amanda. But Ash hadn't done that. He'd turned his back on Nick and left Cherise Gautier dead.

Nor had Ash saved this city from the storm. Up until the night Nick had slept with Simi, Ash had loved this city more than anything. *That* Ash would never have allowed New Orleans to suffer.

But that was before they'd become enemies. Before Nick had taken the wrong woman home.

Now Ash hated him so much that he'd taken everything from Nick.

Everything. Nick winced as he thought about Didymos—the island where Acheron had been born in ancient Greece. The island that Ash had sent to the bottom of the sea in a fit of anger very similar to the one he'd had when he sent Nick through a wall.

"Nice house."

Nick looked up as the driver's voice interrupted his thoughts. Sighing, he stared at the Bourbon Street mansion that had been his home since his graduation from high school.

"Yeah," he said under his breath. "It is."

Or at least it had been when he'd shared this place with his mother. Now . . .

As much as he wanted to be home, he was terrified of entering.

Nick got out of the taxi and paid the fee then pulled his duffle bag from the seat. Slamming the door shut, he looked up at his house and gripped the handle so tight that his fingers ached in protest.

He'd bought this house as a birthday present for his mother. He could still hear her squeal of joy as he handed her the key. See her standing beside him as she stared at him in disbelief.

"Happy Birthday, Mom."

"Oh Nicky, what have you done now? You didn't go and kill someone, did you?"

Her question had appalled him. *"Mom!"*

Still, she'd been relentless as she narrowed her blue eyes on him and stood arms akimbo. *"You ain't been doing none of that drug dealing neither, have you? Cause if you are, boy, love or no love, I'll beat you blue."*

He'd scoffed at her warning. *"Mom, you know me better than that. I would never do anything to embarrass you in front of your church friends."*

"Then how you get all this money, cher? How you able to buy a house this fancy at your age? You still a baby and I couldn't afford two bricks off this place."

"Kyrian put the house in my name, but technically he owns it. He's letting me rent it from him." It'd been a partial lie. Part of being Kyrian's Squire back when Kyrian had been a Dark-Hunter had meant that all of Kyrian's properties were owned by Nick—at least on paper. This house, though, really was Nick's. His salary had been such that he could have easily bought three houses like this, but his mother would never have believed he could make that kind of money without breaking the law.

"Broker, hmmm. That's sounds like one of those euphemisms for drug dealer to me."

"Ah, Mom, c'mon inside and see the book room. I've already got your chair in there so you can read all those romance novels you love so much."

"Baby, you spoil me. You know I don't need anything this big and fancy."

Yeah, but as a kid, he'd heard her crying enough times in the late-night hours that she couldn't do better for him than their run-down rented duplex—that the only job she could find was stripping. *"My baby deserves so much better than this."* Meanwhile her parents had lived in a nice home in Kenner and had money to burn. But they'd disowned her the minute she'd become pregnant with him. His mother had sacrificed everything to keep her son—her dignity *and* her future. And though she cried at night that she couldn't give him the things she thought a boy should have, by day, she was the best mom anyone could have hoped for.

Since the minute he was born, it had been the two of them against the world.

"You've always taken care of me, Mom. It's my turn to take care of you. I got a big house cause one day I'm going to give you enough grandkids to fill it full."

Nick winced as he swore he heard her laughter on the wind right before she'd dashed into the house to inspect it. And as he stood there with his memories, rain began pouring down on him, soaking him to the bone.

All he could think about now was the night he'd found his mother dead in that chair in the library. . . .

Unrelenting pain and grief tore through him with talons made of steel. They shredded every part of him.

How could she be gone, and by such vicious means? Her throat had been ripped out and her body drained of blood. His mother had been a tiny, frail woman. Delicate.

Defenseless.

And she was all he'd *ever* had.

"I can give you vengeance."

That had been Stryker's promise to him. The Daimon lord had told him that if Nick gave him information against Acheron and the other Dark-Hunters and the Squires who served them, then Stryker would give him the power he needed to kill Ash.

That was all Nick wanted now.

Suddenly, he heard Ash's voice in his head. *"You know, Nick. I envy you your mother. She's one hell of a lady. There's nothing I wouldn't do for her."*

He glared up at the dark clouds. "Why did you let her die, Ash?" he snarled under his breath. "God damn you!" But in his heart, he knew who was really to blame for all of this, and that hurt even more. If only he'd been a better son. A better friend. None of this would have happened.

He'd been the one who had signed on to this world where danger was an intrinsic part. Had he just told his mother the truth, then she wouldn't have gone home that night with a Daimon. She would be safe now and happy.

Instead, she'd been killed because of him, and that was a truth that cut to the deepest part of his being.

Unable to stand it, he forced himself to walk to the keypad on the gate and press the code. He half-expected it not to work, but it did.

Nick paused by the petunias his mother kept in a large vase next to the back door and moved it over so that he could get the spare key.

Everything was just as it'd been when he'd been human. . . . Only now everything was different.

Most of all, *he* was different.

His stomach churning, he opened the door and stepped into his house.

His friend, Kyl Poitiers, had told him that there had been some damage to the place during Katrina, but that the house had been restored. Nick had to give them credit—it was pristine. Nothing, other than his mother's spirited presence, was out of place.

"Oh, Nicky, look! It has one of them garbage disposals! I never thought I'd own something so fancy and look at them tiles on the wall. Is that Italian marble?"

Dropping his duffle on the kitchen floor, he glanced to the right, where the Travertine bake center was. *"Only the best for you, Mom."*

He could still see her smiling as she rushed around the room for the first time. *"Oh, you spoil me, baby. You're the only thing right I've ever done in my life. I don't know why God was so good to me that He sent you down from heaven, but I'm glad He did."*

Nick let out a bitter laugh. He wasn't heaven-sent. Like the worthless bastard who'd fathered him, he was hell-born.

Literally.

He laid the key on the countertop. The last time he'd been here, he'd been calling out for his mother. Screaming her name as he ran through the house, trying to locate her.

He'd found her upstairs.

Against his will, his feet took him right to the spot where he'd last seen her. He stood in the doorway, looking at his mother's favorite chair. In his mind, he could see her lifeless body there. But in reality, there was no trace of her death. . . .

Or his own.

He cringed at the memory. Just before where he now stood, he'd called out to the Greek goddess Artemis to make him a Dark-Hunter. When she'd refused and told him he'd have to be dead first, he'd blown his brains out right in front of her.

Afraid of how Acheron would react to his death, Artemis had made him immortal and marked him with the Dark-Hunter bow-and-arrow brand on his face, but he wasn't really one of her army who protected mankind. He had powers greater than the others.

For one, he could walk in daylight while no other Dark-Hunter could.

And now he shared powers with Stryker. . . .

Nick frowned as he saw a half-empty Coke bottle on the side table. His mother had never touched regular Coke, only diet, and he would never have dared left a drink in her secret sanctum.

Someone else had been in the house, and since there was an opened paper from today, he would say that someone had moved in and made themselves at home.

In his house.

Anger tore through him. Who would dare?

Wanting blood, he stormed through the rooms, but found each one empty, with no sign of who had dared trespass here.

"Fine," he snarled. "I'll deal with you later."

First he wanted to visit his mom. He flinched at the thought. He hadn't been to the cemetery since his worthless father had died. Even though he'd passed by the St. Louis Cemetery almost every day, it just hadn't been a place where he'd ever spent much time. It reminded him of his father and of the gang Nick once ran with. A gang that used to rob tourists who dared to enter the cemetery alone.

A gang that had almost killed him when he'd been a boy.

Yet he would go today to visit his mother. He hadn't been here for the funeral. The least he could do now was let her know he still missed her.

His heart heavy, he walked the few blocks that separated his house from Basin Street and walked through the stone entrance of the cemetery. The rains had already moved on, as they often did in New Orleans. But they had left everything sticky and hot.

Since it was morning, the wrought-iron gates were open and chained back. As a Daimon and a Dark-Hunter, Nick shouldn't be allowed to walk in daylight or go anywhere near a cemetery, yet a higher power had spared him *that* curse. Like Ash, he could walk in daylight, and unlike other Dark-Hunters, he could walk in a cemetery and not be possessed by the wandering souls that were trapped here.

Without pausing, he walked toward the Gautier family mausoleum. As he passed the raised tombs that had caused New Orleans cemeteries to be called the cities of the dead, he noted how many of them still bore traces of hurricane damage. Even Marie Laveau's tomb wasn't as colorful as it'd been. Many of the tombs were missing names and stones.

Fear crept into him at what he'd find waiting for him at his mother's resting place. But as he turned the corner toward her grave, he froze.

Menyara Chartier, a tiny, frail African-American woman, was sitting in front of the grave, talking in a whisper to his mother while she arranged bouquets of white lilies. The Voodoo high priestess paused mid-sentence and turned her head as if she knew who would be there.

"Ni—" She frowned, catching herself from saying the rest of his name.

"Aunt Mennie," he said, his voice breaking as he closed the distance between them. She'd been the woman who had delivered him, since his mother hadn't been able to afford a hospital stay. Over the early years of his life, Menyara had been the only family he and Cherise had known. For that matter, his mother had rented a room in Mennie's home until the duplex beside it had been cleared for habitation. "You're still here."

She rose slowly to her feet. Even tinier than his petite mom, she shouldn't have been intimidating to anyone over the age of five and yet there was something so powerful about her that it had never failed to quell him. Without thinking he swept her up into his arms and held her close.

"I knew you would return," she breathed before she kissed him on his branded cheek. "Your mother, she told me to watch for you."

To anyone else, that comment might have seemed odd. But Menyara was a gifted clairvoyant. She knew things no one else did.

Not even Acheron.

"I didn't kill my mother," he said as he set her down again. That was the vicious rumor that had been going around.

She patted his arm. "I know, Ambrosius. I know." She turned and indicated the tomb she'd been tending. "Every day I have come for you, to let Cherise know she's not alone."

He looked down at the stacks of flowers and rosaries that were arranged around the tomb and saw where a small group of black roses were blooming in a tiny patch of earth. "You bring her flowers?"

"No. I only arrange those the dark-haired man sends."

Nick frowned. "Dark-haired man?"

"Your friend. Acheron. Whenever he's in town, he comes and he visits, too. And every day without fail, he sends over flowers for your mother to see."

His blood ran cold. "He's not my friend, Menyara."

"You may not be his friend, Ambrosius, but he is yours."

Yeah, right. Friends didn't screw each other over the way Nick had been screwed by Ash. "You don't know him. What he's capable of."

She shook her head at him. "Ah, but I do. Even better than you. I know exactly who and what he is. I know exactly what he can do. And more to the point, I know what he cannot do. Or what he *dare* not do." Her features softened as she touched his brand, but said nothing about its presence. "All your life, I have watched you. Your mama always say that you react without thought. You feel too deep. Mourn too great. But one day, Ambrosius, you will see that you and your friend are not so different. That there is much of you in him."

"You don't know what you're talking about. I don't walk out on my friends and I damn sure don't hurt them."

She indicated the flowers with a wave of her hand. "He didn't walk out, *cher*. He was here when the devil unleashed his wrath on us. Acheron saved my life and those of many others. He brought food to us when we had nothing to eat and kept your home from being burned. Don't judge him by one bad act when he has done so many good ones."

Nick didn't want to forgive Ash. Not after all that had happened. But in spite of his anger, he felt his heart softening at the knowledge that Ash had been here—that he hadn't abandoned the city as Nick had thought. "Why are you calling me Ambrosius?"

"Because that is what you are now. Immortal." She touched the bite mark on his neck. "My little Nicky is gone. Buried by emotions so great they mock the depth of the ocean. Can you tell me if my baby boy will ever come home again?"

Nick wanted to curse at her. He wanted to shout, but in the end he felt like a lost child who only craved his mother's touch. A deep-seated sob escaped and before he could stop it, he did what he hadn't done since the night he'd found his mother dead.

He cried. All he wanted was for the unrelenting pain inside him to cease. Just for one heartbeat. He wanted time to go back to the way it'd been before—when his mother had been alive and Ash had been his best friend.

But how could it?

Everything was destroyed and every day he hated more. Not just Acheron, but everything and everyone. There was no peace for him anymore. It was as if a part of him had died with his mother.

A part of himself he feared he'd never have again.

His heart.

Menyara pulled him into her arms and held him close. She didn't speak. Still, her touch soothed him even more than words could.

She pressed her lips to the top of his head and gave a light kiss. "You were a good boy, Ambrosius. Cherise still believes in you and so do I. She wants you to let go of your anger. Be happy again."

He pulled back with a curse at her words that reminded him of something his mother would say. "How can I let everything go while my mother is dead?"

"How can you not?" she insisted. "It was your mother's time to leave this world. She is happier now that she can watch over you and—"

"Don't say that to me," he growled from between clenched teeth. "I hate it when people say that shit. She's not happier dead. How could she be?"

Menyara pushed him toward the walkway. "Then go from this place and don't taint her peace with your hatred. It doesn't belong here. Your mother deserves better than that from you."

He opened his mouth to speak.

"I don't want to hear it and neither does your poor mother, God rest her soul. You go on now and get out of here. Don't come back until you get your head on straight and think of someone other than yourself. You hear me? You show your mother the respect she deserves for the decision she made."

Nick narrowed his eyes. He'd argue with her, but he knew her better than that. There was no talking to Menyara when she was in a mood like this.

Disgusted with the whole thing, he turned and left, with no real destination in mind. He merely slinked off toward Conti. The streets were eerily familiar, and at the same time they, like him, were so empty. This time of year, there should have been tons of tourists about. Shopkeepers should have been hosing off the balconies and streets.

Instead there were orange barrels and construction sites all around. The sound of jackhammers had replaced that of morning jazz and beeping horns.

Pain infiltrated every particle of his body. . . .

Until he crossed over to Acme Oyster House on Iberville. God, how many times had he eaten here? How many laughs and beers had he shared with his mother and friends?

It looked the same, only fresher from reconstruction. He stood beside the window, watching the waiters take orders and people chat . . . until his gaze fell to the table in a corner, near the back.

His heart stopped beating. It was Kyrian Hunter and his wife with their daughter Marissa and a baby boy Nick had never seen before. They were laughing and chatting with other people Nick had once called friends—Vane and Bride, Julian and Grace. But what absolutely floored him was the fact that they were sharing a table with Valerius and Tabitha. Since Tabitha was the twin sister of Amanda, that wasn't the shocker.

Valerius was what stunned him.

A mortal enemy of Julian and Kyrian, Valerius's family had tricked and killed Kyrian—then destroyed the people and country the two of them had fought and died to protect. For centuries, they had nursed bitter hatred toward each other.

And now Kyrian was handing his son over to a man he'd once sworn to decapitate. . . .

How had *this* happened?

When had this happened?

How could Kyrian ever sit down at a table with a man whose family had taken Kyrian's wife, destroyed Kyrian's country and caused Kyrian's father to kill himself? Never mind laugh with the bastard.

How could anyone forgive that?

"Nick?"

He jerked at the quiet whisper from behind him. It was Stryker's half sister, Satara. Tall and dazzling, she was the epitome of feminine beauty and grace.

He stepped back so that the others couldn't see him on the street. "What are you doing here?"

"I felt a strange sensation coming from you and I wanted to see what caused it."

He hated that sharing blood with her allowed her to feel his emotions. It was irritating to have someone, other than Menyara, read him so easily. "Nothing. Go home, Satara."

She tilted her head as if looking to see Kyrian and the others inside. "It's interesting, isn't it? Why Acheron brought them back to life after they'd died, but refused to do the same for your beloved mother. I wonder why he chose them over her?"

He ground his teeth. "I don't need you to poke that scab."

"True. I'm sure it's still raw and bleeding."

She had no idea.

"But," she said, stepping close enough to whisper in his ear. "Why should they be here, living happily, while your mother is dead?"

He knew she was intentionally kicking at his groin. Making him bleed internally. "Don't start with me, Satara. That man and his family are all I have left."

She cocked her head. "Are they? What do you think they'll say when they find out you're a Daimon Dark-Hunter? That through you, Stryker can see and hear all *they* do?"

He started away from her, but she pulled him to a stop. Her long nails bit into his forearm.

"The old Voodoo bitch told you that Acheron helped here in New Orleans after the hurricane, but did she tell you who his mother is?"

Nick froze at her words. "Ash has a mother? Alive?"

She smiled. "Ooo, another secret he kept from you, huh? So much for being best friends. Makes you wonder what other things you don't know, doesn't it?"

Yes, it did. He snatched his arm from her grasp. "Who is his mother?"

"The Atlantean goddess Apollymi. But she's better known to the immortal world as the Great Destroyer."

He gaped at her disclosure. "Destroyer?"

"Yes. For no other reason than she was having a bad hair day, she has unleashed unrelenting storms against civilizations for centuries, and she was highly upset that night when Desiderius played havoc here in New Orleans."

Nick couldn't breathe as he recalled that night. Desiderius had been Stryker's agent and he had been the one who had killed Nick's mother.

Satara leaned in to him to whisper again. "She's also the mother of my brother Stryker. You know him. Leader of the Spathi Daimons. Who do you think pulls my brother's leash? Who do you think controls Stryker's army and what they do? Apollymi commands them all to action."

Including the one who murdered my mother . . .

Nick felt rage swell up inside him at all the truths Ash had kept from him and the others. "Ash's mother is the leader of the Daimons?"

"Yes, she is. Now you know why Ash keeps so many secrets from everyone. How would it look to all of you to know his beloved mother is the one who controls your enemies? The enemies who come out every night to prey on you and humanity. That's why Ash hasn't told any of you about the Spathi Daimons, such as Desiderius. Why Ash will always stay out of such conflicts. He's not the big bad. His mother is." She smirked at him. "Face it, Nick. Ash has been lying to all of you from the very beginning. Artemis doesn't control him. He controls her. She lives in complete fear of him."

And as Artemis's niece and handmaiden, Satara would know.

Nick remembered the night he'd killed himself in front of Artemis. Satara was right. The goddess had been terrified of Acheron and his reaction to Nick's death. That alone had caused her to bring Nick back to life.

Still, he couldn't get Menyara's words out of his mind. She was the one person he did trust. Without question or fail. "Menyara has never been wrong about anyone."

"Menyara has never met a god who can alter someone's thoughts and perceptions. Think about it, Nick. How many times have the Were-Hunters tampered with someone's mind to make them forget they saw something preternatural?"

More times than he could count. "But Ash has always profraned doing that."

"That's what he says. Yet how often do people preach one thing then do another?"

Again, she was right.

She leaned against him and rubbed his biceps. "You are blessed with the truth, Nick. Nothing in the Dark-Hunter world is what it seems. Acheron has duped everyone . . . but you. The question is, are you going to let him continue to get away with hurting people for his mother or are you going to stop him? How many more people must die because Acheron is a cruel, sadistic bastard? It's him or us, Nick. Whose side are you on?"

His own. To hell with the rest of them. But he didn't want her to know that. Not yet, anyway.

She toyed with his hair. "Stryker has given you the means for vengeance. The only question is, are you man enough to take it?"

He curled his lip at her. "I'm not a man, Satara. I'm an immortal with god powers."

She inclined her head to him. "And as long as you don't forget that, Acheron is yours."

Nick glanced back at the restaurant and the truth pierced him hard. He would have gladly sacrificed Kyrian and his family to have his mother back. Friendship was one thing. Family was another. Though Kyrian had been like a brother to him, he wasn't blood. Nick had been willing to sell his soul for vengeance and he still was.

"Be true to us, Nick, and we can give you what you want most."

Nick sneered at her. "You don't know what I want."

"Yes, I do. You want revenge and you want your mother back."

"I can get my own revenge."

"True, and we can give you your mom."

He scowled at her. What the hell was she talking about now? The bitch was crazy. "Don't be stupid. My mother's dead. There's no way back from that."

She arched her brow at him. "Isn't there? You're here and yet you were once dead. As was Desiderius." She snapped her fingers. An instant later, a tall, dark-haired man appeared beside them. At six foot four, Nick wasn't used to many men who made him crane his neck, but this one did. And by the luminescent blue eyes, Nick knew exactly who and what this man was.

A Dream-Hunter.

Gods of sleep, they were sent from Olympus to help and protect dreamers. And through a pact with Acheron, many of them were sent to aid Dark-Hunters. To help them heal, especially when they were asleep, so that they could continue to protect mankind from the evil that preyed on them.

This wasn't the first Dream-Hunter to approach him. Nick had sent M'Adoc away as soon as the god had offered to help Nick forget the pain of his mother's death.

He never wanted to forget his mother or what had happened to her.

Nick jerked his chin toward the newcomer. "I don't need his help."

"Of course you don't, Nicky. But Kratos can do the one thing even Acheron can't do."

"And that is?"

"Bring a soul out of its eternal rest and return it to the land of the living."

Nick wasn't stupid enough to buy what she was selling. "At what price?"

"An act of loyalty to us. You bring Kyrian's child Marissa down to Kalosis and we will return your mother to this world."

Still, he was skeptical. "You can't do that."

Satara gave him a smug smile. "Kratos. A demonstration, please."

Before Nick could move, the Dream-Hunter touched him. His grip seared Nick's skin, making it burn and crawl as images tore through him. He saw his mother in a garden, surrounded by roses. Her shoulder-length blond hair was glistening in the light while she laughed at a group of children who were playing around her.

A tear slid down his cheek as he saw her kind face again. "Mom," he whispered.

His mother cocked her head as if she could hear him. "My Nicky," she breathed. "I miss you."

"I can take you into the Underworld," the Dream-Hunter said. "But it won't be easy." He released Nick and the image of his mother instantly vanished.

Nick struggled to breathe. "How do I know I can trust you?"

Kratos shrugged. "I have no emotions. I only do as I'm told. Betrayal is for those who have something to gain."

It was true. The Dream-Hunters had been cursed by Zeus to feel nothing.

Satara smiled at him. "It's too soon, Nick. I know. You go home now and rest. When you're ready to have your mother back, bring Marissa to us."

He nodded before he turned back and did what she said.

Satara narrowed her eyes as Nick vanished from sight. He was being rather willful, but they could still control him. He needed their blood to live, and so long as they had him tied down, there was nothing he could do to escape.

At least nothing that didn't involve him begging Acheron for help, and that was the last thing Nick would do, thanks to her and her half-truths about Acheron and his powers.

"You know I can't bring his mother back." Kratos said.

She scoffed at him. "Of course not. We get Marissa, and both he and his mother can roast in their hell for all I care. But you are another matter. I want you in his dreams, every night, working on him. He has enough anger to feed you well, my Skotos. Play on that anger. Build it higher until he's willing to do anything to free his mother and kill Acheron."

She saw the hesitation in Kratos's eyes.

She curled her lip. "Oh, don't tell me you're going to be a wuss, too. I'm sick to death of weak men around me."

He grabbed her and shoved her against the wall. "I'm not weak, Satara. You'd do well to remember that."

She tsked at him. "For a god with no emotions, you seem rather testy."

He released her. "I'm siphoning off you and your hatred. Even in this realm, it's pungent."

"Leave my hatred alone. I don't want it diminished. Remember, Dream-Hunter, I'm a god, too. Fuck with me and I'll bring down the wrath of Zeus on you."

He scoffed at her. "You're only a demigod, and a servant at that."

"But dear old Grandpa Zeus will take an audience with me and then he'll take your head. Are you willing to chance that?"

He took a step back and gave her a look that let her know she should be on guard while sleeping in the future.

"Just do your part, Kratos, and I'll do mine. The Oneroi don't monitor the dreams of Daimons. You help me keep Nick turned against Acheron and I will give you a playground unimagined by your brethren."

Kratos swallowed at her promise. Three weeks ago, he'd been one of the Oneroi. A servant of the gods who protected humans and immortals while they slept. Then Satara had summoned him in her dreams and had turned him Skoti. She'd seduced him with her body and made him crave emotions like a drug. Now he couldn't stand the emptiness of his existence. He only wanted to feel, and he was willing to do anything to keep his newfound emotions.

She was right. His kind didn't prey on Daimons, and if they were half as enticing as her then he would have a banquet at his fingertips.

And all he had to do was feed the Dark-Hunter's anger and grief. Simple.

"It's a deal, Satara. You give me what I need and I'll give you what you want."

She smiled. What she wanted was simple. Nick Gautier's loyalty and the baby Marissa. With those two things, she could bring down both the Greek and the Atlantean pantheons.

Then she would be a god and she would make Apollymi look weak.

And Nick, Acheron, and Kratos would be her eternal slaves, as would all of mankind.

Where Angels Fear to Tread

1

From humble beginnings come great things.

Zeke Jacobson rolled his eyes as he read the strip of paper he'd just fished out of his broken fortune cookie. "Well, you can't get more humble than me," he muttered as the phone rang.

His stomach clenching in dread of the latest complaint, he picked up the receiver and glanced around his pale gray cube walls. This drab soul-sucking hellhole was where he spent an average of fifty hours a week in absolute effing misery. There were times when he swore he could hear his life ticking away with every swipe of the second hand on the Transformers clock his sister had given him years ago.

Optimus Prime stared at him from his perch next to Zeke's gloomy gray monitor, mocking him with a childhood memory of how he'd thought his life would be once he was a grown-up.

This was definitely *not* his dream.

He sighed and reached for his vat of Tums. "Good afternoon. Taylor Transportation. Claims Division. Zeke speaking. How may I help you?" The worst part of the job? He sometimes heard those words even in his sleep.

The irate woman on the other end laid into him over the fact he'd rejected her dubious claim that their delivery truck had mowed down her mailbox and kept going. If she'd spoken to the driver the way she was speaking to him, she was lucky the driver hadn't mowed her down first.

Her voice held that high-pitched nasal quality that went down a man's spine like a shredder. "You're a pathetic idiot if you don't believe your driver did that."

Zeke didn't speak as she continued shrieking at him.

And for the glorious honor of being bitched at constantly, and the esteemed title of Claims Investigator, he'd given up five years of his life as he went to college, worked three shitty jobs, created a debt his great-grandkids would curse him over, and got the holy honor of MBA. More Bullshit Allowed. Unlike his more intelligent counterparts, he'd actually studied and had graduated with honors, thinking he'd have a bright future. . . .

Yeah, this was his life and he hated every minute of it.

Well, not *every, single* minute. But enough that he dreaded what more wondrous developments the future would hold.

Where oh where is that Pink Power Ranger babe who was supposed to kidnap me and make me part of her merry band?

When he'd dreamed of his future, never once had he seen himself sitting in a cube ten hours a day having people yell at him, while he glibly took it for fear of losing his gargantuan thirty-thou-a-year salary.

The highlights of his life? Drinking beer and playing basketball on the weekends with his friends.

Damn, the woman's right. I am a pathetic idiot.

"Are you even listening to me?" she droned.

"Yes, ma'am. I understand what you're saying. But there's no evidence that our driver did that. I have a sworn statement from him that he didn't hit the mailbox."

"Fuck you, you stupid bastard!"

"Yes, ma'am. You have a good day, too."

She slammed the phone down hard enough for it to ring in his ear.

Hanging it up, Zeke groaned before he put his head to his laminated desk and beat it against the cold, granite-looking finish. *Maybe I'll get a concussion. . . .*

The phone rang again.

He lifted his head to glare at Optimus Prime. It was only eleven in the morning. Was it too much to ask for one little brain aneurysm?

Just one.

His stomach churning, he picked the phone up and repeated his work litany.

"Am I speaking to Ezekiel Malachi Jacobson?"

Zeke cringed at the name his grandfather, a devout Baptist preacher, had cursed him, the only grandson, with at birth. God, how he hated hearing all that said at once. It was a name that had gotten his ass kicked on many an occasion at school. It had even caused one college roommate to move out of his dorm room before Zeke arrived.

Really, I'm not an escapee from Children of the Corn. *I've only thought about mutilating me. Not others.*

"That would be me." *God, don't let this be someone I owe money to.*

I did pay all my bills this month?

Right?

"My name is Robert West. I'm the attorney for your granduncle Michael Jacobson."

Zeke scowled at the unfamiliar name. "Who?"

"He was your grandfather's youngest brother."

That was weird. He'd thought all of those relatives were long gone.

"I'm sad to say that your granduncle passed away a few weeks ago and named me as the executor of his will. Since he wasn't married and didn't have children, he's left everything to you."

Am I being punk'd? Like one of those Nigerian lottery e-mails?

"Left it to *me*? What about my sister?"

"He only named you, son."

Oooo-kay . . . Zeke listened as the lawyer gave him more details about this mystery relative he'd never heard of before. Wow, and here he thought his life was insignificant.

Old Uncle What's-his-face might be the only one to lead a more lonely and pathetic life than Zeke.

Yeah, this was what he needed. Confirmation of how awful his own future death would be.

And as the lawyer continued to talk, he was quite certain Optimus was laughing his Autobot ass off at this new form of hell that was being dumped on him.

2

"Can you imagine how lonely he must have been?"

Zeke paused at his sister Mary's question. At five ten, she was only a couple of inches shorter than him. And like him, she had straight black hair and creepy topaz-colored eyes that their grandmother used to call the devil's gold.

He indicated the brass bed behind her that was covered with an old-fashioned quilt. "Yeah. The lawyer said he died in his bed. Three days before anyone found the body."

She jumped away from the footboard and scowled at him. "Ew! Thanks, Zeke. You're such a sick bastard."

"Apparently so, since that's all anyone ever says to me."

She ruffled his hair. "Oh, poor baby. We have to find you a better job one day."

"Never happen, sis. I sold my soul to the devil for thirty thou a year." Zeke glanced around the room that was litered with ancient artifacts from Egypt, Persia, and other cultures he could only guess at.

Mary wrinkled her nose at him. "What was it Grandpa used to say? You may pawn your soul to the devil, but the good Lord will always bail you out?"

"Something like that."

She paused at the desk by the door before she picked something up to look at it. "What's this?"

Zeke moved to peer over her shoulder. It was a round medallion with what appeared to be an angel and serpent fighting. There was some old-timey script that he couldn't read. "Looks like one of those things from a horror movie that someone uses to summon a demon or something."

She snorted. "Back, Manitou, back. Do you remember that old movie?"

"I remember you making me watch it then telling Mom it had a naked woman in it and getting my ass busted because of it."

Mary gave him a sheepish grin. "Oh, never mind. Forget I said anything." She handed him the medallion. "Maybe you should chant something over it."

"O great Manitou, I want another life. Something completely different than this one."

"Wouldn't it be freaky if the two of us exchanged places? You'd have to go home to my house and make out with Duncan."

Zeke covered his ears with his hands in mock horror. "Ah gah! Eye bleach. Don't put that shit in my head. You're my sister, for Pete's sake. Now I'm going to have to beat your husband the next time I see him for defiling you." He cringed. "I'd rather be at work."

"Oh poo! You always overreact to everything."

"So not true. Trust me. I live a life where people scream at me on an hourly basis, and take it without raising anything more than a jumbo-sized ulcer. The only thing that can make it larger is the cousin ulcer I get from the rampant stupidity on Facebook."

She pressed the medallion to his chest. "One day, your life will change."

"Yeah." He took the medallion as she walked back toward the living room. "One day, I will also be in a pine box, six feet under." He followed her out of the bedroom and had to admit their granduncle was a weird old man. "The lawyer said gramps here spent his younger years as an archaeologist and the last few decades as a total recluse."

Mary nodded as she scanned the bookshelves and tables that were littered with even more artifacts. "It looks like he spent a lot of time bringing that stuff home. You could probably make a killing on eBay."

Zeke didn't really hear her as his attention was taken with an odd coin that was partially covered on the coffee table. Frowning, he walked over to it. Bright and shiny, it looked brand new and yet the markings on it appeared as ancient as everything else.

More than that, it actually felt warm to the touch. "What do you think this is?"

Mary shrugged. "More junk."

Maybe. Then again, a strange sensation went over him. "You think any of this crap could be possessed?"

"No. I think you're possessed of the spirit of creepiness. Put that down and let's go get dinner. This place makes me depressed."

Zeke nodded. He reached out to drop it, but couldn't make himself let go. It was as if the coin somehow called out to him. Whispered to him.

And before he knew what he was doing, he put it in his pocket and followed Mary out to her car and then got into his.

3

You have been chosen. . . .

Zeke looked up from his meatloaf sandwich in the cozy diner they'd found a few miles away to see Mary chowing down on her burger. "What did you say?"

She swallowed before she spoke. "Nothing. I'm eating."

You have been chosen. . . .

"You're not funny, Mary. Stop that."

"Stop what?"

"Throwing your voice."

She gave him a droll stare then ate a fry from his plate. "I'm not throwing my voice, but if you don't stop irritating me, I might be throwing a fry at your head."

You have been chosen. . . .

Zeke looked around the small restaurant. All the surrounding tables were empty. The only other customers were seated at a bar, talking to the waitress. "You didn't hear that?"

Mary scowled at him. "Hear what?"

"You have been chosen."

She screwed her face up even more. "What are you? On crack?"

"Not yet, but I'm thinking it might behoove me to find a dealer . . . except that they make me take a urine test every other day for work, so no fun there."

She snorted. "You're not right, are you? God, I hope that's not genetic, since Duncan and I are trying to get pregnant."

"Again with the ick stuff. Stop!"

You have been chosen. . . .

Zeke growled at the voice. "And that means you, too. Damn. My life is bad enough. The last thing I need is to be schizophrenic."

"I don't know. Given your job, schizo could be fun. . . . No, lady,

I didn't turn you down. That was the voices in my head telling you to shove that claim where the sun don't shine."

"I really hate you," he said with a laugh.

"I know. It's why you tried to feed me Drano when we were kids."

He shook his head at the memory. "Yeah, but you're the one who traded me for a wagon."

She let out an evil laugh then sipped her Coke. "You do know that when you turned sixteen Mom told me we should have kept the wagon."

"I've no doubt." It actually explained a lot about his high school years.

You have been chosen. . . .

Zeke raked his hands through his hair. "Call the shrink. I've lost my mind."

"Sweetie, you lost that a long time ago. Now eat your sandwich. The voices in your head are probably hungry, too."

Zeke rolled his eyes at his sister's curt dismissal. He'd just turned back to his sandwich when something that felt like an electric current went down his spine. It truly felt like a razor blade skimming his soul.

And something inside him raised up like the hackles of a dog. He turned toward the door at the same time a well-dressed man entered. Dressed in a suit and tie, he looked completely respectable.

Cheats on his taxes and wife. Misappropriated funds from his clients earlier tonight. Beats his kids. Total douche. Will eventually spend ten years in jail for fraud. Damned to hell on his deathbed. Nothing will redeem him. His ego won't let it.

Zeke shook his head to clear out that strange voice that wouldn't let up. It reminded him of one of his grandfather's tirades against hypocrites.

"Richard Cheatham."

The man stopped next to him. "Do I know you?"

Zeke looked up and blinked. "Excuse me?"

"You just said my name. Do I know you?"

He frowned at the man. "I didn't say anything."

"Yes, you did. You said Richard Cheatham. I heard you." His dark blue eyes narrowed dangerously. "Did my wife hire you?"

"Dude, I don't know you and I have no idea what you're talking about."

Richard started to grab him.

Zeke caught his hand and whipped it around, twisting Richard's body as he rose. He held Richard against him while the man struggled and cursed.

Stunned, he glanced to Mary who was as shocked as he was. *When the hell did I get my mad ninja skills?* Definitely couldn't be wizard powers . . . he'd lost his virginity at nineteen.

What evoked spontaneous shinobi?

How many hours of Mortal Kombat *have I played?*

He released Richard who then scurried out of the café.

"What the hell was that action?" Mary asked.

Zeke had no idea. He didn't know how to move like that. How to defend himself. God knows, his ass had been kicked enough in his life to prove it to him.

You have been chosen. . . .

Chosen for what?

Psychotic episodes?

Just what I fucking need . . .

"I don't feel good, Mare." He pulled out a ten and dropped it on the table. "I think I need to go home and rest. Thanks for coming with me." He didn't give her time to say a word before he bolted.

He quickly got into his silver Nissan that was parked beside hers, and headed home. For the entire two-hour trip back, he kept waiting for the voices to return.

They didn't.

But his car radio was whacked out. Every time he changed the station, some weird-ass song would play. AC/DC's "Highway to Hell." "Hells Bells." "Evil Walks." Godsmack's "Releasing the Demons." Papa Roach's "Roses on My Grave."

"What the hell is up with my radio?"

Every single station had something to do with death, demons, or hell.

"Well, I know this damn car ain't Bumblebee." For one thing, he'd been driving it for over nine years. If it was an Autobot in disguise, surely it would have transformed before now.

No, this was like one of those *Twilight Zone* episodes they showed on the Syfy Channel.

Maybe his voices *had* possessed his car.

Yeah, right.

By the time he reached his house, he was really starting to freak himself out with psychotic fears that the devil was after him or that aliens were about to pull him on board for an anal probe. This was some kind of freaky *Ring* or *Poltergeist* shit going on.

His heart racing, he left the car in the driveway and got out. Before he reached his door, the neighbor's dog came running up to him to hump his leg.

"What in the world is wrong with you?" He pulled the dog gently from his leg then ran like hell to his door. He fumbled for the keys while Tiny was trying to make time with his shoes.

"I am not your date! Hit up the Chihuahua down the street. I heard she's an easy lay." Opening the door, Zeke slid inside then slammed it shut.

The dog whimpered on the other side.

"This is the oddest day of my life."

"Just wait. It gets stranger."

Eyes wide, Zeke turned at the deep, scary voice behind him to find what had to be a man so beautiful he should have been the lead act in a drag show. Tall, thin, and blond, he had eyes so blue they looked like a cloudless sky. "Who the hell are you?"

"Wrong direction, actually. But my name is Gabriel."

Zeke tightened his grip on the doorknob, ready to bolt outside again. "And you would be in my house to . . ." *Rob me blind and kill me?*

"Explain the current weirdness surrounding you."

Call the cops, Zeke. Now.

That would only be a waste of your time.

He gasped at the sound of Gabriel's voice in his head.

"You have been chosen," Gabriel said in that same spooky voice he'd been hearing.

"For what? Arkham Asylum?"

"To be an avenger for mankind."

Zeke tried to open the door, but before he could, it vanished. Literally.

Anger and fear mixed inside him. "Yo, Hotel California, I want my door back."

"And so it'll return once we have this settled."

"Settled, my ass. I'm not Emma Peel and I'd look like shit in a black catsuit. Find her for your avenger. Now let me go."

Gabriel tsked at him. "You can't fight your destiny, Ezekiel. Besides, you asked for this. We couldn't have fulfilled Michael's choice had you been unwilling."

Unwilling for what? Zeke swallowed as he turned around slowly to face Gabriel. "How did I choose this?"

"You asked for your life to change. You wanted to be special. To make a difference. Michael heard you, and so he chose you to be his replacement."

"Michael's dead."

Gabriel shook his head. "Not dead. After all these centuries of fighting, he's retired. You're the new Seraph who will take on his duties."

Yeah, the dude was on crack. "*What* duties?"

"To maintain the natural order of the universe. Good versus evil. We allow evil a certain latitude to fulfill its part, but whenever the demons take their duties too far, we are the ones who rein them in."

"Bullshit!"

Zeke ran for his bedroom. He slammed the door shut and locked it then froze as he caught sight of himself in the mirrored door of his closet.

His short black hair was now snow white and long. His clothes were gone, replaced by a black shirt and pants and a long, full black leather coat. Three spikes stood out on each shoulder and a red chain was wrapped around his left arm.

Holy shit! I'm a refugee from FUNimation. . . .

Or *Final Fantasy.*

On his right hip was the hilt of a sword that looked like an ancient cross. As he watched the hilt in the mirror, the center opened to reveal two pale blue eyes and a small mouth.

"You can call me Jack."

Zeke screamed and ripped the hilt off then threw it to the ground. He turned to run to the window only to find Gabriel there.

"I see you met Jack. Don't worry. Most men scream like girls when he does that."

Zeke shook his head. "This is a whacked-out dream. I'm going to wake . . ." He trailed off as "Jack" mutated from a cross-hilt into a large, metallic man.

How much Fullmetal Alchemist *have I watched?*

Jack extended his hand. "All Seraph have a minion and a guardian. I'm yours."

Zeke's head whirled at what was happening. *This is not real.* It couldn't be.

"Breathe deep before you hyperventilate," Jack said.

"What are you?"

"I told you. I'm your guardian and your minion. Anything you need that's metal, from transportation to weaponry, I can be. When you need a hand fighting, I look like this." He indicated his armored human form then pounded his hand against his metallic breast. "The best armor in the world. Nothing, except a handful of demonic weapons, can mar me."

Gabriel clapped Zeke on the back. "Welcome to the fold, Ezekiel."

Suddenly something warm swept through Zeke. It felt as if his very blood was on fire. His breathing ragged, he turned back toward the closet. His eyes were a vibrant red and his face was every bit as perfect and ethereal as Gabriel's.

Zeke lifted his armored arm to make sure it was him.

Shit. It was.

Still in shock, he frowned at Gabriel. "What about my day job?"

A bit sheepish, Gabriel glanced away. "There's no payment for being a Seraph. Sorry. But you will have a whole new set of skills. Just wait."

That sounded ominous. "The only skill I want is the ability to wish myself a billionaire."

Jack laughed. "Won't happen. They like poverty."

"They" who?

Gabriel scratched nervously at his neck. "And there's one more thing you should know."

Of course there was. "And that is?"

"Your granduncle Michael notwithstanding, the average life expectancy for a Seraph is . . . two years."

Zeke laughed nervously. "Oh yeah . . . hell to the no. I definitely decline. You can take this crap and stick it."

Gabriel reached behind his ear and pulled out the coin Zeke had taken from his uncle's house. "The minute you willingly accepted the medallion, you sealed your fate. You have been chosen, my brother. The only way out now is death."

Zeke gaped at him. "You're shitting me."

Jack clapped him on the back. "But on the upside, your Seraph form will never age. And the only way to die is by a demon blade. As long as you survive fighting them, you're immortal to the things that would kill a normal human being. Think of the money you'll save on medical bills."

That was so *not* an upside.

Gabriel gave him a gimlet stare. "And there's one more thing."

"Neutering?" That would be Zeke's luck.

Gabriel laughed. "No." He snapped his fingers. An instant later a black mist appeared by his side. It swirled into the small form of a raven. No sooner had the bird appeared than it exploded into the form of a tall, gorgeous woman with long black hair and coal-black eyes. Dressed all in black, she was striking and tough.

Now we're talking.

Gabriel inclined his head to her. "Ravenna is also your helpmate."

"Oh yeah, baby." He reached for her, only to have her grab his wrist and flip him onto the ground, where he landed with a painful *oof.*

She wrenched his arm and put one perfectly spiked heel on the center of his chest. "Keep your hands to yourself or lose them." She pressed the heel in, making him grimace. "And don't call me baby." Then she released him and moved away.

Gabriel's eyes danced with humor. "Ravenna is your contact with the other side. She's also your eyes and ears, both to me and to the demon posse. You guys get acquainted. I have duties to attend." He vanished.

"But—"

"There are no buts, boy," Jack said, laughing. "You, my friend, have been chosen."

Ravenna nodded her agreement. "Always be careful what you wish for. You just might get it."

Yeah, and in this one wish, Zeke had definitely been screwed.

Love Bytes

1

"Could you please tell me what's wrong with me? I swear if anyone else looks at me and snickers, I might go postal."

Samantha Parker looked up from her computer monitor to see Adrian Cole standing in her cube. Or rather towering over it. At six foot five, the man reminded her of a giraffe when he moved around the office.

Not that she minded. Personally, she adored his height, just as she adored those gorgeous eyes of his. Deep and a dark chocolate-brown, they made her melt every time he looked at her.

And the sleek, loose-limbed way he walked . . .

Oooh, just thinking about it was enough to make her burn.

She'd never been particularly fond of blond men, but those dark eyes with his thick mane of tawny curls and lush golden skin just made her ache for a taste. A nervous jitter went over her like it always did when he stood this close to her, and she could smell the clean, spicy scent of him. The man was simply mouth-wateringly scrumptious, and incredibly brilliant.

"Well?" he prompted.

Sam bit her lip as she raked her gaze over his long, lean frame. "Other than the fact you look like your seeing-eye dog dressed you this morning, nothing," she teased. "What did you do to make Heather mad this time?"

He cursed under his breath. It was common knowledge that Adrian had a rare type of color blindness that rendered him completely incapable of seeing any color whatsoever. As a result, he paid his baby sister to do his laundry, and every time Heather got upset at big brother, she took it out on his wardrobe.

"What did she do to me now?" he asked warily.

"Well, you'll be happy to know your red plaid shirt is still red, but the splotchy pink Henley really has to go."

Adrian held his leg out and pulled his jeans up to show her his socks. "What about them?"

"Unlike your shirt, they actually match your Henley."

Growling low in his throat, he buttoned his plaid shirt all the way to his neck. "One day, I'm going to kill her."

Sam laughed at the threat he uttered at least twice a week. She'd met Heather a couple of times during lunch, and though Sam liked her, Heather was a bit self-absorbed.

"So, what did you do?" she asked.

"I refused to let her borrow my Vette. The last time she took it out, she hit a pole and cost me three thousand dollars in damage."

"Yikes." Sam cringed for him. Adrian loved his vintage 1969 Stingray. "Was she hurt?"

"Thankfully, no, but my car is still sulking over it."

Sam laughed again, but then, she always did that around him. Adrian had a dry, sharp wit that never missed a beat. "Well, I'm glad you stopped by. My Perforce is acting up again. I can't get it to integrate my changes." Which meant that the stupid server had her locked out and every time she tried to update a page on their Web site, it refused to let her.

She hated Perforce, and it hated her. But they were required to use it so that upper management could keep track of who made what changes to the Web site, and out of the entire network services department, Adrian was the only one who really understood the program.

"What's it doing?" he asked as he came to stand beside her.

Sam couldn't breathe as he leaned down to read her screen. His face was so close to hers that all she had to do was move a mere two inches and she would be able to place her lips against that strong, sculpted jaw.

"Scroll down."

She heard Adrian's words, but they didn't register. She was too busy watching the way his incredibly broad shoulders hunched as he leaned with one hand against her desk.

He glanced down at her.

Sam blinked and looked back at the screen. "I'm scrolling," she said as she reached for her mouse.

"There's your problem," he said as he read the gobbledy-gook. "You haven't enabled your baseline merges."

"And in English that would mean?"

Adrian laughed that rich, deep laugh that made her burn even more. He covered her hand with his on the mouse and showed her how to choose the right options.

He surrounded her with his masculine warmth. Sam swallowed at the disturbing sensation of his hand on hers as fire coursed through her. He had beautiful, strong hands. His long, lean fingers were tapered and perfect. Worse, every time she looked at them, she couldn't help wondering what they would feel like on her body, touching her, caressing her.

Seducing her.

His cell phone rang. Adrian straightened and pulled the phone from its cradle on his belt. He checked the caller ID, then flipped it open like Captain Kirk. "Yeah, Scott, what's wrong?"

"Radius is down," Scott, their network security specialist, said over the speaker phone, "and I can't get it up and running."

"Did you reboot?"

"Duh."

Adrian indicated her chair with his head.

Sam got up and watched as he set the phone aside, took a seat in her chair, and opened a DOS window on her computer. He tapped swiftly on her keyboard, then picked his phone back up. "It's not cycling."

"I know, and I can't fix it."

"All right," Adrian said with saintly patience. "I'll be up there in a few minutes."

He clicked off his phone, but before he could move his phone rang at the same time his pager went off and the overhead paging system called his name. Adrian answered his cell phone again and checked his pager.

"Did you get the hacker alert?" Scott asked.

"Hang on," Adrian said, then he reached for her desk phone to answer his page.

"Hi, Randy," he said as he tucked the phone between his shoulder and cheek and started typing on her keyboard. "I'm in the process of switching the main databases over to my SQL. We should be ready to fly by five." He paused as he listened and switched her computer from the Windows over to Linux.

Sam watched in awe as he flawlessly entered line after line of stuff she couldn't even begin to follow or understand.

"No," Adrian said to Randy, "our customers won't notice at all, except the searches will take less time." He entered more lines as he listened to their senior director, Randy Jacobs, on the phone.

Another page went off for him.

Adrian nodded as he listened to Randy. "Yeah, I'll get to it. Would you mind holding for just a second?"

He picked up his cell phone. "Scott, it's not a hacker. It's an invalid SID. Someone is using a bookmark with an old Session ID attached to it."

"Are you sure?"

"Positive. I'm looking at it right now."

"Okay, thanks."

Adrian gave her a sheepish smile as he clicked off his cell phone and picked up the other line on her desk phone.

Biting her lips to keep from smiling at the chaos, Sam felt for him. At twenty-six, Adrian was known to everyone in the company as the boy genius. He had taken a billion-dollar corporation from the 1980s mainframe mentality into the twenty-first century Web-based e-commerce. He had single-handedly built the entire programming side of their million-dollar business retail site, and put together a Web design team that was second to none.

Unfortunately, though, everyone in the company turned to him every time something went wrong with the site. Which meant he was always on call and always rushing from one department to the next, putting out fires and trying his best to explain extremely complicated things to people who had absolutely no idea what he was talking about.

Adrian came into the office every morning by five-thirty, and seldom went home before eight at night.

The stress on him had to be excruciating, and yet he was the most easygoing boss she'd ever known. She couldn't count the number of times a day someone was complaining, if not shouting, about something, or begging him to help them, and yet he never let the strain of it show.

"Scott," Adrian said at his cell phone, "go get a cup of coffee. I'm headed upstairs as soon as I finish with Randy." He returned to her phone. "I'm back, Randy." He listened for a few minutes more, then nodded. "All right," he said, pulling the Palm Pilot off his belt. "I'll put it on my schedule."

Sam watched as he added yet another meeting to his already booked calendar.

"Okay," he said to Randy. "I'm on it. See you later."

Adrian left the chair, then hesitated at the opening of Sam's cube as she resumed her seat. In a rare show of uneasiness, he picked up the wooden medieval knight her brother had given her. "This is new."

She nodded. "Teddy got it Thanksgiving when he went to Germany."

"It's neat," he said, putting it back on the shelf with the rest of the knights. She had been collecting them for years. She figured they were as close as she'd ever come to having a real knight in shining armor.

He glanced around her cube at the large Santa and snowmen cut-outs she had pinned up, the small Christmas tree she had next to her monitor, and the stack of holiday catalogues by her keyboard. "You really love Christmas, don't you?"

Sam glanced down at her Santa and reindeer sweater and smiled. "My favorite time of year. Don't you like it?"

He shrugged. "It's a day off, I guess."

Still Adrian hesitated, fiddling with her nameplate.

How odd. It was so unlike him to be fidgety. This was a man who made million-dollar decisions and held meetings with the stars of the *Fortune* 500 without even a minor qualm.

What on earth could he be nervous about?

"Would you mind if I asked a giant favor?"

Her heart pounded. *Oh, baby, ask me anything!*

"What'cha need?"

He dropped his gaze down to her nameplate as he slid it back and forth in its holder. "Since Heather has totally screwed up my clothes again, I was wondering if you'd mind going shopping with me after work? I'd take Randir, but even I can tell *his* clothes don't match."

"I heard that!" Randir said laughingly from the next cube.

Sam smiled. The guys in her department teased each other mercilessly, and it was what she loved most about her job. Everyone got along well and no one minded the incessant quips and taunts that were hurled about as often as Adrian got paged.

"Anyway," Adrian said, ignoring Randir's interruption. "Would you mind? I'll buy you dinner."

Yes! Her heart skipped a beat as she did her best to appear calm, while inside, what she really wanted to do was turn cartwheels. "I don't mind."

"You sure?"

"Positive."

"Great," he said with a slight smile. "Then I guess I better go to Scott before he hyperventilates."

"Okay, see you later."

Adrian took one last look at Sam as she returned her attention to her monitor. He clenched his teeth as he watched her fingers stroking the keys on her keyboard.

That woman had the lightest touch he'd ever seen, and he ached to feel those hands on his body. Ached to take them into his mouth and nibble every inch of them.

Worse, what he really wanted to do was pick her up from that chair, take her into his office, and toss everything on top of his desk onto the floor before laying her down on top of it.

Oh, yeah, he could already taste her lips as he peeled the thick sweater and jeans off her body. Feel her hot and wet for him as he coaxed and teased her body into blind ecstasy.

His groin tightened in pain at the thought.

Stop it! he snapped at himself. He was her team leader, and she was one of his best employees. Company policy stringently forbade dating between management and staff, and violation of that policy meant immediate dismissal.

Yeah, but the woman made him seriously hot.

Dangerously hot.

She always wore her long, dark hair pulled back from her face where it fell in thick waves down to her waist. He'd spent hours at night fantasizing about that hair draped on his chest, or spread out across his pillow.

And she had the palest eyes he'd ever seen. She'd told him once they were green, and it pained him that he had absolutely no idea what that color meant.

But from what he could see, green had to be beautiful.

Her eyes were a bit large for her pixie face, and they were always bright and teasing when she looked at him.

He could stare into those eyes for an eternity.

Adrian ran his gaze over her lush curves, and he hardened even more as raw, demanding desire tore through him. Sam had once complained about her weight, but he couldn't find any fault with it. After growing up with a skinny, frail mother and sister, he couldn't stand to see a woman with no meat on her bones.

Her full, voluptuous body made him absolutely crazy with unspent lust. And for the last year, he'd been forced to learn to live with a raging erection every time he got near her, or heard the sound of her smooth Southern drawl.

Sam paused and looked up at him. "Did you need something else?"

Yeah, I need you to smile at me.

Touch me.

Better still, I need you to climb me like a ladder . . .

"No," he said as another page sounded for him.

Adrian turned away from her and answered the page with his cell phone as he headed upstairs to tend Scott's antsy twitters.

Sam clenched her hands as her computer clock showed ten after five. An anxious tremor went through her as she feared Adrian might have changed his mind about going out with her.

Taking a deep breath for courage, she shut down her computer, then walked the short distance to Adrian's office.

He had his back to her as he typed like lightning on his keyboard while talking on the phone. "It's switched," he said. "Everything is clear . . . No, I ran the logs, and as of yesterday, we've cleared seven hundred thousand dollars in orders since the end of October . . . Yeah," he said with a light laugh. "Merry Christmas to you, too."

He hung up the phone, and she saw him rub his hand over his eyes as if he had a headache. His cell phone rang. Without breaking stride, he answered it.

"Hi, Tiffany," he said to their marketing director. "Yeah, I'll be here for a few more minutes. I was planning on implementing your changeover after Christmas since there's a good chance it could slow down site access." He listened as he worked and Sam shook her head.

The man was simply amazing. She didn't know how he managed to stay on top of everything, but he did.

He pushed his chair back from his computer desk and swung it around to the desk in front of her. As his gaze fell on her, he smiled that wolfish grin that made her blood race. She felt a vicious stab of desire straight through her middle.

Reaching for a stack of reports, he flipped to one of the middle pages. "Okay," he said to Tiffany. "I'll take care of it first thing in the morning."

He clicked off his phone. "Sorry about that," he said to Sam. "I didn't know you were standing there. Just give me a sec, I'll get this finished, and we can leave."

Sam let out a relieved breath. Thank goodness, he hadn't changed his mind. She moved into his office and took a seat against the window as she waited for him. "Have we really done seven hundred thousand dollars off the site since Halloween?"

He nodded. "We should easily hit a million by Christmas." He flashed her another smile. "Should make for nice bonuses."

Money, she didn't care about. So long as she made enough to cover her car and rent, she was completely happy. But she was glad for Adrian's sake. Their business-to-business e-commerce Web site was his pride and joy, and he took a lot of flak from the higher-ups when the site didn't perform the way they thought it should.

Sam looked up as Tiffany stalked into Adrian's office. "Adrian," Tiffany whined as she glanced at Sam without acknowledging her. Thin, tall, and gorgeous, Tiffany should have been a model. All the leggy blonde had to do was bat her eyelashes, and every guy in the building would drop what he was doing and rush to her side.

And every time Sam got near her, she felt like a warted troll in comparison.

"Adrian," Tiffany said again. "I got an e-mail from a customer wanting to know why he has to enter in his password every time he wants to order something. He wants us to fix it so that he can just do a one-click order option. What should I tell him?"

Adrian didn't pause in his typing as he answered. "That it's a safeguard to save his butt should one of his disgruntled employees get ticked off, and decide to order several thousand dollars' worth of merchandise and charge it to his account."

Tiffany rolled her eyes at Adrian's sarcasm. "Well, he says—"

"I don't give a damn what he says," Adrian said calmly.

Sam bit her lip as Tiffany's face flushed bright red. That was Adrian's only flaw. The man didn't pull punches, and he always spoke his mind, consequences be damned.

"Those safeguards are there for his protection," he continued, "and I'm not about to change it since he'll be the first one to whine when he gets burned."

Tiffany stomped her foot. "Would you look at me when you're talking to me?"

Sam arched her brow as Adrian turned around with a look on his face that should have sent Tiffany running. To his credit, all he said was a simple, "Yes?"

"I need a more tactful answer for him than that." She narrowed those blue eyes at him. "Look, I know you think you own this Web site, but the last time I checked, you were just another flunky here like the rest of us."

He took a deep breath as both his pager and phone went off. "I tell you what," he said in a self-controlled tone, "since I'm a flunky here like everyone else, why don't you come in at midnight tonight to post a press release because the man who signs our checks wants it to go live exactly at that time?" He picked his phone off his belt.

He checked the caller ID, flipped it open, and said, "Scott, it's not a hacker. I'm validating the PHP."

Adrian hung up the phone. "Now, Miss Klein, if you want a more tactful response, then please forward the e-mail to me and I will respond to it myself."

Tossing her hair over her shoulder, Tiffany glared at him. "I want a copy of your response."

"Yes, Mom."

Tiffany's nostrils flared. Turning on her red high heels, she stalked out of his office. But as she left, Sam heard her muttering under her breath, "What a friggin' geek."

She couldn't tell if Adrian heard it. He merely checked his pager, then grabbed one of the reports and swung his chair back around to his computer.

"You must get tired of all this," she said quietly.

"I'm used to it," he said simply as he started typing again.

Sam shook her head. Poor Adrian. He wasn't even allowed to get sick. She remembered last summer when he had pneumonia. He'd been forced to drag himself in to work to fix some problem no one else could solve.

The man needed a break.

And how she wished she dared get up from her chair, go over to him and massage those broad, tense shoulders for him. She could just imagine the feel of his lean muscles under her hand, the sight of his handsome features relaxed.

He would be breathtaking.

Sam, you have got to quit fantasizing. Boy-genius doesn't even know you're alive.

Even though it was true, she wished things were different between them. Adrian was the first guy she'd ever met whom she really could see herself having kids with. She'd love to have a houseful of tall brainiacs who were fast on a comeback.

It was a full ten minutes before Adrian finally logged off his computer. He got up to shrug on his faded blue ski jacket.

"C'mon," he said to her. "Let's make a mad run for the door before someone catches me."

She laughed, knowing it wasn't a joke.

He locked his office, then they headed outside to the dimly lit parking lot.

"Why don't you ride with me?" he asked as she started for her silver Honda. "You're the only person in the department who hasn't ridden in the Vette."

Oh, don't tempt me, you cruel man. She hadn't ridden in his Corvette because she couldn't stand the thought of being so close to him and not being able to touch that wonderful body. "Yeah, but you'll have to bring me all the way back here."

"I don't mind."

Sam bit her lip as her pulse raced. *Don't do it! Don't torture yourself.*

But one look at his chiseled features in the streetlight and she was hooked. "Okay," she said with a nonchalance she didn't feel.

He opened the passenger side door for her, then closed it after she got in. Sam drew a ragged breath at his consideration. She'd never had a man do that for her before.

Adrian got in the other side, and she had to bite back a laugh at the sight of him cramming his long body into the car.

"Don't say anything," he said as he put the key in the ignition. "Heather already told me I look like a grasshopper in a peanut shell."

She couldn't help laughing at that. "Sorry," she said, clearing her throat as she caught his sideways glare. "I wouldn't have laughed if you hadn't said that."

Sam leaned back in the black leather seat as she inhaled the warm, spicy scent of him. Good heavens, but that masculine smell made her giddy and hot. She would love nothing more than to lean over, cup the back of his neck with her hand, and kiss the daylights out of those full, sensuous lips.

Adrian started the car and did his best to ignore just how good Sam looked sitting beside him. He ached to reach his hand over to where she had her legs slightly parted and caress her inner thigh.

Oh, yeah, he could already feel the denim and her flesh in his palm. And then, he imagined where he'd like to take his hand next.

Up her thigh to cup her between her legs.

Grinding his teeth, he could see them locked in a kiss, feel her hands sliding over him as he undressed her.

It had been a long time since he'd made out in a car, but for the first time since high school, he found the idea appealing.

A surge of lust ripped through him as he shifted uncomfortably in his seat.

She'd taken that stupid clip out of her hair and brushed her bangs with her hand so that now her hair fell around her face, framing it to perfection. And it was torturing him.

Pulling out of the lot, he headed toward Hickory Hollow Mall. He hadn't even gone a mile when he noticed Sam tensing in her seat. "What's wrong?" he asked.

She flinched as he changed lanes. "You know, Adrian, this isn't a video game, and cars don't evaporate if you hit them. Jeez, you drive like you have a death wish."

He laughed and backed off his speed. "Come on, half the fun of this car is pushing its limits."

She crossed herself. "I hope you have a good life insurance policy."

He did, but there wasn't anyone to reap the benefits of it. And it was one of his biggest regrets. He'd never been the kind of guy to date much. Taking care of his mother, sister, and work left him very little time to socialize.

Not that it mattered. As soon as he opened his mouth and said something, most women got a blank, dazed look on their faces and stared at him like he was speaking a foreign language.

But not Sam. She understood even his most obscure references.

"Adrian!" she snapped as a semi cut them off. "That's a truck!"

He hit the brakes. "Don't worry, I don't dare die before I put the Christmas press release up. And even if I did, I'm sure Randy would be at the funeral home with a laptop asking me to take care of some last-minute thing."

"You're not funny," she said, even though she was smiling. "Do you really have to go in later and do that?"

"Unfortunately, yes." Adrian pulled onto Bell Road. "Want to eat first?"

"Sure."

"What are you in the mood for?"

"Anything."

"How about Olive Garden?" he asked, knowing it was one of her favorites.

"Sounds great."

Adrian pulled into the lot, then went to open the door for her. But by the time he got to her side, she was already getting out. She looked up and smiled. "And they say chivalry is dead."

"You have a hard time letting anyone do anything for you, don't you?" he asked.

"What can I say? My brothers broke me in well."

Adrian shook his head. "I can't believe your mother didn't nag them into doing more for you."

"She might have had she ever been home, but since she had to work all the time after my dad left, it was pretty much just us."

Adrian tucked his hands into his back pockets to keep himself from subconsciously reaching out to touch her.

God, how he wanted her. She barely reached his shoulders and every time he stood this close to her, he had the worst desire to pick her up in his arms and bury his face in her neck where he could inhale the sweet scent of her skin.

Clenching his teeth, he tried to banish the thought of laying her down on his bed, and spending the rest of the night exploring her body. Slowly. Meticulously.

He opened the door to the restaurant and let her enter first. As she passed him, his gaze trailed down the back of her body and focused on her round hips. His groin instantly hardened. Thank God, he wore baggy jeans.

The hostess led them to a booth in the back. Adrian hesitated as Sam sat down. His first impulse was to sit beside her, but he knew it wouldn't be appropriate. The only time he got to do that was when all of them went out to lunch, then he always made a point of being the one to sit closest to her.

His gut tightening as another wave of desire hit him, he forced himself into the opposite booth.

"It's weird to be here without the guys," she said as she glanced over the menu.

Adrian stared at her as she read the menu. He didn't know why she bothered since she always ordered the Manicotti Formaggio, and he loved the way she said it. It rolled off her tongue like smooth whisky.

Sam tightened her hands on the menu as she felt Adrian's gaze on her. Unnerved by its intensity, she tried to cross her legs, but ended up kicking him under the table. "I'm sorry," she gasped as he grimaced.

"It's okay," he said, reaching beneath the table to rub his leg. "I tend to take up a lot of space."

"Don't knock it, I'd kill to be tall."

"I don't know why. I think you're a perfect size."

She glanced up at his unexpected compliment. He cleared his throat and dropped his gaze to his menu.

After they ordered, they sat in awkward silence.

Sam sipped her drink as she tried to think of something to say to him. Normally, they never had a bit of trouble finding things to talk about and laugh over. But tonight, she was just a little too aware of him. A little too nervous about being alone with him, knowing there was no one here to see her if she were to reach over and touch his hand.

No one to see if she . . .

"Did you decide to call that guy about the programming position?" she asked, remembering the résumé he'd given her to review that morning.

"I did, even though my first impulse was to toss it."

"Why?"

"Dear *Ms.* Cole," he said, curling his lip. "I hate it when someone gets my gender wrong. It's the reason I called you so fast when you submitted your résumé. You're the only one who hasn't made that mistake. I knew you had to be brilliant."

She smiled. "Yeah, well, I have to say I was stumped, which is why I wrote 'Dear Adrian.' I figured you had to be a guy, since there are so few women programmers, but just in case you weren't I didn't want to tick you off."

"Thanks, Mom," he muttered bitterly. "It wasn't bad enough she passed along the oh-so-wonderful color-blind genes, but she had to curse me with a godawful name to boot."

"If you hate it so much, why don't you use your middle name?"

"Because it's Lesley."

Sam felt her jaw go slack. "Your mother named you Adrian Lesley Cole?"

He nodded. "She *really* wanted a daughter. When the nurse told her she had a son, she told the nurse to check again. 'That just can't be right,'" he said in a falsetto, mocking a thick Southern accent.

Was he serious?

"You know," she said. "I really like the name Adrian. I think it suits you."

He snorted. "Gee, thanks for the affront to my manhood."

"No," she said with a laugh. There was absolutely *nothing* feminine about him, or his features. "You just have a classical, romantic look to you, like the hero from some period movie."

He looked a bit sheepish at her compliment. Sam dropped her gaze down to his hands again and watched the way he trailed the empty straw wrapper through his long fingers.

Oh, she loved those hands of his.

How she wished for the courage to reach over and cover them with hers. But she was terrified of what he might do. Terrified of him rejecting her, because in her heart, she knew she'd already fallen for him.

She needed to be able to see him every day. Needed to feel his presence even if it was at a distance.

No, she would never chance running him off. He was her boss, and she would have to satisfy herself with just being his friend.

As *soon as* they finished dinner, Adrian drove them up the street to the mall. Sam led him through the men's section of Dillard's, looking for things she thought would be hot on him.

She paused as she found a stack of button-fly jeans. "You know, these would look great on you."

Adrian didn't miss the gleam in her eyes. He hated button-fly, but if Sam liked them . . .

"I need a thirty-two waist and a thirty-six inseam."

"Oh, my God, you're tall."

He laughed. "I know and it's a bitch to find them. But if you can locate a pair in this mess, I'll try them on."

She did. Adrian tucked them under his arm as he followed her around and did his best not to be too obvious in his ogling of her.

"You're not going to put me in anything weird, are you?" he asked suspiciously as she stopped to look at a rack of V-neck sweaters. "I might not be able to see colors, but I know guys don't wear pink, or pastels. And please, nothing in bright yellow because I can't stand light-post jokes."

"I wouldn't do that to you. I'm thinking blacks and dark blues. Maybe red. You look really good in red."

He smiled. "Really? How good?"

"*Very* good." She plucked at his shirtsleeve. "But I don't like your plaid shirts. They make you look like a lumberjack."

She'd noticed him! Adrian wanted to shout in happiness. He couldn't believe she'd actually been looking at him.

"So, what do"—he had to bite back the word *you*—"women want on a guy?"

"Not those baggy jeans," she said, looking at his rear and making him even hotter. Harder.

His breathing tense, it was all he could do not to pull her to him and find out exactly what those lips of hers tasted like.

"I don't know who came up with the idea," she continued, "but ew. Women like to see a man's . . ."

He arched a brow.

"Never mind. I'm having a weird case of déjà vu."

"Why?"

"I used to buy clothes for my brothers and we'd always get into similar discussions." She ran her gaze over him. "No offense, but you could really use a makeover."

Adrian hesitated. Maybe if he let her, she might be a little more receptive to his . . .

You're her boss.

Yeah, but he liked her more than he had ever liked any other woman. She made him laugh . . . made him happy every time she looked up at him.

Better still, she made him burn.

"You feel up to it?" he asked before he could stop himself.

"You'd let me?" she asked in disbelief.

"Sure, just so long as you don't paint my fingernails pale pink."

She frowned at that. "What?"

"Heather did that to me in high school as a joke. One night while I was sleeping, she sneaked into my room and painted my fingernails. I didn't notice until I got to school the next day and people started laughing."

"Why is your sister so mean to you?"

He shrugged. "She doesn't mean any real harm. She's just impulsive, and never seems to think before she acts."

Shaking her head, Sam searched through a rack of black button-down shirts as she thought about what he said. "She really painted your fingernails?"

"Yup."

"My brothers would have killed me."

"Yeah, well, she's my kid sister. My mom always said my one job was to protect her, not pulverize her."

Affected by his protectiveness, she reached out without thinking and touched his arm.

Her heart stopped.

Holy cow!

Up until now, she'd thought he was on the skinny side like his sister, but there was nothing thin about that arm. His biceps were harder than a brick even while relaxed.

"Okay," she said, trying to distract herself from that delectable muscle. "Makeover with no nail polish."

Sam picked out several shirts and more jeans, then sent Adrian to try them on. She was busy looking through another rack when she felt someone behind her.

Turning around, she froze. Adrian was standing at the mirror outside the dressing room with his sweater lifted while he tugged at the back of his jeans. "I don't know about this," he said.

She only vaguely registered his words. Because she was captivated by him. The faded denim cupped a rear so tight and well formed that it made her ache to touch it.

He was wearing a thin, black V-neck sweater that clung to his broad shoulders, biceps, and pecs. And worse, the hem of the sweater was lifted up to where she could see his hard, flat stomach and dark brown hairs curling becomingly around his navel.

Oh . . . My . . . God. The man had the body of a well-toned gymnast. Why he had kept that yummy body hidden was beyond her.

"Buddy, you got abs!" she said before she could stop herself.

Adrian met her gaze in the mirror. "What?"

She closed the distance between them and lifted the shirt hem a tad higher as she stared in awe at that body. "You got abs! A whole six-pack of them." She looked up at him. "You didn't get those on the computer."

"Well, no. I do other things on occasion."

No kidding.

And right then, there was a whole series of other things she wanted to do to him. Starting with those hard abs and working her way up and down that luscious, tanned body. "If I were you, I'd burn all those baggy jeans and oversized shirts as soon as I got home."

"You like these jeans?"

Biting her lip, she nodded.

Suddenly, Adrian liked them, too. But what he liked most was the hunger he saw in her eyes, the feel of her hand against his stomach. It sent chills all over him.

It was all he could do not to kiss her.

Worse, an image of her lying naked beneath him tore through him. He shuttered his eyes as his breathing faltered. He wanted her so badly, he could already taste the moistness of her lips. Feel the softness of those full breasts in his hands.

It was a such a raw, aching need that it sliced through him.

Sam looked up and caught the heated look in his eyes. He had his lips slightly parted. And she became all too aware of the fact she was still holding his shirt in her hand, and was so close to his hard belly that she could feel his body heat.

Her breasts tightened as a wave of lust singed her.

Please kiss me. . . .

But he didn't. He swallowed and took a step back.

Sam sighed. What was she thinking? Smart, gorgeous guys like Adrian didn't date short, fat co-workers. They were friends, plain and simple. There could never be anything between them.

B_y *the time* they finished, Adrian was almost a thousand dollars poorer, but he had an entire new wardrobe. And if it would keep Sam staring at him like she was doing, he decided it was worth every penny.

He changed into a new T-shirt, sweater, and jeans before they left.

Their next stop was MasterCuts. "What's wrong with my hair?" he asked as he sat down in the chair.

"Nothing, Shaggy-Doo," Sam said playfully as she brushed her hand through his hair. His entire body erupted into fire as he savored her light touch against his scalp. "I love the tawny color and curls. With the right cut, you would stop traffic."

Sam watched from the side of his chair as the beautician trimmed his silken curls into a shorter cut that looked incredibly sexy and stylish.

Oh, yeah, now he was cooking. She stared in awe as the woman moussed his hair.

"Now that is a great look," Sam told Adrian. "You get rid of that goatee and watch out."

"Now you hate my goatee?" he asked, aghast.

"For the record," Sam said as she met his gaze in the mirror, "all women hate goatees."

The beautician concurred. "She's right. They're nasty."

Adrian stroked his goatee with his thumb. "Really? You don't think it's manly?"

"Do you think a billy goat is manly?"

"Oh, thanks, *Heather.*"

Sam's eyes twinkled.

Adrian paid for the cut and for the bottle of mousse Sam insisted he'd better use, but personally, he'd rather stick a pair of tweezers in an electrical outlet.

All too soon, the night was over and he had to drive her back to her car.

"Thanks," he said as she got into her Honda. "I really appreciate your taking pity on my clothes tonight."

"It was my pleasure."

God, he wanted to kiss her. He stared at her lips, trying to imagine what they would taste like. He'd give anything to have a single night with her. To sink himself deep between her soft thighs as she held him close and moaned in his ear.

Then again, one night with her would never be enough.

"You be careful," he said, his voice hoarse. "How far is Spring Hill from here?"

"A good fifty minutes."

"Jeez, I shouldn't have kept you out so long. Do me a favor and call my cell phone and let me know when you get home, okay?"

"Okay."

Adrian forced himself to close her car door. He stepped away from her car as she started it. The light from the control panel lit her face as she buckled herself in.

In that moment, he ached for something he knew he could never have.

Her.

She looked up and waved. He returned the gesture, then watched as she drove off.

His heart heavy, and feeling twice as lonely as he had before, he got into his car.

Adrian froze as he reached for the ignition. He could still smell her floral scent in the air. Taking a deep breath, he relished it and dreamed of being able to bury his face in her neck where he could just breathe her in all night.

And in that moment, he made a decision.

Right or wrong, company policy be damned, he was going to find some way to make her his.

2

"Hey, Sam, could you come here for a minute?"

Sam cringed as Tiffany waylaid her outside of the breakroom at ten A.M. "What do you need?"

Tiffany huffed in agitation. "Adrian isn't here yet—"

"That's because he was here from eleven-thirty last night until three o'clock this morning. I imagine he's sleeping in."

"Whatever. I have to respond to the Waverley Valley customer, and he has yet to send me his e-mail."

Sam pursed her lips to keep from laughing. Oh, he'd written the e-mail all right. He'd answered the customer's complaints, point by point, with the most hilarious sarcasm she'd ever read. The last line of it had said, "All hail the goddess Discordia the day we let Lord Bone-Head's twenty-two teenage employees have unrestricted ordering capacity on our system."

Adrian was a riot.

And at the bottom of the e-mail, he'd pasted in the much more professional response that he had sent to their customer.

"I know he wrote it," Sam said seriously. "I'm sure he'll forward a copy as soon as he gets in."

"Well, he better, or I'm telling Randy about it." Tiffany glanced down the hallway, did a double-take, then gaped.

Sam turned her head to see what was going on.

She froze at the sight.

Oh, my.

Like all the other women in the hallway, Sam was transfixed by Adrian and that sexy, loose-limbed swagger of his as he came toward her. Dressed all in black, except for the hint of his white T-shirt peeking out of the V of his tailored black button-down shirt, he was dazzling.

The black leather jacket she had talked him into looked even better on him than she had imagined it would.

His goatee was gone and the new haircut gave a deeply poetic look to his chiseled features. He wore a pair of Wayfarer sunglasses, and when he smiled, she saw deep dimples that had been masked all this time by his thick whiskers.

The man was *seriously* hot.

Regina, the receptionist, was headed to her desk when she passed him. Turning her head to watch him, she stared so intently at his rear that she walked straight into the wall.

Oblivious to the gaping women around him, Adrian made straight for Sam.

"Good morning," he said, flashing those dimples as he took his sunglasses off.

"Morning," Sam said, amazed at how normal her voice sounded given the amount of havoc his new look had on her senses. Now that he was this close, she could smell the leather and his Old Spice after-shave. Yum. Her entire body burned.

"Oh, Adrian!" Tiffany gushed as she twirled a strand of blond hair around her index finger. "We were just talking about you."

Adrian arched a brow at her. "What did I do now?"

"Oh, it was nothing bad. I was just asking about that silly old e-mail, but I know you're busy. So, you take your time and when you're ready, I'll take care of it for you."

My, how her tune has changed, Sam thought irritably. *Why is it, you find a good man, clean him up, and then the vultures start swooping in?*

Life was not fair.

"I sent the e-mail last night," Adrian said.

"How strange," Tiffany said with an obviously practiced frown. "I didn't see it in my in box."

"Did you forget to change it over from your personal e-mail account to the company servers again?"

"Oh," Tiffany said, stroking him lightly on the arm as she giggled and preened. "How silly of me. You know, I just can't keep all this computer stuff straight in my head. I'd really appreciate it if you'd show me how to fix that."

"I'll send Scott down."

His phone rang. Adrian answered it while Tiffany ran a hungry look over his body.

Sam wanted to choke her. "Don't you have something you need to do?" she asked Tiffany.

Tiffany glared at her until Adrian hung up, then she smiled sweetly at him. "You know, if you've got a minute, right now—"

"Actually, I don't. I need to talk to Sam. Excuse us?"

"Oh, absolutely. I'm sure you *guys*—no offense, Sam—" she said, sweeping a hard look to Sam before giving Adrian a worshipful smile, "have computer problems to talk about. I'll see you"—she punctuated the word by touching Adrian on the chest—"later."

Sam had to force herself not to clobber Tiffany.

As soon as they were alone, Adrian bent down to whisper in her ear. "I did put the right colors together, didn't I?" he asked.

"Oh, yeah," Sam breathed as two women who were staring at Adrian collided behind him.

He let out a relieved sigh. "I was having a bad Heather flashback as I came in the door and three women looked at me and started giggling."

Sam could well imagine that. She felt giddy herself.

Adrian stroked his chin with his hand. "And I'm not sure about the face. I've had a beard or mustache since I turned seventeen. I feel really naked."

At that moment, she wished he *were* naked. Naked and in her arms doing the Wild Thing with her. "You shouldn't."

"You're sure I don't look like a girly-mon? Because I really don't want the guys up in design to start following me around."

"Oh, no," she said with a laugh. "There's nothing girly about the way you look."

"All right, but if the guys start harassing me, I might have to fire you."

She laughed at the empty threat.

His phone rang again and Regina paged him.

"It starts already," Sam said.

"Already? Hell, it started two hours ago, which is why I came on in," he mumbled as he flipped open his phone, and headed toward his office.

Sam bit her knuckles as she watched him walk away. She ran a lecherous gaze down his lean back and well-shaped rear. An image of those flat abs tormented her, and it was all she could do not to follow him into his office, lock the door, and keep him there until they were both sweaty and spent.

Y₀, *A-dri-an!*" *Scott* called as he passed by Sam's cube.

Sam cringed, knowing how much Adrian hated for someone to do that to him.

"What?" he snapped as he stuck his head over Randir's cube.

"Oh," Scott said. "You're not in your office. I was wondering what we're doing for lunch today?"

"We haven't discussed it."

"Well, it's eleven-thirty and I'm starving. Let's discuss it."

Adrian peeped over the cube wall to look at her. "Sam, you coming?"

"Depends on where you go."

"Well," Scott said to Adrian, "I was wondering if your sister's working at Chik-Fil-A today. I'm kind of broke, so if she'd spot us again, I'd really appreciate it."

"You mooch," Randir said. "I say we take him out back, and shoot him."

Adrian laughed as he picked up his phone and dialed it. "Hey, Mark? This is Adrian. Is Heather working today?"

"Hey, Sis," Adrian said after a brief pause. "Scott's broke and wanted to know if you'd feed him again? Okay, we'll see you shortly." Hanging up, he looked at Sam. "Chik-Fil-A?"

"Sure, I'll go."

"I'll drive," Jack said from the cube opposite her. "I have the minivan today. But I warn you, it's full of toys."

The six of them gathered their things and headed for the door. Adrian fell in beside her, then reached an arm toward her.

Sam froze in nervous anticipation as it appeared he was about to put his arm around her, then he bent it up quickly and raked his hand through his hair.

Disappointed, she did all she could do not to pout.

Adrian cursed at himself as he realized what he'd almost done. And at work no less . . . Jeez. What was wrong with him?

But then, he knew. Sam had been sneaking looks at him all morning.

And he'd loved every minute of it.

Jack unlocked his van. Sam took the seat behind the driver's and Adrian quickly sat beside her. When she looked up and smiled, he felt like someone had sucker-punched him right in the gut.

"I really like that jacket," she said to him.

"Oh, Adrian," Scott teased from the front passenger seat as Jack started the van, then backed up. "You're just so cute today," he lisped. "Can I have a ride in your special Love Bytes machine after work?"

"Would you guys leave him alone?" Sam said.

"It's all right," Adrian said as he picked up a Game Boy from the seat and turned it on. "I'll just fire his ass after lunch."

Adrian played Centipede while Sam and the guys exchanged insults. He listened to them, all the while glancing sideways at Sam. Man, how he loved the way her eyes sparkled when she laughed.

As soon as they reached the mall, they piled out and headed to the food court. They had just entered the area when Sam caught sight of Heather standing beside a table with a guy dressed in a leather motorcycle jacket. He had three days' worth of black stubble on his face, and a death grip on Heather's arm.

Sam held her breath.

Rage descended on Adrian's face as he rushed toward them.

"Josh," Heather said in a pain-filled voice, trying to pry the man's hand off her upper arm. "You're hurting me."

"I'm going to do more than that if—"

"Let her go," Adrian growled as he grabbed Josh's hand and removed it from Heather's arm. He shoved the man back.

Josh raked a sneer over Adrian's body, but there was fear in his eyes as he took in the size of Adrian. "Look, pal, this is between me and my woman."

"No," Adrian said. "It's between you and my baby sister. And if you touch her again, it's going to be between you and me."

A wave of apprehension crossed Josh's face as he looked from Adrian to Heather. "I thought you said Adrian was a geek."

"He is," Heather said. "But he's a really *big* geek."

Josh angled a finger at Heather. "You remember what I said."

"Let me tell *you* something," Adrian said with a killing glare. "If I find you near my sister again, I'm going to play Picasso with your body parts."

Heather postured. "And he can do it too, he has a black belt."

Josh snarled at the two of them, then stalked off.

"Jeez, Heather," Adrian said as he turned to face her. "Can't you ever find a decent guy?"

"He's not always like that," Heather said dismissively. "He can be really sweet, sometimes."

Adrian's face turned hard, cold. "I better not find you near him again, and I mean it."

"Back off, Adrian. It's none of your business. You know, I'm not eleven years old anymore, and I don't need you coming to my rescue all the time."

"Fine," he snapped. "Then stop calling me every time you get into a jam."

"Fine," Heather snarled back at him. "Mom's right, you are just like your father. Worthless and mean."

Sam held her breath as a dark, angry pain descended over Adrian's face.

It was then Adrian must have remembered they were there, listening, because he looked to his left, saw them and locked his jaw.

Without a word, he walked off.

The guys stayed in the food court to comfort Heather while Sam ran after Adrian. He was halfway down the mall before she finally caught up to him.

"Hey?" she said as she pulled him to a stop with a gentle hand on his arm. "You okay?"

Adrian stared at her as he felt her soothing touch all the way through his body. "Why does she have to act that way?" he asked rhetorically. "I'll never understand you women, and why you're only attracted to pricks who run all over you, then turn on you if you dare open your mouth to defend yourself."

"Not all women are attracted to men like that."

"Yeah, right. Prove it."

Before he knew what she was doing, she stood up on her tiptoes, reached her arm around his neck, and brought his head down for a scorching kiss.

Adrian's head swam at the softness of her lips, of the feel of her tongue against his. He cupped her face with his hands and closed his eyes to better savor the moment.

She had her hand buried in his hair, sending chills the entire length of his body. He felt himself harden even more as a wave of her sweet feminine scent permeated his senses.

In that moment, he couldn't think of anything except taking her home, stripping her jeans and sweater from her body, and keeping her that way until breakfast.

Sam didn't know where she'd found the courage to finally kiss him, but she was glad she had. She'd been dreaming of it all day long. And now that she'd actually done it, it was all she could do not to moan from the incredible taste of his lips. The warm, masculine smell of him.

Until it dawned on her what she was doing. She was kissing her boss less than five miles from work, in the middle of a mall crowded with Christmas shoppers where four of their co-workers could see them any second.

Pulling back, she let go of him. "I'm sorry," she whispered. "I shouldn't have done that."

But Adrian didn't let her get away. He caught her in his arms and pressed her against the store window behind her. Then, he kissed her so fiercely that she thought she might faint from it.

It was raw, demanding, and it made her so hot that she couldn't breathe. Couldn't think as she felt his heart pounding rapidly in time with hers.

Good Lord, the man knew how to give a kiss. Every part of her throbbed and ached for him. And when he ran his hands down her back to press her closer to his hips, she felt his hard erection against her stomach.

He wanted *her*.

In that instant, she felt she could fly.

"Neither should I," he whispered against her lips. "But the bad thing is, I want to do it again."

So did she.

He took a step back and put his hands in his jacket pockets.

"What are we going to do about this?" she asked tentatively.

"I don't know." He looked around them. "You probably should get back to the guys before someone sees us."

She took a step toward the food court, then noticed he hadn't budged. "Are you coming?"

He shook his head. "I'm not hungry. I'll go play at Radio Shack while you guys eat. Just pick me up on the way out."

"I'll stay with you."

He smiled. "I appreciate the thought, but Ms. Hypoglycemic can't go without lunch."

It was so like him to think of her, and that was one of the things she loved best about him. "All right."

He caught her hand before she left him, then kissed the back of her knuckles. "Thanks for coming after me."

"You're very welcome."

He let go and she felt a strange vacant hole in her stomach. Glancing back at him and the striking image he made smiling at her, she headed to the food court.

Sam waved at the guys as she went over to Chik-Fil-A and ordered a value meal.

"Is Adrian okay?" Heather asked.

"No. You embarrassed him."

"Well, you know, it's not my fault. He always has to act like he's Mr. Macho out to defend my honor all the time. It gets really old."

"He loves you, Heather. What's he supposed to do? Sit around and let you get hurt? Jeez, I'd kill for one of my brothers to do the things for me he does for you. I mean damn, girl, you let him go to work, knowing he's the boss, in ruined clothes while he *pays* you to embarrass him. I just don't understand you."

Heather looked away guiltily. "I do love him, you know. I just wish he'd quit trying to parent me all the time."

"Well, from what I've heard, he was pretty much the only parent you had growing up."

"I know," Heather said. "I remember when he was twelve and I was six, Mom couldn't afford a Christmas tree. I was crying on Christmas Eve because I didn't think Santa would come without one, so Adrian rode his bicycle down to the supermarket and talked the tree dealer into letting him work for one."

Heather sighed. "He's always doing really sweet things like that for me. I guess I really do take him for granted."

"Personally, I think a whole lot of people do."

Heather handed Sam her food.

"Wait," Heather whispered as Sam started to leave. She quickly bagged a sandwich, fries, and brownie. "Would you take this to him and tell him I'm really sorry?"

"Sure."

Sam made her way over to the guys who were eating. They were back to their usual bantering, but as she ate, she couldn't get the taste of Adrian's kiss out of her mind. That kiss had really done something to her.

Worse, she kept imagining him as a kid working on a cold Nashville parking lot so his baby sister would have a Christmas tree. It was such an Adrian thing to do.

And she wondered if anyone had ever done such a thing for him. But in her heart, she knew they hadn't.

Adrian took care of the world while no one took care of him.

Sam *cracked open* Adrian's office door. "Hey, I just wanted to let you know that I was leaving."

He turned around in his chair to face her. "Is it five already?"

"Five-thirty, actually."

"Oh." He rose from his chair and shrugged on his leather jacket. "I'll walk you out."

"Okay," she said, her heart pounding as every hormone in her body instantly fired.

There was an awkward silence between them as they walked down the hallway toward the side door where she parked.

"I, um . . . I had something I wanted to ask you," he said as he opened the door for her.

"Sure," she said in dread as she led the way across the lot to her car. "If you're worried about what happened this afternoon, don't be. I'm not going to tell anyone."

"Oh, I don't care about that. I mean, I care about that, but . . . shit," he breathed. "I never was any good at this. So, I'll just do what I do best, and blurt it out. Would you like to go to the Christmas party with me?"

Sam smiled as her heart raced even faster. "Yes, I would. But only if you bring the mistletoe."

His gaze dropped to her lips and she wondered if he was imaging the feel of their kiss like she was.

"Great," he said. "Pick you up at three?"

"Sounds good. I'll give you the directions to my house tomorrow."

"Okay." He bent his head down like he was going to kiss her again, then he quickly shot back upright. "We're still at work."

Adrian watched as she got in her car, and a chill went up his spine that had nothing to do with the cold winter wind and everything to do with her.

She was something else. And he liked it.

She rolled her car window down.

Adrian leaned down to where he could speak to her without someone overhearing them. "You know, I really want to kiss you right now."

"Me, too."

Ask her back to your place. It was on the tip of his tongue, but he didn't dare.

"You better get back in," she said. "It's cold out here."

No, it wasn't. Not when he was standing so close to her. "Yeah," he breathed, "You're probably freezing."

She reached out and touched his hand. "I'll see you tomorrow."

Adrian gave a light squeeze to her hand even though what he wanted to do was hold it tight.

Letting go, he walked away from her, and with every step he took, he cursed himself for the stupidity. Why hadn't he asked her back to his apartment?

But then, he knew. If he had her alone in his place, his hands would be all over her. It was too soon, and the last thing he wanted was to drive her away from him.

He'd never wanted anything in his life the way he wanted Samantha Parker.

Closing his eyes, he did his best to banish the image in his mind of her naked in his arms. The imagined feel of her breath falling across his neck as he lost himself inside her body.

"I want you, Sam," he breathed as he watched her pull out of the lot. "And one way or another, I'm going to have you."

3

"Sam?"

Sam looked up to see Adrian's head poking out of his office door. "Yeah?"

"In my office. Now."

She swallowed at his low, even tone. It sounded strangely like the one he used to crawl all over Scott when Scott did something stupid.

Worse, he'd been avoiding her all day. He hadn't even gone to lunch with them.

Had she done something wrong?

Nervous, she got up and took the five steps that separated her cube from his office.

As soon as she was inside, he closed the door.

Sam's heart pounded. This wasn't good. Adrian never closed his door unless it was time for a major performance talk.

Eyes dark and features grim, he turned toward her.

Sam expected him to tell her to sit, so when he cupped her face in his hands, and pressed her back against his wall, she was stunned.

His breathing ragged, he lowered his head down and captured her lips with his.

And it wasn't just any kiss. It was scorching and demanding. Every hormone in her body jumped to attention. Closing her eyes, she relished the warm scent of him. The masterful feel of his tongue dancing with hers as his hands roamed over her shoulders and back, down to her hips. She wrapped her arms around his shoulders and moaned softly as her desire for him tripled.

He separated her legs with his thigh and cupped her buttocks as he set her down on that taut muscle. Sam groaned at the feeling of him between her legs. Her feet barely touched the floor as he surrounded her with warmth.

Her head light, she throbbed and ached for more of him.

Adrian knew he shouldn't be doing this, but he hadn't been able to stand it any longer. All day long, he'd been unable to think about anything other than the fact that she was only five feet away.

She was so intelligent, so much fun.

He wanted to devour her.

Adrian pulled back from the kiss to where he could nibble her lips as he buried his hand in her thick, dark hair. He laved a trail from her lips to her neck where he inhaled her.

He skimmed his hand up from her waist to the side of her breast. At the sound of her murmured pleasure, he felt his control slipping.

He ached for her. Burned for her in a way he'd never burned before and all he could think of was being inside her.

"I want you, Sam," he whispered.

Sam gave him a chiding stare. "I thought I was in trouble."

Adrian shook his head as he lost himself in those light eyes of hers. "I think I'm the one in trouble. Serious trouble."

He dipped his head to kiss her again.

His cell phone went off.

Growling, he answered it. "Scott, I'm in the middle of a damn important meeting. Send an e-mail."

Someone knocked on the door.

"Just a minute," Adrian snapped, then he brushed her cheek with his fingers, even though what he really wanted to do was lay her down on his desk and alleviate the vicious, throbbing ache in his groin.

Not to mention the one in his heart.

His breathing ragged, he let go of her. "I better let you get back to work."

She nodded, then kissed him hard on his lips.

The knock sounded again.

She smiled. "Duty calls."

Sam *spent the* rest of the day dreaming about that kiss. And as she watched people traipse in and out of Adrian's office, she felt like cursing. Couldn't they just leave him in peace?

"Hey!" Randir said as he came around her cube. "It's snowing really bad outside."

Sam looked up with a start. "What?"

"Oh, yeah, the roads are freezing." Randir stuck his head in Adrian's door. "I'm going home."

Adrian came out of his office. "Tell everyone to head out."

Since she lived fifty minutes away, Sam dialed her oldest brother's cell phone.

"Don't you dare head home," Teddy said sternly. "The roads are awful. I had to leave my Blazer at the bottom of the hill and walk home. Is there some place in La Vergne you can bunk for the night?"

"I guess. Thanks." She hung up.

"Why are you still here?" Adrian asked.

"My brother said the roads are frozen solid. Looks like I'll be spending the night on the cot in the first-aid room."

Adrian frowned. "You can't do that."

Like she had any choice, she thought wistfully. "Sure I can. I have the vending machines and the security guard for company. I'll be fine."

"Why don't you come home with me?" he asked stoically.

Sam hesitated as her heart pounded. If she did that, she had a really good idea what would happen.

But then, how bad would it be to make love to him all night?

She bit her lip in indecision. "I don't know."

At the hurt look on his face, she quickly added, "I bet you get stuck here with me. I'm sure the Corvette isn't any better in this weather than my Honda."

"I'm not in the Vette. I drove my Bronco in."

She arched a brow. "I didn't know you had another car."

"Yeah. I love the Vette, but she's temperamental and she hates snow." He took her jacket off the peg inside her cube and held it open for her. "C'mon. I promise I'll behave."

Her stomach knotted in excitement and fear, she shrugged her coat on. "Okay."

Adrian led her out of the building, across the virtually empty parking lot to an older-model black Bronco and opened the door for her.

After he got in and started the car, Sam sat beside Adrian with her heart in her throat. She was so nervous, she was actually trembling. It'd been a long time since she'd been with a guy. A long time since she'd gone to a guy's place.

And she'd never loved a man as much as she did Adrian.

Should I make a move on him? Or should I wait for him to do something?

What if he thinks I'm fat? He was so well toned and she was . . . well, fleshy. What if it turned him off?

Good grief, her doubts and fears plagued her silly.

Adrian tried to think of something to say as he drove the ten-minute commute to his apartment.

But he couldn't.

His hands were actually sweating inside his gloves. He hadn't taken a girl home with him since college.

Should I make a move on her? Or should I wait for her to do something?

Is it too soon?

He didn't want to scare her off. He really liked her. And the last thing he wanted was for her to bolt for the door.

But he couldn't stand the thought of not having her.

By the time he pulled up next to his Corvette, his stomach was absolutely knotted.

"Do you have a roommate?" she asked as he walked her to his door.

"With the hours I keep? No one would put up with me." He unlocked the door and let her in.

Sam entered the living room, then froze. She'd never seen anything like it in her life.

"Good Lord, it looks like a Circuit City showroom," she said as her gaze darted over the big-screen TV, three leather recliners, DVD player, double-decker VCR, two computers, and a stereo bigger than her car.

His walls were stark white and completely bare. But at least the whole apartment was amazingly clean and well kept.

"Jeez. Adrian, you live like a bear in an electronic cave."

He laughed as he locked the door, then set his keys, security badge, and wallet in a bowl on the breakfast counter.

He shrugged his coat off and hung it up in a closet to her left. Sam took hers off and handed it to him.

"Should I ask about the three recliners?"

He shrugged. "Sometimes the guys come over to watch a game."

"So, why don't you have a couch?"

He looked offended by the very idea. "I'm not sitting my ass down next to another guy. Jeez, Sam, I thought you were raised with five brothers."

"Oh, yeah, how could I forget?" she said as she rolled her eyes at him. "The male and his territory."

He laughed as he gave her a brief tour of his place.

"Do you really need a PlayStation 2, Dreamcast, and Nintendo 64?" she asked. But what really amused her was the small TV next to the big one. She arched a questioning brow.

"Sometimes I play games while I'm watching the big TV," he said as if there were nothing unusual about it.

Sam smiled, until she glanced down at one of the chairs. Then she sobered. "You know, Adrian, you're quite a guy."

He gave her a puzzled frown.

"There's not many men who let their underwear watch TV while they're at work," she said, glancing to the pair in the seat of the chair closest to the window.

"Oh, jeez," he moaned as he grabbed them and rushed to the laundry room in the kitchen.

"I'm sorry," she said as she followed after him. "I didn't mean to embarrass you. I think it's funny. Besides, I used to have to do my brothers' laundry, and all I have to say is—"

He turned around at the same time she took a step forward. They collided.

Adrian's breath left his chest as soon as her breasts touched his arm. She looked up at him with her lips parted and before he could stop himself, he took advantage of it.

Sam wrapped her arms around his shoulders as she kissed him with all the passion and love flowing through her. And in that moment, she knew what was about to happen between them.

This was the moment she'd spent the last year dreaming of.

Scared and excited, she couldn't wait.

Adrian deepened his kiss as his hands roamed freely over her back, pressing her closer to him. Growling low in his throat, he pulled back from her lips and buried his mouth against her neck.

Sam hissed in pleasure as his hot tongue, lips, and teeth nibbled and suckled her. Chills swept through her entire body as her breasts tingled in response to his expert, masculine touch. Heat pooled itself into an aching throb between her legs.

The scent of leather and Old Spice tormented her unmercifully. Gracious, how she wanted this man.

No one had ever made her feel the way he did. Desirable. Beautiful.

And best of all, needed.

Tonight, she would show her love to him. Tonight, she would hold nothing back and she would hope for a time when perhaps he might love her in return.

Adrian's vision dulled as he inhaled the warm, sweet scent of her skin. And he wanted more of her.

He wanted all of her.

That need foremost on his mind, he ran his hand over her breast, and squeezed it gently. He moaned at the softness, and at the feel of her hardened nipple through her Santa sweater.

To his amazement, Sam answered the caress with one of her own as she reached down between their bodies and cupped him in her hand, through his jeans. Adrian growled as she stroked him, teased him, making his entire body quiver and burn for her.

She was bold with her caresses, and more than generous with her lips.

His body on fire, Adrian returned to her mouth as she unbuttoned his jeans, then slid her hand beneath the elastic band of his briefs to take him into her hand.

He sucked his breath in sharply between his teeth as he hardened to the point of pain.

"You are a big man," she whispered against his lips as she gently stroked his shaft.

"You're the only one who does that to me," he whispered. He ran his hands under her sweater, over her smooth, soft skin, to the back of her bra where he released the catch.

His breath caught as her breasts spilled out of the satin bra and into his hands. He reveled in the feel of those taut nipples in his palms and he couldn't wait to taste them. To run his tongue over the tiny ridges as he breathed her scent in.

Her soft flesh filled his hands past capacity and he loved it.

Then, she untucked his shirt and ran her hands over his chest and back, clutching at him in a way that made him dizzy.

The damned phone rang.

"Do you need to answer it?" she said breathlessly.

"To hell with it."

"What if it's work?"

"To hell with it."

She laughed.

He heard his answering machine pick up.

"Adrian?"

He flinched as he heard his mother's nasal, Southern drawl.

"Adrian, this is Mom. Are you there? If you are, pick up, honey. I need to talk to you."

His hormones instantly iced by the sound of his mother's voice, he pulled back. "I better answer it or she'll call every ten minutes from now on and start beeping me."

Devastated by the interruption, Sam licked her lips and tried to pull herself together as Adrian left her and picked up the cordless phone from the counter. He tucked his shirt back in and buttoned his pants.

"Hi, Mom," he said coolly as he left the kitchen, then went to his bedroom, and closed the door while Sam straightened her own clothes.

"Adrian, where have you been? I've been calling for an hour."

Sam went over to his answering machine to turn it off so that she wouldn't overhear their conversation, but it had so many unmarked buttons, she didn't know which one to press.

"I was at work."

"I wish you'd give me your work number. I need to be able to get a hold of you when something comes up."

"What do you need now, Mom?"

"I need you to come over and salt my driveway, so that I won't get stuck here tomorrow."

"Jesus, Mom, it's a forty-minute drive and the roads are iced over."

"I know, that's why I need you to come over, right now."

Sam frowned at his mother's insistence.

"Mom, I can't. I'm busy."

His mother gave a dramatic sigh. "Busy doing what? Playing with your stupid computers again? All I ask is a little, tiny favor and this is the thanks I get. Do you know, I was in labor for thirty-six hours with you? I almost died giving birth."

"Yes, Mom, I know."

"Don't you take that tone with me, young man. I gave my life to you kids, and the least you can do is take care of me in my old age."

"You're only forty-seven."

"Don't you dare get smart with me. It's not like you have anything better to do. God forbid you should actually date and marry someone, and give me a grandchild."

"Would you please lay off me, Mom? I'm not in the mood."

"Fine," she said in a sarcastic tone that made Sam want to choke her. "You just stay there, and let me fend for myself. You're just like your worthless father."

"Would you leave Dad out of this?"

"You're just like him, you know. Selfish and worthless. It's a good thing you don't have a girlfriend. You'd probably just knock her up, and leave her, too."

Sam's heart lurched. Poor Adrian. It was a good thing he didn't have another phone or she'd pick it up and give his mother a piece of her mind.

"Just my luck," his mother continued. "To get stuck with an ungrateful son. I knew you should have been a girl. That's fine, though. I'll just call Heather and get her to do it."

"Jeez, Mom, Heather can hardly drive when the weather's clear and she lives farther away than I do."

"What do you care? At least I can depend on her."

"All right," Adrian snapped. "I'm coming, okay? Don't get her killed because you need your driveway salted."

"Oh, good."

Sam gaped at the sudden change in the woman's voice. Now that she was getting her way, she actually sounded nice.

"Love you, sweetie."

"Me, too." By his tone, Sam knew he had his teeth gritted.

The answering machine clicked off. Sam shook her head. She'd never heard anything like that in her life.

Adrian came out of the bedroom with his jaw ticking. "I have to go out for a little bit."

"Adrian, you can't do that. What if you have a wreck and get killed?"

"Trust me, I'm not that lucky."

"You're not funny."

He shrugged his heavy ski jacket on. Sam zipped it while he fixed the collar. "You be careful," she said, standing up on her tiptoes to kiss him.

Adrian nibbled her lips as warmth spread through him. Only Sam had ever said that to him. "I will. Lock the door behind me."

As soon as he was gone, Sam sighed. Adrian reminded her of a tolerant lion with cubs hanging off him while they nipped his skin. How could he stand it?

Shaking her head, Sam went to get herself a Coke. She opened the fridge and stared in disbelief. It was bare except for an almost-empty gallon of soured milk and a six-pack of beer.

Frowning, she opened his kitchen cabinets, taking inventory. One plate, two mismatched bowls, a cookie sheet, one medium-sized pot, three glasses, two coffee cups, coffee, and two half-empty boxes of cereal. That was it.

Unbelievable. She'd had no idea he lived like this. And now that she thought about it, she realized he didn't even have a Christmas tree in his apartment.

The phone rang again.

Sam ignored it until the answering machine picked up.

"Adrian?" Heather said. "Hey, I need you to call me back as soon as you hear this, okay? Um, I need you, big brother. And please don't yell at me. I had to write a check out for tuition today or else they'd cancel my classes. And I don't have the money to cover it. I'm also two weeks overdue on my rent again. I really need twelve hundred dollars by tomorrow. I swear, I won't ever again ask you for money. I know I said that last time, but I mean it this time. Anyway, please call me tonight. Love you."

Sam ached for him. When he had told her he watched out for his sister and mother, she'd had no idea just what a challenge the two of them were.

"That's *it*," she muttered as she grabbed her coat out of the closet. "It's time someone did something for you."

It *was almost* three hours later when Adrian finally got home. His head throbbed from his mother's incessant criticism. And the woman wondered why no man would ever stay with her for more than a few months.

If he had any sense, he'd take off, too. But he refused to do that to Heather. His sister could barely look after herself, let alone watch after their mother.

Pushing the thoughts out of his mind, he opened the door. He frowned as he caught a whiff of something really good.

Must be his neighbor's dinner again, he thought as he closed and locked the door. He hung up his coat.

"Sam?" he called, not seeing her in the living room.

"I'm right here," she said from the kitchen.

Adrian turned, then froze as his breath left his body. Sam was standing at the sink wearing nothing but one of his flannel shirts. It was huge on her, reaching all the way to her knees.

The sight floored him.

"I hope you don't mind," she said as she pulled at the collar. "I fell on my way back and got mud all over my clothes."

"Fell?" It was then he realized the warm, delicious aroma was coming from his stove. Damn, the thing actually worked. Who knew?

He frowned. "What did you do?"

She moved toward him with a coffee cup in her hands. "Here," she said, handing him hot chocolate. "I'm sure you're frozen."

He had been until he saw her half-dressed. Now, he felt as if he were on fire. "Where did this come from?"

She smiled. "I walked down to the market on the corner."

He was stunned. He'd never in his life come home to such a warm welcome.

And in that moment, he knew he loved her.

Setting the cup down on his breakfast counter, he pulled her into his arms and held her close.

Sam trembled at the contact. He ran his hands down her back, then to her bare hips.

"Oh, God," he breathed. "You're naked under there."

Sam laughed. "I know."

Adrian's thoughts scattered as he touched her bare buttocks. Her skin was so incredibly soft while he was harder than he'd ever been before.

Bending down, he scooped her up in his arms and carried her to the bedroom.

Sam wrapped her arms around his neck, amazed he was able to carry her so easily. And when he laid her on the bed, she smiled, knowing this was what she'd wanted since the first time she'd seen him greeting her in the lobby for her interview last year.

She got up on her knees and pulled his shirt over his head. Her gaze feasted on the sight of all that strong, tawny skin as she ran her hands over his delectable flesh.

Good gracious, the man had a gorgeous body, and she couldn't wait to taste every inch of it.

The way he watched her with his eyes dark and hungry, his breathing ragged, made her burn even more for him. How could a man like this want *her*?

Sam hesitated as she placed her hands on the top button of his jeans. "I want you to know that I'm not easy," she whispered.

"It never crossed my mind," he said as he cupped her face in his hands. He moved to kiss her, but she pulled back.

She met his confused gaze. "I've only been with one other guy. My college boyfriend."

"Okay," he said, dipping his head toward hers.

She laughed as she dodged his lips again. "Would you listen for a second?"

He arched a brow at her.

"I wanted to let you know that I'm not on the pill or anything."

Adrian went rigid. Cursing, he took a step back from the bed. "Well, since we're confessing things, I have to tell you, I haven't been with a woman since college, either. And I threw out my condoms last year after it occurred to me that they were older than I was." Adrian retrieved his shirt from the floor.

Damn it, he was so hard it hurt. And all he could think of was taking her, consequences be damned.

But he couldn't do that. He wasn't about to take a chance on getting her pregnant. In spite of what his mother thought, he wasn't his father.

It figures. Whatever made you think you could have a woman like her, anyway?

Sam frowned as he stalked out of the room. She started to call him back, then reconsidered. He needed to eat first.

She went after him. "You hungry?"

Adrian nodded, but by his face she could tell food was the last thing he wanted.

Sam served him a bowl of chili.

Adrian stood at the counter while he ate it.

Bemused, Sam watched as he refused to look at her. And the only words he uttered were a very brief compliment on how good her chili tasted and a simple thank-you.

As soon as he was finished, Adrian placed the bowl in the sink, then went to sit in his recliner.

Picking up his remote for the stereo, he clicked on his CD player. He had to do something to distract himself from those luscious legs peeking out from under her shirt. He rotated the discs to Matchbox 20.

Suddenly, he felt Sam beside his chair. He glanced at her, then did a double-take as he saw her shirt unbuttoned all the way to her navel. Even worse, the swell of one breast was so obvious that it sent a wave of heat straight through his groin.

"Don't tease me, Sam," he said hoarsely.

With a tight-lipped smile, she lifted up the hem of the shirt to gift him with a glimpse of the dark curls at the juncture of her thighs before she climbed into his lap.

"Sam," he groaned as she reached to unbutton his pants. His entire body burned and, worse, her feminine, floral scent was making him insane. If she didn't get up, he was going to have her regardless of his common sense. "Please don't."

She took his hands in hers and led them to her breasts.

Adrian leaned his head back and moaned at the softness of her bare breasts in his hands.

Sam kissed him then, and he felt something strange in her mouth.

Adrian pulled back to see her with a wrapped condom between her teeth.

The smile on her face was devilish as she removed the package. "I bought them at the store, just in case."

Growling low in his throat, he kissed her fiercely.

Sam gasped as he rose to his feet with her still in his lap. She wrapped her arms and legs around him as he carried her back to his bed with his hands firmly gripping her bare bottom.

He set her on the bed, then pulled his shirt over his head again as she finished unfastening his jeans. She removed his clothes from him.

Sam gaped at the sight of his lean muscles as she saw him naked for the first time. Every single inch of his lean, hard body was toned and perfect. Never had she seen anything like it.

Her face burned as she saw the size of his erection.

She ran her hands over the veins on his forearms, over the strength of a body she'd never dared hope to touch. His skin was so soft, his muscles so hard. It reminded her of velvet stretched over steel.

She'd never imagined her programming genius would have the body of a Greek god. But he truly did.

Adrian hesitated as he stared at her in his bed, wearing his shirt. She was beautiful there. So soft, warm, and giving.

His desire surged through him like lava as he joined her in the bed and laid her back against the mattress. He rained kisses over her face and neck as he did his best to control himself.

His body demanded he get down to business with her, but his heart wanted to savor her for as long as he could. Even if it killed him.

Adrian groaned as she rolled him over onto his back and straddled his waist. He liked her feistiness. But most of all, he liked her on top of him.

She leaned over his chest and ran her tongue along the edge of his jaw, sending a thousand needlelike chills over his body as she rubbed herself against his stomach.

It shook him all the way to his soul.

"I'm so glad you got rid of that goatee," she whispered in his ear a second before she ran her tongue around the curve of his jaw.

Adrian held her against him. "If I'd known you would do this, I'd have shaved it off the first week you came to work."

She laughed.

He buried his lips in the curve of her shoulder, inhaling the sweet scent of her skin. His head swam from the moistness of her on his stomach.

Needing her in a way that terrified him, he unbuttoned her shirt and pulled it from her shoulders. "You are so beautiful," he breathed as he saw her naked.

Her curves were every bit as full and lush as he had imagined. And her breasts . . .

He could stare at those luscious breasts all night long.

His breathing ragged, he reached up and cupped them in his hands. She trembled in response, delighting him even more.

He dropped his gaze down to the moist curls that were driving him crazy, the moist curls that covered the part of her he couldn't wait to have.

Sitting up, he kissed her furiously as he skimmed his hand from her breast, down her smooth, soft stomach to the tangled curls and into the sleek, wet cleft.

Sam hissed at the pleasure of his long, lean fingers stroking her intimately. She'd never felt anything better, until he slid them inside her. In and out, and around, those fingers tormented her with a fiery pleasure she feared might actually consume her.

Shamelessly, she rubbed herself against him, wanting him in a way that went beyond the physical.

Her body on fire, she pushed him back against the bed, then moved to kiss a trail down his chest.

Adrian hissed as Sam brushed her lips against his taut nipple and when she drew it into her mouth he thought he would die from the pleasure of her tongue on his skin.

He buried his hands in her hair, cupping her face gently as he let the love he felt for her wash over him. She was so giving, so kind. Never in his life had anyone taken care of him. Never had anyone cared.

But Sam did, and it rocked him all the way to his heart.

"Touch me, Sam," he breathed, wanting to feel her hand against him again.

She moved herself lower, trailing her tongue and lips down his abdomen, to his navel, his hip, where she tormented him mercilessly with little nibbles that rocked his entire body.

Delirious from her touch, he closed his eyes in painful anticipation as she finally brushed her hand through the curls at the center of his body. She cupped him in her hand.

Adrian arched his back, growling at the softness of her fingers stroking his shaft.

"Yes," he moaned, writhing from the unbelievable sensations that ripped through him.

And before he knew what she was doing, she moved her head lower and licked a slow, torturous path from the base of his shaft, all the way to the tip.

Adrian hissed at the unexpected, blind ecstasy that tore through him.

Sam smiled as she felt him shivering around her. Her only thought to give him more pleasure, she took him into her mouth.

She knew she was making him crazy, and she loved every minute of it. Adrian deserved to be loved by someone who wouldn't take him for granted, and she wanted to show him just how much he meant to her. Just how much she needed him.

Adrian clenched his fists in the sheets at the incredible sensation of her tongue and lips covering him. No one had ever done that to him before, and he couldn't believe just how good it felt.

His body trembling, he couldn't stand not tasting her in return.

He had to have her. Now!

Sam lifted her head as Adrian sat up. His eyes dark and shuttered, he moved until his body was lying in the opposite direction of hers. He ran his mouth and tongue over her stomach as he skimmed a hand down her hips, blazing a scorching trail of heat.

His touch literally burned her from the inside out as he trailed it up her inner thigh, urging her to open her legs for him.

He nudged her legs farther apart, then buried his lips at the center of her body.

"Adrian!" she breathed as he tormented her.

Sam moaned at the sensation of his mouth on her as he nibbled and licked. His tongue and fingers swirled around her, intensifying her pleasure.

Trembling, she returned to torment him the same way.

She writhed as he continued and as she tasted him.

There was such fire and magic in his touch. It scorched her in a way that was indescribable. No wonder she loved this man.

She gave herself to him without reservations or fear. There was something so special in this equal sharing, equal giving. It touched her profoundly and she knew in her heart that she would never be the same.

Sam's head was light as he gave careful consideration to her, and when he slid two fingers inside her body and stroked her, she moaned in ecstasy.

Biting her lip, she closed her eyes as his fingers delved deep and hard inside her, swirling around with the promise of what was to come while he laved her even faster.

Sam's entire body shivered and jerked involuntarily in response to his touch.

Her head spun from the intense sensations. The pleasure was so incredible, so extreme, as it built inside her until she could stand no more.

Suddenly, her entire body exploded as white-hot ecstasy tore through her in ever-increasing waves. Sam cried out as her release came.

Panting, she couldn't move.

"That's it," he said, his skin covered in sweat. "I have to be inside you."

Sam pulled back from him and reached for the condom a few inches from her.

Adrian tensed as she gently slid the cool condom over his hot, swollen shaft. Then she cupped him in her hand. Her touch singed him as his body quivered in response.

How could such tiny hands wreak so much havoc on him?

Needing to feel her more than he needed to breathe, Adrian pressed her back against the mattress, then separated her thighs with his knees.

You are about to violate your Web designer.

He didn't know where that thought came from, but it ripped through his mind as he pressed the tip of his shaft against her core.

What was he doing?

"Adrian?" she asked as she looked up at him with a frown. "Is something wrong?"

"Are you sure you want this?" he asked as he looked down at her. "If anyone finds out, we could get fired."

"Then I'll find another job," she said, lifting her hips toward his.

Joy ripped through him. Taking her hand into his, he stared into her eyes, then drove himself deep inside her body.

They moaned together.

Sam couldn't believe the fullness of him as he rocked his hips against hers. He went so deep inside her, she could swear he touched her womb as fierce, hot stabs of pleasure tormented her.

She wrapped her legs around his lean waist and savored the feel of his muscles flexing in and around her. She ran her hands down his back, over the chills that covered his body as she met him stroke for stroke.

He was spectacular.

"You feel so good," he breathed in her ear as he rocked his hips, hard and fierce, against hers. "I could stay inside you forever."

She was sure she didn't feel half as good to him as he felt to her.

He lowered his upper body to where she could nuzzle his neck as he thrust into her.

Sam wrapped her legs tight about his hips, then she rolled over with him.

Adrian looked up, startled, as he found himself beneath her. She took his hands in hers and placed them on her hips. Then, holding them in hers, she lifted herself up to the tip of his shaft, before she lowered herself onto him.

He growled at the feel of her body on his as she rode him fast and furiously. He'd never felt anything like it.

"You're making my toes curl," she breathed.

"I plan to make more than that curl before the night is over," he said as she released his hands and leaned forward.

Adrian ran his hands over her breasts, cupping them gently as she continued to stroke him with her body.

Why had he waited a year before kissing her?

It terrified him when he thought of how close he'd come to never acting on his desire. What if he had let her get away without ever having tasted her lips? Her body?

And in that instant, a wave of possessiveness washed over him. He would never let her go.

She belonged to him.

Sam watched Adrian watch her. His dark eyes were shuttered, but the look of pleasure on his face tore through her.

She ran her hand over his stubbled cheeks, grateful that she had finally kissed him. This moment far exceeded any fantasy she'd ever had about him.

Her body aching with bliss, she could feel her pleasure mounting again with every forceful stroke she delivered to him. She moved her hips faster as Adrian lifted his hips to drive himself even deeper.

"Oh, my goodness," she breathed as her body became even hotter as massive, wrenching stabs of pleasure tore through her.

Adrian rolled over with her then, and placed her beneath him. His eyes wild, he quickened his pace.

Sam moaned at the feel of him sliding in and out, fast, deep, hard.

And then suddenly, an indefinable ecstasy exploded through her body in resounding ripples. Sam gasped at the same time Adrian threw his head back and roared as he delivered two more long, deep thrusts to her. His entire body convulsed around her as he released himself.

He collapsed on top of her and buried his face in her neck.

Sam held him there, cradled in her arms and legs as she just listened to him breathe. She felt his heart pounding against her chest and sweat covered them both.

This was a perfect, peaceful moment that she wished she could hold on to forever.

"That was the most incredible experience I've ever had," he whispered in her ear as he cradled her gently in his strong arms.

"No kidding," she said as she ran her hands over his hard biceps, then kissed him tenderly on his chest. "You know, I've never done that before."

"Done what?"

"Orgasmed."

Adrian smiled. He was glad he'd been the man who had shown her the full depth of her sexuality. Cupping her head in his hand, he pulled her lips to his for a scorching kiss.

The phone rang.

"I swear, I hate those things," he snarled.

"Oh," Sam said as she let go of him. "I forgot to tell you Heather called."

Carefully, he withdrew from her. "Then I'm sure that's her," he said, reaching for the cordless phone on his nightstand.

"Hi, Heather," he said in a tone that was half a growl.

Sam could hear just a hint of Heather's chattering on the other end.

"Damn, Heather. What do you do with your money? I pay you two hundred and fifty dollars a week to do my laundry and buy groceries for me, and half the time you don't even do it."

She heard Heather chattering again as Adrian ran his hand through his hair and clenched it tight.

Adrian got out of bed and reached for his pants as he listened to her. Biting her lip, Sam admired the perfect shape of his buttocks and rear as he stooped over.

"Give me a break," he said as he fastened his jeans. "I worked three jobs in college and no one ever . . ."

He went rigid. "I'm sorry," he said. "Just stop crying, okay? Heather, please stop crying."

Sam sat up as he walked out of the room.

Frowning, she pulled her shirt on and followed after him.

He wiggled his mouse at his computer. "I'm doing it right now," he said in a gentle voice. He cursed again. "You only have two dollars in your account, did you know that? What are you living on?"

His jaw ticked, but his voice was patient. "All right, I'm transferring two grand over to you, but this is it, Heather. I work too damned hard just to give it away to you because you decide you need a Christmas vacation in Daytona for a week."

He clicked the phone off and tossed it on his desk.

Sam moved to stand behind him. She ran her hand over his back. "You are a wonderful man."

"I'm an idiot," he said under his breath. "I don't know why I put up with them."

"You love them."

"I wonder sometimes. God, I'm just so tired of everyone needing me all the time."

Sam went cold at his words. His dependability was what she loved about him most, and in truth that was what she wanted. Someone she could depend on who wouldn't disappoint her. She was tired of unkept promises.

Sam, you fool. No one is ever going to put you first. When are you going to realize that?

Her father had done what Adrian's had, he'd abandoned them. And her worst fear was to fall in love with some thoughtless, woman-chasing jerk who dumped her for a trophy girlfriend the minute she passed the age of thirty.

She didn't want a little boy, she wanted a man.

And she had hoped Adrian would be that man.

"Is something wrong?" he asked.

She shook her head, then brushed her hand over his whiskered cheek.

Please don't disappoint me, too. The words were on the tip of her tongue. But she didn't dare utter them aloud. Didn't dare give him any more ways to hurt her. He already held a place in her heart where only he could destroy it.

"Why don't we go back to bed?" she whispered.

He looked up at her with those dimples flashing. Then, he scooped her up in his arms and ran with her back to the bedroom.

4

"Hi, Adrian," Sam said as soon as he answered his cell phone.

"Hey, sweet, what's wrong? You sound upset."

God, how she loved the sound of his deep, caring voice. It comforted her on a level that defied explanation.

"My brother forgot to pick up my mom's Christmas tree and she's having a hissy fit. I'm over here at the lot and there's no way I can make it back home and get ready in time. Is it okay if we just hook up at the hotel?"

"Sure. Is there anything I can do for you?"

She felt tears well at his offer. This last week had been the best of her life. After they had returned to work, they had kept quiet about their relationship, but it hadn't been easy. More nights than not, she'd left work first, then gone over to his apartment to fix dinner and wait for him.

He'd even given her a key.

"Thanks," she said, "but I've got it. I'll see you at the hotel."

"I'll be waiting for you in the lobby."

Worried, *Adrian paced* the hotel lobby. The temperature outside was steadily falling, and the news had been calling for a bad snowstorm later that evening. He'd tried to call Sam a dozen times to warn her not to come out this far, but she'd turned her cell phone off.

The door opened.

Adrian looked up and felt his jaw drop as Sam swept in.

She was wearing a Renaissance-style dress with a high waist, long flowing sleeves, and ballerina slippers. Her hair was down around her face and she had a light ribbon braided across the top of her hair with flowers. She looked just like Guinevere.

And he loved it.

No, he corrected himself, he loved her.

Sam paused as she caught sight of Adrian staring at her. He looked gorgeous in his black jeans and sweater. He'd even gone to the trouble of fixing his hair and she knew how much he hated doing that.

Better still, his entire face lit up as his gaze met hers.

"My lady, you are beautiful," he said as she drew near him. He took her hand in his and kissed the back of her knuckles.

The warmth of his hand startled her. He took her coat from her hands and offered her his arm.

Feeling like a heroine in a romance novel, Sam took his arm and allowed him to lead her into the party.

"Wow, Sam," Randir said as he saw them. "You clean up good."

She laughed. "Thanks, I think."

While Adrian went to get her something to drink, she took a seat at the large, round table with the guys from her department.

"Oh, Adrian," Scott teased as soon as he returned. "You're just so thoughtful. Want to go get me a Coke?"

"No," Adrian said as he sat down beside her.

Sam did her best to appear nonchalant and distanced from Adrian, but it wasn't easy when all she wanted to do was lean back into his arms and have him hold her like he did in the early morning hours.

How she loved curling up with him in his favorite recliner, watching TV or listening to music while they fed each other popcorn. Naked.

She'd never been overly comfortable with her body, but Adrian seemed to love it and she loved him for it.

He gave her a meaningful look, then slid his gaze toward the lobby. "I need to go make a call."

Sam waited until he was out of sight before she excused herself to go to the bathroom.

She met Adrian in the lobby where he pulled her into a hidden, dark corner. "Why are we here?" he asked as he pressed her back against the wall.

She trembled at the strength of his chest against her breasts as he cupped her face in his hands and stared down at her with heat in his eyes. "Because it's a free meal?" she asked impishly.

"I'd rather be at home, making love to you."

"Mmm, me, too."

He kissed her then.

"Hey, Adrian!"

They both went tense at hearing Randy's voice.

Adrian stepped out of the corner while Sam pressed herself against the wall, hopefully out of Randy's sight.

"Hi, Randy. How's it going?"

"Great. I meant to tell you that Greg Wilson is going to applaud your team tonight after dinner. We hit the million-dollar mark for the Christmas season this morning. Congratulations. Greg says he's going to double your bonus and give you a raise."

"Thanks."

"So, what are you doing out here?" Randy asked. "C'mon, let's go say hi to Greg. I know he wants to shake your hand."

Sam listened with pride. Greg Wilson was on the pompous side, but he owned one of the largest privately held corporations in the country. For him to want to spend six seconds in your company was a big compliment.

As soon as the coast was clear, she went to the ladies' room.

She had barely closed the door on her stall when she heard Tiffany and a gaggle of her girlfriends sweep into the bathroom.

"Did you see Adrian?" Tiffany said to them.

"Are you kidding?" Barbara Mason said breathlessly. "How could anyone miss such a baby doll?"

"I heard that." Sam didn't recognize that voice.

"Yeah, well," Tiffany said in a loud whisper, "I'm going to nail that boy tonight."

Her friends laughed as Sam saw red. Tiffany better lay off Adrian, if she wanted to keep that perfect nose of hers.

"Right," Barbara said in disbelief.

"I am," Tiffany bragged. "I rented a room upstairs and as soon as I see him, I'm going to get him up there and have my wicked way with him."

They left the bathroom.

Sam clenched her fists. How dare she.

Her eyes narrowed, she left the bathroom and went after Adrian to warn him.

There was no need.

Tiffany had him cornered outside the ballroom. Worse, they were locked in a fiery kiss with Tiffany's hands on his waist and neck.

Sam froze at the sight as pain tore through her.

Her first impulse was to tear them apart and slug Tiffany. And if she wasn't so stunned, she might have actually done it.

But she couldn't move.

Not while her heart was slowly splintering into a million pieces.

And what hurt her most was the fact that Adrian would kiss Tiffany out in front of everyone while he wouldn't even so much as touch her hand when anyone was around.

Her tears swelled, but she blinked them back. She wouldn't give either one of them the satisfaction of seeing just how much damage they had done to her.

God, she was such a stupid fool. How could she have thought Adrian was any different than her own father?

Tiffany pulled away, and handed him a card key. "It's room 316," she said seductively. "I'll see you in twenty minutes."

Sam went numb as even more pain washed over her. How could he? He's a man! Look at Tiffany.

How on earth could you ever compete with that?

Heartsick and aching, Sam rushed back to her table. She gathered her purse and coat.

"You okay?" Randir asked.

"No," she said, swallowing her tears. "I need to go home. I'll see you guys Monday."

A*drian waited and* waited for Sam. Where was she? Had she gone back in when he wasn't looking?

He went to check, and as soon as he saw her coat was missing, a feeling of dread washed over him. "Where's Sam?"

Randir shrugged. "She went home."

"What?"

"She said she didn't feel well."

Adrian pulled his phone out of its cradle and dialed her cell phone. No answer.

Cursing, he ran after her.

A heavy snowfall had started as he reached his Bronco, got in, and went to find her.

S*am wept the* whole way to Spring Hill. She didn't really notice the icy roads until she had to turn onto Nashville Highway to reach her house. Her car started skidding.

Terrified, she held her breath until she landed safely in a ditch.

Her heart pounding, she was glad she hadn't been physically hurt. She picked up her cell phone to call her brothers, then saw the battery was dead.

"Damn it!" she snarled as she slammed her fist against the steering wheel. "What next?"

Angry and hurt, she wiped her eyes, then shoved open her door and started the five-mile walk to her rented house.

A*drian's heart raced* as he realized how hazardous the roads were becoming. Sam's little Honda was about as safe in weather like this as his Corvette.

Why had she left? It didn't make any sense to him.

He turned onto Nashville Highway and saw her car in the ditch. Terrified at the sight, Adrian pulled to the side of the road and got out. Running up to her car, he saw it was empty.

She was out walking in 26 degrees?

He shook his head as he remembered her thin shoes and dress. She would freeze to death. Damn her independence. Couldn't she ever let anyone do anything for her?

He ran back to his Bronco. Getting in, he tried to start it.

"No!" he snarled as the starter clicked without firing the engine. He tried again, but still the car refused to start.

Pulling out his cell phone, he called the only other person he knew who lived in Spring Hill.

"Hey, Trey," he said as his friend picked up. "I need a huge favor from you."

S*am was absolutely* freezing. Her shoes were soaking wet and she had all but lost the feeling in her feet.

Worse, she still had a mile to go to get home. And over and over again, all she could see was Adrian kissing Tiffany.

"Why, Adrian?" she breathed, clutching her coat tighter around her. "Why wasn't I good enough?"

Suddenly, she heard a strange clip-clopping sound coming from behind her.

What on earth?

It sounded vaguely like hooves. Turning around, she saw . . .

No, it couldn't be.

Sam blinked, not trusting her eyes.

The image only got clearer as the snowfall became heavier.

It was a knight. A knight in black leather.

Frowning, she watched as Adrian rode up to her on the back of a white stallion. Her mouth wide open, she looked at him as he reined to a stop by her side.

"Methinks milady damsel doth be in distress."

She shook her head at his fake medieval English way of speaking. Those deep, dark, chocolate-brown eyes stared at her with a heat that instantly warmed her freezing bones.

"Adrian?" she gasped.

"Sir Adrian," he corrected with a smile. He reached his hand down to her.

Without thinking, she took it and allowed him to pull her up to sit before him on the medieval-style saddle. He wrapped her up in two blankets as he adjusted her in front of him.

"What are you doing here?" she asked in disbelief. "I thought you were with Tiffany." As she said the name, her rage ignited.

"Tiffany?" he asked with a frown. "Why would you . . ."

She saw the color darken his cheeks.

"Yes," she snarled at him. "I saw you two. And you took her room key."

"Didn't you see me give it back?"

Sam hesitated. "You gave it back?"

"Yes. A few minutes after she left."

"You kept it a few minutes?" she snarled. "You skunk. How could you do—"

He stopped her words with a heated kiss.

"Don't yell at me, Sam," he said as he pulled back. "It wasn't my fault. I was waiting for you when she grabbed me from behind. At first, I thought it was you. Then she swept around me and put a lip-lock on me so fast I didn't know what to do. In case you haven't noticed, women don't usually do things like that to me. She caught me off guard."

"You looked like you were enjoying it to me."

"I was too stunned to move. And when she handed me the key, it took a full minute before it dawned on me what it was."

"A full minute?"

"I know you don't believe me, but if I wanted Tiffany, then why am I out here on a horse, freezing?"

"I don't know. Why are you here on a horse, freezing?"

"Because I love you, and I wanted to come to your rescue."

Sam choked on a sob. "Really?"

He tilted her chin up to look at him. "Don't ever doubt me, Sam. You're the only woman I've *ever* wanted to take care of."

Coming from him, that meant something.

She smiled as he kicked the horse forward toward the setting sun.

And in that moment, Sam knew she had the best Christmas present ever. She had her knight in shining leather.

Epilogue

Christmas day

Adrian let out a tired sigh as he pulled up to his apartment, just after noon. He'd spent most of the morning at work, alone, doing his best not to call and disturb Sam. She was spending the day with her family, while his had fled. Heather had gone to Daytona, and his mother was on a cruise in Alaska with her latest boyfriend.

But then, there was nothing unusual about that. He hadn't had a family Christmas since he was fifteen.

For the last eleven years, Christmas had meant nothing more than a heated TV dinner eaten in front of bad television shows.

"I hate Christmas," he muttered as he got out of his car, and went to his apartment.

He opened his door. Then, he froze dead in his tracks.

Someone had put a small Christmas tree in his living room and decorated it.

Frowning, Adrian closed the door and took his coat off, then went to the tree where a medieval-looking note card was tied with a ribbon to a branch.

He flipped it open.

Milord, Knight in Shining Armor, methinks thou hast a present in thy chamber.

He smiled at Sam's writing. She must have stopped by while he'd been at work. How he wished she'd called him. He'd love to see her today.

Oh, well, she'd be at work tomorrow.

Holding the card to his heart, he went to see what she'd left for him. He opened the door to his bedroom and went stock-still as his jaw fell open.

Sam was lying on his bed dressed in a teddy that made his mouth water, and she had a bow tied around her neck.

"Where have you been?" she asked with a seductive smile as she closed the book she'd been reading and put it on his nightstand.

Adrian couldn't speak, since his tongue was hanging on the floor.

Her smile widened as she left the bed and moved to stand in front of him. "Carpet got your tongue?" she asked.

He smiled.

Cupping her face in his hands, he stared in awe. "I thought you were going over to your mom's."

"I am for dinner. But I wanted to surprise you."

Adrian pulled her to him and kissed her until he couldn't stand it anymore. He wanted her in a way he had never wanted anything else.

And that flimsy outfit that barely covered her and left nothing to his imagination, was making him way too hard for comfort.

Growling, he pulled his clothes off in record time, then tossed her over his shoulder and deposited her gently on the bed.

Sam laughed.

Adrian ran his hand down the curve of her thigh, amazed at how much he loved her.

Sam kissed Adrian's bare shoulder as he reached into his nightstand for a condom.

He turned to her then, but instead of handing the condom to her as he normally did, he kissed her.

She felt something strange in his mouth.

Pulling back, she frowned as he pulled a ring out from between his teeth and handed it to her.

"I was going to give this to you tomorrow at dinner," he said, looking a bit sheepish. "But since you're here . . ."

Completely stunned, Sam couldn't breathe as she stared at the ring. It was a one-carat, heart-shaped diamond engagement ring in a medieval-style setting that made her heart pound.

Tears welled in her eyes as she blinked in disbelief. "Are you sure about this?"

He ran his hand down her arm. "You're the only thing in my life I've ever been sure about," he whispered before he took the ring back.

He left the bed and went down on one knee beside it, then took her hand into his.

Tears fell down her cheeks at the sight of Adrian naked on the floor.

"Samantha Jane Parker, will you marry me?"

She launched herself at him and knocked him flat against the floor. "Of course I will."

He laughed as she straddled his bare stomach.

Adrian placed the ring on her left hand, then he kissed it. "I love you, Sam."

"I love you, Adrian," she whispered, knowing in her heart that she had finally found her one, true knight in shining armor. And she was never, ever going to let him go.

Santa Wears
Spurs

Prologue

Danger. O'Connell felt it on the back of his neck and deep in his bones as he raced his pinto across the dead winter Texas plains toward a town he'd never known existed.

After all this time, he ought to be used to danger. He had lived his life under its constant stalking shadow, and kept it as his faithful companion. Danger was his ally and his enemy.

It defined everything about him. There had only been one time in his life when he had felt safe. But that was a long time ago.

It was biting cold out, not that he felt it much. His thrumming blood kept him warm as he rode through the night.

"You should have been there, Kid. It was like taking candy from a baby," Pete had laughed. "Hah, now that I think about it, I *did* take candy from a baby. I just wish I could see their faces when they wake up and find their money gone."

Then as now, O'Connell hadn't found the words amusing. He knew Pete could be as cold-blooded as they came—the bullet wound in his arm was testimony to that. But not even *he* had thought Pete would steal from an orphanage just two days before Christmas.

The man had no soul.

There was a time when O'Connell had been just the same. When hatred had strangled his heart and left him unable to feel for anyone save himself.

And then he'd met *her*.

His heart lurched, just as it always did when he thought of her. She had shown him another way, another life, and had changed everything about him in the process. She'd given him hope, a future. A reason to live. And life without her had been nothing more than a bitter hell.

In all honesty, he didn't know how he managed to make it through the endless, miserable days that had turned into years.

Somehow, he just survived. Cold. Empty.

Alone.

God, how he missed her. How he ached for some way to go back and relive just one second of the time he'd shared with her. Just to see her face one more time, feel her breath on his skin.

For a moment, O'Connell let his thoughts drift to the past. And like they always did when he was unguarded, they went to a remembered dream of long dark brown hair and eyes as clear and warm as a summer's day. Of a woman who had told him she loved him without making a single sound.

Closing his eyes, he saw her bright smile and heard the music of her laughter as she lay naked beneath him while he claimed her for his own. He clenched his teeth at the white-hot desire that coiled through his belly. And for a moment he swore he could still feel her hands against his back as she held him tight and cried out in ecstasy.

Not even five years could dull the memories. Or his craving for her touch. He could taste the salty sweetness of her body, feel her hot and tight around him, and smell the sunshine that had always seemed to be in her hair.

Catherine had touched him in ways no one had before or since.

"I remember you," he breathed. But most of all he remembered the promise he had made to her. The promise he had broken. And in that moment, he wished Pete's bullet had gone straight through his useless heart.

Lord above, if there was one last wish he could have, it would be to set things right. He'd sell whatever was left of his blackened soul for a way to go back and change what he'd done to her.

But it wasn't to be.

He knew that.

There was nothing left for him to do except see the money back to the orphans Pete had stolen it from.

After that, he didn't know where he'd go. He'd have to find another place where the law and Pete couldn't find him. *If* such a place existed.

Briefly, he considered trying to find *her*. After all, she had been his safe harbor. His greatest strength.

But then, she had also been his greatest weakness.

No, it wouldn't do to seek her out. Too much depended on him staying away from her. Because one thing his brother, Pete, had taught him years ago—there was no such thing as a second chance.

1

"All I want for Christmas is a man as handsome as the Devil himself. One with a charming smile, at least some semblance of intelligence, and a great, *big,* bulging—"

"Rebecca Baker!" Catherine O'Callahan gasped, shocked at her friend's words.

"Bank account," Rebecca said as she dropped her hands down from the graphic illustration she had been providing. She picked up the frying pan near Catherine, then placed it on top of the black iron stove. "I was only going to say *bank account.*"

Trying not to smile lest she encourage her friend's libidinous conversation, Catherine looked askance at Rebecca as she continued washing dishes.

Rebecca's olive cheeks colored ever so slightly as she walked back to the sink. "Well, maybe I wasn't. *But* as a married woman yourself, you know what I mean. How long am I supposed to go around mourning Clancy anyway? Good grief, it's been almost four years since he died. And I barely knew him before we married."

As was her habit, Rebecca gestured dramatically with her hands to illustrate her next words. "My father practically dragged me to the altar to marry a man almost twice my age. I tell you, snuggling up to a man whose hands and feet are colder than icicles in January isn't my idea of wedded bliss."

Catherine could well agree with that point.

Rebecca sighed dreamily as she idly put the plates on the shelf above her head. "What I'd like to have is a gorgeous, *warm* man I could be cow-tied to forever. A man who could enter the room and make me all hot, and cold, and all jittery." She looked at Catherine and smiled. "Know what I mean?"

Blushing, Catherine grew quiet as she rinsed a large black pot. She knew *exactly* what Rebecca meant. She'd lain awake many a night as memories washed over her of a pewter-eyed demon who had promised her everything, including the moon above.

A man who had made her body so hot there had been times when she was certain she'd perish in flames.

But unlike her friend, she wasn't a widow. For all she knew, her husband could come waltzing up to the front door at any time and knock on it.

As if *that* would ever happen, Catherine chided herself.

When would she give up her useless, unwavering hope of seeing him again? Why couldn't she just put him out her mind?

What was it about him that made her yearn for him after all this time?

Of course, she knew the answer to that question—everything about him. He'd been so wonderful and kind, considerate and giving. Up until the day he left her without so much as a by-your-leave.

She must be insane to still yearn for him.

And after five years, he *might* be dead. Heaven knew, a lot had happened to her since he'd run off. She'd moved to a new town, started her own restaurant and boardinghouse, and created a respectable life for her and her four-year-old daughter, Diana.

Last summer, after the yellow fever epidemic, she and Rebecca had taken in five of the town of Redwood's orphans.

A *lot* had happened.

Rebecca sidled up to her and took the pot from her hands to dry it. "So, tell me, if not a gorgeous St. Nick to come knocking on the door, what *do* you want for Christmas?"

"Oh, I don't know," Catherine said as she reached to wash a pan. "I guess if I had my druthers, I'd like for our money to be returned. It bothers me that someone would steal from the children right before Christmas."

Rebecca agreed. "I know how much you wanted to spend it on them. It's such a shame. I can't imagine what kind of monster could so something so terrible."

Neither did she.

They didn't speak for a few minutes. Only the sound of sloshing water and clanging dishes broke the silence as they worked.

All of a sudden, the hair on the back of Catherine's neck stood up. Turning her head, she saw Rebecca staring at her.

"What?" she asked.

"Is that really all you want for Christmas?"

Catherine handed her another pan to dry. "Why, yes. I'm quite happy with everything else."

Rebecca arched a questioning brow.

"I am," Catherine insisted.

"Methinks the lady doth protest too much," Rebecca said, putting the pan away. "Can you truly tell me that you haven't once given thought to having a handsome man come sweep you off your feet?"

Catherine laughed halfheartedly. "I already had that happen, and I must say I found the experience less than desirable."

Rebecca shook her head. "You know, I came to work here almost four years ago and never in that time have I heard you speak of your husband. That is who you're talking about, isn't it?"

Catherine nodded, refusing to meet Rebecca's inquisitive brown-eyed stare as she moved to pump more water into the sink. "There isn't much to tell."

Rebecca nudged her away from the pump and took up the motion. "Come on, Catherine. All the children are in bed for the night. Why not open up a little?"

Catherine buried her hands back in the suds and sighed. "What do you want me to tell you? Plain preacher's daughter fell in love with the gorgeous stranger who came to work for her father's ranch? He married her a month after they first met, took her off to Nevada, and left her the first chance he got."

"That's it?"

"That's it."

Rebecca paused. Her brown eyes darkened in anger. "I'll never understand a man who could do something so cold-blooded or mean."

"Me either," she whispered under her breath.

"I don't see how you stand it."

Catherine shrugged. "I got used to it. Five years gave me time to lay aside my hatred. Besides, I have Diana to think about. I'm the only parent she has and I decided on the day she was born that I would never mention his name or dwell on what he did to us."

"Well, I respect you for that. Me, I wouldn't have rested until I found the polecat and skinned him alive."

Catherine relished the image of her husband's tawny skin being flayed from him as he screamed for mercy. Now that Rebecca mentioned it, she did rather enjoy the thought of him being skinned. It would certainly serve him right. "You know, I do want something after all."

"And that is?"

Catherine scrubbed her pot with renewed vigor, wishing it were her husband's head she held beneath the water. "I wish I could lay eyes on him one last time to tell him what a no-good, lousy, rabid dog he was for leaving me."

"That's my girl." Rebecca laughed as she patted Catherine on the back. Then, she leaned forward and said in a low tone, "But the real question is, was he any good where and when it counted?"

"Rebecca!" Catherine gasped, trying her best not to think about just how good he had been *there*.

Though why Rebecca's words continued to shock her after all these years of knowing her, she couldn't imagine. Rebecca had never had an ounce of shame in her.

But then, it was her outspokenness Catherine liked most of all. She always knew where she stood with Rebecca. Her friend never held *anything* back. And after having lived with her husband and his secrets, she found Rebecca's candor a true blessing.

Suddenly a knock sounded on the door.

Catherine wrung the suds off her hands, then wiped her hands dry on her apron. "Why don't you go on to bed?" she said, rolling her sleeves back down her forearms and buttoning them against her wrists. "I'll get the door. I'm sure it's just someone needing a room."

"Poor soul to be out on Christmas Eve without a bed," Rebecca said. She inclined her head to the sink. "You sure you don't want me to finish up the dishes?"

Catherine shook her head. "There are only a handful left, and we already have all the gifts under the tree. Why don't you just go and enjoy what's left of Christmas Eve?"

"All right, then. I'll look in on the kids and then retire. Let me know if you need me."

"I will."

Rebecca headed to the back stairs while Catherine took the lantern off the kitchen table and walked down the narrow hallway to the front door.

Through the lace curtains, she could see the outline of a tall man with broad shoulders.

A smile twitched at the corners of her mouth. Perhaps Rebecca would get her wish after all.

Rolling her eyes at the very indecent thought that flicked across her mind, Catherine opened the door.

She took one glance at the handsome stranger, who had his head turned to look at his horse, and dropped the lantern straight to the floor.

O'*Connell cursed as* the lantern's fire exploded on the pine boards of the porch. Reacting without thought, he dropped his black Stetson and saddlebags, and stamped at the flames, his spurs jingling loudly as he stamped. Then, to his chagrin, the flames spread to his boots and set fire to the toes of his left foot.

He hissed in pain as he whipped his black duster off and put out the fire on his smoking boot. Then he quickly used the duster to extinguish the rest of the fire.

Luckily, the fire didn't do much in the way of permanent damage, but the porch and door would need a good washing come morning.

"Good Lord, woman," he snapped as he surveyed the damage. "You ought to be more . . ." his words trailed off as he looked up and met wide, startled brown eyes.

His jaw went slack. Those were the same eyes he'd been dreaming of not more than a few minutes before.

"Catherine?" he whispered in disbelief.

Catherine couldn't move as she stared into the handsome, devilish face that had coaxed her away from everything she had ever known.

Ask and ye shall receive, her father's favorite phrase echoed in her head.

Stunned by his sudden appearance, she took his form in all at once. He was still as handsome as sin. His dark brown hair was short in back with long bangs that draped becomingly into eyes so silvery gray they appeared almost colorless.

Captivating and searing, his eyes could haunt a woman night and day. And she ought to know, since they'd done nothing but torment her since the moment she had first seen them.

That same air of danger still clung to him seducing her, wooing her. Oh, but he was a man to make any woman's heart pound.

His face had grown thinner over the years, adding sharp, angular planes to it. But they in no way detracted from the perfection of his patrician features. Dark brows contrasted sharply with his silver-gray eyes, and his broad nose still had the tiny bump in the center where she'd broken it.

Glory, but he was scrumptious. Completely and utterly scrumptious, like a rare treat of succulent chocolate after a long abstinence.

He'd always possessed a powerful, compelling, masculine aura that was downright salacious in nature. An aura that reached out and captured the attention of anything female within its mighty grasp.

And heaven only knew, she was far from immune to it.

But the Devil would move his home to Antarctica before she *ever* let him know that.

"What on earth are you doing here?" Catherine asked as she finally found her voice.

"Needing a doctor," he said sardonically, shaking his left foot.

Catherine looked down to see the charred black leather in the bright winter moonlight. A rush of embarrassment filled her.

"Why is it," he asked, "every time we meet, I end up needing a doctor?"

She lifted her chin at his playful tone. Her days of finding him amusing were long past. "Are you trying to charm me?"

Not even the dark could mask the wickedly warm look in his eyes. "And if I were?"

I'd probably end up surrendering to it.

But she had no intention of letting him know that, either. *Fool me once, shame on you. Fool me twice, shame on me.* She couldn't afford to let him break her heart again. The first time had been painful enough. And in truth, she wasn't sure if she could survive losing him again.

Instead, she sought to protect herself by putting an end to whatever thoughts might be playing through his mind.

"I'm not a girl anymore, Mr. O'Callahan. I no longer dance to your tune."

O'Connell took a deep breath as he sized her up. He'd almost forgotten his old alias. But the cold tone of her voice chilled him more than the winter wind at his back.

Still, it did nothing to daunt the fire in his gut that her presence stirred. She looked even better than he remembered. Gone was the willow-thin frame of her youth and in its place were the luscious curves of a woman full grown.

She wore her hair in that tight bun he'd always despised. Catherine had such beautiful hair—long, thick, and wavy. He, the man who was wanted in six states, had spent hours brushing her hair at night. Running his hands through it.

And he wondered if it still smelled like springtime.

In that instant, he remembered the way he had left her. Without a word, without a note. He had simply gone off to work and had never returned.

Shame filled him. He should have at least sent a letter. Although, honestly, he had tried to write one a thousand times. But he'd never completed it. What did a man say to a woman he'd been forced to give up against his will?

Especially when he didn't want her to know the real reason he'd left?

Picking his hat up from the porch, he cast a sweeping, hungry look over her body, and wished for the millionth time, that things had been different between them. That he could have had a long life spent by her side, being the husband she deserved to have. "It's good to see you again."

Her look froze him as she untied her apron, then stooped to pick up the broken glass and place it in the cloth. "I wish I could say it's good to be seen by you, but in this case I think you'll understand if I'm a bit cool toward you?"

"Cool" was a mild term for her demeanor. In truth, he suspected icebergs at the North Pole might be a shade or two warmer.

He'd expected more anger from her. The Catherine he remembered would have been cursing him like a slow-walking dog for leaving her.

This Catherine was different. She was composed and serious, not laughing and playful.

Passionate, he realized with a start. That was what was missing. She'd lost the verve that used to have her laughing one minute, sobbing the next, and then kissing him blind two seconds after that.

And without a doubt he knew he was to blame for it. Being abandoned had a way of affecting a person adversely. His gut drew tight. He had a lot to answer for in his life. He just wished she wasn't one of those things he'd messed up.

"Where's your anger?" he asked as he leaned over to help her pick up the mess.

Catherine considered her answer. She should be enraged at him, but oddly enough, once the initial shock of the encounter wore off she found herself completely numb to him.

Well, not completely numb.

In fact, "numb" described his effect on her like "handsome" described Abe Lincoln.

A woman would have to be dead not to feel a vigorous stirring for a man so incredibly handsome as her wandering polecat. Especially a man possessed of such raw, primal appeal.

Everything about him promised sheer, sexual delights. And all too well she remembered the way he had felt in her arms, the strength of his long, lean body caressing hers in playful abandon as he sent her spiraling off into blissful ecstasy.

And right then, with his head just inches from her own, she could smell the raw, earthy scent of him. That leather and musk that had always titillated her. That warm, wonderful smell was a part of him like the innate power and authority that bled from every pore of his body.

And those lips . . .

Full and sensuous, those lips of his had kissed her until she lost all reason, until her entire body buzzed with lust and desire. And those wonderful, sensual lips had teased and tormented her body to the ultimate pinnacle of human pleasure.

Good heavens, how she ached for him. Even after the way he had hurt her.

What are you thinking?

Catherine mentally shook herself. No, she didn't hate him for leaving her the way he had—five years had given her time to lay her hatred aside.

She wouldn't get mad at this point.

She would get even.

He deserved to feel the sting of rejection. Then he would understand exactly what he had done to her. How it felt to be denied and forgotten.

"I got over my anger for you, Mr. O'Callahan," she said tartly, rising to her feet carefully lest she cut herself on the glass in her apron.

She raked a look from the top of his head down to his still-smoking boot, took a step back into the house and spoke, "And then I got over you."

With one last stoic look at him, Catherine closed the door in his stunned face.

2

Catherine's words rang in O'Connell's ears as he stared in disbelief at the closed door.

Well, what did you expect? he asked himself as he retrieved his charred duster from the porch.

Her hatred, in all honesty. That he had been prepared for. But her apathy toward him . . .

Well . . .

It was . . . insufferable.

Anger over her rejection blistered his gut. How dare she dismiss him so. What did she think he was, some lost little puppy come to lick scraps off the floor?

Well, he wasn't a lost puppy. He was a man. A man sought by every woman who had ever laid her eyes upon him. Not that he was vain about it. Not overly so, anyway. It was merely a fact he'd long grown accustomed to. A fact everyone who knew him just plainly accepted.

Women had always been partial to him.

In Hollow Gulch where O'Connell had been working the last few months, the women had singled him out the moment he rode into town—baked him fresh pies, batted their lashes at him. Hell, one gutsy blonde had even snuck into his room and hidden herself naked in his bed while he'd been out drinking.

Not that he had been interested in the blonde or any of the others. Unlike any normal, *sane* man, he'd sent her home as soon as he tossed some clothes on her body. And all the while she'd whispered to him the torrid, lusty things she'd do to give him pleasure.

Her salacious comments had set fire to his loins, but even so, she hadn't appealed to him in the slightest. His heart belonged to Catherine. It always had.

And he refused to sully Catherine's memory by bedding down with any other woman. That was the one vow he'd never break.

Hell, he'd given up everything he valued to see Catherine safe.

And she had banished him from her thoughts?

He saw red.

In the last five years there hadn't been an instant when he hadn't been consumed by thoughts of her. Not a minute he hadn't wondered what she was doing. *How* she was doing.

And she felt nothing toward him.

Nothing.

He didn't even warrant her hatred.

"Fine," O'Connell muttered at the closed door as he shrugged his duster on, then settled his Stetson on his head. He grimaced at the front of the brim that had been partially burned away by the fire. "I don't need you to feel anything for me, woman. I don't need you at all. In fact, I can put you right out of my mind, too."

Spinning on his heel, he took a step for his horse. Pain exploded across his foot and he cursed out loud as he limped away.

The woman had damned near maimed him. And all the while she felt nothing toward him.

Nothing. . . .

W*hat do you* mean, you got over me?"

Catherine turned around to see *him* standing in the doorway. His face awash with shadows, she could feel his angry glare more than see it.

Go ahead and seethe, Mr. O'Callahan. Stew in your rage until your entire body becomes pruney from it.

It was terrible to take such delight in a man's misery, but delight in it she did. Catherine kept her face from betraying her glee. She'd known he couldn't resist her words. That was why she'd left the door unlocked. The last thing she wanted was for him to break it down. And knowing him, he most certainly would have done it had she tried to bar him from her house.

Come into my parlor, said the spider to the fly. He wouldn't escape her clutches until she had exacted five years of rejection from his rotten hide.

"Did you need something?" she asked coolly.

O'Connell forced the emotions from his face as he swept his hat from his head. How could she stand there so all-fired calm and dismiss him like an old shoe?

Well, he wasn't some old shoe, to be cast aside and forgotten. They had been more than merely intimate. The woman had actually touched his unrepentant soul. And after all the years he had tortured himself with guilt over his actions, she had forgotten him?

Oh, he wasn't about to leave here until he made her remember what they'd shared. Stepping into her house, he closed the door behind him.

"What do you mean, you got over me?" he asked again as he closed the short distance between them.

She shrugged casually. "It's been five years, Mr. O'Callahan."

As if *he* needed her reminder. It had been five long, gut-wrenching years of missing everything about her. Of feeling her presence, smelling her scent. Of longing to hear her voice, feel her tender caresses on his flesh.

Like an arrogant fool, he had assumed she'd missed him as well. Obviously, he'd been wrong.

Well, he wasn't going to let her know how much it bothered him. If she wanted to play this with a cool hand, he was certainly one to give it right back to her. He could hide his emotions better than anyone else alive. Indeed, how many times had that trait made her loco?

"You're right, Mrs. O'Callahan," O'Connell said in a deceptively calm voice. "It has been five long years. For the sake of old times, could you at least tell me where I might find a doctor for my foot?"

A becoming pink stained her cheeks as she glanced down to his injured member. "I'm afraid Dr. Watson died a few months back and as yet we have no replacement. But since I'm the one who burned you, I'll tend it."

"Well *it* would definitely appreciate that since it is throbbing."

And now that he mentioned it, the other *it* was throbbing, too. Especially as his gaze dipped of its own volition to her succulent breasts. His body grew even hotter and stiffer as his palm itched to caress the firm round mounds, and his mouth watered to suckle the soft pink tips until they hardened into rippled buds under his tongue.

And she felt nothing for him.

Nothing.

Stifling his growl, he vowed that that would soon change. If it was the last thing he did, he would make her remember how good they were together.

How much pleasure he could give her.

And if any other man had dared enter her bed in the last five years, the law could add the crime of murder to his wanted poster.

"If you're through ogling me," she said, "I keep my medicinal basket in the back."

"I wasn't ogling you," O'Connell muttered, unwilling to admit to her what he'd been doing.

She headed down a narrow hallway toward the back of the house. "Then please forgive me," Catherine said over her shoulder. "I guess after five years, I've forgotten what an ogle looks like."

Biting back his response, O'Connell limped his way down the narrow hallway, past the stairs. He looked around at the burgundy walls and the paintings lining the hallway. She had a beautiful home. He just wished he'd been the one to give it to her.

Even worse, a homey feel enveloped her boardinghouse.

There had been a time once, long ago, when he had dreamed of having such a place to call home. And the thought of sharing such a place with Catherine had been his idea of paradise.

But fate had turned her back on him and he had long given up that delusion. He could never have a life with her. He knew that.

"Nice place you have here," he said.

"Thank you. I made the down payment on it with the money you left behind."

"See?" he said defensively as he limped. "I wasn't all bad."

"Which is why I don't hate you."

O'Connell cursed under his breath. Back to square one. That hadn't helped his case the least little bit.

He wanted her anger, her hatred. He wanted . . . no, he corrected, he *needed* her to feel something for him. Something other than apathy.

There had to be some way to stir her up.

He paused in the doorway of the kitchen as she crossed the floor to put the apron and glass in a wooden trash receptacle. "If you'll sit at the table and remove your boot, I'll be right back with the burn salve."

She disappeared into a room off the kitchen.

O'Connell crossed the floor to the table. He set his hat down on the table, shrugged off his duster, then straddled the wooden bench seat and did as she ordered.

Grimacing in pain, he removed his scorched sock. He had to admit his foot had looked better. And it had most definitely felt better.

He blew air at his throbbing toes, noting the reddish skin that was already showing signs of blistering.

Damn, but it hurt. Even more so than his nose had when she'd accidentally smacked him in the face with a broom handle because of some spider web she couldn't stand being in the corner of the room. Personally, he'd have much rather suffered the spider than the broken nose.

Being around Catherine could be quite dangerous to one's health. Though, to be fair to her, he'd never seen her clumsy around anyone but him.

Then again, he'd never really minded her clumsiness, since she had such wonderful ways of making amends for it.

His breath caught in his throat at the memory of how she had made amends for his nose. Closing his eyes, he could still see her lowering herself down on him, feel her mouth teasing his flesh. Her teeth nibbling him all over.

And his body grew harder, hotter, until he could barely stand it.

Lord above, but she had such a sweet little mouth that tasted like honey and felt like hot silk as it slid over his flesh.

It really was true a body couldn't feel pain and pleasure simultaneously. Because when she teased his flesh with her tongue and teeth, all his pain evaporated like dew on a hot July morning.

Catherine returned to the kitchen, carrying a small wicker basket in her hand. She placed it on the table beside his hat, then leaned over to examine his foot. A stern frown drew her brows together. "Did I do all that?"

"Yes, you did," he said petulantly.

"I'm sorry," she said. "I'd best get some butter for it." As she reached for the porcelain butter jar on the table, she accidentally brushed the wicker basket off the side.

It landed straight on his injured foot.

O'Connell sucked his breath in between his teeth as pain exploded up his leg.

"I'm sorry," she repeated as she bent over to retrieve the basket.

His gaze feasted hungrily on the site of her round bottom as she fished for the basket under the table. Oh, but she had such a nice, round bottom. One that felt incredible under his hands, or against his loins.

He forgot all about his foot until she straightened, teetered ever so slightly, then grabbed his injured foot to steady herself.

This time he cursed out loud.

Color exploded across her face. "I'm—"

"Don't," he snapped, cutting her off. "I know you didn't mean to, just please give my foot time enough to recuperate before you do anything else to it."

Her cheeks darkened even more as she set the basket back on the table. "It's your own fault, you know."

"How is that?"

"You make me nervous," she confessed.

"I make *you* nervous?" he asked in disbelief. If anyone had a right to be nervous, it should be him, since he never knew what injury she might inflict on him next.

"Yes, you do. The way you sit there and stare at me like I'm some prime roast and you haven't eaten anything in a week. It's quite disconcerting, Mr. O'Callahan. If you must know."

He stopped fanning his foot and looked up at her. "Why did you never tell me that before?"

"I used to not mind the way you looked at me."

"And now?"

"I mind it and I wish you'd stop."

O'Connell locked his jaw at her words. There had to be some way to chisel away the ice around her.

Of course, he'd never in his life had to practice chiseling ice away from a woman. Women had always melted in his presence. They had only shown a token resistance before lifting their skirts to him.

Catherine had been the only one he'd ever courted. But then, she'd always been different in his book. Her shy innocence had been what captivated him. The way her smile carried all the warmth of the sun in it.

Pete had mocked him for his love of her. "The woman's as plain as yesterday's bread."

But to him, she'd always been beautiful.

Catherine leaned over him and gently spread the butter on his foot. Her light touch shook him to his core, and a thousand needles of pleasure tore through him.

In spite of himself, he smiled. Her ministrations on his foot reminded him of how they first met.

He'd just turned nineteen and had only been working for her father a few weeks. The main gate to her house had been damaged by a storm and he'd been trying to patch it when all of a sudden she had come riding up over the hill like the Devil himself was chasing her. He had barely ducked out of the way before her horse leapt over him.

The post he'd been hammering into the ground slipped sideways and as he tried to grab it, the hammer had fallen from his hand and crashed down on his toes, breaking the little one. If that hadn't been painful enough, the entire post had also fallen on him.

She had instantly turned around and come back to check on him. Even now he could see her in the dark green riding habit that had no doubt cost more than a year's worth of his pay as she helped him push the post off his legs. Without any thought to her dress, she had knelt down on the muddy ground, carefully removed his boot, and checked on his toe even while he told her not to.

She had insisted that since she broke it, she should tend it.

That had been the first time in his life anyone had ever truly been kind to him without expecting something back in return.

Later that night when she brought out a tray of steak, potatoes, and biscuits to the bunkhouse he shared with the rest of the ranch hands, he'd known he was in love.

She had looked like an angel coming through the door with that large silver tray in her hands.

And that stupid daisy she'd put on it . . . The other men had mocked him for weeks after that. But he hadn't cared.

Nothing had mattered to him, except her smile.

"You're doing it again," Catherine snapped, drawing his attention back to the present as she reached for her burn ointment. Her touch even more gentle, she spread it over his burned toes.

"Doing what?" he asked.

"Ogling me."

O'Connell smiled at her. "Do you know why I'm ogling you?"

"I can't imagine."

"Because you're still the most beautiful woman on earth."

Disbelief was etched onto her face as she straightened and looked at him. "Is that why you left me?"

"No."

"Then tell me why."

3

O'Connell barely caught himself before he spilled the truth out. Now as then, he couldn't stand the thought of her knowing what he'd been.

What he'd become.

He'd never been proud of what desperation and family obligation had led him to. He knew he should have walked away from Pete and his crazy schemes years ago. But every time he thought about hurting Pete, he remembered his childhood, when Pete had been the only thing that stood between him and starvation.

The world was a harsh, cold place for two orphans alone, and filled with unscrupulous people who would quickly take advantage of them. But Pete, who was seven years older than him, had always kept him safe.

If only Pete could let him go. Unfortunately, his big brother saw them as inseparable twins joined at the hip.

And no matter what he did to escape, his brother managed to track him down like some possessed bloodhound.

No, there was no way he could ever have her while Pete trailed him. Sooner or later, his brother would show up and use her as leverage against him—just as he'd done five years ago in Nevada.

O'Connell could only stand strong against Pete when just the two of them were involved.

Catherine made him weak. Vulnerable.

Besides, she was a good woman, with a good heart and he would rather she think him a sorry good-for-nothing lowlife, than ever learn she'd married an outlaw. No good could come of her knowing the truth.

So he answered her question with the first stupid answer that occurred to him. "I don't know."

She arched one dark brown brow at him as she lifted her gaze from his foot to his face. "You don't know?"

"It just seemed like the right thing to do," he offered as a consolation.

By the irate look on her face, he realized too late he should have just kept his mouth shut.

Catherine narrowed her eyes on him. "Why don't you just go and . . ." her voice trailed off.

He waited for her to finish.

She didn't. Instead, she stared strangely at his right arm.

"And?" he prompted.

She stepped around the bench until she rested by his side. She grabbed at the sleeve of his black shirt, and bent down to look closer at it. The contact brought her head right up under his nose. His gut wrenched. She still smelled like springtime. Her hair held that same delectable scent of fresh flowers and warmth.

And right then, all he wanted to do was lay her down on the kitchen table, lift her skirt up, and bury himself deep inside her warm body.

It took all of his willpower not to yield to that desire as the scent of her circled him, making him dizzy. Hungry. Inciting him beyond thought or reason.

A full minute passed before he realized she was staring at his blood on her hand.

"You're bleeding?" she asked.

Unwilling to explain to her that Pete had shot him as he ran off with the stolen money, he rose to his feet. "I probably should be going now."

"Sit!" The sharp tone coming from her was so unexpected and out of character that he actually obeyed.

"Take your shirt off and let me see what you've done now."

"Yes, ma'am," he murmured sarcastically as he unbuttoned his shirt and obliged her.

Catherine opened her basket, then made the mistake of glancing back to him.

His slow, languid movements captured her gaze as those long, strong fingers of his worked the buttons through the black cambric. She had always loved those hands. The way they felt laced in hers, the pleasure and comfort they had always managed to give her.

Her throat dried at the memory.

He opened his shirt, then set to work on the buttons of his white union suit. And with every white button that opened, she saw more and more of his perfect, tawny flesh.

She had forgotten just how nerve-wracking the sight of his bare skin could be. The years had done nothing but make his muscles leaner, more defined. And all too well she remembered what it felt like to slide her hand over those taut ripples. The way his hard stomach felt sliding against her own as he held himself above her and drove her into paradise with long, luscious strokes.

Her body growing hot, it took all her concentration to force herself to reach for the makeshift bandage on his right biceps. His arm flexed seductively as her fingers brushed his skin, and a jolt of molten lust tore through her. There were few things on earth that felt better than those hard, strong biceps flexing beneath her hands.

Catherine clenched her teeth in frustration. How could he make her so breathless after what he had put her through?

Why was her body so determined to betray her? And right then, she wished desperately for an off switch to stop the overwhelming desire coursing through her veins.

Tend his wound, tend his wound—she mentally repeated the words over and over, hoping to gain some control over herself.

I will not succumb to him!

By all that was holy, she wouldn't.

Untying his bandage, Catherine immediately saw the bullet wound. "You've been shot?"

"And can you believe it wasn't by you?"

She stiffened at his playful tone. "You're not funny."

"Not even a little?"

"I told you, Mr. O'Callahan, I'm immune to your charms."

Don't you wish! If only she could live up to those brave words.

"I wish you'd stop calling me that," he snapped at her. "I have a name and you used to use it."

She didn't dare use it right then, because if she did, she had no doubt she would be his to do with as he pleased. Just the sound of those syllables on her tongue would be enough to finish her off.

She struggled to bring herself under control. "I used to do a lot of things with you that I don't do anymore."

"Such as?"

"Use your imagination."

That silver-gray gaze dipped to her breasts, which drew tight and heavy at his heated perusal. "Oh, I'm using it, all right. And I can *well* imagine the sound of your sighs of pleasure in my ear as I nibble the flesh of your neck. Do you remember?"

"No," she lied, her voice amazingly calm.

But in spite of her denials, she felt her body melt against the heat of that silver-gray stare. Even worse, she could smell the warm, uniquely masculine scent of him. It was all she could do not to bury her face in the crook of his neck and inhale the intoxicating scent.

Tend his wound, tend his wound! She forced herself to concentrate on the task at hand.

"Is the bullet still in there?" she asked as she examined the hole in his arm.

"Woman," he said huskily, his gaze never leaving her breasts, "right now I have a loaded gun just waiting to . . ." his voice trailed off.

He finally looked up and met her gaze, but she couldn't read anything in the smoldering depths of his eyes except the raw hunger that scorched her through and through. "Did I just say that out loud?"

She nodded.

He cleared his throat and looked across the room. "No," he said quickly. "The bullet passed clean through."

Disregarding his answer, she gingerly examined the wound to see for herself. As he predicted, it looked to be clean. "It needs to be stitched."

He met her gaze again. Only three inches separated their faces and she could feel his breath on her face as he spoke. "Then by all means, have at it. I'm sure nothing would give you greater pleasure than to take a needle to my hide."

She should take pleasure in it, but she knew she wouldn't. How could she ever delight in hurting the man who had stolen her heart?

But she would never let him know that. Not after he'd hurt her. No, she'd never let him know just how much power he still held over her.

Never.

"Actually, I won't feel anything," she said, reaching for her basket.

O'Connell clenched his teeth in repressed frustration.

I won't feel anything, he mocked silently as she reached for a needle and thread.

You stitch the wound, and when you're finished, I promise you you'll feel something, all right. She was going to remember his touch if it was the last thing he did.

O'Connell felt himself harden even more as she placed the thread between her lips and licked it. The tip of her tongue poked out as she threaded the needle.

I can't stand this. His mind screamed from the needless torment. If he didn't know better, he would swear she did it on purpose.

When she set to work on his wound, he felt no pain, only the pleasure of her soft hands against his bare flesh. Her breath fell against his shoulder as she leaned so close to him he could smell the fresh sunshine of her.

Over and over he could envision letting her hair down and burying his hands in the thick waves. Feeling it fall across his chest as he placed her above him and feasted on those plump, luscious breasts.

Catherine could barely steady her hand as she closed the wound. Her memory of touching his hard, hot muscles couldn't compete with the reality of her hand against him now.

Her head swam at the contact. Worse, she could feel his heat surrounding her, feel his breath against her neck. His shoulder pressing against her right breast.

A thousand chills shot through her. It was all she could do not to moan and demand he take her right then and there. Oh, it was torturous. Especially after all the years she had yearned to see him again, all the years she had lain awake remembering the feel of him lying against her. The feel of him sliding inside her.

After what seemed an eternity, she finished the four tiny stitches that closed the wound. She had barely tied the knot off when he reached up, cupped her face in his hand, and took possession of her lips.

Catherine sighed at the contact.

He'd been the only man who had ever kissed her and the taste of him had been branded into her memory long, long ago.

He pulled her to him possessively and sat her down on the bench before him as he plundered her mouth.

Catherine buried her hands in his silken hair and pressed her breasts against his hot, naked chest. She should stop him, she knew it. But for her life she didn't want to. All she wanted was to savor him like she'd done all those years ago.

Volcanic heat poured through her body, pooling itself between her legs as she ached for him in the most primitive of ways. She wanted him desperately. And only he could pacify the aching heat that demanded his body inside hers.

He was her husband and the part of her that still loved him came rushing to the forefront. Under the assault of his scorching kiss, that part of her took possession of her common sense and forced it to flee her mind.

Before she knew what was happening, she felt her hair fall down around her shoulders and it was only then that he pulled back from her lips to kiss her cheek, her eyelid, the tip of her nose. His lips were hot and moist as they branded a fiery trail over her face.

"My precious Catherine," he whispered in her ear. "Let me love you the way you deserve to be loved."

She felt his hands unbuttoning her shirtwaist. She wanted to tell him no, but in truth she couldn't. The words lodged in her throat because deep down she wanted him. She had always wanted him, and no matter how badly he had hurt her, there was still a part of her that needed him.

And she gave herself over to that part.

He opened her shirtwaist, then buried those hot lips against the tops of her breasts as his hands reached around back to unlace her corset. She sighed in pleasure as she buried her face in his hair and inhaled the wicked, warm scent that was her husband.

O'Connell's head swam from the scent of her as he buried his face between the soft mounds of her breasts and licked her salty skin. It had been so long since he tasted her, felt her, and he knew that he would spend the rest of this night making up for the five years they had been apart.

The five long years he had been without a woman.

In her arms, he had always felt that anything was possible. That he could do anything, be anything. No other person had ever lifted him to the heights of goodness and pleasure that she did.

She was the one truth in his life that he could depend on. The one person he truly needed.

He ran his tongue over the tops of her breasts, delighting in the way she shivered in his arms as he struggled with the corset laces.

And at that moment he despised whoever had invented the cursed thing. It had to be some old, doddering matron seeking to preserve her daughter's virtue, for no man would ever design so inconvenient a contraption.

At last he loosened it to where he could free her breasts to his hungry mouth.

Catherine cupped his head to her as she stifled a moan of pure pleasure. His hand caressed her swollen breasts, drawing the taut nipples so tight she could barely stand it. Heat tore through her body as an ache started deep in the center of her. It was a familiar longing that she only felt in his presence.

No other man had ever aroused her the way he did. No one. And she doubted if anyone ever could.

And then his hands were under her skirt, stroking and teasing as they skimmed over her calves and thighs. One hand cupped her buttocks as he wrapped his other arm around her and drew her up tight against him.

He reclaimed her lips for one hungry, pulsating kiss, then pulled back.

He cupped her face in his hands and tilted her head to look at him. His lips were swollen from her kisses and he stared at her as if he were dreaming.

The need and hunger in that silver-gray gaze mesmerized her. Her breathing ragged, she could do nothing but stare up at him in wonderment.

"Say my name," he demanded, stroking her swollen lips gently with his knuckles.

She hesitated.

But what was the point? She had already surrendered herself to him. And for some reason she couldn't fathom, she wanted to please him.

"Michael," she breathed.

He smiled, then returned to torture her mouth with sweet bliss.

He rose with her in his arms. "Where's your room?"

"In there," she said, pointing to the back hallway and the room on the left.

Limping all the way, he carried her to it then shut the door with the heel of his burned foot. "Where's the lamp?"

Catherine squirmed out of his arms and moved to find her chest of drawers to the left of the door. Too dark to see, she groped along the smooth top as he came up behind her and cupped her breasts in his hands.

She moaned as he toyed with her and heat swept through her body.

"You're making this difficult," she said, then sighed at the feel of his lips on the back of her neck as he pressed his swollen shaft against her hip.

He gave one last possessive squeeze to her breasts, then released her. "Light the lamp," he said, his voice ragged. "I want to see you. All of you."

Quickly, she found the glass lamp. Lifting the globe, she took one of the matches beside it and lit it. She turned the wick down to a low, warm glow that made their shadows dance on the far wall.

Michael came up behind her again and placed a kiss on her shoulder as his arms wrapped around her waist to pull her close to his chest. She leaned her head back, savoring the feel of him. The strength and warmth in his powerful arms. His deep groan echoed in her ears and she sighed contentedly.

Slowly, he began undoing her clothes.

"Michael, what—"

"Shh," he said, placing a finger to her lips. "I want to savor you like a wrapped gift. Slowly. Carefully and with relish."

And so he did. She didn't move as he took her shirtwaist off, then her skirt and petticoats. Her corset went next, exposing her upper body to him. She shivered from the cool air against their skin, but his hot gaze warmed her as he untied her pantaloons, then dropped them to the floor.

She swallowed as she stood naked before him.

O'Connell thought he'd go mad as he stared at her bare body. Not even his memory had been able to hold on to the true beauty that was his Catherine.

And for this one night she was his.

All his.

He reached out and ran one hand over her right breast, delighting in the way her nipple hardened to his touch. Then, he trailed his hand over her abdomen to the curls at the juncture of her thighs. She moaned as he slid his fingers against her.

His mind reeled at the hotness of her body, at the sleek wetness in his hand. She was as ready for him as he was for her, but he didn't want to rush this.

He wanted this night to last a lifetime.

"I am going to savor you," he told her. "Every single inch of you."

Catherine couldn't respond verbally. Her mind numb, she could do nothing more than watch him watch her.

He picked her up again and carried her to the bed, where he removed her shoes, then carefully rolled down her stockings, nibbling her legs as he went.

As she started to sit up, he held her in place with one hand and shook his head. "Let me look at you lying there. I want to see you naked in your bed."

And look he did. His gaze traveled from the top of her head down to her breasts, to her stomach, her hips and legs, and then it returned to the center of her body, which thrummed with a hot, demanding need.

He lifted his hands to her thighs and spread her legs wider.

"Michael—"

"Let me look at you."

So she did, and his look burned even more than his touch. He leaned his head down and placed a tender kiss just below her belly button. His hot breath scorched her as his teeth tormented her flesh. He trailed his kisses lower, down to the inside of her thighs. Catherine closed her eyes and moaned as his lips brushed up against the center of her body.

Then he pulled back.

As if sensing how she ached for him, he quickly shed his own clothes, then climbed up between her legs. His entire body caressed hers in a long, luscious stroke.

She moaned at the erotic pleasure it delivered as her body arched to meet his. She felt him from the tips of her toes to the tips of her aching breasts, all the way to her forehead, where he placed a tender kiss.

His hot, stiff shaft rested on her belly.

Wanting him too badly to wait, she reached down between their bodies and stroked the velvety hardness of him. He hissed in her ear as she cupped him gently, then sought to guide him into her.

But he would have none of it.

Without entering her, Michael rolled to her side before his mouth returned to hers. He skimmed his hand over her body, then buried it between her legs.

Catherine hissed in pleasure as her hips lifted instinctively toward his hand.

He pulled back to stare down at her. "So," he whispered as his fingers toyed with the sensitive flesh between her thighs. He plunged one finger deep inside her, swirling it around and teasing her with pure, unadulterated pleasure. "Do you remember me now?"

"Yes," she gasped as his fingers did the most wicked things to her body.

He teased and toyed, his fingers circling and delving, faster and faster, until she was breathless from her aching need.

"And do you remember this?" he asked as he circled the core of her body with his thumb.

"Yes," she gasped again as her entire body throbbed.

He smiled a tender smile. "Now tell me what you want."

"I want to feel you deep inside me. Now."

He released her.

Catherine whimpered until he picked her up and moved her yet again. "What are you doing now?"

He led her to where her mirror stood in the corner. "You'll see," he whispered in her ear, raising chills on her arms.

He stood her before the mirror, where she could watch his hands as they caressed her body, kneaded her breasts, and masterfully stroked the flesh of her stomach.

He brushed her hair over her right shoulder to where it covered most of her and buried his lips in the curve of her neck.

Reaching up over her head, she buried her hand in his hair and groaned in pleasure.

"You still smell like sunshine," he whispered in her ear before swirling his tongue over the sensitive flesh. And when he plunged his tongue inside her ear, she melted and moaned as her entire body erupted into flames.

Catherine trembled all over as she watched his hands cup her breasts possessively. He pressed them, kneaded them, caressed them until she could barely stand it.

"I want to touch you," she said hoarsely, trying to turn around in his arms.

He stopped her. "You will," he said. "But not yet. Not until I *devour* you."

"Then devour me."

His rich laugh echoed in her ear. "Yes, ma'am," he whispered. "I'm more than happy to oblige you."

And then he trailed kisses down her spine. Slowly, methodically, covering every tiny inch of her flesh. She didn't know how her legs managed to keep her standing, for they trembled until she was sure she would fall.

His warm breath caressed her flesh as his hot, wet mouth teased her skin. He paused at the small of her back, his tongue gently stroking her buttocks. His hands circled around in front of her as he knelt on the floor at her feet.

Then his lips kissed the backs of her thighs, her knees, her calves, and when he got to her ankles, she jumped in erotic pleasure.

He laughed, then nudged her legs farther apart.

Fevered and hot, she did as he wanted and watched in the mirror as he positioned his body between her legs and kissed the front of her knees, her thighs.

He paused at the juncture of her thighs.

Her gaze transfixed by the sight of him in the looking glass, Catherine's entire body pulsed as his hot breath scorched her skin. He ran his left hand through her dark, short curls, kneading her erotically. Then, using both hands, he gently separated the tender folds and buried his mouth at the center of her body.

Tremors of ecstasy shook her.

O'Connell wanted to shout in victory as he tasted the most private part of her. She was his and this part of her was for him alone.

He would never share her! Never.

He ran his tongue over her, delighting in her moans and sighs. In the taste of her body, hot and moist against his starving tongue.

"Please," she begged. "I can't stand any more."

He nipped her tender flesh. "Oh, yes, you can, my love. I've only started with you."

Deciding he had tortured the two of them enough for the moment, he moved to nibble the sensitive flesh of her hip. She buried her hand in his hair. He delighted in the feel of her hands on his scalp.

More hurriedly than before, he kissed his way up her body until he could bury his lips in the hollow of her throat.

He held her tightly against him, reveling in the feel of her naked flesh against his, the feel of her tight nipples burning into his chest.

Catherine lifted one leg up to cup him to her as she arched her body against him, needing desperately to be closer to his heat. His lips burned her throat. She rubbed her hips against his in a silent plea for him to have mercy on her and to squelch the fire scorching her from the inside out.

To her chagrin, he pulled back. Then he took her hands in his and braced them on the frame of the mirror as he moved to stand behind her.

She met his lustful, hot gaze in the mirror. Never had she seen such a look of love and lust intermingled. His breathing ragged, he whispered to her, "I want to see you see me take you."

And then with one powerful stroke he drove himself up inside her. She sucked her breath in sharply at the feel of his fullness stroking her.

"Oh, yes, Michael, yes!" she cried out.

O'Connell thought he would perish at the sound of his name on her lips while she surrendered herself to him.

At that moment, he knew what paradise meant. Nothing could ever be more pleasurable than being with the woman he loved, hearing her sighs, and feeling her body from the inside out.

"Show me," he said in her ear. "Show me that you remember me."

She hesitated only an instant before she lifted herself on her tip-toes, drawing her body up to the tip of his shaft. Just as he was sure she'd drive him out, she dropped herself back against him, wringing a deep-seated moan of pleasure from him. He ground his teeth in the bittersweet torture of her milking his body with hers.

To hell with dreams! he thought rabidly. They were nothing compared to this reality. To the true feeling of her body sliding against his.

Catherine smiled at the look of ecstasy on his face as she watched him in the mirror. Unabashed, she gave him what he wanted and took what she needed. Perspiration broke out on his forehead as he met her gaze in the glass.

She could feel her body starting to teeter, to spiral to the pinnacle only he had ever shown her.

But before she would go there, she wanted something else from him. She delivered one last, long stroke to him, then paused.

He arched a questioning brow.

"Did you ever remember me?" she asked.

"Every minute of every hour. I've never stopped wanting you."

The sincerity in his gaze told her he spoke the truth. Joy spread through her as she again rocked herself against him, then pulled away.

He looked at her questioningly.

"I want to hold you when it happens."

Unwilling to make the short distance to the bed, he laid her down on the floor and again entered her.

Catherine moaned at the sensation of him thrusting between her legs as she encircled his body with hers. Wrapping her legs around his waist, she ran her hands down his spine and cupped his buttocks to her, urging him on. Her pleasure mounted higher and higher until she felt herself slipping again.

This time she let herself teeter over the edge.

Crying out, she shook as tremors of pure pleasure tore through her.

Still he thrusted, deepening her ecstasy until he threw his head back and cried out as well.

With a contented sigh, he collapsed on top of her and she reveled in the weight of him.

It had been too long. Far too long.

O'Connell couldn't breathe or move. Not until the throbbing returned to his arm and foot. "Ow," he breathed.

"Ow?" she repeated.

"My foot," he said as he rolled off her. "It's hurting again."

A blush stained her cheeks. She rose slowly from the floor and reached her hand out to him. "I think I know a way to make you forget about that."

He smiled and rose to her invitation. She took him to the bed and laid him back against the soft, feather mattress.

Surrendering himself to her whims, he watched as she crawled up his body like a naked wildcat. She wriggled her hips and then straddled his body.

O'Connell moaned at the feel of the hairs at the juncture of her thighs caressing his bare flesh as she sat down upon his stomach. She leaned forward, spilling her breasts across his chest as she wiggled that delectable bottom against him.

"Now let's see how much I remember," she whispered before burying her lips just below his ear. "Does this help the pain?"

"A little," he moaned.

She trailed kisses over his skin until she got to his chest. She stroked his nipple with her tongue and he hissed in pleasure. She nibbled him ever so gently.

"And that?" she asked.

"A little better than before," he said.

"Still not gone entirely?"

He shook his head.

"Well, then, let's see what it takes."

She moved to his side and as she bent over him her hair fell against his flesh, raising chills all over him. She lashed his chest with her hair, over and over, and he arched his back against the pleasurable beating.

"Better?" she asked.

"Somewhat."

She arched a brow. "Somewhat?"

He shrugged.

Her smile was wicked and warm. "In that case . . ."

She lowered her head and took him into her mouth. O'Connell pressed his head back into the pillows as his entire body jerked in pleasure.

"Catherine," he said hoarsely. "Next time, you can set fire to my entire body if that's the cure for it."

She laughed against him. "Don't tempt me," she said, looking up an instant before she returned to the part of him that was steadily growing larger. Harder.

Before he could move, she straddled him again and lowered herself on his shaft. "How's that?"

"Hot and wet, just like I like it," he said.

And this time when they came, it was in unison.

O'Connell didn't know what time they finally fell asleep. All he knew was that for the first time in five years, his body had been fully sated. He couldn't remember the last time he had felt this good. This free.

He cradled Catherine's slumbering form against his chest and buried his face in her hair. If he could, he would die right then and there.

Because with the dawn that would invariably come, he knew he would have to leave her. And he would rather be dead than walk out on her again.

But he had no choice.

4

Catherine awoke to the sound and feel of Michael's breathing in her ear, to the warmth of his body pressed against her own. It had been so long since she last had the pleasure of him sleeping by her side.

How could she have told him she didn't remember, when all she did was remember the feel of him? The smell of him? The *essence* of him?

And how could she ever reject a man she loved so dearly?

Catherine opened her eyes and saw him lying on his side, facing her. His left leg snuggled between hers, he had his left arm draped possessively across her body.

Impulsively, she brushed the brown wisps of hair off his forehead and placed a tender kiss to his brow.

"I still love you," she whispered, knowing he couldn't hear her. That was one thing about Michael—once he slept, it would take the end of the world to wake him.

She heard footsteps outside in the kitchen. Afraid it was one of the children or Rebecca, someone who might enter her room to wake her, she quickly got up and dressed.

With one last look to savor the sight of him sleeping naked in her bed, she drew her quilt up over his sleeping form and tiptoed from the room.

Entering the kitchen, she didn't see anyone.

How strange.

She had definitely heard someone a moment ago.

With a frown, she walked into the parlor where they had placed the Christmas tree and toys. To the right of the tree, hidden in the shadows, she found her daughter, Diana, cradling the doll St. Nick had brought her.

Catherine paused, staring at the product of her love for Michael. Diana was a bit small for her four years. She had Catherine's long, wavy dark hair and Michael's silver-gray eyes. It never failed to amaze Catherine that something so pretty and smart had come from her.

Smiling, she approached her daughter who looked up, her eyes brimming with tears.

"Diana, what is it?" she asked, instantly concerned as she knelt by her side. She brushed the dark bangs back from her daughter's face.

"He didn't come," Diana whimpered as a solitary tear fell down her face.

"Of course St. Nick came, sweetling. You have the doll and everything."

"No, Mama, *he* didn't come," she repeated, hugging her doll even closer as more tears fell. "It was all I wanted for Christmas and he didn't come."

"Who, baby?"

"Daddy," she sobbed.

Catherine's breath caught in her throat at the unexpected word. Diana had only started asking about her father a few short months ago, and the fact that he *had* shown up in the night . . .

It was enough to give one the shivers.

"What are you talking about?" Catherine asked her daughter.

"You told me St. Nick could make miracles, remember, Mama?"

"Yes."

"And I told you I wanted a *special* miracle."

"I thought you meant the doll."

Diana shook her head. "I wanted St. Nick to bring me my daddy. I wanted to see his eyes like mine."

Catherine wrapped her arms around her small daughter and held her close. She wasn't sure what she should do. Part of her wanted to take Diana into the bedroom to meet her father, and the other part of her was too terrified of how Michael might react.

She should have told him last night, but she had turned coward.

It was one thing for him to abandon her. She could deal with it. But hurting Diana was another matter.

No, it would be best to wait and tell him about their daughter when Diana wasn't around. That way only she would be hurt if he ran for the door. Again.

With the edge of her shawl, Catherine wiped Diana's eyes. "No tears on Christmas, please?"

Diana sniffed them back.

She kissed the top of Diana's little dark head and squeezed her tight. "I'll talk to St. Nick after breakfast and see what I can do."

"But he's already gone back to the North Pole."

"I know, sweetling, but didn't anyone ever tell you that mommies have a special way of letting St. Nick know what their babies want?"

Diana wiped her tears with the back of her hand. "After breakfast?"

Catherine nodded. "Keep your fingers crossed and maybe he can manage something."

"I will. I promise."

She smiled at those silver-gray eyes that shone with innocence. "Good girl. Now go check your stockings and see what else St. Nick might have left while I go start breakfast."

Diana scooted out of her arms and Catherine rose slowly to her feet.

In truth, she felt ill. Her stomach knotted. How would she break the news to Michael?

Would he even care?

Taking a deep breath for courage, she knew one way or the other she had to tell him. Even an irresponsible scoundrel deserved to know he had fathered a beautiful little girl who wanted nothing more than to meet him.

"Just don't hurt her," she whispered. "Because if you do, I'll kill you for it."

O'*Connell came awake* slowly to the smell of bacon and coffee, and the sound of children laughing outside his door. At first he thought it was a dream.

How many times had he yearned to experience just such a morning?

Many more times than he could count.

"Catherine, do I need to set extra plates for whoever was at the door last night? I didn't know if he, she, or them stayed, or what."

He heard Catherine's mumbled reply through the walls, but couldn't make out any of her words.

All of a sudden the memory of the night before came crashing back through him.

It had been real. All of it. This was no dream. He was, in fact, sleeping in Catherine's bed on Christmas morning.

O'Connell leaned his head back into the pillow as an overwhelming joy ripped through him. He felt like shouting or singing or doing something. Anything to celebrate such a glorious event.

Impulsively, he pulled Catherine's pillow to him and inhaled the fresh sunshine smell of her. Intoxicated, he listened to the children sing "God Rest Ye Merry Gentlemen" as someone jingled china and silverware.

"It's not a dream," he whispered.

He laughed softly as raw euphoria invaded every piece of him. He had his Christmas miracle.

Smiling, he rose from the bed and dressed, then made the bed up. Catherine had always complained he twisted the sheets into knots and she hated a messy bed.

This would be his gift to her.

He left the room warily and made sure no one spied him lest Catherine have some serious explaining to do. The last thing she needed was a tarnished reputation, and the last thing he needed was nosy questions he couldn't answer.

He saw the stairs behind him and made like he was coming from one of the rooms upstairs.

As he drew flush with the kitchen door, he saw Catherine standing in front of the stove, frying eggs.

He delighted at her trim form. She'd left her hair long in the back with a braid wound about the top of her head to keep it out of her eyes. Her dark green dress hugged every one of the curves he had feasted on the night before. And a white shawl draped becomingly over her shoulders.

Never had he seen a more glorious image, and he wished he could stay here forever.

"Rebecca?" Catherine called, stepping back from the stove and looking out the doorway on the opposite side of the room. "Are the children still outside?"

"Making snow angels, last I saw," a woman called as she came into the room. The petite brunette stopped dead in her tracks as her gaze fell to him.

Catherine caught the woman's gaze and turned to face him.

"Morning," he greeted them.

Catherine blushed, and he didn't miss the light that came into the short brunette's eyes.

"Morning," the brunette said warmly, suggestively.

Catherine cleared her throat. "Rebecca, this is our visitor from last night."

"Pleased to meet you," Rebecca said. "Mister . . . ?"

"Burdette," he said, falling into his most recent alias. "Tyler Burdette."

He glanced to Catherine, who took his name in with a frown.

"I'll just go set another place at the table for you, Mr. Burdette," Rebecca said.

As soon as they were alone again, Catherine approached him, waving a spatula dripping with hot grease dangerously near his nose. "Tyler Burdette?" she asked in a miffed tone. "Is there something you need to tell me?"

That was a loaded question and he wasn't sure how to answer it. Luckily another visitor, a man, spared him a few moments to think.

But to be honest, all he thought about was the fact that the distinguished-looking, gray-haired man spent a little too long staring at *his* Catherine.

"Miss Catherine?"

"Marshal McCall," she said, stressing the title, no doubt for his benefit.

And it worked. O'Connell was immediately on guard.

By the look on the man's face, it was obvious he wanted to ask Catherine something of a personal nature. Worse, the man stuttered and shifted nervously before he came out with, "I just came for my morning cup of coffee."

O'Connell's gaze narrowed. The damn man was infatuated with *his* wife.

He flinched as an image of her in the marshal's arms tore through his mind.

Would the insults never cease?

As Catherine moved to fetch a cup of coffee, the marshal glanced to O'Connell. "How do?" he asked amiably enough.

"Just fine, Marshal," O'Connell returned, trying to remain pleasant in spite of the urge he had to choke the man. "And you?"

The marshal frowned as he looked him up and down. "Don't I know you from someplace?"

Probably from about a dozen or so wanted posters, but he didn't dare say that. Instead, O'Connell shook his head. "I don't know any marshals." He made it his habit to avoid them at all costs.

"No?" the marshal asked. "You sure look familiar to me. You got any family in Reno?"

O'Connell shook his head. "Not that I'm aware of."

He seemed to accept that. But still he took a step forward and extended his hand. "Dooley McCall."

"Tyler Burdette," he said, shaking his proffered hand.

"Burdette," the marshal repeated. "Nah, I don't reckon I do know you after all."

Catherine handed the marshal his coffee.

"Thank you, Miss Catherine. I keep telling my deputies no one on earth makes a better pot of coffee than you do."

"Thank you, marshal."

O'Connell didn't miss the blush staining her cheeks. For a moment, he had to struggle to breathe. How dare she blush at another man. So what if he had been gone five years, it still didn't give her the right to do *that* for someone else.

She was *his* wife, not the marshal's.

The marshal nodded, then took his coffee and left.

O'Connell wasted no time sneaking to the doorway to see the marshal sitting in the parlor with a paper, sipping his coffee as if everything were right in the world.

"What the hell is a marshal doing here?" he asked Catherine in a low voice.

She gave him a haughty glare. "He *lives* here."

"Lives here?" he repeated.

"I run a boardinghouse, remember? He's one of my regular tenants."

"Why would you let him live *here*?"

"I don't know," she said sarcastically. "Maybe I like having him here because it keeps out the riff-raff," she said with a pointed stare, "and he pays two months' rent in advance."

Catherine didn't miss the heated glare Michael gave her. Licking her lips, she felt a wave of misgiving run up her spine. Michael was entirely too interested in the marshal.

Something was wrong.

"Are you wanted?" she asked all of a sudden.

He stared at her with those clear silver-gray eyes. "It depends," he said in a serious voice. "I was hoping you'd want me."

Her breath caught. Did she dare hope that he might actually be able to settle down with her and Diana?

"And if I did?" she asked.

He looked back at the marshal. "This is a bad time. I really need to leave."

"Leave?" she gasped. "You can't."

"Why not?"

"Because you just got here. You can't just show up on my doorstep, roll around in my bed, and then take flight as soon as the sun comes up. I thought we had shared something special last night. Or were they all lies again?"

He winced as if she'd struck him. "I've never lied to you, Catherine."

"No. But you lied to my boarder and housekeeper. Is that not true, Mr. *Tyler Burdette*?"

"I—"

"Miss Catherine, Miss Catherine?" An excited boy came bursting through the kitchen with Pete's saddlebags in his hands. The blond head bobbed as the kid jumped up and down. "I just found these outside by the front door, and look," he said, flipping one open. "They're filled with money! Can I keep it?"

O'Connell went cold as everything came together in his mind.

"*I found this little orphanage in a town called Redwood,*" Pete had said. "*You'd probably like it a lot, Kid. It had a real homey feel to it.*"

O'Connell cursed as his stomach drew tight. Pete knew. He had sent him purposefully to find Catherine.

Panic swept through him. That meant Pete wouldn't be far behind. He had to get her to safety before his brother showed up and used her to drag him back into robbery.

But how? She'd never leave her business or her orphans.

"This is bad," he whispered. "Real bad."

Catherine looked into the saddlebags. "Where did this come from?" she asked the boy.

"I was told it was stolen from you," O'Connell said as he doublechecked where the marshal sat.

Looking up at him, Catherine frowned. "By whom?"

"Is it yours?" O'Connell asked, seeking to delay the inevitable explanation of how he'd come by her money. "Were you robbed?"

"Yes, we were. But how did you get it?"

So much for delaying the inevitable.

She looked at him sternly. "Did *you* take it?"

"No!" he barked. "How could you even ask that?"

"Well, what am I to think?" she asked as she set the saddlebags on the table and excused the boy.

She moved to stand just before him, hands on hips. "I thought I knew you, and yet every time I blink I learn something about you that scares me. Now tell me how it is you have my money."

O'Connell didn't have a chance. Before he could say a word, the back door opened to show Pete holding one of Catherine's little girls in his arms.

"Knock, knock," Pete drawled. He flashed an evil grin to O'Connell, then lifted the little girl's face to where O'Connell could see her tear-streaked eyes. "Look what old Uncle Pete found out in the yard."

5

O'Connell felt the air leave his lungs as he gazed into a pair of eyes indistinguishable from his own. They were set in a face that looked identical to Catherine's, right down to the dark brown curls spilling over Pete's arm.

In an instant, he recognized his daughter.

Sobbing uncontrollably, the girl looked to Catherine. "Help me, Mama! Make the mean man let me go."

Catherine took a step toward the girl, but O'Connell grabbed her arm and pulled her to a stop.

No one approached his brother. If Catherine tried to take the girl, there was no telling what Pete might do to her.

"Let her go, Pete," O'Connell said, his calm voice belying the volatile state of his mind and body.

Pete gave an evil smile. "I told you in Oak River, you can't escape me, Kid. Now I ask you again, are you coming with me or what?"

"Oak River?" he heard Catherine repeat under her breath.

That was the town where he'd left her. Only then, Pete had used Catherine as his leverage. It was either go with Pete to rob another bank or see his wife hurt.

After the robbery, O'Connell had lacked the heart to go back to her. He couldn't face her after what he'd done for Pete. Worse, he knew that sooner or later Pete would show up again with the same threat.

And the last thing he wanted was to kill his brother for hurting his wife.

So long as there was life in his body, he would protect his Catherine.

You're my second chance. That's what O'Connell had told her on their wedding night. Catherine hadn't known what he'd meant by it. But he had.

For a time, he had been stupid enough to believe it. But second chances were for fools.

And Catherine could never again be his.

"I'll come with you, Pete. Just put her down."

Pete nodded. "Good boy. I knew you'd see things my way once you saw them again." Pete squeezed the girl's cheeks and tilted her head up to where he could look into her face. "She is kind of cute, isn't she?"

Rage infused every cell of O'Connell's body. "Take your hands off her, Pete, or I'll kill you for it."

His brother met his gaze and for several seconds they stared at each other in mutual understanding. "You know. Kid, I believe you would."

"You can count on it."

O'Connell didn't breathe again until Pete set the girl on her feet, and she ran to Catherine's outstretched arms.

Pete glanced to Catherine and the little girl. "Since it's Christmas and all, I'll give you five minutes with them. I'll be waiting outside by the horses."

O'Connell waited for him to leave before he turned to face Catherine, who cradled the little girl to her chest.

His daughter.

He felt so much pride and delight, he thought his heart might burst. But the joy died as he remembered his brother waiting for him outside.

O'Connell reached a hand out to touch the dark brown curls. The softness of his daughter's hair reached deep inside him, carving a place in his heart.

"She's beautiful," he breathed.

Catherine saw the pain deep inside him and she noted the tenseness of his hand on Diana's hair. "Her name is Diana."

He gave a bittersweet smile. "Named for your mother?"

She nodded.

"Why didn't you tell me about her in Nevada?" he asked, his eyes misting.

"I didn't know I was pregnant until after you left." She narrowed her gaze on him as she finally understood everything that had happened. "You left because of him, didn't you?"

"He's my brother," he said simply. "I had no choice."

"We always have choices."

He shook his head. "No, we don't. You don't know what kind of man my brother is, but I do. I know he's cruel, but I owe him. If not for Pete, I'd have never survived after the death of our parents. He's harsh because that's the way the world made him."

"He's harsh because he's—"

O'Connell stopped her words by placing his fingers on her lips. His heart tearing apart, he leaned over, kissed her gently on the mouth, and whispered, "Until the day I die, I'll always remember you."

He touched Diana's hair one last time, then he turned and walked away.

O'*Connell met Pete* by his pinto, which Pete must have saddled. His brother was as fair-haired and fair-skinned as O'Connell was dark. The two of them had always been opposites in most everything. Even Pete's eyes were a brownish green.

And never before had O'Connell felt so much resentment and hatred for the brother who had once protected him.

"Why can't you just let me go?" he asked Pete. "I've paid my debt to you a thousand times over."

Pete gave him a hard glare. "You're my family, Kid. Like it or hate it, it's just you and me." Pete smiled wickedly. "Besides, you're the only man I know who can blow a safe and not destroy half the money with it."

"You're not funny."

Pete shucked him on the shoulder. "Now, don't get sore on me, Kid. You can do better than her. I told you that years ago. She ain't nearly pretty enough for you."

He grabbed Pete by his shirtfront. "I'm not a kid anymore, Pete, and I'm no longer scared of you. Catherine is my wife and she deserves your respect. If you ever say anything else against her, as God is my witness, I'll tear your hide apart for it."

For the first time in his life, he saw a glimmer of fear pass through Pete's eyes. "All right, Kid. Whatever you say."

O'Connell let him go. He had barely taken a step when he heard the front door of the boardinghouse open.

The marshal strode out across the porch with two men in tow. And all three of them carried shotguns in their arms. By the grim, determined looks on their faces, he knew what they wanted.

Him and Pete.

His blood went cold.

The marshal stared at Pete as he leveled the shotgun on them. "Pete O'Connell," he said slowly. "Never did I expect to receive such a great Christmas present. Imagine the bounty of *both* O'Connell brothers."

Pete swore, then went for his gun.

O'Connell didn't think. He merely reacted. He was tired of his brother's schemes, and tired of the lives Pete had taken for no reason.

It was time for it to end.

He grabbed his brother's gun, and the two of them struggled for it.

Catherine watched the men tussle from the parlor window. She had sent Diana upstairs with Rebecca, then immediately sought out the marshal to let him know there was a possible outlaw outside.

She pressed her hand to her lips as terror sliced through her as she watched the two men fighting for possession of the gun. What had she done?

A gunshot rang out.

Catherine stopped breathing. Michael and Pete froze and locked gazes. Time seemed suspended as she waited.

Who had been shot?

Then Michael staggered back, and she saw the red stain on his shirtfront right before he collapsed on the ground.

"No!" she shouted as tears stung the backs of her eyes. It couldn't be Michael! It couldn't be.

Pete just looked down at him, his face indecipherable.

Dropping her shawl, Catherine ran for the door, down the steps, and across the yard to Michael's side.

His brother stood coldly to the side as the marshal and his men put irons on his wrists.

Sobbing, she knelt by Michael's side. Terrified and shaking, she touched his cold brow.

"Michael?" she breathed.

He opened his eyes and looked up at her. In that look she saw the love he had for her. He opened his mouth to speak, but she pressed her fingertips to his lips.

"Save your strength," she whispered. She looked up to Marshal McCall, who stared angrily at Pete.

"I always heard you were mean, but damn, to shoot your own brother on Christmas? You're a sick man, O'Connell," the marshal said to Pete.

His face blank, Pete glanced down to her and Michael, then back at the marshal.

"What are you, stupid? Do we *look* like brothers?" Pete drawled slowly. "My brother got killed in Shiloh last month during our last holdup. That there's just some stupid cow-poke thinks he's a bounty hunter. Bastard's been trailing me for weeks. I don't even know his name." Pete locked gazes with her, then shocked her with his words, "But I think the lady over there knows him. Ask her who he is."

The marshal gave her a probing stare. "That true, Miss Catherine? You know this man?"

A tremor of panic shook her as she realized Michael's entire fate was in her hands.

What should she answer?

She looked down at Michael's calm, deliberate stare. He expected her to betray him. She could read it plainly in his eyes as he waited for her to denounce him.

But she couldn't. She didn't know everything yet, but before she handed him over to the marshal, she wanted some long-overdue answers. Answers he couldn't very well give her locked up in jail.

"He's my husband," she answered honestly. "Michael O'Callahan."

The marshal gave her a hard stare. "I thought you said your husband ran off."

"He did," she said, looking back at Michael. "But he came home to me last night."

"Farley," the marshal shouted to his deputy. "Help me carry Miss Catherine's husband inside while Ted locks up O'Connell."

The marshal helped her to her feet.

"Where you want us to take him?" the marshal asked.

"To my room," she said, leading the way back into the boarding-house.

Michael O'Connell *didn't* say anything for the rest of the day. His head swam with what had happened.

Why had Pete lied?

Why had Catherine protected him, when she could have easily seen him in prison for the next ten to twenty years?

None of it made any sense to him, and worse, Catherine had avoided coming into the room for him to question her. If he'd been able to, he would have gone after her himself, but he was too weak to do much more than just breathe.

The door to his room creaked open. He glanced over to see a tiny dark head peeking in.

He smiled at the sight of his daughter in the doorway.

When Diana saw him look her way, the little girl smiled from ear to ear.

She fanned the door back and forth as she twisted in the door frame. "Are you really my daddy?" she asked.

"What did your mama say?"

"She said St. Nick brought you to me last night."

O'Connell gave a half laugh at her words, but he couldn't manage any more than that, since pain cut his breath off. Pete had been called a lot of things over the years, but this was the first time anyone had ever referred to his brother as St. Nick.

"Yeah," he said with a grimace. "I guess maybe he did."

Releasing the doorknob, she ran across the room and scrambled to sit next to him on the bed. He winced at the pain she caused by dipping the mattress, but in truth he didn't mind it at all. To have his daughter near him, he would suffer a lot worse than that.

"You sure are pretty for a man."

O'Connell smiled at her words. No one had ever said *that* to him before.

She reached out one little hand to touch his eyelid. "You do have eyes like mine. Mama told me you did."

He cupped her soft cheek, amazed at what he saw in her face. It was so strange to see parts of him mixed in with parts of Catherine.

Never in his life had he seen a more beautiful little girl. "We get them from my mother."

"Was she pretty, too?"

"Like you, she was as pretty as an angel."

"Diana!"

He started at Catherine's chiding tone.

"I told you not to disturb him."

"I'm sorry, Mama."

"She's not disturbing me," he said, dropping his hand from her face.

Catherine shooed her out anyway. At first he thought she'd leave as well, but she hesitated in the doorway.

"Why didn't you tell me who you really were?" she asked.

He stared at her. "I liked the man you saw me as. To you, I was a decent man, not some no-account outlaw drifter. The last thing I wanted was for you to change your mind about me and hate me."

"So you lied to me?"

"Not really. I just didn't tell you everything."

She shook her head. "I always knew you were hiding *something* from me. I was just never sure what. Funny, I used to think it was another woman you loved, not a lunatic brother."

He gave her a hard, meaningful look. "I could never love anyone but you."

"Do you mean that?"

"On my life."

And then she gifted him with one of those loving smiles that had kept him warm on the coldest days. "So tell me, Michael, where do we go from here?"

Epilogue

Christmas Eve. Two years later

"Hey, Pa, where do we go from here?"

Michael looked up at nine-year-old Frank's question. After Catherine had given him his second chance, the two of them had decided to adopt the orphans she'd been keeping. And every day of the last two years, he had spent every minute making up to her for the time they had been apart.

She would never again have cause to doubt him, and he reveled in the blessing of his family and home.

"I think you'd best be asking your mother that question," he said to Frank. "Catherine?"

"It's the big white house at the end of the street," she said as she waddled up to them beside the train station.

Michael grinned at the sight of her pregnant body. He'd missed seeing her carry Diana, but he was definitely enjoying her now.

The way Catherine figured, they had two more months before the baby would join them. Just enough time to visit her parents with their passel of children in tow, and then make it back home in time for the little one's birth.

Four of the orphans still lived with them. Five children total with Diana. Michael smiled as he watched all of them climb aboard the wagon he had rented.

He'd always wanted a big family.

"You nervous?" he asked Catherine as he draped a comforting arm over her shoulders. She hadn't seen her parents since the day they had eloped almost seven years before.

"A little. And you?"

"A little."

Even so, he was too grateful for his life to mind even a lengthy visit at his in-laws'. He still found it hard to believe Pete had lied to save him.

"I've ruined your life enough, Kid. This is one place I think I'd best go to alone," Pete had told him.

Pete would be in prison for a long time to come. Maybe it would make his brother a better man.

All he could do was hope that one day his brother would find the peace that had always eluded him.

Michael placed a tender kiss on Catherine's brow as he took Diana's hand in his and helped her up into the wagon.

Every day for the last two years, he had been grateful that his wife had stood by him, even though it was the last thing he'd deserved.

"Thank you, Cathy," he breathed as he helped her climb into the wagon seat.

"For what?" she asked.

"For making my life worth living."

Her smile warmed him to his toes. "It's been my pleasure, Mr. O'Callahan. Merry Christmas."

And a Merry Christmas it would be, too. For in this life, there were second chances, and this time, Michael wouldn't waste the one he'd been given.

Redemption

A Bonus Scene from The Guardian

Blowing out a frustrated breath, Seth stared at himself in the mirror as he tried to do something with his rebellious hair.

It was useless.

Even worse than the curly mess he couldn't control was the clothes Lydia had picked out for him to wear. The black pants that buttoned on the sides were extremely uncomfortable and they only went to his knees. From there down, he had on white . . . what had she called them? Stockings? And weird buckled shoes that pinched his toes and rubbed his heels worse than his armored boots.

But the thing he despised most was the gold, high-collared, heavily embroidered jacket with a white shirt that had mountains of girly lace cascading down the front. Lydia had called it a cravat. He called it hideous. And that same scratchy lace spilled out at the end of his sleeves, covering both of his hands, all the way to his knuckles.

He'd bitched about this monstrosity the moment she'd shoved it at him. The only reason he'd finally agreed to wear it was that she'd pointed out the fact that it couldn't possibly be any more uncomfortable to wear than his armor—something he empathically disagreed with. Only an outright moron laughed at a man encased in demonic armor. Dressed like this, only an outright moron *wouldn't* laugh at it.

And two—the most important reason of all—he wouldn't have to wear it long. As soon as they were done, she'd promised to rip this heinous outfit off him and make him deliriously happy that he'd humored her.

Little did she know, he'd have worn it for her anyway. All she had to do was smile at him and he was sunk.

Still . . .

"I look like an effing idiot."

Dressed in black tails and tie, Asmodeus snorted from behind him. "I would respond to that, but the fact that you have more powers now than you did when I served you in the Nether Realm, and the fact that I'm fond of my body parts in their current locations, prevents me from saying a single word." He flashed a fanged grin at Seth. "Sorry."

Yeah, right. His expression said Asmodeus was anything but. In fact, that expression said the bastard was highly amused . . . and at Seth's expense.

See. Point taken. Asmodeus had never dared laugh at him when they were in Azmodea and Seth was in armor.

But in *this* . . .

Laughter was a moral imperative, and he couldn't fault Asmodeus for that.

Seth was tempted to offer the demon money to change clothes with him. Unfortunately, Asmodeus was an amorphic demon who could take any form he wanted, and for the wedding, the little creep had decided to be only six feet tall with short white blond hair he had spiked up, all over his head. Then again, Seth could use his own powers to simply change his clothes into something else.

Like armor.

But that would upset Lydia.

For her, Seth would suffer.

Maybe not in silence, but . . .

He stifled a whimper as he met Asmodeus's gaze in the mirror. Those demonic gray eyes were the only thing that stayed the same in all of Asmodeus's incarnations. Eyes that saw far deeper than the surface of any being.

While Seth had been locked in the Nether Realm, Azmodea—the demon—had been the only one, besides Jaden, who'd never harmed him. In fact, it was Asmodeus who'd taught him to paint his face to intimidate the others. And in spite of what Asmodeus had said, Seth had never once done him harm either.

The sad news was that Asmodeus was the closest thing to an actual friend Seth had ever had . . . which was why the demon, who'd been freed from Noir's service a few years back while Seth had been confined, had been asked to be his best man.

Asmodeus moved closer to straighten Seth's cravat. "I have to say that I'm glad you're the only one she wants dressed this way. 'Cause it is epically hideous and you look like a woman in it."

Seth glared down at him. "You better be glad I've mellowed and that you're one of only four guests I have here today."

Asmodeus's grin widened. "Infinitely so, Lord Master Guardian. Besides, you wouldn't want your best demon to have blood on his rented tux at your wedding, would you? It might distress Mistress Jackal."

A wave of anger shot through Seth at the reminder of the slavery in hell he'd barely survived. But for Lydia, he'd still be there, living in torture and chains, and never-ending misery. Even the mere mention of it sent him into a furious state. "I know you're joking with that title, but don't call me that anymore."

Stepping back, Asmodeus inclined his head as if he understood why that reminder stung Seth so deep. "What do I call you then?"

"Seth."

The demon started to chuckle then stopped the moment Seth lifted a questioning eyebrow. "Sorry, Lord Master . . . that which I cannot say."

"What's so funny about my name?"

The demon shrugged. "I just thought you'd have a more sinister one than Seth. Although it does rhyme with death . . . Perhaps apropos after all." Asmodeus clapped him on the back then changed the subject. "Are you nervous about this?"

Not really. Bored. Irritated. Impatient. But definitely not nervous. He couldn't think of anything better than being bound to his Lydia. She was his only master now and he was quite content to be shackled to her for the rest of eternity. "Am I supposed to be?"

"I'm told many are when they go to tie their lives to someone else. I, personally, would be vomitus over it."

"Why?"

"One woman? Forever?" Asmodeus choked himself.

Seth shook his head at the demon. "She's not just any woman." She was unlike anyone he'd ever known. Best of all, she loved him, and *that* he'd never understand. Not even a little.

But he would always be grateful that she, alone, had looked into the eyes of a scarred, broken demon-slave and found a humanity Seth had never known, or even guessed, existed inside him.

Not until he'd been touched by a gentle hand that didn't cause him injury. One that never begrudged or betrayed him.

The demon shrugged again. "That's what they all claim. Then you marry one of them, and they spend the rest of their lives trying to kill you."

"How so?"

Asmodeus checked the list off on his fingers. "Whining. Nagging. Expanding."

Seth scowled at the one he didn't understand. "Expanding?"

"You know, getting fat on you."

Seth was baffled by his reasoning. "Lydia's pregnant, not fat." And that was definitely his fault and not hers.

"Yes, but that weight never goes away. Trust me."

Still, he didn't see how that was a bad thing. "There will just be more of her to love."

The demon made a gagging sound. "Just wait until the demon in her makes a—"

"Asmodeus!" Maahes, the Egyptian god of war and cousin to Seth, snapped as he flashed into the room in all his regal god-finery. "Stop trying to run him off."

"Run him off?" Asmodeus asked indignantly. "I'm trying to save him."

Maahes grinned at Seth. "I don't think he wants to be saved."

Definitely not from Lydia, but he wasn't about to say that to *them*. Neither of them needed to know his emotions. They were reserved solely for the woman who'd given her heart to him.

"Is it time?" Seth asked the god.

"Almost." Maahes squinted at him as he studied his clothes. "You're not actually wearing your hair like that, are you?"

Yeah, okay—that succeeded in making him nervous. "Why? I thought I'd tamed it."

Maahes snorted. "Looks real good, Poindexter."

"Poindexter?" Seth scowled at a reference that had no meaning to him.

Without answering, Maahes grabbed him and turned him away from the mirror so that he could tug at Seth's hair.

Seth tried to pull away, but Maahes wouldn't let him. Then he tried to fend the obnoxious god off. "What are you doing?"

"Put your hands down."

Like hell.

"What in the world is going on here?"

Seth pushed Maahes back at the sound of Ma'at's voice. The Egyptian god of justice and balance, she was so tiny she barely reached the middle of Seth's chest. Her caramel skin glowed with the warmth of her powers and made her green eyes sparkle. An amused sparkle that danced as she watched them.

"Nothing," he muttered.

Maahes flicked at one of Seth's traitorous curls. "I'm trying to make this dark auburn bush that functions as his hair semi-attractive for his bride."

Ma'at arched a brow. "*That* is *not* attractive."

Seth turned to look in the mirror. He'd had his hair kind of smoothed down before Maahes had arrived. Now it stuck out all over his head like Asmodeus's.

Great, I look like I've been given electroshock treatments.

His former owner would be pleased, indeed.

"I wasn't through with it," Maahes said defensively.

Tsking at them, Ma'at came forward to speak to Seth. "Come here, child."

Seth's first instinct was to glare, but he'd slowly learned over the last few months that Ma'at and Maahes weren't his enemies.

They were his family. After all these long centuries, he really did have one.

He still couldn't believe it.

That had been the hardest adjustment for him in this modern, mortal world. Forcing himself to remember that not everyone wanted to hurt him. Not everyone took pleasure in his agony. That there really were people in the world who could love him and not cause him harm.

Smiling, Ma'at patted him gently on the arm. "You'll have to sit or kneel, Seth. I can't reach your hair from here."

Her powers and personality were such that it was easy to forget just how tiny she really was.

Seth knelt down so that she could quickly style his hair.

Once she finished, he rose and went to look at it. The curls were all over his head again. Repulsed by the sight, he reached to straighten it.

She grabbed his arm. "Don't you dare!" Ma'at's voice was as stern as he'd ever heard it.

Seth curled his lip. "I look like a woman."

"No, sweetie, you *definitely* don't. Trust me." She turned a sharp glare toward Maahes and Asmodeus. "And don't either one of you dare contradict me."

Maahes held his hands up in surrender. "I would *never* contradict you. I know better."

"Good." She turned her attention back to Seth. "Lydia wanted a Beauty and the Beast theme for her wedding. I think you look grand."

Asmodeus broke out into laughter.

Once he realized the three of them were glaring at him, he sobered. "Oh c'mon. Don't tell me that went over all of your heads. You know, she's a jackal A.K.A. beast and dressed like *that*," he gestured at Seth, "he looks like the beauty." He laughed again.

Maahes met Seth's gaze. "I can kill him if you want."

"No, don't. *I* want the pleasure of killing the bastard."

Ma'at stopped Seth before he could reach Asmodeus. "Your bride is waiting for you. Do you really want to waste time with an annoying demon?"

"Fine.

But after . . .

"There's one thing I want to add to Lydia's registry." He jerked his chin to Asmodeus. "His head on a platter."

Maahes laughed. "With or without a roasted apple wedged in his mouth?"

Lydia *tucked her* hand into the crook of Solin's elbow. Dressed all in black, her father was stunning and elegant in his coat and tails.

He covered her hand with his and gave her a stern glower. "You know, you don't have to do this. It's not too late to have George take us home."

She smiled at the reminder of his valet who was seated just inside the temple door—ready to run her out to the car should she change her mind.

"Daddy," she whispered to him. "I love Seth."

He picked her hand up and kissed her fingers. "I've waited your entire life to hear you call me that. Thank you." He returned her hand to his elbow.

She kissed his cheek. "I do love you, you know that, don't you?"

"Absolutely. And while I don't like the idea of you marrying that bastard, I promise I will always be polite to him."

Yes, but his idea of polite and hers had a bit of a gap between them. Still, her father was trying, and for that, she'd give him extra points.

Ma'at opened the door that led to the hallway. "He's downstairs, waiting."

Dressed in a pale yellow gown, Ma'at made a gorgeous matron of honor. Since Lydia didn't have a lot of people she was close to and everyone outside of this small group thought her dead, Ma'at had been the best choice.

Ma'at handed her the bride's bouquet . . .

Pink and white lilies. Seth's special nickname for her. Her eyes teared up as she gripped the handle. Seth had insisted she carry them.

"Are you all right?" Solin asked in a worried tone.

"Hormonal." The only thing she didn't like about being pregnant was the fact that she cried over every little thing. It was terrible.

Ma'at led them out of the room and into the main hall of her temple then down to the throne room that had been decorated with more lilies and white crepe.

But Lydia barely saw the decorations or the friend Ma'at had brought in to officiate the ceremony.

All her attention went to Seth in his baroque coat and breeches. She'd known he'd be gorgeous in them, but he defied her best expectation.

Yeah, he was totally lickable and hot.

Her father stopped by Seth's side and hesitated before he kissed her cheek and withdrew to sit beside Thorn and Ambrose.

Seth couldn't breathe as he held onto Lydia's hand and stared down into those brilliant topaz eyes. Dressed in a red gown . . . the color of a traditional ancient Greek wedding gown, she was stunning. The small red veil was attached to her black hair with diamond tipped pins.

Ma'at took her bouquet so that they could approach Savitar who waited for them.

Savitar looked around at the small group that consisted of Ma'at, Asmodeus, Maahes, Ambrose, Thorn, Solin, and them. "Dearly weird and motley beings, we're gathered here today for . . . yada, yada, yada. Seth say something profound and sweet to Lydia."

It took Seth a moment to focus. While he'd never seen a wedding and had no idea what they entailed, Savitar's strange introduction didn't seem right to him. But since Lydia didn't seem to mind, he took a breath to speak the words he'd been practicing to say to her. "My Lydia is like a star rising to guide me through the darkest night." He glanced back at the men and felt a sick rush at speaking the rest in front of them. When he'd written the words, he hadn't taken into account who would be in his audience.

After a minute of Seth's hesitation, Savitar sighed. "Look, kid, I can say the words for you, but I think she'd rather hear them from your lips. Ignore the assholes in the chairs. If one of them laughs, I'll gut him for you."

Seth tightened his hand on hers and remembered what Ma'at had told him. *Most girls spend their entire lives dreaming and planning for their wedding. Whatever you do, don't step on her dream. If you love her, let her have this one day and go along with whatever strange thing she wants you to do.*

Even if it meant dressing like a freak and wearing shoes that pinched his toes.

His gaze went down to her distended belly where their baby was still forming. This was his family and she was all he loved. The others were completely unimportant to him.

Let them laugh and mock. Not a one of them had a woman so fine to call his own.

But he was the lucky bastard who did.

Seth was the lucky bastard Lydia had claimed—the one she'd risked her precious life to save.

He led her hand to his lips so that he could kiss it before he laced his fingers with hers. "When your hand is in my hand, I tremble with an unimagined joy. Never once did I think I could be as happy as I am right now. And every day that I'm with you is better than the one before it. For you, alone, I would bleed and I would die. But most of all, without you, I could never live. So long as I breathe, I will always love you and I will spend the rest of my life making sure that you never doubt the fact that you are the air I breathe."

Lydia pressed her lips together to keep from crying as Seth laid his soul bare to her.

And in front of the others, no less. He wasn't the kind of man who spoke of his feelings and never publicly. If for nothing else, she'd love him for this.

But her reasons for loving him were too many to count.

She laid her hand against his cheek and kissed his lips.

"Hey, hey, hey!" Savitar snapped. "You're jumping ahead, woman. It's your turn to make a vow to him."

She kept her hand on Seth's cheek as she stared up into the steel blue eyes that had stolen her heart and changed her life in ways she'd have never thought possible. He had made her complete. "When I was a child, I learned a poem that was often read to me by mother. Since she couldn't be here today, it seems only fitting that I quote it in memory of her . . . and share her love and mine with you.

"Love is patient. Love is kind.

"It does not envy. It does not boast. It is not proud.

"It is not rude. It is not self-seeking.

"It is not easily angered. It keeps no record of wrongs.

"Love does not delight in evil, but rejoices with the truth.

"It always protects, always trusts, always hopes, always perseveres."

She bit her lip before she recited her own words to him. "While I lived a life without you, Seth, I no longer can imagine one that doesn't begin and end with seeing your gorgeous face. My heart beats only for you, and forever I will stand by your side. No matter the challenge or enemy, I am, and will always be, yours."

Seth couldn't breathe as he heard her oath. Nothing had ever touched him more.

Savitar made a sound of disgust. "Yeah, okay, beings . . . now you kiss."

Seth cupped her face in his hands. He took a moment to savor the beauty of her features before he kissed her. Her stomach brushed against his an instant before their baby kicked him. Laughing, he pulled back to touch her belly. "I hope that was an approval."

She returned his smile. "Definitely."

Savitar clapped his hands together. "All right then, to the handful here, let me present Mr. and Mrs. Demigod Jackal Beings . . ." He frowned at her and Seth. "You know this would be so much easier if some of us had last names."

Ma'at tossed a flower at Savitar. "Would you stop ruining this for them?"

"I'm not ruining it, Mennie. I'm making it memorable."

Ignoring them, Lydia grabbed Seth's hand and started toward the door.

"Where are you going?" her father asked.

Lydia looked at Seth as heat scorched her cheeks. She glanced back at all of them. "I have a promise to keep."

Seth's eyebrows shot up in hopeful expectation.

Wrinkling her nose impishly, she nodded. "Yes, it's *that* one."

Do you love fiction with a supernatural twist?

Want the chance to hear news about your favourite authors (and the chance to win free books)?

Keri Arthur
S. G. Browne
P.C. Cast
Christine Feehan
Jacquelyn Frank
Thea Harrison
Larissa Ione
Darynda Jones
Sherrilyn Kenyon
Jackie Kessler
Jayne Ann Krentz and Jayne Castle
Martin Millar
Kat Richardson
J.R. Ward
David Wellington
Laura Wright

Then visit the Piatkus website and blog
www.piatkus.co.uk | www.piatkusbooks.net

And follow us on Facebook and Twitter
www.facebook.com/piatkusfiction | www.twitter.com/piatkusbooks

piatkus